WISCONSIN

Second Chances Abound in Four Romantic Novels

ANDREA BOESHAAR

BARBOUR
PUBLISHING

The Haven of Rest © 1999 by Barbour Publishing, Inc.
Promise Me Forever © 1998 by Andrea Boeshaar
September Sonata © 2001 by Andrea Boeshaar
Second Time Around © 1998 by Barbour Publishing, Inc.

ISBN 1-59310-164-3

Cover design by Robyn Martins.

Published by Barbour Books, an imprint of Barbour Publishing, Inc., P.O. Box 719, Uhrichsville, Ohio 44683, www.barbourbooks.com

Our mission is to publish and distribute inspirational products offering exceptional value and biblical encouragement to the masses.

ecpa Member of the
Evangelical Christian
Publishers Association

Printed in the United States of America.
5 4

ANDREA BOESHAAR has been married for twenty-five years. She and her husband, Daniel, have three adult sons. Andrea attended college, first at the University of Wisconsin-Milwaukee, where she majored in English, and then at Alverno College, where she majored in Professional Communications and Business Management.

Andrea has been writing stories and poems since she was a little girl; however, it wasn't until 1984 that she started submitting her work for publication. In 1991 she became a Christian and realized her calling to write exclusively for the Christian market. Since then Andrea has written articles, devotionals, and over a dozen novels for **Heartsong Presents** as well as numerous novellas for Barbour Publishing. In addition to her own writing, she works as an agent for Hartline Literary Agency.

When she's not at the computer, Andrea enjoys being active in her local church and taking long walks with Daniel and their "baby"—a golden Labrador-Retriever mix named Kasey.

THE HAVEN OF REST

Chapter 1

Uncle Hal's lawyer, Jim Henderson, had been a family friend for as long as Amie could remember. She'd been in his Wausau, Wisconsin, office only once and she recalled being impressed by its neat and stately appearance. Jim himself was a noble sight, with his bushy, white hair and hawk-like features. He'd always reminded Amie of the second President of the United States, John Adams, with a bit of Albert Einstein mixed in. As a little girl, she had felt thoroughly intimidated around him, assuming he was a stern and intolerant man. But in all of her twenty-six years, she'd come to learn that Jim and his wife, Helen, were kind people and good friends. Even now, as they both sat in her parents' modest but tastefully decorated living room in Chicago's Lincoln Park area, she sensed Jim's concern and compassion as he began reading her uncle's will.

Jim had to have known that traveling to Chicago on a Sunday afternoon was the only way he'd get the busy Potter family together for this somber event. Not all of them had schedules permitting the six-hour drive north to Wausau during the week—and Amie had the tightest timetable of everyone. Her position as a creative consultant for the Chicago firm of Maxwell Brothers' Marketing and Development Company gave her little or no flexibility. And for some reason, Jim stressed the importance of her attendance at the disclosing of Uncle Hal's last will and testament.

"To my sister, Lillian," he read from the document in his hands, "and to her husband, John, I leave ten thousand dollars."

Amie raised her brows in surprise at the generous amount. Her mother, too, looked quite taken aback.

"Mercy!" she exclaimed, shaking her head disbelievingly. "Wherever did Hal get that kind of money?"

Jim smiled patiently. "Investments. He liked to dabble in the stock market and it proved quite profitable for him."

"Well, knock me over with a feather!" Lillian Potter ex-claimed, combing back her silver, chin-length hair with well- manicured fingers. "And to think he's lived like a pauper all these years."

"Don't feel sorry for Hal. He was very happy," Jim stated, wearing a hint of a smile just before his gaze fell back to the will. "And to Dottie I leave my mother's jewelry."

Amie smiled, hearing her twenty-three-year-old sister gasp with pleasure. As girls, Lillian had told them that she and Hal had split their mother's jewels after her death. Grandma Holm had wanted to be fair to both her children, even though she knew Hal hadn't much use for women's jewelry.

"To Stephen, my favorite nephew—" Jim paused to chuckle since everyone knew the youngest Potter was Hal's only nephew. "—I leave my Chevy Caprice."

"Awesome!" eighteen-year-old Stephen declared. His golden-blond hair, the same color as Amie's, shone brightly, and the smile on his face reflected the happiness he obviously felt at receiving such a gift. Stephen had been pleading with their father for "wheels" that he could take to Northwestern University next month when the fall semester started and he'd begin his freshman year. Now he had them.

"And to Amie," Jim stated, causing her stomach to flip in a peculiar way, "I leave my gas station and entire property in Tigerton, Wisconsin."

The room fell silent and all eyes turned on her. Dottie wore an expression of pity, Stephen, a look of confusion, and her parents' countenances scarcely masked their horror. As for Amie, she felt terribly disappointed. Why would he leave her a gas station? Maybe Uncle Hal hadn't liked her after all. . . .

Over the years, Amie had been sure her uncle favored her above her brother and sister. He remembered her birthdays, whereas he tended to forget Dottie's and Stephen's. At Christmastime, all three received gifts from Uncle Hal, but Amie's were always the biggest and the best. It used to be a point of contention among the two other Potter children. And every year around Easter, she would get a card from Hal wishing her a happy "spiritual birthday" because it was her uncle who'd led her to a saving knowledge of Christ when she was twelve years old.

But she must have done something to displease him before his death to warrant such a bequest. Although try as she might, Amie couldn't think of what!

"Oh, I'm sure there's got to be some mistake," Lillian said, turning to Jim with a frown of confusion creasing her silvery brows. "That run-down gas station? He left it to Amie? Why, I don't think it's even in working order."

"Yes, it is. . .for the most part. And there's no mistake," Jim countered emphatically. "Hal told me, himself, even before we'd put anything in writing, that he wanted Amie to have the service station."

"What in the world is she supposed to do with it?" John Potter asked incredulously, sitting and resting his forearms on his knees. As always, he was smartly dressed, wearing a red polo shirt and khaki pants. He shook his white head that, in his younger days, had been as blond as Amie's and Stephen's. "My daughter doesn't know the first thing about running a gas station—not that she'd want to. Look at her. There she sits, sugar and spice and everything nice. Can you see her running a filling station? I don't even think she's put gas in a car in her life. She usually gets Stephen to do it. . .or Dottie. . . or me!"

"Oh, Dad, I've filled my car's gas tank plenty of times," Amie replied, disliking the way her father had just made her sound so inept.

He shot her a teasing grin while Dottie and Stephen burst into hysterical laughter. Meanwhile, she sat by bristling. So she wasn't aggressively competitive like her younger sister, who wore her dark hair short and was majoring in sports medicine. So Amie liked her hair long and softly curled. So she liked feminine-looking clothing, lace and frills; she used make-up, bubble bath, and fingernail polish. So what?

"Princess," her father cajoled, "you've got to admit, it's awfully amusing. You and a. . .a gas station."

Her family laughed again and even Amie had to smile this time.

"Jim, are you certain there's been no mistake?" Lillian asked, doing her best to swallow her merriment.

"I'm positive," the attorney replied. "Hal specifically stated that he wanted Amie to have his gas station and its surrounding acres." Jim shifted his weight in the powder blue wingback chair. "Now, Amie," he said, looking over at her and wearing an understanding expression, "you can sell the place or keep it and hire someone to manage it. There's a fine man who's worked with Hal for the past thirteen years—ever since he was sixteen. Tom Anderson is his name. He roomed with Hal in the two-bedroom apartment above what used to be a laundromat years and years ago. Now it's just filled with junk." Jim grinned. "That was Hal's other hobby—collecting junk. You name it; it's probably stuffed into some part of those two buildings."

He paused, obviously seeing the confusion on Amie's face. "Let me explain. There are two buildings on Hal's property, the service station with an attached garage and a two-story building that houses the laundromat area, along with Tom's and Hal's apartment. . .well, now it's just Tom's place."

A sheepish look crossed Stephen's face. "Was there, um, a particular reason why my uncle and this guy shared an apartment?"

Jim chuckled good naturedly at the implication. "No. They were just good friends. Hal was like a father to Tom ever since he was a teenager." He paused and cleared his throat. "In a way, Amie, you've inherited Tom, too."

"Great," she replied, unable to keep the discouragement out of her voice.

"There, there, take heart, my dear," Jim told her. "Tom is a nice fellow. Honest. Hard working. With his help, you might be able to figure out how to actually make Hal's place into a profitable business." He paused, looking around the room at all the Potters. "I believe you folks met Tom at the funeral a few weeks ago."

"Oh, I know who you're talking about," Dottie said, giving Amie a rap on her shoulder. Leaning toward her, she added, "He was that geek with the dark brown wavy hair and mismatched suit who looked like he'd just stepped out of a rerun of 'The Partridge Family.' "

Stephen hooted. Amie couldn't recall meeting anyone of *that* description.

Jim cleared his throat, appearing slightly agitated. "Look, Tom's a good man. He's intelligent, even though he's only got a high school education. But I know lots of folks with college degrees who don't have a lick of common sense."

"True enough," Helen Henderson agreed, speaking up for the first time in a long while. Round and jolly looking, she possessed a wide, double-chinned face and short auburn hair that was teased back off her forehead. "Tom's a smart fellow. Why, I remember Hal saying he would have been valedictorian of his senior class if it hadn't been for—" She stopped short after receiving a look of warning from her husband. "Oh, never mind," she added, in an obvious attempt to cover her blunder. "It's a long story anyway."

"Tom didn't move into the apartment with Hal until about two years ago," Jim offered, apparently feeling the need to explain the situation. "It was right after his youngest brother turned eighteen and went off to college and Tom sold the family property. Being the eldest in his family and with his mother dead and his father being a. . .well. . .he liked to tip the bottle, to put it politely. Tom kind of raised his siblings, and Hal kind of raised Tom." Jim smiled broadly and glanced at Amie. "Tom will be glad to help you out, whether you decide to sell Hal's station or let him manage it."

Amie sighed glumly.

"I imagine you'll want to at least inspect the place before you make a decision." Slipping his hand into the pocket of his dress pants, Jim pulled out a key, dangling from a chain sporting a plastic rainbow trout the size of a large paperclip. "This is for the safe deposit box at the Tigerton bank. In it you'll find the deed to the property and such."

He handed it to Amie, who turned the key in her palm, still marveling at her inheritance—or curse—whichever the case may be. What was she ever going to do with an old service station filled with junk and an "outdated" attendant?

"Amie?"

She looked up, meeting Jim's serious regard.

"I sincerely hope you'll come to appreciate what Hal left to you. He loved you very much and spoke fondly of you."

"Thank you," she replied halfheartedly. "I hope I'll come to appreciate it too."

❧

The scorching July sunshine beat down on Tom Anderson as he watched the 1980 Caprice drive away, heading south on Highway 45 with Hal's nephew at the wheel. The sun reflected off the red taillights, and as he saw them disappear into the distance, Tom hoped the guy would take care of the vehicle. Hal had babied his eighteen-year-old automobile with frequent oil changes and tune-ups. Tom wasn't so sure Stephen Potter would be as responsible. He'd seen the expression on the kid's face when he first viewed the Caprice—Tom could only describe it as utter disappointment.

Must've been expecting a newer model, he thought dryly.

Turning and heading for his apartment, Tom thought about Stephen's sister Dottie. She'd driven them up from Chicago to get the Chevy. They'd both come to claim their inheritances, and while Stephen seemed dissatisfied with the car, Dottie had appeared wide-eyed and calculating after tucking Hal's jewelry box under one arm. She surveyed Tom's apartment with interested chocolate brown eyes, inquiring over several pieces of wooden furniture, the tea cart, cane-backed chair, coffee table, and matching end tables. Then she asked about their ownership. Hal had purchased them at various rummage sales or found them sitting on the side of the highway with the trash. But Tom had repaired, sanded, stained, and varnished them. They'd both enjoyed them, so he honestly didn't know who possessed legal rights to the items.

"Well, no matter," Dottie had said, lifting her chin haughtily. "Amie owns the place. I'll just ask her if I can have them."

Tom climbed the steep, narrow steps to the apartment he used to share with a man who was more of a father to him than his biological dad. He walked through the kitchen where the red-and-white rubber-tiled floor had obviously seen better days. In the dining room, an aging air-conditioning unit rattled noisily in the window, surrounded by cracked plastered walls. The worn, pea green carpet covering the dining and living room floors needed replacement badly. That was the next thing Hal had wanted to do—rip up the carpeting. But that was before his heart attack last month, and now Tom never felt more depressed in his whole life.

The only consolation he found was thinking about Hal in heaven, walking the streets of gold with the Savior, Jesus Christ. His friend was in a much better place than here in this dumpy apartment, in this nothing little town.

Collapsing onto the green, floral sofa and ignoring the ancient springs' groans of protest, Tom thought about the stocks and bonds Hal had left to him. He supposed he could cash them in, take the money, and run for his life. Leave Tigerton behind along with the nightmarish memories of his life here. But where would he go? What would he do?

In his hopeless state of mind, Tom couldn't fathom that answers to those questions even existed. Picking up his Bible from the coffee table, he opened it and flipped through the Psalms. Finally, he began to read: "The Lord is my shepherd; I shall not want. He maketh me to lie down in green pastures: He leadeth me beside the still waters. He restoreth my soul. . . ."

Chapter 2

A mie had postponed this trip for as long as possible. She'd been dreading this day ever since she'd found out about her inheritance. Dottie said she was "in denial," and perhaps that wasn't too far from the truth. But she had tried to argue the point anyway.

"I'm a creative consultant," she'd retorted. "I am not a financial wizard, nor am I well informed about gas stations!"

"Then just sell it, Amie. What's the big deal?"

What's the big deal? Amie repeated the question to herself now as she drove her red BMW up US-41. She passed farms, wheat fields, cornfields, and Holstein cows, and she marveled at the tranquility that filled her being when she left the bustling city of Chicago behind. Entering the state of Wisconsin, she drove on the outskirts of Kenosha, Racine, and Milwaukee Counties. An hour later, she was just north of Oshkosh when she crossed a long bridge spanning Lake Butte des Morts. Amie smiled at how the sunshine sparkled off the clear blue water as it cavorted around motorboats and fishermen. About fifteen miles later, she exited the interstate in the town of Appleton and found her way to Highway 45.

What's the big deal? Amie sighed, running those words through her head once more. How could she possibly explain to Dottie and the rest of her family that after spending time in prayer and consulting with her pastor, she didn't have peace about selling her uncle's gas station? Her family members were not believers, and Amie had tried discussing other important matters with them in the past, such as her college education. They'd never understood why she'd chosen a Bible college over a state university. And, while her parents thought it was "nice" that she had her "religion," her siblings made it clear that they didn't want any part of Christianity.

Driving on, Amie passed more farms, more cornfields, and then drove through a host of small towns. Finally, she traveled the last stretch of Highway 45 into Tigerton, crossing the Embarrass River on a tiny suspension bridge. To her right, Amie noticed the brand new Amoco gas station and sandwich shop being built on the edge of town. She wondered how her uncle's rundown place would ever compete with such a modern establishment.

Just one more thing to consider, she mused, reaching her destination at long last.

Hot August sunshine bounced off the concrete garage of Uncle Hal's filling station. At one time, the building had been whitewashed, but it now stood in drab gray, chipping and peeling. Amie climbed out of her car and stretched the muscles in her legs while scrutinizing the exterior of the other building. It had always reminded her of something out of an old western movie, with its false, squared-off front that loomed higher than the roof of the second story.

"Can I help you?"

Amie startled at the sound of the male voice coming from behind her car. She pivoted and found herself looking into a pair of the most mournful hazel eyes she'd ever seen.

"Yes, I, um, I'm Hal's niece," she stammered. "Amie Potter." She smiled politely before adding, "That's *Am*ie. . .as in *Am*ish. My mother grew up in Marion. . .you know, the neighboring town? And I was named after her favorite art teacher."

"Yeah, I know who you are."

Surprised at his remark, Amie brought her chin back, considering the man standing before her. Parted down the side, his dark brown hair hung in waves past his ears and had obviously outgrown any particular style long ago. His chin was stubbled, but his arms were smooth and suntanned, their color accentuated by the white tank top undershirt he wore tucked into badly oil-stained blue jeans, and on his feet were soiled work boots. Gazing down at her own sandals, Amie wondered if the guy's toes were frying in his shoes on this ninety-degree day.

She looked back up into his face, unkempt, but not at all unbecoming, and forced a polite grin. "You must be Tom."

"Uh-huh."

She nodded, and then several uncomfortable moments passed.

Amie cleared her throat nervously. "Any chance there's a restroom nearby? I just finished a four-hour drive up from Chicago. . . ."

Tom looked over at the decaying garage. "There's one in there, but the plumbing doesn't work anymore." He shifted his sad, green eyes back to Amie. "You're welcome to use the one upstairs in my apartment, though."

"Oh, well, that's awfully kind of you, but, um. . ." The thought of going into a strange man's apartment—especially if he intended to show her the way—sent a shiver of panic slicing through her.

As if sensing her discomfort, Tom added, "I'm refinishing a piece of furniture around back, but the door to my place isn't locked. Go on up and help yourself. Bathroom's right off of the kitchen."

Amie smiled gratefully, relaxing somewhat. "Thanks."

Walking briskly toward the western-styled building with its green-speckled asbestos-tiled siding, Amie entered the tiny, dank hallway and made her way up the narrow staircase. She found the lavatory easily and marveled at its interior. She assumed the place would be dumpy and dirty—like it was outside. But it was remarkably clean.

Minutes later, she washed up, left the bathroom, and then curiously inspected the apartment her uncle had shared with Tom. Again, she was impressed by its tidiness. There wasn't anything in sight that seemed in need of dusting, and the potted plants in the living room looked adequately watered and healthy. Amie groaned inwardly, thinking of her messy condo in Chicago. She'd left dirty dishes in the sink; the place hadn't been vacuumed in at least two weeks, and any plants she'd ever owned died within a month of her care—or lack thereof. If anyone dropped in on her unannounced, the way she'd done to Tom today, Amie thought she'd die of embarrassment.

Suddenly Amie recalled her sister's pleading for the refinished antiques that added charm to this dilapidated dwelling. Little wonder Dottie wanted them. They were objects of beauty. Carefully, almost reverently, Amie ran her hand across the smooth top of a chest—a hope chest—that sat beneath the dining room windows.

"Did you get lost?"

For the second time in fifteen minutes, Amie jumped. This guy seemed to have a knack for sneaking up on people!

"Sorry," she said, chagrined that she'd been caught snooping through his apartment. "I should have asked for a look around, although you did tell me to 'help myself' if I recall." She gave him a friendly smile, hoping to dispel any irritation he might have with her.

Tom just eyed her speculatively. "I told your sister that I wasn't sure who owned the furniture. Hal bought a lot of it and found the rest, but I fixed it up." His gaze moved past her, to the living room, and he expelled a weary-sounding breath. "But I've decided that I don't care what you take. Take it all, for that matter." He looked back at her and, despite the discouragement in his voice, a slight smile curved his thin but nicely shaped lips. "Except I don't think you're going to get much of anything packed into that little hot rod of yours."

Amie grinned. "Well, I've got a news flash for you, Tom. I wasn't planning on packing anything into my. . .*hot rod*."

He shrugged and Amie all but forgot her earlier concerns about being alone with Tom in his apartment. There was something very disarming about him. Perhaps it was his sorrowful eyes. They were shaped like teardrops that had fallen sideways, and gazing into their aqueous green depths caused Amie to feel a great measure of pity for the man. He had the perpetual expression of one on the brink of a good cry.

"You miss my uncle a lot, don't you?" she asked softly.

Tom's nod was so subtle that Amie barely saw it, and for an immeasurable second, they both stood there staring dumbly at each other.

Finally, Amie's nerves got the best of her, and she gave in to her lifelong, habit of babbling incessantly.

14

"I never really knew my uncle. Not really. I mean, he came to visit during the holidays, and I remember sitting on his knee as a little girl. Once every summer, my family and I made a brief stop here in Tigerton to see Uncle Hal on the way to our lakeside cabin in Minoqua, but that's about as much as I saw of him. And then, after I became a teenager and had my driver's license, I was usually more interested in hanging around with my friends than visiting with an older relative. I don't mean that in any form of disrespect; it's just one of those senseless teenager things." She paused for a breath. "And now I sort of wish I had known Uncle Hal better. Maybe I'd know *why* he left me his property and *what* he intended for me to do with it!"

A slow grin spread across Tom's face. Then, much to Amie's surprise, he actually chuckled. She couldn't help noticing that his teardrop eyes were transformed into little smiles as he squinted when he laughed. A little thrill passed through Amie to think that she'd had something to do with the metamorphosis.

"Hal said you could talk circles around most women."

Amie's surge of joy turned into a huff. "Oh, he did, did he? Well, it's too bad my uncle isn't here so I could properly thank him for the compliment."

"He didn't mean it as an insult," Tom assured her. "Hal thought it was funny."

"I think it's horrible! Not that Uncle Hal thought my chattering was funny, but that I have to chatter at all!" With hands on her hips, she shrugged. "It's a nervous thing with me—especially if I'm around people who don't do much talking. I guess I kind of make up for it, you know? I talk for the both of us. Although, I've got to admit, my rambling does come in handy when I give presentations. Once I had to impress the president of an oatmeal manufacturer with my ideas on building oatmeal's popularity with the general public—kids especially. That was really tough! I mean, what kid do you know who likes oatmeal? I hated it when I was a child. Still do—"

Amie paused midsentence. "See, I'm doing it again."

Pursing his lips thoughtfully, Tom nodded. "Yep, you sure are."

"You could shut me up, you know, by participating in the conversation."

"Participate?" Tom raised dark brown eyebrows. "I haven't been able to get a word in edgewise!"

Amie sucked in her lower lip, wishing she hadn't made such a fool of herself. She sent up an arrow of a prayer: *Lord, help me have a quiet spirit.*

Tom's expression was somber once more. "You want to see Hal's room?"

"Bedroom?" Amie swallowed down a second wave of panic—her other "bad habit." Ever since that night three years ago, she was afraid of being alone with a man, save for family members, of course. Never again, she'd vowed, would she allow herself to get into a vulnerable position. The last one cost Amie her virtue! Yet, it seemed she'd done exactly that today; she'd let down her guard and here she was—alone with Tom, a guy her sister called a "geek," and a man her brother dubbed a "grease-monkey." Worse yet, she knew practically nothing about him or his character.

"No, thanks, Tom. I don't need to see any more of the apartment," she hastily replied. "I really need to get going." She marched toward the kitchen, heading for the door. "I have to go to the bank, check out some things. I'm sure you understand."

Amie heard him silently trailing her, which only increased the alarm pumping through her veins. She practically ran down the precarious stairwell and out to her car. But as she reached the BMW, Tom caught her elbow.

"Hey, are you okay?"

By now, Amie was shaking badly and had worked herself into tears, but she nodded anyway.

"I wasn't making fun of you upstairs or anything." Tom smiled, albeit slightly. "I thought all your talking was rather. . . refreshing." His words faltered as Amie swatted the errant tears, hoping he wouldn't see them. But by the stupefied expression on his face, she knew he had.

"Are you okay?" he asked once more, looking considerably more concerned this time.

"Oh, I'm fine," Amie fibbed. "I get this way sometimes. Must be stress or something." After fumbling with her car keys, Amie managed to unlock the door. "I'd better get to the bank before it closes."

"It's only three o'clock; you've got plenty of time. On Friday nights, the Tigerton Bank doesn't close till seven."

"Good." Amie climbed into the driver's seat.

"Need directions?"

She grimaced. "Oh, yeah, that might help."

Tom explained how to get into town and described the location of the bank. "It's across the street from the pharmacy."

"Thanks."

"When you come back, I imagine that you'll want to see the books."

Amie tipped her head questioningly. "Books?"

Tom nodded. "The financial records on this place."

"Right."

He stepped back and Amie shut her car door. As she pulled out of the ramshackled gas station, she caught Tom's worried frown in the rearview mirror. *He must think I'm totally nuts*, she thought, following his directions to the bank, which wasn't far. *I have to be more careful*, she decided, as she parked and turned off the engine. *I have to quit babbling and stop panicking!* She hesitated before leaving her car, knowing she couldn't do either without God.

"Claim a Bible verse," Pastor Bryant had said when counseling her about the anxiety attacks—even though she couldn't get herself to tell him *why* she'd been having them. "Claim God's promises," he'd advised.

Amie looked at her dash where this week's verse was taped. She'd been trying to memorize Scripture, writing verses on index cards, and keeping them in her car. Currently, she was working on Philippians 4:6–7: "Be careful for nothing; but in every thing by prayer and supplication with thanksgiving let your requests be made known unto God. And the peace of God, which passeth all understanding, shall keep your hearts and minds through Christ Jesus."

"All right, Lord, I'm declaring this passage as Your promise to me."

After several minutes in prayer, Amie sighed, concluding that she felt calmer already. She squared her shoulders. *Now, about Uncle Hal's safe deposit box. . .*

～

Tom eased himself down onto the shaded concrete stoop outside the station and popped the top off a cold soda. Taking a long drink, he stared beyond the old gas pumps and thought about Amie Potter. She was as pretty as her college graduation picture, the one that sat on Hal's dresser—maybe prettier. He took another swig. Definitely prettier! Her hair was the color of a golden wheat field, and her brows were like two upward flaxen slashes above her cornflower blue eyes. And her figure— couldn't say she was fat. And she wasn't too slim. Just somewhere in between. In Tom's estimation, Amie Potter looked like a woman a man could hold onto without breaking in two. He liked that idea, although he sure wasn't any kind of expert on women. With the exception of two younger sisters—who didn't count in the matter of romantic relationships—women were foreign territory to him, especially Amie.

And what in the world happened to cause such a reaction in her? What had she said? Stress? Could be. Or maybe it was one of those female things. His sisters, Lois and Jeanne, used to become veritable barracudas at certain times of the month, and Tom had personally witnessed their transformation. He'd almost been glad when they had run off, one right after the other. However, such glee didn't last long before reality set in: Lois and Jeanne had left him with an alcoholic father and two younger brothers to look after.

Taking another swallow of his cola, Tom wondered where his sisters were. He hadn't heard from them since they left home some ten years ago. He hoped they were happily married and raising packs of kids. He hoped they'd escaped from their childhoods, their pasts.

He wiped the sweat off his brow. At least Matt had a good chance at life. His youngest brother was the first of the Andersons to attend college. He'd gotten a grant and a scholarship—he'd be fine. He'd succeed. On the other hand, his other brother, Phillip, had followed in their old man's footsteps—his drinking and carousing had landed him in jail. Tom went to visit him every couple of weeks, and praise God, Phil had come to a saving knowledge of Christ not long ago. Hal once said that sometimes God had to throw a man into prison in order to save his soul. Perhaps he'd been right.

Tom rose from the cement stoop, drank the last of his cola, and pitched the can into the plastic recycling bin. He decided he'd best pull out the financial stuff so it would be ready for Amie when she returned from the bank. A good portion of the records was on his computer, but he could readily print off anything she asked to see. Turning toward his apartment door, located right next to the closed-down laundromat, Tom entered and started up the steep steps, suddenly wishing he'd been the one to run off at sixteen years old, instead of his two sisters. Sometimes bearing the weight of responsibility was more than he bargained for, especially in a tiny town like Tigerton.

Chapter 3

I n the solitude of one of the bank's offices, Amie read and reread her uncle's letter, marveling at its contents. *He remembered*, she thought with tear-filled eyes. *I had long forgotten, but Uncle Hal remembered. My hotel.*

She swallowed her sadness, smiling now as the memories came rushing back. Amie had always wanted to build and operate her own hotel. As a little girl, she had fantasized about holding tea parties in the beautifully decorated lobby—just as she and her mother had done one year for Amie's birthday at the Palmer House in Chicago. Amie couldn't have been more than five years old at the time, but the grand hotel with its quaint charm had greatly impressed her. Queen of the Hotel, that was the title Amie had always coveted, until she was in her teens and realized the ridiculousness of it all. She had to go to college and learn to do something practical with her life. Hadn't her father drummed that into her brain enough times? And, of course, he was right. She had a marvelous career. Dreams of tea parties and hotels had long ago been stacked away with childhood storybooks and baby dolls.

She glanced at her uncle's letter, still resting on her fingertips. *Use my land, Amie,* he'd written. *Raze the old gas station, laundromat, and my apartment, and build yourself one dilly of a hotel!*

"Oh, right, Uncle Hal," she murmured inwardly, as if somehow he could hear her. "Like this town is ready for a Palmer House." Amie rolled her eyes heavenward. "A truck-stop, maybe. But a hotel? I don't think so. And surely there's a Holiday Inn or something around here."

She studied the letter once more, focusing on the paragraph about Tom Anderson. Her uncle had written: *Tom is my son in the faith. I had the pleasure of leading him to Christ when he was a teenager. He is a good Christian man, and that is why I left him over half of my investments.*

"A good Christian man," Amie murmured aloud, lifting her gaze, contemplating the information. While she hadn't known her uncle well firsthand, she'd known a great deal *about* him. Her mother often spoke of how "religious" her brother was, always adding that she'd never heard a bad word out of his mouth. Amie recalled the numerous times her mother phoned Uncle Hal when she needed encouragement. And her father frequently said his brother-in-law was a good judge of character. If Hal Holm stated that Tom Anderson "is a good Christian man," then Amie felt certain it was true. In the next moment, she realized her earlier fear of the man was unwarranted. A sense of relief swept over her.

She looked back at the letter. *And Tom Anderson inherited over half of Uncle Hal's investments?* she mused incredulously as she simultaneously wondered at the dollar amount.

Suddenly a knock sounded at the office door. "Miss Potter?" It opened to reveal the kindly lady who'd helped her obtain Hal's safe deposit box. "Is everything all right?"

"Just fine, thanks." Amie smiled politely. "I'll be finished up here shortly."

"Very well." The portly woman with curls in her light-brown hair turned to leave. "If there's anything else you need, just give me a holler."

"Thank you."

The door closed and Amie folded the letter. Gathering the contents of the safe deposit box, she realized she possessed the other portion of her uncle's investments—whatever they were worth.

She stuffed the papers and Hal's letter into her shoulder bag, sticking her tiny purse in there too. However, leaving the bank, she didn't feel any closer to knowing what to do with her inheritance than when she first entered nearly forty-five minutes ago.

Amie threw a quick glance up the street. It was obviously the main drag and traffic was picking up. To her left there was a clinic up on the hill, next to the river. The pharmacy was across the street. The next block boasted a sign that read, MARKET SQUARE MINI-MALL. If *that* was a mall, Amie was the queen of England! It hardly compared to anything she was used to shopping at in Chicago. Except she couldn't help noticing the mouth-watering smell of fried chicken emanating from the place or the delicious-looking ice cream cones that four kids were holding as they fairly tumbled out the main entrance.

Gazing farther up Cedar Street, Amie spied an outdated telephone booth on the corner, the likes of which she hadn't seen in at least ten years. Farther yet was RON'S FOODLAND. But what Amie didn't see anywhere was a hotel.

Get it out of your mind, Amie Potter! she berated herself, marching to her car. *This town wouldn't know what to do with a hotel. This town looks poverty-stricken and it's. . .dying!*

An elderly man passed her on the sidewalk and stared openly. "Say," he called after she'd passed him. "Aren't you Hal Holm's niece?"

She stopped, turning slowly. The man had a stocky build and wore a snug-fitting light blue polo shirt. "Yes, sir. I'm Amie Potter."

He grinned broadly and etchings the years had made in his tanned face seemed to deepen. "Well, sure, I recognize you. I remember when you were this high!" he said, holding his hand level with his right hip.

Amie forced a polite smile. "I'm sorry, but I don't remember you."

"Ernie Huffman."

"Pleased to meet you, Mr. Huffman."

He kept grinning. "You visiting?"

"Sort of. My uncle left me his filling station, and I'm trying to get that part of his estate settled."

"I see. Well, I'll leave you to your business, then."

With a polite nod, she continued her short jaunt to the car. Disengaging the alarm system, she opened the door and was met by a blast of suffocating heat. She instantly regretted not opening a window, even slightly. By the time the air-conditioning completely cooled the car, she'd be back at Hal's station. A lot of good it was going to do her then!

Amie drove through town, halting at the junction of Highway 45. The sun bore down on the BMW as she waited for a break in the late Friday afternoon traffic. The road was filled with travelers. Watching them, Amie noticed at least four campers heading north, most likely for the weekend. A couple of cars pulling boats whizzed past, followed by an automobile towing jet skis.

Tourists.

Lots of them.

"I'm not building a hotel in this town!" she said out loud as if debating with someone sitting in the passenger seat next to her. "If I were smart, I'd sell Uncle Hal's property, cash in on those investments, and take a cruise this winter. Chicago winters are pathetic."

A car's horn honked from behind her, and Amie realized the traffic rendered her access onto the highway. She waved in apology and stepped on the accelerator. She had to cross the little suspension bridge again before arriving back at the gas station.

Pulling into the lot, she immediately noticed a car parked at the pumps. Its hood was up and Tom stood beside a gray-haired man, both of them staring at the auto's motor with grave expressions.

"So you can't fix it?" she heard the stranger ask as she walked up to where he and Tom stood.

"Sorry, Russ," Tom replied evenly. "Cars these days have computers, and I don't have the equipment to work on them. Gotta take it back to the dealer in Wittenberg."

"But they'll charge me a fortune!"

He shrugged. "Sorry."

The older man muttered while Tom dropped the hood.

"Why don't you get yourself some of today's modern tools, Tom, so you can fix my car?"

"Guess I'm not interested in fixing cars anymore."

Russ sputtered off a lengthy complaint. It was then he spotted Amie, and the sudden expression on his face seemed to border on shock and curiosity.

Tom inclined his dark brown head in her direction. "This is Hal's niece, Amie Potter."

Russ was immediately all smiles. "Well, how-de-do! Wel-come to Tigerton." "Thanks," she said, unable to keep from smiling herself.

"You know, Tom," he said conspiratorially, yet loud enough so Amie heard, "it's Cash Night in town. If you're inside a local business when your name is drawn, you can win money."

"Yeah, I know, Russ," Tom replied, sounding disinterested.

"Well, I was thinking—the bowling alley's got great burgers. You ought to take her out to eat there tonight. Maybe knock over a few pins while you're at it." He elbowed Tom and winked pointedly. "Match made in heaven, eh?"

Amie puzzled over the remark, then decided to just laugh at the old man's antics. However, one look at Tom's face said he wasn't amused—although he didn't look particularly annoyed either.

Her uncle's words came back to her. *Tom is my son in the faith. . .a good Christian man. . .I left him over half of my investments.*

Amie wondered if he'd like to invest in a hotel.

Except she wasn't building one.

No! She would not build a hotel! The very idea was absurd!

"I think you insulted her, Russ," Tom said, drawing Amie out of the inner battle that was pulling her apart. "She's from Chicago. She doesn't want to eat at some two-bit bowling alley, especially with a guy like me."

He looked over at her, and those sad, green eyes melted Amie's heart.

"I'm not insulted," she quickly replied. "On the contrary. I'm starved. I'd love a hamburger from the bowling alley. No, make that a cheeseburger." She frowned questioningly. "Do they have double cheeseburgers there? And chocolate shakes?"

Half a grin curved his mouth, challenging her. Now she'd have to see him smile—or, better yet, laugh!

Amie put her hands on her hips and lifted a brow in feigned insolence. "And my next question is: Are *you* buying?"

That did it. Tom chuckled, his gaze falling to the cracked pavement beneath his dirty work boots. Then, looking at Russ, he waved an abrupt good-bye. "See you later."

"Oh, yeah, sure." Russ wore that previous look of surprise on his face. "See you later, Tom." He nodded at Amie. "Nice meeting you."

"Same here," she called, watching as he climbed slowly into his car.

When he drove away, Amie turned to Tom. "Did I embarrass you? Sorry if I did."

"No, you didn't embarrass me." His expression had returned to dismal, his hazel eyes so sorrowful. "But I think you'd best be aware of the way talk spreads around a small town like this one. I mean, I wouldn't put it past Russ to spread the word that you and I are. . .dating or something after what just happened."

"Oh, who cares what people say," Amie said with a flippant shrug of her shoulders.

"Well, unfortunately, what people say about you in this town is who you are." With that, Tom turned and walked into the tiny office attached to the garage.

Amie followed. "So, does that mean I have to go find a hamburger by myself?"

Tom didn't reply to her tart remark but found his way to the other side of the counter on which a myriad of papers were stacked, along with a grimy adding machine and telephone. Finally he looked at her with such a probing gaze that Amie was tempted to turn away. But she didn't. She met his stare undaunted.

"Look, Amie," Tom said at last, "I don't think it's a good idea if you go anywhere with me, okay?"

"Why?" she couldn't help asking. And then it hit her. "Oh, I get it. You've got a girlfriend. . .or a fiancée, huh? I understand. I wouldn't come between a couple for a million bucks, even if we are just two friends eating a hamburger at the same table."

"But that's my point. In this town two people can't eat at the same table without folks speculating about something more going on between them."

"Oh. . ."

She glanced out the smeared plate-glass window as unexpected disappointment pricked her heart. She was so tired of eating by herself, save for the "power" lunches she had with clients. It seemed to Amie that everyone had someone special with whom they shared their lives, except for her. All her friends from college were married and raising children. Dottie was engaged. Stephen had a steady girlfriend who was going with him to Northwestern University.

Guess it's dinner for one again, she conceded inwardly. After all, there was no point in agonizing over things beyond her control. She'd just learn to be content as a single woman.

"By the way, I'm not dating. . .or anything."

She pivoted, looking back at Tom. He was pulling out hard-bound ledgers from underneath the counter. "Well," she hedged, "in that case, would it be all right if you and I ordered a pizza and ate it around back where no one could see?"

That slow, half grin reappeared, brightening Tom's countenance ever so slightly. "Amie, I don't care if people see me taking you out to eat. I don't even care if they think we're on a date. I'm just trying to protect your reputation in this town. I owe Hal that much." He shrugged. "But I suppose since you are his niece. . .and everyone knows he and I were friends. . ."

"What do you mean, 'protect my reputation?' Are you implying that being seen with you will ruin it? My uncle told me that you're a fine Christian man."

Tom's face fell, his gaze included. "Yeah, well, he was one of a kind. This town'll tell you that I'm the guy least likely to succeed. Always was. Always will be. You don't need to get pegged with the likes of me."

Amie opened her mouth, fully intending to scold the guy for having his own pity party, but then she remembered what Jim Henderson said the day he read Hal's will. Something about Tom's father being an alcoholic and Tom having to drop out of high school to raise his siblings. No doubt he'd lived a hard life. Then he lost his best friend.

Reaching out, she touched his tanned arm. "Tom, if my uncle said you're a fine Christian man, then I'd believe him over anything other people might say."

He looked up from the ledgers he'd been staring at forlornly.

Amie smiled sweetly. "Will you go get cleaned up and take me somewhere for a double cheeseburger and chocolate shake before I faint from hunger?"

Tom pulled his arm away and nervously scratched the back of his head. "I certainly hope you know what you're doing."

"Does that mean yes?"

"Yeah, sure," he replied, although it lacked enthusiasm. He walked around the counter in acquiescence and headed for the door.

"I haven't had a date in three years," Amie blurted. "And I can tell you right now, Tom Anderson, that you are two hundred times better than the last guy who took me out!"

"You can tell that already, huh?" he asked with a hint of sarcasm.

"There's not a doubt in my mind," Amie stated tenaciously.

He smiled from the doorway. "In that case, I'll even *pay* for your double cheeseburger and chocolate shake."

She laughed, watching as Tom strode purposely for his apartment. Maybe, if she was lucky, he'd even take a shower!

Chapter 4

While Tom cleaned up for dinner, Amie paged through her uncle's ledgers. As far as she could see, everything was in order. She noticed there wasn't much in the way of profits to report, but according to last year's accounting, the filling station didn't appear to be losing money.

Amie closed the hardbound book and began to investigate her newly acquired property. The office and attached garage weren't nearly as well maintained as Tom's apartment. Empty oil cans and various auto parts were strewn about the concrete floor of the garage, while clusters of paper and unopened mail occupied every available flat surface in the office. Amie wondered how a man could work in such a mess.

Stepping outside into the late afternoon sun, she walked next door and attempted a look into the old laundromat. Through a dusty window, she saw that junk and more junk had been piled floor-to-ceiling, from one end to the other.

"Uncle Hal," she muttered inwardly, "what in the world were you thinking when you stored all this stuff in here?"

"He was thinking that it'd be worth something one day."

Startled, Amie turned and found Tom standing several feet away. She narrowed her gaze in annoyance. "Didn't anyone ever tell you that it's not nice to sneak up on a person?"

He shook his head, still damp from its obvious washing, although he hadn't shaved his stubbled chin. Then, putting a hand into the pocket of his clean blue jeans, he withdrew a set of keys. "Would you like to go inside for a better view?"

"No," she replied tersely to cover her embarrassment. "That's not necessary. Besides, I don't think there's room for a human being in there."

"Good point." Tom stuck the keys back into his pocket. "But a lot of decent furniture's in there that could be fixed up, if somebody had the time to do it."

Curious now, Amie peered back into the window. "What kind of furniture?"

"A couple of dressers, a bookshelf, a baby's crib, kitchen table, and matching chairs—some of them have broken legs, though, and I don't know if they're worth salvaging. There's a roll-top desk in there somewhere too."

"Wood furniture?"

"Uh-huh."

"Hmm. . .and here I had thought it was all junk." She turned to face him once more. "Why don't you fix those pieces up, Tom? You've obviously got the capability, from what I've seen of the antiques upstairs that you refinished."

"I've been working at it here and there."

An idea suddenly began to take form. *An antique shop. . .in the hotel.*

"Are you, um, still hungry?"

Amie gave herself a mental shake. "Hungry?" she answered. "I'm starving!"

"Well, let's go, then." Again he pulled out his keys. "I'll take my truck, and you can follow me in your car. We'll eat in Shawano, and then get a motel room."

"Excuse me?"

Tom stopped in his tracks, his face reddening with embarrassment. "For you," he quickly replied. "We'll get a motel room for you. See, there's no motel in Tigerton. Closest one's in Shawano." He cleared his throat uncomfortably. "I didn't think you'd want to drive back to Chicago tonight."

Amie nibbled on her bottom lip to keep from laughing aloud. If she still had doubts about Tom's integrity, they were all gone now. The poor guy was blushing! When was the last time she'd seen a man actually *blush*?

She smiled, swallowing the last of her mirth. "Well, thanks. That's really considerate."

He nodded. "Thought we'd go over the books tomorrow," he added, still looking chagrined. "I've got this year's figures on my computer. I started printing them out, but didn't get finished."

"Sure. Tomorrow's fine."

Tom began walking around the side of the building. "I'll get my truck."

Watching him go, Amie was reminded of a country singer her sister had been madly in love with some ten years ago. Maybe it was Tom's outfit—the navy plaid, light cotton, collared shirt he wore with its long sleeves rolled to the elbow, the faded blue jeans and black cowboy boots completing the ensemble. Coupled with whiskered face and hair wet from shampooing, he looked somewhat cavalier. There was an uncanny resemblance between Tom and that country-boy singer whose picture Dottie had plastered all over her bedroom.

Well, why am I surprised? This town is about as country as it gets, she thought wryly, strolling toward her car. As if on cue, she heard a cow lowing in the distance. *Right. I'm in the land of cows and country boys. Got it.*

Disengaging her car alarm, she climbed into the BMW, and within minutes, Tom pulled up in his red and black Ford Ranger. Amie was amazed yet again, having guessed he'd drive some sort of old rust-bucket.

"Ready?" he called out the window.

"Ready."

The trip didn't take more than twenty minutes, and upon her arrival, Amie noticed Shawano was larger than Tigerton and sported a wide variety of shops, restaurants—and motels. But she couldn't help wondering, as they both parked their vehicles, if Tom's ulterior motive for bringing her here—and taking two cars—was to escape unwanted gossip in his hometown.

"I like this place," he told her when they met on the sidewalk in front of a small, locally owned eatery whose sign read: ALLEN & ROSIE'S KITCHEN, PARKING IN REAR. He grinned slightly. "Hal and I used to come here a lot. Their cheeseburgers are made with real beef, and they make a mean chocolate shake—probably use real milk too."

Amie chuckled at his dry sense of humor before returning a bit of it. "Are you saying you don't care for soybean and artificial dairy products? What kind of an American are you?"

"A healthy one," Tom replied evenly, holding the door open for Amie.

Entering the establishment, she appraised her surroundings. Red-checkered clothed tables lined the small but heavily populated dining room. On the other side of a spindled partition, stood an L-shaped counter, flanked by red and chrome swivel stools.

They waited by the door for a few minutes while a table was cleared, then sat down near the café-curtained plate window.

"This place is so quaint," she remarked. "I get tired of the large chain restaurants. They're all the same in every big city, and the food tastes alike."

Tom shrugged. "Well, as I said before, the food here's real good. They close at eight every night and don't serve liquor. Guess that's what I like best about this place. No liquor."

"Oh. . . ?" Amie glanced around and didn't see a bar, confirming Tom's comment.

"Disappointed?"

She brought her attention back to him as he opened his menu and began studying it. "Not at all," she replied. "I don't drink—anymore. I used to. That is, I'd occasionally indulge in a small glass of. . .something. But then. . .well, it was about three years ago when I gave it up completely. My decision wasn't a result of a religious conviction, although God certainly showed me that bad things can happen when a person drinks and—" Amie paused, expelling a flustered sigh. "And I'm babbling again. Sorry."

Tom lifted his gaze, meeting hers, and she thought she saw a glimmer of understanding in those hazel depths.

Finally, he glanced back at his menu and closed it. "I think I'll have the same thing you're having. Double cheeseburger and a chocolate shake."

"Smart choice," she said, wondering if she'd ever get her irksome habit of babbling under control.

By the time they left the restaurant, it was just past six o'clock. A younger crowd seemed to dominate the streets now and music blared from passing autos. The weekend had arrived in this northern Wisconsin town.

"You want to find a place to stay now?" Tom asked. "There's a motel near the fairgrounds. I can drive you over."

"Can we walk? I feel the need for a bit of exercise after all the food I just consumed."

He nodded. "It'll be a bit of a hike, but sure."

As they turned to go, a burly man approached them. "Well, well, if it isn't Tomboy," he said with a facetious ring in his deep voice. His hair was shiny black, but his craggy beard was the color of charcoal. As Amie stared at the large man before her, she was reminded of Popeye's foe, Brutus. "And who might this be?"

The man shifted his dark-eyed gaze to her, and Amie took a step closer to Tom. She fought down a wave of anxiety and forced herself to smile politely.

"I'm Amie Potter," she replied.

He grinned interestedly. "My pleasure. I'm Al Simonson." The man threw Tom a curious look and smirked. "You two long-lost cousins or something? No girl in her right mind would go out with this guy otherwise. Isn't that so, Tomboy?"

Turning to him, Amie noticed Tom's flushed face, and instantly the desire to thwart *Mr. Bigshot* was too overwhelming to resist. How dare this man belittle one of her uncle's best friends!

She took another step toward Tom. "We're not related at all. Actually, I'm in town for the weekend on business, and Tom was nice enough to take me to dinner tonight." She looked up at him, wearing a sweet smile, and looped her arm around his elbow. "We met over at the gas station in Tigerton."

"You don't say. . .?" He stood there nonplused.

Tom's smile reflected his embarrassment. "Al, she's really—"

"Dying to go for a walk," Amie put in hastily. "Come on, Tom. You promised me a stroll around town." She looked back at the gaping Al Simonson. "Nice to meet you."

She half pulled Tom down to the street corner where she burst out laughing while waiting for the WALK sign. He stared at her, a look of horror on his face.

"Are you out of your mind?"

"Probably. . .oh, now, don't get mad, Tom. That guy deserved it. Didn't you hear how he insulted you? What a jerk!"

Amie released his arm as they crossed the street.

"I've practically grown up with Big Al Simonson," Tom muttered, "and I can't believe what you just did." He glanced over at her. "You don't have a clue, do you? This isn't Chicago, Amie. People talk. Al is from Tigerton, and not only is he a large man, he's got a large mouth. By noon tomorrow, what just happened will be all over town."

"Relax, Tom. He'll find out who I am soon enough and figure everything out. It's not like I lied."

"Purposely deceiving someone is the same as lying, Amie."

She huffed at the rebuttal. "All right. Fine."

Tom stopped in midstride. Amie paused as well. And as she looked up at him, she saw the most miserable expression she'd ever seen on a human being. His gaze was out somewhere over her head, giving her a chance to scrutinize his features without him noticing.

He wasn't at all an unattractive man, she decided as questions piqued her curiosity. "Why wasn't he dating? He seemed like a fine catch—for the right woman, of course.

"Why did that guy say those things, Tom?" she asked softly, so passers-by wouldn't overhear. "Why did he say that no girl in her right mind would go out with you?"

"I thought I explained all this earlier."

"You're the guy least likely to succeed? Bah!" She rolled her eyes. "And now I suppose you're upset because a rude man from Tigerton saw us together and he'll peg me as the woman least likely to succeed. Is that it?" With hands on hips, she lifted a defiant chin. "Well, I know differently, and I don't care what anybody says. I'm successful and you can be too. If God is for us, who can be against us?"

Tom stared back at her in reply, his expression unreadable.

Amie continued her discourse, "I haven't known you for more than a few hours, Tom Anderson, but even if this town thinks you're least likely to succeed, I don't believe it for a minute. You could be anything you wanted to be." She glanced up the street where they'd run into Tom's beefy pal. "But if it will make you feel better, I'll go try to find Al. . . I'll explain everything." She looked back at him. "Will that fix things?"

"Maybe." He narrowed his gaze. "You know, I can't figure you out. You go from feisty to fearful in a single bound. A few minutes ago, I could've sworn you were afraid of Big Al and now you're offering to go find him." He chuckled, looking thoroughly amused. "I suppose you'd take him on single-handedly, huh?"

"I'm a very outgoing, congenial person," she stated, sounding defensive to her own ears. "But every so often I have these moments of. . .of *trepidation*." She turned to walk away, slinging her purse over her shoulder. "In any case, I'm more than able to take care of myself in any given situation. So thanks for dinner and I'll see you tomorrow. And I'll find *Brutus*," she added sassily over her shoulder, "after I check into the motel."

Man, that guy has got to lighten up, she thought in exasperation. However, it only took her a few moments to realize that she had no idea where she was going. She stopped short and turned around, slamming into Tom.

"Oh, sorry."

He lifted his brows expectantly.

She swallowed hard, utterly embarrassed. "Guess I need you to show me where the motel is."

He smirked. "Right this way."

They walked the remaining blocks in awkward silence. Then, upon reaching the Best Rest Motel, she checked in, signed the necessary forms, secured the room with her credit card, and dropped the key to her room into her purse.

"All set," she announced to Tom who'd waited for her outside in the cooling evening breeze.

They hiked back amid the same uncomfortable mood. When they finally reached their vehicles, Amie turned off her car alarm using the mechanism built into her key chain and released the locks in the same fashion.

"Thanks again for dinner," she muttered, opening the door and climbing in. But when she tried to close it, Tom stood in the way.

She looked up at him with uncertainty.

"Do you think we could talk for a little while? I mean, I wouldn't want the sun to go down on our anger."

"I'm not angry."

"Neither am I," he said earnestly. "But, I think it'd be good if we settled a few things anyway."

"What sort of *things*?"

In reply, he reached for her hand, helping her from the car and impressing Amie with his manners once more. She immediately decided that touch of savoir faire made Tom Anderson seem more the gallant gentleman than the backwards country boy she had assessed him as before.

Now, if only he wasn't so melancholy. . .

"Should we go back into Allen and Rosie's for a soda or something?" he suggested. "At least in there we could hold a conversation without being in the public spotlight, and they're open for another half hour."

"Sure."

They entered the restaurant for the second time, and after they were seated, Amie and Tom ordered colas.

"About what happened. . .I'm sorry," she told him. "I should have kept my mouth shut. It's just that Al's insults upset me."

"Why? He wasn't insulting you. Besides, it's no big deal. I'm used to it."

Amie contemplated his answer as she sipped her soda. "That's terrible. You shouldn't have to put up with derogatory remarks from that. . .bully!"

Tom grinned wanly. "Whatever. Can we forget all that? I've decided you're right—Big Al'll find out who you are soon enough, and he'll know we weren't on a date. I actually wanted to talk about the gas station. I meant to bring up the subject at dinner but didn't know how to approach it."

She frowned, puzzled. "What about the gas station?"

"Well," he hedged, "I wondered if you knew what you wanted to do with it."

"No, not yet."

"I suppose you'll need to charge me rent."

"I. . .I don't know. I didn't think about that." She lifted a hopeful brow. "Wanna buy the place from me? I know Uncle Hal left you some money."

"Are you nuts?"

Frowning, she quipped, "I think you just hurt my feelings!"

He smiled, though it didn't quite reach his eyes. "I didn't mean to. It's just that if I buy that gas station. . .well, I'll be trapped. Stuck in a dead end."

"A dead end in a dying town?"

"Something like that."

"I see. . ." Amie thought about telling Tom her hotel idea. Except she really didn't want to be "trapped" either. But even if that wasn't the case and even if she could come up with the funds, which she couldn't, she'd never have the time to oversee such an undertaking.

"There's a lot of traffic on Highway 45," she ventured. Perhaps Tom would want to build a hotel. "I saw plenty of tourists heading north for the weekend."

"I don't want to buy the gas station, Amie, so get that notion out of your head."

"Okay." She sighed. "The truth is, I really never had peace about selling it anyway." She looked down at the ice cubes, swirling around in her glass. "In his last letter to me—the one I found in his safe deposit box today—Uncle Hal told me to raze the buildings on the property and put up a hotel." She lifted her eyes to gauge Tom's reaction. "It was always my dream as a little girl. . .to build a hotel."

"A hotel?"

"Yes. But what's incredible is I've really been thinking about it!"

"Building a hotel. . .in Tigerton?"

"Yep." Amie laughed at his astonished expression, which faded fast. Moments later, Tom seemed pensive.

"Think it would be a profitable business?" she asked.

"Might be."

A spark of aspiration rose up in Amie but dwindled just as fast as it had been ignited. "I don't have the time or money to build a hotel," she confessed, wishing she didn't feel so disappointed.

"Yeah, me neither."

Tom pushed his chair back and stood. Taking it as a hint that their meeting had come to an end, Amie did the same.

"Well, um, I hope you have a good night's sleep," he said, looking suddenly ill at ease. He threw a few dollars onto the table. "I guess I'll see you tomorrow."

"Yes, see you tomorrow."

In silence, they exited the quaint restaurant and without a word they parted, giving Amie the distinct impression that she'd said something terribly wrong.

Chapter 5

W hat a dumb idea. I've never heard anything more harebrained in my entire life!" Tom ranted to himself as he paced the apartment. "What makes you think you can have a hand in running a hotel? You don't know the first thing about it! What are you thinking? As if a woman like Amie Potter would even consider *you* for a business partner." He collapsed into a faded, overstuffed armchair in the living room. "You, a loser. Son of the town drunk. Part of a dysfunctional family unit if there ever was one!"

He sighed, his feelings of depression escalating. He couldn't help thinking that his self-deprecation sounded a whole lot like Big Al's taunts. He'd heard them since junior high, and he was used to it, either way. Combined with the memory of his father's beatings, he didn't have much faith in himself.

"But I've got faith in God," he affirmed out loud, clinging to that delicate thread of hope that kept his head together when circumstances threatened to blow his very mind. Hal, friend that he was, had always told him faith in Christ was the key to everything in life. And he'd been right.

But now he's gone, Tom conceded glumly. He squeezed his eyes closed, shutting them against the onslaught of grief. *Oh, God! Why couldn't You have taken me instead? I'm the one who's so tired of living.*

Suddenly Amie's words from earlier that evening floated back to him. "If God is for us, who can be against us? You could be anything you wanted to be."

Opening his eyes, Tom gazed around his dingy living quarters and smiled sadly. She was so much like her uncle. Always thinking positive. He laughed. Why, she'd even stuck up for him in front of Big Al Simonson, just like Hal used to do. But she'd been scared of him too. Tom hadn't missed that. And he had to wonder—was the incident this afternoon, the one which sent her flying out of this apartment, a result of fear as well?

Naw, he decided. *Why would she be afraid of me?*

With his emotions in turmoil, Tom reached for his Bible. He opened to the Book of Genesis and took up reading where he'd left off yesterday. He didn't have to go far before God spoke to his heart from chapter 39, verse 2: "And the Lord was with Joseph, and he was a prosperous man."

Tom paused reflectively. The Lord prospered Joseph—a man who didn't have the greatest background either. Hadn't Jacob, Joseph's father, deceived Esau into selling his birthright for a cup of soup? Hadn't Jacob displayed favoritism toward his wife Rebecca over Leah, causing great strife between the sisters? Hadn't he done the same with his sons, favoring Joseph over all the rest and generating bitterness and hatred among his family? Yet, God loved Jacob *and* Joseph.

"If God is for us. . ." Tom murmured thoughtfully. Searching the concordance in the back of his Bible, he found the verse Amie had quoted. Romans 8:31: "What shall we then say to these things? If God be for us, who can be against us?"

"Okay, maybe this is a chance at a new beginning." His thoughts returned to the hotel idea, and a yearning such as he'd never experienced began spreading through him, like wildfire through dried brushes. God was with him. The Lord would prosper him. And wouldn't it be something if he could show this town that Tom Anderson could be a successful businessman? What a testimony of Christ's saving power!

All right, Lord, I'll do it, but You're going to have to work out all the details—like convincing Amie to build the place and persuading her to let me be her partner.

❧

Amie toyed with the earring she'd looped around her middle finger while she spoke with her father on the telephone. "I know it sounds crazy, Dad. But after I read Uncle Hal's letter, I just couldn't get the idea out of my mind. I want to build a hotel up here."

"Well, honey, you know I'm all for adventure, particularly if it pertains to business." He chuckled. "I don't call these things 'business ventures,' I call them 'business *ad*ventures.' "

She laughed softly.

"But your mother may not be as supportive as I am, you understand. She hated country living. When we met in college, all she talked about was moving to a big city and staying there so her children would have the opportunities she didn't."

Amie rolled her eyes. She'd heard the story a thousand times if she'd heard it once. "Dad, I'm not talking about *living* here, although there are days when my life is so hectic that I've thought about moving somewhere quiet, slow paced."

"In that case, try North Carolina," he quipped. "I was there on business last week and even the fast food is slow."

"Oh, Dad," Amie chided him, smiling. "Be serious now."

He chuckled. "All right. Well, let's see. . .money? That's your first concern."

"I might have an investor. But I emphasize the word 'might.' " She paused. "His name is Tom Anderson. He's a nice guy. Very helpful, and I think he'd be the perfect person to run the hotel." *I just have to convince him of it,* she added silently.

"Okay, Princess, I trust your judgment."

"And Uncle Hal left me some of his investments. I don't know what they're worth, though."

"Stocks? Mutual funds?"

"I don't know. Let me get them."

Amie fished through all the papers she'd acquired since opening her uncle's safe deposit box yesterday. One by one, she read them to her father who promised to do some research for her.

"I'll also talk to my friend, Bill Reeser, the architect. I'll see if he can come up with a few designs for us to look at."

"Thanks, Dad. Let him know that I want my hotel to include an antique shop, banquet hall, café, and indoor swimming pool."

"Anything else?" he asked on a facetious note.

"Well, rooms, of course."

"Very funny, young lady."

"A veritable chip off the old block, huh, Dad?" she teased.

He chuckled. Then, after a moment's pause, he asked, "Why an antique shop. . .and all the rest? Perhaps those could be added later."

"Oh no, Dad. We'll need those things to draw tourists. Antique shops are big up here, and Tom is fabulous at refinishing furniture. It'll be a great attraction for the hotel. After the tourists stop, we'll have to feed them, so we'll need the café—and, of course we'll have to offer a continental breakfast to our guests. I thought the indoor swimming pool could be a community attraction. We can rent it out for special occasions like kids' birthday parties. The same with the banquet hall."

"Take a breath, Amie," her father joked. "You're going to hyperventilate."

She pursed her lips, realizing she'd been babbling like a silly little brook. "Sorry about that. I guess I'm just excited."

"I guess. But it's not the worst thing in the world to be enthusiastic about a new business adventure, you know."

She smiled. "Thanks for understanding."

"You bet."

"Will you talk to Mom for me?"

"Soften the blow, you mean?"

"Something like that." Amie wondered if her mother would be the next to hyperventilate.

"Yes, I'll speak with her. Don't worry."

"Thanks, Dad."

Amie hung up the telephone and took a deep breath, experiencing God's peace that passed all understanding. This was God's will. She was certain of it.

Ever since last night, after meeting with Tom over colas, she hadn't been able to sleep or even concentrate. It was as if there were a disturbing, nagging swell in her chest that wouldn't go away.

Until she made her decision.

She would build a hotel.

Smiling, she grabbed her purse and left the motel room for her uncle's gas station and yet another meeting with the reclusive Tom Anderson.

❧

"I have to talk to you."

The words were spoken in unison.

Amie giggled. "You first."

"No, no, ladies first," Tom insisted.

"Well, okay."

She climbed out of her car and stood beside Tom, who had immediately met her as she drove into the station. He looked rested and his eyes seemed to have lost some of their sadness. He was dressed better than yesterday when she'd first seen him, and he appeared showered and shaved.

She tipped her head. "Could we talk over coffee. . .and maybe a sweet roll?"

Tom grinned. "You eat a lot for a woman, know that?"

"Excuse me! I haven't had breakfast yet!"

He laughed in a way Amie had never heard. She narrowed her gaze. "Why are you so happy today?"

"I'm not so happy," he replied, a hint of a smile still on his face. "You're just awfully fun to tease."

"Yeah? Well, remind me never to let you and my father in the same room together. He loves to tease me too."

Tom appeared a bit chagrined, glancing at the pavement before looking back at her. "I've got a pot of coffee upstairs and some doughnuts." He assessed her thoughtfully, then added, "If that's okay with you."

She hesitated, but just for a moment. "That'll be fine. Thanks."

As she followed Tom to the front door, a nightmarish recollection flashed through her mind. *Stop it,* she warned herself. But in the next moment, her step faltered as she remembered something more—it was a statement made by one of the women leading a Bible study at church. "Good girls don't get raped," she'd declared adamantly. "It's the girls who put themselves in compromising situations who end up getting hurt."

The woman might have been more sensitive, had she been aware of Amie's past. Nevertheless, those words haunted her. Had she put herself in a "compromising situation" three years ago? Yes. Obviously. And it was all her fault.

Don't think about that now, she chided herself again. But it was no use; she couldn't seem to shake the horrible memory of that night.

"Tom?" Amie reached for his arm, fighting down the sudden panic.

He stopped and turned expectantly.

36

"Do you think we could. . ." She scanned the property. "I mean, it's a nice day, and. . ."

"Want to have coffee at the picnic table around back?" he asked as if divining her thoughts.

She nearly fainted with relief. "That'd be great."

He nodded. "Be right back."

The shaking began as it always did; however, by the time Tom returned carrying a mug of coffee in each hand and a box of chocolate doughnuts under one arm, it had dissipated. Her composure was back. Amie watched as he pulled out packets of powered cream and sugar before sitting down at the picnic table.

"Wasn't sure how you like your coffee," he explained, taking a seat at last.

"Cream and sugar—both." She managed a smile, grateful that Tom didn't treat her like some lunatic. But perhaps he hadn't noticed.

"Okay, you start."

She ripped open a creamer and cleared her throat. "I've decided to build a hotel," she blurted. "And I've decided that you're going to help me. Now, don't argue, Tom. Hear me out, first. I don't mean to be presumptuous; it's just that I *need* you. . .to run the antique shop in my hotel—*our* hotel." She gave him a shy smile. "See, I, um, need your money too."

Tom gawked at her in obvious disbelief.

"I know I'm dumping all this on you, but I really think it'll be a great investment for the both of us." She looked at him askance. "What do you think?"

"I think. . ." He shook his head. "I can't believe what I'm hearing. That's what I think."

Amie winced. "You don't like my idea?'

"No! I mean, yes. Yes, I like your idea." Tom seemed temporarily abashed. But then he grinned. "That's exactly what I wanted to talk to you about. Building your hotel."

"*Our* hotel," she corrected him.

"Our hotel." He scratched his head. "That sounds weird." His hazel eyes suddenly searched her face for several long moments. "I'd like a chance at this," he said earnestly. "I'd like a partnership. I don't know anything about running a hotel and. . .and an antique shop. . ." He paused. "An antique shop." He spoke the words reverently, and an almost dreamy expression appeared on his face.

"I take it you approve of that notion."

"Sure!"

Amie chuckled and sipped her coffee. This was the most reaction she'd ever seen from him.

"I'm a fast learner," Tom continued. "Maybe I could take some management courses to get my feet wet, so to speak. I won't let you down."

"I see," she stated lightly. "You're not a bad salesman, either." Lifting a doughnut from the box, she added, "You're hired."

"So are you," he retorted, extending his right hand. "Partners?"

Amie smiled broadly. "Partners."

Chapter 6

Amie and Tom spent the remainder of Saturday going through the laundromat, sifting through everything Hal had collected over the years. They quickly agreed they were off to a good start in gathering merchandise for their antique shop.

"I know a farmer who'll let me rent part of his shed for storage," Tom said, looking around at all the pieces of furniture. "He won't charge much. I'll start hauling stuff over next week. Obviously, I'm going to have to empty the buildings before we can get a demolition crew out here."

Amie nodded, wondering what she'd ever do without Tom helping her out and offering to be a partner. Besides the financial aspect, her career wouldn't afford her the time to haul and sort. She was glad Tom would be here to do it.

Later, after a picnic supper of microwaved hot dogs—Tom playing the gourmet cook—he allowed her to go up to the apartment alone and box up her uncle's personal belongings.

Entering the bedroom, Amie's gaze immediately fell to the framed photographs on the dresser. One was her own college graduation picture and, next to it, was a photo of Tom, his hair much shorter. He wore a suit that looked as if it had seen better days and, standing beside him, was a younger-looking man in a graduation robe. Both men sported broad smiles.

Setting down the frame, she considered the other snapshots. A woman's black-and-white portrait—probably Hal's wife. Amie recalled hearing the tragic story of the young woman's drowning while on their honeymoon, but it wasn't something her uncle candidly discussed, and as a little girl, she'd often wondered about the incident.

Opening the dresser drawers, Amie emptied them. Then she removed all the clothing from Hai's wardrobe, deciding his garments could go to charity. Glancing around the room, she determined the oak bedroom set that Tom had sanded and varnished could go to Dottie since she'd been coveting some of the furniture. Tom already said he didn't care. Anything in this room was hers to do with as she pleased.

The packing of books on the wooden shelf became her next task. Boxing them up, Amie noticed the three hard-bound journals. *Uncle Hal kept diaries,* she mused, feeling somewhat surprised. He'd never seemed like the kind of man who'd record his thoughts. Marveling at her find, she ran a hand across one volume's smooth red surface. She leafed through it briefly, and then purposed to read all three of the memoirs when she had a free evening or weekend—whenever that might be.

Placing the books into the box, she finished loading the others before gently laying the photographs on top.

Wiping her dusty hands on her colorful broomstick skirt, Amie surveyed the room one last time with a pang of sadness. Much of her uncle's life had just been packed into three large boxes.

❧

Sunday dawned another glorious summer day. Tom invited Amie to attend worship service in a tiny country church in Morris, an outlying, rural community. Amie remembered it well. It was the church in which her uncle's funeral had been held.

Sitting in the hard, wooden pew, she was once again captivated by the charm of the sanctuary, from its polished planked floors to the antiquated pipe organ in the far right corner. Amie found it amazing that the simplicity of her surroundings roused in her an inexplicable sense of inner peace.

Moments later, the youthful-looking pastor began the service with prayer, after which the congregation stood, opened their hymnals to page 270, and sang:

> *My soul in sad exile was out on life's sea,*
> *So burdened with sin and distrest,*
> *Till I heard a sweet voice saying, "Make me your choice!"*
> *And I entered the Haven of Rest.*

Although she'd sung this song dozens of times, today the words touched a tender chord in Amie's heart.

> *I've anchored my soul in the Haven of Rest,*
> *I'll sail the wide seas no more;*
> *The tempest may sweep o'er the wild, stormy deep—*
> *In Jesus I'm safe ever more.*

The pastor returned to the pulpit and delivered an enlightening message, but all the while the hymn's lyrics swirled around in Amie's head.

The Haven of Rest.

Suddenly she knew what to name the hotel—that was, if her partner agreed.

After the service ended, Tom introduced Amie to the minister, his wife, and their four darling little girls, Emma, Carol, Ellen, and Lucy.

"I'm sorry you have to go back to Chicago so soon," Katie Warren, the pastor's wife, said. "I hope you'll visit us again sometime." Her voice sounded as soft as the light brown curls looked in her hair.

Amie smiled. "I'll probably be back in a couple of weeks."

"Oh? Is there more to do in settling your uncle's affairs?"

"Yes, quite a lot more, actually," she replied. "Tom and I. . . well. . ." Amie didn't want to say too much about their hotel endeavor at this point. There were still the legalities to straighten out. "I guess I'm not exactly sure where to start." She turned to Tom. "Probably the Village Hall, don't you think? We're going to need some kind of permit."

"I'll find out," Tom answered. He moistened his lips and looked at the pastor. "There's, um, something I'd like to talk to you about."

Jake Warren's auburn brows shot up in surprise. "Why, Tom, you little sneak!" He chuckled jovially, his gaze moving between the two of them. "Hal's niece, huh?" He whacked Tom on the back affectionately. "I sure was fond of your uncle," he said to Amie. "He spoke of you often. And now you're going to marry our Tom—Hal would have been pleased as punch!"

"I beg your pardon?" Amie gasped.

Tom's hazel eyes were as wide as saucers as he grasped the pastor's meaning. "No, no, Pastor," he quickly tried to explain. "You've got it all wrong. We're not getting married. Not yet. I mean, to each other. . .we're not." He swallowed hard and Amie fought the urge to giggle. "We're building a hotel. Amie and me. . .partners. Business partners. That's what I wanted to speak to you about. You know. . .to get godly counsel."

"Oh, I see." The disappointment on his freckled face was clear, and Amie felt her face flush in embarrassment.

"Oh, I'm sure you two'll end up getting married someday," Katie stated sweetly. Then she frowned. "Oh. I didn't mean it that way. To each other. Necessarily." She cleared her throat uncomfortably. "I meant, I'm sure that someday you'll get married to whomever God has chosen for you."

Amie nodded for the sake of propriety. But, after her past, she'd begun to wonder if there was a decent Christian man alive who'd want to marry her.

Folding her arms tightly, she let her gaze wander around the chapel. "This is such a pretty little church," she murmured, desperate for a change of subject.

"We love it here," Katie told her, her own relief apparent.

"Well, Tom," Pastor Warren began, "drop by anytime and we'll discuss whatever is on your heart."

"Thanks," he said with a slight grin.

They both turned to leave when a plump, elderly lady with tightly coiled gray hair approached them. "Did you say you're getting married, Tom?" she asked. "How wonderful!" Turning to Amie, she added, "Tom is such a nice young man.

It's a pity he's had such a hard life. I'm so glad he's finally found a pretty girl to settle down with."

"Thank you, but, um—"

"We are not getting married, Mrs. Jensen," Tom fairly hollered into the poor woman's left ear. "She's hard of hearing," he explained with a quick glance at Amie.

"Oh."

"This is Hal's niece, Amie Potter," he continued loudly. "She's here for the weekend. . .on business."

The elderly woman frowned. "You're not getting married? Bette Jo Christensen said she heard you were. She heard Pastor Warren say that, just now."

"Good grief," Tom mumbled irritably.

Amie couldn't conceal her mirth a moment longer and burst into a fit of laughter.

Tom shook his head and then hugged the old lady around the shoulders. "A misunderstanding, Mrs. Jensen. Have a good day."

"Thank you, Tom." She pouted slightly. "I just wish you were getting married." With one final glance at Amie, she added, "He really is a nice young fellow."

"Yes, I know he is," she replied, following Tom to the door. When the old woman became preoccupied with talking to another parishioner, Amie turned to Tom. "I noticed *she* doesn't have a low opinion of you."

"Mrs. Jensen was my kindergarten teacher. She still thinks I'm the best finger painter in all of northern Wisconsin."

Amie chuckled softly as they descended the many steps leading to the gravel lot.

"This isn't funny," he told her on a note of exasperation. "Do you understand now what I mean about gossip starting and spreading around here like the Bubonic Plague?"

"Don't fret, Tom," she countered sassily. "Perhaps Pastor Warren will make an announcement from the pulpit next Sunday and dispel the rumors. Or maybe he can take out an ad in the local newspaper."

He shook his index finger at her. "You're gonna be sorry you laughed about this, Amie. Mark my words."

She rolled her eyes. "Lighten up, Tom. It's a hoot." His expression remained grim, so she continued, "You and I haven't done anything to bring gossip down upon our heads. This is harmless—a comedy of errors—and it'll get straightened out soon enough."

"Yeah, sure," he replied, looking none too convinced.

"By the way, I thought of a name for our hotel."

He lifted his brows expectantly. "Oh? And what's that?"

"The Haven of Rest." She smiled proudly.

He repeated it a couple of times. "I like it. The Haven of Rest."

"Great." They stood behind Amie's red BMW. "Well, I guess I'll see you in a couple weeks," she said, opening her purse and pulling out her keys. "I'm sorry I can't get up here sooner. I'm so busy at work."

"That's okay. I've got your e-mail address and phone number, and you've got mine."

A couple of boys, obviously junior-high age, suddenly peeked around the van parked next to Amie's car and began to make smooching noises. Tom took a deep breath, his face reddening with indignation.

Amie didn't even attempt to hide her laughter as she disengaged the alarm system. "Just remember," she said, climbing into her uncomfortably hot car, "self-control! Fruit of the Spirit and all that."

"Easy for you to say, *Miss Chicago*. I'm the one left here to deal with this mess." She gave him a careless shrug, just to tease him all the more.

But then, as she made her way down the little dirt road, heading out to the highway, it occurred to her that not even Tom Anderson, a man who thought of himself as a loser, would want a woman like her for a wife. Chaste and virtuous, that's what single Christian men were looking for in a woman.

Amie thought about the singles group she belonged to at church. They were forever pledging their purity until marriage when the pastor spoke on the topic. But each time the altar call signaled such a response from her, she felt like a hypocrite.

She stepped on the accelerator. Tom was right. This situation was not funny. Not funny at all!

❧

The next week passed quickly for Amie. She barely had time to think, let alone make decisions about the impending hotel project. Her boss, Tim Daley, dumped two new accounts on her, forcing her to put in twelve-hour days at the office and take work home at night. Finally, on Sunday afternoon, otherwise known as "family time," she was able to get her mind off Maxwell Brothers' Marketing and Developing Company for at least a few hours.

"You look a bit peaked, dear," her mother said, furrowing her silver brows in concern. "Are you eating enough?"

"Mom, I could live off my fat for months," Amie teased.

"Nonsense."

"She'll eat tonight," John Potter told his wife. "I'm throwing steaks on the grill."

"Oh, yum!"

Her father winked. "Just for you, Princess. And after dinner, I'll show you the sketches Bill Reeser drew up for your hotel."

"Great." She took a seat in her parents' newly remodeled kitchen. The brightly papered walls added splashes of color to the otherwise stark-white room. Seeing her mother's immaculate countertops made Amie feel like a terrible housekeeper. She'd been too busy and, as a result, her condo was a complete disaster.

"Sweetheart, your father told me all about your plans—and you know how he loves a challenge, but I wish you'd reconsider," Lillian said, pulling a pitcher of lemonade out of the refrigerator. "Property values are rapidly depreciating up there. The community is largely impoverished."

"Then perhaps my hotel will help the local economy."

"Perhaps," Lillian stated carefully as she poured the chilled drink into two frosted crystal glasses. "Or you could lose everything, Amie. You're taking quite a risk."

She shrugged. "Nothing ventured, nothing gained."

Her mother lifted a well-shaped brow. "Nothing ventured, nothing lost."

Amie chose not to reply as she accepted the offered glass of lemonade. She'd known her mother wouldn't be much of a cheerleader. She'd even surmised that Lillian Potter would try to talk her out of building the hotel. However, her mind was made up.

"Mom, look, it isn't like I'm making some rash decision. I've thought about this. . .prayed about this."

"All right, dear," Lillian remarked, looking skeptical.

"Hey, how's Stephen doing?" she asked, attempting to distract her mother from the subject of the hotel. "Does he still like college?"

"Loves it. Got an A on his first biology quiz."

"Good for him."

"He's always done well in school. In fact, when Stephen was in first grade—"

Dottie suddenly burst through the back door, capturing their attention.

"Amie, you've got to be nuts!" she declared loudly. "Dad just told me you're building a hotel in Tigerton. Of all the places in the world, why you'd choose that town is beyond me!"

"Lemonade, dear?" Lillian asked her younger daughter, who nodded as she marched over and stood beside Amie.

"You ought to have your head examined," she rambled on. "And when can I pick up my furniture?"

Amie sighed. So much for a peaceful evening with the folks at home.

Chapter 7

When Amie got back to her condo, she felt somewhat discouraged. She wondered if she had, indeed, made a mistake in deciding to build a hotel. Only her father seemed enthusiastic, but she quickly reminded herself that was the way it usually was with her family. Seldom did her mother and Dottie agree with Amie's decisions, and for some odd reason, their lack of support overshadowed her father's exuberance.

Setting her purse on the kitchen table, Amie walked into the spare bedroom that served as her home office. She flipped on the computer and began to check her E-mail messages, feeling pleasantly surprised to see one from Tom.

Hi, Amie,

Hope you had a nice weekend. Here's the update so far. I got most of Hal's junk cleared out of the two buildings. A lot of it was trash, but the majority of it can be salvaged. I had to rent a storage unit in Shawano. Herb Mahlberg's shed was too small. (By the way, I set aside more furniture for your sister.)

I should be moved out by the end of August. Pastor Jake said I could move into the church basement temporarily. The Tigerton town council meets once a month. If the vote goes through, the property should be ready for demolition some time in October. I talked to a couple of construction companies, and both said they could start building in the spring, provided the plans have been approved by the state. Guess we'd better get the plans together.

Smiling, Amie immediately typed a reply, informing Tom of the structural designs her father's friend had drawn up. She promised to mail him copies and described the layout she liked best. *Nice work, Tom,* she wrote. *You're a fast mover! What would I do without you?*

She clicked on SEND and sat back in her chair, suddenly feeling exited about this endeavor again.

❧

Tom stood across the highway as the last of the golden leaves on the elm trees rustled overhead. The temperature was in the mid-fifties and the gusty wind had a nip to it. He glanced at his booted feet and the surrounding dried vegetation. Fall had arrived, and everything was dying off. Even the October sunshine had grown distant.

At the sound of roaring machinery, he turned his gaze back to the gas station and garage where he'd worked for the past thirteen years of his life. The huge gasoline tanks had been dug out last week and now the final razing of the buildings would occur.

Shaking his head in wonder, Tom forced himself to remember. That's why he'd come here today—to watch and reminisce. One last time, then never again. He caught his breath as the bulldozer slammed into one of the walls. It seemed like a million years ago since he'd walked into Hal's office and asked for employment.

"So you want a job, huh?"

"Yes, sir," Tom had replied, feeling more than a little intimidated. Everywhere he'd applied, he'd been turned down. This was his last chance, and it had taken him over an hour to get his courage up enough to walk in. Halvor Holm, known around town as "Hal," had a reputation for being a harsh, no-nonsense guy. Tom had never known anyone who'd asked him for a job. No one had the audacity! However, Tom felt desperate. He'd been rudely awakened to the fact that if he didn't support his family, nobody else would. It was up to him. His youngest siblings were counting on him—particularly six-year-old Matthew.

"Know anything about cars?"

"Just that you gotta put gas in 'em."

Hal pursed his lips in thought. "Gotta put oil in 'em too. And a few other things."

"Yes, sir." He looked up into Hal's grizzled face, thinking his Norwegian blue eyes were almost startling in contrast. Then they scrutinized him so hard that Tom squirmed.

"Aren't you one of those Anderson kids?"

Reluctantly, he nodded. Once more, his reputation had preceded him. It looked like this job was shot too.

"Your younger brother busted my window the other day. Pitched a rock clean through it."

Tom shifted uncomfortably. "I, uh, didn't know that. Must have been Phillip. I. . .I'll see that he comes back and fixes it."

"Hmm. . .you do that. And I suppose you're not aware that your dad stole fifty dollars from me either. He took it right out of the till while I was fixing the pop machine out front. That guy's got a lot of nerve, I'll say!"

"He stole your money?" Tom's stomach flipped. He'd wondered where the groceries came from. And the bottle of whiskey.

"What's that bruise under your eye? Were you in a fight? Are you one of those kids who uses his fists instead of his brains?"

Any further hopes for a job flew straight out the broken window. "I'd better get going. Thanks anyway."

"Now, hold on a second."

He paused.

"I asked you a question," Hal said sternly, "and I expect an honest answer. Whether you knew about the broken window and the money doesn't matter to me as long as you tell me the truth."

"I didn't pick a fight. My pa hit me," Tom blurted, staring Hal straight in the eye. "But he didn't mean it. He was drunk. He's not a bad man, he's just. . .just not been right since Mom died." He swallowed his shame over what his family had become. "As for the window and the money, I didn't know about either one, till now."

After a moment's deliberation, Hal nodded. "Okay. I believe you." He rubbed his whiskered chin. "You still in school?"

"Uh-huh."

"Can you drive?"

"Legally?"

Hal grinned wryly. "Yeah, legally."

"I don't have my license, but I can drive. Real good too."

"Well, we're going to have to get you your license, son."

Tom's brows shot up. "We are?"

"Yep. I'll need you to fetch parts once in awhile."

"You will?"

Hal extended his wide, oil-stained hand. "You got a job if you want one."

The bulldozer made another hard hit against the side of the apartment building and laundromat, pulling Tom's thoughts to the present. The splintering of wood and the spray of shattered glass echoed in the chill of the autumn afternoon. They weren't unfamiliar sounds, and suddenly he recalled a time when his father hurled a kitchen chair across the room, destroying one of the few framed photographs that hung on the wall, but not before it struck Tom in the shoulder. Hal's place had been a safe haven for him back then—a place where he went to lick his wounds. It was also where he'd come to a saving knowledge of Christ. Under Hal's fatherly and biblical counsel, Tom had learned to forgive. He'd also relearned how to laugh.

So many memories were made and stored up there, Tom reflected, as a good portion of the old apartment building crumbled. *Nearly as many memories as there was junk!*

Even so, he couldn't say he was completely grieved to see the decrepit structures knocked to the ground because with them went his past. There was only one thing left to do now: Rebuild.

❧

Amie climbed out of her car and inhaled sharply when she saw the flattened land that had once accommodated her uncle's filling station. The frosty November wind blew her hair into her face. She pushed it back in vain. She couldn't imagine why she was so surprised to see the buildings gone. Tom, her faithful partner, had phoned her on the day of the demolition. Since then, he'd kept her up to date on everything from finances and town hall meetings to calls inquiring about the state's approval of their hotel plans. Still a little part of her was sad to see her uncle's place actually. . .gone. Only a thin white layer of snow covering two mounds of brown dirt hinted at where buildings once stood on Uncle Hal's property.

"But it's my property now," she reminded herself. "Mine and Tom's."

Glancing at her watch, she gasped. If she didn't hurry, she'd be late for the Thanksgiving dinner at the Warrens'!

Jumping back into her car, she sped down County Highway J and on into the rural town of Morris. Farms, fields, and gently rolling hills stretched out before her. She made a turn and then another, passing the little white country church. Finally, she reached the Warrens' driveway.

Accelerating up the hill, she spotted Tom's truck and cringed inwardly. On several occasions, he'd accused her of living life in the "fast lane," and Amie couldn't deny it. She seemed to rush everywhere she went, and more often than not, she was late in getting there. Recently, however, she'd come to hate her hectic schedule and frequently felt like a caged gerbil, spinning its wheels.

Last night, she'd promised Tom she wouldn't be late today—but she was.

Throwing the car into park, Amie grabbed her purse and coat, then practically fell out of the BMW in her haste. As she reached the front porch of the single-story ranch home, the door opened and Katie Warren smiled kindly.

"Welcome, Amie."

"Thanks," she replied, breathlessly. "Sorry I'm late."

"Oh, you're not late. I just took the turkey out of the oven."

Amie smiled gratefully as the slim brunette hung up her wool, full-length coat. She turned and smiled. "Come with me. I want to introduce you to all our guests."

Following her hostess into the parsonage's modestly decorated living room, she noticed two elderly, white-headed ladies sitting on the couch along with a bald, wrinkled man who was propped at the other end. To her right, an attractive, young, and very pregnant woman with shoulder-length, frosted hair looked as though she'd sunk into the armchair, and Tom was perched on the piano bench across the room.

Amie sent him a subtle wave, immediately aware of his haircut and clean-shaven face. In reply, he mouthed, "You're late."

She grimaced.

"This is Mrs. Helen Baumgarten," Katie began, "and Mrs. Louise Gunderson and her husband, Harold. And over here," she added, indicating the expectant mother, "is Mrs. Nancy Simonson whose husband, Al, is deer hunting. Now, I'll leave you all to get acquainted while I finish preparing dinner. Everything's just about ready."

After Katie left the room, Amie acknowledged everyone with a polite nod and a smile. She strolled over to the piano bench, taking a seat next to Tom who, unlike herself, hadn't overdressed for the occasion. Amie figured they made quite a contrast with him wearing a pair of faded jeans and a navy, long-sleeved shirt and her in a black-and-white checked Christian Dior dress with matching jacket.

She shifted her weight on the hard bench and gave Tom a tiny smile. For some odd reason, she felt suddenly awkward around him, even though they'd been corresponding for months. She chanced another peek in his direction, deciding his facial features seemed much different than she remembered. He looked well-groomed, his handsome features quite apparent now that they weren't hidden behind whiskers and long hair. His hazel eyes didn't seem so sad—so haunted. But curiously, Tom's improved image only boosted her perplexing emotions. Why did she feel shy and self-conscious around him when, by phone or E-mail, she'd been very comfortable? It was as though they'd gotten to know each other a little better on the inside, but they were still strangers on the outside.

"Lots of traffic on the road today?" Tom asked, his arm inadvertently brushing against her shoulder.

Amie gave him a guilty look. "No, I just slept through my alarm."

"I told you. . . ," he stated softly, a teasing light in his eyes.

"I know. I know. . ." She immediately recalled how last night, when she'd telephoned to ask directions to the Warrens' house, he'd warned her not to stay up late, working on her newest account. He predicted she'd oversleep—and she did. "I guess I should have listened to you."

She suddenly caught a whiff of his pleasant-smelling cologne and remembered what he'd said in one of his previous e-mail messages. *It feels strange not to reek of gasoline anymore.*

"So, you guys are getting married, huh?" Nancy Simonson half asked, half stated, her light-brown gaze alternating between the two of them.

"Married?" Amie brought her chin back in surprise. "Is that silly rumor still floating around?"

Tom threw her a dubious glance as his entire countenance reddened.

"I take it that's a 'yes.' "

He grinned wryly. "Yes."

"Yes, you guys are getting married?"

Tom groaned. "No, we're not getting married. Yes, the rumor is still floating around."

Nancy furrowed her brows, looking confused.

"We're just business partners," Amie expounded further, quickly sucking her bottom lip between her teeth so she wouldn't start chattering incessantly.

"Oh," Nancy replied. "Yeah, I guess I'd heard that too."

"If you aren't getting married, are you *engaged* to be married?" Mrs. Baumgarten, the sturdier of the two aging women, asked. "Couples these days seem to have to think about it for a long time." She nudged the frail woman beside her. "Don't they, Louise?"

"Mercy, yes!" she exclaimed shakily. "Why, I just read an article in 'Reader's Digest' on that very subject."

"Well, don't think about it too long, sonny," old Mr. Gunderson at the end of the couch piped in. "You might lose your sweetheart to another fella. Women don't like to wait, you know. They want a commitment."

"Yes, sir, I'll remember that," Tom replied, giving Amie a helpless shrug. It seemed he'd given up trying to explain the circumstances surrounding their relationship.

But the gleam in Nancy's eyes seemed to express her understanding of the situation.

And then Amie began to wonder. . .Simonson. Al Simonson. Where had she heard that name before?

"Have we met?" she asked the young mother.

"You met Al in Shawano," Tom cut in. "Remember? Big Al?"

She thought it over and suddenly the image of Popeye's friend, Brutus, came to mind. "Oh, yes."

"How did you meet Al?" Nancy wanted to know.

"It was last summer. Tom and I were in Shawano. . .on business," Amie stated carefully so no more misunderstandings could erupt. She felt like her nerves were getting the best of her and she decided not to say another word, lest she babble on for hours.

"Al was there for a baseball tournament," Tom explained. "He'd told me about it a couple of days before we saw him. Guess his team ended up winning too."

"Right." Nancy said with a roll of her eyes. "The baseball tournament."

"So you're from Chicago. . .Amie, is it?" Mrs. Gunderson asked.

She nodded.

"Is your family there too?"

Again, she merely gave a nod, not trusting herself to reply in words.

"Amie's folks went to Hawaii for Thanksgiving," Tom informed them, much to Amie's relief. "Her sister is celebrating Thanksgiving with her fiancé, and her brother is away at college." He glanced over at her. "Did I get that right?"

Another nod.

"Oh, my! Well, I'm glad you came up here for the holiday," said Mrs. Baumgarten. "Now you don't have to be alone."

The word "alone" reverberated in Amie's heart. Even as she reminded herself that Jesus always stood beside her in spirit, she couldn't deny the fact that she felt lonely. Sighing inwardly, she came back around to the same conclusion: Singleness was her God-given lot in life. Her cross to bear. But, oh! How she'd love to be married and expecting a baby like Nancy.

Suddenly seven little girls ran into the room, laughing, jumping, and squealing. Four of the children Amie recognized as the Warrens' girls, and the rest, she assumed, belonged to the Simonsons.

"Mama says dinner's ready," Emma announced. She was obviously the oldest of the group, therefore, the spokesperson.

Everyone rose from their places, and Amie watched as Tom politely extended a hand to help Nancy up from the deep-seated armchair.

"Why, thanks." She turned to Amie. "I guess chivalry isn't dead after all." She paused before conspiratorially adding, "You'd never know that by the way my husband acts. When Betsy, our youngest, was born, Al said he hated girls. Can you believe that? He *hates* them!"

With a shake of her head in reply, Amie looked at Tom who was currently helping the senior citizens to the dining room.

Nancy followed her gaze and continued, "Back in high school, Tom had a crush on me. But I didn't know it until a few years ago. He never even asked me out! What was I supposed to do, read his mind?" She paused, gazing at him thoughtfully. "I wished you would have asked me on a date, Tom. I should have married you."

Something tugged at Amie's heartstrings as she wondered whether Tom ever got over his crush. Then she berated herself for even pondering such things! Tom Anderson's personal life was none of her concern. They were partners—professional business partners!

She glanced over at him while he seated Mr. Gunderson. The discomfort Tom obvious felt about this topic was clearly etched on his features.

"Don't even go there, Nancy," he told her. "We're all praying for Al. Once God saves his soul, he'll do right by you and the kids."

"Yeah, sure," she replied doubtfully.

"Now, Nancy," Mrs. Baumgarten said with admonition in her voice, "we're to pray *believing* that God will do all we ask. Why, my great niece had a spouse who was an awful carouser, but once he became a Christian, he turned into a wonderful family man. The same can happen for you."

At that moment, Pastor Jake Warren entered the dining room carrying the turkey, already sliced and on a porcelain platter. Setting it down on the table, he looked over at Amie. "Well, hello! I'm sorry I haven't been much of a host. Katie's kept me busy in the kitchen."

"No need to apologize," she stated, forcing herself not to say any more.

"Now *there's* a family man for ya!" Mr. Gunderson declared. "It's only out of love and sacrifice that the good pastor helps in the kitchen." He laughed, producing a hoarse, wheezing sound.

"Thanks, Harold," Jake replied jovially. Then he clasped his hands together. "Okay, the girls prayed over their food and are eating in the kitchen, so let's thank the Lord and dig in!"

"Amen!" the old man exclaimed.

Everyone chuckled and Katie entered the room. They took hands, Tom holding Amie's left and Nancy, her right. Then the pastor began to pray. But all the while, Amie couldn't stop thinking of how warm Tom's fingers felt as they enveloped her own.

Lord, I'm behaving so foolishly. Help me to control my emotions—and my tongue. Give me laryngitis if You have to, Father God. Do anything to keep me from babbling like an idiot because I'm. . .I'm. . .oh! I don't know what's the matter with me!

When Tom gave her hand a gentle squeeze, Amie knew the dinner prayer had ended. Lifting her head, she opened her eyes and found him gazing at her curiously.

Finally, he indicated the chair he held out for her and grinned sheepishly. "Are you going to sit down or eat standing up?"

She quickly took the seat, her heart pounding in embarrassment, and immediately concluded that this afternoon would be a long one!

Chapter 8

Amie walked out to her BMW in the frozen night air with Tom at her side. A full moon guided their way. "You really didn't have to see me to my car, but thanks."

"Sure."

She looked up, amazed at how sharp and clear the stars appeared without Chicago's city lights and pollution hindering their brilliance. "Wow," she breathed, "get a load of God's creation."

Tom briefly gazed at the twinkling sky. "It's something, all right."

Reaching her vehicle, Amie attempted to disengage her alarm, only to realize she'd never set it. "I was in such a hurry. . ."

"What?"

"I didn't activate my car alarm."

"Nobody would steal your. . .*hot rod* around here," he teased, the moonlight illuminating his features. "In fact, Pastor Jake has a habit of leaving his keys in the ignition when he parks his minivan."

Amie blinked in wonder. "I couldn't do that in Chicago."

"No doubt."

Opening the door, she threw her purse onto the passenger seat.

"Okay, one more time," Tom said earnestly. "How 'bout staying overnight with the Warrens like you planned? It took you a good four hours to get up here, and it's another four to get home. . .that's a long drive for a turkey dinner. Why don't you get some sleep and leave tomorrow morning?"

Amie sighed. "I can't."

"You can't? Or you don't want to?"

"I *can't*. I've got so much work at the office."

"Amie, you've got to slow down. You look. . .worn out."

She rolled her eyes. "And *you* sound like my mother."

He stuck his hands into his heavy jacket. "Well, see, that just proves I'm right."

With a derisive little snort, she climbed into her car and started the engine.

"Hey, let me ask you something before you go."

"Sure." She got back out and closed the door. "I should let my car warm up anyway."

He nodded and seemed to carefully weigh his next words. "Is everything okay, Amie? I mean, you haven't changed your mind about the hotel, have you?"

"No!" She smiled. "I mean, yes, everything's fine and, no, I haven't changed my mind."

"The rumor about us. . .you, know, about us getting married," he stammered, "is it bothering you? I've done my best to set things straight, but folks keep asking me the same questions!" He groaned dramatically. "I just can't believe it!"

"That piece of gossip doesn't upset me, Tom," she stated contritely. "But I do feel badly for you, having to deal with it."

He waved away her comment. "Aw, I don't care anymore either."

"You might if you knew about. . ." Then her words faltered. How could she tell him about what had happened? Shame flooded her and her face grew red. "Oh, never mind."

Amie hadn't ever talked to anybody about what had happened to her three years ago, and the desire to share her past with a friend who'd understand was getting more and more difficult to suppress. After all of their phone calls and E-mails, she was beginning to wonder if maybe *Tom* would understand.

Knock it off, Amie, she inwardly berated herself.

"If I knew about. . .what?" Tom persisted.

"Just forget it."

He narrowed his gaze. "Did Nancy's talk about her marital problems bug you?"

"Not at all." Amie shook her head. "Everything's fine!"

"Well, *something's* wrong!" Tom countered, sounding close to exasperation. "You haven't said more than a dozen words today. That's not like you!"

"I was trying not to babble," she confessed. "You know how I get when I'm nervous. I can't seem to shut up! I didn't want to do that today. I always feel so stupid afterwards. . . ."

She clamped her lips together while Tom chuckled softly.

"Amie, nobody would have cared if you 'babbled,' " he said at last. "Least of all me."

"Thanks."

Tom shifted his weight and the snow crunched beneath his boots. "Well, all right, then. . .um. . .call me when you get home so I don't worry."

"Yes, *Mother,*" she replied facetiously, feeling more like her old self for the first time all day. "Oh, and by the way, I don't think the people of Tigerton look down their noses at you, Tom. Everything I heard about you this afternoon pertained to your good attributes and nothing less." She paused, collecting her wits. "It only affirmed what I already knew."

He glanced at the cold, hard ground, before meeting her gaze again. "Thanks. And maybe you're right—I mean, about the folks around here." He paused momentarily as if collecting his thoughts. "My father was an alcoholic— the town drunk, to be blunt. I always felt like people held me responsible for the bad things he did when he was drinking because I was the oldest. The kids at school never let me forget that the Andersons were 'trash' and somewhere along the line I believed them."

"Oh, Tom." Amie's heart ached for him.

"But I've been counseling with the pastor about it. Got a lot of things settled." He chuckled lightly. "Now that I'm living in the church basement until our hotel gets built, I've had plenty of opportunities to talk with Pastor Jake—while we paint the sanctuary and repair the pews, among other things."

"I'm glad for you. . .that you have someone like the pastor to confide in."

"Yeah."

She smiled, a little envious. "Well, I'd better get going. . . besides, it's freezing out here!"

"Didn't mean to talk your ear off."

"You didn't," Amie assured him. "In fact, I'm glad you told me more about yourself. It helps me get to know you better. After all, we are business partners and business partners should know each other, right?"

"Right."

"And I'm babbling again."

Tom laughed. "I think your habit is rubbing off on me!"

Giving him a hooded glance, Amie climbed into her car again and he politely closed the door after her. Backing out of the driveway, she tooted the horn twice before speeding toward the highway. But for many miles, she speculated whether the day would really come when she could finally tell somebody about that horrible night.

❧

The snow fell heavily and Amie watched it from the third floor window of her downtown Chicago office. Common sense told her to leave work and park her car safely in the underground garage attached to her condominium lest it be buried by a plow. But she didn't dare leave early. Not today. Something was up. Amie sensed it.

All day she'd had a feeling of impending doom, and she knew the reason why. She'd blown an account last week, and although it hadn't been entirely her fault, upper management wasn't pleased. Worse, her ears still burned from her boss's severe reprimand a few days ago. She couldn't blame him for being angry with her. In spite of putting in nearly sixty-five hours a week for two months straight, she hadn't been able to produce an acceptable marketing strategy for Wagg's Dog Food. Every slogan she dreamed up sounded too cliché for her clients' liking. *Your pooch's tail will wag when you serve him Wagg's Dog Food.* She sighed inwardly.

It had been the best she could do, but it was far below her usual standard. Even Amie knew that.

Just then Tim Daley, director of the marketing department, entered her office, and she solemnly turned from the window.

"It's a winter wonderland out there," he stated, wearing a plastic smile. It was a sure sign that unpleasant business followed.

"What's up?" she asked, her heart hammering anxiously.

"We—ell," he closed the door and sat down in the adjacent chair, "I had a long talk with Kirk Maxwell, and we've decided that in the best interest of the company we. . .we have to let you go. I'm so sorry. And here it's right before Christmas too."

"Let me go?" Amie suddenly felt as if her whole world was crashing down around her.

"I tried to go to bat for you," Tim insisted, "but Kirk was adamant. . .and you know Kirk."

"Okay, I know I blew a big account," she said desperately, "but it won't happen again. Give me another chance. I'm a hard worker. Haven't I proved that to this company?"

"You *were* a hard worker. You were one of our best creative consultants." He shook his golden head sadly. "But I've been watching you lately. You're here, but you're not. Your mind is elsewhere. Personally, I think you're distracted by that hotel nonsense. It's all you talk about."

"My hotel has nothing to do with my position here," Amie stated vehemently, wondering why she felt the need to defend that part of her life. Except she wanted to save her job with Maxwell Brothers' Marketing and Development Company.

"I disagree."

She closed her eyes, seething inside.

"Look, I'm sorry," Tim said. "I wish things were different. But there is good news: Kirk prepared a severance package that'll get you through the holidays."

"Great," she replied evenly. Rising from her desk chair, she scanned the small office through tear-filled eyes. "I guess I'll need some boxes so I can pack my things."

"Sure. I'll go see what I can find." He stood and walked out of the office, leaving Amie with a bitter taste in her mouth and a sinking feeling in her heart.

≈≈

Tom glanced at his watch and realized Amie had been talking for a half hour straight! He shifted the telephone receiver to the other ear. Shortly after Jake summoned him to the phone and Amie told him about losing her job, a complete and utter helplessness engulfed him. What could he say to console her? *Help me, Lord,* he prayed silently.

"Can you even believe such a thing? Those jerks!"

"Listen, you've got to calm down. You're only going to make yourself sick by rehashing everything that happened this afternoon."

"I can't help it. I just had to talk to somebody. That's why I called you. Oh, maybe I shouldn't have bothered you with this."

"No, Amie, I told you before; it's okay."

"What am I going to do?" she lamented. "I'm ashamed to tell my family that I got. . .*fired*. How humiliating!"

He heard her begin to weep softly and his heart broke. "Aw, Amie, don't cry. Everything'll be all right. Things might look bad, but God's still in control."

Tom knew the words were trite and overused, yet they were the only ones he could think of.

"How will I pay my mortgage? How will I live?"

"Sell that condo and move up here!" he blurted. An instant later, he wanted to bite off his tongue for saying such a foolish thing.

"Sell my condo?" Amie sniffed. "Yeah, I guess I could do that."

"Well, think about it," he said lamely. "Pray about it."

She paused momentarily. "You know it might work, Tom. I could sell this place and live with my parents until the hotel is built. Maybe God wants me to put all my energy into our venture, instead of killing myself for those ungrateful scoundrels at MBMD."

"Yeah, maybe. I'll admit, I've been worried about you, burning the midnight oil and all."

"Yeah, and a lot of good it did me!" She paused. "Do you think we could work together, Tom?" she asked in a broken little voice that tugged on his sensibilities in the most peculiar way.

"Of course," he replied adamantly. "We're already working together."

"But I mean. . .if I moved up there?"

"Sure." *Except the architectural plans include just one apartment,* Tom wanted to remind her, since he had no intention of living in the church basement forever. On the other hand, he didn't want to make her feel any worse.

"I always thought of myself as the proverbial 'silent partner,' " she admitted. "I figured I would continue with my career in Chicago and just check on my investment from time to time while you'd run the hotel."

Tom didn't know how to reply. He'd assumed much the same; however, the thought of having Amie around wasn't an unpleasant one, other than they'd have to decide which of them got the apartment. "Everything will work out."

"Promise?"

"Promise." He detected in her voice that she needed to hear something that she could hang onto, and suddenly a Bible verse came to mind. " 'All things work together for good—' "

" 'To them that love God,' " she finished for him, " 'to them who are called according to His purpose.' Romans 8:28."

Amie breathed a sigh, sounding much more relieved. "Oh, Tom, I knew you'd make me feel better. You're becoming such a good friend! Thanks."

"You're welcome," he said, his confidence on the rise. "Anytime."

Chapter 9

*T**he hurt won't go away. I can't sleep at night because every time I close my eyes I see my beloved Rachel bobbing in the ocean, gasping for breath. Why couldn't I have reached her in time? Why did she have to die? She was a good swimmer. . .how could she have drowned? We'd only been married nine days. . .*

Amie reached for a tissue and dabbed her eyes. Reading the first volume of her uncle's journals was not the light entertainment she'd needed. Although, from his writings, she was able to learn much about him. It seemed he was a very sensitive man, one with big ideas, but at the same time straight-forward, even blunt, when it came to voicing his opinions. Amie felt proud of him when she read how he'd rallied against a wealthy citizen of Tigerton who wanted to build a shameful dance hall at the end of town—and Uncle Hal won!

But that was before World War II. He'd been twenty-six years old when he enlisted in the Air Force. He got shot down and spent several months in a military hospital in London. There he'd met Rachel.

I never had much use for religion, Hal had written, *and now I wonder if there even is a God, because if He really existed, He wouldn't have taken away the one person who meant everything to me.*

Mulling over what she'd just read, Amie realized her uncle must have become a believer later in life. No doubt the Lord used that tragedy to bring Uncle Hal closer to Himself.

The telephone rang, startling her from the colorful floral-printed sofa. She rose from her comfy position, berating herself for not having her portable phone within an arm's distance, and walked to it where lay on the dining room table.

She pressed the TALK button. "Hello?"

"What are you doing, you bum? Lying around, eating bonbons, and watching soap operas?"

Amie rolled her eyes. "Hi, Dad."

He laughed. "Say, Princess, one of the guys at work here had a secretary quit. Want a job?"

"Secretary?" She wrinkled her nose distastefully. "No way."

"But why?

"B.O.R.I.N.G."

"Now, Amie, I'd like you to at least consider this tremendous employment opportunity. Buzz is a great guy to work for."

"Oh, yeah," she replied smartly, walking over the lush, off-white carpeting and making her way back to the couch, "then why'd his secretary quit?"

"She didn't get enough roses on Secretary's Day; I don't know why she quit! But, just between you and me, she was something of a ding-dong."

"I don't know, Dad." Amie collapsed into a pool of multicolored throw pillows. "I really just want to concentrate on building the hotel, and then I'll work there. Tom suggested that I run the café while he manages the antique shop, and we'll both check in guests. Of course, we'll need to hire other personnel too."

"Well, that's just peachy, but you can't even *start* building until at least. . . what, June? And then it will take months to actually construct the place." Her father paused. "Amie, you'll be lucky if you're able to hold a grand opening next Christmas Eve. That's a year from tomorrow. What are you going to do with yourself till then?"

She smirked. "Lie around, eat bonbons, and watch soap operas."

"Very funny, young lady!"

This time *she* laughed.

"Now, look, I'm serious—"

"Thanks, but no thanks."

"Paid benefits and eight dollars and fifty cents an hour."

"What? I can't live on that!" She shook her head, marveling at her father's ludicrous proposition. "That's a mere third of my salary at MBMD."

"Honey, let me remind you that you're selling your condo and moving in with Mom and me."

She relented somewhat. "Yeah, I suppose I won't have too many expenses—"

"Any money you make you can put toward your hotel adventure. Buzz is aware that you wouldn't be around forever."

"Hmm. . ." Amie paused and began to consider the offer. "Can I pray about it?"

"Of course. I'll give you till five o'clock." With that her father hung up.

Amie glanced at the mahogany grandfather clock in the corner of her posh living room. *Thanks, Dad,* she thought sarcastically.

It was four-thirty.

❧

Tom sat at the dining room table of the Warrens' home and sipped his coffee.

"Dessert?" Katie asked.

"No, I'm stuffed after that meatloaf dinner." He smiled graciously. "You're a great cook."

She blushed, looking pleased. "Why, thank you."

"Yeah, sure beats frozen entrees, hon," Jake teased his wife.

"Oh, you!" she replied with a tiny laugh before walking into the kitchen.

The girls had finished eating long ago and were now playing in their bedrooms. Periodically a high-pitched giggle floated down the hallway, and as much as Tom dined with the Warrens lately, he was used to hearing it. He was also getting a taste of how a healthy family behaved, although up until the age of twelve, his home life wasn't the dysfunctional mess it had become after his mother died.

"All set for the holidays, Tom?"

He lifted his gaze to the pastor. "I think so."

"Did Amie decide whether she's going to drive up for Christmas?

"Yep. She said she'd come." He sipped his coffee. "Her family doesn't know the Lord, and they celebrate by going to Florida for a couple of weeks."

Jake furrowed his auburn brows. "Weren't her parents recently on vacation in Hawaii?"

"Yeah, but I guess that was more business than pleasure. Amie's dad had to work, so her mom just went along."

"I see." He sat forward, his forearms on the table, as a lock of his reddish-brown hair flopped onto his high forehead. "And Amie doesn't want to go to Florida with her family?"

"Nope. Guess she never does. She told me she usually finds someone from her church family to spend Christmas with, but this year she didn't have the time to ask around. So it all worked out that she'll come up here."

A surge of anticipation coursed through Tom's veins—as it did whenever she phoned or e-mailed lately. He wasn't quite sure what to make of these tumultuous feelings he'd developed for Hal's niece. He hadn't experienced anything like them since high school. Surely he was too old to have a crush on Amie like he'd had on Nancy. Regardless, he didn't think any more than a professional friendship was warranted, under the present circumstances. Besides, Amie Potter was a woman way out of his league.

"So," Jake said, his cobalt eyes gleaming with mischief, "are you planning to take Amie. . .out. . .somewhere?"

He smirked. *Suddenly half the town is playing matchmaker*, he thought cynically. Glancing at the pastor, he answered, "I'm not planing any candlelight dinners, but Amie and I have an appointment on Saturday to see an attorney and legalize our partnership. That's about as 'out' as I'm taking her."

"Tom, you old romantic, you!" Jake razzed, getting up from his chair. "An attorney open on Saturday, huh?"

"It's Jim Henderson, Hal's lawyer, and I guess he's doing us a special favor since Amie will be in town and because he'll be on vacation for the next two weeks."

"I see; well, it's good to hear that Amie can spend Christmas with us, anyway," Jake stated more soberly now. "I know Katie will look forward to having her around for a few days. It's nice that she doesn't have to rush right back to Chicago."

"Uh-huh." Tom stood, following the pastor's lead; however, a host of clamorous emotions still wreaked havoc in his heart. He went from infatuation with Amie to grieving Hal's death—and seemed to stop at everything in between!

"You ready to take a look at my van?"

Tom gave himself a mental shake. "Ready when you are."

"Great. I can't get the thing started. Don't know what it could be. . ." Jake paused, giving him a friendly slap on the back. "It sure is a blessing to have you around."

"No, Pastor," Tom replied sincerely, "it's a blessing to *be* around. You and Katie make me feel like part of your family. Thanks."

"You are a part of our family. You're my brother in Christ and we're all in God's family."

"Right. But it's kind of hard when a guy loses his best friend. Especially around the holidays. I mean, Hal was my best friend *and* my family—except for Matt."

"And what a blessing that your younger brother can take time from his job and college education and visit us at Christmastime too. But I understand your sense of loss," the pastor said, throwing a fraternal arm around Tom's shoulders as the pair walked to the garage, attached to the parsonage. "It's going to be painful for a while."

Tom inhaled deeply as they reached the minivan. "Yeah, painful is right!"

❧

The trip to Tigerton wasn't as hectic as the last time Amie had made it. In fact, it wasn't rushed at all. In the past four days, since her termination from Maxwell Brothers', she'd been able to relax, read through two of her uncle's journals, and now she felt thoroughly rested and all set to celebrate the Savior's birth!

She passed the future site of the hotel, now covered in a thick blanket of snow, and a thrill of expectancy traveled up her spine. The construction company Tom had painstakingly chosen said a crew could probably start excavation as soon as the end of March or early April. But already Amie was ordering catalogues, anxious to select the decor.

Minutes later, she pulled into the Warrens' driveway. Climbing out of the BMW, she opened the back door and withdrew several colorfully wrapped boxes.

"Welcome, Amie!" Katie called from the opened garage. "Want some help?"

"That'd be great. Here. . ." She immediately filled her new friend's arms with boxes.

"What's all this?"

"Presents!" Smiling, Amie shrugged helplessly. "I always go overboard at Christmas."

"Oh no. . .you shouldn't have!"

"Maybe not, but I love to buy gifts. I hope Tom likes his. . .oh! and wait till you see what I got the girls!"

Katie rolled her honey-brown eyes. "You'll spoil them—"

"I bought you and Pastor Jake something too."

"You'll spoil all of us!"

"Good. You deserve it." Amie paused, and the gratitude that filled her being threatened to spill over in the form of sentimental tears. She'd been so certain that she would have to spend Christmas alone. Either that or endure a Florida vacation with her family, listening to her mother, Dottie, and Stephen badger her endlessly about how foolish she was for building a hotel in this hick town. "Thanks for inviting me to share your holiday."

"Oh, you're welcome. This will be so much fun!"

After attempting a no-handed hug, Katie laughed softly while Amie turned to extract the remaining presents from the backseat. With her arms filled, she met Jake near the porch. He took the packages from her and scolded her the same way Katie had only moments ago.

"You shouldn't have done this!"

"But I wanted to! Besides, my mother taught me that guests who show up empty-handed are rude. . .and I already disobeyed her at Thanksgiving."

"All we expected you to bring, Amie, was yourself."

"And here I am," she replied lightly, returning to the car and opening her trunk. "Along with a few other things. . ."

"You mean there's more?"

"Uh-huh. But I think I can get the rest."

She removed the last three Christmas surprises and then lifted out her luggage. As she followed the pastor into the house, she could hear the girls' excited exclamations, and already, she knew this would be a Christmas she'd never forget.

Chapter 10

After Pastor Warren left the parsonage to prepare for the night's Christmas Eve Vespers Service, the girls managed to coerce their mother into allowing them to open one present. Of course they chose Amie's gifts—the newest under the evergreen tree decorated with handmade ornaments.

Amie watched in delight as eight little hands excitedly tore at the colorful wrapping paper, revealing the clear plastic boxes containing Madame Alexander dolls, each representing one of Louisa May Alcott's *Little Women*.

"Oh, Amie, how generous of you!" Katie exclaimed, looking as impressed as the girls.

"I couldn't help myself," she replied, hunkering beside little Ellen and freeing *Beth* from her plastic restraints. "When I saw these dolls at a boutique in Chicago, I just knew I had to buy them for the girls."

As Katie began explaining to her daughters about the dolls' value and that they weren't toys but keepsakes, Amie wondered if she'd ever have a little girl of her own. At twenty-six years old, she still had plenty of child-bearing years ahead of her—

Suddenly a horrid memory flashed through her mind. An empty sanctuary filled with her uncontrolled weeping. "Please, God, don't let me be pregnant!"

A heavy sadness spread across her chest when she had stood. The Lord had honored her request, yet her heart ached and tears threatened at what she perceived as His punishment. While she had friends who were blessed by their singleness, Amie felt cursed.

No husband.

No children.

"Amie, are you okay?"

She snapped out of her musings to find Katie and the girls staring at her with concerned expressions. She forced a smile and swatted at an errant tear. "Oh, I'm fine. I just. . ." She swallowed. "I'm just so glad the girls like their gifts."

"Oh, we do!" cried Emma, obviously trying to make her feel better.

Amie felt like a fool as she glanced around the living room adorned with the children's drawings and cut-out snowflakes from red and green construction paper. Her new friends were likely to think she was a nut case—and maybe she was. Why else would those haunting remembrances plague her in the midst of a joyous celebration?

"Well," she said, looking back at Katie and shifting uncomfortably, "I guess I'll go change for church."

"You do that. Feel free to lie down if you're tired."

"Thanks. I think I'll do that."

"And, Amie?"

She turned back around. "Yes?"

"Don't be too hard on yourself. . .I mean about whatever's troubling you. You're probably still recovering from working all those long hours."

Amie blinked back an onset of fresh tears but could only manage to nod in agreement.

"You've got so much to look forward to, what with building that hotel. Why, the entire town is buzzing with excitement!"

This time Amie actually smiled.

"And I can't begin to tell you what your partnership has done for Tom. It's like he's a. . .a new man." Katie took a step closer. "What I mean is, he's been a believer for years but he never stepped out in faith before. He was always too afraid of what people might say to give in to God's promptings. But now he's trusting the Lord to direct his paths, instead of letting that old insecurity stifle him. Isn't that wonderful?" She grinned impishly. "Just for the record, I'm not tattling or gossiping. Tom himself stood up and gave that very testimony during the last mid-week worship service. Jake and I were so encouraged. We think God's going to use what Tom said to light some fires in other Christians' souls!"

"How amazing," Amie replied, slightly envious that her partner could experience such inner healing. At the same time, she was happy for him. His melancholy was what she'd liked the least about him when they first met. But lately it seemed to be the very thing she liked the least about herself. Up until now, she'd kept so busy she never had time to think about her past. Oh, she remembered well enough. But she quickly suppressed each awful memory as soon as it took form, locking it tightly inside herself. Perhaps, that secret hiding place had begun to overflow. Perhaps her panic attacks were the result. . . .

If I could just talk to somebody, she thought as desperation tweaked her heart. *Another Christian—but not some indifferent psychologist and not dear, sweet Katie who'd probably faint in horror, or my pastor's wife who'd most likely shun me for being a bad girl in the wrong place at the wrong time.* She sighed inwardly. *I just have to find someone who'll understand.*

"I'll stop foaming at the mouth," Katie announced in her soft voice, penetrating Amie's thoughts. "You rest and change clothes. I'll knock on your door when we're ready to leave."

Amie nodded and resumed walking down the hall.

The bedroom she would occupy during her stay was, in actuality, a nook that served as a sewing room too. Pattern pieces were stacked neatly beside the machine, and portions of material lay in an orderly fashion on half of a long, narrow table. The other half sported Amie's suitcase.

Opening it, she pulled out the clothes on hangers, hoping they hadn't gotten too wrinkled from the trip. She hung them on the brightly colored plastic hooks, mounted on the wall since the room didn't have a closet.

Dear Lord, she prayed silently, lying down on the single bed, intending to take just a short fifteen-minute rest, *I know You are good and everything You do is good. I know You are love and that You love me—enough to die for me. But I have so many questions and so many feelings boxed up inside. I need You to answer them, Lord. Please help me.*

Amie dozed, awaking with a start a half hour later. She swung her legs off the bed and grabbed the long, full black skirt she planned to wear tonight along with a belted red, silk tunic and black vest. After she dressed, she pulled up her blond hair, fastening it on top of her head with a red ribbon and allowing it to spill down in a chic mess of curls. She was just putting the finishing touches on her makeup, using a small hand-held mirror, when Katie knocked.

"Ready to go, Amie?"

She opened the door. "Ready."

"Oh, you look pretty!"

"Pretty. . .what?" she teased. "Pretty ridiculous?"

Katie giggled, putting a hand over her mouth, and Amie noticed her simple red dress with its white lacy collar. "You look pretty *pretty*," she replied, still smiling. "But we'd better leave now if the girls are going to be on time."

The walk to church was a short one since the quaint structure was located just beyond a row of pine trees that separated the cemetery from the Warrens' home. Inside, the place bustled with activity as they hung their winter coats in the cloak room. Excited voices echoed from little children, hustling to the front of the sanctuary to receive last-minute instructions from the music director. In her haste to get out of the kids' way, Amie nearly bypassed Tom, who was standing in the doorway, passing out programs.

"Merry Christmas," he said pointedly, leaning slightly forward.

"Oh!" She felt herself blush. "Merry Christmas. I didn't see you there. . . ."

Katie was right behind her. "Did you save us some seats, Tom?"

He nodded, handing each of them a program. "First pew on the left."

"Thanks." She gave him a grateful smile before looping her elbow around Amie's. "This place is packed on Christmas and Easter," she remarked, as they glided forward, little Lucy in tow. "Jake always wishes he could get the same crowd in every Sunday."

"I'll bet."

Reaching the pew, marked as saved by a row of hymnals, Amie was hard pressed not to turn around and take a second, more appreciative glance at Tom. In his khaki tan slacks, forest green dress shirt and tan, red, and green speckled tie, he looked quite the "new man" as Katie had said earlier.

Meanwhile, the church filled rapidly. Then, at precisely six o'clock, Pastor Warren stepped up to the pulpit. "Merry Christmas, ladies and gentlemen. Tonight is a special service with special music and readings from our children. But first, let's open in prayer."

Amie bowed her head, eyes closed, and after the last "Amen!" she looked up to find Tom beside her. They ex-changed polite smiles before sitting down, Tom positioned on the end. With him next to her, Amie experienced that same awkward feeling she had at Thanksgiving. It almost seemed as if each time she and Tom saw each other, they had to get reacquainted. Phone calls and E-mails just didn't match face-to-face communication.

A group of kindergarten-aged children were lined up on the stairs below the podium. They began to sing "Silent Night," their cherubic voices ringing throughout the small sanctuary. Amie smiled just as Katie nudged her.

"Can you move over?" she whispered. "The Morrisons need a place to sit."

Nodding, Amie scooted down, causing Tom to slide over.

The children finished their song and stepped off the makeshift platform as the next group came up. Amie guessed they were the elementary group.

"Amie, can you move over a little more?" Katie asked softly, pulling Lucy onto her lap. "Here comes Mr. Morrison."

Nodding, but skeptical, since the aisles were filled with people in folding chairs, she inched closer to Tom. He had no place to go but up against the end of the pew. "Sorry," she told him under her breath.

Beneath the dimmed lights, she caught a slight accommodating grin as he shifted his weight to one side and stretched his arm along the top of the pew. She knew it was a necessary gesture if he hoped to obtain any measure of comfort, yet Amie got so flustered, she barely heard the children's chorus of "Away in the Manger." She kept imagining Tom's arm around her in a display of affection, though it was hardly that. She stiffened, then slowly realized it felt rather pleasant to sit so close to him.

The tension in her muscles ebbed as a group of junior- and senior-high kids spread out on the stairs and began reciting select Scripture passages from the second chapter of Luke. "And it came to pass in those days, that there went out a decree from Caesar Augustus that all the world should be taxed. . .and Joseph also went up from Galilee. . .To be taxed with Mary his espoused wife, being great with child. . .And she brought forth her firstborn son, and wrapped him in swaddling clothes, and laid him in a manger. . ."

By the time the young people were ending their segment with an enthusiastic rendition of "God Rest Ye Merry, Gentle-men," she had relaxed against Tom. But it was hardly the romantic setting it might have been since Katie and Lucy were fairly lounging against her too, causing Amie to feel like the middle domino. But at least she was no longer so uptight about the seating arrangement. She only hoped Tom wasn't getting squashed!

Minutes later, Jake stepped forward and gave a brief message, encouraging unbelievers to "repent and be saved."

"Just as our teens sang only moments ago: 'Remember Christ our Savior was born on Christmas Day to save us all from Satan's power when we were gone astray. . . .'" He paused momentarily. "I urge you folks who aren't born again to make this Christmas a celebration to remember for all eternity. Ask the Lord Jesus, Who came to this earth as an infant and died as a man so our sins would be forgiven—ask Him into your hearts today." He smiled at the congregation. "Let's bow for prayer. . . ."

The Christmas vespers service ended and everyone rose from the pews as the woman at the old pipe organ played "O Come, All Ye Faithful." Amie finally turned to Tom.

"I hope you weren't totally squished for the last half hour."

A little smile curved his lips and his face reddened slightly. "I think I survived. Thanks."

Deciding he'd been as uncomfortable as she in the beginning, Amie dropped the subject. She turned and started making her way toward the center aisle when she bumped into Nancy Simonson.

"I was just coming over to say Merry Christmas to the Warrens," the expectant mother said. Her light brown gaze did a quick assessment of Amie's attire before she smiled. "Nice to see you again."

"Same here." She looked at Nancy's protruding middle, covered by the green maternity sweater. "I never did ask—when's your baby due?"

"The end of May."

"And it better be a boy too!" Al exclaimed, emerging from seemingly nowhere. He now stood blocking half the aisle and staring at Amie through a dark, piercing gaze that sent a shiver of fright up her spine.

Then in one sudden motion he leaned toward her, his right hand extended, and she stepped back anxiously. As she did, her heel landed on someone's foot. Fighting for balance, she felt a pair of strong hands steady her.

"Well, Tomboy, Merry Christmas."

"Same to you."

Amie heard his voice just behind her ear before he leaned forward and shook Al's hand, still dangling out in front of him.

She breathed a sigh of relief.

Just then Katie appeared. Nancy gave her a hug and the two began to chat.

"Sorry I stepped on you," Amie stated over her shoulder.

"Not a problem," Tom replied easily.

Big Al smirked. "Don't worry, he's used to getting stepped on. Whole town used to step on him, till he inherited a lot of money. Now suddenly Tomboy's not such a loser."

Amie stood there, aghast. She'd never met anyone so blatantly rude.

Al laughed. "Aw, I'm just kidding." He moved sideways and rapped Tom on the shoulder. "Me and him's known each other since seventh grade."

Amie opened her mouth to retort but thought better of it. The last time she'd smarted off to "Brutus," Tom hadn't appreciated it.

A few moments of uncomfortable silence passed and then Al commanded Nancy to the car. He turned and left, allowing his pregnant wife to gather up the children and follow behind, pausing only to get them bundled before heading out into the cold.

Feeling disgusted, Amie turned to gauge Tom's reaction and found him observing Nancy with an intent expression. Were those clouds of compassion in his hazel eyes, or was that something else she saw?

He's still in love with her? Amie thought, wondering why she should even care. Tom had his own life to live. So did she! They were just business partners!

Finally he glanced her way and grinned solemnly. "Guess I'd better help Pastor Jake pick up the folding chairs."

She just nodded, watching him walk away.

Chapter 11

S now flurries danced crazily in the night air, illuminated only by the church's solitary yard light as Amie and Tom trudged to the Warrens' house. Katie and the children had gone on ahead, but the pastor was still in the sanctuary, counseling a parishioner.

As they walked the short distance, a weighted silence hung between them, and Amie found herself wishing vehemently that she didn't care so much about Tom. Moreover, she wished she didn't enjoy the feeling of sitting so close to him. Then, of course, there was the way he always seemed to understand. He was the first man she could ever remember talking to so candidly about everything—well, *almost* everything.

They reached the gravel driveway of the Warrens' home, and suddenly Tom paused. "Amie, can I ask you something?"

"Sure."

He tarried an instant more, as if collecting his thoughts, while a faint bulb beside the front door cast a shadow across his features. "Amie," he began again, "are you afraid of men?"

The directness of his question stunned her, and she groped for a reply. "Well, it. . .it's not so much that I'm afraid of men per se," she stammered. "It's that I get. . .well, just sort of. . .oh, I don't know. . .I get edgy, I guess. . ."

He rubbed his jaw, and even in the darkness, she saw his thoughtful concern. "So, in a word. . .yes."

She shrugged, unable to disagree. But then, in an effort not to appear the weak, simpering female, she quickly added, "I'm not afraid of *all* men, just some men. . .until I get to know them. A single woman can't be too careful, you know. The world is filled with lunatics!"

"Well," he stated, looking down at his booted feet, "I don't think you're afraid of me—at least not anymore."

"No. . ."

An idea began to form as she watched the snowflakes accumulate in Tom's dark brown hair. Perhaps he would be the one who'd understand. . .about that night. . . .

Tom lifted his gaze. "And I don't think you need to be afraid of Al," he continued. "You heard him tonight. We've known each other since junior high, and

70

I'll admit he gets to me sometimes, but I can tell you firsthand that Big Al's bark is all he's got. There is no bite."

Any hope of confiding in Tom shattered like a piece of fine Baccarat crystal. *Didn't you see that look in his eyes?* Amie wanted to scream at him. But she didn't utter a sound. He'd never understand. No one ever would.

Beneath her red wool, full-length coat, her shoulders sagged in defeat. She turned away from him and began walking toward the Warrens' front door.

"Amie, hold on."

She quickened her pace and managed to enter the house before Tom could stop her. He arrived just an instant later.

"There you two are!" Katie exclaimed. She looked past them. "But where's Jake?"

"He'll be along shortly," Tom said, panting slightly. "Someone at church cornered him after the service."

Katie sucked in her lower lip, looking troubled. "Was it Mr. Tucker?"

Tom nodded.

"Oh, that poor man. His wife is in a nursing home, and he just doesn't know what to do without her. Fortunately, he does have a sister who lives nearby."

Amie hung up her coat, ignoring Tom's gesture to help, and walked on ahead into the living room.

"By the way, the girls are upstairs, changing into their nighties," Katie informed them. "When Jake gets home, he'll light the fireplace, and then we can open presents. Meanwhile, I'll finish getting supper ready."

Amie was quick to volunteer in the kitchen, and Tom supposed she was angry with him. *Don't have to hit me over the head with a brick*, he thought sardonically, taking a seat on the sofa.

He tried to think of what triggered her "cold shoulder." Defending Al? Why would that be such a major deal? Big Al could be surly, and he rarely had a good word to say about Tom—especially in front of others, but he'd never hurt anybody, at least not physically.

Tom picked up a magazine, flipping through it sightlessly. He thought about Nancy, who had only recently become a Christian. Al's shameless insensitivity was hurting her, no doubt about it. It was painful for their whole congregation to watch, and yet, in seeing the Simonsons' misery, he'd come to realize those feelings of desolation didn't just belong to him. If he trusted God to pull him up by his bootstraps, couldn't he then be used to help others? Like the Simonsons?

Lord, make me a success story, he often prayed these days, *so I can be a blessing to others.*

Now, if he could only figure out what to do about Amie.

Tossing the periodical back onto the coffee table, Tom wondered over their growing friendship. Was it just a friendship? Perhaps, on her part; however, tonight in church he could scarcely concentrate on the Christmas program, what with Amie sitting right up beside him. A few nights ago Jake had teased him about asking her for a date, and since then he'd done little else but imagine doing exactly that. How was he ever going to run a hotel with her around?

Amie entered the room, causing Tom a good measure of trepidation. He hated the thought of any sort of confrontation, yet he longed to set things straight. Sitting forward with forearms on his knees, he watched her settle in the adjacent armchair. As much as he tried to catch her eye, she wouldn't look at him.

He cleared his throat. "Um, Amie. . .look, I'm sorry if I offended you."

She glanced down at her lap, picking at her black skirt. "You didn't offend me."

"Okay." Tom sat back, puzzled. "Well, could you tell me what happened then? I mean, everything seemed fine until I mentioned Big Al."

Her blue-eyed gaze snapped to his. "I don't *like* him," she said vehemently.

Tom nodded. "Yeah, I sort of got that impression." He rubbed his rough chin contemplatively. "To tell you the truth, he's not exactly one of my favorite people either."

"Then why do you insist on defending him? Personally, I think you ought to punch him in the nose." She sat back with a huff. "Or maybe I will."

He grinned, trying to imagine that. "Listen, Amie, we're supposed to turn the other cheek as Christians, not retaliate. I don't like what Al says about me—I'll admit it's humiliating. But I'm trying to keep the whole picture in mind. Nancy's a new Christian, and she wants Al to get saved too. If I treat him the same way he treats me, what's that going to prove?"

Amie blushed, looking properly chagrined.

Tom shifted self-consciously, having to tell her the next bit of information. "Um. . .I suppose you best be aware that it's Big Al's company I selected for the construction of our hotel."

"What?" At this she stood, fists clenched at her side. "Are you out of your mind? That. . .that *brute* doesn't deserve our business!"

Tom rose from the sofa and swallowed hard. "I didn't deserve God's saving grace, but I got it anyway."

"That's different."

"Maybe. But the Simonsons need the money."

"Oh, so that's it. You're hiring Al for Nancy's sake. Why didn't you just say that in the first place!"

He was momentarily taken aback by her venomous tone—mostly because he didn't know where it came from. "I thought you liked Nancy."

She closed her eyes for a brief instant, then shook her head apologetically.

"I'm sorry. I do like Nancy. I don't know what's the matter with me."

Lowering his chin, Tom blindly studied the coffee table as some of the old insecurities and discouragements came prowling back. Should he have consulted her first? She'd only met Al once. She told him to choose the construction company. . . but maybe she was right. Maybe he shouldn't have selected Al's corporation.

"I prayed about it," he stated, looking over at her again. It was the truth, yet it sounded so lame.

She folded her arms. "I don't like him," she said once more. He saw her chin quiver slightly and guessed she was still afraid.

"Al does a good job," he tried to assure her. "And you won't have to see him often. He stays mostly in his office."

She rolled her eyes. "I suppose you've signed the contract."

He nodded. "Right after I had Jim Henderson look it over."

"Well, what's done is done. I'll just have to deal with it."

She crossed the room, glanced out the door, walked back, and stood right in front of him, glaring into his face. Positioned just inches away, Tom decided she was the most beautiful woman he'd ever seen. Her indigo eyes sparkled with unshed fury, and her cheeks were heated to a lovely color that nearly matched her red blouse.

"Tom, I don't like this. I don't like Al! He gives me the creeps! I think you should forget about—"

"You're so pretty when you're angry," he mumbled, barely aware that he'd voiced the thought.

She gave him a quelling look, putting her hands on her hips. "Don't try to change the subject."

Tom felt entranced. Was there even a remote possibility? No. He didn't have a chance with a woman like Amie Potter.

"Will you listen to me?" She was obviously working hard to stay angry. But a moment later, she burst into a fit of giggles, surprising Tom right out of his catalepsy. "Oh, you nut!" she said between chortles. "You are just like my dad. Every time he gets me upset and I try to give him a piece of my mind, he ends up making me laugh!"

Combing his fingers through his hair, Tom was relieved that she wasn't perturbed anymore, though he was more than a little baffled about this whole thing—his feelings for Amie included.

She sighed, her mirth fading. "We'll work it out, won't we?"

"Yeah. . .sure we will."

The front door suddenly opened, and Pastor Warren stepped into the house, shaking the snow out of his auburn hair and brushing it off the shoulders of his black wool coat. "It's really coming down out there," he said in a robust tone. Then, just as heartily, he added, "I hope supper's ready. I'm starved."

Katie's voice echoed from the dining room. "It's all set. I'll just call the girls, and we can eat."

Supper consisted of homemade vegetable soup and freshly baked bread. The girls barely touched their portions, being so excited about the gifts under the tree. But Jake made them sit politely while the adults finished up, and Amie was impressed by their good behavior.

When at last the meal was finished, everyone ambled into the living room, Emma, Carol, Ellen, and Lucy running on ahead. Katie dispersed the gifts, making piles for her enthused daughters. When her laden arms deposited a couple on Amie's lap, she glanced up in surprise.

"For me?"

Katie nodded, smiling and appearing almost as excited as the children.

Sitting at one end of the sofa, Jake dug right in and ripped open his gift with fervor. "A coffee mug!" he exclaimed, proudly showing it off. "Thank you, Amie. I'll pray for you each time I drink my morning coffee from it."

She smiled. "You're welcome."

Tom opened up his present. It was a thick, quality knit sweater, predominantly green in color but having other shades interwoven throughout. She had selected it with his hazel eyes in mind.

"Thanks," he said, looking over at her from the adjacent arm chair. "Just what I need."

"Good," she replied, feeling a bit embarrassed.

"That, um, top one's from me," he informed her, raising his voice slightly to be heard above the din of the four little girls, squealing with delight.

Amie looked down at the large, square, neatly wrapped box in her lap. "From you?" She carefully lifted the taped edges and then removed the colorful candy cane decorated paper, inhaling sharply when she spied what lay beneath it. "Oh...," she breathed, viewing the darkly stained wooden jewelry box. It was intricately carved on the sides and on top. She opened the lid, discovering the quilted patchwork piece embedded within its depths. "It's beautiful."

Crossing the room, Tom hunkered beside her chair. "I discovered this when I was cleaning out the laundromat," he explained. "I remembered when Hal found the thing. It was in old Mrs. Thorbjorg's attic. The box was dried out, the bottom of it severely cracked. When she died, her family stuck it in a heap of rubbish on the side of the road, and that's where your uncle picked it up."

Tom fingered the etchings. "You told me when we first met that you wished you'd known your uncle better; well, he was a man who saw beauty in things that other folks had long decided were trash. Like this little jewelry box." He lifted his gaze to hers, his eyes taking on their sorrowful appearance. "Like me."

Amie felt hot tears threatening as she looked back at the now expertly varnished creation.

"You remind me a lot of Hal," he whispered.

That did it. A surge of emotion streamed down her cheeks. She was touched to the heart by his words and, at the same time, riddled with guilt for her earlier fit of temper. Suddenly she saw things in a different light, realizing there were a lot of people like this box, in need of repair and the Master's touch, and a vision of Big Al came to mind.

"Oh, Tom," she sniffed, holding the piece of artistry to her. "You're so thoughtful. I'll treasure this forever."

He gave her a warm smile, rising to his feet, and Amie was suddenly aware that the room had become deathly still. One quick glance around told her the entire Warren family was watching on with tender expressions—even the children.

Wiping her eyes, she gave them each a shy smile.

"I was impressed with Tom's work," Jake said. "I saw the box before and after." He shook his head. "Amazing."

"Mrs. Jensen was kind enough to make the padding inside," Tom said.

"Thank you," Amie told him as gratitude flooded her being once more.

The girls resumed tearing at their gifts. In addition to the dolls, she'd bought them one book each and a video to watch. One by one, they came over to give her a "thank you" kiss on the cheek.

Katie opened her gift, a bottle of perfumed body lotion, and then Amie unwrapped the present from the Warrens. It was a wall hanging that Katie had made with the words THE HAVEN OF REST embroidered along the top, and beneath it, Matthew 11:28: "Come unto me, all ye that labour and are heavy laden, and I will give you rest."

"This is wonderful! I'll hang it in the lobby of our hotel!" She flashed the fabric mounting at Tom, who smiled and nodded approvingly.

"Well," Katie said, getting up from the sofa, "it's time for all little girls under the age of ten to go to bed."

"Awwww. . . ," the four children replied in unison, sounding utterly disappointed. But after a pointed look from their father, they readily complied and marched off in the direction of their bedrooms.

Tom rose from his chair. "I'd better leave too. Matthew's supposed to arrive bright and early tomorrow morning."

"Matthew?" Amie asked curiously.

"My younger brother," he explained. "He's driving up from Madison. He's attending the university there—a junior this year."

Jake slung a friendly arm around his shoulders. "Spoken like a proud papa," he teased. Turning to Amie, he added, "Tom has been like a second father to Matthew."

Nodding, she recalled her uncle mentioning the young man in the beginning of his third journal.

"Jake," Katie called from down the hallway, "can you give me a hand?"

"Coming, hon." He turned to Tom. "See you tomorrow for. . . brunch?"

He grinned sheepishly. "I'll be here. And hopefully Matt will too."

The pastor left the room to help his wife, and Tom walked to the front door, pulling his coat out of the hall closet.

"See you tomorrow, huh?"

Amie nodded, leaning against the half-wall that divided the rooms. "Sorry about before. . .losing my temper. I hope you don't think I'm some kind of shrew."

"No, I don't think that at all," he said with a little chuckle.

"I see what you mean now. . .about trying to help the Simonsons."

A tiny smile curved his lips. "All's forgiven."

Their gazes locked briefly before Amie looked away. He wasn't in love with Nancy. That was apparent. She'd jumped to a false conclusion earlier tonight. One she regretted. Tom was a empathetic man with a deep understanding of the human heart. She briefly wondered if he would understand her. . .if she trusted him enough to tell him her whole story.

"Well, I'd better go," he said, opening the front door. "Merry Christmas."

"Merry Christmas, Tom."

Once he'd gone, she stared out the window after him until the falling snow covered his footprints.

Chapter 12

When Matthew Anderson arrived, he livened up Christmas Day with his quick wit and hearty laughter. It was obvious that Tom felt proud of his younger brother's achievements, and likewise, it appeared Matthew had the utmost respect for his eldest sibling.

With the men gathered in the living room, Matt talked animatedly about his latest college experiences while Amie helped Katie in the kitchen. Once the pork roast was cooked to perfection, everyone took a seat around the expanded dining room table, and Jake prayed over the food.

"This looks great!" Matt exclaimed, shoveling a fork full of mashed potatoes and gravy into his mouth. "Mmm. . .tastes even better."

Katie blushed pleasingly. "Well, thank you."

"The stuff at the university is like cardboard." Then, very suddenly, he set down his fork. "Okay, okay, you guys, something's driving me nuts. I've been waiting all afternoon for you to tell me, Tom, but since it doesn't look like that's going to happen, I'll just have to ask."

"What's that?" Tom replied, munching on his salad.

Matt smirked. "We–ell," he drawled, "I stopped by the Kelsigs' on my way into town to say hello to Laura, and what do you suppose her dad tells me?"

Tom shrugged. "What?"

"What? What, you say?" Matt threw his hands in the air in mock exasperation, causing Emma and Carol to giggle at his theatrics. "He tells me you two are getting married!" he replied, looking first at Tom, then at Amie, and back at his brother. "You don't even tell me yourself, you goon! I gotta hear it through the Tigerton grapevine! What kind of brother are you?"

Sitting across the table from him, Amie did her best to hide a smile. Tom groaned, and Jake chuckled openly from the far end.

"It's a rumor, little bro."

The younger man's face fell. "Yeah? I thought maybe you were going to tell me. . .you know, sort of my Christmas present. . . ." Matt turned to Amie. "He hasn't proposed yet?"

"Will you knock it off!" Tom told him, sounding genuinely agitated. "The Warrens might understand your warped sense of humor but Amie doesn't, and you're making her feel uncomfortable."

"Oh, sorry." Matt gave her a penitent grin. "But, um, seriously. . .Ron Kelsig really did tell me that." He looked back at Tom and resumed eating. "I figured it was just talk since you hadn't said anything to me. I mean, you've told me about your plans for the hotel and all."

Amie watched Tom nod as his gaze met hers. She noted the apology pooled in his eyes and sent him back a reassuring smile. The talk didn't bother her. In fact, she wished there was a fraction of truth to it—perhaps even more than a fraction— and the silent admission surprised her.

"I think Amie's getting used to this particular piece of gossip," Jake inferred.

Her smile grew, as did her embarrassment. It was as if the dear pastor had discerned her very thoughts.

"As for the hotel," he continued, "it's been one miracle after the other, what with all the red tape that goes along with trying to build a new establishment. But there hasn't been a single snag."

Tom agreed. "It really has been amazing."

"And while there are those in town who'll always be critical of somebody trying to do something new," Jake stated, "most everyone else is excited about Tom and Amie's new business venture."

"My father calls it our *adventure*," Amie said, chuckling lightly. "But I have to admit that Tom has done all the work so far." She turned to Matthew. "He's been absolutely wonderful. He's managed everything." She stabbed a few green beans with her fork. "Frankly, I don't know what I would have done without him."

Matthew eyed her for a moment, then turned to his brother. "You sure you haven't proposed to her yet?"

Tom scowled at him.

"I mean, if you don't want her, *I'll* marry her!"

Amie nearly choked on her dinner.

"Oh, I can just hear the gossip mill grinding on this new tidbit," Jake moaned, a sound that ran contrary to the amused twinkle in his Irish-blue eyes. "Quick, Tom, let's send this hooligan back to Madison where he belongs!"

A sudden outburst of laughter spouted from the men while the two eldest Warren girls gazed on, wide-eyed, and Amie wondered if her incredulous expression mirrored theirs.

"All right, that's enough," Katie scolded. "Poor Amie—I wouldn't blame her if she never wanted to have dinner with us again!"

"It's okay," she murmured, somewhat astonished at her soft-spoken friend's spurt of gumption.

But Katie wasn't through with her reprimands. "Now, girls, you will *not* repeat this to anyone, understand? Matthew was just joking."

"Yes, Mama," they said, their honey blond heads bobbing in unison.

The men seemed properly put in their places and, after that, no more wise-cracks ensued around the children—or Amie.

A good portion of the remaining evening was spent around the piano, Katie at the keys, singing Christmas carols and favorite hymns. Amie sat on the couch with Ellen and Lucy curled up beside her. From her vantage point, she observed the Anderson brothers undetected.

She'd heard a lot about Matthew from Tom and decided the two resembled each other in many ways—the well-defined jawline and slight cleft in the chin, the tear-shaped, hazel eyes, and dark brown hair. But where Tom's features looked almost worn beyond his twenty-nine years, Matt's features appeared rather juvenile for twenty.

Amie then remembered her uncle's journal. *Tom's the fall guy in his family,* he'd written. *Makes me sick. His childhood is gone. The boy's only seventeen years old, but he looks and acts twice his age!*

Uncle Hal hadn't given any specifics, but Amie guessed there had been physical abuse in the home. Tom openly admitted his father's alcoholism, and the diary confirmed it. Still, Tom's background didn't lessen her opinion of him. It was just as Hal had penned: *Tom isn't responsible for his father's bad decisions. Just because old Norb goes and gets drunk every night of the week, doesn't mean his oldest kid'll do the same. Tom knows the Lord now. He's got a lot of character for one so young, and I'm convinced God will guide his path. The boy knows right from wrong. He's seen the effects of his father's sin, and I don't believe Tom'll touch a drop of booze in his entire life. But there are a few strong voices in this town that go around slandering less fortunate folks who don't meet up to their hypocritical standards. It's a crying shame that Tom believes what comes out of their mouths.*

A sad chord plucked Amie's heartstrings when she thought of all Tom must have suffered. Conversely, she was grateful her uncle had been his advocate and his mentor. No wonder Tom missed his fatherly friend so much. She wondered if this Christmas holiday was especially difficult for him, then berated herself for being so insensitive that she'd never asked.

The two girls rose from the couch to play with their new toys, and Tom strolled over from where he stood near the piano.

"You look deep in thought," he said observantly, sinking into the sofa.

She sighed, unable to deny it. "Ever since I got fired, I've been so introspective."

"That's not always a bad thing."

"Maybe not, but I'm getting myself depressed."

Tom turned toward her. "About what?"

She shrugged, still unwilling to share.

"I suppose getting canned from any job is a major letdown. But you had a career, Amie. Can't really blame you for feeling bummed out about losing it."

"Thanks. . ."

"But, like we talked about before, the upside is now you can concentrate on. . . what does your dad call it? Our 'hotel adventure'?"

She smiled. "Yes, and my father also got me another job in the meantime."

Tom furrowed his brows, eyeing her curiously. "I thought you were moving up here."

"I am. . .eventually. But until construction on our hotel begins, I've got to do something with myself."

He nodded. "Yeah, I suppose. . ." After momentarily studying his folded hands, dangling off his knees, he shot her a teasing grin. "Just don't get too comfy at this new job, huh? I've gotten rather used to the idea of having my partner around."

"Don't worry," Amie replied on a slight note of sarcasm, "it's a secretarial position. You'd realize that was funny, Tom, if you had any inkling as to how disorganized I am. Besides, the job only pays eight dollars and fifty cents an hour. I'm practically working for free!"

"Eight-fifty an hour?" He shook his head, smiling slightly. "That's a better-than-average wage up here."

"Well, I don't know. Maybe it's a better-than-average wage in Chicago too. . . for a secretarial job. But it's a far cry from the salary I used to earn."

"Welcome to the real world," Tom replied facetiously.

Amie bristled, but was then reminded of the chasm between her world and his. She'd grown up with money, a stately home in a posh neighborhood, and two sophisticated parents who had handed her their elite social status. He'd grown up with nothing and no one. . .save her uncle. And yet, she couldn't say that she was any better off, or any happier. Besides, couldn't their faith bridge that social gap?

"Better rethink this partnership," Tom said, gazing at her intently, "before it's too late."

"What?" Amie felt confused.

He seemed pensive for a few long moments as he peered over at the Warrens and Matthew still singing around the piano. "I mean, Tigerton is a whole lot different than Chicago. Might even be backwards to a woman like you. Maybe you won't like living up here."

"Maybe," she replied carefully. "But I don't like living in Chicago all that much anymore. There's nothing for me in that city, and I think I've sensed it for a long time." She paused, considering him and concluding that the look on his face was one of worry. "I'm tired of living my life at such a break-neck speed, Tom. I'm looking forward to the change up here. But, I will admit, it'll probably take some getting used to."

"What about me?" he asked challengingly. "I've got a GED and in a few months I'll have three managerial courses under my belt. But that's it. I'm not exactly your typical Harvard graduate."

"And praise the Lord for that!" she exclaimed, smiling at the comment. "Just remember, you've got a lot of wisdom gleaned from life experiences. You're also honest, forthright, and a Christian. . .as well as one of the best friends I've ever known. Who else would put up with my babbling?"

He chuckled and sat back, appearing more at ease and. . . even confident. "Okay, then, Amie. Seems your fate is sealed."

"I hope so."

He paused. "Yeah, me too."

His gaze met hers, searching her face intently, and a tiny breath caught in her throat as she slowly comprehended the meaning in his expression, the desire shining plainly in his hazel eyes. *He wants to be more than just my friend*, she realized. Oddly, she didn't feel panicked in the least but filled with a wondrous sense of anticipation.

❧

"I'm telling you, she's interested," Matt said, his voice carrying in the darkness from a few feet away where he lay on the double bed.

Stretched out on his back on the inflatable mattress, hands behind his head and gazing at a ceiling of nothingness, Tom couldn't believe what his brother was saying—and yet he'd detected it as well.

"I mean, there you two were, sitting on the sofa tonight and giving each other calf eyes." Matt sighed dramatically. "If that ain't love. . ."

"We were not giving each other. . .*calf eyes.*"

"Oh yes, you were. We all saw it."

Embarrassment stabbed at Tom's gut.

"You've got it bad, dude," his younger brother continued. "I've never seen you so taken with a woman before—not unless you include Nancy Chesterfield."

"It's Nancy *Simonson*—and has been for the last nine years."

"Yeah, but who's counting, right?" Matt laughed.

Tom rolled his eyes. "I got over Nancy before dropping out my senior year."

"I know. I'm just giving you the business." The younger man hesitated momentarily. "So. . .are you really interested in Amie? I mean, romantically? I don't hear you denying it."

"Oh, I'm interested, all right. More than I should be." Tom heard the bed springs creak as Matt shifted his weight, and he imagined his brother had rolled onto his side.

"Seems she's good for you—you look a lot better than the last time I saw you."

Tom knew that much was true. "You saw me right after Hal's funeral when I was down in the dumps."

"Down in the dumps? Try clinically depressed. I was worried about you."

Tom couldn't help but grin. "I was worried about me too."

"And then Amie comes along. . ."

Tom's grin broadened. "When she first showed up at the filling station, I assumed she was going to be like her greedy siblings and take everything of value. I figured she'd be one of those high-society snobs, but instead she. . .she wasn't." Tom chuckled reflectively. "She talked me into taking her to dinner, and that night we ran into Big Al. He started up with his usual slams, but Amie put him in his place."

"You were down and out, so God sent an angel to cheer you up."

Tom laughed again. "Yeah, something like that." He went on to relay the story of how he came into the partnership, and how he and Amie had been corresponding for months, with the exception of Thanksgiving, when they'd actually seen each other. And now Christmas. "I guess that's where we're at."

"So, you gonna ask her out? I mean, *officially?*"

"Been thinking about it."

"Take her to the bowling alley, why don't you?"

"Yeah, right," he said, amusedly. "Somehow I don't think my Chicago angel would appreciate the place."

"Well, okay, how 'bout a concert? Laura told me about one in Wausau tomorrow night. It's a four-man ensemble that plays classical music—guitar, two violins, and a flute, I think. You know, kind of boring, but the stuff females think is romantic. I can't go because I'm due back in Madison tomorrow night for work. But I could get the details for you."

"A concert, huh?" Tom's mind went into a tailspin. They'd be in Wausau anyway to see Jim Henderson. . .maybe they could just stay for dinner. . .a concert. . . their first date. . .

"Tom? You dreaming before you even fall asleep?"

"Very funny." He rolled over and plumped his pillow. "Yeah, find out the specifics for me."

"Sure." A moment of silence passed between the brothers. "Hey, Tom? About your wardrobe—"

"I'm working on it."

"Okay. . ." Matt paused. "Uh, well, if you're not above taking some advice from your little bro, I could share what I learned in that business class I had last semester. We spent weeks on the subject of dressing for success. We were even assigned partners and had to go shopping for the best deals on clothes."

"Sure. I'm open to hearing whatever you've got to say on the subject." Tom grinned into the darkness of his makeshift apartment. "As long as you passed the class, that is."

An unseen, hurled pillow suddenly landed on Tom's chest, and he chuckled. "I'll have you know I aced it!"

"Well, that's a relief," Tom replied, tossing the thing back at Matt. "But how 'bout you play professor tomorrow morning? I'm beat."

"No problem," he quipped. "Gives me time to plan my lessons."

Tom gave his brother a derisive snort and turned onto his stomach. A hush fell over the room, and soon he heard Matt's light snoring. Still, sleep eluded him as he imagined scenario after scenario of his possible date with Amie. Then, grimacing, he wondered how he'd ever ask her out.

Chapter 13

Tom's palms were sweaty, his stomach rolling, and his mouth felt as dry as an old soda cracker. Was asking Amie out really worth all this? As if in divine reply, Amie strolled into the Warrens' living room and gave him a sunny smile that melted his trepidation. It was worth it, all right.

"Believe it or not, I'm finally ready," she stated brightly. "Are you all set to go?"

Nodding, Tom rose from the couch where he'd been waiting for her. "Say, um. . . ." He glanced around to be sure everyone was out of earshot. "Would you, um, well, what I'd like to know is. . .would you go out with me tonight?"

Her blond brows shot up in surprise. "You mean like. . .on a date?"

He hesitated. Maybe mixing business with pleasure wasn't such a good idea after all.

"Sure," she said, before he could reply. "That'd be fun. What do you want to do?"

Relief flooded his being. Then, feeling more surefooted, he said, "I thought we could go to dinner and a concert in Wausau. We'll be there anyway for our meeting with Jim Henderson this afternoon."

"Am I dressed okay for the concert?"

Tom felt himself flush as he gave her attire the once-over. In a denim skirt, multi-colored sweater, and cream-colored turtle-neck underneath it, she looked perfect. "You look great," he finally replied.

"So do you."

He could feel his color deepening and decided to thank Matt for lending him the navy dress slacks and gray corduroy jacket. He'd never paid much attention to his wardrobe and only bought new blue jeans, underwear, socks, and shoes when the old ones wore out. His sweatshirts, T-shirts, few dress shirts, and the one suit he owned, he'd acquired. But since the end of October, he had become more aware of the way professional men dressed, and as he told his brother last night, he was working on upscaling his apparel. If he was going to be manager and half-owner of a hotel, he figured he'd better look the part.

Amie pulled her coat out of the hall closet, and Tom politely helped her into it. Then they left the house for his pickup truck.

"When did you buy this vehicle?" she asked, strapping herself in the seat. "It looks rather new."

"I try to take care of it." Tom started the engine and backed down the gravel drive. "A couple of years ago, after my dad died, I sold our property," he explained, heading for the highway. "I put some money away for my sisters, whom I haven't seen in years, gave my brothers a portion, and put down a chunk on this truck." He smiled wistfully. "Hal was the one who insisted I buy something with my share of the sale, even though I had intended on giving it all to Matt for college."

"Hmm. . .so you have two brothers and two sisters?"

Tom nodded, wishing she wouldn't ask too much about his less than admirable family background. But he knew, if she did, he'd tell her.

"And Phillip was always the troublemaker, huh?"

He turned toward her in a quick, jerking motion. "How'd you know that?"

"Well, ah, my uncle told me."

"He did, huh?" Tom returned his gaze to the road ahead and submitted to the informal interrogation. As much as he disliked talking about it, he didn't want any of the past ever coming between Amie and him—even if their relationship didn't develop into anything beyond a strong friendship. "Yeah, Phil always had a knack for getting himself into all sorts of predicaments. Wound up in jail and still has a couple more years to serve. I try to visit him a couple times a month."

"That's so sad," she lamented. "That he's in jail, I mean. But perhaps his life will be much different once he's released."

"It better be. Now that he knows the Lord, I guess he's got a fighting chance at a decent life after he gets out."

From the corner of his eye, he saw her nod in agreement.

"And your sisters, Lois and Jeanne, they got married awfully young, didn't they?"

"I guess you could say that. . .yeah." Discomfort mounted in his chest. Had Hal really told her all this? When? More importantly. . .*why?*

Silence filled the truck's cab.

"Am I asking too many questions, Tom?" Amie queried.

"No, it's okay."

More silence.

"My family background is different from yours," she began in her typical sweet, babbling way. "But there are similarities. For example, we're both the eldest of our brothers and sisters, and I suppose a good measure of responsibility goes along with that rank."

"I suppose," he conceded cautiously.

"I was always the black sheep of my family, since I got saved in junior high. It was Uncle Hal who found a church for me to attend outside of Chicago, and he'd check on me every so often to make sure I was really going." She chuckled lightly. "And there's another similarity between you and me, Tom—my uncle called us his 'son and daughter in the faith.'"

He grinned. "That's right."

"Did he ever talk about me?"

"Uh-huh. All the time."

"What did he say?"

Tom had to think about it for several long moments. "It's hard to remember the specifics," he said at last, "but I can recall the time you were in a high school play, and Hal got all worried you'd be so wonderful on stage you'd run off to Hollywood and ruin your life. He wanted me to pray you'd be a flop."

Amie giggled. "Did you?"

"Sure."

"Well, it worked." She laughed again. "When it came time to say my lines, my mind went totally blank. Right in front of a packed auditorium! I was so humiliated that I never tried out for another production." Leaning toward him, she gave his shoulder a playful swat. "So you see, your prayers probably saved me from a becoming another Marilyn Monroe, complete with tragic ending and all."

"Whew! That's good." Tom grinned, feeling more at ease now that the topic was off of him. "Tell me some more about your family."

"No way!" she replied teasingly. "I don't want to scare you off before we even have our first date."

"Yeah, right." His grin broadened. "I don't scare that easily, Amie. Besides, I already met your brother and sister."

"Oh yes. . .Dottie and Stephen. They can be difficult. They're not easily impressed with anyone—unless you're, like, some top exec of a Fortune 500 company. But I think you'd like my dad. I've told you about him."

"A practical joker?"

"I guess that sums him up, yes." Amie smiled broadly. "I'm sure you'll meet him eventually; after all, we are business partners."

Tom nodded.

"Now, my mother. . .she's another story."

"Hal mentioned her. What did he used to call her again? The socialite?"

"That's her." Amie paused. "I love her dearly and I pray for her soul, but she and I rarely get along. My dad sort of plays mediator." She sighed. "Mom's very different from Uncle Hal. You'd never guess they were even related."

Tom pondered the remark. "Kind of funny how people turn out like that. . .so different, given the fact they've got the same parents."

His own words convicted him. If Hal and Amie could be different from their siblings, couldn't he also be dissimilar from his family—all except Matt, anyway? It occurred to him then that he judged himself unfairly. The measuring stick he used on others was long and marked with understanding, while his was short and scored by self-condemnation based upon who his father had been: the town drunk.

Shaking himself mentally, Tom tuned in to Amie's congenial prattling. He smiled, thinking he'd never known a woman who could talk as much as she did and still be coherent. But it didn't annoy him. Rather, he found it endearing somehow.

Lord, is she the one? he silently asked. *Is she the woman You would have me marry someday?* The questions sounded incredible to his own soul; however, he couldn't help wondering as his feelings for Amie grew beyond their business association and friendship.

Nearly an hour later, they arrived in Wausau, a city of some thirty-eight thousand people. Tom parked his truck, and then he and Amie ambled into the building that housed Henderson's Law Office. They took the elevator to the fourth floor and only had to wait a few minutes for Jim to finish up with another client.

The meeting went well. Several loose ends were tied, their limited liability company established, and some unfinished financial predicaments solved. Jim proved infinitely helpful when it came to several confusing forms and permits that Tom had been unsure of how to handle. As it happened, with the money Hal left his "children in the faith," there was a good chance they wouldn't have to take out a building loan.

"Watch your pennies," the attorney advised. "It's doable."

At the end of the conference, Jim stood and wished them a Happy New Year.

"We've got a couple of hours to kill before dinner," Tom announced once they'd left the office building. A chilling gust of December wind blew against Amie's face, causing her eyes to tear.

"Is there a shopping mall around?" she asked, as they walked back to his truck. "I can easily pass the time away in there."

Tom nodded slightly. "Okay."

Upon arriving at the mall, it soon became apparent that December twenty-sixth was *not* a good shopping day, at least not in Tom's opinion. The stores were crowded with customers returning gifts and hastening to purchase sale items. Amie, however, was hardly intimidated, being accustomed to competing with other Chicagoans, and she managed to coax him into a few shops. But after a while, they sat down in the middle of a thoroughfare, conversed, and watched people pass by.

When at last it came time to leave the mall for the restaurant, a comfortable, easy ambience had settled between them.

"It's strange," Amie began, "but I feel like I've known you my whole life."

He nodded: "I can relate to that."

"You can?' she asked as the cold winter wind took her breath away.

"Sure. Except for Hal, I can't ever remember telling anybody the things I've told you."

Amie smiled. "I'm flattered."

Flashing her a look of chagrin, Tom shrugged, and she felt guilty for bringing up things she'd read in her uncle's journal. It really hadn't been any of her business, and Amie was grateful that she hadn't offended him. In truth, his candidness amazed her.

Leaving the truck parked near the mall, they walked down Third Street, heading for the old Wausau hotel and the Chinese restaurant located inside. Once they arrived, Amie curiously surveyed the high-vaulted ceilings, accentuated with thick, polished wooden beams.

"This used to be a hotel," Tom informed her, "but now it's more of a rooming house. The lobby is still intact; it's on the other side."

Amie nodded as she continued to take in her surroundings with fascination. The walls were decorated with rococo C-and-S scrolls and shells in gilt gesso, framing panels of photographs of China. White linen cloths covered the tables, and a large marble fireplace stood in the center of the far wall. "This restaurant is so. . .charming," she stated at last.

Tom looked pleased as the hostess showed them to a table. "Just don't get any ideas," he stated jokingly as they sat down.

"What do you mean?"

"I mean, like our café." His hazel eyes scanned the room. "It sure won't look like this."

Amie grinned. "No, I suppose it won't. I'll just have to wait to expand our full-scale restaurant after we're wealthy entrepreneurs, selling franchises all over the world."

Tom let out a soft, slow whistle. "Amie, you're a big dreamer, you know that?"

"Dreaming is fun."

He paused, looking over the dinner selections. "And what if your dreams never come true? Then what?"

"They're just dreams."

"You're not going to get disappointed, are you?"

"Probably."

He looked at her askance. "You really want to be a wealthy entrepreneur?"

She considered the question while taking a sip of water from the long-stemmed glass goblet. "Actually, Tom, I don't care a whole lot about money. Perhaps that's because I've never been without it. But, no, I'm not aspiring to earn some great fortune. I just want to do something fulfilling—something that's mine. God gives all His children *something*. . .a ministry of sorts." She paused reflectively. "Maybe it's our partnership and building the hotel, but I think that's really only the first step—to what, though, I'm not sure."

"A dreamer and a deep thinker." Tom shook his head. "You are so much like Hal it's spooky!"

She smiled. "Except he needed a levelheaded business partner."

"He sure did."

"Someone who could have helped him develop that gas station and laundromat into a profitable business," she murmured, trying to decide on either the sweet-and-sour chicken or the shrimp and snow peas. "He had such visions for the place when he first purchased it, after his wife died."

Tom sat back, and immediately Amie knew she'd said too much. She could feel his penetrating stare.

"You told me the day we first met that you never really knew your uncle."

"And that's true. But I've been finding out more and more about him." She cleared her throat uncomfortably and then took another sip of water.

"Where are you getting your information, if you don't mind me asking?"

"From my uncle." She almost laughed, realizing how ridiculous that sounded, but she knew she'd backed herself into a corner by giving her tongue free rein. While her predicament was somewhat amusing, she prayed Tom wouldn't hate her for what he might perceive as snooping.

He sat forward once more, hands folded over his menu. His countenance was a mask of disbelief. "Your uncle?"

Amie gave him an apologetic look and confessed. "I've been reading Uncle Hal's journals."

His green eyes lit up with understanding. "Ahh. . .I wondered where those went."

"Please don't be angry, Tom. I wasn't prying into anyone's past. . .except, perhaps, my uncle's. But that's only because I wanted to know who he was and what he was like."

"And that's how you found out about my family."

"Yes," she admitted, feeling like a naughty child. "But it's only been in this third diary that he's talked about you. I won't read any more, if you don't want me to. I'm not even halfway through."

"I never read them," Tom mumbled as he gazed off in the distance. "But I saw him writing from time to time. He said it helped him sort things out." He glanced back at her. "I thought I'd accidentally pitched his journals in the trash when I emptied the apartment."

Amie shook her head. "No, I packed them up with his other books and the photographs that were on his dresser." She fretted over her lower lip. "Tom?"

"I'm not angry, and I guess I don't care if you read the rest or not." His features softened, and Amie sighed audibly with the relief she felt. Then he took her hand, holding it between the two of his, and the mantle of warmth that suddenly enveloped her was startling. "I've got no secrets from you," he told her, wearing a tender expression. "You're my business partner and my friend and my. . .well,

I guess there comes a point in every relationship where you either trust the other person or you don't. And, Amie. . .I trust you."

"Oh, Tom." That was about the sweetest thing she'd ever heard, because she knew the words came straight from his heart. Her lips parted to speak the same thing back to him—*I trust you*. And yet the utterance refused to take shape.

Finally the blond waitress who'd introduced herself as Tracy approached their table, ready to take their orders, and Amie realized she had more of a decision to make than simply which entree to select.

Did she dare share it? Her dark secret?

Tom's words reverberated within her soul: *I guess there comes a point in every relationship where you either trust the other person or you don't.*

It seemed she'd arrived at that very crossroad.

Chapter 14

Dinner was delicious and the musicians, playing with heart and soul, wooed the couple with their romantic serenades. During the ride back to Tigerton, Amie and Tom fell into an easy conversation.

"I'll send you Uncle Hal's journals," she promised, "just as soon as I finish reading the last one. But I have to warn you, I'm a slow reader. Might take me a good week or two."

"No problem. Send them when you're ready."

"I've really enjoyed reading them. I feel like I've gotten to know what kind of man my uncle was and. . .I'm proud to be his niece."

"I'm glad. He was a good man."

At last Tom pulled into the Warrens' driveway, and an awkward hush filled the inside of the truck's cab.

"I had a really nice time tonight. . .today. All day," Amie said, breaking the silence.

"Yeah, me too." He cleared his throat. "Um. . .I'll walk you up to the house."

Smiling in reply, Amie opened the door and jumped down out of the pickup. Tom met her halfway around, and in the still and frosty night, they walked side-by-side to the small front porch. Little flutters of nervousness welled up in Amie, and she decided that the end of any first date always seemed uncomfortable. Except the one three years ago. That finale was a nightmare! But tonight, she shoved aside those horrible memories and focused on her present companion. The thought of Tom's embrace was not at all unpleasant, and the idea of his mouth lingering on hers in a sweet kiss sent shivers of excitement through her. Somehow he'd captured her heart in a very special way.

They stopped by the front door, and she watched as indecision flittered across his face. She guessed he was debating whether to kiss her good night. It felt like eons before he decided. Finally he leaned forward. She lifted her chin and pursed her lips ever so slightly. Her eyelids drifted shut in dreamy anticipation.

"Amie. . ."

She blinked. "Yes?"

"I. . .I'm falling in love with you," he stammered. Beneath the porch light, his face shone with a boyish innocence.

"Tom, you're so sweet. . ." She smiled. "But aren't you supposed to kiss me and *then* tell me you're falling in love with me?"

"I don't need to kiss you to know that."

His expression was one of adoration, and Amie knew he meant every word. Suddenly she longed to throw her arms around his neck and smother him with the unshed emotion building within her.

"But, I hope you'll understand. . ." He stuck his hands into his jacket pockets. "About eight years ago, I made a decision not to kiss a woman until she was my wife. I probably sound like some dumb country hick," he said, shuffling his feet nervously, "but I know that conviction came from God, and I can't break my vow to Him."

"I wouldn't want you to," Amie stated sincerely, and given her past, she could see the wisdom in that resolution. She wished she'd been a stronger Christian a few years ago.

Tom momentarily looked down before returning his gaze to hers. "It's not that I don't want to kiss you—"

"It's all right. Really."

He nodded. "I've watched so many of my peers, Christians included, date and kiss women, only to break up and move on to someone new. Then I got to thinking that what they were doing was the same as. . .well, kissing somebody else's wife, since a lot of those ladies wound up marrying other guys." He paused and cleared his throat. "I made a decision to keep myself pure until marriage."

Something deep within Amie began to wither.

He shrugged, looking chagrined. "I guess I just wanted to share my heart with you on this. . ."

"Oh, I'm glad you did," she replied readily, although it lacked genuine enthusiasm. Inside, that old familiar ache of sheer and utter discouragement quickly choked any hopeful feelings of love she might have begun to entertain.

"You're a fine Christian man, Tom," she said matter-of-factly, opening the door to the Warrens' house. "You made a godly decision. I pray you will never go back on it." A flash of confusion crossed his features, but Amie didn't bother to explain. "Good night, and thanks. . ."

Entering the house, she closed the door on his murmured " 'Night" and stood in the little foyer. Everything was dark and quiet; obviously the Warrens were already sleeping. In the silence, she stood there pondering the events of the last few minutes. How ironic that on the way back from Wausau tonight she'd determined to share her hurtful past, certain that Tom would be the one who'd understand. And he would, no doubt about it. But he wouldn't want her after learning about her shameful secret. If he considered kissing "impure," what would he think of. . .

Amie put her face in her hands, feeling the need to weep until she could no more. And once her tears had dried, she'd begin her life again. Single. Forever on her own. The curse.

I can't stay here, she hastily concluded. *How can I ever face him again? I can't lead him on. Nothing good will come of it.* Moving away from the front door, she crept down the hall to the little sewing room where she quietly packed her things.

❧

Tom couldn't believe it.

"She must have left some time during the night," Katie told him once the worship service had ended. She opened her purse and pulled out a slip of paper. "This is what I found just before I made breakfast."

He took the proffered note on which a simple *Thank you for the memorable Christmas!* was penned, signed by Amie at the bottom. Looking back at Katie, he was speechless.

"Why don't you come over for lunch today," she suggested. "We can talk about it then."

"Thanks. . .sure, I'll do that. But I think I'll go downstairs and give her a call first."

"That's a good idea." The look on Katie's face mirrored the confusion in his heart.

Leaving the sanctuary, Tom's puzzlement over Amie's swift departure mounted. *Did I offend her? But how?*

In his makeshift apartment, he picked up the extension in the kitchen area and dialed her phone number, only to get her answering machine. "Hi, Amie, it's me," he began, leaving a message. "Give me a call back when you can."

Hanging up the receiver, he decided to try her parents' home. He knew that number from memory too. But again, only a machine answered and he chose not to leave a message there.

Concern and frustration plagued him as he walked back into his bedroom/ living room area. He glanced at his computer and decided to check his E-mail. Much to his relief, Amie had left a message; however, it was short and revealed nothing about why she left. *Don't worry. I got home all right. I'm sorry, Tom. It's not you. It's me.*

"What does *that* mean?" he asked aloud, staring in utter confusion at the words on the screen.

Clicking on the REPLY TO AUTHOR button, he responded with: *Glad you made it back to Chicago okay, but would you mind telling me why you left?* He thought about asking more, but settled on one question at a time. He only hoped she'd respond. Soon.

Shutting down his computer, Tom made his way over to the Warrens', where, after lunch and out of the children's ear-shot, he divulged to Jake and Katie the entire conversation he and Amie had on the porch last night.

"She said I was sweet," he relayed. "I don't get it."

"Perhaps she's a person who fears commitment," Jake suggested.

"I don't know; she agreed to our partnership readily enough."

"Yes, that's true," Katie said, looking at her husband as though he possessed the answers.

"But you know," Tom began, "she does have a curious fear of men. I've seen it. She panics—at least she does until she gets to know them. But she's not afraid of me, and I don't think I did anything last night to change her opinion of me."

"Hmm. . .a fear of men?" Jake inhaled deeply, then stood and strolled to the coffeepot, pouring himself another cup. "I hate to even speculate as to what that could mean." He returned to the table and sat down. "We'll, of course, keep her in our prayers."

Katie agreed, her soft brown eyes looking sad. "She's a special young woman, Tom. The girls and I enjoyed her company. I'm so sorry she left."

He nodded. "Me too."

"Maybe I could give her pastor a call tomorrow and try to get some insight from him," Jake offered.

"Naw, don't bother. I'd rather hear about whatever's bothering Amie straight from her," Tom said, pushing his chair from the table. He looked at Katie. "Thanks for the lunch. I don't know what I'd do if you decided not to feed me."

She waved a hand at him as though it were nothing.

"See you guys later."

" 'Bye, Tom," Jake called as he made his way to the door.

Lord, Tom prayed on the way home, *You're gonna have to close the door with a bang and build a cement wall so high I'll never get over, if You want me to forget about Amie. But I don't think You do. Besides, what would I have done if Hal hadn't taken a chance on me?* Tom walked into the church building and went downstairs. *But You'll sure have to give me the smarts to deal with this thing—whatever it is—because I have no idea where to even start.*

Chapter 15

One of the first things Amie did after she arrived home was pack up her uncle's journals and ship them off to Tom. She didn't think she could bear reading any more about his life. The mere thought of him caused her heart to ache. She felt as though she were mourning the death of something that hadn't had the chance to even be born.

The days passed, and Amie managed to skirt Tom's phone calls and refused to reply to his E-mail messages, deleting them before she even read them. She knew his questions and words of concern would break her heart all the more, and she prayed that in avoiding him altogether, he'd change his mind about falling in love with her and lose interest in her romantically. Then perhaps by spring, they could resume a platonic business partnership during the construction process; however, she doubted her plans to move up to Tigerton now. . .which meant she couldn't sell her condo. . .which meant they'd most likely have to take out a mortgage on the hotel. Suddenly everything seemed highly complicated.

New Year's Eve came and went with Amie choosing to stay home. Friends tried to coax her to church and New Year's parties, but she didn't feel up to it. Then, the following Monday, she began her new job.

"Okay, let me get this straight—all you want me to do is answer this phone?"

"That's it. For now." Buzz chuckled. "Don't want to overwhelm you on your first day."

Buzz Felton, her new boss, was a short, squat, jolly man who laughed at just about anything. Amie wondered if he'd been moonlighting as Santa Claus during the holidays.

"Go ahead. Have a seat," he told her. "Just answer the phone. The other girls will answer your questions."

Amie made herself comfortable at the end of a large U-shaped desk. It was part of what the company called The Information Center, and two other secretaries worked side-by-side as they greeted customers and answered calls.

The phone began to ring, and Amie soon discovered her job consisted largely of taking messages and listening to Buzz's customers complain. Her only reprieve came at noon when her father invited her to lunch.

"You'll love working here, Princess," he said as they dined in the company's cafeteria.

"Dad, I can't afford to love working here." Amie poked at the salad she'd ordered, pushing the lettuce around her plate. "I'm going to have to find a job that pays as much as MBMD did."

Her father's whitened brows went up in surprise. "What about your hotel?"

She shrugged. "I don't know."

"Hmm. . ." He munched hungrily on his hamburger.

Amie chafed at her father's ambivalent attitude, although she told herself she ought to be used to it. While he was the only one in the family who encouraged her, she sometimes wondered if he only did so to escape dealing with her feelings, not to mention her "religion."

Even so, she made an attempt. "Tom and I. . .well, our relationship started to develop beyond a mere partnership."

"Oh, really?" He took a drink of his coffee. "Pass me the ketchup, will you?"

Amie nodded and handed him the round red bottle at the end of the table.

"Well, you know the old saying," he said, pouring the condiment onto his burger, "don't mix business with pleasure."

"Yeah. . ." She sighed woefully. "I kinda wish I hadn't."

His blue-eyed gaze met hers, and she hoped he'd inquire further. She needed to talk so badly. However, her hopes were soon dashed when her father changed the subject.

"Say, would you like some dessert? The cheesecake down here is out of this world. But don't tell your mother. She thinks her cheesecake is the best. . .and it's close. Real close."

But Amie had long since lost her appetite. "No. . .no, thanks, Dad."

❧

Tom's business management and accounting courses began in mid-January. After a few weeks, he found a job at a motel in Shawano, working a split shift, six o'clock in the evening until two A.M. He didn't plan on keeping the position long, but determined to learn everything possible about running the place. And even with his busy schedule, he faithfully e-mailed Amie once, sometimes twice, a day. He wasn't sure if she read his messages, even though he tried to keep them light and friendly. She never wrote back.

Lord, he prayed early one morning before falling into bed exhausted, *only You know a woman's mind, that's for sure! But I'm not giving up.*

❧

Valentine's Day decorations cluttered The Information Center where Amie worked, causing her to hate the job all the more. She'd sent out at least a dozen resumés but hadn't gotten a single response.

"Say, Amie, are you doing anything special this weekend?" Nora Craig, another secretary, asked. "I mean, Valentine's Day *is* Sunday, you know."

"How could I forget?" she quipped, glancing at the cardboard cupid dangling from the ceiling, close to her head. She sighed. "No, I'm not doing anything special."

Lifting her gaze from the fingernail file she held and raising her penciled eyebrows, Nora frowned. "Your boyfriend isn't taking you someplace romantic? Why, my Ronald is taking me away for the weekend, except he won't tell me where." She laughed gaily. "He's such a Casanova—even after twelve years of marriage!"

"That's really special," Amie replied in an apathetic tone. She glanced at her wristwatch. Two more hours to go. Could she last till five o'clock? The afternoon had dragged on until she couldn't stand this place anymore. No way was she coming back Monday. Not a chance. Her father and Buzz could beg her blue, but she'd refuse to step a foot into this office again!

At that moment, Amie looked up to see a delivery man walking into the building carrying a large bouquet of red roses.

Casanova strikes again.

"Ooh! Who are these for?" Charis, the main receptionist, asked.

The delivery man read the name on the attached envelope. "Amie Potter."

Her two associates gasped with pleasure.

"She's right here!" Nora grabbed the boxed blossoms and brought them to Amie.

"They're probably from my dad," she said facetiously, as her face warmed with embarrassment.

The ladies "oohed" and "ahhed" as they took charge of setting the flowers aright in their accompanying cut-glass vase. With a roll of her eyes, Amie opened the card. Liquid numbness spread through her veins as she read the words: *I love you, Amie. Tom.* For several moments, she stared at the note in her hand, feeling as though she couldn't breathe.

How can he still love me? she wondered. *I've given him the cold shoulder for nearly two months.*

"Well, now, honey," Nora crooned, "are you sure you're not doing something special this weekend?"

Amie finally conceded a laugh.

The last couple of hours passed quickly that afternoon, and Amie found herself actually enjoying the conversation between herself and her coworkers. Since her first day on the job, she'd been cool to the ladies, ignoring their attempts at friendship. But somehow today her icy facade cracked, and it wasn't long before she told them about her hotel "adventure" in Tigerton, Wisconsin, and gave them a vague rundown on Tom.

"Marry him quick, Amie," Charis advised, her eyes a too-bright shade of green from her colored contact lenses. Shaking her bottle-blond head, she continued, "There's not many of those kind of guys left these days. And I should know! I think I've dated every eligible bachelor in the Chicago area under fifty years old."

"Well, try frequenting the senior citizen centers," Nora shot back jokingly. "You're no spring chicken anymore."

The ladies, both twenty-plus years older than Amie, cackled and teased each other, making her giggle until her sides ached.

That night, as she made her way through the front door of her condo, her arms filled with fragrant roses, she wondered what to do about Tom. She supposed she could be blatantly honest with him regarding her past so he'd change his mind about her once and for all. Get it over with. Quickly. Or she could break his heart and lie, telling him she didn't love him and that she never would.

With her winter coat hung up and the flowers on the coffee table, Amie walked to her office and booted up her computer. She sat down in front of the monitor and decided she couldn't hurt Tom for the world nor could she lie and hurt her Savior. She'd rather hurt herself. But if he rejected her, once he knew the truth, could she ever face him again? And yet, what did she have to lose? Could she really feel any more miserable?

Oh, Lord, she prayed, *I'm so scared. . .*

It was then the Lord spoke to her heart from 1 John 4:18. "Perfect love casts out fear."

Jesus Christ loved her so much that He died for her. In these past several weeks, she'd felt as though she'd grown closer to the Savior. It was His love that kept getting her out of bed every morning and His love that gave her hope for the future—with or without Tom.

"Perfect love. . .all right, Lord. With Your help, I'll tell him. I don't know how or when, but I'll share my past with him. You'll have to orchestrate it all and prepare Tom's heart. But I won't be afraid of his reaction anymore, I'll just think about You. . .and how much You'll still love me. . . ." She wiped an errant tear from her eye. "Even if Tom changes his mind about his feelings for me."

It was as if that Still Small Voice replied to her soul, "One day at a time, beloved. One day at a time."

Taking a deep, cleansing breath, Amie accessed her server and downloaded seven E-mail messages—two of them from Tom.

The first message from Tom gave his work phone number, "in case you misplaced it."

Amie frowned, confused. Work number? Where was he working?

She read the second message. *And just in case you forgot, I don't get to work until six o'clock. Dinner break at eight. Call then.*

Her frown increased until she figured out that somehow Tom knew she hadn't read any of his E-mails for the last seven weeks. He obviously hoped she'd read these, no doubt since he'd sent her the roses and the simple, yet poignant, Valentine's Day card.

He knows me too well, she mused with a slip of a smile.

Then she replied to his last message on a lark he'd get it before he left for work. *Thanks for the roses, Tom. I'll call you around eight.*

Chapter 16

Tom glanced at the octagonal wall clock stationed behind the check-in desk. Seven fifty-five. Would she really call?

Before coming to work, he'd checked his E-mail just to see if Amie had sent him a message. Much to his immense elation, she had. Would she keep her word?

At eight, Tom turned to his coworker Rosa. "I'm going on my break. Will you watch the desk?"

She bobbed her graying curls and smiled easily.

"Oh, and I'm expecting a phone call. . ."

"I'll patch it through to the lounge," she finished for him.

"Great."

Down the hallway, Tom entered the small break room. Opening the slim refrigerator he extracted the sack with the supper Katie graciously prepared for him, then he moved to the round veneer-topped table and plunked down in a swivel chair. Physically, he felt exhausted. Emotionally, he could run the Olympic mile. He glanced at his wristwatch. *Eight-o-three. Anytime now, Amie.*

He reminded himself that she always ran late. Ten minutes ticked by. *No, she's not going to call.* Filled with a huge sense of disappointment, he started picking at his sandwich, ham and cheese on a hard roll. He popped the top off a soda can and took a swig.

The phone rang and he nearly choked in his haste to answer it. "Staff lounge," he said, the receiver to his ear.

"Tom?"

His heart sped up in the most peculiar way. "Yeah, hi, Amie." He pulled the long, coiled phone cord across the table and sat down again. "It's nice to hear your voice."

He heard her soft exhalation. "I guess it's been a long time coming, huh? I'm sorry, Tom, for being so. . .so. . ."

"Forget it. I'm just glad you're okay." He paused, feeling a twinge of concern. "You are okay, aren't you?"

"Actually, no. I've been miserable. I hate my job. I'm not exactly multi-task oriented. But who in their right mind can answer five incoming phone calls at once? And my father certainly doesn't help matters. He taunts me with his dumb-blond jokes. So, I'm not secretary material," she huffed. "Excuse me!"

She's nervous, he realized. Still, he wasn't about to dismiss matters. He'd waited too long for some answers.

"Is that all you've been miserable about?" he queried gently. "A job that you never intended to stay at anyway?"

"No." She took a ragged breath. "I guess you and I need to talk, Tom. . .but not tonight. Not over the phone."

"All right," he agreed, curiously. . .warily.

"Thank you for the roses," Amie said quietly. "And the card. Actually, it was the card that touched my heart. You're really sweet."

"Last time you told me I was sweet you didn't talk to me for two months."

Silence. "I'm sorry, Tom. It's me—"

"What does that mean, Amie? *It's you?*" He fought to control his mounting frustration. "Are you trying to tell me that you don't share my feelings? Is that it? You know, I think I could handle point-blank honesty better than all of this."

"No. . .no, in fact. . ." She paused, her voice wavering slightly, and Tom instantly regretted his impatience with her. "In fact," she began again, "I feel very much the same way you do, Tom. But, see, that's why this whole thing started."

"I don't get it," he stated flatly, sipping his soda. "I love you. . .you share my feelings. . .shouldn't we be. . .*rejoicing?*"

"Yes." There was a smile in her voice now. "And I hope we will be. . .rejoicing. . .soon."

"You hope?"

"Uh-huh. That's why we've got to talk. Except, until today, I haven't been ready to discuss anything. Maybe I've been feeling sorry for myself on top of being so frightened, I don't know."

"Frightened? Of what?"

She hesitated. "Do you remember when you said that you were afraid I'd change my mind about our partnership once I heard the gossip regarding your family?"

"Yeah," he replied cautiously.

"Okay, well, that's sort of how I'm feeling now. I'm afraid you're going to change your mind about. . .about me. . .after I share something from my past."

That's it? Tom shook his head in wonder. "Amie, there's nothing you could ever say to change the way I feel about you. I'm hopeless. The only cure is. . ." He balked, not wishing to broach the subject of marriage over the phone. "I guess we'll have to talk about that too."

"Are you working this weekend?" she asked. "And what in the world are you doing at the Best Rest Motel?"

"On-the-job training."

"Oh."

"You would know that, if you read all the E-mails I sent you."

"Sorry. . ."

She sounded satisfactorily remorseful, so Tom didn't rub it in further. "And, yeah, I'm on this weekend. I'm working a double shift tomorrow, filling in for the manager."

"Good going. As soon as you figure out how to run a hotel, you can teach me."

He laughed. "You bet. Well, my break's just about over so I'd better hang up. But, Amie?" He softened his tone. "Don't stop talking to me. Whatever's bothering you, we'll work it out."

"All right." She still sounded skeptical.

"Promise me."

A moment's pause—or was it reluctance? "I promise."

"Can I call you early Sunday afternoon before I go to work?"

"Yes. I'd like that." Her voice returned to its honeyed tone.

Neither spoke for several seconds.

"I love you," Tom said at last, cringing slightly at how trite his admission might sound to the average hearer. He figured those three words were probably the most overused and misused in the English language, yet the most profound when spoken earnestly, as he'd intended.

For most of his teenage years, he'd longed to say them to that "special someone." But, shortly after his twenty-fifth birthday, he all but convinced himself he'd never fall in love—that he was unlovable. And then Amie babbled her way into his heart.

He grinned.

Fleetingly, Tom wondered if he ever told his father he loved him. He hoped so. It was true—he'd loved his father enough to stick with him year after year, hangover after hangover, until finally the booze he cherished more than his family killed him. Still, Tom had refused to give up, praying his dad would trust the Lord with his soul. And he might have.

Even so, Tom saw more suffering than he cared to remember while living with his father. He'd survived horror stories that would intimidate Hollywood film makers.

No, whatever the secret Amie harbored, it could neither shock him nor change his feelings for her a mite. He *loved* her.

"Tom. . .?" Like a healing balm, her soft voice penetrated each scabbed wound. "I love you, too."

❧

Within a week, Tom and Amie had more than made up for the past two months of not communicating. However, because of his classes and work schedule, it soon

ecame apparent that the earliest they'd be able to spend time together was Easter
eekend.

And so it was planned. Tom would come to Chicago and meet Amie's family,
nd they'd talk—face to face. Despite the forty days she had to wait to see him, Amie
idn't feel anxious in the least over sharing her three-year secret. Not anymore. It
lmost seemed as if it didn't matter if she told Tom or not; he insisted his feelings for
er were unconditional. But she'd tell him anyway. He had to know, and she needed
o confide in the man she loved.

However, there was another matter causing her mild apprehension, and that
vas telling her family about Tom and his upcoming visit.

Two weeks before Easter, on a sunny March afternoon, Amie finally found
he nerve to address the subject at the family dinner table.

Upon hearing the news, Dottie dropped her fork. It clanged loudly against
he expensive Haviland dinnerware. "The gas station geek! You're kidding!"

"Tom is *not* a geek," Amie stated, giving her younger sister a furious look.

Beside her, Dottie's fiancé shifted uncomfortably. "He works at a. . .*gas sta-
ion?*" He said the last two words in a manner of distaste with a perfectly wrin-
led nose.

"No, Gregory," Amie corrected him, "Tom is my business partner."

"Amie, dear," her mother crooned from one end of the long, polished dining
oom table, "what happened to that charming young man. . .Wanda Carter's son?"

"He wasn't all that charming," Amie quipped. The truth was, she'd met Kevin
Carter only once, very briefly—and she hadn't been impressed.

Besides, she loved Tom.

"Now, listen everyone," John Potter told his family from where he sat at the
head of the table, "we owe it to Amie to at least *meet* this fellow before we pass
judgment on him."

"Thanks, Dad," she muttered, picking at her veal cordon bleu.

"After all," he continued, "Tom did inherit quite a bit of money from Hal.
Let's not forget that."

Amie groaned inwardly, wondering how she happened to be born into this
money-minded family. Except she knew God never made mistakes.

"I met him," Dottie stated flatly, "when Stephen and I drove to northern
Wisconsin to claim our inheritances. He was. . .a dirty-fingernailed car mechanic
with long hair and a stubbled face." Her brown-eyed gaze zeroed in on Amie. "Are
you out of your mind?"

Amie shot a quick glance across the table at Gregory, his soft, shiny baby-
face grinning amusedly, and thought she might ask Dottie the same thing. Of
course, Amie hadn't judged her sister's fiancé on appearance alone. It was his bad
temperament, moodiness, and sickening habit of whining that made her dislike

him. Dottie's attraction, however, seemed to stem from the fact that marryir Gregory ensured her a position within the wealthy Bradford family.

Lillian cleared her throat. "Just how. . .serious are you about this man, Amie Her mother's white-winged brows were knitted together in concern.

The room fell deathly quiet and all eyes turned on Amie. She took a dee breath, feeling overshadowed by her family's expectations. They'd never under stand. They never did.

Gazing back at her mother, who looked as she always did, very dignified, ver regal, Amie began. "I'm quite serious about him. Tom is probably the best frien I have on earth and I. . .I'm in love with him."

Dottie shook her head, looking disgusted. "You have flipped your wig! You'r going to ruin your reputation. What are people going to say when they find ou you're involved with a. . .a grease monkey?"

"He is not a 'grease monkey,' and I couldn't care less what anybody says, Amie replied sharply, scooting her chair back and rising from the table. "Tom is warm, caring person with a good head for business. He's a hard worker and. . .oh never mind. I don't want him to meet you. . .any of you!" Tears of humiliatior filled her eyes. "I would be ashamed for him to discover how shallow my family really is!"

With that, she tossed her linen napkin onto her barely touched plate, ignoring the gasp from her mother and the appalled expression on Dottie's face. Leaving the room, she grabbed her purse and walked into the wide foyer, her heels clicking smartly on the Spanish tile. There she opened the closet and pulled out her coat.

"Amie, don't leave the house like this," her father warned, coming up behind her.

Casting a look of disappointment his way, she yanked open the front door and marched out to her car parked in the circular drive.

By the time she arrived back at her condominium, Amie felt ashamed at her outburst of temper. It was one of the things she couldn't stand about Gregory, yet she'd behaved the same way.

"Lord, I don't think my actions glorified You to my un-saved family, did they?" she muttered, kicking off her shoes with more force than necessary. She walked to the answering machine and checked for messages.

"Hello, Miss Potter, this is Dennis Templeton of Templeton Realty. Good news. I believe I've sold your condo this afternoon. I told you it wouldn't take long. . ."

Good grief! Amie thought, smacking her palm against her forehead. *Now I'll be forced to actually live with my parents!*

The telephone rang and she checked the Caller ID. Seeing it was her parents' number, she decided against answering it.

"Amie, darling," her mother's smooth voice lilted through the machine. "I'm so sorry we hurt your feelings this evening. Of course we want to meet Tim."

"Tom," she grumbled, rolling her eyes in aggravation.

"Now, you just tell me when he's coming, and we'll all be on our best behavior." A pause. "Honey, I want you to be happy, it's just that. . .well, you know, I grew up near Tigerton, and I've always wanted better for my children. People are so. . .so *backwards* up there, and. . .oooh!" she moaned, "my worst fears have been realized. My daughter. . .romantically involved with someone from the small town I endeavored to escape." She sighed dramatically before her voice took on a steely tone. "It's a good thing Hal's already dead because if he were here, I'd wring his neck for starting all this trouble! I knew it was a mistake for him to leave you that gas station!"

A decisive click, and then Amie collapsed into a nearby armchair. She couldn't allow Tom to come to Chicago. There was no way. She wouldn't put him through it!

❧

"All right, people, listen up." Amie watched her father trying to get his family's attention. They were all gathered in the living room, including Stephen, who'd come home from college on spring break. "We've promised Amie we would be polite, and I will not tolerate any rude remarks or condescending comments about her. . .friend. Got it?"

Dottie clucked her tongue and cozied up next to Gregory on the love seat. "Oh, Dad, you make us sound like naughty children."

If the shoe fits, Amie thought wryly, folding her arms.

For the past week, she had pleaded with Tom, begging him not to come for Easter weekend. However, he seemed bound and determined no matter what she said. Amie even phoned Pastor Warren and explained the circumstances, only to have him side with Tom.

"He's going to have to meet them eventually, Amie. Trust God to work in the hearts of your family members, and let Tom face the challenge. It'll be good for him—for both of you."

But she had her doubts. And, now, as she gazed around at the faces here in the living room of her parents' home, she felt so sorry for Tom. Her siblings and Gregory looked like felines ready to pounce. Her mother, situated comfortably in one of the two matching powder blue wingbacked chairs, filed her fingernails indifferently. Only her father appeared to be making any sort of attempt.

A car door slammed outside and Amie startled. Dottie peaked out the side of the off-white pleated drapes covering the large picture window. "He's he–ere," she crooned.

"Be nice," John Potter cautioned her.

"I'm always nice," Dottie replied irritably, while Stephen and Gregory snickered.

Oh, Lord, help! Amie prayed silently as the front doorbell sounded. "I'll get it," she said quickly.

Hurrying into the foyer, she checked her reflection in the antique wall mirror. With a deep breath, she pulled open the large front door.

Tom smiled a greeting.

"Hi," she said. "Come on in."

As he stepped into the house, she impulsively threw her arms around his neck in a hug of welcome. "I've missed you so much," she murmured. His cheek felt cool against hers as a rush of nippy spring air blew into the house.

"I've missed you too."

Amie pulled out of the embrace and shut the door. Turning back to Tom, she asked, "May I hang up your coat?"

He nodded, shrugging out of the handsome camel's hair coat and handing it to her. After tucking it in the closet, she gazed at him, taking in his every feature. Four months apart had certainly dulled her memory of him and how incredibly handsome he was. His dark brown hair was neatly cropped, although, for the moment, it looked windblown. As if divining her thoughts, he quickly combed his fingers through it. Their gazes met, and Amie decided his hazel eyes no longer seemed sad, as they stared back at her with adoration sparkling in their depths, leaving no doubt in her mind as to how he felt about her. She noticed, too, that he wore the sweater she'd given him at Christmas and a pair of khaki trousers. He looked terrific. He might even impress Dottie!

Amie smiled almost apologetically. "Can I introduce you to my family?"

He nodded. "Lead the way."

Chapter 17

S o, what line of work is your father in?"

Amie cringed at the barrage of questions being hurled at Tom, although he seemed to be holding his own.

"My father's dead, Mr. Potter," he replied politely. "But he worked for the railroad for almost fifteen years."

"The railroad? Hmm. . .I had a cousin who worked for Union Pacific." Tom nodded, looking interested.

"Anderson. . .I'm trying to think if I went to school with any Andersons," Lillian stated, drumming a well-sculpted fingernail against her chin pensively. "You wouldn't happen to be related to Margaret Anderson, would you?"

Tom smiled patiently. "Not that I know."

"So, um," Stephen began, sitting forward on the sofa, "like where are you working now that my uncle's filling station is gone?"

"I'm the assistant manager of a motel in Shawano."

"Assistant manager, huh?" John Potter looked mildly impressed.

Amie was aware of the promotion and felt proud of him. The national motel chain knew Tom planned to move on but advanced him anyway, citing his outstanding work ethic. Within just a few months of his employment! She wished he'd tell her family that piece of information, but figured he'd probably consider it bragging, which wasn't at all Tom's nature.

The interrogation continued; however, it wasn't long before Dottie and her fiancé grew bored and left, claiming they had dinner reservations. Stephen, too, made his excuses and exited the house.

"Our dinner will be ready shortly," Amie announced.

"She's making lasagna for us," her father added, looking at Tom. "Took over our kitchen so she could impress you with her culinary skills."

John Potter laughed, and Amie shot him a dubious glance, while Tom's face reddened slightly.

"Amie could make peanut butter and jelly sandwiches, and I wouldn't care."

She was touched by Tom's kind remark—and even her parents looked a bit taken by it.

"So, how's this hotel adventure coming along?" her father asked, clearing his throat.

"Excavation has already begun," he replied. "And if the mild weather keeps up, the foundation could be poured as early as next month."

"Don't count on it," Lillian said. "I can remember snow storms up there occurring as late as May."

Tom agreed courteously.

John drew his brows together. "How'd those architectural drawings work out for you?"

"Would you like to see the plans, Mr. Potter? I've got a set out in my truck."

"Sure!" he boomed on a enthusiastic note.

Tom fetched the drawings, and while he explained the layout for the hotel, café, and antique shop, Amie made the final preparations for their dinner. At last they sat down to eat, and although her parents' questions persisted, the focus now centered on the business adventure instead of Tom's personal life.

Amazingly, the evening progressed at a comfortable pace, and by the time her father turned on the late edition of the news, Amie was sure he liked Tom. Even her mother behaved sweetly toward him now.

"Tom, dear, the guest bedroom is all ready for you."

"Thanks, Mrs. Potter."

She yawned, placing a delicate hand over her mouth. "Gracious! I'm tired. See you all in the morning. Amie, you will be here for breakfast, won't you?"

"Yes." She planned to drive home tonight but return bright and early tomorrow. "Good night, Mother."

Lillian blew her a kiss as she left the family room.

The night wore on and Amie began to wonder if her father would ever get sleepy and allow her some time alone with Tom. But when Stephen arrived home and settled down in front of the television, she gave up.

"Guess I'll go home," she finally announced. Glancing at Tom, she added, "I hope you don't mind me abandoning you this way."

"Not at all," he replied graciously. "I'm in good company."

"G'night, Princess," her father called from his recliner.

"See ya, sis," Stephen mumbled in between a fist full of corn chips.

Tom offered to walk her to the door.

"Will you be all right here?" she asked feeling uneasy.

"I'll be fine. I like your family."

Amie smiled. "They like you too. I can tell."

He grinned.

"I thought we could eat lunch over at my place tomorrow," she said, praying they'd have time to talk then. "Later we've been invited to some of my friends' house for fellowship and board games." Amie shrugged into her coat with his mannerly assistance. "Does that sound okay?"

"Sounds great."

She paused, longing to kiss him but remembering his vow to God. Somehow that special promise made her feel secure, evidencing that Tom was a man of his word.

"Well, good night."

His expression softened. " 'Night, Amie."

For lunch the following day, Amie created peanut butter and jelly sandwiches *extraordinaire*. While eating, they laughed together about Tom's first racquetball experience. Her father had insisted he come to the club that morning, along with Stephen and Gregory, and a highly competitive game ensued between the four men.

"I still can't believe your dad and I won," Tom remarked as they moved to the living room after their meal. "I mean, I never played before!"

"You must be a natural."

He laughed. "Right."

Amie watched him walk to the grandfather clock and appraise the piece with admiration.

"Nice," he said. "You've got a really nice place."

"Thanks."

He pursed his lips, looking momentarily thoughtful. "Do you think you'll be happy living in a small country town like Tigerton after. . ." He waved his arm, indicating their surroundings. "after living like this? Plush carpet, expensive furniture, fine paintings, knickknacks. . ."

She shrugged. "Sure? Why not? Can't I take this stuff with me?"

Tom grinned wryly. "Why do I have visions of Zsa Zsa Gabor on that TV show 'Green Acres' when I think of you living in Tigerton?"

Laughing, Amie picked up a throw pillow from the colorful floral-printed sofa and threw it at him. "So, you've been watching those old late-night reruns at work again, huh?"

His grin broadened.

"Well, I'll have you know, Tom Anderson, that I don't need any of these *things* to be happy."

"No?"

"No." She stepped closer, feeling as though her now-sober expression matched Tom's. "I'm a single woman who, up until recently, made a lot of money. I bought what I wanted, but I never needed any of this." She cast one quick glance around the well-decorated living room before her eyes came back to his. "I've learned that it's the Lord who puts joy in my heart, but Tom. . .just being with you makes me happy."

"You're sure about that?"

She tipped her head, puzzled over all the questions. "Yes, I'm sure."

"Well, in that case. . ." Tom reached into his blue jeans pocket and pulled out a diamond solitaire, set in sterling. Slipping the ring onto her left-hand finger, he got down on one knee. "Will you marry me, Amie?"

Gazing at him, she didn't know whether to laugh or cry—so she conceded to both. The most she could do was nod a reply.

Standing to his feet, he chuckled lightly. "Does that mean yes?"

"Yes," she fairly choked, throwing her arms around his neck.

He pulled them back, then held both her hands in his. The expression on his face was of a sorrowful apology. "I don't think it'd be a good idea to have a. . .a real long engagement."

"Oh, but, Tom," she pleaded, "wouldn't it be wonderful to have our wedding reception at our new hotel?"

He looked skeptical. "We're talking September, October. . .?"

She nodded, adding, thoughtfully, "Otherwise, we'll both be living in the church basement."

"Not necessarily. There's an apartment for rent above the funeral home."

Dropping her hands to her side, Amie lifted an incredulous brow. "Funeral home?"

"It's spacious," Tom continued, wearing a sheepish smile. "And it'd be. . .quiet."

She winced. "It'd be creepy. No. No way! We wait till fall."

Smiling, he walked to the sofa and sat down. "I figured you'd say that."

She seated herself on the other end, leaving a generous amount of space between them. In that moment, she wanted his convictions to be her convictions, and she made her own vow to God.

Heavenly Father, I will not tempt this man to break his promise to You. She'd love to kiss him and knew herself to be somewhat impetuous at times. Like now, when passion overruled her common sense. *Lord, help me keep my feelings for Tom in check until after the wedding.*

In that same, prayerful state of mind, Amie realized it was time to share her heart.

"Tom, before we start seriously discussing our future, there's something you need to know about my past."

"It doesn't matter, Amie," he insisted. "I read Hal's journals. You never finished them, did you?"

She shook her head.

"Well, I'm not completely done myself, but I got far enough along to have figured out that something pretty soul-shattering happened to you about. . .four years ago."

"How could that be in my uncle's diary?" she asked, frowning heavily. "He never knew. No one did. . .or does."

"He knew *something* happened. He wrote about his visit with your family over Easter. He'd looked forward to it because the holiday always reminded him of your spiritual birthday, and we both know Hal felt like a proud papa in that respect."

Amie smiled slightly at the comment, trying to recall that particular time in her life, yet wishing vehemently she could wipe away the event from her mind forever.

"Hal wrote that he saw you at supper and everything seemed fine," Tom relayed. "You talked about going to a company party later in the evening. You were smiling and happy, but the next day you'd completely changed. You appeared. . . 'skittish,' and he caught you crying your heart out a couple of times. Hal stated your mind was a million miles away. He asked you if something was wrong and if you wanted to talk, but you refused and pretty much stayed in your room the rest of the weekend. Hal said in his journal that it appalled him none of your family members acted concerned about you. But, to use his words, 'something happened. . .something bad.' "

Listening to Tom's recitation hurt more than Amie imagined anything in life ever could. His words were like a searing brand upon her memory, so hot and horrid that she wanted to scream from the pain. She rose from the sofa and walked over to the front windows and stared out over the soggy spring lawn.

"Look, Amie, you don't have to tell me any more than what I learned from Hal's writings."

"But I want you to know," she said tearfully. "I *need* for you to know everything because I need to share this. . .with somebody. With you."

Tom sat back. "Okay, I'm all ears."

She brushed away a tear. "I did go to that party," she stated with a sniff. "I had the afternoon off but went back to work because everyone at Maxwell Brothers was celebrating the acquisition of a large account and I didn't want to miss out on the. . .fun. Besides," she added, fighting against the all-consuming humiliation, "there was a business consultant there whom I'd been flirting with for months, and it was his last night with our company so, of course, I wanted to say. . .good-bye."

Avoiding Tom's probing gaze, she folded her arms tightly, peered at her cream-colored carpeting, and continued. "I was such a little fool. I don't know what I was thinking. . .well, that's just it: I wasn't thinking. I never bothered to find out if he was a Christian, and I had allowed my coworkers to delude me into believing coquettish behavior was an acceptable part of having a good time. I know how wrong they were. . .how wrong I was."

She sighed ruefully. "But that night, I accepted a couple glasses of champagne against my better judgment. Then when he asked me to drive him back to where he was staying since he'd relinquished the keys to his company car, I jumped at the opportunity.

"After we arrived, he asked me up to his place, and I willingly followed him inside. It was very romantic at first." Amie swallowed painfully, urging herself to go on. "He put on some soft music and I let him kiss me. Th—then everything happened so fa—fast," she stammered. "It was like he turned into a different person, so rough and demanding. I tried to stop him. I said no, but—"

She choked on a sob and squeezed her eyes closed. Every muscle in her body felt taut as the rest of the horror washed over her. When she looked up again, Tom was standing in front of her, his face a mask of pity, coupled with something indefinable.

"Did he rape you, Amie?" he asked in a tone filled with such incredulity that it sent a chill right through her.

Nevertheless, she managed a nod as the familiar trembling began.

"Did you report the incident? Tell police?"

She shook her head. "He said I deserved it. . .and I did."

"What are you talking about?" He gave her a mild shake. "No one *deserves* to be raped."

"I was hardly the innocent victim. I led him on." Scalding tears of shame streamed from her eyes.

"You were naive. But, even if you weren't, it still doesn't excuse the guy's actions. What he did to you was criminal!"

Amie couldn't reply, so overcome by emotion was she. Tom gathered her into a comforting embrace.

"You know," he said, after a few long moments passed, "I thought I'd prepared myself for everything. But I didn't prepare myself for this."

Pulling back, she saw an angry muscle working in his jaw, and his hazel eyes glistened sharply.

"Do you want your engagement ring back?" she sniffed.

He blinked, the dark clouds of wrath dissipating. "No. . .no, I love you, and nothing will ever change that."

However, the truth about her past changed his heart about something, and for the remainder of the weekend, Amie sensed a barrier between them. While Tom had been two hundred and fifty miles away, he'd never seemed so distant as he did now.

It was the very thing she'd feared the most.

Chapter 18

Amie drove fast along the last stretch of highway, the windows of her BMW open to let in the early summer air. She'd given the situation six weeks to change, and she wasn't about to wait any longer. Oh, Tom had maintained a terrific facade—too bad she could see right through it. But after today, it'd be all over. She fully intended to break their engagement. As for their business partnership—she'd have to decide what to do about that later.

One hand on the steering wheel, Amie finger-combed her wind-blown blond hair back off her face with the other. Making the turn onto County J, she saw that the hotel's construction was well under way—its foundation poured, the wooden skeleton of its walls erected. Tom had kept her posted on the progress—and he'd even recently inquired about starting wedding plans, but Amie sensed his heart wasn't in the latter.

"And I'm not playing any more games!" she declared to an empty car. She'd had four hours of solitary driving to get herself worked up into a fitful state that would not be abated until she had had her say.

She turned onto the gravel road and sped toward the church. At three-thirty on a Friday afternoon, she'd been hoping to catch him, and thankfully she spotted Tom walking from his truck. Curiously, she watched his expression as he saw her car. His eyes lit up in surprise and he smiled broadly.

Amie's resolve wavered.

"What are you doing here?" he asked, walking up to her car as she parked. His grin hadn't lessened.

Opening the door, she climbed out. "I want to talk to you."

He looked amused. "You couldn't phone or e-mail?"

She shook her head stoically. "Not for this."

"Okay." Tom's expression changed to one more earnest. "Something wrong?"

Amie took a deep breath and glanced around her. The tops of the tall pine trees swayed gently on the tepid June breeze. Beyond them, she could hear laughter from the Warren girls at play in their yard. In that very moment, she almost wished she could pretend, like Tom.

Steeling herself against those expressive hazel eyes, she slipped off her engagement ring. "I'm letting you off the hook." She took his hand and set the ring in his palm, ignoring the look of shock on his face. "You're a fine Christian man, Tom, and I know you'd never go back on a promise. So, I'm doing it for you."

"Amie—"

"You don't have to say a word," she prattled, feeling impotent. "I know you changed your mind when I told you about. . .my past. I can't blame you, and if you'll remember, I expected it. But, you know, you could have saved us both some heartache if you would have left things alone back in December."

"It's that obvious, huh?"

His admission startled her and all she could do was nod.

"Here," he gently admonished her, "put this back on. . .and don't you dare take it off again." He slipped the ring back in place. "It's not what you think, Amie. I haven't changed my mind about marrying you." He paused and she watched his Adam's apple bob with emotion. "I love you. It's just that. . . I'm so angry. Not with you. With. . .well, let's just say I'm glad you didn't mention any names, because I'd probably kill the guy who hurt you!"

Amie felt taken aback by the severity of his statement, yet, in some strange way, it consoled her too. "You're the most chivalrous man I've ever met," she finally whispered. "You'd fight for my honor? How sweet!"

"It's not *sweet*, Amie. I never get angry," he announced. "That's why this has been so hard on me. I watched anger destroy my father. He was furious with God for taking Mom, and he vented his wrath on us kids. Afterwards, he comforted himself with a bottle of whiskey. I vowed when I was thirteen that I'd never get mad—at anything. I swore I'd let nothing and no one push me to commit an act of violence against another human being. But here I am. Right where I vowed never to be."

Amie empathized with his inner struggle. "But, Tom, I'm glad you told me."

He shrugged. "I s'pose I should have been up-front with you from the start. It's just that I felt so. . .ashamed." After giving her a long look, he glanced at his wristwatch. "Listen, Amie, we'll have to finish this discussion later. I'm sorry. But I'm meeting a building inspector at the construction site." He shook his dark brown head ruefully. "Something's not right. I can tell—except I don't know enough about building to pinpoint the problem. Then, again, maybe this is all my imagination."

"*What* is all your imagination?" Amie asked, puzzled.

He grinned sardonically and looped an arm around her shoulders. "Well, as long as you're here, *business partner,* you might as well come along and find out."

❧

When they arrived, the construction crew was packing up for the day. The men cast curious glances at them, especially after they met up with the building inspector. Amie noticed ominous stares from two in particular.

"Who are those guys, Tom?" she whispered as they walked into the site.

"Keith Reider and Tyler Johnson. They're Al's buddies. We all went to high school together."

"They look mean."

"They're probably hot and tired from working all day."

Amie was tempted to argue but decided against it and turned her attention to the inspector. He had a very round head, and his dark gray hair was buzzed, except for the very top where he'd gone completely bald. Wearing tan trousers and an off-white short-sleeve dress shirt and brown-striped tie, he possessed a military-like appearance, even though he barely stood five feet five inches tall.

He poked at pipes and rattled wooden beams, scrutinized the cement foundation, asking minimal questions. Then every so often he'd pause to consider Amie, who was growing increasingly uncomfortable.

Finally, he said, "Don't I know you?"

She shrugged.

"I'm Ed Holm," he stated, even though introductions had already been made.

"My mother's maiden name was Holm," she replied, "but I really didn't think anything of the similarity, since it's a common last name around here."

He snapped his fingers. "Lillian's daughter—Halvor's niece."

She smiled, somewhat relieved to know the reason behind his earlier observations of her. "That's me."

"I'm Lil and Hal's cousin."

"Oh." She gave him a polite smile.

"Sure. But I'll bet it's been at least ten years since I last saw you."

She nodded. "I'll tell Mom I ran into you."

"Do that." Cousin Ed began studying Tom.

"This is my fiancé," Amie told him.

"I worked for Hal at the filling station."

"Right." Ed chuckled. "I thought you looked familiar too. Small world, eh? You request a building inspector and you get me!" He glanced around the construction site. "So, you two are going to get hitched and then run a hotel together, huh?"

They nodded.

"Be good to have more family up here." Ed gave Amie a look of approval. "Well, listen, kids," he said more soberly now. "There's nothing here that's in any code violation, but the workmanship stinks. Who's the contractor?"

"Simonson's Building and Lumber."

"Big Al? Well, he usually does an okay job," Ed stated, pulling up the front of his trousers by the belt buckle. "Maybe he's got a new crew this year."

"Don't think so. I recognize most of them."

"Then money must be tight; he's using seconds. Look here. The quality of wood isn't the greatest; pipes are cheap; foundation looks sloppy."

"I noticed the foundation," Tom muttered and Amie stifled a surprised gasp.

"But, believe it or not, it's up to code." Ed grinned wryly. "The big bad wolf'll just be able to huff and puff and blow the place down."

"Great," Tom replied sarcastically.

Ed crossed his arms and looked at them earnestly. "You two are family. Normally, I don't do this, but I'm going to give you some advice." He tapered his stare. "Hire a different builder."

Later, sitting beside Tom in the pickup truck, Amie guarded her tongue against any "I told you so" remarks. He seemed miserable enough without her adding to it.

"Do you have to work at the motel tonight?" she asked.

"Yeah," he replied flatly, turning onto the church road.

Feeling a case of nerves on the rise, she decided to change the subject. "I quit my job this morning," she announced. "Poor Buzz. I thought he was going to have heart failure. The other secretaries actually started to cry because I was leaving." She shook her head, still amazed. "They knew I wasn't going to stay forever. But these past few months we kind of got to be friends. The ladies even came to church with me one Sunday."

Tom reached across the truck's cab and took her hand. "Amie, I can tell you're upset. But don't worry, all right?"

She took a deep breath and chastened herself for babbling. "Are you going to terminate Al's contract?"

He dropped her hand. "I don't have a choice, do I? I gave him a chance, but. . ." He paused, looking almost hurt. "I don't get it. What did I ever do to make him hate me so much that he'd try to ruin our hotel?"

"Do you think this is a personal thing, Tom? Maybe Al's funds are just low and he's cutting corners."

"His funds *are* low, but it's personal."

"You're sure."

"I'm positive."

Amie wanted to inquire further, but they'd reached the Warrens' drive.

"I'll let you off here 'cause I've got to get to work. I know Katie will be happy to see you. She and Pastor Jake can fill you in on everything else."

"Everything else?"

Tom gave her a guilty nod.

"You mentioned your run-ins with Al, but you haven't told me the whole story, have you?"

"No. I didn't want to worry you."

"Worry me? It's that bad?"

"Katie can explain, and I'll call you on my break."

His hazel eyes pleaded with her until finally she acquiesced. Opening the door, she jumped down from the truck.

≫≪

After the four young Warren girls were tucked snugly into bed, Katie and Jake were able to join Amie in the small living room of their home where they could talk uninterrupted.

"Thanks for putting me up tonight," Amie stated, "although I suppose I could have stayed at the Best Rest in Shawano and bothered Tom all night by calling him at the front desk every fifteen minutes." She laughed impishly.

"Oh, you could never *bother* Tom. I'm sure he would have enjoyed your staying there," Katie said, smiling. "But we're a lot cheaper than the Best Rest, not to mention the fact that we love your company too."

Amie felt herself blush at the kind sentiment. "Okay, tell me," she began, putting all humor aside for the time being, "what's going on with Big Al?"

The Warrens gave each other a quick look, and then Jake spoke up. "We don't have any evidence that anything's going on with Big Al. It's just that things have happened—"

"What *things*?"

"Well, a few weeks ago, Tom was on his way home from work. It was about two-thirty A.M. and the highway was pretty much deserted. But then he noticed an old rusty pickup truck tailing him. Finally, it passed him and Tom noticed there were three men inside, but he didn't get a look at their faces. All he can swear to is that they wore ball caps of some sort." Jake paused thoughtfully. "After the truck got ahead of him, it slowed down, and when Tom tried to pass, the other driver sped up—even crossed lanes so Tom couldn't get ahead of him. That lasted all the way until Tom turned onto the church road out here."

"Intimidation," Amie muttered.

"Exactly."

"But then there was an accident at the site last week which really started to concern us."

"First tell Amie about Nancy," Katie interjected.

"Oh, yes, Nancy gave birth to another girl. Did Tom tell you?"

Amie nodded. He'd e-mailed her about a month ago with the news.

"Well, that sent Big Al into apoplexy. He'd had his heart set on a boy, and I don't know. . .Nancy told us he thinks fathering all females is some kind of insult to his manhood." Jake spread his arms wide. "I've got four daughters, and I feel blessed! I tried to share as much with Al, but he refused to listen, and finally he became so hostile toward Nancy that this past weekend she packed up the girls, moved out of their home and in with her parents for safety reasons."

"Right around the time the accident at the site occurred," Katie said.

Amie raised an inquiring brow. "Accident?"

"Tom got the notion things weren't going exactly right with the construction of the hotel," Jake informed her. "As you said, it's just what the building inspector confirmed this afternoon. But last Saturday morning, Tom was nosing around, thinking he was alone at the site, when suddenly a generator fell from a crane where it'd been strung up for safekeeping. It nearly hit him. In fact, he got a gash that needed a couple stitches on his elbow from flying debris. But God, in His infinite mercy, protected him from real harm."

Amie folded her arms, feeling slighted. "Tom never said a word about it."

"He didn't want you to worry," Katie said. "But he planned to tell you eventually."

"And no one saw anything?" Amie's question sounded more like a retort.

"Not so. Big Al saw the whole thing. In fact, he took Tom to the hospital."

"Big Al?" Amie replied incredulously.

Jake nodded. "He said he was driving down Highway 45 when he saw the generator crash. That's why he stopped. Told Tom it was one of his most expensive pieces of equipment. Couldn't understand how it fell from its perch."

"But Tom doesn't believe him?"

"No, Amie. And, unfortunately, neither do I. There are too many questions unanswered. Such as, why was Al's minivan near the crane? If, indeed, he'd seen the accident and pulled into the site off of 45, he would have been out in front, not around back."

"Are the police involved?"

Jake shook his auburn head.

"They're not?" Amie was shocked.

"There's no proof and, for Nancy and the girls' sakes, we're keeping quiet until more evidence surfaces. . .if it ever does."

Rising from the comfortable armchair, Amie strode to the bay window where she viewed the eastern sky's reflection of the setting sun. She shuddered inwardly, suddenly fearing for the life of the man she loved.

Chapter 19

Amie pensively tap-tap-tapped the end of a pencil on the dining room table until Tom's hand covered hers, putting a stop to her fidgeting.

"Yes or no, Amie? We're all waiting."

"Yes!" she declared at last, smiling into his eyes. "Yes, yes, yes! This'll be great!" She glanced at Katie and Jake who were all smiles now also. "If I move in here until the wedding, I won't have to live with my folks!"

"Is that the only reason?" Tom asked with an injured expression.

"Of course not," she replied, thinking he was about the most sensitive man on earth. "If I move in with the Warrens, I'll get to see you everyday—that's the biggest blessing of all!"

He grinned.

"Well, Amie, you handled that just right," Katie teased. "We, ladies, must always be mindful of our men's fragile egos."

She and Katie shared a good-natured chuckle, while Tom and Jake gave each other leveled looks.

"All right, all right," the pastor said, his hands up as if in surrender, "our fragile egos aside for now, the best reason for Amie moving in is so that the four of us can begin discipleship classes twice a week." He narrowed his gaze in earnest. "From what you've both shared, I sense you'll be bringing a lot of baggage to this marriage unless certain issues get settled before the wedding. Delving into God's Word will help you give your pasts over to Him."

"I agree," said Tom.

"Me too." Amie looked over at him, glad they'd confided in Jake. It became apparent during the weekend that they both needed to learn how to communicate and better address their insecurities.

Jake scooted his chair back from the table and stood. "I'm whipped. Good night, people."

Katie rose as well. "Am I a terrible hostess if I turn in before you, Amie?"

She laughed. "Not at all. Besides, I won't be a 'guest' for long."

"True enough."

The Warrens ambled off for the night, and Amie considered the pad of paper before her. Picking up the pencil again, she jotted down several more notes about the hotel. After the worship service that evening and just before the conversation had turned so personal, they'd been discussing the business and how to handle their current predicament.

"Do you want me to call these other construction companies in the morning?"

Tom nodded. "We'll need estimates." Looking weary, he combed a hand through his hair. "And I've got to tell Al I'm backing out of our contract."

"Did you get a hold of Jim Henderson?"

"Yeah, and he's taking care of the legalities, but now it's back to square one."

Amie nibbled her lower lip in consternation. "Do you think the hotel will still be ready to open before the wedding in October?"

"I hope so." He gave her a smirk. "Those invitations go out yet?"

"No," she replied guiltily. "They're printed, but. . .well, I was holding off mailing them until I talked to you this weekend."

Tom shook his head. "You thought I'd change my mind." He reached out his hand to her. She took it before he continued. "In reality, I was just too afraid to confess my angry feelings."

"But that's all over with now. We're taking measures to correct things." She smiled. "I'm relieved. We've really got a chance, Tom. Our whole future is filled with promise. If God is for us, who can be against us?"

"Amen."

Amie giggled. She hadn't meant to preach. It was just that a bright sense of hope had been renewed in her—a far different feeling than the one she'd had on Friday, or the past few months for that matter. As far as the situation with Big Al, she felt encouraged about taking steps to rectify it too. She only prayed that once they canceled their contract with him, he'd stay out of their way for good. Perhaps he'd concentrate on reuniting himself with Nancy and their children.

"But you know what I wish?" Tom said, standing and stretching with arms behind his head. He sighed, suddenly sounding as tired as he looked, light shadows lining his lower lids. Amie was glad he didn't have to go in to work tonight.

"What do you wish?" she replied to his question.

"I wish our wedding was a lot sooner than October." He grinned sheepishly. "How am I supposed to stand firm on my convictions with you around all the time?"

"Need a chaperone out there, Tom?" Jake called from the other end of the hallway.

Amie swallowed a laugh.

Looking thoroughly abashed, he shook his head. "No, sir, I'm just on my way out."

"Good. I want to get some sleep."

Tom chuckled. Then, after gazing at her for a few long moments, a pining light in his eyes, he told her good night and departed, leaving Amie wishing their wedding was sooner too.

❧

Monday morning, God sent a thunderstorm, so none of Al's crew showed up at the construction site. By the end of the day, Jim Henderson had terminated The Haven of Rest, LLC's contractual agreement with Simonson's Building and Lumber Company. However, Tom still felt he owed Al an explanation or, at the very least, a phone call. Getting the big man on the line, he got five words in—"Hi, Al, it's Tom Anderson"—before the profanity began. Finally Tom hung up on him.

"You did what you could," Jake told him. "Now it's up to the Lord."

Tom nodded his agreement but couldn't seem to rid himself of a nagging fear that something would happen to destroy his new-found joy with Amie before they even made it to the altar. *Heavenly Father, help me trust You more,* he prayed. *Strengthen my faith.*

❧

With her condominium sold and most of her belongings moved into a large storage facility in Shawano, Amie began to relax and enjoy the summer. After just a few weeks, she adjusted to country living and learned to perform amazing feats, such as weeding Katie's vegetable garden and hanging clean laundry on the clothesline to dry. Such simplicity, yet so foreign to Amie, who had lived her whole life in a bustling city. Her mother had never hung clothes out to dry, neither had she cared for gardening, thus Amie hadn't given such chores much thought. But, lately, when she lay in bed, preparing for sleep, she could smell the sunshine in her linens and feel a healthy freshness in her skin that tanning booths couldn't ever achieve.

"You look. . .happy, Amie," Katie remarked one evening as they stood at the kitchen sink, washing dishes.

"I am. I'm very happy."

Katie smiled. "I've been meaning to ask if you've met more people. I feel bad that the neighborhood Bible programs have been keeping me so busy. I've neglected introducing you around."

"In this town, introductions aren't necessary," Amie replied with a little laugh. "Even Judy at the grocery store knew who I was. She said, 'Aren't you the one marrying Tom Anderson?' And I said, 'Yep. I'm the luckiest girl in the whole world.' Then Judy told me she'd marry Tom, too, since he inherited all that money." Amie chuckled lightheartedly. "But I set her straight by informing her that Tom is flat broke—and so am I. Our hotel is taking every cent and then some!"

Katie laughed. "What did Judy say to that?"

"She asked if we were hiring. . .and we are. Eventually." Amie sighed. "It's one of the million things still left to do."

"Did Nancy Simonson talk to you about a job?"

Amie nodded, recalling the conversation vividly. Al's company had taken a financial nosedive. He was barely supporting himself, let alone his wife and four kids. Nancy's parents were picking up the slack while she was living with them. Meanwhile, the Simonson's house was pending foreclosure.

Tom had mentioned seeing Al stumbling out of the local tavern on more than one occasion—and in the middle of the afternoon. But, where Tom continued to feel bad for backing out of their deal, Amie felt justified. Big Al's problems were consequences of his own actions. No one else's fault.

However, she didn't have a problem with offering Nancy a position at their hotel—specifically in the café. In dealing with her insecurities, Amie had stopped speculating over Tom's teenage crush on the other woman, and as a result, her friendship with Nancy was blossoming.

Once the dinner dishes were dried and put back into the long, wooden cupboards, Amie gathered her catalogues and sat down on the front porch steps, while Katie and Jake put their girls to bed. As she leafed through the pages of motel room decor, sounds of animated voices and girlish giggles floated to her through the screen door. She marveled at how bedtime was such a family affair in the Warren household, and she vowed to make it the same in hers, should she and Tom be blessed with children.

Momentarily forgetting the colorful, thick books in her lap, she gazed out over the emerald green cornfield across the gravel road and got lost in a daydream about life after marriage. Tom would make a wonderful husband. He'd be gentle, passionate. Oddly, the latter didn't scare her in the least, as it used to when she thought about marriage. Tom had already proved his love for children. Amie prayed they'd have their own brood of Andersons some day, each with their daddy's hazel eyes.

The sound of tires on the dusty road drew Amie out of her reverie. Tom was at work, and not many cars passed by this way, unless they had business with the pastor. Curiously, she watched as a black minivan with a red pinstripe running along its side came into view.

Big Al. . .what does he want? she wondered as her stomach did a nervous flip.

The van slowed to a crawl in front of the Warrens' house, and Amie inhaled sharply when she saw Al's expression. Pure, unadulterated hatred emanated from his dark, burly features. Standing, she slowly backed up to the front door, then he sped off, the wheels of his vehicle spitting gravel in their wake.

Amie clutched the catalogues to her chest, her heart still pounding fearfully.

"What was that all about?" Jake asked from behind her, his voice wafting through the screen door.

She shook her head. "I don't know."

Later, in the wee hours of the morning, Amie awakened to a loud bang and a shout.

The front door?

Tom's voice?

Definitely.

"Jake?" She heard Tom calling in the hallway. There was no mistaking the urgency in his tone.

Fully roused now, Amie sat up and swung her legs off the bed. She grabbed her robe, tied it about her waist, and then opened her bedroom door where she collided with Tom, who was obviously on his way in.

"Are you okay?" he asked almost breathlessly.

"I'm fine. What's going on?"

"Good question," Jake said from behind Tom.

He pivoted. "Are you guys all right? The girls?"

The pastor didn't waste any time in checking on his children, Katie right beside him. When they discovered them unharmed, they turned back to Tom who sighed audibly with relief and sagged against the door frame of Amie's room.

"Something happen tonight?" Jake inquired, flipping on the hall light. Amie saw the concern etched upon the pastor's freckled countenance.

Tom nodded, his eyes suddenly looking so sad and mournful that Amie took his hand. She gave it a little squeeze as a sense of dread filled her being.

"I just got home from work and. . .well, you'd better come back to the church with me, Pastor." With reluctance, he added, "Have Katie call 911."

Chapter 20

Amie was still seething as she took the last of Tom's clothes out of the dryer at Brown's Laundromat in town. The horrid vision of white, spray-painted swastikas on wooden pews, walls, and outside on the church's front doors caused Amie's muscles to tense in anger. Several stained-glass windows had been cracked, and Tom's living quarters. . .totally ransacked, his computer smashed on the floor, and his clothes strewn about and trampled upon with soiled boots. There was no doubt in her mind who was responsible for the desecration of the sanctuary and the destruction in Tom's apartment. Big Al, although it'd be hard to prove it. The sheriffs who had answered their early morning call tried in vain to obtain fingerprints.

At least it was only Tuesday, and they'd have most of the week to repaint and repair before Sunday services. Pastor Warren was already making alternate plans for tomorrow's Wednesday night worship service.

Folding Tom's things neatly into a large plastic laundry basket, Amie was glad that she could help him in this small way. She'd taken his shirts and miscellaneous other items to the dry cleaners in Shawano, and it looked as though his washables had scrubbed up nicely.

She slung her purse over her shoulder and lifted the basket, carrying it out to her car on one hip. Walking down the nearly deserted street, she stopped short, spying Al Simonson perched on the hood of her BMW. On the edge of the sidewalk stood two men whom Amie recognized as his mean-looking friends from the construction site.

Lord, help me, she silently prayed, grappling for composure as she approached. Al just sat there, watching her with an amused grin.

"Get off my car," she said tersely.

He put his hands out as if to forestall her. "Hey, no problem." Sliding one tree-trunk-like thigh off the hood, he smirked. "Me and the boys're just wondering how that hotel's coming along?"

After checking for scratches on the hood, Amie unlocked the driver's side door, wishing she would have activated the alarm. Setting the basket into the backseat, she bit back a snide reply and prayed for control over her mounting temper.

"Guess she's too good to talk to the likes of us," Al re-marked to his friends. He grabbed her elbow and spun her around. "Miss High 'n' Mighty."

"Let go of me!" she said, wrenching her arm free. "Why don't you guys start acting like men instead of delinquents?"

Al hooted at the retort. "Like you know real men, eh? What a laugh! You wouldn't be marrying Tom Anderson if that was true."

Something inside Amie snapped, and she all but forgot her fear of the large man looming above her. Before she knew it, her palm connected soundly with his cheek. "Tom is more of a man than you'll ever be!"

Al scowled, unable to mask the animosity blazing from his dark, beady eyes. He was as poised as a rattlesnake, and Amie fleetingly wondered if he'd strike her back. She braced herself but couldn't back down.

One of his friends suddenly stepped between them. "Forget her, Man. She ain't worth it." Turning to Amie, his gaze signaled an unspoken warning: *Get in your car and get out of here!*

Amie didn't wait for a second urging. Climbing inside, she started the engine and peeled away from the curb.

When she arrived back at the church, she was trembling. She couldn't imagine what had come over her. She'd slapped Big Al so hard, her arm now ached. By the time she entered the sanctuary where Tom and Pastor Warren were busily painting walls and revarnishing wood, hot tears were streaming from her eyes and hysteria was welling in her chest.

Tom glanced up from between two pews and dropped his brush. "Amie, what in the world. . .?"

With an expression of concern, Jake scampered down the ladder on which he'd been working and jogged over to them.

It took Amie several long minutes to get her emotions in check and relay the story. "Am I going to get arrested for assault and battery?" she cried, feeling miserable hanging onto Tom.

"I doubt it," he replied, attempting to comfort her.

"Amie, I am very proud of you," Jake told her. "Not for losing your temper, even though Al might have deserved the whack upside his noggin, but. . .I sense God is at work here."

"What do you mean?" she sniffed.

"Well, don't you think the Lord has just proved that you don't have to be afraid of men. . .or anything else? Of course, bad things can happen to all Christians, but we're not to live in fear, Amie. This is exactly what I've tried to explain during our discipleship classes, although I haven't felt very successful. I've been asking the Lord to help me describe trust to you." Jake chuckled softly. "But He had to show you Himself—just now with Big Al."

She thought it over, then looked up at Tom. "God protected me," she murmured.

He nodded, widening his hazel eyes emphatically. "I'll say!"

Later, that evening, just after supper, Amie spotted one of Al's buddies pulling into the Warren's driveway.

"Pastor Jake? Tom? I think we might have problems."

Katie ran into the living room, looking alarmed. "I'll send the girls to the basement playroom for a while."

Tom squinted as he peered out the window. "That's Keith Reider."

"He's the one who fended off Al so I could drive away this morning," Amie informed him.

Pastor Warren stepped outside and met the man on the lawn. After a few minutes of conversing, they both entered the house.

"Mr. Reider has something to tell us," Jake announced.

The man nodded a brief greeting to Tom, although his expression was one of chagrin.

"Have a seat," the pastor said. "Everyone."

Reider seemed to grow uncomfortable with all eyes on him. "Listen," he began, "I don't want any trouble. My wife is expecting our second kid, and I've got a good chance at steady work in New London. That's why I came over here tonight." Leaning forward in the armchair, he folded his hands and allowed them to dangle between his knees. "It's Al. I don't know what's happened to him. It's like he's gone berserk. I think it started back when you, Tom, bought that pickup truck. Al got real jealous, said no Anderson ought to be allowed to drive something that nice. So he went out and bought himself that Chevy minivan, which put him and Nancy into debt."

Tom shook his head as if he couldn't fathom it. "Al's got no cause to be envious of me."

"Oh, it don't stop there," Reider continued. "A year ago, when you inherited Halvor Holm's money, Al saw red. He kept saying that no Anderson deserved to have that kind of loot. And then, of course, we all heard you were getting married." He nodded toward Amie. "Al figured she was just marrying you for your money, but then Nancy said it was love, all right. She'd seen it with her own eyes on Thanksgiving Day."

Amie blushed, and one glance at Tom told her that he felt equally embarrassed.

"For some odd reason," Reider went on, "that was a real kick in the head for Al. He couldn't get over it. He brought it up all the time. Tom Anderson, a guy from a no-account family, marrying a high-class babe from Chicago. . ." A look of concern crossed his lean, chiseled features. "The fact is, Al was jealous of you— or at least that's what it seemed like to the rest of us. Then he started taking it out on Nancy, and their marriage started really going down the tubes."

Amie groaned inwardly, feeling nauseated. Suddenly she knew why Al

Simonson had given her the creeps from the first day she met him.

"And then. . .about the church and your place, Tom," Reider continued, looking apologetic. "We all left the tavern together. . .I was there, but I swear I didn't do any of the damage. Big Al did it. . .and Tyler Johnson helped him some. He didn't want to. He's just more afraid of Al than I ever was." The man shook his sandy blond head and a disbelieving look crossed his features. "But then when this little lady over here gave Al what-for. . .I'll tell you," he added, looking right at Amie, "I was ashamed of myself after that. If a woman can stand up to Al, I should be able to."

Amie lowered her gaze, feeling very much aware of God's handiwork. She found it incredible that Keith would make this confession as a result of her earlier altercation with Big Al. Jake had been right: God was at work—in more ways than one.

"And, Tom," Reider added, "I don't have anything against you. Never did. Not even when we were in high school. The only reason I sided with Al is because he's my friend, and he hated your guts—just like his dad hated your father. But, see, that's the kind of men those Simonsons are. They're like politicians. They can make a whole host of people see things their way. I'm not trying to excuse my wrongdoings." Shaking his head, he added, "If my boy ever did something like this, I'd switch him. But. . .well, I'll bet there's lots of folks in town who can't stand the sight of an Anderson, only they don't know why. They just heard the talk for too long and now they believe it."

Amie found herself fairly gaping at his statement. Such ignorance boggled her mind.

Keith stood. "I told the pastor that I'm willing to talk to the police and help with the cleanup. Like I said, I don't want to bring any trouble down on my family." Then to Amie he added, "I'm real sorry and. . .well, I wish you guys the best."

Everyone rose almost simultaneously, and Tom stuck out his right hand. "I appreciate your honesty."

Reider shook it. "About time, huh?" With a rueful smile, he left the house, and Jake followed him out.

Amie looked over at Katie who lifted her hands helplessly. "I don't know what to say. I'm. . .stunned."

"I'm not," Tom replied thoughtfully. "I don't claim to understand Al's hatred, but having lived with it practically all my life, it's nice to hear somebody acknowledge it. Up until tonight, the prejudice in this town against my family has been something undefined and ignored. . .and accepted."

Amie stepped close to him, slipping her arm around his elbow. "Well, I don't care about any of it. I love you with all my heart."

"I love you too," he said, tweaking her nose affectionately. "Truth is, I can't imagine where I'd be today if God hadn't brought you into my life."

⤟

The October sunshine shone through a clear blue sky and warmed the day to a pleasant seventy-five degrees. Down in the church basement, where Tom's living quarters had been up until a week ago, Amie gazed into the large bathroom mirror and smoothed down the lace on the full-length skirt of her antique-white wedding dress.

"Will you stop fidgeting?" Dottie, her only bridesmaid, told her. She stood behind Amie, clad in a burgundy satin gown. "You look fine."

"What about my hair?"

"The French twist is gorgeous. Don't touch it—there's not a strand out of place."

"Better not be," she quipped, "after all the hair spray you put on it."

Hearing high-heeled footfalls descending the wooden steps, they both turned and exited the tiny restroom. Nancy Simonson appeared, her frosted hair falling to her shoulders in permanent waves. "The church is packed," she announced. "It's like Christmas or something!" She grinned. "But I wanted to give you a hug, Amie. . .before you walk down the aisle."

They embraced, and Nancy placed a kiss on her cheek. "I'm so happy for you."

"Thanks, Nance." Considering her friend's weary countenance, she frowned slightly. "Are you holding up all right?"

"Yes. God has really been looking out for me. I thought that after Al spent thirty days in jail for defacing property, he'd want to get his life back together. I'd been praying he'd want to give his heart to Christ. But nothing's changed. These past few weeks have been awful."

Amie gave her a knowing nod. She had employed Nancy's help in decorating the café and preparing it for the Grand Opening. Nancy had often brought her children with her to their meetings or on shopping trips when they went to pick the perfect decor. Subsequently, Amie had grown close to Nancy and her daughters and understood the stress they'd all been under because of Al's behavior.

"I keep trying to remember him as he was on our wedding day," Nancy said with a sad smile. "Believe it or not, Al was quite handsome and charming."

"There's still hope."

"Yes and I'm not giving up." She hugged Amie once more. "I'm just glad you and Tom are building the foundation of your marriage on your faith. Al and I didn't have that start." She suddenly chuckled. "And Tom's so funny. . .I just saw him. He just cannot wait until you're Mrs. Thomas Anderson." Leaning forward conspiratorially, she added, "He'd probably like to skip the reception altogether and get right to the honeymoon."

"Oh no!" Amie exclaimed, ignoring her sister's chortles over the remark. "My mother and I practically killed ourselves—and each other—getting that banquet room ready for this evening." She sighed. "It's such a shame the entire hotel won't be completed for another month or so—which is not entirely Al's doing."

"I know, I know. . .I'm just glad your apartment is finished."

The old pipe organ began the first strains of the wedding march, and Nancy made a hasty departure back to the sanctuary. Following her up the stairs, Amie and Dottie paused in the tiny vestibule where they were met by their father and Matthew.

"You're lucky, you know?" Dottie whispered, just before taking Matt's arm. "You're marrying a guy who really loves you."

Amie agreed, feeling as though she could start bawling already. . .and the wedding hadn't even begun! It wasn't the first time her sister had made such a comment, and she sensed Dottie's heart was softening.

"You look like a million bucks, Princess!" John Potter declared, taking her hand and wrapping it around his elbow.

She smiled. "Thanks, Dad."

The procession began. The wedding party consisted of a maid of honor and a best man, so Amie didn't have long to wait for her turn to walk up the aisle. As she made her way on her father's arm, she paid little heed to the many well-wishers crowded into the tiny country church. All she could see was Tom waiting for her expectantly, his eyes captivated by her every step. At last her father gave her away, and she linked arms with Tom, feeling his nervous warmth radiating from beneath the black tuxedo.

The ceremony proceeded, and the vows were pledged, Amie choking on her emotion when it came her turn to speak, then crying softly as Tom promised to "love, honor, and cherish." Time had no bearing on Amie, and it seemed only moments passed before Pastor Warren looked at Tom, and said, "You may kiss your bride."

She turned to her new husband, suppressing the urge to giggle like a school-girl at his eager expression. Tom gently cupped her face with his hands and lowered his mouth to hers, touching her lips lightly at first, then steadily deepening the kiss until Jake cleared his throat. Chuckles and "Amens!" emanated from the congregation. Amie felt herself blushing profusely before deciding Tom's kiss was the best she'd ever experienced. *Pretty good,* she thought, *for a guy who's never done that before!* She glanced at him in mild amazement as they walked back down the aisle, sporting the new title of Mr. and Mrs. Thomas Richard Anderson.

The remainder of the afternoon was spent taking pictures. Then Amie and Tom changed clothes in their apartment above the hotel in preparation for the evening's reception, and later, their escape. They planned to catch a midnight flight out of Green Bay, heading to Key West, Florida, for their honeymoon. The trip was a gift from Amie's parents, and both she and Tom were looking forward to it.

Tom cornered her as she made her way from the large master bedroom to the bathroom where she intended to perfect her makeup. He pulled her into a close embrace and kissed her thoroughly. "I love you so much," he whispered next to her ear, sending delicious shivers down her spine.

But just as they thought they'd found scant precious time alone, curious friends and relatives filed into the apartment, begging for a tour of the hotel.

"It's a couple of months from being completely finished," Tom explained; however, no one seemed to mind.

Amie smiled wistfully as she watched him lead the way out. Tom was so proud of their endeavor—so was she! The place still smelled of new wood and fresh paint and much of the cabinetry and decorating hadn't been completed, but it was definitely a hotel.

And it was theirs.

Chapter 21

Well, darling, I had my doubts," Lillian Potter said as her gaze wandered around the banquet room. "But it's turned out to be quite a lovely reception."

Amie smiled. "Thanks, Mom. I couldn't have done it without you. You're the best interior decorator ever!"

"Oh, go on with you!" Her mother appeared embarrassed, but Amie could tell she was pleased with the final result.

The room's motif was Early American, intermingling Colonial-blue wainscoting and dark brown and blue patchwork papered walls. All the woodwork had been painted in the same blue trim, and the drapes, hanging on the multi-paned windows, matched the wallpaper. The carpet was a durable, stain-resistant woven fabric of taupe and seemed to pull all the colors together.

"I love you," Amie said, leaning over and placing a kiss on her mother's press-powdered cheek.

"I love you too. I just hope you'll be. . .happy up here." She cleared her throat, indicating she still found the whole idea quite distasteful. Then, painting a smile on her face, she left to mingle with the guests, most of whom were relatives.

After her mother waltzed away, Amie scanned the reception for Tom. She spotted him standing in the corner near the windows, pointing toward the little creek that ran through the middle of their property. No doubt he was explaining to Ernie Huffman and Russ Thorbjorg that he'd promised to build Amie a gazebo out there next year. The two elderly men nodded their gray heads, looking interested.

From a small platform on the other side of the room, an all-female musical ensemble began to play their next piece. They were local talent, referred to Amie by the Warrens. One of musicians, Katie said, was a teacher at the grade school. She'd had Emma in her class last year.

Smiling contentedly, Amie made her way toward Tom who had now been waylaid by her mother's cousin Ed, the building inspector. It had become apparent of late that the older gentleman loved to tell stories about "the good ole days," and Amie had a hunch that unless she rescued Tom soon, he'd be listening to Cousin Ed the rest of the night. She got about four steps into the middle of the banquet room when Matthew burst through the side entrance that led into the hotel's still unfinished lobby.

"Fire!" he yelled. "Everyone out the back way. Fire!"

Initially, Amie sent a scolding frown at her brother-in-law, thinking this was his idea of a joke. But then the instantaneous mayhem that broke out, coupled with the steadily increasing smell of smoke, forced the harsh reality upon her. The hotel was on fire!

"Tom!" she called, but he was nowhere in sight.

The alarm system sounded, heightening the panic in the room, which had suddenly grown much too small. Amie guessed the sprinkler system had already been activated. The fire would be extinguished in no time. . .wouldn't it? If everyone would just stay calm—

Her brother, Stephen, caught her around the waist. "C'mon, Amie, we gotta get outta here."

"I can't leave without Tom."

He ignored the argument and fairly dragged her outside. The October night air had grown cold and Amie shivered. Her view from the side of the building revealed a sickening orangish-gold reflection.

"Get out there with everyone else and stay put," Stephen commanded. "I'm going back in to make sure all those old folks get out okay."

"Stephen, wait!" Amie felt icy fingers of terror grip her heart.

"Go on!" he yelled.

Someone grabbed her arm and propelled her forward. Meanwhile, the hotel's alarm continued to ring out into the chilly darkness, resounding within Amie's very soul. Reaching the front of the structure, she turned and beheld a nightmarish vision. Hot flames shot out of the front doors and windows and licked upward greedily, pursued by billows of black smoke. Why wasn't the sprinkler system working? How did the fire get so out of control? And where was Tom?

Tom!

"He's in there!" she shrieked. "Tom's inside!" Mindlessly bolting for the hotel, Amie was swiftly overtaken by three concerned men who hung onto her despite her attempts to break out of their grasps. "Let me go!" she cried. "He's in there. I know it!"

"Tom's not in there," one of them said, pointing toward the side of the building from where she'd just come. "Look."

Sure enough—it was Tom, along with Stephen, Matt, and her parents. A quick survey of the parking lot told her everyone had exited the burning building unscathed.

Amie sighed with relief. *Thank You, Lord. . .thank You. . .*

In the next moment, she was turned loose and ran to Tom, throwing her arms around his neck.

"I thought you were inside," she said, trembling with a mixture of terror and joy. "I. . .I thought you were. . .inside."

She clung to him, inhaling the acrid smell of smoke from the flames he'd tried in vain to subdue.

"It's okay, Amie. It's okay."

The fire department seemed to take forever in coming, and then it felt like another eternity until the blaze was finally extinguished. The damage looked so extensive that it made Amie sick with grief.

"Our hotel, Tom. Look at it. It took so long to build, and now our plans, our future. . .it's gone."

Taking a hold of her shoulders, he gave her a mild shake. "It's just a hotel, Amie," he said tightly. "It's wood, hay, and stubble in comparison to you and me and what *really* got built this last year. Look at us. Look what we've got—something nobody, nowhere can ever burn down. We've got Christ. We've got each other!"

She gulped down a reply as Tom's lips gently touched hers. He was right. She knew it, and yet. . .

Stepping back, he took her hand. "Come on. We're leaving."

"Leaving? We can't go anywhere now!"

Amie saw his terse expression beneath the red and white revolving lights of a fire engine. "May I remind you, *Mrs. Anderson*, that this is our wedding night?"

"But—"

Tom wouldn't hear another word and, after voicing instructions to Matt, he led Amie over to where her BMW sat parked in the far corner of the hotel's lot. "Good thing I stuck our luggage in the trunk earlier this afternoon."

"Tom, I don't think—"

He pressed his forefinger against her mouth and silenced her protests. Then he gathered her in his arms and held her, laying his cheek against her forehead. As the moments passed, Amie somehow sensed he was praying. Very slowly, her anguished spirit quieted within her.

At last Tom inhaled deeply, kissed her, then opened the car door. Amie crawled in, waiting only seconds until he unlocked the other side and climbed behind the wheel. She had to smile, remembering how much he enjoyed driving her car—her *hot rod*.

"Think we'll make it?" he asked, starting the engine. "Our flight's in three hours."

"We'll make it," she replied, forcing enthusiasm into her voice.

He sped down the highway, heading for the Green Bay airport, and Amie compelled herself not to look back.

❧

Ten days later, Amie peered out the window of the airplane as it flew the last stretch of sky back to Wisconsin. Beside her, Tom stirred and she glanced over at his snoozing form. No matter how many times she'd flown in the past, she'd never relaxed enough to fall asleep—how did Tom manage it? This was only his second time in the air!

Shifting in her first-class seat, she thought back on her honeymoon. Her parents had purchased their airfare and rented a room for them at a hotel on the ocean in Key West. The weather had been gorgeous—perfect—and each passing day, she'd fallen even more deeply in love with Tom.

On occasion, she wondered whether she'd gained a husband or a playmate. He would tackle her in the ocean or tickle her until she couldn't breathe. Each time she was tempted to admonish him for his roughhousing, she'd recall the words her uncle had penned: *Makes me sick. His childhood is gone.*

Amie grinned reflectively, deciding Tom had certainly made up for lost time. And yet, when the situation lent itself to intimacy, all rowdiness ceased. Moreover, his tenderness vanquished the horrid memories from her past.

"What are you smiling about?" he asked lazily, startling Amie out of her reverie.

"I was thinking of how much I love you," she replied in a soft voice.

"Well, I love you too." He sat up a little straighter and stretched. "You know what Pastor Jake said? He said he loves Katie a hundred times more than he did on their honeymoon." Taking her hand and weaving his fingers through hers, he added, "Think about us. . .can you even begin to imagine loving each other more than we do right now?"

"It is hard to fathom," she agreed. Then, with a teasing smirk, she added, "But I'll definitely remind you of those words in about five years when the kids are screaming and the bills need to be paid."

He grinned, looking chagrined. "Okay, Amie, you do that."

The plane landed and they gathered their luggage, packing it into the trunk of the BMW. On the drive back to Tigerton, their lightheartedness grew suddenly heavy, and Amie knew it was because of what awaited them. A burned-out hotel. Damaged dreams.

Then, just after they crossed the little bridge over the Embarrass River, Tom pulled the car onto the shoulder of the road and stopped.

"Let's promise each other something," he said, his arm across the back of her seat, his hazel eyes searching her face. "Let's promise not to let any circumstances at home kill the joy that's in our hearts right now, all right?"

Amie nodded timidly, wondering if she could really own up to such a vow.

"I've never been happier in my life than I have been in the past ten days."

His candidness touched her very soul, causing her to remember what was really important in this life—the eternal.

She smiled. "I promise, Tom."

Satisfied with her reply, he maneuvered the car back onto Highway 45, and within the next mile, the hotel came into view—along with the hundreds of people milling about like ants on a sugar cube.

"Tom, look at that!" Amie gasped and sat forward in her seat. "What's going on?"

"I don't know." There was a wary note in his tone.

Pulling into the lot, the sound of buzzing electrical saws and drills made melody with the many banging hammers. As Amie and Tom climbed out of the car, they stared in wonder at the sight.

"Hey, Tom, welcome back," someone called from the roof.

He looked up. "Thanks."

"Who's that?" Amie whispered.

"Don Satner—a guy I went to high school with."

"Oh. . ." She frowned. "What's he doing on our roof?"

"Fixing it, looks like." Tom glanced around at all the commotion, looking as confused as Amie felt.

Just then, old Mrs. Jensen approached them. "Did you two have a nice time in Tahiti?"

"We were in Key West, Florida," Tom shouted into her deaf ears. "What are you doing here? What's going on?"

The woman produced a silent laugh. "All of us in Tigerton decided to rebuild your hotel. We took up a collection and bought some supplies, figuring the insurance company will come through for the rest, and the lumber company in town donated the wood. And the Ladies Aid from Immanuel Bible Church," she added proudly, "fixed up lunch here everyday for the past week."

"The whole town?"

"Pretty near."

Tom's face was a mask of incredulousness. Combing fingers through his hair, he gazed at the old lady before him. "Thanks, Mrs. Jensen," he said loudly once more. "I'm grateful."

"Oh, I know you are, Tommy," she said, patting his cheek affectionately as if he were five years old again and in her kindergarten class. Then she ambled off.

Chuckling softly, Tom took Amie's hand and together they walked toward the hotel, waving back at those who called greetings.

"Well, well," John Potter said, exiting the building. The burned wood had been torn away from the main entrance and new bare wood replaced it. "I see you two finally decided to come home."

Amie couldn't suppress a little giggle. "Hi, Dad. What are you doing here? I thought you'd be back in Chicago by now."

"Took some vacation time and. . .hey! Would you believe we've just about got

135

your apartment shipshape? And your mother and Dottie are just about finished up with the café."

Amie's heart swelled with love for her family. "Thanks," she replied, unable to find the words to adequately express her feelings.

"The second floor didn't suffer too badly. Mostly smoke and water damage. But the lobby and Tom's antique shop were completely destroyed." He shook his head. "What a shame."

"Any news on what caused the fire?" Tom asked. Amie felt him tense at her side.

He nodded. "A man's in custody. Seems he got burned pretty badly on his face and hands when he lit the blaze. After he gets out of the hospital, he'll go right to jail. Your brother knows who he is—said he's been undermining the hotel's construction since day one."

Tom grimaced. "Al Simonson?"

John snapped his fingers. "That's him." He frowned. "Must have some mental problems, huh?"

"Yeah. . .and some spiritual ones too," Tom muttered.

"Well, good thing your pastor is on the ball. He's been with him at the hospital for the last couple of days, from what I heard."

"That's good," Tom replied, his expression teetering somewhere between disgust and sorrow.

Amie squeezed his hand supportively, feeling grateful that no one else had been hurt.

At that moment, she caught sight of a pile of rubbish, heaped at the far end of the lot. It made her sick to see all the beautiful new items she'd purchased for the hotel and their apartment lying there in utter ruin.

Suddenly a flash of red, poking out from beneath the mound, caught her eye and she gasped. "Uncle Hal's journals!"

"Sorry, Princess, all your books got wrecked."

She ran over to the garbage and pulled out the diary. It was badly warped and the pages were smeared beyond recognition, but she managed to identify it as the final log. "I never finished reading it," she lamented, doing her best to swallow down a lump of emotion.

Tom gently took it from her fingers and assessed the damage. Then he flipped to the back page, took several long moments to read it over, before throwing his head back in a laugh. "I don't believe it! Here," he said, amusedly, "finish it right now."

The last paragraph was amazingly legible and Amie noticed it was dated three months before her uncle's death. *When I look at the photographs on my chest of drawers, I can't help but think Tom and my niece Amie would make a nice match. Her bouncy personality alone would give him hope, and Tom, being so kind, would help Amie forget whatever happened to her a few years back. Oh, those two are worlds apart, all right, and I don't know how God will ever manage it, but I just can't get the notion out of my head and I pray about it everyday. But, like I told the boys at the bowling league Tuesday night, God always answers my prayers. I told them they best expect a wedding in the near future. . .*

"Uncle Hal, you stinker!" Amie said, gazing down at the journal. "So he's the one who started the rumor!"

She chuckled softly before looking back at Tom. A little tear had formed in the corner of his eye.

"God answers prayer," he stated simply.

"He sure does." Wrapping her arms around his neck, she kissed the sadness from his face before fastening her mouth to his.

"Hey, Tom," a voice boomed from the balcony above the hotel's front entrance. Parting, albeit reluctantly, they glanced up to see Keith Reider grinning at them. "Honeymoon's over, pal." His wave beckoned them. "Come and take a look at this new carpet."

With a sigh, Tom turned to Amie. "Shall we?"

She nodded, and as they walked hand-in-hand toward the hotel, a feeling of excited anticipation surged through her veins. "You know," she said, as he opened the new front door for her, "I'm going to like living in Tigerton. Look at how this community pulled together for us. You just wouldn't find that anywhere else in the whole world. I think we've really found our Haven of Rest, Tom—in more ways than one."

He smiled broadly. "Very well stated, Mrs. Anderson."

SEPTEMBER SONATA

Prologue

Milwaukee, WI—May 2000

Icy fear gripped Kristin Robinson's heart as she raced down the emergency room's stark corridor.

A dark-haired woman in blue scrubs stepped into her path. "Can I help you?"

"I. . .I'm looking for my husband," Krissy panted, halting in midstride. "His name is Blaine Robinson. He's a fireman, and he was injured—"

"Yes, I know who you mean. Follow me."

The nurse led her into a bustling area where doctors, nurses, and secretaries conducted business matters around an island containing desks and computers. Reaching the last room in a row of six, the woman opened a sliding glass door. There, right before Krissy's eyes, lay her husband, stretched out on a hospital gurney. His face had been blackened with soot and his hair and skin smelled singed by the hungry flames that had obviously sought to devour him.

"Blaine," she choked, rushing to his bedside. She noticed the blue and white hospital gown he wore, and the lightweight blanket covering him from the waist down. "Are you all right? I came as soon as I could."

"I'm okay, Honey." He peeked at her through one open eye. "I fell through the roof and injured my back. Looks like I might have cracked a couple of vertebrae."

"Oh, Blaine, no!"

"Now, don't worry. It's not as bad as it sounds. Could have been worse. I'm praising the Lord that my spinal cord is intact. I can move my feet, wiggle my toes. . .sure hurts though." He winced as if to prove his point.

"Blaine. . ."

With tears pricking the backs of her eyes, Krissy lifted his hand and held it between both of hers. In all their twenty years of marriage, this is what she'd feared the most: An injury in the line of duty. How many endless nights had she lain awake worrying that he'd never come home again to her and their two daughters? She knew too well that firefighters faced the possibility of death each and every time they responded to a call and by now, Krissy thought she'd have become accustomed to the ever-present threat. Today, however, when she'd

141

received the phone call informing her that Blaine had been hurt, it was like living the nightmare.

"Hon, I'm going to make a full recovery," Blaine assured her, his eyelids looking heavy with whatever the nurses had given him for pain. "The ER doc said the orthopedic surgeon on call is coming to speak with us. I'll probably have to have surgery to help my back heal, and after a few months of recuperation, I'll be as good as new." He paused, grinning beneath the filmy soot covering his mouth. "Maybe even better. . ."

Chapter 1

Three months later

"A re you sure you're up to driving?" Krissy asked Blaine as they headed
north in their minivan. They'd dropped their twin daughters off at a
Christian college in Florida and had been traveling most of the day.
According to Krissy's calculations, they had another seventeen hours to go before
they reached Wisconsin. Since Blaine was still recovering from his back surgery,
she didn't want him to overdo it. "Would you like me to take the wheel for
awhile?"

"I'm fine," he replied, "but I think we'll stop at a motel in Knoxville."

Krissy nodded, knowing her husband wasn't all that "fine" if he intended to
stop for the night. Not Mr. Drive-'til-we-get-there Blaine Robinson. His back
was most likely aching from all the activity last week. He'd loaded and unloaded
the girls' belongings in and out of the van and carried items into their dormitory
that he probably shouldn't have lifted.

Krissy glanced over at the profile that, in the past two decades, had become
as familiar as her own face. Blaine's chestnut-brown hair was tinged with just a
hint of gray above the ears, and in the last five years, he'd developed a bald spot at
the crown of his head that the girls liked to kiss just to irritate him. His skin was
tanned from the summer sunshine since he took advantage of convalescing out-
doors. His neck and shoulders were thick with muscles he'd developed lifting
heavy fire hoses and other equipment while he'd been on the job, although his
midsection was getting awfully thick these days. Krissy didn't want to mention it,
but she figured he'd put on about twenty pounds in the past three months. Worse,
it seemed to her that he'd gotten lazy and slack when it came to his appearance.
All these years, they had both tried to take care of themselves and keep fit, but
lately Blaine seemed to have let himself go. It was rather disappointing.

Still, she loved him. He was the man with whom she would spend the
remainder of her life. . .but why did that suddenly sound like such a long time?

"It's kind of weird without Mandy and Laina around," Krissy stated on a
rueful note.

"Yeah, I think the girls chattered the entire way to Florida."

Krissy grinned. "They did. . .and now it's too quiet in here."

143

Blaine apparently decided to remedy the matter by turning the radio on to a syndicated talk show.

"Must you really subject me to this?" Krissy complained. "You listen to this guy every day."

"Yeah, so?" Blaine took his eyes off the road for a moment and looked over at her through his fashionable sunglasses.

"I don't care for some of his views."

"Well, I do, and with the presidential election coming up in November, I want to stay informed."

Krissy gritted her teeth and leaned back in the seat, closing her eyes and trying not to listen to the male voice booming conservative credos through the stereo speakers. While she considered herself a conservative Christian, she simply found the popular radio talk show host, in a word, annoying. In the last twelve weeks, while Blaine recuperated, Krissy had tolerated his penchant for the program. But now, as a captive audience, she felt resentful. Trapped.

She opened her eyes and leaned forward abruptly. "Blaine, can't we compromise? Surely there's another news station we could listen to."

"Relax. This show is only on for another hour and then I'll change the channel if you want."

Won't be any reason to change the channel then, she silently fumed.

Krissy turned her head toward the window and watched the scenery go by. It was only late August, but already some treetops were turning gold, orange, and russet. Autumn had begun in the Smoky and Appalachian Mountains. And next week Krissy would be back at school, teaching third graders. She mulled over everything she had to do in preparation. This year would be much different than the past twelve since Grace Christian School, the elementary school in which she'd taught, had merged with a larger institution due to financial constraints. Krissy expected changes, but she tried not to worry about them. Monday would come soon enough.

The minutes ticked by and finally the ragging on the liberals ceased. Blaine pressed the radio buttons until he found classical music. Krissy's taut nerves began to relax.

"Better?" Blaine asked, a slight smirk curving his well-shaped mouth.

"Much. Thanks." Krissy couldn't seem to help the note of cynicism in her reply. Then she paused, listening. "I don't recognize this piece."

Blaine gave it a moment's deliberation. "I believe it's one of Mozart's sonatas, obviously for the violin and piano."

"Obviously." Krissy quipped, smiling. She had acquired a taste for classical music over the years but hadn't ever learned to discern the various artists' styles, let alone the titles. "And tell me again how a sonata differs from, say, a waltz or serenade."

"A waltz is basically dance music written in triple time with the accent on the first beat."

"Ah, yes, that's right."

"A sonata is written in three or four movements."

"It's coming back to me now," Krissy said.

Blaine chuckled. "After hearing this music for twenty years, you should be an expert."

"Yes, I suppose I should."

"Well, after another twenty," Blaine stated in jest, "you're bound to be a fine critic of classic music."

An odd, sinking feeling enveloped Krissy. Symphonies and overtures were Blaine's forte, not hers. He was an accomplished musician himself and played the piano, although he hadn't practiced in years. Regardless, she had developed knowledge and respect for the art because of him and had to admit that Brahms, Beethoven, and Mozart did have a way of soothing her jangled nerves after a long day at school. Nevertheless, she enjoyed other types of music as much or more. In fact, she and the girls liked to attend musicals, both in Chicago and Milwaukee. They had seen *Show Boat* and *Phantom of the Opera*. . .

But the girls are eighteen years old and in college now, Krissy thought. *Blaine and I have the rest of our lives. . .together. Alone.*

The reality of her situation suddenly struck with full force. There were no more children to care for, fret over, shop with, or cook for. No more parent-teacher conferences to attend, basketball and football games to watch as her lovely daughters cheered on their high school's team. Although Amanda and Alaina were twins, they weren't identical, and each had her own fun personality that Krissy now realized she would sorely miss.

Tears began to well in her eyes and spill down her cheeks. She sniffed and then reached for her purse to find a tissue.

"What's the matter?"

"Oh, nothing."

"What?" Blaine pursued. "It's not the talk radio show. . . ? It's over now."

"No, no. . .it's the girls. They're gone." Krissy's tears flowed all the harder now. Her babies. Grown up. Living far away from home. Why, she'd been so preoccupied with helping them prepare and pack for college, not to mention nursing Blaine back to health, that she hadn't realized the impact the girls' departure would have. "They grew up so fast," Krissy said, blowing hard into the tissue. "Where did the years go?"

"Oh, for pity's sake. . ." Krissy heard the exasperation in her husband's voice. But then he reached across the built-in plastic console in the center of the two front seats and stroked the back of her hair. "Sweetheart, the girls'll be back. In just a few months it's Christmas. A few months after that, they'll be home for summer vacation. . .and you'll never have the telephone to yourself again."

Krissy managed a smile. "You're right," she said with a little sniffle. "I'm being silly." She thought it over, then sighed. "I just wish we would have had more children."

"That's a ridiculous wish, and you know it," Blaine said, removing his hand and placing both palms on the steering wheel. "We tried, but God didn't see fit to give us any more kids. Instead, Mandy and Laina were a double blessing. Still are. Always will be."

Krissy couldn't argue. Their twin daughters were a special gift from God.

"Think of it this way," Blaine continued, a smile in his deep voice, "we're still young. You and I have the rest of our lives together."

Krissy winced, and fresh tears filled her eyes. How could she tell Blaine that the very words he just spoke to cheer her up depressed her? She wasn't exactly feeling like the godly, submissive wife of which the Bible speaks, yet her feelings were real, and she didn't know how to handle them. True, she and Blaine had the rest of their lives, but what would they do with all those years together? She loved him, but somehow that didn't seem like enough. In the past twenty years, Blaine had been gone more than he'd been home, and Krissy had been a busy mother and schoolteacher. Of course, she and Blaine would continue to have their work. But was that all their lives together amounted to? Separate occupations? Separate lives, joined together by a vow to have and to hold, for better or for worse. . .'til death do us part. . . ?

❧

"What's eating you?" Blaine asked later as he lay on one of the double beds in the motel room. He was clad in a white T-shirt and navy-printed boxers, and beneath his knees, Krissy had placed three pillows to ease his back discomfort. Unfortunately, she couldn't do anything about the atmosphere. Coupled with her melancholy, the air-conditioning unit wasn't working well, and the room felt hot and stuffy on this sweltering August night in Knoxville, Tennessee. "You haven't said more than five words since we stopped for supper."

"Oh, I'm just tired." Krissy decided that had to be it. Exhaustion. Sitting in a nearby floral-upholstered armchair, she stared blindly at the newscast on television. Maybe once she got back home and fell into a routine, teaching during the day, correcting homework in the evenings, she wouldn't miss the girls so much.

"Go take a cold shower," Blaine suggested. "That made me feel better."

"Yeah, maybe I will."

She looked over at him again, noticing for the first time that his brawny frame took up most of the bed. They slept on a king-size mattress at home. Last night, they'd rented a motel room with the same size bed. But tonight, this room with two doubles was all the desk clerk could offer them if they preferred a non-smoking environment—which they did. If Blaine weren't healing from back surgery, Krissy wouldn't hesitate to tell him to move over, but it appeared as though tonight she'd sleep alone.

Separate lives. Separate beds. What a way to start the rest of their lives together.

Chapter 2

Blaine watched Krissy back the minivan out of the driveway, then accelerate down the street. He couldn't figure out what had gotten into her. She'd been glum for the past few days. He'd first concluded that it was because the girls were gone, but after listening to her talking on the telephone with them yesterday afternoon, hearing her encourage their daughters, Blaine had to assume there was more to Krissy's doldrums.

So he questioned her.

In reply she had merely shrugged and admitted she didn't know what was wrong.

Maybe after today she'll feel more like her old self, he thought, moving away from the living room windows. After today Krissy would be teaching school again.

Walking into the kitchen, Blaine smiled at the red apples on green vines that Krissy and the girls had papered onto the walls not even a month ago. They had urged him to stay out of their way while they pasted and hung the wallpaper, giggling and chattering all the while, and Blaine had no problem finding something else to do.

Females. After living with three of them for nearly two decades, Blaine still couldn't figure them out half the time.

He continued grinning as he poured himself a cup of coffee. Taking a sip, he thought over Krissy's odd mood swing, then recalled what she'd said about her new school, its principal, and the other teachers. He figured she was most likely suffering from a case of nerves. Or maybe it was getting to be that time of month. Well, whatever bothered her, she'd snap out of it.

Blaine glanced at the clock and realized he had to hurry and shower in order to make it to his physical therapy appointment. Pushing thoughts of Krissy from his mind, he set down his coffee mug and headed for the bathroom.

❧

Krissy glanced around at all the enthusiastic faces in the conference room of Wellsprings Academy and realized she was one of the older teachers here. Surrounding her were five other women, all appearing to have just graduated from college, and three men, who couldn't be any older than the academy's principal, Bruce Sawyer, who looked about thirty-something. As Mr. Sawyer detailed his plans for the upcoming year, Krissy wondered if she really belonged at this place.

"I'd like every teacher to get personally involved with his or her students' education this year," the principal said, and when his gaze came her way, Krissy noticed how blue his eyes were, how strong his jawline seemed, how tall he stood, and how broad his shoulders looked beneath the crisp, white dress shirt he wore.

I wonder if he's married. In the next moment, she berated herself for even allowing the question to take form in her mind. *I'm married and I love my husband,* she silently reaffirmed. However, it was disheartening that she found another man attractive.

Oh, Lord, what's wrong with me? Nothing has seemed right since Blaine's accident.

Krissy sighed. When no divine reply was forthcoming, she gave herself a mental shake and forced her thoughts back to the meeting.

At the midmorning break, Krissy helped herself to a cup of steaming coffee from the long, narrow refreshment table which had been set up in the hallway. She looked over the delectable treats which were also on display and chose a small cinnamon muffin.

"Those are my favorite."

Krissy turned to find Bruce Sawyer standing directly behind her. Then he reached around her and plucked a muffin from the plastic plate.

"Well, what do you think so far?" he asked.

She smiled. "I think your staff is very young."

He grinned and took a bite of his muffin. Chewing, he looked around at the other teachers congregating on either side of them. "They're all qualified educators, believe me."

"Oh, I'm sure they are. It's just that. . .well, I don't see any of the teachers I worked with last year."

"They seemed competent and experienced. I read each one's resume. Unfortunately, we only had need for one third grade teacher since Leslie Comings got married this past summer."

Krissy couldn't believe her ears. "You mean to tell me I'm the only teacher who didn't lose her job?"

"Combining two schools isn't as simple as it might appear, I'm afraid. There were no easy decisions for the board members. The truth of the matter is, the merger didn't warrant extra teachers—even with the addition of Grace Christian School's populace."

"I see." She suddenly felt very badly for all her former colleagues.

"But we're glad you're here. . .Kristin, isn't it?"

She nodded.

"I've always been partial to the name. If I'd have had a daughter, I would have liked to name her Kristin."

She smiled nervously, unsure of how to respond. "Well, thank you, Mr. Sawyer."

He grinned. "Call me Bruce. We're all in this together, and I think we should be on a first name basis, don't you?"

"Sure." She'd been on a first name basis with the principal of Grace Christian School. The solidly built, gray-headed man had been a father figure to her when situations arose in the classroom and Krissy wanted advice. But somehow she couldn't imagine herself running to Bruce Sawyer's office for morsels of wisdom and seasoned counsel. The guy was too charming. Too. . . threatening.

"So you, um, have no daughters?" Krissy ventured, thinking that bringing up his family life would deter her attraction to him. "You and your wife have sons?"

"I have neither a wife nor children," Bruce said as a rueful expression crossed his handsome features. "My wife is dead. She died very suddenly about three years ago."

Krissy sucked in a horrified gasp.

"It's no secret around here," Bruce continued, "and I find being open about the tragedy has helped me recover."

"I'm so sorry. . ."

"Thank you." He paused and took another bite of his muffin. "My wife suffered with severe stomach problems. The medicine she took caused her to feel tired and depressed much of the time. Finally, she conceded to have surgery to fix the problem but something went horribly wrong and she never regained consciousness despite the doctors' best efforts."

"How tragic," Krissy said.

Bruce nodded and finished the rest of his baked treat. "Yes, but I'm comforted to know that my wife was a believer. I like to imagine that when she met the Savior, He put His loving arms around her and. . .and wiped away all tears from her eyes. He probably assured her that there would be no more death, neither sorrow, nor crying, and no more pain."

Krissy recognized the paraphrase from the book of Revelation, saw the faraway, mournful look in Bruce's gaze, and marveled at the depth of his sensitivity.

"Well, I hope you'll enjoy your year at Wellsprings Academy," he said, snapping from his reverie and pulling Krissy from hers also.

"Thanks." She gave him a smile.

"And I'll look forward to getting to know you better," he added with a light in his blue eyes.

"Same here." The words were out of her mouth before Krissy even realized she'd spoken them.

❧

Blaine groaned in pain as he lowered himself onto the padded lawn chair in the backyard. His physical therapy session had taken a toll on him today; he'd used muscles in his back he hadn't realized he possessed. Unfortunately, instead of feeling better, he felt more disabled than ever. Glancing around the yard, he wished he could pull out the weed-whacker and get rid of the some of the growth inching upward through the patio blocks. He wished he could mow the lawn. This summer Krissy and the girls had taken turns and, while they did an adequate job, they didn't mow it the way Blaine liked. But he didn't complain. How could he? He'd been little more than vegetation, supervising from the lawn chair.

"Hi, Blaine." The cool feminine voice wafted over the wooden fence from the yard next door. "It sure is hot this afternoon."

Lifting an eyelid, he saw his neighbor, Jill, wearing nothing but a little halter top and a skimpy pair of shorts. He closed his eyes again. "Hi yourself. Pardon me for not being a gentleman and getting up. The truth is, I can't move."

He heard his neighbor's soft laugh. "Give me a break. Even flat on your back you're a gentleman."

Stretched out in the shady part of the yard, Blaine grinned at the remark. He felt complimented.

"I wish Ryan was as much a gentleman as you."

Hearing the anguish in her voice, Blaine's heart filled with sympathy. His neighbors weren't exactly the happily married couple that he and Krissy were. During the summer months with the windows open, sounds of their feuding drifted over the property line nearly every night. Blaine and Krissy had shared the Good News with the couple, inviting them out to attend a Bible study and church, but Ryan and Jill had vehemently stated they weren't "into religion." Regardless, prayers continued on their behalf.

"Did the girls get off to college all right?" Jill wanted to know.

"Yep. They called this weekend and seem to be doing fine. They like their roommates."

"Think they'll get homesick?"

"Probably."

Jill laughed and Blaine prayed she'd quit her chatting and tend to the toddler he could hear yelping inside the house. Nothing grated on his nerves more than a bawling child. Krissy said the neighbors' bickering bothered her more than listening to their kids throwing temper tantrums. Blaine, on the other hand, had no problem tuning out the arguing, but the kids' fussing made him edgy.

"I'll sure miss Mandy and Laina," Jill said. "They were such handy baby-sitters."

"They'll be back."

"Yeah, but my sanity might be gone by then." The child's wailing increased. "Well, I'd better go. See ya later."

"Sure, Jill. See ya."

Blaine opened his eyes in time to see his neighbor stoop near the sandbox and retrieve two small navy-blue sneakers. She shook the sand off of them, then entered the house.

Left alone to relax once more, Blaine suddenly felt glad those days of sand-boxes, diapers, and crying children were behind him. He recalled how he had enjoyed leaving the house for work just because he knew he wouldn't be back for thirty-six hours. Thirty-six hours without listening to kids cry. Krissy, of course, handled things much better than he; she never complained. Not once. She never seemed to get upset or impatient with the twins. They turned out to be sweet young ladies largely because of her, although Blaine had made it a point to be part of their lives as much as possible. He'd enjoyed his daughters from the time they were about six years old on up. He coached their girls' softball team in the summertime and gymnastics team during the winter months. He involved himself with the youth group at church and chaperoned outings and events whenever his schedule permitted. He had fond memories of his daughters' growing up years. But he felt glad they were over.

Off in the direction of the garage, a car door slammed shut and Blaine realized Krissy had arrived home from work. He heard her enter the house and wondered how long it would take before she found him languishing in the yard. She'd have to help him out of the lawn chair. He hadn't been lying to Jill when he said he couldn't move. Minutes later, much to his relief, Krissy appeared.

"Must be nice to lounge around all day," she quipped, her hands on her slender hips. The tepid autumn breeze tousled her blond hair, causing it to brush lightly against the tops of her shoulders.

"Hey, you're a sight for sore eyes. Can you help me out of this chair?"

Krissy wagged her head, obviously over his pathetic state, and walked toward him. When she reached the edge of the lawn chair, she held out her hand. Blaine took it, but instead of allowing her to pull him up, he tugged, causing her to fall against him. Then he kissed her soundly, albeit awkwardly.

"You're real funny," she said, working herself into a sitting position on the side of the chair near Blaine's knees. "The two of us are liable to break this flimsy thing and then you'll really have back problems."

Blaine sighed. "I suppose you're right."

"As always." Krissy discreetly tucked her denim dress beneath her.

"How was your day?" he asked.

"Not too bad. And yours?"

"In a word. . .painful."

"Sorry to hear that." Krissy stood and helped Blaine to his feet. Lightning-hot pain bolted down his lower spine and thighs, blinding him for about ten seconds.

"Are you all right?"

"Yeah." He forced a smile, not wanting to worry his wife. "What's for supper?"

"I don't know. What are you hungry for?"

"Not sure."

"We're a decisive team."

Blaine grinned, then looped his arm around Krissy's shoulders, leaning on her as they walked toward the house. He didn't inquire further about her day. Didn't need to. His wife seemed to be her old self again.

Chapter 3

"Mind if I use you for a pillow?"

"Do I look like a pillow?"

Blaine grinned. "You're soft and curvy. You'll do."

Unable to help a grin, Krissy scooted over and made room for Blaine on the couch. He stretched out, his head at the far end, while he lifted his legs onto her lap.

"I've got to have something under my knees when I lie down," he explained. "I think that's why I couldn't get myself out of the lawn chair earlier."

"I'm honored that you've selected me as your cushion," Krissy replied on a note of sarcasm. "Nice to know I'm good for something around here other than cooking, cleaning, and playing nurse and taxicab driver to a convalescing husband."

"Playing nurse is my favorite," Blaine shot back with a mischievous gleam in his eyes. "I only wish I could enjoy it more."

Shaking her head at him, Krissy lifted her feet onto the coffee table and set aside her now-empty paper plate. She and Blaine had decided to order out tonight. He wanted Italian and she wanted Chinese and neither would compromise, so Krissy ended up making two stops.

"How was your supper?"

"Great," Blaine replied. "Yours?"

"Marvelous. Sweet and sour chicken is my ultimate favorite."

"The stuff gives me gas. Are you sure it's chicken that Chinese place uses? Hard to tell with all the breading and sauce."

"Oh, quiet. Of course it's chicken."

Blaine chuckled, and Krissy rested her hands on his navy wind-pants. "One of the guys at work told me this joke about a Chinese Restaurant."

"I don't want to hear it."

"Something about a cat in the kettle at the Peking Room."

"Blaine, I said I don't want to hear it!"

He laughed while she bristled. Why did he always have to poke fun at the food she ate? She would never do such a thing to him. . .not that he'd let an unsavory joke spoil his appetite.

Still fuming, she tried to squelch her irritation by allowing her gaze to wander around their lower-level family room. The walls were paneled with knotty pine and decorated with various family snapshots that ranged from

Blaine and Krissy's wedding to the twins' first steps to their graduating from high school last May. As she recalled each special event, a wave of nostalgia crashed over her.

Her exasperation forgotten for the moment, she turned to Blaine. She'd intended to engage him in a match of "remember when" but noticed that he'd begun to doze. Disappointed, Krissy looked back at the television set. As she watched the handsome, syndicated talk show host, she decided he had the same strong jawline as Bruce Sawyer and a little smile tugged at the corners of her mouth.

Yes, the principal of Wellsprings Academy could certainly dub for a celebrity with his good looks and charming manner. Krissy couldn't help but wonder why he didn't remarry. She imagined Bruce would most likely say it was because he hadn't "found the right one." That seemed to be a standard line among single people these days. However, Krissy noticed that there were a number of unattached, pretty females teaching at the academy and she guessed it wouldn't be long before the "right one" walked into Bruce's life.

Within moments, her musings took flight and she speculated on the sort of woman it would take to win Bruce's heart. Obviously, he'd been devastated when his first wife died, so the next woman to enter his life would have to somehow dispel all the hurts and fears born from such a tragedy. Krissy thought she knew what she'd do if she weren't married. She'd cultivate a friendship with the man, learning all his likes and dislikes, and she would be quick to point out the interests they shared. Like reading for instance. This afternoon while Krissy acquainted herself with her new classroom, Bruce had stopped by with a novel in his hands.

"Have you by any chance read this book?"

Spying the cover, Krissy recognized it, nodded, and rambled off an impromptu quote that could have come straight from the book jacket.

"Yes, that's the one." Bruce grinned. "I'm enjoying it very much."

"I recall it was a very touching story."

"Quite. And this entire series. . .have you read it?"

"Every book."

"What's your take on the novels?"

For nearly an hour, they had discussed books and shared their perspectives on various authors, styles, and story lines. Krissy found the conversation refreshing, since she'd been trying for two decades to get Blaine interested in books. But he only liked to read if the topics pertained to sports or firefighting, and he couldn't appreciate anything longer than a feature article.

She glanced over at him now, expecting to find him snoozing. But to her outright chagrin, she discovered Blaine staring back at her.

"What are you thinking about?" he asked softly. His eyes seemed to scrutinize her every feature.

Krissy felt her cheeks redden with embarrassment. "Books. I was thinking about books."

"Mmm. . ."

Blaine's gaze was like a weighty probe, searching into her heart, her soul. Suddenly she felt like the wickedest woman ever to roam Wisconsin. Here she ought to be enjoying her husband's company, but instead she was dreaming of capturing another man's heart.

Forgive me, Lord, she silently prayed. *What's wrong with me?*

Krissy crawled out from under Blaine's knees, then placed a large throw pillow beneath them in her stead.

"I'm tired. I think I'll turn in."

"Sure. Good night, Hon."

" 'Night."

Heavyhearted and feeling more than just a tad guilty, Krissy made her way upstairs to the master bedroom.

❧

That was weird, Blaine thought, watching Krissy's departure. He'd never seen such an odd expression on his wife's face. She'd been daydreaming, that was obvious. But about books? No way. If she would have said she'd been thinking about the girls and remembering some silly thing the three of them had done together, Blaine would have bought it, lock, stock, and barrel. Unfortunately, he didn't buy it at all, and a slight foreboding sent a chill up his already aching spine. What was with Krissy these days?

Time to find out.

With a determined set to his jaw, he roused himself from the couch and made his way upstairs. He walked down the hallway, heading for their room. When he reached the doorway, however, he stopped short, seeing Krissy on her knees at the side of the bed, her Bible open on the floral spread in front of her. Silently, Blaine stepped backward, retracing his steps to the living room where he decided to put off any discussion until she finished her devotions.

Nearly twenty minutes later, he heard the bathroom door close followed by sounds of the shower spray.

Great, he thought, *she'll be in there all night.*

Well, fine, he would just wait for Krissy in the bedroom. Once more he ambled upstairs and down the hallway and entered their room. Lowering himself onto the bed, Blaine threw a pillow under his knees, turned on the small television, and began his vigil.

❧

Krissy heard him before she ever saw him. Blaine. Snoring loudly. On top of their bed. And with her pillow under his knees, no less. Had he worn those

156

wind-pants all day? To physical therapy with a lot of sick people around? Wonderful. Like she really wanted to place her head on it now!

Irritation coursed through her veins as she slipped into her nightie. Did Blaine ever once think of her? Couldn't he respect her feelings on anything, be it carry-out food or books or her own, personal pillow?

With a huff, she grabbed the remote from where it lay on Blaine's T-shirt encased stomach and turned off the TV. Next, she switched off the lamp and stomped out of the room, intending to sleep in one of the girls' beds tonight. She wanted to slam the door but refrained from doing so. Still, she wasn't quiet about putting clean sheets on Mandy's bed.

Regardless, Blaine never awoke.

Chapter 4

Blaine yawned and stumbled into the kitchen. "How come you slept in Mandy's room last night?"

Krissy threw him an annoyed glance, then whirled around and finished preparing a pot of coffee. She had already dressed for school and Blaine thought she looked quite attractive in the blue and green plaid cotton skirt and hunter-green T-shirt. The outfit complemented her blond hair and tanned skin.

"All right, Krissy, spit it out. What's up with you these days?"

She flipped on the coffeemaker and it began to brew. Turning to face him again, she folded her arms in front of her.

"Well?" Blaine demanded.

"Nothing is 'up with me.' "

"Nothing? It's hardly nothing, Kris," he said, easing himself into a chair at the kitchen table. "You've been acting so strange. . .ever since the girls went off to school. I mean. . ." He searched his mind for the right words. "Sometimes I feel like I don't even know you anymore. Like last night. I've got a feeling you weren't daydreaming about books. So what was going through your head?"

He watched as she blushed slightly before lifting her chin. She appeared almost defiant—another trait unlike the Krissy he'd married.

"I think you said it all," she stated softly, "when you said you don't know me anymore. In all honesty, you don't."

"What in the world are you talking about?"

"It's true," she said, avoiding his gaze, her voice wavering. "We never talk like we used to and when I try to discuss a topic of importance to me, you never listen. You don't even know what's going on in my life these days. You think you do, but really you don't."

Minutes ticked by as they regarded each other in silence. Then, once the coffee finished brewing, Krissy turned and poured two mugs. She crossed the room and placed one in front of Blaine.

Sipping it, he tried to think how he should handle this situation. Maybe hormones were to blame. Sometimes when she got this way it was just a matter of riding out the storm.

As if she'd read his mind, she spat, "And don't think this is just a PMS thing. It's not. This is something I've been aware of for a long time now. An intricate part of our marriage is gone, and it's never been more prevalent than it has since your accident. You and I, Blaine, have nothing in common. We're two people who are married and live under one roof, but we're not one flesh. Not anymore."

Blaine narrowed his gaze, feeling more than just a little disturbed by what he'd just heard. "Krissy, are you. . .are you thinking. . .?"

He couldn't get himself to say the word "divorce." Thinking about it caused his gut to knot up.

"Krissy," he began again, "you and I made vows to each other—"

"I'm not about to break my wedding vows," she shot back.

"Well, that's good."

"We're just stuck with each other. . .for the rest of our lives."

Blaine felt his jaw drop slightly. "Stuck with each other?"

Krissy had the good grace to look chagrined.

"Stuck? Is that how you see it?"

"I'm going to be late." She marched quickly past him and grabbed her bagged lunch and purse.

Blaine rose from the chair. "Wait."

She didn't. "See you tonight."

She fled out the side door before he could stop her. As a feeling of disbelief enveloped him, Blaine listened to the van door slam, the engine roar to life, and the sounds of Krissy backing the vehicle out of the garage and down the driveway.

"Stuck with each other," Blaine whispered incredulously. Next came the tidal wave of hurt that threatened to submerge him in a mixture of sorrow and rage. He didn't feel "stuck" with her. He loved Krissy—loved her with all his heart. He'd do anything for her. But she felt "stuck" with him.

First the rage. *How can she be so selfish, thinking only of herself and what she wants? And what does she want anyhow? She's got everything. A house, a job she enjoys, a husband who loves her, two nearly perfect daughters. . .*

He fumed all the while he dressed. Then, as he drove to his doctor's appointment later in the morning, the agonizing sorrow gripped his heart. *She doesn't love me anymore. What does a guy do when his wife doesn't love him anymore? When did it happen? How come I never noticed?*

Blaine had heard of marriages crumbling once the kids were grown and gone. He would believe it'd happen to his next door neighbors, but not to him and Krissy. They were Christians. This stuff wasn't supposed to happen to godly couples.

Perplexed, he drove into the clinic's parking structure, found a spot, and pulled his truck to a halt.

"So how's the back?" Dr. Lemke asked about thirty minutes later. The man's bald head shone like a brand-new plastic toy under the fluorescent lights in the exam room. Blaine would wager the short, stocky physician weighed about three hundred and fifty pounds, and he prayed he'd never end up fat and bald in his old age.

"Back's not so good. I'm still in a lot of pain."

The doctor glanced up. "Yes, so I see from the physical therapist's report. He states you're unable to do some pretty simple stretching and bending exercises."

"True, but don't think I haven't been practicing at home just like the therapist told me," Blaine stated in his own defense. "But the exercises aren't working."

"Hmm. . ."

Blaine watched the pen tip wiggle as Dr. Lemke scratched down what they'd discussed. Since the man was employed by the City of Milwaukee, Blaine figured he wanted to write out a return-to-work slip as soon as possible and spare further workers' compensation. In truth, Blaine wanted that too. He was growing bored at home all day.

"You're going to have to see a specialist," the doctor said at last. "Go back to the surgeon who operated. I'm afraid I can't do anything more for you."

"Sure. Whatever."

The doctor scribbled out the referral and his medical assistant made the appointment for Blaine. Sheet of paper in hand, he left the clinic and climbed into his pickup truck. He didn't care a whit about himself as he made the drive toward home. He kept thinking about what Krissy said that morning.

We're stuck with each other.

Blaine knew she meant it, too. They'd said things to each other before that they didn't mean, just like most other married couples. They'd apologized for it, then prayed together and asked for God's forgiveness, too. But given Krissy's odd behavior of late, he could tell those words had come from the very depth of her being.

Lord, what do I do? he prayed as he pulled into the driveway. Tears welled in Blaine's eyes, and he couldn't even remember the last time he'd cried. *Lord, please help me. Please save my marriage. I'm nothing without Krissy.*

Did you ever tell her that?

The Voice wasn't an audible one, but it had replied to his heart just the same.

Sure I told her. Millions of times.

Millions?

And trillions.

Blaine shifted, feeling uncomfortable since he suddenly couldn't recall when he'd last shared his heart with Krissy.

How many times does a guy have to tell his wife the same old thing?

Millions and trillions.

Blaine grinned and gazed up through his sun roof and the blue, cloudless sky. "All right, Lord. I get it. You don't have to hit me over the head with a brick."

Exiting his truck, he grimaced as a shooting pain blasted down his leg. "On second thought, maybe You did."

⌘

"Mrs. Robinson, you have a phone call." Turning from the bulletin board she was decorating, Krissy forced a smile at the secretary. "I would have used the intercom system," the woman continued, "but it doesn't seem to be working. We'll have it fixed by the time school starts though."

"Thanks. I'll be right there."

The tall, slim, redhead whose age seemed unfathomable nodded and exited the classroom. Krissy had heard Mrs. Sterling was pushing sixty, yet she looked and acted no older than thirty-five. Secretly, Krissy hoped she'd be in such good shape at that age.

Setting the stapler down on her desk, Krissy followed the secretary through the hallway. They entered the office suite, Mrs. Sterling returned to her desk, and without even picking up the receiver, Krissy knew Blaine would be at the other end of the line. What had possessed her to throw such hateful words at him? She'd felt badly all the way to school and then Bruce's morning "challenge" to all the teachers had really touched her heart.

"Hello?" she answered somewhat timidly.

"Hi, Hon, what do you want for supper tonight?"

Blaine sounded like his same old self for which Krissy felt grateful. "Um, I really hadn't thought about it."

"Well, do you mind if I whip up something?"

She grimaced. Blaine was famous for his three-alarm chili at the fire station. Unfortunately, it wasn't one of Krissy's favorites. But she'd hurt him enough for one day. "Sure, make whatever you want."

"Okay."

"And, Blaine?"

"Yeah?"

Krissy glanced over her shoulder to be sure no one could overhear. Mrs. Sterling was nowhere in sight. "Sorry about this morning. . . ."

"Honey, all is forgiven, and we can talk about it tonight if you feel up to it."

"We can?" Holding the phone several inches away, Krissy stared at it like the piece of equipment had just grown a mouth of its own. "Well, all right," she said at last. "I'll see you in about an hour."

"Sounds good. And Kris. . .I love you."

She smiled, feeling guilty as she hung up the phone. Why was Blaine acting so nice after she'd been so mean? Of course, he wasn't a guy to stay angry or hold grudges, but he wasn't always so agreeable either.

"Everything all right, Kristin?" Pivoting, she glanced across the office suite in time to watch Bruce walk out of his private office. "You look like you might have had some bad news."

"No, no," she assured him. "I think the doctor just gave my husband some different pain medication. He didn't sound like himself."

"Hmm. . ." Bruce gave her a curious frown. "Pain medication for what?"

"For his back. Blaine was injured at work. He's a fireman and he fell through the roof of a two-story house. Cracked a couple of vertebrae and had surgery to repair a couple of discs that ruptured in the process."

"How horrible. When did that happen?"

"This past May."

"I see. Well, I'll pray for him. It's my belief that chonic pain often leads to drug addiction. My wife nearly became addicted to her precription drugs. It's one of the reasons she opted for the surgery."

Krissy sucked in a breath, hoping such a thing wouldn't befall Blaine. But she quickly shook off her misgivings, realizing her husband hadn't been depressed a day in his life. As for an addiction to pain medication, he rarely took the stuff—even when he legitimately needed it.

"I didn't mean to frighten you," Bruce said, looking earnest.

Krissy snapped from her musing. "You didn't. You just gave me something to think about."

"One thing I learned from the situation with my wife is that life is short. Too short to waste on unhappiness."

Krissy couldn't help agreeing. She'd felt dispirited for over a week and it wasn't any fun.

Bruce gave her a compassionate grin. "You can talk to me anytime. I'll be here for you."

Krissy felt a blush creep up her neck and warm her cheeks. "That's very kind."

"I mean it."

"I know you do. Thanks."

Their gazes met and Krissy's traitorous heart began to hammer so loudly she felt certain Bruce could hear it. She was only too grateful when Mrs. Sterling reentered the office, carrying a stack of papers.

Krissy quickly made her exit.

Chapter 5

Krissy turned the van into the driveway and groaned at the sight of her next door neighbor, Jill Nebhardt, standing near the patio wearing khaki shorts and red T-shirt. Next she noticed the cloud of gray smoke billowing into the air and guessed that Blaine had fired up the grill. Now Jill was most likely chatting his ear off while he barbequed.

Well, at least he didn't make his three-alarm chili, Krissy mused gratefully as she killed the engine. Grabbing her purse, she climbed out of the van.

As she strode toward her husband and neighbor, Krissy experienced a twinge of guilt for not feeling very friendly. She supposed she should have compassion on the poor woman since Jill was terribly discouraged in her marriage. On the other hand, Krissy felt tired, and she and Blaine had their own issues right now.

"Hey, you're home," Blaine said as a smile split his tanned face. "I didn't even hear you pull in." His gaze flittered to Jill in explanation, and Krissy understood immediately.

"I was just telling Blaine about Ryan's new work schedule. He's gone twelve, sometimes thirteen hours a day. When he comes home, he's so crabby the kids and I can't stand to be around him. Worse, he expects dinner on the table and the house to be spotless."

"I told Jill I know the feeling since that's what you expect too, right Hon?"

Krissy rolled her eyes. "You haven't done housework in twenty years, Blaine."

"With three women around, why should I?" Pointing the metal spatula at her, he added, "And you haven't changed a flat tire in all that time. Or shoveled snow."

"You won't let me use your snow blower, otherwise I would." Krissy leaned toward Jill. "This argument could go on all night."

The younger woman chuckled. "I'm so glad to see you two aren't perfect. You seem like it sometimes. I'm really envious of your relationship." She peered into Krissy's face with teary brown eyes. "You don't know how lucky you've got it, Girlfriend."

"I remind Krissy of that at least three times a day," Blaine said.

Sudden shouts from the adjoining backyard brought Jill to attention. "Uh-oh. . .sounds like Grant and Royce are at it again. I'd better scoot. Talk to you guys later."

"See ya, Jill," Blaine replied.

"Bye." Krissy watched their neighbor jog around the house before looking back at Blaine. "Hi."

"Hi." He stepped around the smoking grill and gave her a kiss. "Have a good day?"

"Yeah, and you?"

"Okay."

"What did the doctor say?"

"He wants me to go back and see Dr. Klevins."

"The surgeon? How come?"

"Because my back isn't improving at the rate he'd like."

Krissy nibbled her lower lip in momentary contemplation. "Do you think another operation is ahead of you?"

"I doubt it. I've had a fusion, what more can the surgeon do?"

"I don't know."

Blaine looked down at whatever he was cooking.

"What are you making for supper?" Krissy asked, curious.

Bringing his gaze back to hers, he grinned. "Beef tenderloin. One of your favorites."

The news made her smile. "I've been hungry for a grilled steak. And here I had assumed you concocted your famous chili."

"You hate my chili. Why would I make it when it's just you and me for supper tonight?"

"Well, I—"

"See, I know you, Krissy. Better than you think." He raised an eyebrow as if to make his point.

"Touché." Hitching her purse up higher onto her shoulder, she couldn't help grinning. "I'm going inside to change."

"Slipping into something more comfortable, are you, Darling?" Blaine asked in a feigned British accent.

"Oh, like right." Krissy shook her head at him and walked to the side door. "I've got a mountain of things to accomplish tonight."

Entering the house, a swell of disappointment rose inside her when she realized she could sure use a romantic evening. Then, much to her shame, a vision of Bruce Sawyer and his tender blue eyes flittered across her mind.

❧

"You're not eating."

Krissy looked up from her plate. "Everything is perfect, Blaine. The steak, the salad, the dinner rolls. . ."

"But?"

164

"But I feel a little down all of a sudden. I can't explain it. It's just weird."

"Maybe it's the company," Blaine quipped, setting his fork down none too gently.

Krissy stared at him ruefully. How could she make him understand what was going on inside her when she didn't understand it herself? "Blaine. . ."

"You know what," he said, an earnest light in his dusky, blue-gray eyes, "I've been in love with you since we were juniors in high school."

Krissy had to smile as mental snapshots of the past flashed through her mind. "I know. . ."

"And when you agreed to go to the prom with me that year, I felt like the luckiest guy alive. I mean, Krissy Marens. . .*the* Krissy Marens, prettiest girl in school. . .going to the prom with me. . .and I wasn't even on the football team."

Laughing, she sat back in her chair and folded her arms. "I thought you were awfully cute."

Blaine's smile faded. "Change your mind lately?"

"No. . .I mean. . ." She sighed. "I don't know. . ."

She began picking at her salad again, not willing to see the pain she probably inflicted on the man she was supposed to love unconditionally. She felt guiltier now, trying to be honest, than if she'd have just stuffed these feelings in the deepest part of her and somehow tried to forget them there.

"I can't help it that my hair is thinning," Blaine said. "This bald patch on the back of my head seems to get bigger every year."

Krissy glanced at him and smiled. "I like your bald spot. And I think your thinning hair makes you appear. . .distinguished."

"Hmm. . ." He rubbed his jaw, looking perplexed. "Maybe my five o'clock shadow bugs you, is that it?"

"No, I like your five o'clock shadow. I wish you had it all day."

"Want me to quit shaving?"

Krissy rolled her eyes. "No."

"Help me out here, Woman," Blaine cried in exasperation, holding his arms out wide. "I want to please you, but how can I when I don't know what it is that's displeasing you?"

"The paunch hanging over your belt turns me off. There. I said it."

"Thank you." Throwing his gaze upward, he shook his head. "For your information, I plan to get rid of my. . .paunch. . .just as soon as my back heals up."

"That's what I figured, so I didn't want to make a big deal out of it. But you've been wearing such sloppy clothes lately."

"My blue jeans are a little snug. Besides, they're hard to pull on with my back killing me half the time."

Krissy shrugged.

"Okay, okay, okay," he said, his palms out as if to forestall further debate. "I'll lose some weight. I'm not pleased with this extra twenty pounds either."

"You'll feel better, too. That's twenty pounds off your aching back."

Blaine humbly agreed. "Now, I need to ask you something else," he said, standing and taking his silverware and half-empty plate to the sink. "Something important."

Krissy felt horrible for ruining his dinner. "What's the question?"

"I want a totally honest answer. No beating around the bush." After depositing his dishes near the sink, he turned and faced her.

She rose and cleared her place, setting everything on the counter next to Blaine's utensils. Standing in front of him, she looked up into his eyes, unsure if she trusted herself to be as forthright as he requested.

"You still love me, Krissy?" Her brawny husband wore an expression of boyish vulnerability and the sight moved her to tears.

"Yes, I love you. Of course I love you. It's just that. . ."

"What?"

"It's just that in so many ways, Blaine, we're strangers."

"That makes no sense. We've been married for twenty years. We've known each other since high school. How can we possibly be strangers?"

"Because since the twins were born we put all our energy into raising them. We did a good job, too. But, when the girls were in first grade, I went back to school and finished my degree and from that point on, I had my career, you had yours, and our home life consisted of our daughters and maintaining a house."

Krissy expelled a long breath, hoping she was getting through to him. "I don't regret any of the sacrifices we made for Mandy and Laina, except for one. Our relationship. We lost touch, you and I, and now there's a distance between us that I don't know how to bridge."

Working the side of his lip between his teeth, Blaine seemed to be considering everything she said. Then he sighed, shrugged, and gathered Krissy into his arms. "If we love each other, which we do," he stated at last, "then we can pray about these things and work on spanning whatever gap exists."

Resting her head against the lower part of his shoulder, Krissy could hear the strong, steady beat of Blaine's heart. She could smell smoke on his T-shirt from the outside grill. It was a scent she'd become well-acquainted with over the years because of his occupation. She associated the odor with an unsettled sensation and realized that, even though they'd grown apart, she'd always concerned herself with his safety. She had fretted and prayed for him during those hours following his accident. Wasn't that love? Of course it was!

Blaine placed a light kiss on her forehead. "Everything'll be all right."

She nodded and tightened her arms around his waist. "Fall always seems like a time of change and adjustment. A different school year, new students—and this year another school altogether for me, and now Mandy and Laina are gone."

"Honey, they're not 'gone.' You make it sound like they're dead. They're just away at college. It's a temporary thing."

"Like the season."

"Right. Life's full of seasons."

Krissy nodded, wishing this one would pass quickly.

Chapter 6

It was the last day of the week and first day of September. Warm sunshine spilled through the partially cloudy sky and onto the black asphalt where Krissy's third graders were at play. Shiny new equipment in bright yellows and reds beckoned children of all ages to its monkey bars, slide, and swings. The little girl inside Krissy felt tempted to join the kids each time she heard their squeals of laughter.

"I wish they would have made gym sets like that when I was growing up," fellow teacher, Erin Latrell, said. She stood to Krissy's right, observing her second graders.

Krissy laughed. "I was thinking along those same lines." Tipping her head, she considered the young woman. Krissy guessed Erin wasn't much older than the twins, with her peaches-and-cream complexion and blue-eyed innocence framed with shoulder-length, reddish-brown hair that fell in soft curls past her shoulders. "Mind if I ask where you attended college?"

"Not at all. I stayed right here in Wisconsin. I lived at home. Still do, but I'm getting married soon. Next summer, in fact."

"How nice." Krissy smiled, suddenly wishing she would have insisted that Mandy and Laina live at home while going to school. But as she mentally replayed the conversation she'd had with each of her daughters last night, she realized the girls were happy and enjoying campus life. Besides, they truly needed this time to blossom and grow into the young women God intended them to be.

Wistful, she returned her gaze to the children at play. *Blaine was right*, she thought, *this is just a season. . .a stormy one. And it's storming in my heart.*

The sound of hard sole shoes tapping against the pavement drew Krissy out of her reverie. Glancing over her shoulder, she saw Bruce Sawyer, dressed in a light brown suit, striding toward them. Reaching her and Erin, he grinned.

"Nice day."

Krissy smiled. "It certainly is."

Erin nodded in agreement.

"I wanted to deliver these personally," he said, handing each of them a white, sealed envelope. "They're invitations to my annual Labor Day party this coming weekend. Time got away from me, and I didn't trust placing them in teachers' inboxes." He paused, bestowing a warm smile on Erin, then Krissy. "I'd be honored if you would both attend."

Krissy glanced down at the envelope in her hand, not wanting to look up into Bruce's blue eyes. She was a married woman and to flirt would be very wrong, but if she wasn't mistaken, Bruce sought out her company. . .and Krissy felt more than flattered. Worse, she enjoyed it.

Oh, Lord, this is a bad situation, one I can't give in to even if I'm tempted to. . .

"May I bring my fiancé?" Erin asked.

"Of course. I'd love to meet him," Bruce replied graciously. "And, Kristin," he added, turning toward her, "I hope you'll bring your spouse."

Why had that just sounded like a question? Did Bruce care one way or the other?

Pushing her ponderings aside, she tried to attack the issue pragmatically. Would she bring Blaine? Or rather, would he deign to accompany her? In all probability, he'd elect to stay home. He abhorred attending social functions that included Krissy's coworkers. He said teachers were boring and tried to one-up each other as proof of their intellect. Of course, the same could not be said for Blaine's colleagues who played tug-of-war over mud pits and blasted each other with fire hoses on their company picnics. Over the years Krissy had gone to each and every one with Blaine, and she did so without complaint.

Mustering her courage, she glanced up at Bruce and gave him a formal grin. "I'll pass the invitation on to my husband. Thanks."

"Great," he said, but Krissy sensed the answer lacked Bruce's usual enthusiasm.

As he walked away and reentered the school, she felt her heart take a plunge from the weight of the guilt she'd been carrying around for almost two weeks. Yet, she hadn't done anything to feel ashamed about, except entertain thoughts of impossibilities. She wasn't about to leave Blaine in order to have a fling with her new principal. She was a Christian. She loved her husband. He loved her.

Krissy sighed. *So what in the world is my problem?*

❧

Blaine wasn't sure how he felt as he drove home that Friday afternoon. Disappointed, scared, and irritated all at the same time. He'd seen the orthopedic surgeon, and after hearing the bad news, he checked in at the fire station to say hello to the guys. Next, he conversed with the captain for a long while, and at last, Blaine saw the wisdom behind taking the permanent disability the city offered, along with a compensation package the union procured for him. The surgeon had stated that Blaine would never return to work. His back wasn't ever going to be as limber and as strong as it had been before the accident. However, his physician ordered him to swim and lose weight. . .that is if he didn't want to turn into a mass of plump vegetation. Blaine knew it was sound advice, and he'd been watching his diet lately. He'd even shed a few pounds, but he had many more to lose. So, after the fire station, Blaine's next visit was to the local health club where he purchased a membership. He figured a workout would use up an hour or two, but how would he spend the rest of his days?

Lord, there has to be a job out there somewhere that I can do. A man doesn't work, he doesn't eat. . .

Blaine pulled into the driveway and parked behind Krissy's van. Climbing out of his truck, he entered the house and the aroma of sautéing garlic immediately met his senses. He followed his nose to the kitchen where he found Krissy at the stove.

"Smells great in here," he said, placing his hands on her slim hips and kissing her neck. "What are you making?"

"A stir-fry. . .with real chicken," she replied emphatically.

Blaine chuckled. "Your version of Chinese food is always tasty, Hon. It's the order-out stuff that rouses my curiosity."

"What did the doctor say?" Krissy asked in a no-nonsense tone.

He chewed the side of his lip and considered her. Was she in one of her moods again? She didn't even acknowledge the compliment he'd just paid her.

She looked at him askance. "Well?"

"I've got six months to live."

Krissy gave him a quelling look. "Don't even joke about such things, Blaine."

"Well, maybe that's what you'd like to hear," he blurted. He was getting tired of catering to her whimsical ups and downs. Didn't she care a whit about him?

Setting down the spatula, she faced him, hands on hips. "I'm not up to sparring with you, so just tell me what the doctor said, okay?"

Blaine exhaled and fought against the frustration welling inside of him. "He said I can't go back to work because I'll never be able to function in the capacity the fire department expects. So, I stopped by the station and accepted the permanent disability offer and comp package. I'm no longer a firefighter."

Krissy's jaw dropped slightly. "You're out of a job? Just like that? Can't they give you some more time to recuperate?"

"It's been three months, Kris."

"But—"

"Look, the doc said it and my captain agreed. I'm no longer physically able to perform my job. And I won't be. Ever."

Blaine saw Krissy swallow hard. "We can't live on my salary. . .and help the girls through college."

"I'll have money coming in. And I plan to find something else to do besides sit around here all day watching soap operas."

"You've been watching the soaps?"

Blaine laughed at her horrified expression. "I meant that figuratively."

She nodded, looking relieved, and began slicing the boneless chicken breasts and adding the pieces to the oil and garlic.

"Honey, don't worry. Things are going to be fine. The Lord will take care of us. He'll find me some sort of work that I can do to supplement the disability payments."

"Yes, I. . .I'm sure you're right."

Blaine folded his arms and watched his wife prepare their meal with lack-luster efforts. It just wasn't like her. Up until a few weeks ago, she'd had an unsurpassed zest for life, but now a kind of dreariness clouded her eyes. He wished he could get inside her head for five minutes. Maybe then he could understand whatever it was that bothered her. . .other than what she'd previously admitted to. He had a feeling the problem was more than just his extra poundage and the girls being away, although the combination might have been the boiling point.

"Hard day at school, Kris?"

"Not exactly."

"Well, what *exactly* is bugging you right now? Me?"

"No. . .not you. It's just that I was thinking about quitting my job until you came home with your news."

Blaine brought his chin back in surprise. "Why do you want to quit your job? You don't like the new school?"

"I don't know. . .maybe I'm just tired of teaching altogether. Maybe I've lost what it takes to be a good educator."

"That's not what you said Monday night. You said the kids seemed to adore you and that they were excited about their new third grade teacher. I really thought you were starting to snap out of this depression. . .or whatever you want to call it."

Krissy began chopping celery, onions, and mushrooms. Next she tossed the vegetables into the wok on the stove. "There's just this person at school who. . ." She swallowed and Blaine sensed she was trying to carefully select her words. "Well, I don't know if it's. . .healthy for me to work near this person."

Blaine frowned. "Not healthy?"

"Emotionally speaking."

"Hmm. . ." He thought it over. "So this person is verbally abusive or threatening?"

"Threatening," Krissy replied on a decisive note.

"You're kidding? This person is making threats? Let's call the cops!"

"No, no, Blaine, not that kind of threatening. I mean, he's not threatening me, he's just a threat to me."

"Like he wants to take over your job?"

Krissy turned thoughtful. "Something like that, I guess. He wants to take over something."

"Man, you wouldn't think that kind of competition existed in Christian day schools, but I suppose it's everywhere." He paused, thinking it over. So all this was about her career? Well, that made sense. "Listen, Kris, if after bathing the matter in prayer, you feel you need to quit your job, go ahead. You'll find another one. Probably a better paying one, too." With that he closed the distance between them and kissed her cheek. "See? Problem solved."

∼∾

Krissy watched her husband's retreating form as he left the kitchen and entered the living room. Next she heard the rustling of the paper and knew he'd taken to reading the daily local news.

Blaine thinks the problem's solved, she thought, jabbing at the stir-fry with the wooden spatula. She then placed the cover on top of the wok and allowed it to cook. *The problem is not solved. It's far from being solved. But what do I say? I'm bored with our marriage and I'm attracted to Bruce Sawyer?* Krissy shook her head. Blaine would hit the ceiling. What husband wouldn't? And here she was supposed to be a good, Christian wife.

Her spirit plummeted deeper with discouragement and shame. Not only was she a lousy wife, but she was a sorry excuse for a Christian woman as well.

Chapter 7

Krissy sulked around the house for the rest of the evening, and Blaine didn't even bother trying to cheer her up. Frankly, he hadn't the slightest clue what more to do for her, other than leave her alone and allow her to come to her own conclusions about whether she should quit her job. Meanwhile, he started his new swimming routine on Saturday morning, and after completing several laps he could tell the exercise would strengthen his back muscles. Maybe he'd take off this extra weight quicker than he anticipated. The idea encouraged him.

On Sunday morning, he and Krissy attended their usual Bible study and the service that followed. When the pastor gave an altar call, Krissy went forward, looking more miserable than Blaine had ever seen her.

Lord, I feel helpless, he silently prayed, stepping into the aisle and allowing Krissy back into the pew after she'd knelt and prayed up front. It comforted Blaine to know she, at least, communed with their Heavenly Father. God had the answers that he lacked, and the Lord would guide Krissy's steps.

Back at home, she seemed. . .happier.

"Everything okay?" Blaine asked as they stood in their bedroom. He unknotted his tie, then yanked it out from around his neck.

Krissy smiled and nodded as she changed her clothes. "Everything's fine."

"What do you want to do this afternoon?"

She stopped and glanced at him, her expression one of surprise. "You want to do something?"

"Well, yeah. . .why is that such a shock?"

Krissy laughed softly and hung up her dress. "Because you usually like a nap on Sunday afternoons."

"That's when I was a hardworking man. Now I'm footloose and fancy-free."

"Oh, brother!" She rolled her eyes.

Blaine chuckled. "And tomorrow's a holiday, so you don't need a nap either."

"We sound like two old fogies."

"We are two old fogies. So what do you want to do this afternoon, *Granny?*" Judging from her wounded expression, Blaine instantly knew he'd said the wrong thing. "Honey, I was only kidding. The granny-thing was supposed to be funny."

"I know. . .I guess it just struck me the wrong way." She gave him an

173

earnest stare. "I'm not ready for old age."

"Well, we're not getting any younger. I mean, think about it. We could be grandparents in the next couple of years."

"Bite your tongue!"

Blaine laughed at her incredulous expression. Then she threw one of the bed pillows at him. He caught it and whipped it back, hitting her in the shoulder.

"All right, that's it. The war's on."

"Now, wait a second, here. I've got an injured back, remember?"

"Too bad. All's fair in love, war, and pillow fights. . .even when you're wounded."

Blaine grinned broadly. He hadn't seen Krissy this feisty in months. Clad in her lacy white slip, she made a fetching sight as she gathered her ammunition. He gave her enticing curves a long, appreciative glance.

Then suddenly the phone rang, intruding upon their special moment.

"Let's not answer it," Blaine said.

Krissy frowned. "But it might be the girls."

He thought it over. "We'll call them back."

She worried over her lower lip, and Blaine knew he had to answer it and put her mind at ease. Ignoring the pangs of disappointment, he lifted the portable phone from the bedside table and pushed the TALK button. "Hello, Robinsons'."

"Yes, may I speak with Kristin?" the male voice at the other end asked.

"Who's calling?"

"Bruce Sawyer. I'm the principal of Wellsprings Academy."

"Oh, right. Sure. Hang on a sec." Covering the mouthpiece, he held the phone out to his wife. "For you."

"Who is it?" she asked, sitting back on her haunches on top of the bed.

"Your new principal."

Blaine watched as Krissy paled in one second and blushed in the next. In fact, she turned scarlet right down to her collarbone. He narrowed his gaze, trying to gauge her odd reaction.

"What does he want?"

"Beats me," Blaine replied. "Should I tell him we're, um, busy?"

Krissy nodded, looking almost afraid to take the call.

Blaine put the phone to his ear. "Sorry, but Krissy's unavailable. Can I give her a message?"

"Yes, please. Ask her if she'd mind bringing a pan of brownies to the picnic tomorrow. My caterer's mother got sick, so I'm trying to put together an impromptu potluck."

Blaine pursed his lips and looked at Krissy who was staring back at him curiously. "Sure, I'll ask her."

"If there's a problem, tell her to give me a call. She's got my number."

She does? Blaine swallowed a tart reply. There was just something in this guy's tone he didn't appreciate. "Okay, I'll relay the message."

"Great. Thanks."

Blaine pushed in the OFF button with his thumb. "Who's this Bruce Sawyer anyway?"

❧

Krissy felt as though there was a hot blade piercing her insides. Inadvertently, she placed her hand over her stomach, but then she told herself she'd done nothing to feel ashamed about. "Bruce's the principal of Well-springs Academy," she answered honestly.

"Yeah, that's what he said. And he wants you to make a pan of brownies for tomorrow's picnic. Did I know about this picnic?"

"No, because I wasn't planning to go."

"Hmm. . .well, you'd better call the guy back and tell him. He said you've got his phone number."

Krissy frowned. "I have his number. . . ?" Then she realized what Bruce meant. "Oh!" she said with a good dose of relief. "We all have it. It's in the staff directory."

"So, why do you look so guilty, Kris?"

"I don't know. Do I look guilty? I shouldn't. I haven't done anything wrong."

Blaine sat on the edge of the bed. "Is this guy hitting on you or something?"

Krissy shook her head and glanced at the printed spread. The last thing she wanted to do was discuss Bruce Sawyer with her husband.

"He's not the one threatening you and making you feel like quitting your job, is he?"

"Bruce isn't making threats against me, no," Krissy said. How could she possibly describe the kind of threat the man posed? Bruce walked into her classroom and she suddenly felt sixteen again, all weak-kneed and nervous. When he sought out her company, she felt flattered, honored. They shared many common interests, and Krissy sensed the mutual attraction. Still, he knew she was married. . .so what was he thinking? The same thing she'd been thinking? That in another place, another time, they might have pursued a romantic relationship? But the fact remained: she was married. Very married. . .and Krissy planned to stay that way, despite her wayward emotions.

Blaine cupped her chin, bringing her gaze up to his. "Everything okay?"

"Yes," she replied, unsure if it were the truth or a lie. She felt so troubled in her heart, so stressed. Hadn't she gotten all this settled during the worship service?

"All right. If you tell me things are okay, then I believe you."

Krissy forced a little smile before Blaine leaned over and touched his lips to hers. It was like salve on a painful red welt, and she closed her eyes at its sweet familiarity.

But then all too soon, he ended the kiss. "You never answered my question," he said, wearing a silly smirk. "What do you want to do this afternoon?"

Krissy grinned as her hand clutched the corner of a pillow and before he could duck, she whacked him upside the head.

Chapter 8

Krissy leafed through the staff directory, found Bruce's phone number, then picked up the telephone and began to punch in the digits. Before she could finish, however, Blaine came up behind her and stole the phone out of her hand.

"Hey, I've been thinking. . .why don't we go to this picnic tomorrow?"

Krissy dropped her jaw. "You? Want to go to a picnic? With a bunch of teachers and their spouses?" She held her hand over her heart, feigning cardiac arrest.

He shook his head. "You'd starve to death if you went into acting."

She shrugged.

"But I'm serious. Maybe we should go. I mean, it's your new school and you're debating whether God wants you there. . .perhaps He'll show you at tomorrow's picnic."

Nice try, Krissy wanted to say. She wasn't that dumb. She knew the reason behind Blaine's interest in attending. He was curious about Bruce. She likened it to the times she and the girls would return from an afternoon of shopping and Blaine would ask, "How much money did you spend?" to which Krissy replied, "Not much." Then Blaine would say, "Lemme see the checkbook." It wasn't that he didn't believe her or didn't trust her. He'd made that much clear over the years. And he never once berated her for overspending. Simply, he liked to see the facts for himself. In all probability, the same held true now with the principal of Wellsprings Academy. Obviously Krissy hadn't adequately hidden her feelings when Bruce phoned earlier, so now Blaine wanted to appraise the situation for himself. Unfortunately, it made Krissy feel terribly uncomfortable.

"Blaine, I don't want to attend this picnic."

"Free food. You don't have to cook. . .except for a pan of brownies."

"I'll make you your own personal pan," she promised. "And I'll make your favorite cream cheese brownies, but only if we can stay home."

"Sorry, Babe, I'm on a diet." He patted his tummy for emphasis. "Besides, you accused me of not enjoying the same things you do, so here's our chance to do something together. Something you enjoy."

Krissy inhaled deeply, then let out a slow breath.

Blaine tipped his chestnut-brown head. "Want to tell me why you're so dead set against going to this little shindig?"

She considered the request. It would be nice to clear the air. But at the same time, she didn't want to hurt Blaine by admitting her attraction to another man. Would he ever trust her again?

"Don't you think I'll understand?" he asked, his expression soft, earnest.

"No, I don't think you will."

"Well, why don't you try me and see?"

"Because I don't want to take the chance. Besides, whatever I'm going through is something very personal. It's between God and me."

Blaine folded his arms. "I feel kinda left out."

She tried to ignore the pained look on his face. "Want to go to the zoo this afternoon?" she asked, purposely changing the subject.

"Not particularly."

"I thought maybe we could even ask Jill if we could take her kids. You know, get them out of the house for awhile so she and Ryan can have some time alone."

Blaine grimaced. "I'd rather go to fifty school picnics than take a bunch of whining kids to the zoo."

"Oh, come on, Blaine, it'll be fun."

He puffed out an exasperated sigh. "How'd you manage to come up with this harebrained scheme?"

"Harebrained? Thanks a lot."

"The idea, not you, Krissy."

She folded her arms, trying to stifle her irritation. "For your information, I heard Jill and Ryan arguing at one o'clock this morning. They were in their kitchen with the window open and they woke me up. I couldn't fall back asleep, and I started thinking about how we could help them. We can't enroll them in Christian marital counseling or a Bible study because they're opposed to anything religious. But then, during the worship service, I came up with. . .with this *harebrained scheme* of taking their kids to the zoo. It's a way to reach out to our neighbors."

"The zoo, huh?"

Krissy nodded.

Blaine rubbed his stubbly jaw in consideration, then finally agreed. "Okay, I'll go to the zoo this afternoon, but only if we can go to the picnic tomorrow."

"I'll think about it. I mean, I can always phone Bruce later with our regrets."

Blaine shook his head. "No picnic. No zoo. I drive a hard bargain."

Krissy stared hard at him, and Blaine stared right back. She could see the spark of determination in his dusky eyes. Against her better judgment, she relented. "Oh, all right. We'll go to the picnic. But I don't want to hear one complaint about being bored."

He grinned wryly. "Got it."

"And you don't have to tell every stupid joke you know and embarrass me."

"Me? Tell stupid jokes? C'mon, Hon, my jokes are always hilarious."

"Yeah, right." Spinning on her heel, she marched toward the front door. "I'll go ask Jill if we can take the kids."

"Sure. And I'll be here on my knees praying she says no."

∞

Krissy felt pleased that Jill agreed to allow her four children to go on the outing. In addition, Jill promised to spend some quality time with Ryan.

"I'm sorry we disturbed you last night," she muttered, looking embarrassed.

Krissy gave the woman a warm smile. "I wasn't so much disturbed as concerned, and I hope you don't think I'm a nosy neighbor trying to butt into your business."

"Are you kidding? You're a godsend. With the kids out of the way this afternoon, I might even accomplish a thing or two around the house and that'll make Ryan happy. He's forever complaining about the messes. But I just don't have any time to clean."

Krissy thought Ryan had better lighten up. But then she reminded herself that there are two sides to every situation, and she didn't know the other half of this one.

Sitting on a step in the back hall, she helped baby Haden on with his shoes. Then she lifted him into her arms, thinking he was about the cutest thing she'd ever seen, with his blond curls and deep brown eyes.

"Wanna go to the zoo?" she asked the eighteen month old.

"Zoo. . .Mama. . ." He pointed at Jill and Krissy wondered if he was going to cry when she took him home.

"Don't worry," Jill said as if divining her thoughts, "Haden will go anywhere with anyone—especially if his brothers and sister are along."

"Okay, then, let's go." Krissy carried the youngest on one hip while the three other kids followed her back to her house.

"I guess I wasn't praying hard enough," Blaine mumbled when she entered.

"Hi, Mr. Robinson," the oldest said cheerily. At eight years old, he was a red-haired, freckle-face kid with a smile that displayed a future need for orthodontics. "You coming to the zoo with us?"

"Yep. Mrs. Robinson is making me."

"She is?" The boy looked at her curiously.

"He's teasing you, Grant." Krissy gave Blaine a stony look.

He grinned back at her in reply.

"I like the aminals at the zoo," four-year-old Chelsea announced. Her coloring was similar to little Haden's. "I 'specially like the bears."

"I like the snakes," Royce interjected. The second-oldest, his features were a mix of his siblings'. He had reddish-brown hair and brown eyes but only a smattering of freckles.

"I like the snakes, too." Blaine grinned and pulled out his car keys. "Mrs. Robinson hates snakes, so we'll have to make her stay in that part of the zoo the longest."

"Yeah!" the two older boys agreed.

"Oh, fine," Krissy retorted, "but then I'll make you all go to the gift shop where I'll stay for hours!"

"Yeah! We like the gift shop, too!" Royce said.

Blaine laughed and headed out of the house. Krissy and the children trailed behind him. When they reached the van, the kids piled in and Krissy converted one of the back passenger benches to a child's harnessed seat into which she strapped Haden. With the task completed, she made sure the others were belted in safely before she took her place up front.

Blaine gave her a sidelong glance from where he sat behind the wheel. "You sure you want to do this?"

"Too late now."

With a sigh of resignation, he started the engine and backed out of the driveway.

They arrived at the Milwaukee County Zoo, parked, and Blaine paid the admission fee, grumbling under his breath about the cost of four children and something about highway robbery. Krissy ignored the remarks, knowing that he was only half serious anyway, and entered the gates with the children. The welcome sign proclaimed that this particular zoo was considered one of the finest in the country, and it housed approximately twenty-five hundred different animals. Krissy remembered from bringing her third-grade class here on field trips that it was virtually impossible to see everything in a span of a couple hours.

"Okay, what animals should we look at first?" she asked.

"Can we go on the train first?" Royce replied, and in the next moment the calliope-like blare from the down-sized steam locomotive heralded its arrival at the midget station.

The children were all in agreement; the train ride which circled the zoo had to come first. Blaine murmured a little louder this time as he bought the six tickets, but he seemed to enjoy the ride on this sunny September afternoon.

Krissy enjoyed it, too. Moreover, she relished holding a little one on her lap again. Her once-a-month nursery duty at church never seemed to completely satisfy the longing she'd harbored for years to have another child. Well, it obviously wasn't in God's plan. She would have to wait for grandchildren.

After the train ride, they visited the polar bears and sea lions. Then it was on to see the snakes and sundry other reptiles, all of which made Krissy's skin crawl. Next the alligators, and they finally moved on to the monkey house.

"Now you boys'll feel right at home," Blaine said as they entered the area where the chimps were swinging from tree limbs, jumping around, and picking at each other. "This reminds me of you guys playing on your gym set."

"Uh-uh," Grant said, an indignant frown furrowing his auburn brows. "We're not monkeys."

"It's a joke," Krissy assured the boy. "Mr. Robinson is always making bad jokes."

"Uh-uh," Blaine mimicked juvenilely.

"You're more trouble than these kids," she whispered, giving him an elbow in the ribs.

"Oh, yeah?" He caught her arm in fun and drew her tightly to his side. "Well, just for that little comment, you get to buy us all popcorn and soft drinks."

She shrugged, figuring it was the least she could do. Overall, Blaine was being a good sport.

A half hour later, they sat on a park bench, munching on popcorn and watching the children who were preoccupied with the elephants.

"You know, that little guy is awfully cute," Blaine remarked.

"Haden? Yes, he sure is."

"I used to often wish I had a son. . .not that I ever felt displeased about our twin daughters. But I prayed hard and long for a boy. Guess God answered that prayer with a 'no.' "

Krissy whipped her gaze around and stared at him. She would have never guessed Blaine harbored such a desire all these years. He had never said a thing. "We could have adopted. We still could, I suppose."

"Naw, I don't have the energy or the patience for kids anymore."

"That's just because you're out of practice."

"Yeah, maybe."

A rueful smile tugged at the corners of her lips while she studied Blaine's profile. Did he have any other regrets? The very question seemed like evidence enough that she really didn't know this man the way she ought to.

Two sides to every situation, she thought, recalling her speck of wisdom concerning her neighbors. And in that moment, Krissy realized how one-sided, how self-focused she'd been. Blaine was hardly some amoeba, like the kind scaling the aquariums here at the zoo. He was a man with emotions, ideas, feelings, and. . . disappointments.

"I'm sorry I never gave you a son," Krissy said. "I would have loved one, too."

He glanced at her, and with his sunglasses hiding his eyes, she couldn't quite make out his expression. But if she had to guess, she'd define it as surprise. "It's not your fault." He turned his line of vision back to the kids. "Just wasn't meant to be. I accepted that a long, long time ago."

Acceptance.

Oddly, the word seemed to cling to Krissy's heart for the remainder of the afternoon.

Chapter 9

Blaine groaned and then stretched out on the sofa and placed his head in Krissy's lap. "I think I outdid myself at the zoo today. My back is killing me."

"Oh, I'm sorry," Krissy replied, feeling guilty for insisting they go. "Sometimes I forget you're recuperating."

"Sometimes I do, too, and therein lies the problem."

Smiling at the retort, she ran her fingertips through Blaine's chestnut-colored hair. It felt thick and coarse, and although he kept it cropped short for the most part, he really had quite a lot of it around the sides and on top of his head.

"Say, Blaine, can I ask you something?"

"Sure you can." He peered up at her expectantly.

"I've been thinking ever since you said you wished we'd had a son. . .well, do you have any. . .regrets?" she asked on a note of hesitancy.

"Regrets about what? Our relationship or life in general?"

"Life in general."

"Sure I do. Who doesn't?"

Krissy grew more curious. "What do you regret?"

"Not becoming a Christian sooner in life for one thing. The girls were, what, in second grade or something when we accepted the Lord?"

She nodded, recalling how the twins had gone to vacation Bible school one summer and how at the closing program she and Blaine had heard the gospel preached for the first time. Neither had any trouble accepting the Word of God as truth. Each had been raised to revere the Bible and God; however, they had both trusted in something other than Jesus Christ for their salvation.

"On occasion I think that if we'd known then what we know now. . ." He chuckled. "What's that old cliché? Hindsight is twenty-twenty vision?"

Krissy had to agree. "What about our relationship, Blaine? Any regrets there?"

"None whatsoever. And you?"

"No. . ." She hedged slightly.

"That didn't sound very convincing, Kris."

Contrition filled her being. "Sorry. It's that I'm a different person today with different interests, likes, and dislikes. I'm not the same woman you married."

"Tell me one person who stays the same over twenty years' time." Blaine frowned.

"But that's what I mean. . .if we had to do it all again, would we?"

"That makes no sense," Blaine said on a note of exasperation. "The fact is, we can't do it all again, so why even bother speculating?"

"You're right."

"You know as well as I do that we can't change what's happened in the past. We can only go forward."

"True."

Krissy continued to caress his scalp, running a finger down the side of his face and around his ear. It obviously felt good because Blaine closed his eyes, looking like he might fall asleep. She wondered if he were right that perhaps she had begun to dwell on things beyond her control. . .and imagine things she had no right thinking about, such as Bruce Sawyer. Try as she might to rid her thoughts of the tall, broad-shouldered man with a sparkling blue gaze, it seemed impossible. Was she obsessed, or was this something that happened to people at one time or another during their marriage?

"Can I ask one more thing?"

"Shoot."

"In all the years we've been married, were you. . .well, did you ever find yourself attracted to another woman?"

Blaine cocked one eye open. "Nope."

"Oh, come on, you're a red-blooded man and you're not blind."

"Sure, but I don't allow myself any appreciative glances. It's like Pastor once said from the pulpit. The first look is accidental, the second look is sin." Blaine grinned. "On my life, Kris, I never needed to take a second look. I've got it too good at home."

His words should have comforted her, but instead they caused Krissy to feel even more guilt-ridden.

❧

Blaine pushed himself into a half-sitting position and searched her face. "Are you feeling insecure about us? I mean, you don't think I'm doing something I shouldn't. . .do you? Was it because Jill came over that day I was grilling? Honestly, I wouldn't dream of—"

She placed her fingers over his lips. "The thought never even entered my mind. I trust you. Completely. The truth is, I trust you more than I trust myself."

Confusion swept across him. "What's that s'posed to mean?"

"I. . .well. . .I. . .I guess I don't know how to explain it."

"Try." He narrowed his gaze speculatively. "Does it have something to do with your not wanting to go to this picnic tomorrow?"

"Yes."

A glacier of fear suddenly began to slide from his forehead, down his face, neck, chest, and spread to his limbs. What was Krissy getting at? Was she trying to tell him that she'd been unfaithful?

Tamping down his anxiety, he knew he had to stay calm. If Krissy sensed his upset, she'd shy away and wouldn't confide in him.

"Tell me, Krissy," he whispered.

Tears filled her eyes. "I want to tell you, Blaine, because after today I realize that I. . .I need your help."

"Okay." He felt willing to help her any way he could.

She swallowed hard. "But I'm afraid you'll hate me if I tell you. I hate myself."

Blaine thought this might be as bad as he feared. Swinging his legs off the sofa, he stood and walked to the large picture window on the far wall of their living room. He stared out across the lawn, noticing that the leaves on the trees were starting to change colors.

Change. It was frightening, and Blaine felt like he had an icy death grip around his neck. Prayer seemed impossible. But after several long moments, he took a deep breath and turned back around. "Honey, I could never hate you," he said sounding more composed than he actually felt. "You're the love of my life."

Rising, Krissy strolled slowly toward him, wiping a tear off her cheek. "You know I've been in this funk since the girls went away to college."

Blaine nodded.

"Well, then I began teaching at the academy where I met. . .the principal, Bruce Sawyer. Almost immediately we discovered that we had common interests. What's more, Bruce listened to me and validated my feelings, and he wasn't so macho that he couldn't share his. . .and he did."

Blaine bit his bottom lip, struggling to keep his temper in check. He suddenly felt like hopping in his truck, driving to the guy's house, and knocking his block off. "So how far did it go?" he heard himself ask.

"How far did what go?"

"The affair."

A look of horror crossed Krissy's features, and Blaine felt mildly relieved. "You didn't have a fling with this guy? That's not what you're trying to tell me?"

"No, Bruce has never touched me."

"You gave me heart failure for nothing?"

"It's not 'nothing.' " Krissy threw her hands in the air. "See, that's what you do. You make light of everything important to me. I'm torn in two over this. Doesn't that matter?"

"Of course it does. I'm not taking any of this in stride. I'm merely trying to understand."

After an audible sigh, Krissy sniffed back the remainder of her tears. "I'm attracted to Bruce. I know it isn't right and our friendship is inappropriate at best, but there's this part of me that enjoys his company. . .and I know he enjoys mine. That's why I don't want to attend the picnic tomorrow. I don't want to see him and be reminded of all these crazy things I feel—and I certainly don't want them to develop. You're my husband, Blaine, and I'm committed to our marriage no matter what. It's just that. . ."

"It's just that your heart isn't in it anymore," he finished for her.

Looking ashamed, she bobbed her head in silent affirmation, and Blaine felt tears prick his own eyes. The admission wounded him; however, it wasn't nearly the travesty he'd first imagined. For that he felt grateful. But even if it were, he would have fought for his marriage, and with God on his side, he would have won, too.

Tell her that.

The inner prompting was so strong, Blaine didn't dare ignore it.

"Come here, Sweetheart," he said, although he didn't give Krissy a choice in the matter as he pulled her into his arms.

"You must be so angry with me."

"No, not angry. . ."

"I'm sorry, Blaine. I didn't want to t—tell you be-cause I didn't w—want to h—hurt you."

"It's all right," he said, kissing the top of her head while she sobbed into his sweatshirt. "I'm glad you told me. I love you and I want you to be happy." He pushed her back slightly and gazed down into her tear-streaked face. "But I want your heart, Krissy. It belongs to me and I want it back." With his thumb, he gently brushed away the sadness marring her lovely countenance.

"I want you to have my heart, too, Blaine."

"Okay, well, your willingness is half the battle, I guess. . ."

He pulled Krissy close to him, feeling like an apprehensive soldier. The war was on. . .

But could he win?

Chapter 10

The sound of children laughing outside her bedroom window awoke Krissy from a sound sleep. It took a moment, but then she realized the kids next door were playing in their yard.

With a yawn, Krissy rolled over and glanced at the alarm clock on the bedside table. Surprised, she lifted her head from the pillow and stared hard at the glowing numerals. Could it really be 10:30 in the morning? She looked at the vacant place beside her and the obvious registered; Blaine had gotten up already.

Climbing out from under the bedcovers, she strolled to her closet and pulled on her robe for warmth. The house felt chilly, but since it was only September, Blaine wouldn't want to turn the heat on yet. However, it wouldn't be long. Winter was rapidly approaching.

She stopped in the bathroom, freshened up, and brushed out her hair. Then she made her way to the kitchen where she found Blaine, standing in front of the sink, holding a cup of coffee in his hands, and gazing out the window.

"G'morning."

He turned around and gave her a tiny smile. "It's about time you woke up, Lazybones."

Krissy scrunched her countenance in a sassy reply and walked toward him. "Any more coffee?"

"Uh-huh." He handed her a mug from the cupboard.

"Blaine," she began, as she poured the fragrant dark brew from the carafe, "you haven't said a whole lot since our discussion yesterday evening. Does that mean you're upset?" Taking a sip of coffee, she turned to view his expression. It was thoughtful, serious.

"What guy wouldn't be upset?"

Krissy grimaced. "I know. . ."

"But I'm glad you told me. And I've given the matter a lot of thought. I didn't sleep much, and with every lap I swam this morning, I asked the Lord what I should do about the situation."

"And?"

"Well, first let me tell you what I *wanted* to do. I wanted to phone Sawyer and tell him that not only are we unable to attend his picnic today, but that you aren't returning to work tomorrow. . .or ever." He sighed. "It took every ounce of strength I had not to give in to the urge. But the Lord showed me that I really need to trust you and let you decide how to handle this situation."

Krissy's heart warmed to his words. "I've got good news for you. I'm not going back to the academy. I've already decided that much. I'll call Bruce today and let him know, and I can clean out my desk tomorrow morning before school starts." She paused, encouraged to see a look of relief on Blaine's face. "But I want you to know that I could probably face anything now, knowing that you're praying me through it." She took a step closer. "With you and God on my side, I can do anything."

Again just a hint of a smile. "I'm glad you're feeling better, Hon."

"But you're angry, aren't you? I can sense it."

"Yeah, I'm angry. . .at him! The jerk." A muscle worked in Blaine's jaw. "He knew you were married all along. He should have kept his distance."

"I'm not exactly innocent. I should have kept my distance, too."

"True, but I've got a hunch that guy wouldn't have minded busting up our marriage."

Krissy didn't agree. She rather thought Bruce fell into the situation just as she had. It wasn't a premeditated thing. The attraction, the chemistry between them, had been apparent from the beginning.

"Listen, I'm a man, so I know how men think. The thrill of a conquest and all that. But as a Christian, Sawyer shouldn't have ever befriended you. I mean, if I sensed a woman was attracted to me, I wouldn't go out of my way to discover all the great things she and I had in common."

Mulling it over, Krissy had to admit he had a point. She took another sip of coffee and recalled the many times Bruce had sought out her company. She'd rationalized it away, feeling badly for him because of what he'd gone through with his wife. She thought he merely wanted someone to talk to—a comrade; however, she'd mistakenly opened her heart to him when her heart belonged to Blaine.

Krissy shut her eyes and anguished over this whole mess. "I'm so sorry." Sudden tears threatened to choke her. "Can you ever forgive me? Can you ever trust me again?"

"I can, yes, on both accounts."

She peered forlornly into her black coffee. "But it'll take time, won't it?" When Blaine didn't answer, she looked up at him.

"It's going to take more than time, Kris," he said, his dusky eyes darkening in earnest. "It's going to take patience, communication on both our parts, commitment to our relationship, and. . .last but hardly least, it's going to take a lot of love."

Krissy felt oddly impressed by his answer. It sounded rehearsed, but that only meant he'd really been giving the matter his utmost attention. Finally, he was taking her thoughts and feelings—he was taking her!—seriously!

"I'm willing," she said, setting down her mug on the counter. She slipped her arms around Blaine's midsection and smiled despite her misty eyes. "I do love you. And I think you're pretty terrific to put up with me."

He set his forearms on her shoulders, coffee cup still in hand. "And I think you're pretty. . .period."

She tipped her head, feeling both flattered and surprised. "You really think I'm still pretty?"

"No, actually I think our girls are pretty. You're. . .beautiful."

Her smile grew. "It's been a long time since you told me that."

"I tell you all the time."

"No, you don't."

"Well, I *think* it all the time."

Krissy shook her head. "Too bad I can't read your mind."

Blaine looked properly chagrined. "Okay, so I should say what I'm thinking more often. I'll try."

"That's all I can ask for."

He nodded. The pact was sealed. Then, as Blaine regarded her, a tender expression wafted across his features and deepened the hue of his eyes. Slowly, he lowered his mouth to hers. On contact, she closed her eyes, deciding this was most pleasurable kiss he'd given her in a long while. Gentle, undemanding, yet heartfelt and sincere.

After several long moments, Blaine lifted his chin and kissed the tip of her nose, then her forehead.

"You smell like chlorine," Krissy blurted.

"From the pool."

"Kind of a different smell for you." At his questioning frown, she added, "I'm used to you smelling like smoke."

"Those days are gone."

"And I'm glad. No more fretting over you fighting fires."

A wry grin curved the corners of Blaine's lips. "So now that we're both unemployed, what do you want to do with all the time we're going to have together?"

"The rest of our lives," she murmured. Funny how the thought didn't seem so oppressing anymore. She grinned up at him. "Blaine, I'm sure we'll think of some way to amuse ourselves."

❧

That evening, Krissy watched Blaine stack kindling in the fireplace and light it. Then she glanced across the dimly lit room at their neighbors who sat together on the love seat, sipping hot cocoa, and she marveled at the turn of events this afternoon. While Blaine had manned his post at the grill, slopping thick barbeque sauce on fat spare ribs, Ryan had sauntered over and began complaining about wives, kids, and marriage in general. After a lengthy discussion, Blaine had invited Ryan and Jill and their brood over for supper.

That was the first thing to blow Krissy's mind. Blaine had always acted more irritated by the Nebhardts than concerned for them and their marriage.

The second thing that sent her reeling was when Blaine suggested the younger couple get a sitter and come over after their children were settled. Surely, he would have much preferred to plant himself in front of the television tonight rather than entertain Jill and Ryan.

But when Blaine sat down at the piano and began to play for their guests, Krissy's head really began to spin. She hadn't heard him play in years.

"I wrote this piece just after I left for college," he'd announced. "I hated leaving Krissy behind. So I composed this sonata. I called it 'September Sonata.'" He grinned over his shoulder at his audience. "It was the very piece that made her say, 'I do.'"

His fingertips danced across the ivory keys of the baby grand in the corner of their living room and Krissy's face flamed with self-consciousness. The stirring melody evoked a host of memories that she didn't feel like reliving in front of her neighbors. That sonata—an instrumental musical composition consisting of three or four movements—how like their relationship it seemed. From falling in love to their perfect wedding day, to becoming parents and watching their daughters mature into lovely young women, their song of life had now begun to play a tune of rediscovery.

Suddenly their future together looked more than promising. It seemed downright exciting.

Krissy felt proud of Blaine, and the Nebhardts seemed impressed with his talent and applauded when he finished playing. Suddenly embarrassed, he announced he'd make a fire.

Brushing the wood dust from his hands now, Blaine walked over and claimed his place beside Krissy on the couch. It may have been her imagination, but she thought his blue jeans fit a little better and instead of wearing one of his usual, worn-out sweatshirts, he wore a dark gray pullover which he had neatly tucked into his pants. Making himself comfy, he stretched his arm out around her shoulders.

"You guys are so cute together," Jill remarked. "Like newlyweds or something."

"Well, we are. . .kinda," Blaine said, giving Krissy a meaningful wink.

"So you survived raising kids, huh?" Ryan asked.

"Just barely," he replied. "And if I've learned anything, I've learned I need to cherish my wife." Looking at her, he added, "If I ever lost her, I'd have nothing. I'd be nothing. I only wish I would have realized it years ago. I wish I would have made time for her. . .for us. . .in spite of our hectic schedules."

There beside him, Krissy felt like her wanderlust heart had come home. Blaine wasn't a man to make public professions, especially when they pertained to his personal life. He had sincerely meant every word he'd just spoken.

She glanced up at him in a measure of awe, and for the first time in years, she felt unmistakably loved—and, yes, even cherished.

Epilogue

Icy fear gripped Blaine Robinson's heart as he raced down the hospital corridor. He'd been conducting a routine insurance inspection for the company at which he'd been employed for the past year when he'd gotten Krissy's page. He had left right away, but was he too late?

A nurse in lime-green scrubs and a matching cap stepped into his path. "Can I help you, Sir?"

"My wife," he panted, "her name is Krissy Robinson."

"Right this way."

Blaine followed the woman through a set of doors and down another hallway. "If you want to go in with her, you'll have to put a gown over your clothes."

"Fine." Blaine didn't care what he had to do; all he wanted was to be with Krissy.

The woman handed him a blue printed gown and he immediately pulled it on and tied it at the back of his neck.

"Okay, you ready?" The nurse smiled.

"Ready as I'll ever be, I suppose."

"Aw, come on now," she said with a teasing smile, "you've got the easy job."

"Yeah, so I've been told."

She laughed and escorted him into the birthing room where Krissy reclined in a specialized delivery bed.

Blaine rushed to her side. "I got here as soon as I could." He noticed the beads of perspiration on her brow as he bent to kiss her forehead.

Krissy held out her hand, and he took it. "The contractions came on so fast."

"No kidding. You were fine this morning."

"I know. . ."

Her body suddenly compelled her to bear down hard, and she was helpless to do otherwise. A moment later, she collapsed against the back of the bed, letting go of the hand grips.

"Okay, this is the big one," Dr. Herman announced, her soft voice carrying a note of excitement to Blaine's ears. Despite Krissy's routine ultrasound exams, they had decided against learning the sex of their unborn child. "Another push. That's it."

But this was the part he hated, those agonizing last few minutes. Standing by Krissy's side, he knew his "job" was to encourage her, except it was hard to get past the feeling of utter helplessness.

Krissy squeezed his hand and cried out in final travail before falling back against the bed again. Blaine brushed the hair from her face and then the newborn's squall filled the room. Exhausted, Krissy went limp.

"I'm too old for this."

Blaine grinned, then looked at the doctor with anticipation coursing through his veins. "Is it a he or another she?"

The woman's round face split into a smile. "It's definitely a he!"

"Are you sure?" After he'd spoken those words, Blaine felt like an idiot. The doctor's incredulous glare only confirmed it.

"Of course I'm sure!"

"Don't mind him, Dr. Herman," Krissy said. "I think my husband is just overwhelmed."

"To say the least," Blaine admitted. He had to take several quick swallows in order to keep his emotions in check. He and Krissy had prayed for a son ever since they discovered she was expecting. Now that God had answered that fervent request, Blaine could scarcely believe it. He never thought this day would come and over the past seven months, he had found himself praying like the man in the Gospel of Mark: "Lord, I believe; help thou mine unbelief."

One of the nurses placed the baby on Krissy's abdomen. She clamped the cord in two places, then offered the scissors to Blaine. He took it and cut the umbilical cord, feeling glad that the hospital staff allowed men to take such an active role in the birth of their children. He'd read everything he could find on the Internet pertaining to pregnancy and childbirth, he'd monitored Krissy's diet, and he had even attended the birthing classes with her. But now he felt cheated because he'd arrived so late. He had looked forward to assisting with the delivery.

However, his disappointment paled beside the joy he felt at having a son. Putting an arm around Krissy, he watched as she cradled him. Blaine reached out and touched the infant's tiny hand, marveling at God's phenomenal creation of life.

"Let's call him Luke," Blaine said.

"Sounds good to me."

Leaning forward, he gave Krissy a kiss. "I love you," he whispered in her ear.

"I love you, too." She placed one hand against Blaine's face. He kissed her palm. "This is one of the happiest moments of my life."

"Ditto."

Krissy smiled. "We have our little boy at last."

Blaine's eyes grew misty.

"And you know what else?"

"Hmm. . . ?"

"You're my very best friend, and I couldn't stand the thought of bringing our baby into the world without you by my side. I tried my best to hold back the labor, but I couldn't fight the inevitable for long."

"You did just great, and God saw fit to get me here in the nick of time." He gave her shoulder an affectionate squeeze. "And for the record, Kris, you're my best friend, too. Want to know something else?"

"What?"

"It's going to stay that way, despite diapers, bottles, and frenzied schedules. Neither your day care center nor my part-time job. . .nor our precious children will come between us as long as I'm alive and have something to say about it."

Krissy smiled and glanced down at their latest little blessing who had fallen asleep. Looking back at Blaine, she said, "That's a promise I'm going to hold you to."

"Good."

Several moments passed before Krissy spoke again. "This marks a whole new season of life for us. We've got a baby again."

"You're just realizing that now?" he teased, although he knew what she meant. God was still composing their life's sonata. . . .

And this was simply the next interlude.

PROMISE ME FOREVER

Prologue

June 16

The little country chapel in Lyon, Illinois, was modestly, but tastefully decorated. Fresh floral arrangements stood in glass vases, white roses tied with emerald bows, near the altar and pleated paper wedding bells hung about. The pews were filled with enthusiastic friends and relatives who had come to share this special day. A wedding day, uniting for life Julia Rose McGowan and Mark Thomas Henley.

In the small dressing room in back of the chapel, Julia smoothed the skirt of her formal white lace gown which her Aunt Louise had sewn especially for this day.

"You look beautiful, dear," Julia's mother, Caroline, said with a proud smile. Then tears gathered in her green eyes. "You're the most beautiful bride I've ever seen."

"Oh, Mom, don't cry," Julia chided her gently. "You'll ruin your makeup. Don't forget pictures afterward in the park across the street."

Nodding, Caroline dabbed her eyes with a tissue. Her dark auburn hair, streaked with strands of gray, had been swept up in a regal bun.

"Can you believe it, Juli?" her best friend and maid of honor, Kathy, asked. The slim brunette fussed over Julia's lacy veil. "You and Mark. . .married." Kathy sighed, looking dreamy. "What a fairy tale. High school sweethearts, married forever!"

Julia was smiling, too. She had been in love with Mark Henley ever since the Junior Prom—that was two years ago. Julia was eighteen years old now and had just graduated from high school last month. Mark was a year older and, though some people said they were too young to make a life-long commitment to each other, Julia and Mark knew they were so much in love that it didn't matter. They promised each other that together they would conquer any obstacles brought on or compounded by their youth. After all, they had each other. . .what more did they need?

"I'm glad that we'll be sisters," Teri Henley said. Blond like her brother, she was sixteen years old and one of Julia's bridesmaids.

"I'm doubly glad!" declared fifteen-year-old Jenny Henley. "Now we've got the Henley men outnumbered!" She smeared gloss on her lips, then tugged at the forest-green bridesmaid dress she wore.

"Yeah, it was a draw before. Mom, Jenny, and me, Tim, Mark and Dad—that is, before Dad left. . . ."

At Teri's words a cloud of despair seemed to settle over the room.

"What on Earth makes a man go so crazy that he up and leaves his wife and kids for some other younger woman and a job transfer to Oregon?" Teri continued.

Julia shook her head sadly. "I don't know, Teri. A mid-life crisis, maybe."

"Now, let's not spoil this special day with troubled thoughts and grim speculations, all right?" Caroline McGowan smiled at her daughter first and then at the Henley sisters. "This is a happy occasion, and there isn't a thing you can do about your dad today."

"But he wouldn't even come for Mark's wedding," Jenny said with a large pout.

"His loss!" Julia exclaimed. She was angry with Mark's father for what he had done to his family. It was a scandalous thing, especially in this close-knit, rural community in central Illinois.

Kathy suddenly held out a tube of pink lipstick. "I think you need some of this so when Reverend Ritter tells the groom 'You may kiss the bride' you can smooch Pink Passion all over Mark's face." She laughed. "That'll make a great wedding picture!"

"Okay." With an impish grin, Julia turned to the mirror and smoothed on the lipstick. Then she rubbed her lips together.

"Oh, that's a pretty color," Caroline remarked.

"Yeah," said Kathy, "it'll look great on Mark, too!"

Giggles went around the room. Then, minutes later, the females in their lace and satin ruffles, left the room to line up for the procession as planned at the previous night's rehearsal.

Julia's father was already waiting in the vestibule, wearing a light grey tuxedo. He looked so handsome out of his greasy work clothes that Julia's eyes grew misty. Her daddy. . .all dressed up to give her away.

Suddenly Tim Henley, Mark's older brother appeared. He seemed anxious.

"You okay, Tim?" Julia asked.

He took a deep breath. "I've got to speak with you," he said in hushed tones. "It's important."

"But the wedding march is going to start and—"

"Juli, really. . ."

She looked at him with a concerned frown, but then nodded. "All right."

Lifting her hem slightly, Julia followed Tim away from her parents and bridesmaids and back to the far corner of the vestibule.

"What is it?"

"It's Mark."

"Mark?"

Tim nodded. "He's gone, Julia."

Her eyes widened. "Gone?" She didn't understand. "What do you mean. . . gone?"

Again, Tim took a deep breath. "Juli, he called me from the airport about half an hour ago." He looked down at his rented tux then. Blond and blue-eyed like Mark, he had been chosen as the best man. "I didn't know what to do. . ."

"What?" Julia's head began to spin. "What are you talking about?"

Tim pulled a letter from out of the inside pocket of his jacket. "I think this will explain everything," he said in a gentle voice. "Mark wrote it last night. After the rehearsal dinner. I found it in my tux pocket after he called."

Tears filled Julia's eyes as she unfolded the sheet of lined notebook paper. She read:

> *Dear Juli,*
>
> *I can't go through with it. I'm not ready for the altar. I can't work at a gas station the rest of my life! I wouldn't be able to stand it! I appreciate your dad giving me the job, but I want to do more with my life. My dad was right when he said I'd never be happy working as a greasy auto mechanic forever. And it's true. I want a career. Like the one Dad has, working for one of the biggest insurance companies in the nation.*
>
> *But I know my mom won't understand. She's a romantic. She always said, "love never fails," but, considering her and Dad, I guess it did anyway.*
>
> *Maybe marriage isn't such a good thing, Juli-bean. My sweet, sweet Juli-bean. I promise I'll always love you, but I'd probably end up breaking your heart. . .just like my old man did to my mom. Just like I'm doing right now. . .*

A sob escaped from the innermost part of Julia's being and she let the letter slip from her fingers. It fell to the worn, wooden floor of the old chapel along with the first of many tears.

"Mark went to live with my dad in Oregon," Tim informed her in somber tones. "He's decided to go to college. Dad said he'd pay for it. . .if Mark called off the wedding. . ."

The news was as crushing to Julia's heart as an iron wrecking ball to a fragile, crystal champagne glass. Mark. Julia loved him so! So much, in fact, she had given him the most precious thing a woman could ever give a man—herself.

"What's going on here?" Roy McGowan asked, suddenly standing beside his daughter. He put a parental arm around her. "What's happened. . .Julia?"

"It's M–Mark," she sobbed, turning and throwing her arms around her father's neck. "He left me, Dad!" she cried into the shoulder of his tuxedo. "He left me!"

Fifteen minutes later, the father of the bride walked up and stood before the guests. His shoulders sagged as he made the sad announcement. "Dear friends," he began, "I'm afraid there's not going to be a wedding today. . ."

Chapter 1

The alarm startled Julia awake at five-thirty. She rolled over sleepily and shut it off. Then, yawning and stretching, she crawled out of bed and padded to the windows. Peonies, she thought, spotting the abundance of pink and white bushes lining the tennis courts. It's late springtime when the peonies are in bloom.

The past month had been so rainy and cold that Julia was almost hoping spring would never come—as if the seasons could pass from winter right into summer. Late spring was not pleasant for Julia, at least it hadn't been for the last twelve years. Once it had been her favorite time of year, but it was now a difficult season to endure. Peonies and spring brought to mind a certain wedding day so long ago—and a ceremony that never took place. It was twelve years ago yesterday.

Turning from the windows, Julia shook off her melancholy, changed into her nylon wind-suit and began her habitual morning jog. She forced herself to count her many blessings and, of course, Jesse was one of them. At eleven years old, her son meant the world to Julia, and if she hurried, she would be back at their apartment before he awoke.

After Mark Henley left her for a college education and ideas about a fabulous career, Julia discovered that she was pregnant. Her parents were terribly disappointed in her, and Julia felt so ashamed. She had known her intimacy with Mark was wrong, but she convinced herself that since they were getting married it was all right. It wasn't. And, consequently, Julia found herself alone and in a terrible predicament.

Finally the decision was made that, to avoid a scandal in their small-town community, Julia would go to live with relatives: Barb and Glen French who resided in Menomonee Falls, Wisconsin. The plan was that Julia would put her baby up for adoption; however, after Jesse was born, she couldn't bear to part with him. He was, after all, the result of her intense love for Mark—even though Mark never knew about the baby. Neither did his family who had moved to Springfield to escape the gossip surrounding Mark's father's absence.

Stop dwelling on the past! she chided herself. But between Jesse and the time of year, the reprimand seemed preposterous. She could no more stop thinking about Mark Henley right now than she could stop breathing.

Re-entering the apartment, Julia poured herself a generous glass of orange juice. "Jesse, it's time to get up," she called as she turned on the television.

Then, while her son, blond and blue-eyed, stumbled to the kitchen and sleepily poured himself a bowl of cereal, Julia showered. By seven o'clock, she was dressed in a smart yellow silk blouse, black linen skirt, and black and yellow checkered linen jacket. Slipping into black pumps, Julia returned to the bathroom where she pinned up her shoulder-length, wavy, auburn hair. Then she applied a subtle amount of makeup—just enough to accentuate her teal-blue eyes. With a hand mirror, she considered her reflection and nodded with satisfaction. She looked businesslike. Professional.

"What time are you coming to get me at Aunt Barb and Uncle Glen's house?" Jesse asked. He had pulled on blue jeans and a red polo shirt.

"About eight-thirty," Julia replied. "I'm still working on that computer program for Customer Service."

"You'll get it right, Mom, don't worry," Jesse said with a confident look on his face.

Julia smiled. "You have more faith in me than my associates do, Jess." She gave him a curious look then. "Speaking of faith. . .did you have your devotions this morning?"

"Nope, but I'm going to do them with Uncle Glen. We pray together, too."

Julia nodded, though she felt the pinch of hypocrisy. When was the last time she'd had her devotions? Much to her dismay, Julia couldn't even remember. Lately God seemed far away, although it hadn't always been that way.

Before Jesse was born, Barb helped Julia come to a saving knowledge of Christ. She had been so excited about it, too. Forgiveness. No more guilt and shame over past sins. She was forgiven! And it was as if she could feel God's presence in every aspect of her life. It was exciting.

Then Julia had shared her newly found faith with her parents and brothers, and they too became Christians—all except for her father, that is. She was still praying for him. They all were. And Jesse. . .he was a special boy. At least, Julia thought so. He had understood his need for the Savior when he was just six years old.

"C'mon, Mom," he was calling from the side door. "I'll race you to the car!"

Laughing together, mother and son ran from their apartment to the hunter-green, Buick Park Avenue which was housed in a heated garage under all the units.

"I win!" Julia teased.

"No way. I got to the car first!" Jesse cried.

Julia had to laugh, knowing she had lost, fair and square. Unlocking the car door, she climbed in and opened the passenger side for Jesse. They drove the distance to the Frenches' home on the north side of Menomonee Falls and, by eight o'clock, Julia was entering the well-groomed property of Weakland Capital Management Corporation.

As Julia drove into her assigned parking slot and then entered the double glass doors of Weakland Management, she mentally prepared herself for her role as Manager of Information Systems. At work, Julia was cool—if not distant—but polite, intelligent, and always a professional. Relationships, she had learned, were risky, especially at work—especially in her position. Distance, she had discovered, was safe.

Julia's heels clicked smartly on the tile flooring now, as she walked through the women's locker area, and her stomach growled as she headed toward the cafeteria-style restaurant. Already she could smell the delicious aromas coming from its kitchen.

"Good morning, Juli," Stacie Rollins, the manager of Customer Service, said with a little smile. "I sincerely hope your people are going to have my program up and running today. It's been a horrible mess since Thursday."

"Conversions usually are." Julia stepped in beside Stacie and waited to place her order with Walter, the proprietor—or "Sir Walter" as he was fondly referred to at Weakland Management. He was from England and frequently entertained employees with his tales of London, during which his accent became more apparent than ever. However, his abilities in the kitchen were far more impressive than his English accent.

Julia ordered an egg bagel, strawberry cream cheese, half of a grapefruit and a serving of strawberries for her breakfast. Stacie ordered bacon and eggs.

"May I join you?" she asked, after Julia had taken her usual place in the dining room. Julia was fond of sitting next to the windows where she could look out over the vast gardens and evergreens behind the little pond while she ate.

Looking at Stacie, now, she simply nodded.

"Have you heard the latest?" Stacie asked, lifting a well-sculptured blond brow. "Bill has hired a consultant."

Julia nodded. "I heard."

Stacie looked surprised. "When?"

Julia just smiled. "Late Friday afternoon. Bill told me."

Stacie swallowed her obvious indignation at not being the first to hear. "Well," she said, shaking out her napkin and setting it in her lap, "I think it's a preposterous idea. We don't need a consultant around here. Everything is running smoothly." Stacie gave Julia a pointed look. "Except for my computer program, that is."

Julia chuckled softly. "We'll get it right. Don't worry. It's an excellent program. I think you're going to be very pleased. Give us a chance."

"Do I have a choice?"

Julia shrugged, though she detected a hint of a smile on Stacie's full, red lips. But she wasn't too concerned with Stacie's criticisms. Bill Weakland, the CEO and president, had been impressed with Julia's presentation of the new Customer Service computer program.

"Well, anyway, I met him this morning."

"Who?" Julia asked, distracted by her breakfast and thoughts of computer programming.

"The business consultant. I met him this morning." Stacie rolled her eyes and gave Julia a look as if to say, Pay attention, will you?

Smiling inwardly, Julia asked, "What are your first impressions?"

Stacie seemed eager to give them. "He's tall, blond, blue eyes, broad shoulders—Evan-Picone and Lagerfeld all the way."

Julia couldn't help an amused grin. "Don't underestimate our new consultant, Stacie. Underneath those popular name-brands is a man to be respected. I mean, Bill wouldn't have hired him if he wasn't top-notch."

Stacie lifted a brow. "We'll see." She set down her fork and, leaning back in her chair, she considered Julia through narrowed lashes. "I suppose you've heard the rumors. Large sums of money are missing and now the books aren't balancing. Jerry Fein is pulling out his hair—what's left of it, anyway."

Julia nodded. She'd heard. Of course, it was only speculation.

Stacie leaned forward. "But I still don't think we need a consultant, rather a new accountant. Consultants downsize. Now it's middle management that'll most likely get cut—and that's you and me, Juli!"

Julia didn't reply, but she had heard a similar rendition of the state of Weakland Management's affairs from Ken Driscoll, one of the Portfolio Managers.

Looking a her wristwatch now, Julia made her excuses to Stacie. "Your computer program awaits. . .gotta go."

"By all means," Stacie retorted. "Oh, and let me know what you think of Mr. BC."

Julia frowned, puzzled. "Mr. BC?"

"Business Consultant."

With a thumbs-up sign and a wink, Julia nodded. "Got it. Code names, right?"

Stacie laughed. "Right."

Smiling, Julia deposited her dishes on the conveyor belt in the kitchen area and then made her way toward the elevators.

Weakland Management was housed in a building three stories high. On the first floor were the locker rooms, Sir Walter's Restaurant, the mail room, and security office.

The second floor housed Customer Service, Data Processing, Information Systems and Public Relations.

Finally, on the third floor were the executive suites where Bill Weakland, his vice president, and all six of the portfolio managers worked. From their computer terminals, they kept track of the Dow Jones averages and, by phone, they bought and sold stocks and bonds all day long. The company's sole accountant, Jerry Fein, worked up there, too, and on some days the stress level was so incredibly high that no one in his right mind ventured farther than the second floor.

Julia reached her department by eight forty-five and had fifteen minutes in which to plan and organize her day. Her office, located in the back of the department, was tastefully decorated, though devoid of any personal items. Julia strived to keep her personal and professional life as separate as night and day. It was all part of the distance she had decided on so long ago. The fewer questions about Jesse the better.

At nine o'clock, Julia's employees began to stroll into the department. Angela Davis, her Assistant Manager, was the first to actually enter the office. She was short in height and on the heavy side, though she wasn't at all unattractive. She dressed well and had long, dark brown hair and large, mournful, brown eyes.

"These are for you," Angela announced with a smile as she set down a vase of white peonies on the glass-protected surface of Julia's desk. "First pick of the season."

Julia nearly groaned aloud. More peonies.

"You okay?" Angela asked, looking concerned. "I mean, you're not allergic to these things, are you?"

Julia forced a tight smile. "In a way, I guess I am. Would it be all right if we set the vase next to the coffeepot?"

"Oh, sure." Angela picked up the flowers and left the office. With a heavy heart, Julia watched her go, hating the fact that she'd never gotten over her feelings for Mark Henley. Every spring, memories of what she and Mark shared flooded back like April showers—and they lasted until July! And then, of course, Jesse was a constant reminder.

"What, daydreaming already? It's only five after nine."

Julia looked over at her office door and smiled when she saw Ken Driscoll standing there. He was attractive—almost pretty actually, with his light brown hair, big green eyes, and slim physique. Ken was most definitely on his way up the corporate ladder. He talked of little else. His career meant everything to him—and that was about all he and Julia had in common: their career goals.

"I worked all weekend," he was saying now. "What about you? Did you have a nice weekend also?"

Julia nodded. "I worked as well, but from home using my computer modem."

"Good for you. I tried to call you several times, but only got your answering machine." Ken paused, curiosity alighting his large, almond-shaped eyes. "You must have been out."

Julia nodded, remembering that she and Jesse had gone over to the Frenches' for dinner on Saturday evening.

Suddenly voices and laughter outside of Julia's office caused Ken to stand up a little straighter and wear a more serious expression.

"It's Bill," he said in hushed tones. "And he's got his consultant with him. They're making the rounds this morning, meeting all the employees. I had my turn already." By the look on Ken's face, Julia surmised that Ken's territory had somehow been tread upon. She'd seen it before whenever macho ego clashed with macho ego—like two oncoming locomotives on the same track.

Bill poked his head into her office. "G'morning, Juli."

"Good morning." She pushed a smile onto her face.

"Do you have a minute to meet Weakland Management's new business consultant?"

"Of course." Julia knew the question was a mere formality. Bill expected she'd always have "a minute" at his request. He owned the place, after all.

The consultant stepped into the office, and Bill made quick introductions. "Mark, this is Juli, the Manger of IS. . ."

Her jaw fell slightly as she viewed the man before her. Sandy-blond hair, cropped short and worn carelessly, framed the handsome face of the man who haunted her dreams. Weakland Management's new business consultant was none other than Mark Henley!

Like an automatic gesture, he held out his hand. "Nice to meet you, J—"

He paused abruptly, his bright blue eyes now taking in every feature, every contour of her face. He smiled, looking rueful at first and then. . .delighted?

"Julia," he said, making her name sound like a caress, "it's. . .it's good to see you again. . ."

"You two know each other?" Ken asked at once.

Mark nodded, his eyes never leaving Julia's face. "We were. . .we went to high school together."

Julia felt the air returning to her lungs. Her heart, pounding before, was slowing to its normal pace; however, she couldn't think of one single intelligent thing to say. If she thought Mark Henley was handsome before, he was ten times more so now. His once youthful, ruddy complexion was now rugged and mature, but he possessed the same wolfish grin she always remembered.

And then it surprised her to realize just how angry she felt at seeing him again. Mark, standing here in her office. This was her office, her career, her new life since he'd left her standing in the chapel so long ago. How could this be happening?

Bill cleared his throat, looking suddenly uncomfortable. "Yes, well, perhaps you two can get reacquainted over lunch."

"It's a date," Mark said with that charming smile of his. And before Julia could tell him that she never took a lunch, he and Bill were gone.

Turning back to her desk, Julia never saw the scowl on Ken Driscoll's face. In fact, she had forgotten all about him!

Chapter 2

"So who is Mark Henley to you, anyway?" Ken asked for the second time.

"What? Oh, I'm sorry, Ken. . .what did you say?"

"How do you know him? Our new business consultant?"

Julia shrugged her shoulders in what she hoped was a flippant manner. "Mark is just some guy from high school. That's all."

"That didn't seem like 'all'." Ken searched her face until Julia turned away.

"Ken, I have work to do. . ."

"Of course. I guess I just want to know that Henley isn't anything more than a friend."

After he left, Julia began to fret. She thought of Jesse, and a little chill passed through her as she imagined Mark discovering that he had a son. She knew she should tell him before he heard it from somebody else. Would he be angry? Would he feel cheated out of fatherhood or would he want nothing to do with either of them? The latter was what Julia feared most. Jesse would be devastated to learn he had a father and then feel the sting of his father's rejection. Julia simply couldn't let that happen.

Julia somehow worked her way through the morning. She managed to push aside her tumultuous feelings for Mark—until noon-time arrived and so did Mark.

"Are you ready for lunch?" he asked, walking into her office with a galling air of confidence.

"I didn't get a chance to tell you," Julia replied coolly, "but I generally work straight through."

"Okay. No problem." But instead of leaving, Mark walked farther into her office and shut the door.

From behind her desk, Julia stood, her heart hammering once more. "What do you think you're doing?"

Mark smiled, though it didn't quite reach his eyes this time. It was a sad-looking smile. "It's good to see you, Juli," he said softly.

She produced a curt smile. "I wish I could say the same, but I can't."

"I can accept that."

"Good. Now, if you'll excuse me, I have work to do."

Mark, however, didn't make a move. "For years I pictured you happily married

208

with a pack of kids somewhere."

"Well, if you remember, that was the original plan."

"Touché, Juli."

She closed her eyes against an enormous wave of pain. "Please, Mark. . . ."

"All right. I'll go."

He moved toward the door, then paused, his hand resting on the doorknob. "I've been trying to track you down for years, Juli." He turned around to face her. It was all she could do to hold her emotions in check. "It seemed you had disappeared off the face of the earth, but I never gave up hope in all my searching."

"You can't possibly expect me to believe that."

Mark shrugged. "It's the truth, although you're obviously not ready to hear it yet. But someday, Juli, I'm going to tell you all of it."

She forced a smile. "I would be happy to talk to you as one professional to another, but that's where I draw the line. Now, if you'll excuse me—"

"But I need to tell you, Juli. I must." Mark paused once more, this time raking a troubled hand through his hair. "And for both our sakes, you're going to listen."

With that, he walked out of the office, leaving Julia fuming over the threat.

❧

"I've been a wreck all day," Julia admitted as she and Barb sat on the wide front porch of the Frenches' home. Jesse and his "Uncle Glen" were away on errands. "I couldn't concentrate on anything."

"Oh, I imagine you had quite a shock today, honey," Barb replied. She was a short, jolly woman with a sweet disposition and, though she had never born any children, she was as motherly as they came, and Julia loved her.

"What am I going to do, Barb? It's Mark. I never thought I'd see him again. And what about Jesse? I've managed to forestall him every time he's asked about his father. But do I tell him now or do I wait and talk to Mark first?"

Barb clucked her tongue. "You're in a pickle, all right."

"I'll say. And can you believe that Mark had the audacity to say he's been trying to track me down for years? What a lie!"

"Are you sure it's a lie?"

"Of course I'm sure." Julia shifted uncomfortably then. "No, I take that back. Barb, I'm not sure of anything right now."

"Well, let's think about this for a moment." She paused, doing just that. Then she met Julia's stare. "I remember when you first moved in with us. You told me how hurt you were when Mark left you on your wedding day. And then to discover Jesse was on the way. . .you didn't know how things were going to turn out."

Julia nodded sadly. It had been a very bad time in her life.

"But what did you do then? What brought about a change?"

"I turned to God," Julia replied easily. "You know that. You're the one who led me to Christ."

"And you've still got Him, Julia," Barb said with an affectionate smile. A gentle breeze wrapped around them. Strands of her strawberry-blond hair threatened to come loose from the chignon she wore. "He's only a prayer away."

At Barb's reply, something tugged on Julia's heartstrings. When was the last time she'd gone to the Lord with a problem? Too long, she supposed. But there was a time when she conversed with God on a daily basis. When had it stopped? Julia didn't know. However, one thing seemed certain—if she ever needed God back in her life, now was the time.

❧

On Wednesday evening, Bill Weakland invited his employees to a business dinner at the country club. It was an annual company event, occurring every June, and various topics of interest were discussed. Typically Bill led the meetings, although he was known to invite guest speakers or elect different department heads to the podium. Tonight, Mark was scheduled to speak.

Parking her car, Julia entered the club and headed for the reserved banquet room. As she neared the doorway, she spotted Mark and her step almost faltered. She lifted a determined chin and marched straight ahead, refusing to let him intimidate her and despising the fact that he did anyway.

For the past two days, Julia hadn't seen much of Mark since Bill Weakland occupied most of his time. And that was just fine with her. The less she saw of him, the less he could affect her. However, tonight he stood, greeting employees as they entered the banquet room, and there was no way Julia could avoid him.

Mark nodded politely. "Good evening, Juli."

"Good evening," she replied coolly. But then she turned and smiled a greeting at Bill.

"Juli, you're prompt as always," he said. "You'll be sitting at my table tonight."

"Thank you, Bill."

Then, without a glance in Mark's direction, Julia set out to find her assigned table. Off-white linen tablecloths covered their surfaces and matching napkins had been carefully laid at each place.

Julia sat down and greeted some of her co-workers. They were all from various departments. It was Bill's effort at forcing acquaintances and, as Julia listened to one of the women talk about the woes of dictation, she glanced curiously at the name card on her right side. Ken Driscoll. And, on the left. . .

Julia groaned inwardly. Of course. It would have to be Mark Henley.

Dear God, she silently prayed, *I've been asking You what to do for two days, and I've been reading my Bible, but I'm just as confused as before. And now this.*

Stacie Rollins suddenly showed up and took her assigned place across the table from Julia. "Well, well," she crooned, "isn't this just the sweetest little setup."

Setup is right, Julia thought, wondering if Mark had anything to do with the seating arrangements tonight.

Stacie cleared her throat. "Will you be going to the Brewer's baseball game on Friday the twenty-first, Juli? It's a company event, really, and the tickets are inexpensive."

Julia shook her head. "Maybe next time." She had taken that very afternoon off since her parents were coming to pick up Jesse and take him up north for a week. She didn't use much of her vacation time, but somehow it had all worked out for which she was thankful.

Bill was suddenly standing at the podium. "I'd like everyone to take their places," he announced. "Our food will be coming shortly."

Minutes later, dinner was served—grilled pepper steak, sautéd vegetables and rice pilaf. Normally Julia would have enjoyed the expertly prepared food; however, with Mark sitting beside her, she had to choke down every bite.

"So tell us about yourself, Mark," Stacie ventured. "Where did you acquire your education?"

"UCLA."

Surprised, Julia glanced over at him. She had assumed that he stayed in Oregon all these years, finished college and then worked with his father. Questions filled her heart as Mark caught her eye and smiled.

"Are you a home-grown California boy?"

He chuckled at Stacie's question. "No, actually I'm from the Midwest."

Julia's heart began to hammer. *Don't say it Mark,* she pleaded inwardly.

But he did. "In fact, Juli and I grew up together in Lyon, Illinois."

"Is that so?" Stacie drawled, giving her a speculative glance.

"I think we met on the playground," Mark replied, "when Juli was in Mrs. Craig's first-grade class."

"You remember her name?" Julia asked incredulously.

Light laughter frittered around the table.

Mark nodded. "I remember a lot things," he said, looking directly at Julia. His expressive blue eyes darkened with emotion and the underlying meaning of his words rang in her heart, fostering an unbidden hope. . .which annoyed her to no end!

How can this man incite all these different feelings in me at the same time? Julia wondered.

Bruce Johnson, from the Public Relations Department, began asking Mark some more questions about his education. As Mark replied, Julia discovered he had earned his Bachelors and Masters degrees, both in Business Management.

"And he's working on his Doctorate," Bill interjected. "Just needs to finish up that old dissertation." He gave Mark a friendly slap on the back. "Right?"

Mark grinned. "That's right."

"Mark comes highly recommended from a good friend of mine," Bill added. "I've got a world of confidence in him."

"Thanks, Bill." Mark suddenly looked a little embarrassed by all the fuss being made over him.

"Well, well, isn't that impressive," Ken said in a tone that made Julia wonder—it sounded sarcastic at best.

The conversation shifted to hobbies. Mark liked boating, golfing, biking—and he loved hiking in the mountains. Suddenly Julia wished she could go home. She didn't want to know what Mark loved.

"My very favorite hobby, though," he admitted sheepishly, "is working on cars."

Julia brought her head up quickly, and Mark met her gaze.

"It was Juli's dad who taught me everything I know. . .and that's how I worked my way through college. Working on cars, rebuilding engines."

Julia swallowed hard, and it took everything in her to tear her gaze from his. Then, in an attempt to hide her discomfort, she looked at her wristwatch. She wished Bill would begin the meeting.

Someone changed the subject and suddenly separate conversations ensued around the table. Julia caught snippets, but wasn't really listening carefully to anything particular.

That's when Mark nudged her. "Help me with something, will you, Juli?"

She gave him a suspicious look. "That depends."

He smiled at the tart reply. "Listen, I'm a Christian and. . . well, I've been looking around. . .can you suggest a good church for me around here?"

Julia pulled her chin back in surprise. "A. . .church? For you?"

Now it was Mark's turn to look surprised. But then his expression changed to apparent regret. "Is that really so hard to believe, Juli? That I'm a Christian man now?"

She shrugged, deciding to answer his first question and ignore his last. "There's a Bible-believing church right up the road from Weakland Management. It's the one I belong to."

Just as soon as those final six words tumbled out of her mouth, Julia could have bit off her tongue. The last thing she wanted was for Mark to show up at church and invade her faith as well as her life. However, she couldn't retract the offer now with any semblance of dignity.

A slow smile began to spread across his face. "Are you a believer, too?"

She nodded.

"That's great. . .really great. When did it happen for you?"

Julia took a long, pensive drink of her mineral water. She didn't think it would hurt to tell him. "About eleven years ago."

"Happened for me about six years back." Mark paused. "Were you praying for me, Juli?"

The question momentarily threw her. Praying for him? Why, she'd done nothing but rue the day she'd ever met him—except, of course, where Jesse was concerned.

Fortunately for her, Julia never had to reply. Bill began the business meeting and the dinner dishes were quickly cleared.

"Thank you all for attending tonight," Bill stated. "As you're aware, we have a new business consultant and he'll be reporting directly to me. Some of you may already know that Dave Larkey, our Vice President, resigned—"

Gasps of surprise echoed around the room while Julia and Stacie exchanged curious glances. Julia, herself, had had no idea that Dave resigned and, by the expression on Stacie's face, it appeared she hadn't known about it either.

"That's only one of the many changes that'll occur," Bill continued. "Mark has been hired to reorganize and restructure Weakland Management, so I'd like him to stand and say a few words."

Gliding his chair back, Mark stood and walked to the podium where he began a very eloquent presentation, complete with an outline that was handed to every employee.

"If you turn to page five," Mark was saying, "you'll see my itinerary. For the remainder of this week and all of next week, I'll be working closely with Bill, learning more about the company as a whole. Then, I'll be spending one week with each department, evaluating its efficiency. I'll report my findings to Bill and then we'll reorganize accordingly."

He's likely to be here till Christmas! Julia realized with dismay. She had been half-hoping that Mark's stay would be very temporary.

Julia sighed. Then, looking back at the outline, she noticed that Mark planned to start with Customer Service. Her department was third on his list, but Julia was fretting already. It had nothing to do with her department, per se; she ran a tight ship. Everything was in order. No, Julia's fretting came straight from her heart.

"Inevitably," Mark continued, "there will be changes, just as Bill mentioned, so I'm counting on everyone's cooperation. Cooperation, in fact, will be essential to my work and for the good of the company."

The meeting ended at nine o'clock sharp and, while the employees with questions gathered around Mark and Bill, everyone else went home. Julia was part of the latter crowd.

"So, what did you think?" Stacie asked as they walked to their cars.

Julia smiled. "About the meeting? Or Mr. BC?"

"Why, Mr. BC. Who else?"

Julia laughed. "Well, I think. . ." She paused. Actually, Julia didn't know what to think. Finally, she said, "He puts on a fine presentation."

Stacie lifted a brow. "I asked your opinion on him, not his presentation. I mean a girl would have to be in coma not to notice the man. He's gorgeous! And the looks he was sending you. . ."

Julia felt her face warming red, and she wondered if her flaming cheeks matched this evening's earlier sunset.

"Well, in any case," Stacie said, "it's just too bad that he's married."

"Married? Who?"

Stacie turned to give Julia an exasperated frown. "Mr. BC, that's who."

"Mark?"

"Come on, Juli, didn't you see the wedding ring on his left hand? I mean, really, that's the first thing I look for, and he's wearing one."

"I didn't notice."

Stacie shrugged. "Well, here's my car. I'll see you at work tomorrow."

As she watched Stacie drive away, Julia's heart plummeted. She tried to convince herself that she was glad Mark was married because now she could harden her heart against him and not feel guilty about it. Furthermore, she told herself that Mark didn't deserve to know about Jesse; he wasn't worthy of the title "Father."

However, Julia Rose McGowan had lied to herself before, some twelve years ago, and she knew the sting of consequence. She had to face the cold, hard facts: Mark was married. . .and he still had to be told about Jesse.

Chapter 3

The following morning dawned cold and rainy; however Julia decided to take her habitual run in spite of the weather. It was a challenge, too, considering that she'd tossed and turned for most of the night. She'd been so tired and yet she hadn't been able to fall asleep—not with the words "Mark" and "married" hammering away at her subconscious.

I don't care, Julia told herself for the umpteenth time as she jogged her last quarter of a mile, heading for home. She was soaked to the skin and the rain kept falling, but to Julia it felt refreshing. The cold rain did wonders for her swollen eyes and tear-streaked cheeks. Memories, like ugly demons, continued to surface, and Julia couldn't seem to steer her mind clear of them. Mark. She had loved him so much. Mark. He had been her best friend. . .even better than her girlfriend Kathy. They had talked and dreamed together, planned their future together. . .

So what? That was twelve years ago. I don't care if Mark is married! Julia declared inwardly as she entered the condo. *I've got my own life. I've got my work. . . and Jesse.* Julia was only too glad that her son hadn't witnessed her fitful night since he stayed over at the Frenches' because of the meeting at the country club.

In the back hallway, Julia began to peel off her soaked wind-suit. Then she pulled on her bathrobe, which she had strategically laid over the kitchen chair. She swallowed down a painful lump and willed herself not to shed another, single tear. What had she expected? How absurd it was to think that Mark would have stayed faithful to her memory all these years when he couldn't even show up at the church to fulfill his promises! And yet, Julia had stayed faithful to Mark's memory. . .except, she had to admit, it hadn't totally been by choice. She simply had never met another man to whom she was willing to give her heart.

That's because Mark stole it, the rat!

She showered, and more memories assailed her then. This time, memories of Jesse. He had been a good-natured baby, one who didn't mind being left for college classes and part-time jobs. Then he grew into a good-natured boy. It had taken Julia six years to earn her Bachelors Degree, after which she'd obtained the Information Systems position at Weakland Management. She didn't know what she would have done without the love and support of Barb and Glen. They nurtured her through her pregnancy, and they loved Jesse almost as immediately as Julia had. Then they had helped raise him.

Julia's parents, too, had been a great source of encouragement and, over the years, they became close friends with the Frenches. So, with her family cheering her on, Julia worked her way through college, determined to make something of herself.

Feeling that same self-determination growing inside of her, Julia dressed for work. She dried her eyes and carefully applied her makeup. Then, just as she was on her way out the door, she saw her Bible on the coffee table. *My devotions. I didn't have them this morning.* She really didn't feel like having them this morning, either; however, her heart seemed to prod her onward, toward the coffee table.

The devotional book and her Bible in hand, Julia took in the daily reading and then followed up with the coinciding passage from Matthew 11:28–30. "Come unto me all ye that labour and are heavy laden, and I will give you rest. Take my yoke upon you, and learn of me; for I am meek and lowly in heart: and ye shall find rest unto your souls. For my yoke is easy, and my burden is light."

Those words were like a soothing salve to Julia's heart. Her emotions were in such a tangled mess that she did, indeed, feel "heavy laden." She needed that "rest" that Jesus promised. Why had Mark reappeared in her life after all these years? Why did he say that he had been trying to "track her down" when he was married? He had promised to love her forever, except he married someone else! The realization of it hurt terribly, yet she knew she had to be honest with herself and at least admit that, yes, it hurt.

Picking herself up, Julia gathered her attaché case and purse. She was pensive as she left her apartment and drove to work. Part of her felt spiritually uplifted because of her devotions, yet Jesus seemed very far away. Where was He in all of this? Didn't He care that she was miserable?

Walking into Weakland Management, Julia met up with Angela Davis. "Everything all right, Juli?" she asked, trying to pull her from her meditative mood. "Our handsome new business consultant doesn't have you worried, does he?"

"Yes, he does," Julia replied tightly, as they walked through the locker room. "But not in the way you think."

Angela seemed to ponder the remark momentarily. "I heard you guys grew up together," she commented, walking beside Julia as they headed for Sir Walter's Restaurant.

"We did."

"So this situation is like. . .too close for comfort, huh?"

Julia forced a smile. "Yeah, something like that."

"Well, as always, if there's anything I can do to help, let me know."

"Thanks, Angela. As always, I appreciate your offer."

Julia surveyed the food and then selected her breakfast—a warm, flaky croissant and a sliver of Brie cheese. Angela had fruit salad, served in the shell of half a cantaloupe. Together they sat down near the windows and began to eat.

"Good morning, Juli. . .Angela."

Julia managed a smile. "Good morning, Ken."

"Mind if I join you lovely ladies?" Without waiting for a reply, Ken pulled out a chair and sat down. "These waffles are my favorite! And I absolutely must eat them with an indulgent serving of Sir Walter's famous strawberry syrup."

Sitting across from Ken, Angela shook her head. "How come men can enjoy their 'indulgent servings' but we women pay for ours. . .in inches to our hips?"

Julia grinned.

"Now, listen here," Ken replied with a slight smile curving his pretty-boy, handsome face, "I like a woman with a little meat on her bones. Indulge away, Angela."

"Not a chance," she retorted. "I've worked hard to take off that last twenty pounds. No indulging for me!"

"Such a pity." Ken sent a wink to Julia. "And how about you?"

"I indulge on the weekends only."

"Really?" Ken suddenly looked very interested. "What do you indulge in?"

"Chocolate *anything*." Julia couldn't hold back a soft chuckle.

Ken was smiling warmly at her now, and Julia grew uneasy. She could tell he was interested in her romantically and thought she should say something to discourage him. However, she figured Ken would lose interest in her as soon as he found out about Jesse. It had happened before, an interested man who lost interest as soon as he found out there was a child attached to her. Fortunately, Julia was never too heartbroken about it. She hadn't been the one interested, after all.

Glancing at her wristwatch then, she said, "You'll have to excuse us, Ken, but Angela and I are going to be late for work if we don't get going."

Nodding, he waved the ladies off while enjoying a mouthful of strawberry-saturated waffles.

"What do you think of him?" Angela asked, walking beside Julia as they headed for their department. "I'm just curious."

"Ken?" Julia smiled. "Oh, he's very dedicated."

"So are you," Angela observed.

Julia agreed. "I guess we have that much in common."

"Are you thinking of. . .dating Ken?"

"No," Julia replied, shaking her head. "I never liked the idea of dating my co-workers."

"Even if they beg and plead and turn on the charm?" Angela's chuckle had a cynical ring. "Juli, how could you resist? I don't think I could."

"Resist Ken?" Julia shrugged. "It's easy for me here at work. My career is very important to me. In fact, it's more important to me than dating a begging and pleading co-worker, okay?"

Chuckling together, Julia and Angela rounded the corner. Then, entering the department, they met Mark who was obviously on his way out. In fact, all three of them nearly collided in the doorway.

" 'Mornin', Juli," he said good-naturedly. Looking at Angela, he said, "Good morning to you, too."

Angela looked suddenly uncomfortable, but mumbled a greeting before scurrying off to her desk. Julia just folded her arms tightly across her chest and lifted her chin. She was determined not to let her personal feelings affect her professional stance.

"Can I help you with something, Mark?"

He nodded, still wearing a charming smile. "I need a PC hooked up. Bill wants me to have access to every program you've got up and running. I have an office now—upstairs. It used to be the small conference room." He paused, his gaze roaming over her in a quick head-to-toe motion, his expression saying he liked what he saw. "So what do you think?"

I think your wife ought to know about the looks you're sending me, Julia fumed. However she replied, "I have to iron out some kinks in Customer Service's new program this morning, but I'll have your PC installed this afternoon."

"Good enough."

Julia gave him a dismissive nod and then made her way to her office. But, as she unlocked the door, she discovered that Mark was right on her heels.

"How 'bout dinner tonight?" he asked, entering the office behind her. He closed the door, much to Julia's aggravation. "I'll pick you up about seven o'clock. Just give me your address and phone number."

"You've got to be kidding!" She glared at him with arms akimbo.

A puzzled brow marred Mark's handsome face. "What do you mean? Of course I'm not kidding." He paused, looking thoughtful. "I figured we broke the ice last night at the business meeting. It seemed like we did, anyway."

Julia fairly gaped at him. *He's married and he's asking me out. What a jerk!*

"Look, Juli," Mark said softly, seriously, "there's a lot you and I have to talk about. There's so much unsettled between us and I. . .well, I need to see it settled."

Julia narrowed her gaze suspiciously. "Okay, let me get this straight. You're asking me out for the sole purpose of seeing things settled between us. Correct?"

Mark seemed to weigh her words before nodding. "Correct. Look, Juli, you're a part of my life that I've never been able to resolve, and I can sense that it's the same for you, too."

He smiled, his blue eyes softening, and Julia knew he was determined to get his way. Some things never changed!

"Come on, Juli, what do you say? Dinner tonight. It's perfectly harmless. I promise."

Julia rolled her eyes. "Yeah, sure, I've heard your promises before."

Mark seemed to grow suddenly very serious. "Juli, that's why we need things settled between us. I owe you an explanation and an apology and I. . .well, I desperately need your forgiveness."

The way in which Mark said that caused Julia to wonder if he was having marital problems, and all because of their past. Then she wondered if it was really her responsibility to help Mark lay it to rest.

"Juli," he asked softly, "what do you say? Let's talk over dinner tonight."

"I'll think about it," she replied, turning away from him and sorting through some mail on her desk. She hoped she sounded bored and distracted even though she was anything but.

"Well, that's all I ask," Mark said, "just that you think about it."

With that he left her office, leaving Julia alone with her tumultuous thoughts.

Chapter 4

It wasn't until two o'clock that Julia found enough time and resolve to hook up Mark's PC. She wheeled the color monitor, hard drive, and keyboard to the elevator on a cart. As she entered his office upstairs, Mark stood immediately and helped her unload the equipment. Julia was both surprised and impressed when Mark began plugging the PC components together with their proper cables.

And then a flash of silver from his left hand. So, it's true.

Julia's heart felt like it was going down for the last time and, in effort to save it, she forced herself to concentrate on the business at hand.

"I'm going to program your PC into a community printer that's located near the portfolio managers," she told Mark.

"That's fine."

"And I downloaded everything from my PC to yours. . .but only because Bill requested it. I'm not pleased about it at all."

"Why's that?" Mark asked with a slow smile that was so charming it caused Julia to bristle all the more.

But, to him, she merely replied, "It gives me an uneasy feeling to know that other co-workers—make that consultants—have access to my programs. It's kind of like too many cooks in the kitchen. The more people entering into the Program Manager files, the more potential there is for error."

"And I agree," Mark said, still smiling. "I promise I won't mess up your computer programs, Juli."

Another promise.

Taking a slow, deep breath then, Julia determined not to let Mark get to her anymore. She needed to put aside her personal feelings. After all, this was the work place, and she had a job to do.

Julia cleared her throat. "If you'd like to pull up a chair, Mark," she offered in the politest tone she could muster, "I'll give you a briefing of the system."

He nodded and pushed a chair in beside her; however, with him so close, Julia could scarcely concentrate. She could smell his cologne, like leather and spice, and there was an aura about Mark that commanded respect, not in a military sense, but in a professional one. Yet he was quick to smile, seemed eager to be friendly, and he had an athlete's look about him.

Jesse would like him, she thought, wondering simultaneously what in the world she was ever going to do.

"Juli?" Mark gave her a nudge with his elbow. "Wake up, lady!" he said, grinning.

Julia shifted in her chair, feeling embarrassed. "I'm sorry. I was thinking about something else."

"That's okay." He chuckled softly. "Now what about this new program that you wrote for Customer Service? Tell me about it. Show me how it works."

"All right." Julia signed onto the program and showed Mark the basics as she gave him an overview.

"I see." Mark seemed thoughtful. "Weakland Management is certainly a rapidly growing company."

With a nod, Julia smiled inwardly. She felt quite pleased with her accomplishment. She rather thought that Mark looked impressed, too. And wait until she unveiled her new software ideas for the portfolio managers. Ken had been a big help to her in that regard, during the early stages of her program's development.

Mark suddenly reached over with his left hand and pointed to the computer screen. "So this is where the callers' names and addresses go, huh?"

"Right."

As Julia looked at the monitor, she couldn't help but look at Mark's wedding ring. It was, after all, right there in front of her nose. And when she focused on it and not what Mark was pointing at, a vague sense of familiarity arose in her until at last it took hold of her recollection. *That's our ring!* she realized. *The one Mark bought for our wedding. . .it had belonged to a set. . . .*

"Juli, honestly, are you with me or not?"

In reply she stood up abruptly, sending the wheeled chair rolling backwards. "You're despicable!"

"Excuse me?" Mark stood as well, arching questioning brows.

"You heard me, you lowlife snake in the grass!"

Mark brought his chin back at the insult. "Juli, what in the world. . . ?"

"In fact, you're lower than a snake. You're a worm!"

"Julia," Mark's voice beheld a hint of warning, but she ignored it.

"Bad enough that you're married and sending me suggestive glances, but that you couldn't even buy yourself a different wedding set. . .that's inexcusable, unforgivable. . .and just plain old bad taste!"

Mark turned on his heel and headed for the door. Julia fully expected him to storm out of the office or, at least, slam the door, but Mark did neither. He simply closed it softly and then walked back over to where she stood, still smoldering.

Sitting on the corner of his desk, one leg dangling over the side, Mark gave her an earnest look. "I'm not married, Juli," he said. "Never was."

She folded her arms across her chest and lifted a defiant chin. "Yeah, that's what they all say."

Mark grinned. "All of them?"

Julia gave him a leveled look. "A figure of speech, Mark."

His grin broadened, and Julia realized that he was teasing her. . .and it hurt. Tears threatened in the backs of her eyes, but Julia willed them away.

"Mark," she began in voice that sounded broken to her own ears, "that was our wedding set. How could you flaunt it in front of me? How could you flaunt it in front of everyone here at Weakland Management? My co-workers think you're married now. In fact, it was Stacie Rollins who pointed out your. . .our. . .wedding ring, and—"

"And she's probably a good example of why I'm wearing it, too!" Mark interjected. "At least a good example of one of the reasons I'm wearing it."

Puzzled, Julia could only stare back at him.

"I put this ring on," Mark explained gently, "after my first consulting job. I was a novice, and I didn't want anything—make that, anyone—distracting me from my work. Besides, I wasn't interested in a romantic relationship, and I figured wearing a wedding ring would forestall any predatory females," he said emphatically. "It usually works, too."

Julia stood there, wondering whether to believe him.

"I'm not married, Juli," Mark said, in a low, sincere tone of voice. Then he took her hand. "I wouldn't purposely hurt you. . .not again. I can tell that you're still hurting over what happened twelve years ago."

Julia fought the urge to yank her hand away, except that would only prove his point.

"Besides," he added, "how could I ever marry someone else when I could never forget you? Which brings me to the other reason I'm wearing this ring."

This time she did pull her hand away. "I don't want to hear it. You were always such a sweet talker. I can still see you sweet talking poor Miss Lamont in English class. I don't think you ever had to write an English paper."

This time Mark laughed, nodding. He obviously remembered, too. "All right, I'll admit that I was a sweet talker. But I sincerely meant what I just said about never being able to forget you."

She narrowed her gaze suspiciously.

"Look, I have no dark, ulterior motives, I guarantee it. But I do think we need to talk. Tonight. Over dinner." Mark's voice was soft and persuasive. Standing, he guided her toward the door, placing his hand on the small of her back. His blue eyes shone with promise. "I'll pick you up at seven o'clock."

Before Julia could utter a single reply, Mark had ushered her out of his office. She decided to leave peaceably, since she didn't have much choice. She was in the hallway now, right across from the portfolio managers' workstations with Ken Driscoll staring holes right through her.

Julia gave him a quick smile. But then, walking toward the elevators, she realized that she hadn't given Mark her address. Turning, she walked back into his office.

"Forget something?" he asked.

"No, but you did," she replied tartly.

"And what's that?"

"My address."

Mark grinned mischievously. "Got it right here," he said, pointing to the computer screen. He turned the monitor so she could see it. "The personnel file. Too bad there's only demographic data on these things, though. I would have liked to have more information on each employee."

"Such as?" Julia ventured.

"Such as a resume—something to give me background info on everyone." Mark shrugged. "I suppose I'll have to hit the guys in Human Resources, huh?"

"You mean Public Relations."

"No, I mean Human Resources." He smiled lazily as he sat back in his swivel chair. "The first major change I'm going to suggest to Bill is that we create a Human Resources Department. Instead of the PR Department doing the hiring and keeping tabs on employees, Human Resources will do it. Bill can hire experts who know the State's labor laws. PR can't manage it any longer."

"I see," Julia said, feeling suddenly a little concerned for her own position. What if Stacie was right? What if middle management was on its way out? But this was her career! Her life's blood! How would she and Jesse ever survive?

Just then, Mark looked up and smiled warmly. "I'm going to do a little playing on my new PC," he said sheepishly. "I'm a bit of an egghead, so don't worry." He lowered his voice then. "See you tonight, Juli. Okay?"

Still feeling troubled, she could only nod as she turned and left his office.

❧

I can't believe I'm doing this, Julia thought as she changed from her three-piece suit of skirt, vest, and matching jacket, into a light-blue silk dress. *I can't believe I agreed to go out to dinner with Mark!*

Julia was only grateful that Barb had no reservations about keeping Jesse overnight for the second time this week. Jesse, too, hadn't seemed bothered when Julia spoke with him on the phone. He said his friend, Sam, was going to sleep over and that Uncle Glen was going to take them both fishing in the morning.

"Just don't forget that I'm taking a half-day off tomorrow because Grandpa and Grandma are coming to get you on their way to Minoqua."

"I can't wait!" Jesse had declared. Julia smiled, knowing how he loved to vacation with her parents up in northern Wisconsin.

"Well, Jess, I'll miss you," she said at last, "but it'll only be for a week. Then I'm on vacation, too, and I'll ride up with Aunt Barb and Uncle Glen."

"Are you going to stay the whole week, Mom?" Jesse had asked. "Or are you gonna have to go back to work early. . .like usual?"

Julia had felt a stab of guilt at the questions, but determined to stay up north the whole week. Jesse was glad to hear it, too. With that, she told him she loved him and hung up the phone.

Vacation, she thought now as she brushed out her auburn hair, *the word does have a nice ring to it.* Unfortunately, the week after vacation would be her week with Mark, one on one in IS. Julia decided she couldn't think that far ahead. Dining with Mark tonight seemed foreboding enough.

He was prompt, ringing her front doorbell at precisely seven o'clock. Julia let him into the front hall of the apartment. Hers was a modern, bi-level unit with entrances leading directly outside.

"Come in," Julia invited. Then she reached for her raincoat hanging on the hook of the wooden coatrack.

"You look beautiful as always," Mark commented, helping her with her coat.

"Thanks," she murmured. Turning then, her gaze met Mark's and something warm and familiar passed through Julia. How natural it would be, she thought, to walk into his arms and feel his lips on mine. Her heart fairly skipped a beat at the mere thought of Mark's kiss. "Are you sure you're not married?" she asked weakly. She didn't want to be experiencing these emotions for someone else's husband.

Meanwhile, Mark was hooting at her question. "Juli, there are two things I'm certain about in this world, my salvation and that I'm not married." He laughed once more. "Let's go. I'm hungry."

She allowed him to take her hand as they walked outside to where Mark had parked his car on the street.

"This?" Julia asked when he was about to open the door for her. "This is your car?"

"She's a beauty, isn't she?"

Julia had to smile as she surveyed the light blue, two-door Chevy Impala. She would have thought Mark would be driving a sporty little red thing. But instead he drove a relic!

"My dad would love this car! What year is it?" she asked, climbing into the front seat.

"It's a '66," Mark replied, closing the door.

As he walked around to the other side of the car, Julia was amazed at how big the front seat was. Blue upholstery with vinyl trim, it seemed as large as her living room sofa!

"She was a wreck when I first bought her," Mark said, starting the engine. The car purred like a giant cat. "I rebuilt the engine, polished up the interior, which included replacing the old, torn vinyl seats with these. I found them at a junkyard. Then came the paint job. Now this baby's as good as new."

"My father would love this car," Julia repeated.

"You know, I thought about your dad a lot while I was fixing it up."

Julia didn't reply, knowing how her father felt about Mark.

"So where am I going?" Mark asked. "Where's a good restaurant around here?"

"There's a steak house right up Appleton Avenue."

"Let's give it a try."

They drove to the restaurant in foggy weather. After they arrived, the waitress led them to their table—a quiet corner booth with a rounded seat. Julia slid in on one side and Mark on the other. After they had ordered two coffees, the waitress left them to study their menus.

"So, tell me about yourself," Mark ventured. "Where did you go to college?"

"The University of Wisconsin, here in Milwaukee."

"Major?"

"Computer Science."

"I figured." Mark grabbed a warm bread stick out of the linen-covered basket which had been set on the table. "Bachelors? Masters?"

Julia paused. "Bachelors." She wondered if her position at Weakland Management would be jeopardized when Mark discovered that she didn't have as much education as some of the other managers.

He didn't, however, seem concerned about it for the time being. "Why did you leave Lyon?"

The question didn't surprise Julia in the least. In fact, she was ready for it. "I wanted to start a new life." She reached for a bread stick of her own.

"Kathy told me you were sick when you left."

Julia tore at the warm bread. "I was." The sickness Mark referred to had been due to her pregnancy. Kathy, of course, hadn't known about it. No one had. "I got better."

"That's good. Nothing serious, huh?"

Julia just shrugged.

"Can I tell you what happened to me after I left Lyon?" Mark asked. "I think after all these years you deserve an explanation."

Julia looked up from her plate. She really didn't want to talk about this. It was still much too painful.

"Please, Juli," Mark persisted, "let me offer up an explanation and an apology."

After a moment's thought, Julia nodded. She should, at least, allow him that much. . .shouldn't she?

Chapter 5

I was a very confused young man when I arrived in Oregon," Mark began. "My parents were the mainstays in my life. When Dad left us, it shattered my security and my faith in people. . .and relationships."

Julia nodded. She had guessed as much from Mark's last letter.

"So I ran away. That's really what it was," Mark admitted candidly. "I was scared, Juli. I knew I loved you, but I started feeling claustrophobic in Lyon. I thought my future looked like a dead-end street."

"Well, that's fine," Juli replied, trying to keep the edge out of her voice, "but it would have been nice if you had said something sooner than our wedding day. In fact, it would have been nice if you would have said something. But you left me with a. . .a lousy letter and a church full of people!"

This isn't going to work, she decided, tossing her linen napkin onto the bread plate. She would have left the table, the restaurant, too, if the waitress hadn't shown up and blocked her way out of the booth. And she would have refused to place an order except Mark took the liberty of ordering "tonight's special" for the both of them.

"Juli, please, hear me out," he pleaded after the waitress walked away.

"I don't know if I can," she replied honestly. The twelve year ache in her heart had surfaced, and it hurt as much as if it had happened only yesterday.

Mark's expression softened as he moved closer to her. He put his arm around her shoulders while taking hold of her elbow with his other hand. It was like some gentle warning that she couldn't run from what he wanted to say to her tonight.

"I should have taken you with me," Mark whispered, causing tears to form in the backs of her eyes. "I just wasn't thinking straight at the time. But I tried to come back for you. . .later."

When Julia didn't reply, Mark continued his explanation. "I worked for my dad's company that first summer as I prepared to go to college in the fall. I wanted to contact you, Juli, but I was still running scared. When fall came, the company downsized and cut my dad's entire division. He decided, then, that he couldn't afford to pay my tuition, even though he had promised. I got angry and we had a terrible fight. It was then that my eyes were opened to how wrong my dad's lifestyle was and how wrong I had been to think every married man ended up like him. Within the week, I had moved in with a friend from work. When he went back to school at UCLA, I went with him. He was in his third year and he helped me get registered and apply for student loans.

"That's when I decided I wanted you with me, Juli," Mark told her, his mouth still close to her ear. "I wrote you letters, begging you to come to California and I tried to telephone on numerous occasions. Your father intercepted all my phone calls, and I imagined he did the same with my letters. So I tried to get to you through Kathy. That's when she said that you were sick all summer and left Lyon."

Julia just nodded, but she couldn't bring herself to tell Mark why. Not just yet. Not when she was feeling so vulnerable.

"I tried to find out why you left town and where you'd gone, but no one would say, and your father kept me away from your family."

"He was trying to protect me," Julia said in his defense. "My father knew how hurt I was and—"

"I know," Mark replied. "I know that now, and all I want is to make things right somehow."

A few moments of silence followed, and Julia took the opportunity to shrug out of Mark's hold and move away—but only slightly. On one hand she liked being close to him, remembering how much she once loved him—or, perhaps, she still did. But she couldn't think straight with his nearness.

"Throughout my college years, I tried to contact you. I wrote letters. I tried to call." Mark pursed his lips in the way Julia always remembered. He had a way of doing it, too, bringing his bottom lip out and up at the same time, which made him look stately and important. Mrs. Baker used to encourage Mark to use the gesture during debate class. She said he looked like a politician. "Have you ever been able to forget me, Julia?" he asked softly. "I've never been able to forget you."

Julia could only shake her head in reply. How could she tell Mark that every springtime he crept into her thoughts? How could she say that every time she looked at Jesse, she was reminded of his father?

"As I told you," Mark began once more, "I became a Christian about six years ago. That changed my perspective on a lot of things, and it somehow made me more determined to find you."

Julia looked over at him, wondering if he really meant it. She couldn't think of why he'd lie, but she was afraid to believe him. She was afraid he'd hurt her again. However, his face, so close to hers, his charming ways and warm, endearing words, were more wonderful than anything she'd ever dreamed of.

"Then I ran into your brother Rick last summer," Mark explained. "It was at a camp in South Carolina. I was in Charleston on business and got invited to a revival meeting at this camp." Mark chuckled. "And what a surprise to learn that Rick is a youth pastor in Indiana. Unfortunately, he and his youth group had been at camp all week and were leaving the same night I arrived. I did, however, manage to talk to him for a little while. He's a fine man, Juli."

She nodded. She was very proud of both her brothers; however, she was now curious as to how much Rick had shared. Did Mark know about Jesse? And why didn't he let on if he knew?

"Rick told me that you were living in Menomonee Falls, Wisconsin. He couldn't remember the name of the company you worked for, but he told me you were doing something with computers. So I began to pray that the Lord would find me a consulting job in the area—Milwaukee, preferably, but I would have taken something in Chicago. Then things began to develop through a friend of a friend and, here I am." Mark laughed. "But, Juli, when I was praying, I only expected God to take me somewhere in the vicinity of where you were—not the same city or the same company. God most certainly does do exceedingly, abundantly above all we ask!"

"I guess He does," Julia replied skeptically. She wasn't at all convinced that Mark's being here was answered prayer. "What else did Rick say?" she couldn't help but ask then.

Mark only shrugged. "He said just about all he could say over a quick cup of coffee in the lodge. We didn't have much time together."

Julia felt pacified for the moment. She thought she'd like to verify Mark's story with Rick later.

A tossed salad was served and then dinner arrived. As they ate, their conversation was light, Mark relaying stories of his "college days" at UCLA.

"I love California," he said. "Have you ever been there?"

Julia shook her head in reply. She couldn't bring herself to say that being a single parent took all her free time and most of her extra money. Even so, Julia knew she'd never have it any other way. She loved Jesse with a mother's fierce, protective love and, from the day he was born, Julia knew that he was a very special blessing.

"Did you know that my parents got back together?" Mark asked.

Julia nearly choked. "Back together?"

Mark nodded. "They've been together for the last eight or nine years now."

Julia raised astonished brows. "Your mother took him back? After what your father did to her?"

Mark nodded. "Incidentally, my parents are both believers now, too. They have been for years, although Mom has been a Christian since she was a teenager. I never knew that until after my own conversion to Christ. Mom said she had gotten away from the Lord for a while."

Julia felt amazed.

Finally they finished eating and left the restaurant. It was still drizzling outside, and there was a damp chill to the early summer air.

"I'll turn on the heater," Mark said, after they had climbed into his car.

"Thanks." She couldn't contain a shiver.

The ride back to Julia's apartment was quiet, save for the mellow pianist playing on the car stereo. After parking in front of the apartment complex, Mark leaned over and shut off the music.

"So, what do you think?" he asked.

"What do I think about what?"

"About what I said tonight."

Julia shrugged. "I don't know what to think, Mark, and that's the truth."

He nodded. "I suppose I should give you time to sort everything out. Here," he said, reaching across her lap and opening the glove compartment, "I want to give you my phone number just in case you need to get a hold of me after work."

He scribbled down his number. When he handed the slip of paper to Julia, she stuffed it into her purse.

"Thanks. And thanks for dinner tonight," she said, reaching for the handle. She opened the car door and climbed out. Mark did the same and met her on the sidewalk. It was obvious that he meant to walk her to the front door which sent Julia's heart beating wildly. Would he kiss her good night? Would she be able to stand it if he did? What if her knees gave out right there on the front walk? What if he wanted to come in. . .?

But Mark surprised her on all accounts. "G'night, Juli," he whispered, placing a firm, but gentle kiss on her cheek. "See you tomorrow."

She nodded, feeling somehow disappointed. Then, as if he sensed it, Mark said, "I know what your kisses are like, Juli-bean They're like those potato chips advertised on TV—I could never have just one."

Julia managed an embarrassed grin. Even with all the years between them, Mark could still read her so well. "Good night," she said at last.

He waved and Julia watched him walk back to his car, marveling at this side of Mark she'd never seen before. Years ago, he would have taken what he wanted despite the consequences, be it potato chips, a kiss, or much, much more.

Inside her apartment, Julia changed into her most comfortable clothes. Then she plopped herself on the sofa, reflecting on the entire evening. She glanced at the telephone and picked it up, impulsively dialing Rick's number. Julia had a good relationship with her younger brother, in spite of the gap in their ages. She knew he'd understand the reason for her call. She knew Rick would listen and then answer in all honesty. And she just had to know for sure. . .

"Sorry, I know it's late," Julia said when her brother answered, sounding sleepy.

"That's okay, Juli," Rick replied. "What's up?"

She paused. "I had dinner with Mark Henley tonight."

"Oh, yeah?" There was a smile in Rick's voice. "You two kiss and make up?"

"No. I guess Mark is too much of a gentleman for kissing."

"What?"

Julia chuckled. "Never mind." Again, she paused. "Mark said he saw you last summer, Rick, is that true?"

"Yep. We had a nice talk, hasty as it was. I answered every question Mark asked me, too. I just decided I wasn't going to lie anymore. You really need to talk to him about Jesse, Juli. You know, in many situations, keeping silent is the same as lying in my book. Jesse has been a secret for too long. It's only right that Jesse be allowed to know about his dad."

"I know. . ." Julia was momentarily pensive, feeling the burden of her responsibility. Telling Mark and Jesse about each other wasn't going to be easy, yet she knew she had to do it. But for now, she was preoccupied with questioning Rick and, for the next few minutes, he confirmed everything Mark had said as truth.

Finally, he added, "I think our family needs to practice some forgiveness, and I think all dark secrets need to see the light of truth for a change. That's my opinion, Juli—my two cents worth."

After a moment's pause, Julia replied, "I appreciate your straightforwardness, Rick. I'll consider what you've said."

Julia said her good-byes and then hung up the phone. Feeling a myriad of emotions, she made herself a cup of herbal tea. Back in the living room, Julia telephoned her mother, inquiring over the letters Mark claimed to have written.

"It's true, dear," Caroline said. "Mark wrote to you on numerous occasions. I. . .I saved the letters."

"You did?" Julia was actually quite glad about that. She thought she'd like to read them.

"It wasn't my place to throw them away, Juli," her mother said. "Your father would have insisted, though. . .if he had known about them. Perhaps I was wrong in keeping them a secret, but. . .I just didn't think it was right to throw your mail in the garbage."

"Mom," Julia asked softly, "will you bring the letters with you tomorrow when you come for Jesse? I've got the whole afternoon off. . .I guess I'd like to read them."

"Of course. I've got them in a stationary box. I'll pack them in my suitcase."

"Thanks."

"You're welcome. Now tell me how your dinner with Mark went."

Julia had to smile as she recounted the evening. "And he didn't even kiss me good-night, Mom," she concluded. "Well, he did, if you call a little peck on the cheek a kiss. He's different. I'm beginning to see that."

"We all make mistakes, Juli," Caroline said.

"I know."

"I think it's time we forgive one another." Caroline paused. "And in that regard, please continue to pray for your father, Juli. I've thought for years that the bitterness in his heart against Mark—and the whole Henley family—has been in the way of his accepting Christ."

"Really?" Julia hadn't ever thought of something getting "in the way" of her father's salvation.

She promised to keep praying, and then they made some last-minute plans regarding the trip up north. Finally Julia hung up the phone and prepared for bed. Crawling beneath her sheets and thick down comforter, she listened to the rain as it splashed against her bedroom windows.

She replayed the two telephone conversations in her mind. The words "bitterness" and "forgiveness" seemed to pluck a sad cord in Julia's heart. Had she, like her father, been harboring a bitter spirit all these years? Perhaps without realizing it? Had she only thought that she forgave Mark?

"Of course I forgave him," she muttered, turning into her pillow. "I'm a Christian."

Suddenly Julia recalled her conversation with Mark last Wednesday night at the business dinner. "Were you praying for me, Juli?" he had asked. *No, I never prayed for him,* she had to answer in all honesty.

Many pensive moments ticked by, and Julia had to finally admit it—she had never forgiven Mark. And, though she loved Jesse with her entire being, he had been a constant reminder of the pain Mark inflicted upon her when he left her so long ago.

She had never forgiven Mark for that.

"Oh, Lord," she breathed into the darkness of her bedroom, "I want to forgive Mark. Help me forgive him."

Then, moments later, she knew what she had to do.

Julia threw off the bed covers and walked into the living room. Grabbing her purse, she fished through it until she found the slip of paper with Mark's phone number. Then she picked up the telephone and dialed.

"Mark. . .?"

He paused. "Juli? Is something wrong? What is it?"

She had to smile at the sound of concern in his voice. "Nothing's wrong. . .I just have to tell you something. You know how, as Christians, we're not to let the sun go down on our anger?"

"Yes."

"Well, I've been letting the sun go down on my anger for twelve years."

Mark didn't reply.

"And I haven't been acting like much of a Christian this week, either," Julia admitted. "It was. . .well, it was such a shock to see you again."

"I understand. You know, I always planned to telephone you first, once I finally found you." He chuckled. "Sorry, but I never got the chance."

Julia smiled in spite of herself.

"Well, I'm sorry, Mark," she finally managed to say. She marveled at saying it, too. Last week if anyone would have told her that she'd be apologizing to Mark Henley, she would have laughed her head off! However, her behavior of late warranted an apology. There were times this week when she'd been downright rude to Mark.

"I forgive you," he said easily. "No problem."

"And. . .and I forgive you, too, Mark," she said, softly, earnestly. She swallowed a sudden painful lump. But instead of willing it away, she chose to deal with it. "It hurt so badly," she confessed, "and sometimes it still hurts. . ."

"Juli, I'm so sorry." Mark's voice was soft, as if it somehow hurt him, too. "Apology accepted."

There was a smile in his tone when he said, "Juli, those words are music to my ears."

"I'm glad. Well, good night."

"Good night, Juli," Mark replied. "Sweet dreams."

As Julia put the receiver in its cradle, she felt as though a load had been taken off her shoulders. She realized, then, that unforgiveness was a heavy load to tow. Now that it was gone, however, Julia felt the joy of the Lord returning to her heart. *So that's why He seemed so far away. With so much bitterness in my heart, there hadn't been room for Jesus!*

Crawling back into bed, she knew that there were a great many things still unsettled between herself and Mark. But, at least she seemed to be headed in the right direction now.

Chapter 6

G'morning, Juli," Mark said jovially as they met in the hallway at work the next morning. "Lovely weather we're having."

Julia smiled a greeting, but rolled her eyes. There was a torrential downpour outside, the skies were gloomy and gray. . .but, sure, it was "lovely weather." Then Mark walked right into her, sending the memos in her hand flying. His right arm circled her waist as he pretended to be surprised. Julia immediately recalled how Mark used to do this to her in high school. It had started by accident but quickly turned into one of those silly games that sweethearts played.

"You nut!" she cried, laughingly. She noticed, however, that Mark's arm around her felt firm and secure. Then his gaze met hers and for a long moment she was reminded of the love she'd seen shining from his blue eyes so many times. Could it be? There again. . . ?

Suddenly uncomfortable and confused, Julia stepped out of his embrace and stooped to pick up the colored memos. Mark joined her, chuckling. "You're just lucky no one was around to see that!"

"Why do you think I did it?" He chuckled again. "Really, I couldn't help it, Juli," he admitted. "I saw you coming and the temptation was just too overwhelming."

Smiling, Julia shook her head at him.

"Need some help?"

Looking up, she saw Ken Driscoll standing over her. "No, I'm all right. Thanks." She hoped he couldn't see her cheeks warming pink over the less-than-professional incident that had just occurred.

"Guess I've got to watch where I'm going," Mark said with a sheepish grin.

They stole an amused glance at each other, and Julia had to bite the inside of her lip in an effort not to smile.

At last the memos were collected and Julia and Mark stood at the same time. "Here, I might as well give you one of these now," she said, handing a memo to Mark. "It'll save me a trip up to your office."

"What is it?"

"Print-outs of the week's stock market activity," Ken replied. "All employees receive one every Friday morning. I'll take one, too, Julia. Thank you." He scanned it and then looked back at Mark. "Of course, this is just a briefing."

Mark nodded, looking over the memo in his hand. "Thanks for the info, Ken," he said politely. Then to Julia, he smirked and said, "Nice running into you."

Julia didn't reply except to give Mark a pointed stare since Ken was still standing beside her and obviously had no intentions of moving until she did.

"I see you and our business consultant are getting along better," he commented lazily as they walked toward Customer Service. "And, come to think of it, I don't believe I've heard you actually laugh out loud the entire six months I've worked here."

Julia paused. "You mean. . .you heard me just now?"

"All the way down the hallway."

Julia grimaced.

"Angela told me you were quite stressed out for a few days, so I'm glad to see you've overcome whatever was bothering you."

Julia smiled. "Yes, I did." Then she quickly changed the subject. "Will you take these upstairs for me?" She counted out several memos.

"What do I look like, the mail boy?" But Ken took the memos anyway and headed for his office. Julia walked into Stacie Rollins' department.

"Good morning."

Stacie sighed, looking harried. "Listen, Juli, if I can't figure out this new computer program by Monday, my goose is cooked. . .and so is yours!"

Julia set down the memos. "What's the problem?"

"This thing won't let me sign-on, that's what's the problem."

Patiently, Julia took a chair and began to manipulate the keyboard while Stacie paced in frustration.

Julia smiled. "Okay, you're in. And I think you'll find that, once you get used to it, this application will be easier than the old one. Maneuvering the mouse will be easier and faster than using the keyboard."

"Yeah, sure it is," Stacie replied on a facetious note. "I had just better be able to impress Mr. BC with my looks, because I certainly won't impress him with my computer skills."

"Mark knows it's a new program," Julia replied, getting up from the chair so Stacie could take her rightful place. "I'm sure he'll be understanding."

Stacie lifted a brow. "You're singing a different song this morning, Juli. Yesterday you were wailing about having to let Mr. BC in on all your computer secrets." She tipped her head slightly. "What gives?"

Julia shrugged. How could she possibly explain?

"He's married, Juli," Stacie sang on a note of warning.

Again, Julia didn't know how to reply. She didn't have Mark's permission to say that he wasn't married.

"And aren't you one of those born-again people?" Stacie charged with a toss of her blond head. "I thought you told me you were "born again" that time your kid was selling tickets to some band concert at his Christian school. Doesn't the Bible say something about not getting involved with married men?"

"Yes and yes," Julia replied honestly to both questions. She found it interesting that even an unbeliever knew born again Christians were Bible-believing people and that one of God's commandments warned against committing adultery. Julia understood that she had a testimony to uphold. "You're right, Stacie, because of my faith I would never enter into a relationship with a married man."

Stacie turned away with a little shrug of satisfaction and, as Julia made her way back to Information Systems, she knew she needed to be careful. As long as it was assumed that Mark was married, she had to distance herself. On the other hand, she had to get close enough to tell Mark about Jesse—and before he heard it from someone else.

⁊

"Jesse? Are you ready to go?"

"Yep!"

Julia grinned broadly as her son came out of his bedroom, pulling behind him the largest suitcase she owned. "Are you sure you've packed enough stuff?"

"I got everything."

"I'll bet you do," she said with a little chuckle. Julia looked at her parents, sitting at her dining room table enjoying a cup of coffee. "I think he's ready."

Roy McGowan stood and stretched. "Tell me again, when are you driving up?"

"Next Friday," Julia replied, "after work. I'll ride up with Barb and Glen."

He nodded in satisfaction. "And what's going on with that Henley kid?"

Julia and her mother exchanged glances over Jesse's blond head.

"He's hardly a 'kid' anymore, Dad. . .and we'll talk about him some other time." Julia looked at Jesse then back at her father. "All right?"

Roy nodded. "Come on, Jess," he said, "you can help me repack the car. Why on earth your grandmother needed me to pull her suitcase out of the car, I'll never know."

"Thank you, Roy," Caroline said with a sweet smile to end his complaints. Then, once he and Jesse were out of the room, she added, "The box of letters from Mark is on your dresser." She paused, looking thoughtful. "I'm going to tell your father about them and how I saved them for you. I think he'll be angry, but I feel so dishonest. I shouldn't have kept them from you either, but I knew you wouldn't accept them."

"You're right. I wouldn't have even a week ago."

Julia grinned. "Tell Dad, and I'll talk to him, too, when I get up north next week. Between the two of us, we ought to be able to soften his heart."

Caroline laughed. "It's always worked that way before, hasn't it?"

Nodding, Julia smiled and hooked arms with her mother as they walked outside. Her father and Jesse were already in the car and waiting to go.

Caroline kissed her cheek. "Good-bye, sweetie," she said, "see you next week."

"Okay," Julia replied, watching her mother climb into the car. "Bye, Jesse. I love you."

"Love you, too, Mom," the boy called from the backseat.

Julia stepped back as the car pulled away from the curb and waved as it disappeared down the street. With misty eyes at her son's departure, Julia watched the vehicle until it was swallowed in the fog and gloom. Then she ran back to her apartment and set the tea kettle to boiling. There was a chill in the air today and dampness had a way of seeping into her joints. This weather belonged to March or early April. Hardly appropriate for the end of June. Julia shivered.

Then she remembered the letters.

With eager steps she walked to the bedroom and picked up the stationery box from where her mother had set it on the dresser. It wasn't a small 6 x 9 inch stationary box, as Julia had presumed, but a 10 x 12 inch box that had obviously held business-size envelopes. Opening the lid, Julia counted and quickly guessed that there were at least one hundred letters in the box. All addressed to her, all from Mark.

With a cup of tea in one hand, the box of Mark's letters in the other, Julia made herself comfortable on the couch and began reading. She was amazed that her mother had kept them in order. All the envelopes were still sealed.

Dear Juli,

I'm taking a chance in writing to you. I don't know if your father will even let you get this letter, but it's worth a shot.

I love you, Juli. I can't live without you. I should have never left you behind. We belong together. Soul mates, remember? That's what we always said...

Julia groaned. This wasn't going to be easy. How did she ever come to believe that she could read Mark's letters the way she read computer programming material—emotionally unaffected? It was impossible. By the fourth letter, Julia was in tears. By the tenth she'd decided she couldn't read any further, and she had ninety more to go!

She cried and amazingly it felt good. She allowed it, the crying, the cleansing. How long had she swallowed these tears? How long had she stuffed her feelings so far and deep inside herself, willing them never to surface? For years and years, she admitted inwardly.

With renewed resolve, she picked up letter number eleven. It was dated November 4, 1986. Mark wrote about school, his distant relationship with his father and some friends he met.

> *Juli, please come. You would love California. I've got a small apartment, but it's big enough for the two of us. We'll get married...*

Promises, promises. No, this wasn't going to be easy. Christmas cards, birthday and Valentine's Day cards. "I love you, Juli," Mark had written inside them. More letters. "Please answer me. I made a mistake and I'm sorry. I only hope your dad won't intercept this letter. He hates me, but I don't care. Until you say to my face that we're through, I'm going to keep on loving you..."

As the dates on the letters progressed, they gave testimony to Mark's education. He began using longer, more complicated words and sentences. Then, instead of handwritten, his letters were done on a typewriter or computer. However, they always said the same thing. "I love you." "I miss you." "I'm sorry."

Then Mark wrote about his conversion to Christ. The peace in his heart, the freedom in the Lord's forgiveness. Several letters later, Mark shared the Gospel and stated he was praying for her salvation. Little did he know, that she had been saved by grace nearly six years before he had.

Then Mark wrote about "Roberta" and Julia's heartbeat quickened. She read the letter anxiously, as though she were reading the latest, best-selling thriller.

> *I met someone. She's a Christian...but I need to settle things between us before I can begin a relationship with her. You must have received at least one of my letters—your lack of response indicates your disinterest in rekindling anything we might have shared in the past....*

A series of letters followed. Three in six weeks' time. Mark stated that he had tried to telephone her, only to have her father answer. He tried to explain himself, but Roy McGowan wouldn't hear a word of it. Mark phoned a few more times before the phone number was changed to an unpublished one.

Julia remembered when that had happened. Her father said in was due to "prank" phone calls. And here, all along, it had been Mark trying to reach her.

There was a wide gap in the letters, then. No more came for over a year. The next, a Christmas card, was signed very formally, "Love, Mark." But not "Love, Mark and Roberta."

The rest of the letters had come in the form of cards, Christmas, birthday; however, there were no Valentine's Day cards. No more words of love. No more pleas for their reunion. Then the frequency of his letters slowed dramatically until they all but stopped. Mark's last Christmas card came a year and a half ago, and there hadn't been anything since.

So whatever happened to Roberta? Julia knew it was none of her business, and she told herself she shouldn't care. . .but she did. And that was her biggest problem: she still cared for Mark. Very deeply. However, along with the admission came the fear of being hurt again. She could still feel the pain and devastation of his leaving and the horror of discovering she was expecting a baby. Julia didn't think she could ever live through his rejection again.

And so, with guarded heart, she folded up the last of Mark's letters and put it into the stationery box. She then carried the box into her room and set it on the top shelf of her closet. It fit among her shoe and hat boxes. It blended right in and soon she'd forget it was even there. At least she hoped she'd forget. However, it looked like Mark Henley was back in her life to stay—and what was she ever going to do about that?

Chapter 7

Julia pulled on her favorite denim skirt completing her Saturday attire. She wore a light-blue, scoop-neck T-shirt with long sleeves, light-blue stockings and her most comfortable denim slip-ons. Walking from her bedroom, Julia paused in the living room and picked up last night's newspaper from the coffee table. Then she searched for the time the art festival on the Lakefront began. Ten o'clock. *Good, I'll have plenty of time to get there.*

Julia enjoyed arts-and-crafts shows. She had dabbled with the idea of being an "artist" someday. She liked to draw and paint; however she knew she wasn't good enough to make any kind of living at it. As Barb had told her while she was in college, "You don't often hear of starving computer programmers, but you hear of starving artists all the time!"

Smiling at the recollection, Julia made a small breakfast and poured herself a cup of coffee. In her sunny yellow kitchen, she read her daily devotion and its Scriptural application. It helped ease her insecurities. She now felt prepared to face the day.

Julia rose from her place at the small table and cleared her dishes. After rinsing them, she grabbed her dry-cleaning and the garbage while she juggled her purse and left the apartment by way of the back door. With her hands full, however, she only managed to knock over the aluminum garbage can as she struggled with the lid.

"Want some help?" a male voice called from behind her.

Julia swung around and met Mark's smiling face. "What are you doing here?" she asked, surprised.

He shrugged. "I was ringing your front bell when I heard the garbage can ensemble here. I had a feeling it might be you."

"It's me, all right. I guess I took on more of a load than I could carry." Gratefully, Julia accepted his help with the garbage, noticing his attire. He wore a red, plaid, cotton shirt with a band-collar and beige twill pants.

Mark turned and smiled. "Got plans?"

Julia nodded. "I'm on my way to an art festival."

"Want some company?"

She didn't, of course; however, the way he was looking at her reminded her of Jesse. *It's the eyes,* she decided, *and that Henley smile is irresistible.*

"Sure, come on along," she finally conceded.

Mark's smile broadened. "Where are we going?"

"I told you. It's an art festival."

"Yeah, but where?"

Julia stopped short on the narrow walkway between hers and the apartment building next door and laughed aloud. If Jesse wasn't his father's son! Mark's last question sounded like something that would have come right out of Jesse's mouth.

How will I ever contend with the two of them? Julia wondered, smiling at Mark.

"What's so funny?" he asked.

"Can I tell you later?" Julia lost some of her smile. "Seriously, Mark, there's something I need to tell you."

"Okay."

His blue eyes seemed to grow soft with compassion, an expression that belonged to this "new" Mark standing before her. It was all Julia could do to keep from blurting out her twelve-year-long secret—Jesse.

"Just don't tell me you're romantically involved with Ken Driscoll," he said, sounding like the Mark she remembered, "or I'll—"

"Or you'll what?" Julia demanded, shocked by his response.

He smiled, but his eyes lost all compassion, and suddenly he was that hard-line business consultant who intimidated Julia to no end. "I'll tell Bill to fire him."

"You wouldn't!"

Mark chuckled while Julia momentarily chewed on her lower lip. She couldn't say for sure what Mark would do. In the end, she merely shrugged. "Well, no matter," she replied, "I am not romantically involved with Ken."

"Good," Mark said in way that made Julia wonder if he'd been teasing her all along. After all, he probably didn't have the authority to tell Bill to fire anybody. Now, suggesting that he eliminate middle management. . .well, that could be different.

Wearing his prized wolfish grin, he took Julia's dry-cleaning from her as they continued to walk toward the front of the apartment complex. "I'll drive," Mark offered. "You can navigate since I'm new in town."

"Sure." Julia felt a little uneasy. It bothered her that she couldn't tell when Mark was teasing. "Hey, Mark," she asked suddenly before climbing into the car, "how did you pick up on Ken and me? I mean, there's nothing to pick up on, really. . .except that. . .well, I've suspected that Ken is interested in me."

"It wasn't too hard. He follows you around like a puppy. And I caught him hanging around your department at least ten times last week. Most times you weren't there, though. And once, Juli, he was in your office."

"In my office? What on earth was he doing in there?"

"Snooping, maybe. I don't know. Perhaps you ought to start locking your door when you leave your office."

"I can't. My employees need to get to the file cabinets and program manuals."

"Then maybe you ought to give one of them a spare key," Mark suggested. His eyes suddenly twinkled with mischief. "Now get in the car and we're not going to talk about work anymore today. Got it?"

"Got it," Julia replied on a note of resignation. Then she sighed. This wasn't exactly how she had planned to spend her Saturday.

❧

Lake Michigan stretched eastward as far as the eye could see, a body of blue trimmed with whitecaps that lay beyond the park where artists had set up their work. The grass was soggy underfoot since yesterday's rain had saturated everything. Today, however, the weather looked promising. Partly sunny skies and warm breezes.

Julia and Mark walked through the rows of sketches and paintings, marveling at many and pondering over a few.

"What do you think it is?" Mark asked softly.

"It is very abstract, isn't it?" Julia replied, tipping her head from one side to the other. "A seascape, maybe."

"Seascape? How do see that? Looks like a scrapyard."

"Oh, hush," Julia admonished him on a teasing note. "You never had an eye for art. What do you know?"

"I know that's not art, okay?"

Julia chuckled under her breath and moved on. She had to admit, Mark could be fun company. It had been a long time since she felt comfortable enough around someone to joke and laugh. Her best friends were Barb and Glen French, despite their age differences. While the Frenches were looking forward to retirement, Julia's career had really just begun.

Mid afternoon, Julia and Mark finally stopped for lunch. Purchasing hotdogs and nachos from a vendor they wandered closer to the lake and found a vacant picnic table.

"Very pretty area," Mark commented, his gaze scanning the lakefront.

Julia agreed. "It's a very popular area, too. And look that way, Mark, to the south of here is where all the ethnic festivals are held. Polish Fest, Irish Fest, German Fest, African World Festival and Indian Summer. But the biggest festival is called Summerfest. It's usually too rowdy for my liking."

Mark nodded, seeming to be content at letting Julia babble.

"I like the State Fair." She caught herself before adding that it was Jesse's favorite, too. She took a bite of her hotdog instead.

Mark had finished his in two bites. "How are your folks, Juli?" he asked, changing the subject.

"Just fine. Enjoying their retirement."

"Good. Mine, too."

A moment passed. Then another. Finally, Julia decided to tell him about the stationery box in her chest. "My mother saved all your letters," she said, hoping she wasn't dropping an ugly bomb on this perfectly lovely afternoon. Then, again, "the bomb" was going to come sooner or later.

Mark narrowed his gaze. "Saved them? My letters?"

Julia nodded. "She didn't feel right about throwing them away and, for that reason, she kept them from my father."

Mark shook his head, looking rueful. "It's a shame your mother didn't do more than just save my letters, Juli. I wish she would have given them to you."

"No, Mark. Back then, I would have never accepted them. I would have most likely torn them to shreds without even opening them. I was determined to forget my past, which included you. . .us. I wanted to start a whole new life."

"And it seems as if you have."

"Yes, I have."

"Are you happy, Juli?"

"Of course I am," she replied a little too quickly. "I stay busy. . .my work is very important to me."

"So I've gathered. In fact, it seems you have a whole different set of values. . . to go along with your new life, I mean. . .since I knew you last. . ."

The crowd from the art festival had diminished and, except for some brave sea gulls loitering around the picnic table. She and Mark were free to hold a private conversation without anyone else overhearing.

"I'm not the same person you left behind in Lyon," Julia told him.

"And I'm not the same person who left you."

"I can tell from your letters." She smiled at his shocked expression. "Mom and Dad have a cabin in Minoqua," Julia explained, "and they stopped yesterday on their way up. Now that they're retired, they spend their entire summers up north and don't go back to Lyon until about October.

"Anyway, I asked Mom to bring me your letters and she did." Julia looked up from where she had been picking at a tortilla chip and met Mark's intent gaze with one of her own. "I read them last night. Every one."

"And?"

"And, I believe you. I mean I believe that you told me the truth on Thursday night."

Mark looked momentarily hurt. "Did you think I'd lie?"

"I don't know. Forgiving you and believing you are two very different things. I forgave you last Thursday night, but I wasn't sure I believed you."

"And now?"

"Now I know you told me the truth."

Again, the awkward silence. Julia thought of how ironic it was that nature could be so noisy at a time like this. Lake Michigan's rushing waves slapped the shoreline and the sea gulls, circling above, gawked at each other, paying no heed to the intensity of their conversation.

Finally, Julia couldn't stand it any longer. "Can I ask you something personal, Mark?"

"Sure," he said easily.

"It's really none of my business."

"Ask away."

Julia paused. "Who's Roberta? I mean, I understand who she was. . .well, that you were interested in her. I guess I'm wondering what happened."

Mark gave her a gentle smile. "We dated for about a year, but when it came time to make a decision about marriage, I didn't have any peace about it. Our relationship came to an end because I couldn't promise her a future. I wasn't convinced that Roberta was the woman God had chosen for me."

"Hmmm. . ." Julia was momentarily pensive. Then suddenly she sensed that now was the time. She had Mark's undivided attention. They were talking about the hurtful past. . . .

"Mark, I've got to tell you something. Maybe I should have told you sooner," she said quickly so she couldn't change her mind. "Perhaps I should have told you years ago, but the truth is, I never thought I'd see you again. I really believed you didn't want anything to do with me."

"Not true."

"Yes, well, I know that now. And this whole thing seems more and more like a Shakespearean tragedy."

Mark grinned slightly. "Tell me, Juli. What's on your mind?"

"Well, when I left Lyon, I wasn't just sick, Mark. Oh, I was heartsick and depressed, and my parents were worried, but when I became physically ill, they took me to old Doc Kramer. That's when I learned that I. . .I was pregnant."

Julia looked down at the cheap paper plate in front of her. She was afraid of what she'd see in Mark's expressive blue eyes. Disappointment? Disdain? Both?

"I kept the baby," she continued, "even though my parents and I had planned to give him up for adoption. But I couldn't do it. The very moment I looked into his little face, I knew he was mine. . .ours, and I loved him immediately. Giving him away would have been like cutting my very heart out."

Finally, Julia felt brave enough to chance it. She lifted her gaze and, much to her wonder, she saw tears pooling in Mark's eyes. The sight was enough to make her cry, too, since the Mark Henley she had known back in high school would have rather died than let anyone see him shed a tear.

"Please, go on, Juli," he said, blinking back his emotion.

She nodded. "His name is Jesse, and he's a terrific kid. He knows the Lord. . . wants to do right. . .and he favors you in looks."

For a long, long time, Mark said nothing. He just sat there with his elbows on the picnic table, his hands folded tightly in front of him, his mouth resting on his knuckles. Finally, he said, "I always thought that was it, Juli. . .the reason you left Lyon. Your brother only confirmed it. You see, I've known about Jesse for almost a year."

Julia was stunned. "Rick? He told you?" At Mark's nod, she felt betrayed by her own brother. But then she recalled him saying, *I answered every question Mark asked me. . . Jesse has been a secret for too long. . . .*

"Yes, he told me. And, Juli, you can't begin to imagine how many times I wanted to see you. . .and our son, once I found out where you were. I nearly went crazy all these months. But I wanted the timing to be right. Perfect. And I wanted God to direct my every step. I knew how hurt you were, and still are, to some extent."

Julia's jaw dropped. "You knew? You knew all this time. . . ?" Angry now, she grabbed her purse and rose from the picnic table. "You could have said something, instead of playing games, Mark. I've been a nervous wreck ever since you came to town, wondering how on earth I'd explain that you have a child. Here you knew all along!"

"Juli, I only wanted you to trust me enough to tell me yourself."

"Trust has nothing to do with it. It's called honesty!"

Suddenly Julia wondered over Mark's motives for showing up in Menomonee Falls. What if the only thing Mark wanted to settle between them was custody of their son?

"Juli. . ."

But it was too late. She turned and ran toward the bustling Lincoln Memorial Drive. It wasn't long, however, before she realized how futile her attempt at escape really was. She had come here in Mark's car!

Minutes later, he caught up and fell into step beside her on the sidewalk.

"Juli, would you stop? Can we talk about this like two mature adults?"

"Don't worry," she shot at him, "I have no intention of denying you your parental rights."

"I'm not worried. Come on, Juli, we were getting along so well."

She slowed her pace, but only to move aside and let a young man on roller blades whiz by.

"Come on, Juli, let's keep up the dialogue," Mark said. Several minutes passed as they kept walking. "Look, there's a bench over there in the shade. Let's sit down."

By now Julia had worked out some of her frustration, and she realized she was going to have to talk with Mark sooner or later.

With a reluctant nod, she followed Mark across the street and walked beside him through the park toward the brown, wooden bench. It was near one of the park's steep ravines and with the buds of spring all around them, they sat down.

Mark stretched his right arm across the top of the bench behind Julia, while she folded hers tightly across her chest.

Finally, Mark asked, "What's his middle name? Jesse's?"

"It's Mark. After you. . ."

He smiled. "Well, thanks for that. It tells me a lot."

Mark's arm suddenly moved from the bench to her shoulders. Julia's first impulse was to shrug it off, but she couldn't deny the comfort of his touch.

"Jesse Mark. . .McGowan, huh?"

Julia nodded.

"I'd like to change that. I mean, I'd like my son to have my last name."

She fretted over her lower lip. "He doesn't know about you, yet. I've got to tell him."

"When?"

"He's up north with my parents."

"When will you tell him, Juli?" Mark's tone was insistent.

"I don't know. Don't pressure me. I'll tell him as soon as I can."

Mark shook his head. "Not good enough."

Julia turned, looking at him in all her surprise. "What do you mean, 'not good enough'?"

His eyes bore into hers. "I'm not waiting another twelve years to meet my son."

"He's eleven," Julia stated sarcastically. "And you wouldn't have had to wait at all if you would have shown up at the church twelve years ago like you were supposed to!"

Mark ignored the reply. "You've got ten days, Juli. After that, I'll tell Jesse myself."

She glared at him. "Don't you dare threaten me."

Mark smiled charmingly. "Juli, I wouldn't threaten you. That's a promise."

"Well, what a relief," she said with a bitter laugh. "For a minute there, I was worried. But you, Mark, make empty promises, so I guess I have nothing to fear."

Standing, Julia slipped the strap of her purse over her shoulder and turned and walked away. "I'll tell Jesse when I think the time is right. . .and I'll take a cab home."

Mark let her go.

Chapter 8

Julia sipped her herbal tea while the incessant pounding at her front door continued. She knew it was Mark, but she refused to open her door. However, she was softening, minute by minute. The pounding had been going on for ten minutes now. What would her neighbors think?

"All right, all right, I'm coming," she called at last. Walking to the front door, she slipped back the chain and unlocked the door.

"You are one stubborn woman!" Mark declared once she opened it.

"Whatever."

Mark narrowed his gaze. "Did you ever stop to think about anyone else through all of this, Juli? Did you ever think that maybe I was hurt, too? Well, I was. . .and I still am. I've missed so much of my son's life—Jesse's first smile, his first baby steps. . .throwing a football with him. . . Little League Baseball. And my parents. . .did you ever think of them? My mother loved you like a daughter—she's always felt bad over what happened. But that you never thought to let her in on Jesse's arrival, it broke her heart. My dad's, too."

"For your information, Mark," Julia said, hands on hips, "I purposely didn't tell your mother because I didn't want to add to her shame and suffering. She was already contending with what happened between her and your dad. You're the one, Mark, who doesn't think of anyone else but yourself!"

He leaned against the doorframe, looking weary. "Listen, I didn't come here to argue with you, believe it or not. I really just wanted to make sure you got home all right." He paused. "Good night, Juli."

As he turned and walked away, something caught in her heart. A shred of sympathy for the man. Perhaps it had been his admission of hurt feelings or maybe it was his remorse over all the years he'd missed with Jesse. In any case, Julia didn't want to let him go away like this.

"Mark?"

He paused at the end of her walkway and turned a questioning gaze in her direction.

Julia stepped out of her front entrance and walked to where he stood, leaving the door behind her wide open. "I know it's hardly compensation for everything that's happened," she began, "but. . .well, maybe we could call a truce and you could join me for supper tonight at Barb and Glen's. I'm sure they'd like to meet you. They're like my second parents, and they were a great support to me after I left Lyon. They're aware of the situation, Mark, but I can guarantee they'll remain objective. On the other hand, Barb's a great cook, and I've got stacks of photo albums full of Jesse's baby pictures. I could bring them along. . ."

She held her breath, awaiting Mark's reply. She felt foolish for propositioning him like this, and yet, for some crazy reason, she hoped he'd accept the offer.

He did. "I'd like that, Juli," he said softly.

She smiled. "I'll get my things and we can go."

"Oh, look! This picture was taken at the Milwaukee Country Zoo," Barb said, sitting beside Mark, explaining each snapshot of Jesse's life. "There's this little train that goes around the zoo, and Jesse just had to ride on it. In fact, we used to take him for a ride on the train first thing just so he wouldn't beg the entire time we were trying to see the animals."

Sitting across from them, Julia smiled and stifled a yawn. They were on the fifth photo album and Barb was still going strong.

"Jesse loved trains. He still does, doesn't he, Glen?"

Her husband nodded quietly from where he sat in the other armchair.

"Oh, and this picture was taken at a family reunion that same summer. . . ."

Julia smiled though she was struggling to keep her eyes open. She sensed it was a losing battle and, next thing she knew, Glen was gently shaking her awake.

"It's after midnight, Juli," he was saying, "and Mark is leaving."

She roused herself and then pulled her stiff body out of the cushioned armchair. "Sorry to be such bad company," she told Mark. "I didn't mean to fall asleep."

"That's all right." There was a light in Mark's eyes that was soft and genuine.

Julia smiled back at him.

"I told Mark you'd be staying over," Barb was saying. "You might as well."

Julia nodded. She had extra clothes here and frequently spent the night, especially when Jesse was home and they all had plans for the weekend.

"I'll see you tomorrow, Juli," Mark said, surprising her by taking her into his arms. He hugged her, kissing the side of her head.

"Good night, Mark," she replied, giving him a little hug and telling herself that this embrace meant nothing; it was just something from one friend to another. Her heart, however, seemed to beat contrary to that notion.

"And Mrs. French," Mark said, having released Julia, "I thank you for a wonderful meal. Best I've had since Christmas when I was home." Taking her hand, he patted it affectionately. "The meal was almost as wonderful as the company. Thanks for sharing your memories with me."

"Oh, my pleasure," Barb replied, blushing profusely. Her rosy cheeks spread to the tips of her ears.

Julia grinned. Mark Henley could charm the birds right out of the trees!

"And Mr. French, it was good meeting you."

"Same here."

Then after a firm handshake, Mark left.

"He's coming to church tomorrow," Glen told Julia, closing the front door.

Barb nodded in delight. "What a nice young man," she crooned.

Julia nodded for lack of a better reply. Mark could turn on the charm when he wanted to, although, she had to admit that tonight had been extremely enjoyable.

Yawning, Julia walked down the hallway to the spare bedroom. Barb was right behind her and Glen stayed back to turn off all the lights.

"Good night, dear," Barb said in a motherly way as she kissed Julia's cheek. "You know, I'm experiencing a sense of peace over this situation. I've heard you speak about Mark through the years, and I know how much you've been hurt, honey, but I truly believe things are different now."

Julia had to agree; she'd seen the difference in Mark, too. "But I have to proceed with caution." If anyone understood her, it was Barb French. "As you're already aware, Mark is a consultant at Weakland Management for the next few months, and everyone thinks he's married since he insists on wearing that stupid wedding band!"

Barb's merry laugh rang through the hallway. "Oh, wasn't that the story, though? But I suppose there are unscrupulous women in this world who would like nothing better than to ruin a man's career, not to mention his Christian testimony."

Julia shrugged, too tired for further debates, especially where Mark was concerned.

Barb was standing beside her now. "I don't want you to think I'm taking sides, dear," she said, putting a large, comforting arm around Julia's shoulders, "but if you could have seen the way Mark looked at you while you were sleeping in that chair tonight, you wouldn't be so wary around him." Barb chuckled. "You did look awfully sweet, too, all curled up and sleeping peacefully. You looked like an angel."

Julia clucked her tongue in embarrassment.

"Glen saw it, too," Barb continued. "Mark couldn't take his eyes off of you."

"You're exaggerating."

"Why, I am not! In fact, I'd go so far as to say that Mark Henley is still in love with you!"

"All right, that's enough," Julia said lightly. "Time for bed. You're obviously delirious with exhaustion."

"Humpf!" Barb said, feigning indignation. She strode toward the bedroom door. "Suit yourself. Find out the hard way." She shook her finger at Julia then. "But I know love when I see it."

Julia rolled her eyes and saw her out. "G'night, Barb."

Closing the door, Julia turned and leaned against it. She had tried to cover her emotions in front of Barb; however, now that she was alone, there was no mistaking the tumult in her heart. *Mark still in love with me?* Julia shook her head disbelievingly. She didn't want to entertain such a thought because she feared it might grow into a precious, fragile dream that was sure to end up in pieces at her feet.

Not again, Lord, she pleaded. *Please protect me from getting hurt again.*

And with that simple prayer came the realization of just how dangerous a man Mark really was. He could take everything she held dear. Her career, her son. . .and her very heart!

Chapter 9

D id you have a good weekend, Juli?"

Standing in line at the restaurant, waiting for her turn to order with Sir Walter, Julia merely nodded. How could she tell Ken that she'd spent Saturday and Sunday with Weakland's business consultant? Very simply, she couldn't.

"I worked all weekend," Ken was saying.

Julia turned to look at him. "Did you get a lot done?"

Ken nodded, and Julia realized this last weekend was the first in many that she hadn't worked. And that little bit of time away had helped Julia see things differently—in a healthier perspective, perhaps.

"Maybe some Sunday you could come to church with me, Ken," she impulsively offered. "There's a Bible study for single people, too."

"Not interested," Ken replied in a bored tone as he gazed over the food. "I'd rather work than go to church."

"Do you believe in God?"

"I believe in myself." Ken turned her way and his green eyes scanned her face. His expression was hard, even cruel—so much so, in fact, that Julia found herself taking a step back.

"I'm sorry, Ken. I shouldn't have put you on the spot that way."

He shrugged. Then, an instant later, his dark expression was gone. "God and church are not for me."

His simple reply somehow saddened Julia. However, when her turn came to order, she did so with fervor. Bacon, scrambled eggs and an English muffin. Normally she never ate this much in the morning, but for some odd reason she was hungry today. Perhaps it was due to the basketball game she and Mark had played in the rain last night.

Julia smiled inwardly, remembering. At ten o'clock, in the pouring rain with thunder rumbling in the distance, Mark had challenged her to a basketball game. Barb and Glen had laughed till their sides ached, watching from the dry, covered front porch. It was the stupidest thing she'd done in a long time, but it had been so much fun! And she'd nearly won the game, too, which came as no surprise to Mark. He said he remembered how good she had been when she played on the girls' basketball team in high school. Now if only she didn't catch pneumonia. . . .

Julia chose a table near the windows and sat down. Despite the rain last night, the sun shone brightly this morning.

"I had hoped you would show up this weekend," Ken said, taking a seat on her right.

"Oh, well. . .I was. . .busy."

At that precise moment, Mark appeared, a tray of food in his hands. "May I join you?" he asked, setting down his tray.

"By all means," Ken replied, though his countenance hinted at the contrary. He sat back lazily.

"Good morning, Juli."

"Good morning," she said with a smile.

"Say, Ken, I've been meaning to congratulate you," Mark said moments later. "I heard you acquired the Paxton account."

Ken's face immediately split into a huge grin. "I worked very hard on getting that account, thank you."

Mark chewed, swallowed, then pursed his lips thoughtfully. "It's a multi-million dollar deal, isn't it?"

"Sure is."

Julia considered each man as he spoke. She sensed that while Ken seemed proud and enthusiastic, Mark appeared to be troubled. She couldn't figure out why, until she suddenly remembered. The Paxton account. . .wasn't that the one George Simmons, another portfolio manager, had been trying to secure? Julia was puzzled. What was Ken doing with the Paxton account?

"Nice people, the Paxtons," Ken was saying. "And they're very eager to invest."

"Great."

"I've given them several investment options and they're presently deciding on which is the most suitable."

"How did you hook them. . .the Paxtons, I mean?"

Julia suddenly felt as if she was watching a Ping-Pong match.

"Oh, I have my ways," Ken replied mysteriously. "However, I will say that I've got other irons in the fire."

Mark paused and looked up from his breakfast. "If you play with fire, Ken, you might get burned."

He laughed. "I think you've missed my point."

"Well, just so you don't miss mine, okay?"

Julia shifted uncomfortably. The atmosphere was suddenly laced with tension, and she debated whether she should excuse herself. But, then, she didn't have to. In a single, abrupt motion, Ken picked up his tray and left the table, making a racket as he deposited his dishes. Other employees in the restaurant looked over at Mark as if for an explanation. He offered none.

"Oh, boy," Julia muttered, nibbling on her bacon, "troubled waters ahead."

"And the boat's got a leak."

Julia frowned. "Ken?"

"I don't know," Mark replied. "I'm not sure what I'm dealing with quite yet."

Julia nodded for lack of a better response. Then she watched as Mark pushed around the food on his plate and for the first time since his arrival, Julia sensed the amount of pressure he was under at Weakland Management. *It can't be easy,* she mused, finishing the last of her breakfast. Mark had to insinuate himself into the company, knowing that some employees would be hostile to the changes he proposed. Julia had learned that that was why Dave Larkey resigned: he had been opposed to making changes.

Minutes later, they disposed of their trays and dishes. Julia noticed that after the incident with Ken, Mark hadn't eaten much more. Her heart went out to him, which surprised her. The man was in a position to advise Bill to cut middle management, he could sue her for custody of their son—and she was feeling sorry for him?

I do need a vacation, she decided as they left the restaurant.

"See ya later, Juli," Mark said as he headed for Customer Service.

She nodded and, watching him go, she couldn't say who she pitied more at that moment, Mark. . .or Stacie Rollins.

❧

As usual, Julia didn't take a lunch break. She was too busy. Her paperwork was piling up and computers were going down. She was constantly interrupted and called away from one job to another. A program error here, an equipment problem there. Julia was only too glad for Angela, who followed her with spare keyboards, while Julia pushed a cart filled with extra monitors and hard drives.

"If Joan Miller spilled soda on her keyboard again, I'm writing her up!" Julia fumed.

"No, it's her monitor, this time," Angela replied.

Julia sighed. She'd never get to her paperwork today. After replacing the malfunctioning equipment, she had to check on a program error in Customer Service. Apparently, the "bugs" weren't all out of the new program yet. And here, Julia had thought she'd gotten everything up and running perfectly.

She wondered what Mark would have to say about her less-than-efficient program. Perhaps he would side with Stacie and insist the old program be reloaded. Except the new program had so many more capabilities. . . .

It was nearly five o'clock when Julia got to Customer Service. "Sorry I'm late in getting here," she told Mark sincerely. "I've had some equipment problems."

"That's okay. The program error, whatever it is, doesn't seem to be getting in anyone's way for the time being."

She nodded. That's what one of Stacie's employees had said when they made the initial call for help, so she had put it last on today's priority list.

Sitting down at a vacant workstation, Julia proceeded to enter the computer system. Then, out of the corner of her eye, she spotted Stacie and turned to say hello. The sight that greeted her, however, stopped any words from forming. There, sitting across the aisle at another workstation, was Stacie Rollins, wearing one of the tightest, shortest skirts Julia had ever seen on a woman. Her low-cut, sheer blouse was equally remarkable.

It was then that Julia recalled Stacie saying she hoped to impress Mark with her looks since she wouldn't impress him with her computer skills.

"It's about time you got here, Julia!" Stacie declared, suddenly taking notice of her. In spite of her words, Stacie was smiling and seemed in a good mood.

"Not to worry," Julia said, recovering from her initial shock. "I'll fix the program error. I hope it didn't cause too many problems for your department."

"We worked around it." Stacie walked across the aisle and leaned over the side of the mahogany-veneered workstation. Julia forced herself not to grimace at the thought of Stacie's short skirt creeping any higher. "Mr. BC isn't such a bad guy," she whispered.

"Oh, well, that's good," Julia replied rather generically while she wished that Stacie wouldn't lean forward quite so far. Then she wondered how Mark had endured Stacie and her mini skirt all day. She was attractive in the outfit, even if it was grossly inappropriate for the office.

Obviously Mark handled things well enough, Julia decided, if Stacie isn't insulted. Maybe he even enjoyed working with Stacie today. Julia's sarcastic thoughts caught in her heart—she had already sensed Mark's deep love for the Savior and his desire to obey God's Word. So how had Mark handled the likes of Stacie Rollins today?

Julia worked on the PC while Stacie walked off to gather her things.

"Well, it's almost five-thirty," she stated minutes later, slinging her delicate, leather purse over a slender shoulder. "Good night, Julia."

"See you tomorrow."

Julia looked for Mark as Stacie left the department. Two workstations away, he was sitting beside a male customer service representative, looking engrossed in whatever the other man was saying. Somehow Julia felt relieved that Mark's gaze hadn't followed Stacie.

Julia fought to bury her personal struggle and concentrate on the job before her. She managed to work diligently, and the next time Julia glanced at her watch it was nearly seven o'clock. She had corrected the program error—or at least she was reasonably sure she had. Time would tell. If the second-shift employees didn't have any problems, she would know she had been successful.

Mark came over as Julia stood, preparing to leave. "All done?"

She nodded, thinking that Mark looked tired. "Have you had a hard day?" He shrugged.

"Stacie seemed to have fared all right. She told me you're not such a bad guy after all."

Mark grinned. "I do my best—at not being a bad guy, that is."

Julia smiled and then momentarily contemplated as she chewed on her lower lip. "Can I ask you something, Mark? Something. . .personal?"

"Sure. Fire away."

"Well. . .how did you handle it today? I mean. . .as a single man, a Christian man. . .and Stacie, dressed as she was. . .?"

Mark's smile waned. "She really wasn't a distraction to me, Juli, if that's what you're getting at."

Julia was momentarily thoughtful. "Does that type of thing happen often? Business women trying to impress you with their looks instead of their diligence?"

Mark shrugged. "Now and then."

She nodded, coming to understand the reason behind the wedding ring he insisted upon wearing. "It must be very difficult for you sometimes," she murmured, lowering her chin. She ran a finger over the keyboard in front of her, as her heart went out to him for the second time that day.

"Yes, it is sometimes. But as a single, Christian woman, you must experience the same thing from time to time. Take Driscoll for instance."

Surprised, Julia looked up. "I'm not interested in Ken."

"I know you're not. And I have no interest in Stacie, other than to get her input on how this department functions as a whole."

Mark smiled so tenderly into her eyes then, that Julia felt as if her heart was out on a line and he was reeling it in. Slowly, ever so slowly.

"Will you have dinner with me, Juli?" he suddenly asked.

"I'd love to."

❧

The evening was warm and smells of early summer were in the air—budding trees, blooming flowers, and smoke from backyard grills.

Julia walked beside Mark as they strolled back to Weakland Management. They both had left their cars in the parking structure and decided to walk the mile or so to the restaurant since the evening weather was so delightful.

"So, you're on vacation next week," Mark said, though it sounded more like a question.

Julia nodded. "I haven't been on a week-long vacation for years," she admitted. "I always make plans, but then something happens with the computer system and I end up either cutting my vacation time in half or not going at all. But

I always manage to give Jesse a vacation. A few days here, a few days there. We sort of 'vacation' all summer long."

"Well, that's good. But aren't any of your employees capable of managing the computer system for a week?"

"Sure, they're capable. I just feel guilty for leaving them with the problems, I guess."

"For shame, Juli," Mark admonished her lightly. "Even you need a good chunk of time away from your work."

She grinned. "That's what Barb said, too. So, okay, I'm going on vacation, already!"

They shared a laugh and continued walking as an amiable silence fell over them. Julia resisted the urge to slip her hand into Mark's. How often had they walked together like this during their high school days? Except they would be holding hands. . . .

Julia shoved hers into the pockets of her suit jacket instead.

"Do you think you'll tell Jesse while you're on vacation?" Mark asked, breaking her silence.

"Yes, I'll tell him," she replied, noting the edge in her own voice. She tried to swallow it down. "He's going to have to learn about his father sooner or later, may as well be sooner." She paused. "Are you still holding that threat over my head?"

In the dusk of the evening, Julia saw him purse his lips thoughtfully. "No, I'm not going to hold that threat over your head. I'm sorry I ever made it." He paused. "I'm just anxious to meet my son. Is that unreasonable? It seems I've waited forever for the day to come. Even though I knew about Jesse a year ago, I wanted to wait until I talked to you before I entered his life. Like I said, I wanted you to tell me about him, Juli. I wanted to hear about our son from you."

Julia sighed. "Well, now you know."

"And you're not happy about it, are you?"

"I never said that."

"Juli, what are you afraid of, anyway?"

"Afraid. . .?" She let the word hang between them in the evening summer air as she wondered how she could ever voice her innermost fears to him. Hadn't she shared her heart and soul with Mark before? And look what happened then. He betrayed her trust.

"Guess I hit a nerve, huh?" Mark finally said when she didn't reply.

"Sort of. Look, Mark, I forgave you. I even believe you, but I guess I'm just not ready to trust you yet. That's going to take a while."

The silence, no longer amicable, seemed to grow between them, lasting until they reached Weakland Management. Then finally Mark said, "I'm not a monster,

Juli." His voice sounded weary or maybe heavy with emotion, she couldn't tell. And she couldn't see his face because of the encroaching darkness of the night.

When she didn't reply, Mark said roughly, "Come on. I'll walk you to your car."

Chapter 10

Julia arrived at work shortly after eleven-thirty the next morning due to a downtown business seminar. She was still making some mental notes when Mark came up behind her.

"G'morning, Juli. It is still morning, isn't it?" Beside her now, he looked at his wristwatch. "Yep. It's still morning."

Julia gave him a curious look, noting that he didn't look very happy.

"Where have you been?" he wanted to know.

"At a seminar." She frowned now because he was frowning so hard.

"Did I know about this seminar?"

"I don't know. Were you supposed to? I mean, I was scheduled to attend it months ago. Bill knew about it."

"He didn't have it written down on his calendar and he was looking for you."

"Oh. . .well, I'm sorry about that. I'm sure I cleared it with him. In fact, Weakland Management prepaid my way. . . Mark? What's wrong?"

"Was Driscoll at the seminar, too?"

"Ken?" Julia shook her head. "It was a seminar on technological advancement in computer programming. Why would Ken attend?"

"He's not here."

"Well, Ken wasn't with me."

They had reached IS now and Mark continued to walk with her all the way to her office. He waited while she unlocked the door and then he followed her inside.

"Do you have a syllabus or something from this seminar?"

Setting her attaché case on her desk, Julia whirled around to face him. "Do you think I'm lying? And what's it to you, Mark? You're not my supervisor."

Mark lifted his brows. "I'm curious. Why are you so defensive?"

Julia paused, considering him. "I guess I just don't appreciate you questioning me like this."

Mark closed her office door. "Juli, I didn't know where you were this morning. Bill asked me if I had seen you and, since I hadn't, I began to wonder. Besides, that program error is still popping up in Customer Service."

"Oh no. . ." Julia leaned against her desk.

"I think I might know how to fix it, but I didn't dare do anything without you here."

Julia sighed. "Well, thanks for that, anyway."

He nodded. "So, when can you get to that program error?"

"Why are you attacking me?"

"Why are you taking it personal? This is a business and there's a department with a programming error."

Julia swallowed her retort and took a deep, calming breath. "I'll get to it right away," she said, forcing a soft tone of voice. Then she crossed the room and opened the door.

"Juli?"

She turned.

"Aren't you going to put this stuff away?" Mark asked, nodding toward her purse and attaché case.

She shrugged. "I'll put it away later." On that, she left her office with Mark still standing there.

❧

Two o'clock that afternoon, Julia was in Sir Walter's, pouring herself a strong cup of coffee. She normally didn't drink coffee this late in the day, but it looked like it was going to be a long night. The program she had created for the Customer Service Department had all but crashed, and Julia was disappointed and frustrated.

Having filled her ceramic mug with the freshly-ground, steaming brew, Julia walked slowly back toward Customer Service and the workstation she'd been at, laboring diligently. She sat down and began to work on the computer program when Mark pulled up a chair beside her.

"Listen, Juli," he fairly whispered, "this isn't small-town Lyon, Illinois. You've got to lock up your stuff—your desk drawers, credenza and your office door from now on. Okay?"

She looked at him, puzzled. "Why?"

"Don't ask questions. I can't answer them right now. Just take my advice, okay?"

"You're serious, aren't you?"

"Extremely."

She nodded, feeling a little worried now. What was going on that had Mark whispering and acting suspicious? "Can I question you after hours?" she asked on a hopeful note.

Mark shook his head. "Sorry. You'll just have to. . .trust me, Juli." The statement had a ring of sarcasm to it.

Then he looked at her computer terminal. "Want some help?" he asked, his voice its normal pitch again.

"With trusting you or with the computer program?" she asked tartly.

Mark's expression said he wasn't amused. Standing, he walked off to the other side of the department.

The night wore on. Finally, around ten o'clock, the computer program was up and running, but very slowly. The second-shift employees were frustrated because they couldn't get their work done. Adding to their stress was the fact that Mark, for whatever reason, had decided to hang around. After the business dinner last week, several of the more rebellious employees dubbed him the company "spy" since he had access to Bill's "listening ear." Julia suspected that those same employees were the ones working tonight, in Security, Customer Service, and Data Processing—the only departments that had a second shift. And they did not look happy.

"So what happens if the computer crashes at eleven-thirty some night?" Mark asked, following her back to Information Systems.

"I carry my pager at all times. Security notifies me if something goes wrong."

He nodded, pursing his mouth and looking pensive. "Do you have backups?"

Julia nodded. "Downstairs. Behind Security. The Central Processing Units, or CPUs, are in a standard climate-controlled room. That's where much of our information is stored."

"And only authorized personnel are allowed in there?"

Julia turned to look at him. "No, we don't lock it up. Employees from the Data Processing Department have to get in there. I've trained them to start certain programs on certain nights so the jobs can run all night and not hang up the computers during the day."

"Then maybe the employees from DP ought to lock it up," Mark suggested. "As a matter of fact, that's next on my list of recommendations. Locks."

"But, Mark, security officers are sitting right there."

"Would they stop an unauthorized employee from entering the CPU room?"

Julia shrugged. She honestly didn't know. She'd never had a reason to question anyone here at Weakland Management. Who would want to go into the CPU room anyway? Half the time, she and her employees had to practically beg the people in DP to go in there and run the programs.

Entering her office, Julia gathered her things and prepared to go home. She was suddenly glad that Jesse was up north with her parents, although there had been other late nights when he stayed at Barb and Glen's house. In any case, she missed him. The apartment was much too quiet without him around.

As she left her office, Mark stepped aside so she could lock the door. Then he followed her through the department and waited while she locked the outer door.

"I'll walk you to your car."

"I can manage."

"I insist."

She gave him a curious glance, but his expression revealed very little. "Did you ever find Ken today?"

"Yes. Apparently he had a 'power brunch' with some clients and didn't bother to let Bill know about it. He's still upstairs. . .working, I guess. Frankly, I don't know what he's doing. Shuffling papers, maybe." He looked over at her as she struggled to understand where all the animosity was coming from. "That's why I'm escorting you to your car, Juli."

She lifted her brows. "Because of Ken?" Smiling, she shook her head. "He's harmless, Mark."

He laughed tersely. "So he's harmless, but I'm a monster?"

"Mark, I never said you were a monster."

"You didn't have to," he told her as they reached the parking lot. "Your actions speak louder than words."

Julia didn't reply. She was too tired to spar with Mark.

❧

"Oh, come on, Juli, you need to be spiritually fed," Barb told her the next night. "Come to the worship service tonight. Glen and I will pick you up."

"But I just got home from work. It's six-thirty."

"You've got a whole half hour to get ready."

Julia sighed, but she knew trying to talk Barb out of dragging her to the midweek worship service was futile. Unless she had a legitimate business meeting, was sick or dying, Barb accepted no excuses.

"We can be at your place by seven."

"All right," Julia said in a note of resignation.

She shrugged out of her navy blue, linen suit jacket and walked into her bedroom. There she changed from her matching linen skirt and peach-colored silk blouse into a full denim dress and casual flats. The midweek worship service wasn't formal. Next Julia brushed her hair out and wondered if Mark would be there tonight. He had enjoyed the Sunday service?

Mark. What was with that man anyway? Julia hadn't a clue. Since yesterday he had been curt with her to the point of being downright unfriendly. And Ken. . .

Julia sighed, touching up her makeup. Ken was going out of his way to flirt with her which only seemed to fuel Mark's already fiery temperament.

Men, she thought with a sigh. *Can't live with 'em, can't live without 'em. . .*

Barb and Glen were precisely on time, Glen at the wheel of his GMC Suburban.

"Hi, you guys," Julia said, climbing into the backseat.

"Hi, yourself," Glen said with a smile. "Barb has been thinking about joining the choir again, so she's been warming up."

"There's practice tonight," she said informatively.

Glen snorted. "Guess that means you and I will have to fellowship after service tonight, Juli."

"Okay." She smiled, squelching the urge for an early night at home and a hot bubble bath.

For the remainder of the drive to church, Barb sang "It Is Well With My Soul" while Glen hummed along, and Julia was reminded of how much she loved these two people. They had provided a firm foundation for her at a time when she thought her whole world was falling apart. How could she ever repay them? She couldn't. It was a simple as that! Julia knew the Frenches wouldn't want any payment, at least not in the monetary sense. *Dear God, please show me a way that I can repay Barb and Glen for all they've done for Jesse and me over the years.*

They arrived at church and Glen let the ladies out before he drove back into the lot and parked the Suburban. Julia followed Barb into the church, then to a pew where they sat down. The service was about to begin.

Glen appeared and when Julia looked up and prepared to make room for him in the pew, she saw that Mark was with him. He gave her a tight smile before sitting beside Glen.

"I'm glad you came, son," Glen said.

"I almost didn't," Mark replied, causing Julia to wonder. She exchanged looks with Barb who smiled back at her lovingly.

The worship service began with singing praises to God, followed by a brief, life-application message from the Bible. Next, requests were taken from those who had special burdens or needs and then everyone broke into small groups for prayer. When it was over, Barb went to choir practice and Glen was called away by a fellow parishioner.

"Can I speak with you for a few minutes, Juli?" Mark asked, standing at the end of the pew.

"Sure."

They walked outside, where the evening sun was just beginning to set. They made their way through the parking lot, toward Glen's Suburban. The church had been built on the outskirts of Menomonee Falls where there were still a few farms and fields left.

"This kind of reminds me of Lyon," Mark murmured.

Julia nodded. She had been reminded of Lyon, too, after she first started attending this church with Barb and Glen.

When they reached the truck, Mark turned and faced her. "Juli, I'm sorry for the way I've been acting the last couple of days." He looked down at the pavement for several long moments before his gaze met hers again. "I know you've never called me a monster to my face, but that's the way you make me feel sometimes. My intentions are honorable. Really. I've tried to show you that, but you still seem suspicious."

Julia didn't know what to say. She supposed he was right: she was suspicious. But that was only because she had so much to lose.

"Look, Juli, I don't want to fight anymore." Mark took a step closer. "When you and Driscoll didn't show up for work yesterday morning, I imagined you two were together somewhere and it riled me."

Julia gave him an incredulous stare. "Mark, I told you. . . there is nothing between Ken and me."

"I know, I know. But I was. . ." He paused as if struggling with what he wanted to say. "I was jealous, okay?" he finally blurted. "I'll admit it. . .and quit laughing!"

"I'm not laughing," Julia said, biting her cheek. "Okay, I laughed a little. Sorry. But, Mark, it's so silly. I mean, Ken and I. . ." She shook her head. "He's not my type, all right?"

Mark smirked. "What kind of man is your type?"

She shrugged, feeling a mixture of embarrassment and discomfort. She had always thought that Mark was her type. Lately, however, she wasn't so sure. She didn't know him anymore.

"There's that silence again. Like a wall." Mark shook his head. "Juli, you build them better than Nehemiah."

"Will you give me some time?"

"Time to fortify your walls and keep me out for good? I do want a relationship with my son, you know. It would be nice if you and I could at least be friends."

"I agree. But I need time to get reacquainted with you."

Mark considered her for a few moments through a narrowed gaze. "All right, that's fair," he finally said, heaving a tired-sounding sigh. "Maybe I did come barreling into your life. I suppose I should apologize for that along with my over-zealousness about meeting Jesse." He smiled then, and it was so charming and sincere that Julia's heart raced. "Guess I need to be like Joshua, huh? If I'm patient and trust God, those walls will come tumbling down. I'd do that for you, Juli. No problem."

She was touched by Mark's sensitivity.

"As for our close proximity at Weakland Management. . . well, I'd resign, but Bill has a lot of money invested in me."

Julia tipped her head to one side. "So what do you propose?"

"I propose a strictly professional relationship at work and a. . .well, whatever develops after that on our personal time."

Julia lifted a brow. "That means no running me over in the hallway."

Mark laughed. "Oh, all right." His tone beheld a note of feigned reluctance.

Julia smiled. "Okay, your proposal sounds reasonable to me."

"Should we shake on it?" Mark held out his right hand.

Julia slipped her hand into his. "You've got a deal, Mr. Henley."

His grip tightened. "But you've got to promise me that you'll be very careful at work right now, Juli, all right? No more working late by yourself. Lock up your belongings and your office. . ."

"Mark, you're scaring me."

"I don't mean to. I just wanted to give you a warning. Be aware." Still holding her hand, he pulled her closer to him. "It's just commonsense stuff, really—and I can't explain it right now. But I will someday. Someday soon." His blue eyes darkened with seriousness then. "Promise me, Juli. Promise me you'll be careful."

Looking up into Mark's face, she momentarily contemplated his request. It wasn't outrageous, only confusing. But what harm could there be in promising Mark she'd be "careful" at work? She was always careful!

"Juli. . . ?"

She gave him a little smile. "All right, Mark. I promise."

Chapter 11

When her office door slammed shut, Julia looked up suddenly from her computer. "Stacie. . .?"

"I wanted you to be the first to know," she said with a toss of her head and wide grin. She shoved a memo at Julia.

"What's this?"

"An announcement. Read it."

Julia did and when she finished, she looked back at Stacie and smiled. "Congratulations. You've been promoted to the Director of the Customer Service Department."

Stacie smiled back at her. "I told you middle management is on its way out. But we've got one smart business consultant, Juli. He's advising Bill to make us all directors!"

Julia laughed softly. "How's that suppose to save Weakland Management any money?"

"Beats me. But as long as it's not my job in jeopardy, I don't care."

Julia rolled her eyes. Typical response from Stacie.

"Well, TGIF and have a good weekend," she said, moving toward the door. "You're on vacation next week, aren't you?"

Julia nodded.

Stacie chuckled. "Better rest up. Your week with Mr. BC is coming."

"Thanks for reminding me," Julia said facetiously.

"You bet."

On that, Stacie left the office and Julia forced her thoughts back to her work. She had to get her department's payroll done and handed in by the end of the day, and she didn't want to stay much after five o'clock. Today was Friday, after all, and Barb and Glen would be waiting for her since they were driving up to Minoqua tonight.

Their last conversation weighed heavily on Julia's heart once again. "Ask him," Barb had urged. "Ask Mark to come up for a few days."

Julia stared blankly at the computer screen. She'd been debating the idea ever since Barb had suggested it, crazy as it was—or was it? Since Wednesday night, she and Mark had been getting along very well. They had eaten dinner with the Frenches last night and then they went for a walk.

Julia pushed her thoughts away and finished the payroll. She printed out the information, locked her office door, and took the report up to Jerry Fein. Then she entered Mark's office.

He glanced at his watch. "Four fifty-seven, Juli. Barb will tan your hide if you're late tonight."

She grinned. "I've still got three minutes."

He chuckled.

"Mark, I, uhm, wondered if I could ask you something." Julia lowered her voice. "Something personal."

"Sure. What's on your mind?"

"Well, you know I'm on vacation next week. . ."

"Yes."

"And Barb thought that it might be nice if you came up for the Fourth of July. I'll talk to Jesse immediately, of course, but I don't expect a bad reaction. He's curious about you—his father."

Mark pursed his lips thoughtfully as he considered the offer. "What about you? This is your vacation, Juli, do you really want me to impose?"

"You're not imposing. I'm inviting."

"Because Barb put you up to it?"

Julia paused for a long, pensive moment. She thought about their walk last night and how they had laughed over fond memories. "No. I. . .I'd like you to come," she finally said. She could feel her cheeks warming pink, and she hoped she didn't look as stupid as she felt—like a sixteen-year-old girl asking the cutest boy in the class to the "Turn-A-Bout" dance, where the girls ask the guys.

"Well, thanks, Juli."

She shrugged, wanting to appear nonchalant. "I sort of figured you'd be working Friday—"

"I can take Friday off."

Julia couldn't help but smile.

"Do you think Jesse is really going to be all right with the news about me?"

She nodded, feeling confident about at least that much. "Jesse is a well-adjusted kid, Mark, and you and I have been getting along—"

"And I think that's important for Jesse to see."

"Exactly." Julia rose from the chair. "How about if I call you on Wednesday night? We can confirm our plans then."

Mark shook his head. "Call me Wednesday afternoon. . . better yet, I'll call you."

Mark grabbed a pen, and Julia gave him the phone number. He seemed so excited that Julia had to smile, even though there was trepidation pumping through her veins with every beat of her heart. What if Jesse preferred Mark to her and decided he wanted to live with his dad? What if Mark decided he wanted complete custody? What if, because he was in child care so much with her working her way through school and her career, Mark found her mothering skills lacking?

"Change your mind?" Mark asked as if divining her thoughts.

Julia shook her head. She didn't know how to voice her silly insecurities. And, yes, they were silly. Yes, she was insecure. . .and, yes, she was frightened!

"I wish you'd talk to me, Juli," Mark said wistfully as he walked around his desk and stood beside her. "I feel like a wall is going up before my very eyes."

Julia managed a smile and shook her head. "No, Mark, I'm entertaining ridiculous thoughts which I shouldn't even be thinking."

He frowned. "Hmm." Then a smile broke through, re-minding Julia of a sunbeam on a cloudy day. "Well, stop it," he teased. "Let's have fun next weekend!"

"Okay," Julia smiled broadly in spite of herself.

Mark was smiling, too, as he walked her to the door. "Take care."

She nodded and left his office.

Then she caught a glimpse of Ken from the corner of her eye. She turned and saw that he was watching her intently so she waved. "See you in a week. I'm going on vacation. I mean, I'm really going this time. And not just for a day or two, but a real vacation!"

"I'm very disappointed in you, Julia," he replied, lofting a brow.

She chuckled inwardly at the sarcasm, knowing it came from a workaholic who would probably never think of taking time off from his career. Julia knew the feeling well.

"Have a good weekend anyway, Ken," she quipped before walking away.

She never saw the exchange that went on behind her back between Mark and Ken—the look of warning, the glare of open resentment.

❧

"Mom, the lake is freezing up here!" Jesse declared the next morning at breakfast.

Julia smiled at her son. "We've had a cold and rainy spring, Jess. I guess that explains it."

"Fishing's good, though," Roy replied, taking a bite of his homemade cinnamon roll. "We've had fish twice this week for supper. Isn't that right, Jesse?"

The boy nodded. "They were big ones, too, Mom. Really big."

Julia furrowed her brows. "Sounds like a fish story to me."

Her parents chuckled while Jesse insisted that the fish were "really big."

"And how are things at work, Juli?" Caroline asked, taking a sip of her coffee.

"Much better, Mom."

Roy looked across the table at her from beneath his bushy gray brows. "I hate to even ask what that means."

Julia sobered. "It means it's time to forgive and forget, Dad."

Roy narrowed his gaze. "Never!"

"What are we talking about?" Jesse wanted to know. "And how come you're so mad all of a sudden, Grandpa?"

"Never mind, son," Roy replied. He glanced back at Julia. "I've worked very hard to protect you all these years. I don't want to see you get hurt again—or any of us get hurt again." He nodded sideways at Jesse. "I especially don't want to see him getting hurt."

"Me? Why would I get hurt?" Jesse asked, obviously trying to understand the adult conversation. "Are you talking about the time I went down to the lake by myself, Grandpa? But I know how to swim."

"No, no, son. . ."

"Jesse, will you go out to Uncle Glen's truck and bring in the rest of my things?" Julia asked sweetly. "I'm sure I left something in there last night. It was dark and I couldn't see to grab everything."

Reluctantly, the boy nodded, though he looked a little confused. "Can I say hi to Uncle Glen and Aunt Barb, too?"

"Sure."

Julia watched him go, waiting for him to get down the hill before she turned back to her father. "Mark wants to be part of Jesse's life, Dad, and I think that's only fair. He's Jesse's father. He has that right."

Roy's face reddened with anger. "Don't talk about rights where Mark is concerned. He forfeited his rights twelve years ago."

"That's how I felt too initially, but Mark is a different man these days." Juli smiled, shaking her head at the irony. She was defending Mark, of all people!

She stood and walked over to the coffeemaker which was on the counter next to the sink. She filled her mug. "Dad, I think you should know that I've invited Mark to spend the Fourth of July with us. . .up here."

"You. . .what!" Now Roy was standing. He shook his head adamantly. "No. Absolutely not!"

"He'll stay with Barb and Glen," she continued despite his reply. "They were actually the ones who thought it would be a good idea. And I agreed. Mark and Jesse can get acquainted."

"Bad idea, Juli." Roy still shook his head. His gray hair was thinning on top, even though he combed it back in an effort to conceal the fact. He was a large man, with broad shoulders and muscular arms from years of heavy lifting and hard work. But beneath the gruff, Julia knew there was a man of sensitive heart and spirit, though he didn't share her Christian faith—yet. Julia knew that she could probably talk her father into buying swamp land in Florida if she truly had her mind set on it.

She sipped her coffee, considering him as he stared out the screen of the back door. "Mom said she told you about the letters."

"Yeah, she told me. You two are ganging up on me. . .as usual."

"We are not ganging up on you, Roy," Caroline said, still enjoying her breakfast despite the commotion around her.

"Look, Dad," Julia said carefully, "you may as well get used to the idea. Mark is in our lives to stay. . .at least I hope so."

Roy swung around and glared at her. "You hope so?"

"For Jesse's sake," Julia clarified.

"Oh, and I suppose the next thing you'll tell me is that you're still in love with him."

Julia lowered her gaze to the coffee mug between her hands, hoping to hide her sudden discomfort. Part of her wanted to debate the comment, yet she honestly couldn't do it.

"I don't believe it!" Roy murmured.

"Dad, please, will you give Mark just one more chance? For Jesse's sake."

"And who's going to tell Jesse?"

"I will."

Caroline had finished her breakfast and was now clearing the table. "I think Jesse is going to be excited about meeting Mark." She looked up then, and her mind seemed far away. "You know, I can remember when Mark was Jesse's age." She smiled fondly. "He was such a sweet boy."

"What do you mean, 'sweet boy'?" Roy asked, frowning heavily. "He and his older brother were always getting into trouble."

"Oh, they were not!" Caroline declared. "They were just being boys. Ours were just as mischievous, Roy."

"No, they weren't," he muttered irritably.

Julia had to chuckle. "Yes, they were, Dad." A moment of silence passed. "Did Mom tell you that Mark and his family are Christians now and that his parents are back together?"

"Yes." Roy shook his head once more. "Who would have ever called that one, huh?" He paused, then, and considered Julia thoughtfully. "So you're really going to allow Mark visiting privileges?"

Julia nodded.

"And he's really coming up here for the Fourth of July weekend?"

"That's right, Dad, although I wish that you'd concede to it."

"Oh, I'll concede to it," Roy said with a glint of warning in his eyes. "But I'm going to threaten that boy within an inch of his life. If he ever does anything to hurt my family again, he'll have to deal with me! Won't matter if he runs off to the other side of the world this time, either. I'll find him!"

Julia smiled.

❦

The next afternoon was warm and the sunshine glistened off the lake, making the water look like fine crystal. From where Julia sat on the pier next to Jesse, she could feel the warm rays penetrating her skin like a deep-heating massage. It felt comforting.

She turned to Jesse now, wondering what he was thinking. She had just begun to tell him about his father.

"So you and. . .my dad went to school together?"

"That's right. And your dad was on the football team. He was the best, too, and that's when I fell in love with him."

"Then what happened?"

"Well, your dad finished school a year before I did and he went to work for Grandpa at his gas station and garage. The next year, after I finished school, your dad and I planned to get married." Julia paused, thinking that telling Jesse about Mark wasn't nearly as painful as she had thought it would be. "Well, the time came for us to get married, but then your dad changed his mind. He decided he needed to go to college before he got married. So he went away and we never got married, and that's when I learned that I was going to have a baby."

"Me?"

Julia nodded. "You see, Jesse, your dad and I. . .well, we sinned because we. . . Well, we were acting like a husband and wife, except we weren't married, and that's sin. We made a mistake, but, Jesse," she said emphatically, "you were never a mistake. Do you understand that? You have always been a very special blessing to me. . .and all of our family, too." Julia smiled. Then, putting an arm around his shoulders, she leaned over and kissed his cheek. "I loved you from the minute you were born!"

The boy shrugged, looking embarrassed. "Aw, Mom. . ."

Straightening, Julia concluded her story. "I never told your dad about you because I thought he didn't care. But he does. And now he wants to meet you. What do you think?"

"I don't know." Jesse seemed thoughtful as he gazed down into the water. "Is my dad nice?"

"Yes."

"Is he rich?"

Julia thought about it. "I guess I'm not sure if he's 'rich,' but he's probably doing all right financially."

"Do you like him?"

"Yes," Julia replied carefully.

"Do you love him?"

Julia rolled her eyes. How come she had a feeling Jesse would ask her that?

But she was prepared.

"Jesse," she began, "my feelings for your dad don't matter when it comes to your relationship with him. Your dad wants to be part of your life, and I think you should at least meet him and give him a chance."

Jesse seemed to think it over before he starting on his next series of questions. "What's his name?"

"Mark Thomas Henley."

"Hey, Mark is my middle name!"

"You were named for your dad."

"What's he look like?"

"Well, he's about as tall as Grandpa, and he still sort of looks like a football player. . . ."

"Grandpa looks like a lineman."

Julia bit her lip in effort not to chuckle. Her father did have a bit of a tummy on him now, due to his retirement and her mother's good cooking. "Your dad isn't that big, Jess," she finally replied. "And you kind of look like him."

"Does he like jokes?"

"Loves them."

"Does he have a dog?"

"I don't know, but you could ask him."

Jesse's questions didn't stop for the next three days, and he took turns following the adults around, asking them about his dad. Julia was only too grateful for her mother who provided Jesse with story after story about Mark's growing up years. And, when he finally called Wednesday afternoon, Jesse behaved as though he knew his dad very well.

"Mom says you've got a real neat old car," Jesse told Mark, holding the receiver to his ear as Julia sat by, watching, listening and praying that all would go well. "Uncle Glen says he's got some fireworks that we can set off on the Fourth of July." Jesse paused and then his eyes grew round. "Mom!" he whispered, holding his hand over the phone, "Dad says he's got some fireworks, too!"

"That'll be fun," Julia replied with an encouraging nod.

"Okay, here's Mom." Jesse handed her the telephone unceremoniously before running off to inform his grandparents about the fireworks.

"Hi, Mark," Julia said, putting the receiver to her ear.

"Did I hear correctly? He's calling me 'Dad' already?" There was a note of amazement in Mark's voice.

"Yes, well, he's got the scoop on you now." Julia chuckled and explained about Jesse's inquiring mind and how Grandma McGowan was stimulating it with stories of days gone by. Minutes later, Mark was chuckling too.

"Well, I can't wait to meet him, Juli. He sounds like a neat kid."

"He is."

"My parents will be thrilled. They can't wait to meet Jesse, either. I haven't really thought that far ahead, but I'd like to take him to Springfield sometime."

Tiny prickles of apprehension climbed Julia's spine at Mark's words "take him," and yet it only seemed logical that Mark would want his parents to meet Jesse. She had decided to share him, and now she would just have to follow through on her decision.

Mark asked for directions to Minoqua then, and Julia gave them. "I'll see you later this week," he promised. "I'm leaving here right at five o'clock, so I'll get up there around ten-thirty or eleven. I hope that's not too late."

"No, it's not too late," Julia replied, swallowing the urge to ask how things were going at Weakland Management. This week Mark was sitting in with Jon Maxwell and the data processing department. But she was on vacation. She wasn't supposed to think about work. "See you later, Mark."

Julia hung up the telephone, and when she turned, her father was standing there in the kitchen, eyeing her speculatively.

"You're setting yourself up for a fall, Juli," he said. "I can see it coming and, just like the last time, I'll have to pick up the pieces."

"No, Dad, don't say that." Without even knowing it, Roy McGowan had voiced her darkest fear.

As she watched her father walk away, Julia noticed the slight bend to his shoulders. It seemed like a sad bend, too, like one that had carried an enormous burden for a long, long time.

Oh, dear God, I just want to do the right thing by Mark and Jesse. Please don't let this be the second biggest mistake of my life.

Chapter 12

It was nearly eleven o'clock when Julia heard Mark's car pull onto the gravel road. Sitting in the kitchen, she and Jesse had been waiting up for Mark, playing "Crazy-8s" to pass the time. But when his car's headlights briefly flashed through the kitchen windows, Jesse looked across the table at her, wearing an anxious expression.

"Mom. . .?"

"Don't worry, Jess," she said with a smile. "You'll like your dad. You'll see." Julia felt somewhat apprehensive, but she wasn't about to let her son know it. "Come on. Let's go meet him."

They walked outside, Julia's arm around Jesse's shoulders. After days of excitement, the boy seemed suddenly shy and reluctant as Mark climbed out of his car.

"Welcome," Julia said neighborly. "I'm glad you found the cabins all right."

"You gave great directions." Mark looked at the boy now standing in front of him. "You must be Jesse."

He nodded and an awkward silence ensued.

Julia decided to break the ice a bit. "This is your father, Jesse, Mark Henley." She looked back at Mark, his features barely visible under the yard light.

He held out his hand. "I'm glad to finally meet you, Jesse."

The boy considered, first the outstretched hand, and then the man. Finally he clasped Mark's hand. "I'm glad to finally meet you, too." His voice sounded stiff and formal.

Julia turned to Mark. "You'll be staying with Barb and Glen. Jesse and I can help you with your things, and then we'll walk you down to their cabin."

"Sounds good. Here, Jesse, will you carry the bag of fireworks for me?"

Julia smiled. Mark couldn't have picked a better task. Jesse perked right up.

"Wow! You brought all these?"

"Uh-huh."

"Can I help you set some off?"

"I think you probably can. . .if your mother says it's all right."

"Is it, Mom?"

"Well. . .is it really safe, Mark?"

"Sure. I'll be right there with him."

"C'mom, Mom, plee-ease."

Julia laughed softly, deciding that she could now sympathize with her father and how he must have felt all those years being constantly coerced by the two women he loved most. "Well, we'll see," she finally replied.

Jesse turned to Mark with an air of confidence. "Whenever my mom says 'we'll see' that means yes."

Mark chuckled. "Is that right?" He looked at Julia who was shaking her head at the both of them.

"Jesse, let's get your dad to Aunt Barb and Uncle Glen's cabin. I'm sure he's tired."

"Okay."

Jesse led the way with Mark trailing behind Julia. He wouldn't let her carry anything so she walked empty-handed down the narrow dirt trail that led to the cabin.

"Barb and Glen are sleeping," she whispered to Mark as they entered the dimly lit kitchen/dining room area. "You're in the back bedroom and the bathroom is right across the way."

Mark set down his suitcase. "I'm kind of keyed up from all the driving. Would it be okay if we just sat outside for a while?"

"Sure. Would you like something to eat first?"

Mark shook his head. "I stopped at a fast-food place on the way up."

"All right. . .well, let's all go sit on the pier for a while. It's so peaceful out there."

"Yeah, and I'll get my fishing pole!" Jesse declared. Then he stopped short. "Hey, do fish sleep?"

Julia furrowed her brows. "I don't know." She turned to Mark. "Do they?"

He smiled, looking amused. "Naw, fish don't sleep."

"Good!" Jesse was gone in an instant, promising to bring a flashlight along with his tackle box.

Julia sighed as she and Mark stepped out of the cabin. "He'll be up all night at this rate."

Mark chuckled. "Well, maybe he'll catch something and it'll be worth it."

The narrow dirt path continued from the Frenches' cabin on down to the lake. The moon was only a half-sliver in the sky, but a relatively sufficient guiding light.

"There's a long bench on the end of the pier," Julia said, pointing straight ahead. She noticed that Mark hadn't even changed after work—he wore a light-blue dress shirt, navy pants, and fine leather shoes.

"How's everything going at Weakland Management?" she couldn't help but ask. "Any new developments?"

Mark looked at his watch. "Fifteen minutes."

Julia paused, standing in the middle of the pier. "What?"

"Fifteen minutes. I was wondering how long it would be before you brought up the subject of work. You waited a whole fifteen minutes. Good for you."

Julia tossed her head in indignation, putting her hands on her hips. "How would you like to take a swim, Mark Henley?"

Beneath the moonglow, she saw him grin. "If I go swimming, Juli-bean, you're coming with me."

She considered the challenge, smiling all the while. Oh! but she would like nothing better than to push Mark into the freezing cold lake with his dress clothes on! Of course, if he pulled her in with him, that wouldn't be so fun.

She sighed a dramatic breath of resignation. "All right, you win. . .for now."

Mark chuckled. "Know what? I can tell we're going to have a great time this weekend."

Julia was still shaking her head at him when Jesse returned, fishing pole in one hand, his tackle box in the other. "Hey, wanna see all my lures?" he asked Mark enthusiastically.

"Sure."

Mark held the flashlight, while Jesse pulled out each lure, one by one, explaining where and when he got it and how many fish he had caught with it.

Julia looked on, marveling at the scene before her. Mark was here. . .with her. . .and Jesse! The makings of a family right before her eyes. But what would become of it?

Julia pushed her thoughts away and glanced out over the still, dark lake. She was afraid to pay the price for dreaming. She couldn't afford it.

"Hey, Juli, you falling asleep on us over there?"

She smiled from where she sat on the bench at the end of the pier. "No, I was just thinking."

"No thinking allowed. You're on vacation, remember?"

Julia laughed softly as Mark walked over and sat down beside her. Jesse was sitting a few feet away, his legs dangling off the pier while he fished.

"This is almost perfect, isn't it, Juli?" Mark murmured, his arm stretched out behind her, resting on the top of the bench.

He turned to her and, though Julia couldn't make out his features clearly, she sensed the intent expression on his face. He's going to kiss me, she thought, her heart pounding in anticipation and, yes, even longing.

"Hey, are you sure that fish don't sleep?" Jesse called over his shoulder, breaking the intensity of the moment.

Julia didn't know whether to feel disappointed or relieved.

Mark was chuckling under his breath. "I've never known fish to sleep, Jesse," he teased the boy, "but, in any case, I'm sure you just woke them up."

"Good!"

Mark chuckled again and even Julia had to laugh. It was obvious, Mark and Jesse were going to get along just fine.

They stayed on the pier for a good hour, until the wind felt cold and Julia's eyelids refused to stay open. She and Jesse said good-night to Mark at the Frenches' cabin and then climbed the hill to their own. Inside, Julia helped Jesse put away his fishing gear and then insisted that he wash up before going to bed.

"I like him, Mom," Jesse said, twirling the bar of soap between his hands.

"That's good," Julia said as a yawn escaped her. "Hurry up, Jess. I'm tired."

The boy finished in the bathroom and then Julia planted a good-night kiss on his cheek. She watched him walk into the bedroom next to her parents' and knew that he'd be up bright and early in the morning. He would most likely want to see his dad first thing.

A wry grin curved her mouth, and she hoped Mark was prepared to be awakened in about five hours.

∾

The Fourth of July dawned bright and beautiful. The sun shimmered off the lake and the treetops waved in the warm breeze. Just as Julia had predicted, Jesse awoke and ran down to the Frenches' cabin to see his father. Barb came in about eight o'clock, chuckling all about it.

"And Mark seems impressed with Jesse, too," she said, looking pleased. "What a blessing."

Julia just nodded as she stood at the sink, drying the breakfast dishes while her mother washed them. Her father had been stomping around the kitchen all morning and she feared a positive reply would be like waving a red flag in front of an angry bull. Finally Roy announced that he and Mark were going to have "a talk" and, with that, he left the cabin.

Julia glanced at her mother, feeling a good measure of alarm. "Should you stop him?"

"I should say not!" Caroline exclaimed and Barb agreed.

"Glen can keep Jesse occupied. It's high time Mark and your father had a talk." Caroline seemed momentarily pensive. "You know, Juli, after Mark left, there were those times when you were up in your bedroom crying your heart out, and all of us, your brothers included, felt just wretched for you. But your father. . .well, I think he felt it even more deeply than the boys and me. I believe, in fact, that he was just as hurt as you were when Mark left. He thought of Mark as one of his own boys. So much so that he was willing to leave his service station to him—and that business meant a lot to your father."

Caroline washed a plate, still looking thoughtful. "But what I remember most," she continued, "is that your father would stand at your closed door, Juli, with tears falling down his cheeks. He was crying right along with you, but he didn't know how to comfort you because he was so hurt himself."

Julia had never heard this before and she was touched to tears. No wonder her father's anger at Mark had matched her own. No wonder he was so unwilling to let Mark back into their lives. He had been affected the same way she had. The only difference was, Julia knew the love of the Savior now, her father did not. Forgiving Mark hadn't come easily for her, but it had been possible because of Christ.

Barb sniffed, looking teary-eyed herself. "Oh, I just pray that Mark and Roy can work things out."

Julia nodded, still struggling to put her own emotions to rest.

Many long minutes passed, and she resumed drying the dishes and putting them away. Then she tuned in to Barb's merry chatter about the picnic this afternoon. And then, of course, the fireworks tonight.

"Oh, this will be so much fun," Barb crooned. Together the two older ladies sat down at the kitchen table to prepare the menu.

Listening to her mother and Barb, Julia had to smile. They were planning a veritable feast.

Then suddenly she spotted Mark and her father walking casually toward Mark's car. "Mom. . .?" Julia wondered if her father were insisting that Mark leave, except he didn't have his suitcase and. . .and they were both smiling!

"What is it, dear?" Caroline came to stand beside her.

"Look."

"Oh. . ."

Barb was at Julia's other side now. She chuckled at the sight of Mark and Roy lifting the Impala's hood. "Looks like a budding friendship to me."

"Yes, and now the real discussion begins," Caroline added with a satisfied smile. "I've heard it before and it's amazing what men can talk about beneath the hood of a car."

Amusement danced in Barb's blue eyes. "Solve the world's problems, do they?"

"And then some!"

The women all laughed. Julia was downright amazed—if Mark could win her father, he must be sincere. Perhaps even trustworthy. After all, Roy McGowan was no fool—not even for a refurbished '66 Chevy Impala!

We'll see, she told herself. We'll just see. . .

❧

By the time Mark and Roy came in from outside it was after noon, and Jesse and Glen were sitting at the kitchen table, eating sandwiches. The party didn't start till three o'clock, so the "boys" insisted upon a "snack."

"Are there more of those?" Roy asked, nodding at Jesse's plate. Then he tossed Mark a clean rag with which he could wipe off his hands. "I'm starving."

"Coming right up," Caroline replied. "You too, Mark?"

"Yes, thanks."

Julia couldn't resist sending Mark a questioning look. She was eager to learn what happened between him and her father. But when Mark smiled at her, sending back an affectionate wink, Julia decided things must have gone well.

The rest of the afternoon was as pleasurable as the weather. Warm friends and sunny conversations. Glen took Mark, Jesse, and two of the neighbor boys for a ride in his motorboat. They cruised around the lake and, once they returned, all "the guys" sat on the pier and fished until it was time to fire up the grill.

After a supper of grilled hamburgers and bratwurst, baked beans, Jell-O, and chocolate brownies, the adults settled into lawn chairs near the lake and visited while the kids lit sparklers on the beach. One of the neighbor girls was in high school so she was awarded the job of holding the matches; however, adult super-vision wasn't ever far away. Then, later, Mark and Jesse would set off the fireworks.

Julia noticed that Mark fit right in. The guests liked him and Jesse had already come to adore him. Mark was suddenly his hero and, likewise, Mark seemed captivated by his son.

Watching this, Julia had to admit she felt a stab of jealousy. But then she imagined how complicated it could have been if Mark and Jesse hadn't taken a liking to each other. She would have felt badly for the both of them, so she allowed herself the joy of witnessing father and son together, having a good time.

"Want a roasted marshmallow, Juli?" Mark asked, sitting in the lawn chair next to her. "Jesse's cooking."

She smiled. "Sure."

Mark nodded and cupped his hands around his mouth. "Make one for your mom, Jess," he called.

"Okay, *Dad.*"

The way Jesse said "dad" was so cute it made Julia grin. It was a new word in his vocabulary, and he used it whenever he got the chance.

"Having fun?" Mark asked, turning to Julia.

"Yes, I'm enjoying myself today."

"Me, too. Especially since your dad and I talked things out. He hasn't said he forgives me—I think he's going to make me prove myself." Mark shrugged. "But I accept the challenge. Making amends with you and your family is that important to me."

Julia appreciated the remark. "I'm glad."

Mark sighed, looking around. "It's pretty up here."

She nodded.

"Do you get to come here often?"

"Oh, maybe a few times each summer."

"I think I'd be up here every weekend."

Julia shrugged. "I'm often on-call during the weekends."

"Which is going to change," Mark said emphatically.

She looked at him, raising questioning brows.

Mark sat back in his chair and crossed his legs. He wore faded blue jeans and a red-and-white striped T-shirt—very appropriate for the holiday. On his feet, he wore the latest, fashionable brand of athletic shoes, causing Jesse to want a pair just like "Dad's."

"Listen, Juli," he began, "you've got three employees, two of which can take turns carrying that pager."

"But—"

"And Jon Maxwell's department is going to help. In fact, Bill decided that Jon is going to—"

"He's going to. . .what?" Julia asked with a frown.

Mark paused. "Forget it, Juli. Let's not talk about work any more."

Julia opened her mouth to protest, but then Jesse presented her with a charred marshmallow.

"Here you go, Mom."

"Thanks," she said, looking at the burned thing. "You know, Jesse, I prefer my roasted marshmallows a golden brown. Could you cook another one for me?"

Jesse shrugged. "Okay."

Being a good sport, Mark volunteered to eat the burned one.

"Now, what about Jon's department?" Julia wanted to know after Jesse walked back toward the brick barbeque pit.

"Juli, let's not discuss it now. There will be plenty of time next week for us to discuss all the changes, all right?"

"All the changes. . .?" Julia's voice trailed off as she considered what those words meant. "I missed a lot this past week, huh?" Insecurity suddenly gripped her heart.

"You didn't miss anything you can't catch up on next week."

Julia folded her arms across her chest and turned pensive. Jon Maxwell had his Masters Degree; she only had her Bachelors.

"Quit worrying, Juli," Mark whispered. "I'm sorry I even brought up the subject of work. You were actually beginning to relax."

She sighed and had to admit Mark was right. She had been slowly unwinding from all the day-to-day stress, but now it seemed pressing again.

"Lighten up, Juli," Mark teased her, "or I'll throw you in the lake."

She bit the inside of her cheek in an effort to keep from smiling. How could Mark do that to her? From worry to amusement in a single bound.

She looked over at him, meeting Mark's gaze. "You know? I'm glad you came up here," she said softly.

He smiled back in a way that made Julia's heart hammer. "So am I," he replied. "So am I."

Chapter 13

The next day, Friday, was as pleasant as its predecessor. Mark learned that there was a public stable off the main highway and wanted to take Jesse horseback riding. Jesse, of course, was all for the idea, especially since it was Mark who suggested it.

Then Mark insisted that Julia come along. He seemed to be working very hard at including her, and she appreciated his efforts. After all, he could demand that, since she'd had their son to herself for eleven years, he was entitled to at least a few hours. But he didn't. In fact, Mark was a perfect gentleman the entire afternoon.

Later that evening, after supper, Jesse fell asleep early. Julia's parents and the Frenches were playing their own simplified version of bridge at the kitchen table, which left Julia and Mark to themselves.

"Would you like to go for a walk?" she asked. "I'm feeling kind of restless."

"I'm feeling exhausted," Mark replied, looking sheepish, "but I'll go for a walk anyway."

Julia smiled as they left the cabin and slowly walked down the gravel road. The air was mild and the sun was just beginning its descent in the western sky. There was still a good hour of daylight left.

"Are you really too tired, Mark?" Julia hoped he didn't feel obligated.

He shook his head. "No, I'm fine. In fact, I think the walk will do me some good. Stretch out my leg muscles. I have a feeling I'm going to be a little sore tomorrow."

"Sorry to hear that, cowboy," she quipped with a teasing smile.

Mark's expression was one of chagrin and Julia had to laugh. "You sure are sassy."

"Yes, so you've told me before."

They turned off the gravel road and onto the pavement of another, seldom-used road. On either side, a dense grove of trees grew so tall they seemed to touch the clouds. Julia inhaled deeply. The air felt so clean and fresh.

"You like it up here, don't you?"

She nodded. "I wish I'd make myself come up here more often."

Mark seemed to consider her comment for several long moments as he gazed around them, wearing an appreciative expression. Julia could tell he liked it up here, too.

"I'm having a nice holiday," Mark said at last. "And you're a lot of fun to be around."

"Thanks. So are you."

Mark smiled. "I'm glad you feel that way. I guess I'd like to think we're friends." He paused. "Hey, Juli? Can I ask you something personal?"

She shrugged. "Sure."

Mark paused once more, seemingly to collect his thoughts. Finally, he asked, "Are you romantically involved with anyone? I mean, I asked about Driscoll, but. . . well, is there someone else? Someone in your Bible study perhaps?"

Julia figured he was asking because of Jesse. "No, I'm not involved with anyone."

"How come?"

"What?"

"How come? I mean, you're a lovely person, Juli. I'm actually surprised more men at Weakland Management aren't pestering you."

She smiled, feeling a bit embarrassed by his comment. "Oh, they used to, especially right after I started working there. But I wasn't interested in dating." She bent to pick a wild flower at the side of the road. "Relationships take so much time and effort," she said frankly, "and I just wasn't willing to make that kind of investment."

"Hmmm. . .so, let me get this straight. You haven't had a date in twelve years?"

Julia thought it over and then nodded. "Pretty pitiful, isn't it?"

Mark furrowed his brow, and Julia couldn't help but suddenly wonder if he were inquiring over her morals in order to gauge what kind of mother she'd been. Would Mark find her lacking? Did he think she was lying about not dating?

They walked for a few moments in silence and then Mark changed the subject completely.

"So how did you get interested in computers?"

"Well, after Jesse was born, I got a job as a clerk in a small computer store. I got interested in programming, so I decided to go to college. I figured programming would allow me to use some of my creativity. And it does."

Mark nodded. "Ever wish you weren't a. . .a career woman?"

Julia expelled a curt laugh. "Mark, I stopped wishing a long time ago."

His expression changed, and she sensed she'd somehow hurt his feelings. She hadn't meant to; she was just being honest.

She gave him a sweet smile, trying to console him. He smiled back then, and the tension between them vanished. They continued to walk down the road which circled around the property and ended up back on the gravel driveway. But when they reached the cabins, neither Julia nor Mark seemed to want to say good night, so they strolled down to the lake and onto the pier where they sat on the long wooden bench.

Mark stretched his arm out along the back of the bench behind her, and Julia felt warm and secure sitting so close beside him. She thought that something deep within her was awakening after being dormant for so very long. And that something, she decided, was a little frightening.

She folded her arms tightly in front of her, suddenly feeling terribly unsure of herself.

"Cold?" Mark had obviously noticed the cool breeze coming off the lake.

But Julia shook her head. "No, I'm okay."

Silence settled between them as they listened to the loons. And all the while, Julia was very aware of Mark's presence. She realized, then, that she had virtually turned off her feelings twelve years ago in effort to protect herself from ever getting hurt again. She had lied to herself, telling her heart she didn't care about Mark anymore. But, the truth was, she had loved Mark all along.

"You're awfully quiet," he remarked. "You didn't fall asleep on me, did you?" His arm fell onto her shoulder and he gave her playful shake.

Julia smiled. "I'm awake, I'm awake!"

She turned to consider him, his face just inches away, and her smile faded as an intense wave of emotion gripped her heart. Likewise, his blue eyes darkened with ardor.

"I never stopped loving you, Mark. I never stopped. . ." Tears pooled in Julia's eyes at the admission.

"Why are you crying?" Mark asked, wearing a confused frown. "What you just said is a wonderful thing. Juli?"

She was shaking her head. "But I don't want to love you."

Mark's frown deepened and there was an obvious look of hurt in his eyes, so Julia rushed on to explain.

"I'm afraid, Mark."

"Of what? Of me?" His tone sounded suddenly impatient.

"Yes! Mark, I don't want to get hurt again."

His features softened. "I won't hurt you, Juli. I've told you that already."

She swallowed the last of her emotion and wiped away an errant tear. "I'm having a hard time trusting you. I mean, I trusted you once before, and—"

"Juli, that was twelve years ago." Mark shook his head, looking exasperated. "I was nineteen and very confused. . .Juli, we've been through all this. I've apologized and you said you forgave me. What else is left?"

She chanced a look at him, then momentarily fretted, chewing on her lower lip. "What about Jesse?"

"What about him?"

She lifted her chin, remembering Mark's earlier questions about her dating experiences. "Are you going to fight me for custody?"

Mark's eyes widened as if he couldn't believe what he'd just heard. "Fight you?"

"I mean, if that's your plan I would like to know so I can prepare—"

"Julia!" He shook his head incredulously before his eyes bore into hers. "Juli, look at us. I'm sitting here with my arm around you, the moon is coming up over the lake, you just said you're still in love with me. . .we should be enjoying this moment. But instead you've poisoned it with your ridiculous suspicions!"

"I was trying to be honest with you, Mark. I was sharing my heart—"

He stood, the magic of the moment gone. "No, you weren't. You were slinging the past in my face—again."

"Not intentionally." She stood now, too. "I was merely trying to tell you my fears—so I can put them to rest." Anger suddenly overtook her emotions. "But you don't care about that, do you? All you care about is what you want, which is. . .oh!" she cried, throwing her hands in the air. "I don't even know what you want—and that's the problem!"

Even in the dimness of the evening, Julia could see Mark's eyes narrowing to dangerous slits. With hands-on-hips, she glared right back at him.

"How'd you like to go for a swim, Julia Rose McGowan?"

Her eyes widened at the question—the same she'd asked him two nights ago. She tipped her head saucily. "If I go swimming, Mark," she mimicked, "you're going with me."

He stepped forward, obviously undaunted.

"Mark, I'm serious." She pointed a warning at him. "Stay where you are."

Another step.

"I was nice to you and backed down," she said, feeling testy now since Mark seemed bent on throwing her into the lake. "I didn't push you in even though I would have loved to—Allen Edmonds and all."

One step closer.

Julia looked behind her heels then and realized that she was at the very edge of the pier. Maybe she'd jump and rob him of the satisfaction of pushing her in.

But the idea came too late. Mark suddenly grabbed her around the waist and he gave her a toss, but not before she got a good hold of his T-shirt. They both fell into the lake with a giant splash and flailing limbs.

Julia surfaced with a cry of indignation, while Mark was laughing heartily just a few feet away.

"I thought you needed to chill out, Juli," he teased her.

"Yes, well, I'll be lucky if I don't get pneumonia," she shot right back. "Then I'll have to call in sick, and you'll have to explain why I'm not at work."

"I would be honored," Mark said, feigning a stuffy English accent. He sounded like Sir Walter.

Floating on his back now, Mark looked as if he hadn't a care in the world. With her palm, Julia hit the water, sending a large splash in his direction. Her aim was perfect, but he just laughed, irritating Julia all the more.

"I'd like to see you explain, Mark," she huffed. "Explain about me, about our son. You, the Christian man who is supposedly *married*—which is another source of irritation for me, I'll have you know."

"Juli, I never told anyone I was married."

"You didn't have to since you insist upon wearing that cheap ring."

"Hey, it's not cheap!" Mark brought himself up and began treading water. "This wedding set cost me a lot of money!"

"Twelve years ago, you didn't have a lot of money."

Julia began swimming for shore. By now night had fallen and the air was especially cold now that she was soaking wet.

Mark swam up behind her and then they walked to shore side by side in the shallow part of the water. When they reached the small stretch of beach, he grabbed her elbow and turned her to face him.

"Juli," he said on a serious note, "about your trying to be honest with me—"

She pulled out of his grasp. "Don't worry," she told him, unable to conceal her irritation, "it won't happen again."

Chapter 14

Saturday arrived, another beautiful summer day. Mark took Jesse to ride the go-carts and, afterwards, to find a fast-food place for lunch. Julia refused the offer to join them since she was still smarting over last night's confrontation. Instead, she sipped her coffee on the back porch and read a book, trying to get her thoughts off Mark and their situation.

At last he and Jesse arrived back at the cabins around one o'clock. Almost immediately the two made their way down to the lake. Glen had consented to drive the motorboat while they water-skied.

Another barbeque was planned, but this time it would be family members only—and this included Mark, of course. It was to be a special picnic, since this was Julia's last full day up north. Tomorrow afternoon she would leave for home. But, instead of enjoying another sunny afternoon by the lake, Julia decided to stay in the cabin and cook up some homemade potato salad. It would save her mother some work since this was, after all, Caroline's vacation, too. On the other hand, staying inside the cabin was a nice way to avoid Mark, or so Julia had thought.

"What? Do I have to throw you in the lake again?"

Julia started at the sound of Mark's voice. "Didn't anyone ever tell you that it's not nice to sneak up on a person?"

"Who? Me?" Mark grinned. "I walked right through that back door, Juli—didn't even try to be quiet about it." His gaze went to the bowl of diced potatoes, mayonnaise, chopped celery and onion. "That looks good."

"I'm not done yet."

Mark took a finger full anyhow. "Aren't you coming out?" he asked, smacking his lips.

"Well, yes. . .I'll come out in a while," she stated on a note of resignation. "I just have to finish up here."

Mark leaned against the counter and, though she wasn't looking at him at the moment, she could feel the weight of his stare.

"Hey, Juli, let's be friends," he finally said.

She turned to look at him now, and he continued, "I have absolutely no intention of fighting you for custody of Jesse. I'm just sorry the thought ever entered your pretty head!"

She ignored Mark's attempted charm. "I'm sorry, too," she said stiffly. "Next time I'll keep my thoughts to myself."

Mark sighed. "Look, Juli, I want you to be honest and open with me. I really do. But it hurts me when you act as though I'm just waiting for the moment when I can ruin your life. That's so totally opposite of what I'm all about. The whole idea behind my trying to get in touch with you all these years was so that I could somehow right all the wrongs between us. Won't you just give me a chance?"

Julia considered what he said. "Do you really care about my feelings?"

"Of course I do."

She searched his face, his eyes—windows to the soul—and all she saw was sincerity. "You know what, Mark? I believe you. I really do."

He smiled broadly. "I'm glad to hear that. And as for the wedding ring, I've been wearing it for years, as I told you before. It's like a part of me, so I'm not taking it off."

Julia shrugged, turning back to her potato salad. She added some chopped green pepper, and began blending it in. "The decision is and always has been yours, Mark."

He leaned closer to her. "Aren't you even going to ask me why I'm being so stubborn about this?"

Julia stopped her stirring and looked at him.

"You've challenged me over lesser things."

She sighed impatiently. "You already told me why you're wearing that ring."

"I told you in part. You wouldn't let me finish."

She quieted. She'd let him finish today.

"It reminds me of you, Juli," Mark told her softly. "I never stopped loving you, either. I tried—just like you tried to stop loving me. It didn't work, though, did it? With either of us?"

Julia shook her head as Mark's soft voice and sweet words penetrated her heart.

She put down her spatula and wiped her hands on her apron. She considered Mark under careful scrutiny and, again, saw that light of sincerity in his blue eyes. Julia knew then that they were more than just sweet words.

"You mean it, don't you?"

"It pains me that you even have to ask, but, yes, I mean every word." He shook his head, looking troubled. "Oh, Juli. . ."

Mark hesitated for a moment, then pulled her into his arms. Julia couldn't deny the warmth of his embrace. It seemed to melt the years of loneliness in her life. Slowly, her arms went around his neck and she buried her face in his shirt. He smelled good, like the wind off the lake and the North Woods.

Mark's arms were around her waist, holding her tightly. "Juli, Juli," he murmured against her hair, "I've waited so long to hold you in my arms again. . .to kiss you. . ."

She heard his husky sigh, but instead of a kiss, Mark pushed her away slightly. "But we've got to be careful," he told her with a sudden, pleading look. "Do you understand?"

She understood completely. Their Christian testimony was at stake. Her father was watching them closely to see if all this talk about faith, love, and personal holiness was for real. And their co-workers would be watching, too.

Mark's smile broadened, and Julia decided that he looked relieved.

Reluctantly, she let her arms slide from his shoulders, and Mark's arms dropped from around her waist.

Just then Caroline entered the cabin and walked into the kitchen. She smiled happily. "How's the potato salad coming along, Juli? It was so nice of you to offer to do this for me."

"My pleasure. It's just about done."

"Tastes like it's already done to me," Mark said, snitching another finger full. This won him a smack on the hand with the spatula and Caroline chuckled.

"Oh, you two," she said, shaking her head at them. "You act as though you're the best of friends." Caroline's smile broadened. "Twelve years may have gone by, but some things never do change, do they?"

"Nope," Mark replied, looking over at Julia.

She met his meaningful gaze for a long moment before turning back to the potato salad. And she couldn't deny the burst of joy, permeating her heart of hearts.

❧

After the morning worship service the next day, Barb and Glen made the announcement that they were staying another week.

"We'd like Jesse to stay with us," Glen said to Julia. "You have to work all week anyway."

"Since Mark is driving back," Barb added, "we thought you could ride home with him today instead of us."

Julia looked over at her son who was frowning heavily. "Will you stay another week, Jess?"

He shook his head. "I want to go with Dad."

Mark smiled and put an arm around Jesse's chair. They were both still sitting at the kitchen table, having just finished their lunch. "Listen, Jesse," he explained, "I've got to work all week just like your mom. So, it's fishing and swimming this week for you and, boy, am I jealous!"

Jesse grinned.

"We'll come back up next weekend and get you," Mark promised. Then he looked at Julia. "How about it?"

"I'm supposed to have the pager next weekend, but I'm sure I can work something out."

Nodding, Mark looked back at his son. "We'll see you next weekend."

"I guess so." Jesse sounded doleful as he peered out at Julia. "You'll still call me every night, though, right, Mom?"

"Right."

He turned to Mark. "Will you call me, too?"

"Sure."

At last Jesse seemed pacified. He was staying.

Julia loaded her luggage into the backseat of the Impala feeling a bit melancholy. She didn't want to leave Jesse—she didn't even want to leave. This vacation had done wonders for her mind and spirit, and now it would be difficult to go back to Weakland Management and confront the daily routine.

And then, of course, there was Mark. It would be awkward to work with him, and though she loved him, she wondered if she could trust him. To Julia, trusting meant letting go and, in this case, it meant letting go of all those heart matters she had reined in so tightly, both at work and in her personal life. Could she really let them go so easily?

Julia hugged her parents good-bye, then the Frenches, and finally Jesse. "I love you." She planted a kiss on his cheek.

"Love you, too, Mom," Jesse replied automatically. "Bye, Dad." He looked up at Mark adoringly.

"Good-bye for now." Mark embraced his son, and Julia wondered if it was the first time ever. Then, in a manly effort to conceal his emotion, she watched as Mark tousled the boy's hair. "See you next week."

Julia's heart lurched as the two pulled apart. Father and son, they had missed so much of each other's life.

Mark turned toward her then, and she saw a tumult of emotions cross his face. "Ready?" he asked.

She nodded.

With family members waving good-bye, they pulled away from the cabins and drove down the gravel road.

Julia was silent for the first mile. So was Mark. In fact, they both seemed to be struggling with the same sort of things—regret from the past, apprehension for the future.

Finally, she looked over at Mark and said, "I'm really sorry that I didn't try to find you years ago and tell you about Jesse. I should have. You had every right to know about him, but I was. . .well. . ."

"Juli, don't bring that up again. The past is dead and gone. So forget it, okay?"

"No, it's not okay. The past might be dead and gone for you, but I'm still wrestling with the beast."

Silence again for the next few miles. Then, finally, it was Mark who spoke. "You know, Juli, I think that's your biggest problem. You won't let go of the past."

"My biggest problem?" she asked, lifting a brow. "You mean there are more?"

Mark glanced at her. "And you're defensive, too."

Julia swallowed a tart reply, knowing it would only prove his point. But as she stewed in silence, it occurred to her that Mark was right. She knew she wasn't "letting go." Let go, let God, she reminded herself.

Mark sighed wearily. "I suppose we're at war again, huh?"

"No," Julia replied softly. "In fact, I agree with you, Mark. You hit my problem right on the head. But, believe it or not, I'm working on it."

She chanced a look at him, saw his astonished expression and almost laughed out loud. There's quite a lot to say for blatant honesty, she thought, if it leaves Mark Henley speechless!

∼❧∼

Two and a half hours later, they stopped for supper at a little restaurant called Buckey's, just outside of New London. It was a quaint little diner that served up family style meals, complete with homemade pie for dessert.

Then it was back on the highway.

It was after seven o'clock when Mark pulled up in front of Julia's apartment complex. "I'll help you with your luggage."

"Thanks."

She had wanted to say that it wasn't necessary for him to help her since she had been carrying her own luggage for years, but Julia was practicing the fine art of conciliation.

"Where do you want them?" he asked entering the foyer, a suitcase in each hand.

"Would you carry them upstairs?"

"Sure."

Climbing the stairs, Mark stopped just outside the living room and deposited the suitcases in the hallway which led to the two bedrooms. "Nice place," he remarked, looking around.

Julia smiled. "Thank you. It's nothing fancy, but it's home."

"It feels like a home. . .except for the weird art hanging on your walls." Mark tipped his head to one side, examining the painting over her couch. "What is this supposed to be?"

Julia laughed. "It's not supposed to be anything. It's just the colorful product of the artist's imagination."

Mark was shaking his head. "I always think a painting is supposed to look like something. A beach, a vase of flowers, some historical building or landmark. . . something like that."

Julia said nothing but still sported a grin.

Mark turned to her then. "Guess we'll never agree on artwork."

"Guess not."

He was looking at her so intently now that Julia's pulse quickened.

"I had a great weekend," Mark said, taking a step closer.

"Me, too," Julia replied, gazing back at him and marveling at how he could affect her so.

"Well," he said, looking down at the carpet, "I'll see you tomorrow."

Julia nodded.

Mark walked down the stairs to the foyer and Julia followed. "Oh, and about tomorrow," he said, his hand on the knob of the heavy, wood-paneled front door. He looked at her with a softness in his blue eyes. Then he touched her cheek with the back of his knuckles. "Just remember I love you, okay?"

She frowned. "What do you mean? What's going to happen tomorrow?" She tried to keep the worry out of her voice.

"Juli, you're just going have to trust me on this one—and I mean really trust me."

She swallowed hard. "But, Mark—"

"We'll talk tomorrow, all right?"

"But—"

Leaning forward, Mark's lips touched hers ever so briefly. It was, however, long enough to cause Julia to forget her immediate thoughts.

He grinned. "Good night, Juli-bean."

After his car pulled away from the curb, Julia let out an exasperated moan. Mark had kissed her to shut her up.

Worst of all, it had worked!

Chapter 15

Monday morning's meeting was in Mark's office, since it used to be the conference room and since it was the most spacious "office" currently in the building. Mark had informed her about the meeting just before breakfast, though he wouldn't say what it was about.

Entering Mark's office now, Julia immediately noticed Bill Weakland and Jerry Fein sitting across from Mark's desk. Then she spotted another man whom she didn't recognize sitting in a chair beside Bill.

"C'mon in, Juli," Mark said, wearing a serious expression; however, there was a softer light in his eyes. "And, please, close the door."

Following Mark's instructions, Julia walked over to the vacant chair which was positioned at the foot of his desk.

Then Mark made the introductions. "You know Jerry and Bill, of course, and this is Frank Houston. He's with the FBI. Frank. . .Julia McGowan."

The well-groomed man, dressed in a dark suit, stood politely, and Julia noticed that he wasn't very tall. "Pleased to meet you, Miss McGowan."

She nodded and shook his hand, wondering why someone from the FBI would be here at Weakland Management—and why he'd sit in on this meeting.

She looked expectantly at Mark, then at Bill.

"While Mark was browsing through your programs, Juli," Bill began, "he stumbled across something that didn't make a whole lot of sense. . .at first. He came to me with it, and I had Jerry do an audit. Our findings were shocking. Here, take a look at these."

Bill handed her a stack of green-and-white statements, and Julia looked each one over. Her trained, technical eye scanned the names, addresses, column alignments, and balances in the bottom boxes. It seemed to her that the statements had printed out just fine.

"What's the problem?" she asked at last.

"The arithmetic is the problem," Jerry Fein interjected, earning a sharp glance from Mark. He closed his mouth and sat back in his chair, folding his arms over his chest.

"Juli, the percentage that Weakland Management charges its customers in commission fees doesn't equal the amount charged on the statements." Pulling out a small calculator, Mark demonstrated his point. "The figures are off by about one and a half percent."

"Actually, they're off by a little more," Jerry said, "and it hardly seems significant. However, when you consider the millions of dollars this company invests, that extra percentage adds up to quite a tidy sum."

Julia was still peering at the statements. "How can that be? That particular software package isn't capable of what you just described."

"No, but the program you created is," Mark interjected.

Julia stared at Mark in disbelief. "The one I created. . . ?"

He nodded. "You loaded it onto my PC along with all the other programs. I found it, as Bill said, while I was 'browsing.'"

"But that's not a live program," Julia replied, referring to the one she was working on for the portfolio managers. "It's still in the developmental stages."

"I didn't know about this program," Bill said.

Julia turned to him. "I had every intention of coming to you with a software presentation, but I hadn't worked out all the bugs."

"Maybe not, but you certainly worked out a nifty way of giving yourself a little spending money," Fein stated sarcastically. "Your computer program sets up bogus accounts and then transfers money right into them."

"What?" Julia couldn't believe what she was hearing.

"Juli, watch what happens when we post the payments off these statements." Turning to the computer, Mark showed her how, instead of creating a credit on the accounts, since the statements were overcharging clients, the balances were zero. The extra funds were being automatically deposited into bogus accounts.

Julia's jaw dropped slightly.

"So what we want to know, Miss McGowan," Frank Houston said, "is to what extent you're involved."

Julia had come around to stand behind Mark so she could see the computer screen better, and she was still staring at it in awe. "I. . .I don't know anything about this."

"Come now, Julia," Bill said testily, "you wrote the software. How can you not be involved?"

After a long, pensive moment, Julia shrugged helplessly.

"Did you have a nice vacation?" Jerry Fein asked with a hint of disdain in his voice.

Julia put her hands on her hips. "I went up north, Jerry, not on a shopping spree to Paris!"

"Can you prove it?"

"That's enough," Mark told him.

Julia clenched her jaw angrily. Then she glanced at Bill Weakland who had clouds of suspicion in his eyes as he looked back at her. Seeing it, Julia's indignation turned to a heartfelt pain. *He thinks I'm stealing money from the company,* she realized. *After all my long hours and hard work. . .*

"Sit down, Juli," Mark said gently.

Still looking at Bill, she shook her head. "I think I'll go call my attorney instead."

"You need an attorney, Julia?" Bill asked sardonically.

She lifted her chin. "I do if you're going to accuse me of theft."

Mark stood. "No one is accusing anybody." He looked at Bill who dropped his gaze from Julia.

"Miss McGowan," Frank Houston began, "all accusations aside, the facts remain. Funds are being embezzled from Weakland Management, and the perpetrator is using your computer program to do it. You are, of course, the prime suspect."

Apprehension shot through Julia as she slowly looked over at Mark. He was staring blankly at the statements on his desk with his lips pursed thoughtfully. Did he think she was guilty, too?

Then she recalled what he had said last night. *Just remember I love you.*

Yeah, right, she thought cynically. *I'll be in jail and he'll take Jesse!*

Julia entertained the thought that, perhaps, Mark had even set her up in order to take what he wanted and to get her out of his way and another blast of panic left her unable to reason.

"The idea does seem rather ludicrous, though," Houston said, and Julia momentarily wondered if she had spoken out loud. Then she realized that the man was referring to her as a suspect. "Whoever is doing the embezzling is somehow making transfers from the account here to another bank and, since one of those transactions occurred from Miss McGowan's terminal and—"

"What?" she asked incredulously.

"It's true, Juli," Mark said. "We've investigated it thoroughly. Your PC was used to make an illegal transfer. The other two were made from the CPU room. Altogether, there were three transfers made in the last two months and the dates coincide to the dates that you were on-call. Furthermore, your initials and password are all over everything."

"I don't believe it," Julia murmured.

"I guess my thoughts are," Houston continued, "that if you were going to embezzle money, Miss McGowan, you'd be intelligent enough to use someone else's PC, initials, and password and not your own." He looked around. "She's much too obvious a target."

"I agree," Mark said, but Julia couldn't bring herself to look at him. "Juli has access to everyone's passwords. Why would she use her own?"

"Perhaps because this is the very guise Juli had hoped for all along," Fein replied suggestively.

Julia glared at him for a long moment before looking over at Mark. "Why can't we trace the three money transfers?" she asked, struggling to keep her voice calm and even.

"We've tried that already," he replied. "But the accounts that received the transfers were already closed. We'll have to do a little more digging. Why don't you sit down, Juli, so we can discuss a plan of action?"

Reluctantly, she sat.

"Bill? You wanted to begin?"

He nodded. "Basically, you have two choices, Juli. You can resign from Weakland Management or you can step down from your managerial position." He glanced at Mark. "I'm in favor of terminating your employment—"

"What about my idea, Bill?" Mark interjected.

"I don't know. . ."

Julia felt sick as she thought over Bill's ultimatum. After all these years of faithful service, how could he think she'd steal money from the company?

Then, stubbornly, she made up her mind. "I'll resign, thank you very much." She stood and turned for the door.

"Hold on, Juli," Mark said, grabbing her upper arm. She shrugged out of his grasp, and he gave her a curious look. "Let's not overreact, here, all right?" He turned to Bill. "If Juli is innocent, which I know she is—which Frank thinks she is—how is her resignation going to help? Why don't we tap her resources as a programmer instead—so we can find the real culprit?"

"I don't think so." She glared at Bill, swallowing down the last of her indignation. "For years I've dedicated myself to Weakland Management," she said in a fierce but steady tone. "I've sacrificed time with my son—with my family—so that I could make sure things were running smoothly here. I've done over and above for this company, and my track record proves it! But you, Bill, are free to think what you'd like."

With that she left Mark's office, willing herself not to slam the door.

Twenty minutes later, she deposited her letter of resignation on Bill Weakland's desk. He wasn't in his office and, as she passed by, she noticed that the door to Mark's office was still closed.

Back in Information Systems, she said nothing to her employees after she telephoned for a security guard. She knew the rules stated that a guard had to watch employees, resigned or terminated, pack their things. Julia was certain that she was no exception. The security guard would also have to escort her from the building. Then, later, someone would have to come for her company PC and modem at home. It was all very humiliating.

"Your services won't be necessary after all. You may return to your own department. Thank you." Julia looked up when she heard Bill Weakland's voice. Next she watched the security guard leave her office, after which Bill closed the door.

She stopped packing her desk.

"I came to apologize," he said stiffly. "I can't deny that you have an outstanding history with Weakland Management." He took a deep breath. "I would like you to rethink your resignation. Take a couple of days if you must."

"And if I stay?"

"If you stay, you'll be offered a new position. Because of the situation, you can't run IS. Things need to change, and Mark has some very good thoughts on the subject. I think they'll work."

Julia folded her arms. "But you think I'm stealing money."

"Look, Julia, *someone* is stealing money, and if this person isn't caught soon, I could be brought up on criminal charges. As owner of Weakland Management, I could be found personally responsible for the stolen money. Fortunately, I informed the authorities before any clients filed complaints with the DA's office. But if the public finds out before we can correct the problem. . ." Bill shook his head and sighed wearily. "Reputation is everything in this business and the slightest murmur against us will be critical."

Julia chewed her lower lip thoughtfully.

"Why don't we go back upstairs and discuss this situation, and your new position, with Mark. I hired him for his ideas and he's full of them."

Julia softened, sensing that Bill was under an enormous amount of pressure. Over the years, she'd had the utmost respect for him, and it was hard to see him bowing beneath this burden.

"All right," she said at last, "I'll agree to, at least, a discussion."

She followed Bill out of her office and managed a smile for her employees. She turned to her assistant. "Angela, continue to cover for me, okay? I'll be back in a little while."

Angela nodded and the look on her face spoke of her relief. Obviously she'd sensed that something was amiss and the security officer had only confirmed it.

Julia locked her office door and then continued to follow Bill to the elevators. As she waited beside him for the car, her thoughts turned to Mark. It was most likely because of his influence that Bill apologized. In all the years she worked for him, Julia could never recall Bill Weakland apologizing to anyone—except, perhaps, an irate client.

Then she remembered back to when Mark first told her to be careful and lock up her belongings and her office door. He must have suspected that something like this was going on then, and suddenly Julia felt guilty for ever imagining Mark would set her up so she'd go to jail. How hurt he'd be if he knew that, while he had thought the best of her, she had thought the worst of him. She had accused him of everything from wanting to break her heart again to fighting her for custody of Jesse. And even with the evidence stacked against her, Mark believed she was innocent.

Julia and Bill rode the elevator in silence and then walked down the hallway to Mark's office. He smiled as they came in.

"Did things get straightened out?"

Bill nodded curtly. "Julia has agreed to hear your ideas, Mark."

"Good."

Julia gave him a smile, feeling quite humbled. Then she noticed that Jerry Fein and Frank Houston were gone. "Where are the other two?"

"They went back to work," Mark replied. "Frank said he'll check in with us in a few days." He pulled a chair over and sat down. "Ready to hear my ideas, Juli?"

"Ready as I'll ever be."

Mark grinned. "What do you think about an Operations Department?"

Julia lifted an inquiring brow. "Operations?"

Mark nodded. "It'll be a brand-new department here at Weakland Management, and you would be the one to implement it."

"What about my current department?"

"Bill can select someone else to take it over."

Julia shrugged, not exactly thrilled with the Operations idea. She thought it was something of a setback, as far as her career. Still, she understood that, in order to clear herself of any wrongdoing, she would have to accept the changes. It was either that or resign, which was still a possibility.

"Now about our new Operations Department. . ."

Julia listened for the next hour as Mark explained his ideas. The position wasn't anything she would ever apply for since there wasn't any programming involved. She would be working primarily with the hardware and only monitoring the software. She was not to work with any of the programs themselves. She could only advise from a distance.

"It's for your own protection," Mark explained.

Julia understood. If she wasn't using the computer system and the embezzling continued, she couldn't be a suspect. Furthermore, the thief wouldn't be able to use her as a cover.

"What do you say, Julia?" Bill asked.

She looked at him, then at Mark, weighing her options. She wasn't exactly strapped for cash. If she resigned, she'd have about five weeks coming in vacation pay. She had a savings account and during the summer months she wouldn't have to pay the tuition for Jesse's private Christian day school. Perhaps she and Jesse would make it until she found another place of employment.

On the other hand, she wasn't quite ready to give up her career with Weakland

Management—not when Mark and Bill were offering her a chance to clear her name. Besides, she had a lot of time invested in this company.

"Juli? What do you think?" Mark widened his gaze and nodded slightly as if it was the decision he wanted her to make.

Julia smiled. "Yes, all right. I'll give it a go."

Chapter 16

"I almost had a heart attack when you told Bill Weakland off this morning!" Mark exclaimed. He collapsed onto Julia's couch with a throaty moan. "Here I had been tiptoeing around Bill, negotiating, mediating. . .and then you tell him off!"

"Well, it's not as though I planned it," Julia stated in her own defense.

Mark relented. "I know." He grinned. "You're just as sassy as they come, that's all."

Shaking her head at him, Julia smiled and set down her purse and attaché case. They had just walked in, having eaten dinner at a local Greek restaurant. "Should we call Jesse now?" she asked, taking off her red blazer and throwing it carelessly over the other end of the couch.

"Give me a few minutes. . .I'm exhausted."

Still smiling, Julia sat in the adjacent swivel-rocker. She was filled to the gills after devouring a Gyro sandwich with the works, and now she was feeling like a beached whale. But, overeating aside, the evening had been a very pleasant one.

"Thanks for dinner," Julia murmured.

"My pleasure."

A few minutes of amicable silence passed during which Julia couldn't help but consider Mark as he lay stretched out on her couch. There was a placid expression on his face—a face that was tanned with just a hint of golden stubble around his jawline and chin. A lock of blond hair had fallen rakishly onto his forehead, and his chest, beneath the light blue dress shirt and blue-and-tan speckled tie, rose and fell slowly, methodically. Then he started to snore.

"Hey! You're not falling asleep, are you?"

"No! No. . .of course not," Mark replied a little too quickly. "I'm just resting my eyes."

Julia chuckled. Who did he think he was fooling?

Then Mark cleared his throat and sat up, among the living again. His gaze met hers with blue intensity. She smiled back.

"Honestly, Juli," he sighed, "I thought you'd hate me right about now. I thought that you'd somehow blame me for what happened today. I worried that everything good between us would fall to pieces." Mark sighed once again. "I didn't sleep a wink last night."

Julia's heart went out to him, and she couldn't bring herself to confess that she'd nearly succumbed to all he had feared.

"Mark," she said softly, "I don't blame you at all. And thanks so much for believing in me. With the evidence stacked against me, you could have easily thought the worst."

He shook his head. "I could never believe the worst of you. No matter what."

Touched to the core of her being, Julia smiled. She sat there, looking at Mark, unable to speak. Then, needing something to dispel her discomfort, she stood and picked up the cordless phone. "Ready to call Jesse?"

Mark nodded and she dialed the number to her parents' cabin from memory. Jesse answered at the other end.

"Hi, Mom. I knew it was going to be you."

"Your father is here, too."

"Good. Can I talk to him?"

Feeling a tad slighted, though it was short-lived, Julia passed the telephone to Mark.

"Hi, Jesse. . ."

While Mark chatted with their son, Julia kicked off her heals and walked stocking-footed into the small kitchen. She set a kettle on the stove for some tea. . .perhaps peppermint, she decided, to help digest all that food she'd consumed.

She yawned, only half-listening to Mark answering what had to be a barrage of questions from Jesse. The water boiled and she poured it into a mug, adding a tea bag and carried it back into the living room.

"I agree, Jesse, and I think that'll probably happen someday."

Sitting, Julia wondered over Mark's grave expression. She hoped Jesse wasn't getting too personal. Perhaps she'd have to talk to him about that.

"Yes, I do, Jesse. Very much." Mark's voice was soft. Then suddenly he looked at Julia and smiled "I'm going to hand you back to your mom, okay? Okay."

Mark shook his head, still smiling, and gave Julia the phone.

She and Jesse conversed for a few minutes and then Julia shut off the phone and set it on the coffee table.

"It rained all day up there," Mark said with a smile, "so Jesse had eight hours to. . .think."

"So I gathered."

Mark just chuckled. "The kid's a thinker, that's for sure. Must be like his mother."

Smiling, Julia took a sip of her tea but then remembered her manners. "I'm sorry, Mark, would you like a cup of tea? Or a soda? Anything?"

Mark shook his head. "No, I should be leaving."

He stood and Julia set down her mug before following him to the front door.

"What were you and Jesse talking about?" she couldn't help asking.

Mark considered her for a long moment, his lips pursed in contemplation. Finally, he said, "Jesse told me about his friend Sam and how his parents were divorced. Jesse said that Sam has to spend alternate weekends with each parent and he wondered if we were going to do that to him."

"What did you say?" Julia asked in a whispered voice.

"I told Jesse I had to talk to you." He gave her a gentle smile. "Guess you and I have a lot of talking to do."

"Yes, I suppose we do."

"When you're ready."

Julia lifted surprised brows. "When I'm ready? What do you mean?" The question wasn't defensive, just curious.

Mark chucked her under the chin. "I mean, you've got enough stress in your life right now without me adding to it. There's time ahead to make decisions. But I promise, I'll never make any unyielding demands on you regarding our son. In fact, I plan to support you. . .him. But there's time to talk about all of that."

Julia felt grateful to hear he wouldn't push her. "I appreciate your sensitivity, Mark. I really do. And, yes, we'll talk later."

He gave her an affectionate wink.

"One more thing?" she asked softly, when he opened the front door.

"Shoot."

Julia cleared her throat, forcing herself to speak of the fear that was steadily growing in her heart. "Could I go to jail? I mean, what if the embezzling stops now? What if the thief isn't ever apprehended?"

Mark was shaking his head. "You're not going to jail. I won't let that happen. Besides, Houston said that since someone has gone to a lot of trouble to steal this money, he or she is not going to give up easily."

Julia nodded thoughtfully. "The love of money is the root of all evil."

"You got it. And don't worry. I'm going to do everything in my power to protect you."

"I love you, Mark," she whispered.

"I love you, too. Ever since I was seventeen."

Julia smiled.

❧

The following morning, Mark sent a memo to all employees, announcing the changes within the company. "Angela Davis has been promoted to the Director of Information Systems," it stated, "while Julia McGowan has been named Director of Operations, a brand-new department."

"I'm impressed, Juli," Stacie said later as she watched the mahogany "pod" being erected in the area which would house Operations. The pod was an octagonal thing that enclosed four spacious workstations. Similarly, the portfolio managers worked out of a pod since it enabled communication between them without having to leave their workstations or the happenings in the stock market.

Stacie looked at Julia. "I heard from Ken that you got a little heated at the meeting yesterday and stormed out of the office." Stacie lifted a winged brow. "They didn't give you what you wanted, so you fought to get what you deserved."

Julia frowned slightly. "That's not what happened, Stacie. It was a misunderstanding. That's all. I overreacted."

"And you got a promotion? How amazing." Her expression said she didn't believe a word of it. "If you had overreacted, Juli, we would not be standing here on the third floor this afternoon. Bill despises emotional counteractions. He's strictly business, so you must have had some leverage."

Julia turned to face her. "None, Stacie. . .except for having the Lord on my side. I suppose that's all the leverage one needs."

Stacie donned a very bored expression as she continued to watch the workers erect the pod, which was nearly finished now.

Suddenly Julia felt impulsive. "Stacie, our church has a midweek worship service every Wednesday night," she ventured carefully. She'd never asked a co-worker to church before; however, lately, Stacie seemed more like a friend than a co-worker. "Would you like to go?"

"Are you asking me out on a date?" she retorted with a teasing gleam in her eyes.

Julia bit her lip in effort not to grin, but then she gave into her feelings and laughed. Even Stacie chuckled softly.

"Oh, maybe I'll think about it," she said at last.

Julia nodded, glad that Stacie hadn't refused her offer of the worship service altogether.

However, refusing Ken's flirtations was a-whole-nother story. He walked over to Juli's area every chance he got, trying to engage her in conversation, which, of course, didn't sit well with Mark.

Then, on Wednesday morning, a giant bunch of long-stemmed red roses was delivered to Julia's workstation. She couldn't help but smile when the flowers arrived. . .until she read the card: *Congratulations, Julia, and please have dinner with me tonight. Love, Ken.*

She sighed, not even chancing a look in the direction of the portfolio managers' area. Why was Ken pursuing her?

Glancing in the other direction, Julia spotted Mark standing in his doorway. His arms folded in front of him, he was leaning casually against the doorframe, but it was his probing regard that unnerved Julia. He obviously saw the roses.

And he was angry.

She shrugged helplessly, and Mark turned back into his office.

Oh, brother! she thought dryly. *The testosterone level up here is going to kill me!*

Later, she ventured into Mark's office, closing the door behind her. "Have a minute?"

"A minute." He didn't even look up from the papers on his desk.

Julia cleared her throat. "You're angry with me, Mark. I can tell. But it's not my fault that Ken keeps pestering me. And, if it's any consolation, I'm planning to return his roses and let him know I'm not interested in him, his flowers, or his dinner invitations."

Mark looked at her, pursing his lips in thought. "It's about time. Why didn't you do that sooner?"

Julia shrugged. "I thought he'd lose interest in me when he found out about Jesse, so I figured there was no need to say anything."

Mark softened his expression. "Look, I'm sorry, Juli. I'm struggling with jealousy—it's a real demon. What can I say?"

"Say you'll conquer it," she retorted.

He nodded reluctantly. "Easier said than done, but. . .I'll work on it."

"Good."

Mark gave her a helpless shrug.

Leaving his office, Julia had one more piece of evidence that Mark really did love her. His act of jealousy just now seemed to etch his words of love upon her heart. After all, Mark wouldn't be jealous if he didn't really care.

But did he care enough? Did he love her enough to last a lifetime? Or would he change his mind again?

Trust, the Lord's voice seemed to whisper in Julia's ear.

I'm trying, her heart seemed to reply.

Chapter 17

Julia could hardly believe it. She wanted to pinch herself to be sure it was true. Here she was, sitting in a pew with Mark on her left side and Stacie Rollins on her right. If someone would have predicted this very moment a month ago, Julia would have thought the person was crazy, to say the least. Yet, here they were. Mark, back in her life after twelve years and Stacie, sitting beside her in. . .in church!

But God's timing is always perfect, Julia reminded herself. God knew the precise timing of her reunion with Mark—a time when she would accept his apology, forgive and go on, even though she and Mark still seemed to have unfinished business between them. But God was bigger than unfinished business.

And God knew the exact worship service Stacie needed to attend.

The latter seemed so obvious, since the testimonies given were poignant illustrations of God's mercy and grace. Those who stood and shared their stories described how they had been delivered from backgrounds that included marital problems, drug abuse, immorality, alcoholism and more. Furthermore, before the service had even begun, Mark and Julia had told Stacie about their pasts, God's grace, and deliverance in their lives. . .and then they told her about Jesse. Surprisingly, Stacie wasn't shocked or judgmental, but awed.

Glancing to her right now, Julia noticed that Stacie was sitting straight and still, hardly breathing, it seemed, as she listened intently. These testimonies were for her.

Except Julia could not deny the affect of these testimonies in her own heart tonight as well. That these fellow believers spoke about their painful pasts so candidly amazed her. It was obvious that they had truly been set free. And it seemed that, while Julia had tried to run from her past, those giving testimonies had allowed God to use theirs to reach others. After all, one couldn't have a present or future without a past—and look how her past had touched Stacie's heart!

Lord, I was wrong, she silently prayed, her eyes closed reverently. *I should have given my past to You a long time ago. I should have given You my hurt, my loneliness, my insecurities, my fears. Just like my career, I thought I could control my personal life, too. But I can't. And I can't change the past, either, but I can take care for the future. I can give it all to You. It's Yours anyway. My ambition, my heart. . . my life.*

When Julia opened her eyes, an errant tear fell onto her cheek. She didn't even bother to wipe it away. This, she decided, was a time to be honest before both God and man.

It occurred to her, then, that sitting beside her, were two people who represented her past and present. Mark and Stacie, even though Mark represented a little of both. And, in her heart, Jesus Christ held her future.

The pastor came up and stood at the pulpit. He delivered a brief message and then called for an invitation. Those who had made decisions were invited to share them, while those who needed salvation were urged to come and get that matter settled once and for all.

Since Stacie didn't appear to want to go forward, Julia went by herself. She knelt at the altar, silently rededicating her life to the Lord. Then she filled out a decision card—something she had always been too prideful or too stubborn to do before.

When she returned to the pew, Stacie was gone.

"Did she leave?" Julia asked, concerned.

Mark shook his head and pointed to the other end of the pew, where Stacie sat with a man who looked "thirty-something." He was obviously pointing out the way of salvation to Stacie from the open Bible in his lap.

"I've been praying for her," Mark said.

Julia nodded. She had been praying, too.

When the service ended, Julia and Mark walked out into the lobby where they stood around, chatting with other believers and waiting for Stacie.

Once the crowd thinned, Mark turned to her. "You know, I was really impressed by your decision tonight, Juli. Good for you."

She smiled. "I've never gone forward before," she confessed. "It seemed disconcerting to have something so personal read out loud to the entire congregation. But I had left my first love, Mark, and now I've come back to Him. My public profession tonight was like spiritual cement, sealing my relationship with Christ."

"That's wonderful."

Stacie finally emerged. The same gentleman who had counseled her walked beside her. When they reached Mark and Juli, Stacie made the appropriate introductions.

"Tell your friends what happened tonight," the man prompted. He had been introduced as Dr. Ryan Carlson. He was a nice-looking man with an easy smile.

Stacie seemed a little embarrassed, however. "I prayed," she announced. "I believe. . .well, I believe what Ryan showed me in the Bible tonight. . .about Christ. I believe it."

Ryan was grinning from ear to ear. "You got saved, Stacie."

"Right. That's what it's called. Saved."

Mark chuckled joyfully as Julia hugged Stacie. "We're sisters in Christ now," she whispered.

Again, Stacie looked chagrined, and Julia recalled how overwhelmed she had felt as a new believer.

"Well, I've got to be on my way," Ryan said, shaking hands with Mark. He turned to Stacie. "I'll look forward to seeing you on Sunday. I hope you'll come."

Stacie's face turned as pink as a tea rose. Then she nodded a reply to Ryan while Julia had to force herself not to gape at the sight. Stacie Rollins? The sophisticated blond from Customer Service, blushing?

Julia turned and looked up at Mark who seemed quite amused.

After Ryan departed, the three of them ambled out into the parking lot.

"I guess there are some decent single men left in the world," Stacie remarked, speaking of Ryan. She glanced at Mark. "No offense, but up until tonight, I thought you were married."

"No, I'm not married."

Mark looked over Stacie's head and met Julia's gaze in a meaningful way—except Julia wasn't sure what the meaning was. His eyes may have said, "I'll never get married as long as I live!" Or they may have implied that Mark intended to marry her. . . .

Lord, You're in control, Julia prayed silently. *I gave my future to You and I won't take it back!*

❧

The next couple of days passed quickly for Julia. At work she stayed busy interviewing applicants for the three Operations positions. Internal applicants were given first priority, but only a handful had expressed interest.

"Here are the last of the interviews, Juli," a young woman said, handing her a printed sheet of paper. "You can begin interviewing outside candidates next week."

"Thanks." Julia paused. "You're Darlene, right?"

The woman nodded.

"I thought so. We haven't formally met, but I understand you're developing the Human Resources Department."

Darlene nodded again and managed a tired-looking grin. "I think I bit off more than I can chew."

"I know how you feel!"

They chuckled together, then Darlene left for her own department.

❧

Later that Friday afternoon, Julia spotted Ken entering Mark's office. He closed the door behind him, and Julia glanced at her wristwatch in dismay. It was four-fifteen and she and Mark had decided to leave Weakland Management precisely at five o'clock so they could get up to Minoqua before midnight. Jesse would no doubt be waiting for them.

Five o'clock came and went, and Julia left a telephone voice-mail message for Mark, saying that she would wait for him at her apartment. He finally showed up at six-thirty.

"What in the world. . . ?"

"Sorry, Juli."

She let him into the front hallway where her suitcase stood. "Is everything all right?"

Mark nodded. "I'll tell you all about it on the way up north."

He picked up her suitcase and Julia followed him outside, locking her front door behind them.

"Well, as you probably guessed," Mark began as he pulled onto the expressway, "Ken and I had a long talk today. He gave me some song and dance about being misunderstood. The Paxton account was only one of those 'misunderstandings.' There are others, but I'm not free to discuss them at this time."

"Okay. But. . .you don't believe what Ken told you this afternoon?"

"I don't know, Juli. There's just something about that guy that makes my skin crawl."

"You're not still jealous, are you?"

Mark sighed. "I don't think so. I think I'm confident enough about where I stand with you now."

Julia smiled at his reply. Then, seriously, she said, "I think Ken is a workaholic who's hurting and needs the Lord desperately."

"Oh, yeah? And you know what you are?"

With raised brows she turned to him. "What am I?"

"You're a bleeding heart, that's what. I'll bet you'd bring home every stray dog and cat in the neighborhood if your landlord allowed it."

"I would not!" Julia retorted. She mulled over the comment and shifted uncomfortably. "Well, maybe not every stray dog or cat. . ."

"Aha! So you admit it!"

"Sort of," Julia said on a defensive note.

"Man, have I been going about this all wrong," Mark muttered.

"What do you mean? Going about what all wrong?"

"You. I should have gotten you to feel sorry for me, and then I would have had your bleeding heart right in the palm of my hand."

Julia huffed. "Fat chance."

Mark feigned an expression of pure affliction. "Oh, Juli, I've had a tragic life. . ."

"Oh, quiet."

"I've been used and abused. . ."

"With good reason," she teased.

"My parents never understood me. My friends have forsaken me. Even my dog doesn't like me."

"You don't have a dog."

"That's because he ran away," Mark improvised. "It was very traumatic."

"I'm sure it was, you poor thing," she crooned dramatically.

"Are you feeling sorry for me yet?"

"Absolutely," Julia replied facetiously. Then she added, "Not!"

"Well, then I'll have to lay it on heavier." Mark cleared his throat. "Oh, Juli," he began again, "my heart is crushed. I'm. . . I'm just a bug on the windshield of life."

Julia laughed. "That's pathetic, Mark!"

He sobered. "Yeah, I know, but it's timely." Manipulating the windshield wash and wipers, Mark cleared his view. "Ah, that's better." He smiled.

Julia just shook her head at him, still chuckling at his shenanigans.

Chapter 18

The following Sunday night Julia stood beside her son, helping him unpack from his two weeks up north. This past weekend had gone much like the weekend before. Sunshine, blue skies, and a crystal-clear lake for swimming, fishing, and water-skiing. And, if it were possible, Julia thought she'd fallen even more in love with Mark Henley.

"Hey, Mom?" Jesse began as he put a clean shirt away in his dresser drawer. "Do you think you'd ever marry Dad?"

Julia stopped her unpacking. "Why do you ask?"

Jesse shrugged. "Just wondering."

She smiled. "Well, first of all, your dad would have to ask me to marry him, and since that hasn't happened yet, we shouldn't even speculate on the 'what ifs.' "

"But—"

"Now, Jesse, you heard what I said."

"But let's pretend Dad asked you. Would you marry him?"

Julia chewed her lower lip in momentary thought. "Jesse, I love your father. I really do. But let's see what the Lord does with the future."

"If you love him, you should marry him," Jesse muttered irritably.

"But I can't marry him if he hasn't ask me," Julia replied.

"But if he did—would you?"

"Oh, Jesse. . ." Julia sat down on the twin-size bed covered with a blue bedspread with baseball players scattered about. The question of marrying Mark had entered her head dozens of times, but always a bit of fear put a check in her heart when she remembered how he had left her at the altar. But that was more than a decade ago and the past belonged to God to use as He saw fit. And she did love Mark. She had been dreaming of spending the rest of her life with him, as his wife.

Looking at her son, his wondering blue eyes staring back at her, Julia smiled. "You know, Jess, if your dad asked me to marry him, I'd probably say. . ." She paused just to tease him.

"What would you say?"

"I'd say. . ."

"What!"

"I'd say. . .yes!"

"Hooray!" Jesse said, throwing a sweat shirt into the air.

Julia stood and caught it. Then she pointed a warning at her son. "But your dad hasn't asked, and I don't think either of us should get our hopes up. Okay? I mean, what if your dad doesn't want to get married?"

"Oh, he does."

Jesse suddenly looked like the Cheshire cat and Julia narrowed her gaze. "Okay. Spit it out. What do you know?"

"I can't tell," Jesse said. "I promised."

Julia rolled her eyes. "Then you shouldn't have said anything, Jesse, because now I'm going to be nervous."

"Don't be nervous, Mom," Jesse coached her. "Just say yes."

Julia lifted a brow. "So he's going to pop the question, huh? When?"

"I don't know. Dad said he had to wait for the perfect moment."

Julia handed the boy a few more articles of clothing to put into his dresser.

"Dad says he wants us to be a real family. That's what I want, too. And I think he'll be a good dad, once he gets the hang of it."

Julia chuckled softly. "Well, I just hope you thanked your father for those cleats he bought you on the way home today."

"I did. They're the best, aren't they?"

"For that price, they'd better be!" Julia mumbled. She had told Mark not to spend so much money on shoes that would most likely be wrecked by August, but since Jesse had wanted them so badly, he gave in.

With the unpacking finished, Julia closed the suitcase and then left the bedroom so Jesse could change into his pajamas. Once he was dressed for bed, Julia tucked him in, kissing his forehead and wishing him a good night.

Undressing in her own bedroom now, Julia thought over the conversation she and Jesse had about Mark's alleged impending marriage proposal. The idea of planning a wedding sent terrors through Julia.

Oh, Lord, she whispered, *why can't I get over this? Mark left me once, but he wouldn't do it again. He's a different person altogether. . .*

Besides, Mark wouldn't dare leave me twice. My father would have him flogged!

But even with that bit of "assurance," Julia couldn't seem to find peace in accepting Mark's marriage proposal.

Then she laughed at her presumption: Mark hadn't even asked her! What was she thinking?

Forgive me, Lord, for running ahead of You again. . .

❧

The next morning, Julia took her habitual run. The day was bright and sunny, but hot and humid. The air was thick, making Julia's exercise more of an effort than usual. Re-entering her apartment then, she praised God for central air conditioning.

"Jesse, time to get up," Julia called in the direction of his bedroom.

"I'm up. I'm up."

She smiled. His voice didn't sound "up." It sounded sleepy.

"Your vacation is over," she told Jesse as they walked to the car later. "It's back to reality for you, which means you're up and dressed and then we're both out of the apartment by seven-thirty."

"You don't have to remind me." Her soon-to-be twelve year old seemed crabby this morning.

"Have fun at practice," Julia told him, leaving him off at the Frenches' house.

"Bye, Mom," he muttered.

At work, Julia was surprised to discover that her son wasn't the only crab this morning. The tension was so thick on the third floor that finally Julia decided to see how Angela was doing with her reorganizing of IS. On the way over, she met Stacie.

"What's the matter, Juli," Stacie cooed in a sarcastic manner. "Can't take it up there with the big boys?"

"You got that right."

Stacie laughed at the admission. Then, more seriously, she asked, "Is it really that bad up there?"

Julia nodded. "It's a big trading day."

"Wonderful. I hope we make lots of money!"

Julia headed for Information Systems with Stacie walking beside her.

"I went to church yesterday," she said, looking somewhat abashed. "I had lunch with Ryan afterwards."

"Oh?"

"Yes. I never knew a Christian man could be so charming and so polite at the same time. And a doctor. . .I think I'm in love!"

Stacie laughed, and Julia smiled as they parted at the door of IS. Walking to the back of the department, Julia entered the rearranged office. Angela had moved the desk and the credenza.

"This looks nice," Juli remarked.

Angela smiled slightly. "I decided on a change. Actually, lots of changes. . . but some I don't have a say in."

"Mark?"

"Bingo. And he'll be here shortly. This is our department's week with him. Remember?"

Julia couldn't help but grin. "Sorry I won't be here to help," she teased.

Angela cocked a brow. "We know where to find you."

They shared a laugh.

Julia looked down at Angela's desk, then, and spotted two stacks of green-and-white statements. "What are these doing here?"

"Mark gave them to me. I'm supposed to key-in the correct payments which leave a credit balance on each account. Then Weakland Management has to reimburse the clients."

Julia nodded ruefully.

"There must have been a problem with the computer program, right?" Angela's large, brown-eyed gaze searched Julia's face.

"There was a big problem, Angela. Didn't Mark tell you about it?"

"Some. . .which, uhm, program was it?"

"A new one I was working on. It wasn't even a live program, or so I thought. Someone tampered with it. He or she interfaced it with the current portfolio managers' program and did some embezzling."

Angela paled visibly. "How. . .how was that discovered?"

"Mark found it."

"I see." Angela turned suddenly pensive.

"Don't worry," Julia assured her, "this isn't going to affect your taking over Information Systems."

"But that's why you got moved?"

Julia nodded. "That news is just between you and me, Angie, okay? I thought you should know since you're taking over here. They wouldn't have given you the job if they didn't trust you."

She nodded. But then her gaze darkened and a troubled look crossed her features.

"What is it, Angela?

She shrugged.

"Tell me." It was more a gentle prompting than a command.

Angela sighed. "It's our business consultant. . .it's Mark."

"What about him?"

"Well, I walked in on him rummaging through your desk. It was the Saturday after his first week here. I had left my wallet in my desk drawer and, since I was having breakfast with friends, I needed to stop by Weakland Management and get it. It was only seven-thirty in the morning, but there he was, shuffling through all your files and anything else you might have had in there."

"Why didn't you tell me this sooner?" Julia asked.

"I was afraid. He saw me. I feared for my job. I mean, there were rumors flying that half of Weakland's employees were going to get the ax. But when nothing happened, I began to relax. . .except it's always bothered me. And now, you say, he's the one who found the embezzling program. . ."

"But it's been going on for months," Julia countered. "Mark couldn't be involved, if that's what you mean."

Angela shrugged. "I heard he did off-site work for Bill before coming here. I suppose he could have used a modem—"

"Highly unlikely."

"But not impossible."

Folding her arms in front of her, Julia wondered what this meant. She suspected Mark's "rummaging" through her office was just all part of that "investigation" he had mentioned last Monday. One illegal money transfer, after all, had been made from her PC.

Julia shrugged it off. "Don't lose any sleep over it, Angela. Whoever stole the money will be discovered sooner or later."

"Okay, if you say so," she said waveringly.

Julia smiled more confidently than she felt. "I'd better get back to work, Angie. See you later."

Julia returned to the third floor about a half hour after she'd left. The tension hadn't lessened, but she did her best to ignore it and went about her own business. She did her best to discount Angela's news, too; however, it sat in her mind, lurking like a dark shadow that she couldn't shake.

Mark, she noticed, was out of his office almost all day, consulting with the IS department. But, finally, Julia got a chance to speak with him at the end of the afternoon when he ambled over to "check in."

"Everything going all right?" he asked, peering over the side of the workstation.

"Well. . ." *Now is not the time to discuss what Angela told me,* she decided. "Yes, everything is fine," she finally replied with a smile. "I hired two of my three employees today."

Mark looked surprised. "You don't waste any time, do you?"

She laughed and shook her head. "They're the ones for the job. I just know it."

He smiled and glanced at his wristwatch. "I'd like to take Jesse to a baseball game tonight," he said, changing the subject. "Want to come along?"

"What time?"

"Oh. . ." He looked at his watch again. "As soon as we can change clothes and pick him up at Barb and Glen's. We can grab supper at the stadium." He grinned. "I just love those stadium hot dogs. They just have that. . .taste, you know?"

Julia grimaced. "I don't know about the hot dogs, but Jess will love going to the baseball game tonight."

"You, too?"

She grinned. "Only if I can have a cheeseburger."

Mark chuckled. "I guess we can make an exception for you. I'll meet you over at Barb and Glen's place, okay?"

Julia nodded and Mark walked back to his office.

❧

"You're awfully quiet tonight," Mark said as they sat in the bleachers, watching the Milwaukee Brewers.

"It was that hot dog!" Julia declared teasingly. "I shouldn't have listened to you."

"I enjoyed every bite."

"I know. You ate four." Julia shook her head. "So did Jesse. . .and if he gets sick in the middle of the night tonight, I'm calling you."

"I won't get sick!" Jesse said from on the other side of Mark.

Julia smiled and turned back to the game. She hoped her feelings of discomfort didn't show—her true reason for being especially quiet tonight. The fact was, Angela's news had begun to trouble Julia greatly, and now she wasn't sure what to do. If she mentioned it to Mark, would he take offense? Julia didn't want that. She and Mark had come so far.

Forcing her disturbing thoughts aside, Julia decided all she could do was try to enjoy the rest of the evening.

The game ended and the crowd dispersed to the parking lot. From there it was slow going until Mark accelerated onto the expressway. Jesse talked most of the way home, comparing his baseball teammates with the Brewers.

"And Sam can hit a ball as good as Cirello, but I can pitch like Cal Eldred."

"Who?" Mark teased him. "I'm a White Sox fan, Jess."

"Oh no." Jesse turned around and looked at Julia who had graciously volunteered to sit in the backseat. "Did you hear that, Mom? He's a Chicago fan!"

"Mark, how could you?" Julia said, shaking her head in mock disappointment. "Well, don't worry, Jess, we'll convert him this summer."

"You think so?" Mark commented. "I don't know. . . ."

The amiable banter continued until Mark parked his car in front of Julia and Jesse's apartment complex.

"Thanks, Dad," Jesse said as he opened the car door and jumped out. Then he ran to the front door.

"There are days," Julia told Mark, "when Jesse goes to bed with more energy than I wake up with."

"I believe it."

Mark walked her to the front door where Jesse stood waiting.

"Would you like to come in for a while?" Julia asked, fishing in her purse for her keys.

"No, I've got to be on my way."

"Will you come to my first baseball game on Friday night?" Jesse asked Mark. "You bet."

Julia smiled. "Good night, Mark, and thanks."

"Sure. See you tomorrow, Juli. . .'night, Jess."

"Hey, aren't you guys even gonna kiss? Sam's mom kisses her boyfriend when they—"

"Get yourself in the house," Julia said on a note of admonishment as her cheeks warmed with embarrassment.

She glanced at Mark who looked thoroughly amused. He did, however, have the good grace to turn and walk back to his car. "Before I get to thinking too hard about Jesse's question," he called over his shoulder. "I might want to do something about it then."

Julia smiled. "Good night."

Chapter 19

The rest of the week passed quickly for Julia. She stayed busy organizing her new department. Two employees were scheduled to start next week and the third employee would begin the week after that.

With one situation taken care of, Julia went onto the next. She wrote and assembled a training manual since she had been allowed a word processing program on her PC. Much of the information she used had belonged to the original manual in the IS, so Julia found herself in Angela's department on several occasions, searching for things she'd left behind. Angela didn't seem to mind her presence, though she was distant to the point of being unfriendly. However, Julia was relieved when Angela didn't say another word against Mark. She had all but convinced herself that it was a misunderstanding on Angela's part and, slowly, Julia forgot about the incident.

The following Monday, Julia glanced at her wristwatch. Four-thirty. She stifled another yawn and looked over at her two new employees. They were browsing through the training manuals. Julia had decided to give them a break for the last half-hour of the day. It had been a busy one, but both employees would be outstanding team players. Julia could tell already. They were perfect for the job.

But am I? she couldn't help wondering.

It occurred to Julia today as she began training the new employees that, once they knew what they were doing, she wouldn't have anything to do. The thought of growing bored and useless wasn't appealing in the least.

At five o'clock, the employees left with a hearty "See you tomorrow!" Julia smiled and nodded. She felt exhausted. Looking across the way at Mark's office, she smiled as he waved her over.

"Tough day?" he asked as she walked in.

"Sort of," Julia replied. "I didn't sleep well last night."

Mark frowned, looking concerned. "Why not?"

She shrugged. How could she tell him that she hated her new job?

"You weren't worrying about things here at work, were you?"

Julia shrugged once more.

"Well, you should be!" Jerry Fein cut in, entering the office unannounced. He dropped a pile of invoices on Mark's desk. "Anyone else, Juli, would have been out on her ear. Proof or inconclusive proof. . .doesn't matter. You're a suspect in this embezzling thing—your job should have been terminated." Jerry narrowed his gaze. "But since you and our business consultant are so friendly, you get to keep your job. You even got a promotion. . .sort of." He smirked.

"Can it, Fein," Mark said, seemingly unaffected. "Now what's all this that you dumped on my desk?"

As Jerry explained about the corrected invoices, Julia had to swallow down her tears of indignation. She was innocent. Jerry had no right speaking to her that way! And yet, something inside Julia wondered if he wasn't right. Bill treated her differently now, as though he didn't trust her anymore. The light of respect was no longer in his eyes when he spoke to her. Was Jerry Fein just crass enough to speak what Bill really thought of her?

Turning, Julia left Mark's office, packed her things and headed for the elevator. As she glanced across the way, she watched Mark's office door close—with Jerry Fein still inside. Part of her hoped Mark would defend her, but the other part thought that, perhaps it really didn't matter. How could she work at Weakland Management when its President and CEO didn't trust her?

Julia climbed into her car and drove out of the parking lot. Heading for the Frenches' place, where she'd pick up Jesse, she couldn't help but rehash the situation in her head. Trust was essential to any working relationship. The give and take was disproportionate if the element of trust was missing.

Then suddenly Julia realized that her thoughts on professional trust could well be applied to personal relationships, too. Trust. Wasn't it the key to salvation? Trusting in the shed blood of Jesus Christ instead oneself or one's religious works? And in friendships trust was an awesome factor. What would she have done if Barb and Glen hadn't been trustworthy? And her parents, her brothers. . .Jesse.

"And Mark," Julia said aloud as she pulled into the Frenches' driveway. Jesse and his friend Sam were playing basketball. "How can I claim to be in love with him and still not trust him completely?"

Getting out of the car, Julia smiled a hello to the boys before walking into the house. Barb was cooking something that smelled delicious.

"You look beat!" Barb exclaimed when Julia entered the kitchen.

"Thanks a lot," she quipped.

Barb chuckled. "Oh, you know what I mean, honey. You look so tired. . .want to lie down and rest before supper?"

Julia shook her head. "I've got too much on my mind to lie down and rest. What are you making, anyway?"

"Glen is grilling hamburgers and I'm creating a pasta salad."

"What smells so good?"

"Probably my rhubarb squares in the oven."

Julia's mouth was watering already.

"As soon as Mark shows up, we'll eat."

Julia nodded. Lately it seemed Mark was over here as much as she was, and she couldn't say she minded it, either.

"Hey, Barb, do you. . .well, do you trust Mark?"

"Well, sure I do." Barb frowned. "Don't you?"

Julia momentarily chewed her lower lip. "I want to. I guess I'm just afraid to let go and trust this thing between us now."

Barb smiled in a motherly way. "Mark is a wonderful man, honey, and he loves you very much. Why, it thrills my heart every time I see the way he looks at you."

Julia's heart swelled with emotion. It was a joy to hear that from Barb. It was like affirmation from above.

Dinner was ready at last and Mark walked in with Jesse. He had been playing basketball with the kids in the driveway, suit and tie and all.

"Are we still going to the State Fair tonight?" Jesse asked, biting into a hamburger which was oozing with ketchup.

Mark looked at Julia. "Are we still going?"

She shook her head apologetically. "I'm exhausted. But you two can go."

"Can Sam come along, Dad?"

Julia saw Mark's expression register the disappointment he felt; however, he recovered and told Jesse to bring his friend.

"I'm sorry, Mark," she told him later. Jesse and Sam were already in his car waiting for him. "I'm just so tired that I don't feel like walking around the fairgrounds tonight."

He smiled. "That's all right. We'll just have to go again." With a chuckle, he added, "I don't think Jesse will mind that a bit."

"No, I'm sure he won't."

Mark climbed into his car. "I'll have Jesse home by ten o'clock."

"Aw, that's too early!" the boy exclaimed.

"Not for me, it isn't," Mark replied, grinning. "I've got to get up early tomorrow."

"So do I," Jesse countered.

"Yeah, but you have more energy than I do." Mark and Julia exchanged amused glances.

"Have fun, you guys. I'll see you at home."

She waved them off and walked back into the house. Gathering her things, she told Barb and Glen good-night. On the way out, however, she decided to grab the want ads. Just for a look.

"Can I take some of your Sunday newspaper?" she asked Glen.

"Sure. It's still on the table in the TV room."

Julia entered the room. It was decorated with a masculine touch, from the paintings of hunters on horseback, which hung on the dark paneling, to the sculptured carpet in various shades of brown. The tan, woven-fabric of the couch was worn, but still comfortable. It had once been in the living room until Barb insisted on new furniture. A large-screen TV and entertainment center had been placed against an adjacent wall and a gun case stood in the corner. This was Glen's favorite room while Barb enjoyed her sewing area in a finished section of the basement.

Julia smiled. The Frenches loved each other, but desired their own "space" too. *I wonder if Mark would want a room like this,* she mused. She couldn't seem to help it. And then she imagined father and son watching baseball games together, and football games while she baked cookies with their daughter.

Julia shook herself. *I'm getting delirious.*

However, Julia couldn't deny that part of her found the idea of home and family—having more babies—quite appealing. On the other hand, until Mark proposed, her dreams were about as attainable as catching a falling star.

Looking through the newspapers now, scattered across the coffee table, Julia found the employment section and folded it under her arm. She hadn't paged through this part of the newspaper in years—not since before she'd been hired at Weakland Management. She had always thought she'd stay with the company forever. There had been security in that idea, but no more. The Lord was her security now. She clearly saw how wrong she'd been to give her heart to her career.

Once Julia got home, she changed clothes, pulling on a "skort" which was a combination of a skirt and shorts all in one. Next she pulled on a matching T-shirt. Folding her long, tanned legs beneath her, she sat on the couch and paged through the employment section. Much to Julia's amazement, there were plenty of opportunities for which she was qualified. Getting up from the couch, she found paper and pencil and began writing down names and addresses of companies in the Milwaukee area. She'd update her resumé and send it out.

Julia was still at her task when Mark and Jesse showed up.

"Hey, Mom, look what I won!" Jesse burst into the living room, carrying a large stuffed panda bear.

"Goodness! Do people really win those things?" Julia smiled at her son, then at Mark. "I always thought those games at the midway were big rackets and that no one ever won the nice prizes."

"Well, I won. . .with Dad's help."

Mark grinned. "It was a basketball game."

"Good thing we were practicing before we went to the fair?"

"Good thing," Mark agreed. Then he spotted the want ads and Julia's notes spread all over the couch. He frowned. "What's all this?"

Julia paused, not wanting to discuss it in front of Jesse. "Time to hit the shower, Son."

"But, Mom—"

"Don't argue," Julia warned him.

Looking like a puppy with his tail between his legs, Jesse moped all the way down the hallway. Then Julia turned to face Mark.

"I was just looking. . .trying to get a feel for what kind of career opportunities are out there."

Mark regarded her through a narrowed gaze. "Why? Because of Jerry Fein's thoughtless remark this afternoon?"

Julia shrugged. "That's part of it—maybe even most of it."

"I didn't think it bothered you," Mark said softly. "You handled it well in my office, and you didn't seem upset tonight."

Swallowing the sudden urge to cry, Julia forced herself to say, "I hate to admit it, but I think Jerry was right. Anyone else in my situation would have been fired."

Mark was shaking his head. "Not necessarily. It's a judgment call. Each situation is unique, and Fein had no right to make a blanket statement like the one he made today. Forget it, Juli. Don't let it get to you. . .oh, and don't cry. . ."

Julia swiped at the errant tear as Mark pulled her into his arms.

"I'm sorry he hurt you," Mark whispered against her ear. "But he's not right. Bill made the decision to put you in charge of Operations, I merely suggested the idea."

"But he wanted to fire me," Julia sniffled against his shoulder. "Bill admitted it."

"Well, sure. . .at first. He was angry." Mark gently pushed her from him, holding her by the shoulders at arm's distance. "One of Bill's employees is stealing money from his clients, Juli. Can you blame Bill for being upset?"

"I don't blame him, but I can't make him trust me either. I'm the prime suspect. You heard Frank Houston."

Julia pulled out of Mark's grasp. Walking over to the windows, she peered out onto the well-lit tennis courts. "Besides," she added, "I don't like my job anymore."

"Why's that?" Mark's tone indicated his surprise at her statement.

She turned back to face him. "I'm a programmer, Mark, but I'm not allowed access to the computer system because Bill doesn't trust me. Once my employees are trained, which won't be long, I'm not going to have anything to do."

"In a company that size, there's always something to do."

"Secretarial stuff, I imagine. But I don't want to be a secretary. I'm a computer programmer."

Looking pensive, Mark picked up one of Julia's notes. He read it over before bringing his blue-eyed gaze back to her. "It won't be difficult for you to find another place of employment," he said at last. "You're intelligent and a conscientious worker. You're organized and you carry yourself in a professional manner."

"Thanks," she said skeptically as Mark walked slowly toward her.

"But will you put off this job hunt for a while longer?"

"Why?"

"Because I'm asking you to."

Julia lifted her chin stubbornly. "You'll have to come up with a better reason. I'm sorry, but this is my future we're discussing. With God's help, I want to map it out, whether it means staying at Weakland Management or not."

"And how will it look if you quit now? Frank Houston said that if our embezzler even senses that we're onto him. . .or her, he or she will most likely quit."

Julia frowned. "I didn't think about that."

"Hang in there, Juli, all right? For just a while longer? Let's ask God to bring this sin to the surface. Then the thief will be apprehended and your name will be cleared."

"And that will be great, but I still won't like my job in Operations any better."

"One step at a time." Then he chuckled at her sigh of impatience. "Waiting isn't easy, is it? When I first found out where you were living and that I had a son, I wanted to jump the first airplane heading in this direction. Twice I even made weekend reservations, but each time God put an undeniable check in my heart. He didn't want me to go. It wasn't His time yet. And now I'm so glad I waited."

Mark took both her hands in his. "This will work out too, Juli. You'll see." Then suddenly he snapped his fingers with an idea. "I know. We'll talk about all this job business tomorrow night. Let's go out to dinner. Just you and me. A nice place. Fancy. Romantic. . ."

Julia immediately knew what was coming. A marriage proposal. . .just like Jesse had said. She wanted to smile and cringe at the same time. On one hand, she loved Mark and wanted to marry him, but, on the other, she knew what it meant to have a "check in her heart" because it was there in her heart right now. If only she could be sure that Mark wouldn't change his mind again. If only she could be guaranteed somehow that he'd never leave her behind.

"What do you say, Juli? Is tomorrow night okay?"

At last she nodded, unsure if she could speak.

Then, as she walked Mark to the door, Julia decided that, proposal or no proposal, she needed to be honest with him tomorrow night. No more walls for self-protection. She didn't need them; she had the Lord.

"G'night, Juli," Mark said, kissing her cheek softly. He paused before adding a whispered, "I love you."

Looking into his eyes, so blue and sincere, Julia smiled.

Chapter 20

The next screen gives you the client's past history with us," Julia explained, sitting in between her department's two new employees. Amazingly, she had been given permission to acclimate them on various programs, even though they'd be working mostly with the hardware. "Now, the next screen—"

Julia paused, hearing Mark clear his throat. She looked at him, leaning over the side of the pod. "May I help you, Mr. Henley?" she asked in feigned formality.

He gave her a quick look of warning, although he was grinning all the while. "Can I speak with you a minute?"

Julia nodded and followed Mark into his office.

"I'm going to have to postpone our dinner tonight," he said softly. "I've got a meeting and it's not going to let out early."

"All right," Julia replied, hiding her disappointment. She had been starting to look forward to a romantic dinner with Mark.

"Maybe Thursday night."

Julia nodded. "I think Thursday is okay."

"Me, too, but this is going to be a bad week."

"Well, whenever, Mark. We can have dinner any time." Julia folded her arms. "What's going on? Can you tell me?"

Mark sat on the corner of his desk, his one leg dangling over the side. "Bill decided to get rid of all the security staff and start from scratch. A memo will be circulated tomorrow, telling everyone about the change."

Julia was surprised. "Why?"

"Because the department was being run far too loosely and none of the employees seemed very eager to change their practices. Most of those guys are college students and thought this was a great job since they could do their homework while they worked. They weren't paying much attention to what was going on around them."

Julia was sorry to see a whole department go, and yet Mark's explanation made sense. He was a good business consultant, and she had come to respect his judgments.

"Frank Houston is going to train the new security officers," Mark added. "However, no one else here is aware that he works for the FBI. That's still 'top secret,' as they say."

"Oh, my." Julia grinned impishly. "Is a barbed wire fence going up around the building, too? That'll be great for the morale around here."

Rubbing the back of his neck, Mark chuckled. "No barbed wire." He shook his head at her. "You know, I can't figure out who's sassier. . .you or Stacie Rollins."

"Oh, it's Stacie, of course," Julia said facetiously. Then she rolled her eyes and left Mark's office with a broad smile.

The next morning, just as Mark had said, a memo was circulated stating that a whole new Security Department would be established.

"Hmm," Ken Driscoll said, leaning against Julia's pod, "I wonder which department is the next to go." He crumpled the memo and tossed it into a nearby wastebasket. "Must be nice to be a consultant. You wreak havoc and then go your merry way, never looking back at the damage you've done."

"I think the changes in security were Bill's idea," Julia stated in Mark's defense.

"But on whose suggestion?" Ken countered.

Julia didn't reply but marveled at the level of Ken's animosity toward Mark. She looked at her two new employees and wondered if they noticed it. By their expressions, she gathered they did.

"Well, my clients' money awaits," Ken said offhandedly. "Talk to you later."

As he walked away, Julia glanced at Mark's office door. She was glad it was closed because Mark still didn't like her talking to Ken, and she still couldn't avoid it.

Turning back to her employees, Julia smiled. "Shall we begin? We're going to get through two programs today."

❧

Wednesday night was the mid-week worship service, and Julia was disappointed when Mark didn't make it. He said he had another meeting. Stacie came, however, and she sat with Julia, Jesse, Barb, and Glen. Stacie listened to the pastor intently, Julia noticed, and she even followed along when he read Scripture passages. She had purchased a Bible for her own use and it made Julia smile in satisfaction to see how reverently she handled her new treasure.

When Julia arrived home that night, the telephone was ringing. Jesse ran to answer it.

"It's Dad," he hollered from the next room. Then he took ten minutes to tell Mark every detail of his day.

Julia smiled as she listened, and then Jesse handed the telephone to her.

"Hi, Mark," she said jovially.

"Hi." His voice was flat. "Look, Juli, we heard some disturbing news today, and I asked Bill if I could be the one to confront you about it. He was agreeable."

"What is it?" she asked, sensing the seriousness of what was to come.

"Someone tried to make another illegal transaction today," Mark said. "It didn't go through from what we can find, but when we investigated further, another employee said she saw a woman in the CPU room." Mark paused. "She said it was you."

"Me? But I haven't been near the CPU room. Ask my employees. Except for an occasional trip to the ladies room, I've been with them all day."

"You were working with computer programs today?"

"Not working with them, Mark. I was paging through them. . .and my employees were there with me."

"All right." Mark's voice still sounded down and troubled.

"You don't believe me?"

She heard him let out a slow breath. "Juli, if you tell me that you weren't anywhere near the CPU room today, I believe you."

A moment's pause as they both digested questions and answers.

"Mark, who said that it was me?"

"Doesn't matter. The important thing is that she was wrong. Okay? I'm going to hang up now. Good night."

Julia heard the decisive click on the other end before turning off the portable phone. She wondered if Mark really believed her, but then realized that she couldn't do anything about the thoughts going around in his head right now. She had told him the truth, now he'd just have to trust her.

Trust her. . .

Julia got up from the chair she had been sitting in and walked to the patio windows. She pulled the draperies closed on the last of the setting sun. *With all odds against me, I'm insisting that Mark trust me. I haven't proven that I'm worthy of his trust. All I've given is my word. And yet, Mark has proved himself over and over. He's a different man. God changed his heart. It's obvious. But I still hold back on trusting him all the way.*

Julia shook her head sadly. She felt like a hypocrite, saying one thing, expecting another. And, ironically, she couldn't say that she'd blame Mark if he changed his mind about marrying her a second time.

❧

At Weakland Management the next day, things were so tense on the third floor that Julia could barely concentrate. She considered taking the afternoon off, since her employees were doing well on their own; however, she was more than just a little intimidated about taking the idea to Bill. He looked preoccupied, serious, and very unapproachable.

Jerry Fein, on the other hand, seemed completely harassed. He walked briskly from one office to another, slamming doors and speaking loudly, and he glared at Julia each time he walked by. It occurred to her that if Mark was defending her, while Bill and Jerry thought she was guilty, he was putting his own reputation on the line. That troubled her. A lot.

Finally, five o'clock came, and Julia didn't waste a minute in gathering up her things and leaving. On the way out, she paused in front of Mark's office. "Good night," she ventured.

He looked up and smiled briefly. " 'Night, Juli."

Walking to the elevators, she thought of their plans for a "romantic dinner." But, given the day and Mark's expression just now, Julia knew it wouldn't be tonight.

As usual, she dined with Barb and Glen. Their love and friendship soothed Julia's misgivings over what was happening at work. She did, however, miss Mark's presence and Jesse, of course, wanted to know where his dad was and why he didn't come over tonight. Julia explained that he was having a busy week, and Jesse seemed satisfied with that. After all, his mother had had years of "busy weeks" in the past.

Once at home, with Jesse reading a book on the couch, Julia changed clothes and then sat outside on the patio with her Bible in her lap. The air was hot and humid, but it felt nice after being in cool air conditioning all day. She re-read this morning's devotional and Scripture application. One verse in particular stuck out at her: "A word fitly spoken is like apples of gold in pictures of silver."

Julia read it five times before deciding what to do with it. Re-entering the apartment she picked up the phone and dialed Mark's number. No answer. Then she tried him at his office, and found him.

"What's up, Juli?"

He sounded tired and Julia almost backed down from what she intended to say. Almost.

"I just called to tell you that. . .well, that I love you, Mark."

The words came straight from her heart—precious words, as precious as gold and silver. But, still, Julia held her breath, wondering over his reaction. This was the first time in twelve years that she reached out to Mark—without his prodding or prompting. It was all on her own.

"Thanks, Juli," he finally replied. "You'll never know how much it means to hear you say that. I'm glad you called."

She smiled, relieved. "Are you all right? You sound exhausted."

"I'll be fine. . .and I'm sorry for being such a bear lately. How's Jesse?"

"Terrific. He's reading a book."

"Wish I were reading a book."

Julia chuckled softly.

Mark heaved a weary-sounding sigh. "Do you have a few minutes? Can we talk?"

"Sure."

"All right. Tell me what you know about Angela Davis."

"Angela? Why?"

"Because she's the one who said it was you in the CPU room."

"Angela?"

"Uh-huh."

Julia paused to consider the news. It couldn't possibly be a case of mistaken identity; Angela knew very well what Julia looked like. So why would she lie?

"Tell me about her, Juli."

"Well, she's been with the company for almost a year. She's always been a big help to me. She even took the pager for me on a couple of weekends so that I could go to Jesse's soccer games and—"

"What did you say?"

"She took the pager for me. . ."

Realizing the implication of what she'd just said, Julia felt like her heart stood still. Hadn't the embezzler made the illegal transactions on the days when Julia was to have had the pager? But Angela had covered for her.

"This is all very interesting, isn't it?"

She sank onto the couch. "No, Mark, it's not Angela. She wouldn't steal money."

"Then why did she tell me that it was you in the CPU room?"

"I don't know."

"She didn't want me to tell you that she made the ID, either. Maybe she worried that we would talk to each other."

Julia was momentarily pensive. "You know, Mark, Angela told me that she caught you rummaging through my desk the very first Saturday you were here. I wasn't going to say anything to you because I figured it was just some mix-up."

Mark laughed. "Really? She said that? Funny thing, but I haven't worked a single Saturday since I came to Weakland Management." His voice grew serious. "All right, now we've got two blatant lies from Angela Davis."

"But she seems so sweet, Mark, and I really don't think she's capable of embezzling money."

"Maybe not. . .at least not on her own. But teamed with someone like. . .say, Ken Driscoll—"

"Ken and Angela?" Julia laughed. "No way! Besides, we already discussed Ken and—"

"And I always thought he was a shyster. Listen, Juli, in the six months he's worked for Weakland Management, Driscoll has stolen four accounts from other portfolio managers. What does that say about his character? Furthermore, Houston did background checks on every employee and Ken's is sketchy."

Julia didn't know what to say.

"There's something else. On one of my first days with Weakland Management, Ken told me that you were a. . .well, let's say he called you the company flirt."

"What!" Julia could only imagine the real terminology Ken had used. "You should have knocked him out—you still should! And if you don't, Mark, I will!"

He laughed. "You're in enough trouble. How about if we just figure out how to nail these two. I'm sure they're in it together. Angela had access to your PC, your desk—"

"My password, my initials." Julia sighed. "All my employees knew my codes. They had to in order to work on some of the data files."

"And then there's Driscoll who really did snoop through your desk. I saw him with my own eyes. And, as for Driscoll's trailing you everywhere when he should be paying attention to the Dow Jones average instead. . .well, nothing personal, honey, but I don't think he's really as smitten with you as he acts. I think he just wants to make sure that you haven't found out what he and Angela are up to."

"But it's so hard to believe. I feel. . .betrayed."

"I'm sure you do. But, Juli, you're going to have to overcome those feelings and help Houston prove that Angela and Ken are the real embezzlers."

"How?"

"I don't know," Mark said, his voice sounding weary once more. "I just don't know. But, Juli? Please be careful."

Chapter 21

Seven days later, Julia wiped the beads of perspiration off her forehead as she waited for Mark in the shade just outside the church's front doors. At seven o'clock, it was still a sultry eighty degrees on this first Wednesday evening in August.

"I got us a seat," Jesse said, coming to stand beside her now. "Are you sure Dad is coming?"

Julia nodded. "He said he had to work late, but he said he'd be here in time for the worship service."

Jesse nodded. "Hey, did Dad pop the question yet?"

"What question?" Julia replied, playing dumb.

"You know, *the question.*"

Julia shook her head. "Not yet." She grinned while Jesse frowned in disappointment. "You'll be the first to know, Jess. Not to worry."

He shrugged, his blond head now at Julia's eye-level. Her son had grown a few inches in this summer's sunshine.

"Sam's mom said that she's never getting married again," Jesse confided. "She said she's having too much fun. I told her that you never had fun until Dad came along."

Julia had to laugh. "Thanks a lot, kid!" she teased him.

"Well, I didn't mean it in a bad way. I just mean that you're. . .happier now that he's here. You smile more. . .and you laugh more, too."

Julia agreed. "Yes, I am happier. I love your dad, that's true, but God is the One who put the joy back into my heart."

"Yeah, I told Sam's mom that part, too. Hey, look! Dad's here!"

Jesse ran out into the parking lot to meet Mark while Julia smiled in his wake. Then father and son walked back together.

"You guys sure are a sight for sore eyes!" Mark declared with a wink at Julia.

"Is that good or bad?" Jesse wanted to know.

"It's good. You and your mom are a good sight for my sore eyes." Mark chuckled.

"Anything new?" Julia asked hopefully as they walked into the vestibule. "How did your meeting go this afternoon?"

"No, and fine," Mark replied, answering both her questions. "We can talk later."

Julia nodded and slid into the pew next to Barb. In front of her, sitting beside Ryan Carlson, Stacie turned around. "Hello, Mark. Long time no see."

He grinned at the facetious remark. "Hi, Stacie." Then he nodded a friendly greeting to Ryan.

The pastor's message was short and then prayer requests were taken and testimonies given. Afterwards, the congregation was encouraged to break into small groups for prayer. Julia, Mark, and Jesse made up one group with Mark leading them through all the requests.

As she listened to him pray, Julia was awed by the depth of Mark's faith. His love for the Savior was obvious as first Mark praised Him, then thanked Him for an abundance of blessings, which included Julia and Jesse. Finally Mark interceded for other Christians, his words heartfelt, and an overwhelming sense of security enveloped Julia as she prayed along with him.

And at that very moment, she knew she could trust this man. She could trust him, because she trusted God—the same God who lived in Mark's heart!

❧

The next morning at work, things seemed unusually tense. It wasn't like a busy stock-market-day tenseness. It was a quiet tenseness, like the calm before the storm.

Frank Houston was hanging around, going in and out of Bill's office, and Julia couldn't help but recall what Mark had said at breakfast. "Today's the day, Juli. I've just got the feeling. . . ."

Julia hoped he was right. She hoped Houston would apprehend the thief, or thieves, very soon. She was getting nervous, working in such close proximity to Ken, and Julia had to constantly be aware of what she said or did so she wouldn't give the investigation away. On the more positive side, Bill didn't seem to distrust her anymore and even Jerry Fein was acting civil toward her again.

"Who is that man, Juli?" Ken asked, leaning his forearms on the wooden pod now. "I've seen him here before, but I thought he was just some flunky helping out Jerry Fein."

Julia pulled herself from her musings and wondered how to answer Ken's question without divulging the truth, but without lying either.

Finally, she said, "I don't know what his title is. . ."

"Hmm. . ." Ken's intense green-eyed gaze followed Houston as he picked up the telephone in Bill's office. Then he looked back at Julia and a softness entered his eyes. "I have to leave. . .a meeting. . ."

She nodded.

"Well, I. . ." He shrugged. "Good-bye, Juli."

She smiled. "Have a good day, Ken."

As he turned and walked back to his work area, a strange feeling came over Julia. Ken's good-bye had sounded so final.

Glancing across the way, Julia watched him pack up his attaché case. Then he looked around his desk as if making sure he hadn't forgotten anything. Nothing strange about that, since he'd said he had a meeting to attend. However, as Ken's gaze came back around to Julia, he gave her a slow, sad smile, and she immediately knew he was leaving for good. Fleeing, most likely.

Her eyes widened at the realization.

His gaze darkened in warning.

Oh, Lord, Ken knows I know. . .

Julia turned back to the training manual that she had been preparing for her newest employee. Apprehension tingled her every nerve. She stared at the words in front of her, without seeing them, as she contemplated what to do next.

She glanced at Mark's office. . .empty. He was working with Public Relations this week. She looked over at Frank Houston. He was within shouting distance—

"Don't even think about it," Ken said softly, as he leaned over the pod and put his hand on Julia's shoulder. "I want you to stand up and follow me. Don't try anything stupid, because I have a gun and I'll use it."

She looked at him in wondering horror. "Ken. . .?"

"Get up," he whispered.

She did, glancing at her two employees who were engaged in a conversation about computer components.

"Come on, Juli." Ken's tone was insistent now.

Hesitantly, she walked around the work area.

"Going for coffee?" one of her employees asked suddenly.

Julia opened her mouth to speak, but nothing came out.

"Mid-morning coffee break," Ken said with a forced smile. He looked at her. "Come on, Juli."

As she walked toward him, Julia wished she could come up with some clever way to get Frank Houston's attention. But she was so frightened, she couldn't even think. *Oh, Lord, please help me!*

Ken grabbed a hold of her upper arm, his impatience very evident now. "Move, Juli," he hissed, "I haven't got a lot of time."

He pulled her forward, and she had to run a few paces to get in time with his quick steps.

At the elevators, he released her arm. She rubbed it.

"I'm sorry," he said stiffly. "But just do as I say and everything will be fine, all right?"

Reluctantly, she nodded.

The elevator doors opened and Ken ushered her inside. Looking up at the camera in the left-hand corner, Julia wished that Bill hadn't fired all the security guards. One might have come in handy right about now.

She looked over at Ken who was watching her thoughtfully.

"How much do you know?" he asked.

Julia shrugged, but figured it was ridiculous to play dumb at this point. "I know that you tampered with my software and embezzled money."

A little smile curved Ken's mouth. "Took you long enough to figure it out."

Before Julia could reply, the elevator doors opened. They were on the first floor now. Using the phone just outside the Mail Room, Ken dialed a number and held the receiver to his ear, all the while holding Julia's hand. She wanted to pull out of his grasp, but she didn't know where he had the gun.

"It's time, Angie," Ken said into the phone. "Now!" Slamming down the receiver, he turned to Julia. "Come on. You're going to ensure our escape."

"What are you going to do with me?"

Ken smiled. "Once Angela and I are on our way out of the country, I'll let you go."

Julia sighed, praying she could believe him. "So Angela is really involved? I had hoped she wasn't."

Ken chuckled. "Angela is the mastermind behind all our plans."

Julia could barely believe it.

"We're married, you know."

"You and Angela?" Julia would have stopped dead in her tracks at the news, if Ken wasn't pulling her behind him. "But I thought Frank Houston did a background check on you and—"

Ken stopped so quickly that Julia almost fell over him. "Who is Frank Houston?" His hand tightened around hers in a bone-breaking grip.

She winced. "He's with the FBI."

Ken muttered an oath. "I knew it!" He turned and kept walking, pulling Julia along with him. "I told Angela that I smelled trouble, but she just had to try one more transfer. She couldn't resist."

They reached the double-glass doors which led out to the parking lot and Ken leaned against the wall, waiting for Angela. Julia wiggled her hand out from under his.

He looked at her, but let her go.

Minutes passed, and Ken grew restless. After fifteen minutes, he was pacing the corridor like a caged animal. Finally, Angela appeared, although she was standing out in the parking lot. Just standing there. With her hands behind her back.

"What in the world. . .?" Ken grabbed Julia's elbow and pushed her through the doors. "What are you doing out there?" he shouted to Angela. "I was waiting for you in—"

"Watch out, Ken!" she cried. "Run!"

The next seconds were a blur of shouts and shuffling feet as, first, Frank Houston grabbed hold of Angela's arm, though she was already handcuffed, and two other men took Ken down, handcuffing him. This left Julia standing in the middle of the chaos, feeling stunned and more than just a little frightened.

Finally, when Ken and Angela were loaded into a waiting car, Houston approached her.

"You okay?"

Julia just stared back at him, dumbstruck.

"I realized you were in trouble," he explained, "when I saw Driscoll holding you by the arm and leading you toward the elevators. I summoned my men and we got to Angela before she could get away. She was amazingly compliant. We used her as bait, so to speak, in order to apprehend Driscoll. Worked out nicely, I think." Houston narrowed his gaze. "Are you sure you're all right, Miss McGowan?"

She managed a nod, although she felt as if she had just gotten off a spinning ride at an amusement park.

"Would you like to sit down?"

"I'll be all right."

And then she saw Mark. He was running toward her from around the other side of the building. Seeing her, he paused, taking in the outcome of the situation. But then he closed the distance between them, pulling Julia into his arms.

"Thank God you're not hurt," he said, his lips brushing against her ear. "When Bill told me what was happening, I. . . I panicked, Juli. I don't know what I would have done if something happened to you."

Julia wanted to tell him that he was holding her too tightly—that she couldn't breathe. But she just as soon decided that she'd gladly die in Mark's arms this way. He loved her and she was unharmed. God had answered her prayers.

❧

"It's a beautiful night, isn't it?" Mark said as they strolled along Lake Michigan's breakwater walkway. Two weeks had gone by since Ken and Angela had been arrested and changed with theft.

Julia nodded in answer to Mark's question. It was a beautiful night. The temperature was mild here by the lake, and a sliver of moon shone in the sky surrounded by hundreds of stars. "Beautiful."

"Dinner was good, don't you think?"

"Very good."

Julia bit the inside of her cheek in an effort to suppress her giggles. Poor Mark. He had been making small talk all night when what he so obviously wanted to do was "pop the question."

"That was a very elegant restaurant," Mark said. "I'm glad you suggested it."

"Me, too. I had never been there before."

"What was the name of that place again?"

"Pieces of Eight." Julia smiled, wondering if she should help Mark out. They could go on like this all night.

Deciding she ought to, she strategically slipped her hand into his. "It was very romantic, Mark. The candlelight, the view of the lake as we ate. . ."

He nodded, and Julia could feel the clamminess on the palm of his hand. *He's nervous. How sweet!*

They reached the end of the walkway and Mark turned to her. Julia could clearly see his features beneath the soft glow of the street lamp several feet away. She watched as he seemed to struggle with what he wanted to say. Then he took a deep breath.

"You're not going to throw me in the lake, are you?" she teased, trying to put him at ease.

"No, not tonight," Mark said seriously, in spite of her attempt at humor. He took another preparatory breath, and Julia bit the inside of her cheek again. *Don't laugh. Don't even smirk.*

Her mirth faded, however, as she remembered that Mark didn't have this much trouble proposing twelve years ago. He's serious this time, she realized. This is forever, and he knows it.

"I love you, Juli," he said, taking both her hands in his as he leaned against the painted, metal rail behind him.

"I love you, too."

Mark nodded. "I know. . .and I've been doing a lot of thinking about. . .us."

"Yes?"

"And Jesse. I mean. . .I've been thinking about what's best for all of us."

Julia nodded, wishing he'd just spit it out.

"I'm leaving for Colorado after Christmas, and—"

"You are?"

Mark nodded. "Look, Juli," he said, sounding more like his old practical self. "I need a business partner, okay? I want someone organized, intelligent, educated and, well, you fit the bill."

"Business partner?" she asked in disbelief. "You want a. . .*a business partner?*"

"We'd make a great team, don't you think?"

"Well, yes, but—"

"You'll travel with me and. . .well, we could see each other all the time—have romantic moon-lit walks like this every night if we want to. And I could see Jesse all the time—"

"Business partner?" Julia's ire was up now. So he wasn't talking commitment. He was talking— "Business partner!" She yanked her hands free.

"Well, there is just one condition."

With arms akimbo now, she glared at him. "And what might that be?"

"You'd have to marry me." Mark grinned.

Julia blinked. He got her. He got her good, and he knew it. Mark laughed and laughed.

"Very funny," she said dryly.

"I'm sorry, Juli," he said between chortles, "I couldn't help myself."

And here she had tried so hard not to laugh at him!

Folding her arms in front of her, she allowed Mark to chuckle it out. Finally, he grew serious again.

"I'm sorry I teased you. But you see, I just had to lighten up the moment. I was getting too nervous in all the seriousness." Mark paused, swallowing hard. "Except, I am serious. Will you marry me, Juli?"

"You going to show up this time?"

Mark looked chagrined. "I knew you were going to say that." He grinned. "Yes, I'll show up this time. I promise."

"You know what, Mark? I believe you. And I trust you. Completely."

Then, an earnest expression on his face, he got down on his knees. "Juli, I promise you forever—as much of forever as God allows me to give. Will you marry me?"

Julia's heart melted at the sight. "Yes," she replied, "I'll marry you."

Epilogue

December 21

The church in Menomonee Falls, Wisconsin, was modestly, but tastefully decorated. Fresh floral arrangements stood in glass vases near the altar and pleated paper wedding bells, in a variety of pastels, hung about. The pews were filled with enthusiastic friends and relatives who had come to share this special day. A wedding day, uniting for life Julia Rose McGowan and Mark Thomas Henley.

In the dressing room in back of the church, Julia smoothed the skirt of her formal off-white, tea-length gown which she'd purchased especially for this day.

"You look beautiful, dear," Julia's mother, Caroline, said with a proud smile. Then tears gathered in her green eyes. "You're the most beautiful bride I've ever seen."

"Oh, Mom, don't cry," Julia chided her gently. "You'll ruin your makeup. Don't forget pictures afterward in the Mitchell Park Domes."

Caroline nodded, dabbing her eyes with a tissue.

Then, as if tears were contagious, Barb dabbed at her eyes, too. "This is one happy day," she muttered. Then to Julia she said, "You once asked what you could do to payback Glen and me for all the years you lived with us. Well, honey, this wedding is all the pay-back I'll ever need or want. You and Mark. . .oh, it's so wonderful to see what God can do!"

"Thank you, Barb," Julia said, giving her a hug. "Thank you so much."

"You're welcome. Now, smooth your hair and let me fix your veil. I think I bumped it."

Turning around, Julia allowed Barb to fuss over her for a few minutes.

"You do make a beautiful bride, Juli," Kathy said sweetly.

Julia smiled her thanks. She and Kathy hadn't seen each other in over twelve years, but when Julia phoned her, it was as if they'd never been apart—best friends once more. Kathy, her husband, and four children had come up from Illinois for the wedding.

"And the gown is stunning, Juli," Stacie said, handing her a pair of pearl earrings. "But these will make the whole outfit."

Julia took the earrings and smiled. "Thank you, Stacie. How thoughtful."

"Well, aren't you supposed to have something borrowed and something blue? Those earrings are borrowed, Juli, and I want them back before you leave for Colorado."

Julia laughed. "Good as done."

"So what are you going to do with Jesse?" Kathy asked. "All that traveling Mark does, and your going with him. . .what about Jesse's education?"

Julia smiled. "I'm going to home-school," she announced. "I'll be Jesse's teacher, and he'll be able to study anywhere we go. I'm excited about it."

Mark's sisters, Teri and Jenny, stood by and smiled. They had come for the wedding with their spouses and children, too.

"Next to Teri," Jenny remarked, "I couldn't ask for a better sister than you, Juli."

Now Julia's eyes grew misty. She hugged Jenny. "I love you. I really do." Then she embraced Teri. "You, too."

"This should have happened a long time ago," Teri said, teary eyed.

But Julia shook her head. "God knew what He was doing. Mark and I had to give our lives to Him before we could give our lives to each other."

Teri nodded, wiping away her emotion.

Peggy Henley suddenly stuck her head into the dressing room. "Everybody ready?" She smiled at Julia. "Oh, darling, you look gorgeous!"

"She'd better," Stacie said facetiously. "We've been working on her for two hours!"

All the ladies laughed and any melancholy vanished.

"I can't wait to see Mark's face when you walk up the aisle," his mother said. Her white-blond hair was pinned elegantly in a chignon, and her emerald green dress accentuated a rosy hue that all the excitement had put into her cheeks.

The prelude sounded and Peggy's eyes grew wide. "That's the cue. Time to go."

They all left the dressing room and stood in the vestibule while the "mothers"—all three of them—took their places in the front pew. They were the last to be ushered forward by Julia's brothers before the wedding procession began.

The matron of honor, Kathy, walked up the aisle with Tim, Mark's older brother. Next, Teri with her husband, and then Jenny with hers. Stacie followed, escorted by Dr. Brent McDonald, a long-time friend of Mark's and, finally, Jesse, the ring bearer, made his way to the altar.

Taking her father's arm, Julia smiled. "You look great, Dad."

He was beaming. "You're not so bad yourself." Roy cleared his throat. "I'm proud of you, Juli, and I'm proud of Mark. Oh, and he wanted me to tell you something."

Julia lifted a brow. "Uh-oh. I don't know—"

Roy chuckled. "You'll want to hear this, I think." He paused momentarily, collecting his thoughts. "I accepted Christ as my Savior, Juli. Mark and your brother Rick talked to me and I saw my need. . ."

"Oh, Dad, that's wonderful!" Julia couldn't contain her happiness and threw her arms around her dad's thick neck.

"Easy now, honey, you'll wrinkle my tux."

Julia let him go. "Sorry about that." She straightened his lapels.

And then it was their turn to go forward.

Step by step, they walked up the aisle as cameras flashed and friends and family smiled. All Julia could see was Mark, waiting for her and wearing an expression that bordered on awe and anticipation. He was the most handsome man she'd ever seen.

Stepping around her, Roy "gave her away," slipping Julia's hand into Mark's elbow. Then the vows were spoken, the promises made. A commitment for a lifetime. They were united as man and wife.

"You may kiss your bride," the pastor said with a good-natured grin.

Mark smiled at her and Julia's knees grew weak. "I've been waiting a long time to do this," he murmured, his lips touching hers. Then he kissed her with a passion that Julia felt to the tips of her toes, and the congregation applauded.

"Allow me to present," the pastor said, "Mr. and Mrs. Mark Henley."

Second Time Around

Prologue

The sun was just beginning to set in the smoggy Los Angeles sky when Korah Mae McDonald got off work from her second job. During the day, from seven A.M. to three P.M., Kori worked in the Medical Center's admitting department. Then, from four to nine, she worked a part-time job as a waitress.

But it will be worth it someday, Kori reminded herself. *Just as soon as Brent finishes his residency. One more month. Then he'll be a doctor. Dr. Brent McDonald.*

Kori was so proud of her husband. Proud, but exhausted! Brent had been in school, on and off, for the last fifteen years and Kori had supported him for over a decade.

She and Brent had met in college twelve years ago. Kori was a freshman and Brent, a junior. They married two years later when she was twenty years old and he was twenty-four. Then, after Brent was accepted to medical school, Kori abandoned her own studies for a job so Brent could continue with his education. His goals seemed more important than her business degree. Brent had a passion for medicine, just as he had a passion for everything else he did in life, and Kori couldn't deny the world the best doctor it would probably ever know.

So she worked and worked hard. Brent, too, had held various part-time jobs whenever he could; however, the bulk of the financial burden had fallen on Kori's shoulders. But she didn't mind. Brent was worth it!

Juggling her purse, tote bag, and keys, Kori unlocked the door to the apartment she and Brent shared. The small unit consisted of only a living room, kitchen, and bathroom, but Kori had done her best to make it feel homey, decorating it with her handiwork. Framed needlework, sayings and scenes, hung on walls in nearly every room. "Love Is Forever" met Kori as she entered the apartment. "Home Is Where You Hang Your Heart" was the next proclamation, hanging in the hallway near the kitchen.

However, the next sight that greeted Kori wasn't all that pleasant and it was becoming far too familiar—as were the sounds accompanying it. Brent and four of his "doctor" friends crowded the small living room, the room that also served as the bedroom once the couch was pulled out. It irritated Kori that she couldn't just relax after her long day, but she was determined to be nice. . .for Brent's sake.

"Hi, everyone," she said, forcing a smile.

The greeting was ignored, or perhaps unheard, beneath the raucous laughter. Kori walked into the kitchen area feeling more discouraged now than tired. She had a hunch that Brent's friends didn't like her. They habitually discussed topics that were over her head, though Kori caught on to more than they realized because of her experience in the admitting department. And the other day she overheard Meg Stark refer to her as "the country bumpkin." But worse was the fact that she'd seen Brent smirk at the remark. He didn't bother to defend her where once he would have. Once she and Brent had been the best of friends, but lately Kori felt forgotten.

With a weary sigh, she kicked off her shoes and unpacked her tote bag. A thermos, a Tupperware lunch box. Next she filled the sink and began to wash the dishes that Brent and his friends had accumulated.

I'm glad he found some supper, she mused, washing Chinese food off the plastic plates. But she couldn't help wishing that Brent would have thought to save her a bite. She was hungry since she didn't get a chance to grab anything at the diner tonight. Looking out over the counter and into the living room, Kori wished Brent would try to include her. . .the way he used to. But he didn't anymore, and things had been getting progressively worse between them in the past several months.

Kori continued to clean the kitchen until, at last, Brent's friends roused themselves and headed for the door. Kori heaved a breath of relief. Finally she could put up her tired feet and watch a little television.

"Oh, hi, Kori," tall and lanky Max called. Then, with a sardonic twinkle in his hazel eyes, he added, "Bye, Kori."

"*Au revoir,* Kori," Joe, another of Brent's buddies, said. Light brown hair and blue eyes, he was as handsome as the day was long. Unfortunately, he had an ego to match.

"*Arrivederci,* Kori," came Meg's parting shot as she swung several strands of her long blond hair over her slender shoulder. Pausing near Brent, she coquettishly whispered, "Just remember, Brent, there's fifty ways to leave your lover."

His friends all chuckled.

"Shut up, you guys," Brent said irritably. Then Kori heard him mumble something about not making things easy. . .

Finally Brent closed the door on all of them.

"Mind telling me what's going on?" Kori asked warily. She could sense something. . .something very wrong.

Brent sighed, raking a hand through his straight, jet-black hair, an ancestral trait. He was part Native American and his swarthy features revealed his heritage. The other part of his makeup was Irish and his zest for life lent credence to that nationality as well. But now, as he stood before her, Kori saw a tumult of emotions cross his handsome face. Then a sort of hardness entered his mahogany-colored eyes.

"What is it, Brent?"

"I don't know," he hedged. "It's you. . .it's me. It's us." He turned away and walked into the living room, leaving Kori standing at the edge of the kitchen area.

"I think it's your friends," she said calmly. She understood him well enough to know that he was easily swayed. Every cause that came his way, Brent wanted to stand for it, fight for it. That part of his character was, in fact, the reason he had taken so long to finish med school. He was easily distracted. But Kori. . .she was his voice of reason, or so Brent told her on many occasions.

"Leave my friends out of this, Kori. They've got nothing to do with my decision—"

"What decision?"

Brent paused momentarily before turning to face her again. "I'm leaving you, Kori. Tonight. I'm moving in with Brad Henschel. I can't put it off any longer."

"You're leaving me?" she asked incredulously. "I. . .I don't understand. . . ?"

"It's not too difficult," Brent replied in a patronizing tone. "A child could figure it out. I'm leaving. Period."

Kori walked slowly toward him, stunned that he could be so casual about something like their life together. "Why don't you think this over?" She reasoned. "We've been through some hard years together, but they're almost over. The best is yet to come. I suggest you stay away from your friends for a week and—"

"No," Brent said adamantly, shaking his dark head. "It's over. I. . .I just don't love you anymore."

His words cut straight to her heart, piercing it through with an unimaginable sorrow. *I just don't love you anymore.* And all she could do was watch tearfully as Brent packed his things and left their apartment.

❧

Three months later, Kori sat on one of the park benches outside the hospital where Brent now worked. He had been hired by a group of emergency physicians almost immediately after completing his residency. But that came as no surprise to Kori. Brent was the best physician she knew. What did surprise her, however, was the fact that he was determined to get a divorce. She had been so sure that he'd change his mind. . .

Looking across the hospital's front yard, Kori suspected Brent's reasons involved Meg, the "other woman." She couldn't prove it, though. Nor did she care to. There was definitely some truth to that old cliché "ignorance is bliss." Kori couldn't stand to think of Brent and Meg together. Except it made sense. Meg Stark was prettier, with her stylish, blond "bob" hair style and willowy figure. Kori, on the other hand, did what she could with her long, naturally "brassy" blond hair. She hadn't the money to spend in the professional salons. . . like Meg. And Kori's figure, though not "fat," was full. She was soft and round where Meg was straight and firm. Kori was a farm girl. Meg was a city slicker. Obviously, Brent decided he preferred the latter.

*I just don't love you anymore. . .*Kori thought those words would haunt her till the day she died!

With a breaking heart and her world crashing at her feet, Kori read Brent's latest note of instruction.

> *Go see Tom Sandersfeld. He's handling our divorce and taking care of the paperwork. He needs your signature.*

Kori folded up the letter. She remembered Tom Sandersfeld. He and Brent had met at school a couple of years ago. Tom had been a friend—to her as well as Brent. But now he was Brent's attorney and obviously Brent's friend, not hers.

Kori sighed. She supposed she should be compliant and sign the divorce papers; however, before she signed anything, Kori wanted to talk to Brent one more time. Perhaps he would have a change of heart after all.

Still sitting on the bench, she waited patiently until he finally emerged from the hospital. She watched him walk toward the adjacent parking structure that housed his brand- new, little red sports car. Ironically, Kori thought that the new car matched Brent's new, careless lifestyle as a single emergency physician. Attracting women wouldn't be a problem if and when he tired of Meg—and the idea sent a wave of heartsickness through Kori.

"Brent!" she called just before he disappeared into the parking structure.

He stopped and she ran toward him. "What is it?"

Kori reached him, hoping against hope that he would change his mind and want her back.

"I got your letter," she began. She held it up so he could see. "But I. . .well, I don't want a divorce." Tears gathered in her eyes. "I love you, Brent. Can't we work this out? I'll do *anything*."

He shook his head. "Kori, there's nothing you can do. My mind is made up."

Her heart took a plunge. "But I thought we were happy together."

"That's just it. You were happy and I wasn't."

"You weren't? But I thought—"

"You thought wrong," Brent replied irritably. Then he paused and began to address her like he might a very slow child. "Look, Kori, I don't love you anymore and I want out of our marriage. Is that too much for you to comprehend?"

"No," Kori murmured, her tears threatening to choke her. "I understand more than you think. You want Meg, not me."

"Leave Meg out of this."

Kori smiled bitterly, meeting Brent's dark gaze straight on. "It's a good thing you realized how *unhappy* you were with me *after* I worked two jobs and put you through med school!"

At that Brent merely smirked. Then he turned and walked away, heading toward his new sports car.

❧

"Oh, Kori, I'm so sorry to hear about you and Brent," her older sister Clair crooned over the telephone line later that day. "Why don't you move to Wisconsin? You can live with my roommate Dana and me. What's keeping you in California?"

"My two jobs, that's what."

"You could get a job—make that *jobs* right here."

"I don't have any money. My old, beat up car won't make the trip and I can't afford airfare." Discouraged, Kori plopped down on the couch. "How's that? Three reasons right there."

"Mere technicalities," Clair replied in her usual optimistic tone. She was always outgoing and very practical, whereas Kori was serious and somewhat intro-spective. "I'll wire you the money."

Kori smiled, knowing her sister could afford it, too. Clair had a wonderful job with a national firm. She'd gotten transferred to Wisconsin over three years ago—and she loved it there.

"Mom and Dad will help you. . .as much as they can, anyway." Their parents lived in a rural, little-nothing-town in Idaho. "Call them."

"I did. Dad wants me to come home."

"Oh, bother!" Clair replied, sounding like Winnie the Pooh. "You'll never have a moment's independence if you move back with Mom and Dad. Mom will mother you to death and Dad will give you an eleven o'clock curfew."

Kori laughed, but Clair was right. Their parents would always see them as girls and not grown women. Kori didn't want to go home.

"So what do you say? Wisconsin or bust!"

Kori thought it over. "But what if Brent decides to reconcile?"

"Leave him your address and phone number."

"But what if—"

"Kori, stop it. Stop building false hopes. The reality is: Brent is gone. You've got to start your own life now and what better way to do that than to move and begin all over again here in Wisconsin? Besides," Clair added, "California is too hot in the summer. Wisconsin is beautiful! Come for a few months. You'll see. And, if you don't find a job or you don't like it here, I'll pay your way home, too."

Tears gathered in Kori's eyes. "You'd do that for me, Clair?" After all these years of "doing" for Brent, it was nice that someone wanted to take care of her for a change.

Clair was laughing. "Of course I'd do that for you. Big sis to the rescue. Now, pack your bags, darlin'," she drawled, "and get yourself on the next flight out."

"Yes, Ma'am," Kori quipped. Her decision was suddenly made: she would start a brand-new life—without Brent!

Chapter 1

Eighteen months later

The busy, ever-growing Westpoint Medical Clinic, in West Allis, Wisconsin, was winding down for the weekend. At five o'clock on this Friday afternoon, it was already dark outside. Doing the preliminary work, Kori had taken her last patient's blood pressure and now Dr. Ryan Carlson had gone into the exam room.

Back at her desk, Kori completed the route slips for the day. As Ryan's medical assistant, Kori had patient contact and paperwork galore, but she loved her job. Ryan had hired her two years ago as a secretary, promising to train her for the medical assistant position. In the meantime, Kori attended the area's technical college and took the courses required for the certification exam. She passed and, with Ryan's help, she was promoted to a certified MA.

Ryan Carlson was a joy to work for and the two of them got along quite well. His manner was unpretentious and amicable, even if he was somewhat of a religious fanatic.

Ryan was one of those "born-again" people and he never hesitated to tell Kori about the love of Jesus—mere words, she thought; however, Ryan's warm, friendly, and very Christian-like conduct gave her pause. In fact, she was almost envious of his new love interest, a woman by the name of Stacie Rollins whom, he said, he had met at church.

Imagine meeting someone at church, Kori thought, gazing at the picture of Jared Graham, her fiancé. Blond and brawny, he was posed on a lake pier, holding the tail of the fish he'd just caught. She had to admit the fish was something, too. The thing looked nearly as long as Jared was tall, and Jared's countenance told of his pride over his catch.

Kori smiled, remembering how she and Jared had met at Clair's company picnic last summer. Jared worked for one of the affiliated divisions and he was handsome in a rugged way. He was a "man's man" who hunted, fished, bowled, played baseball, basketball. . .the list seemed never-ending. And he was rather impatient when it came to female sensibilities, but Kori tried not to mind that aspect of his personality too much.

The upside, she told herself, was that Jared would not be easily persuaded by each and every female who crossed his path. In fact, Kori doubted that he would have noticed her—except she had literally run into him at the picnic, spilling a thirty-two-ounce cola down the front of his shirt. That was when he *noticed* her, and he had obviously liked what he saw. They started talking, Kori offering to have the shirt laundered and Jared insisting it wasn't worth it. By the time the picnic was over, Jared had asked her out on a date—and they'd been seeing each other since.

Then last month he proposed marriage. Kori accepted, though she couldn't say that she actually *loved* Jared. But maybe she didn't really know what love was anymore. Since her divorce, Kori had been questioning many things—including love.

But Jared wasn't anything like Brent. Jared was practical, sensible, and. . . stable. No more chasing one rainbow after another. Not with Jared. But that's what life had been like with Brent.

Shaking herself out of her musings, Kori went back to her route slips, but it wasn't long before her thoughts returned to Jared. She wondered if, perhaps, she shouldn't have accepted his marriage proposal. Maybe it wasn't fair, Jared being in love with her and Kori so uncertain about her feelings. Furthermore, Ryan had voiced friendly concerns, and now his misgivings were somehow causing Kori to have doubts. Why couldn't she just fall in love with Jared? Why was love such a complicated matter?

Love. It was what Kori longed for in this world. She was so incredibly lonely, even with her sister Clair and their roommate Dana around. Kori's longing for the love of someone who would cherish and protect her was like an abyss in her soul, aching to be filled. And she hoped Jared was that someone who would teach her how to fall in love again.

Kori forced her thoughts back to the present and finished her paperwork. At six o'clock, she punched out, leaving the clinic for the weekend. She walked through the darkened parking lot, heading for her 1986 Chevette.

She had bought the car for a thousand dollars from a friend of Clair's. Ryan had called it "answered prayer" since Kori was, at the time, in desperate need of transportation. The apartment she shared with Clair and Dana was in New Berlin, a western suburb just outside of Milwaukee County. However, there wasn't a handy bus route, making getting to and from work a hardship. But with a car, it was easy and, within ten minutes, Kori was pulling into the parking structure of the apartment complex in which she lived.

"Hello? Anybody home?" she called minutes later, unlocking the door and entering the apartment. When no one answered, Kori dropped her purse and took off her winter coat, hanging it up in the closet. Then she sorted through the mail that had been set on the little table in the front hallway by Dana, who habitually came home for lunch.

Claiming a few bills, Kori walked into her bedroom and put them on the desk.

Next she changed from her uniform to black stirrup pants and a large sweatshirt that came to her knees.

Comfortable now, she padded through the tastefully decorated living room. Clair, whose hobby was interior design, had done it in mauves, blues, and greens, and one piece of furniture complimented the next, pulling the whole room together. But how Clair ever came to be an insurance adjuster, Kori would never know!

And then there was Dana, the beautiful, intellectual, personable banker by day and the gourmet chef by night. She said cooking helped her relax, but her delicious creations made dieting next to impossible. In fact, one of Dana's meals necessitated a good half hour on the treadmill!

Turning up the heat, Kori headed for the kitchen just as Dana Taylor burst through the front door.

"Hiya, Kori. Have a good day?" Dana's straight, blond hair hung to her shoulders, flaring slightly from the static electricity in the air, and the cold outside seemed to have turned her eyes a brighter blue.

"My day was all right. How 'bout yours?"

"Pretty good." Taking off her navy-blue wool coat, Dana walked through the apartment and met Kori in the kitchen. "Did you get my message?"

"No. What message?"

Dana laughed. "Oh, it's right here. On the counter. I meant to put it in with your mail." She handed the slip of paper to Kori. "Some guy called for you."

And that's just what the note said, too. It read: *Some guy called for you.*

Fighting the urge to laugh, Kori nodded her thanks.

"Sorry to be such a bubblehead," Dana said apologetically. "I should have asked for his name, but he said he'd call back. It wasn't Jared, either. Probably some salesman," her roommate continued as she opened the refrigerator and pulled out a can of cola. She popped the top. "Those guys always call at lunchtime or around the dinner hour." Dana sipped the soda before grinning mischievously. "You're not two-timing poor Jared, are you?"

Kori gave her a quelling look. "Me? Please! Jared is the first man I dated since coming to Wisconsin." She smiled then. "But I think Jared is a keeper."

Dana returned her smile just as the telephone rang. "I'll race you."

Both women pounced on the poor cordless phone, which had been tossed haphazardly on the sofa. But it was Dana who picked up the call.

"Oh. . .it's just you, Jared," she said, disappointed. "Yeah, she's here." Dana handed the phone to Kori.

"Come on, Dana. Smile. Your sweetheart will be the next caller."

Dana tossed her blond head. "He'd better be, if he knows what's good for him!"

Kori laughed, putting the receiver to her ear. "Hi, Jared."

"Hey, how's my best girl?" he asked jovially.

Kori was still smiling. "I'm great. Are we going out tonight?"

"Sure. My bowling team needs a scorekeeper. How 'bout it?"

"Scorekeeper?" Kori hid her disappointment. She would rather go out to dinner and a movie alone with Jared than share him with his bowling team. However, Kori knew she'd better get used to it.

She forced a smile into her voice. "Sure."

"Great. Afterwards we can rent a movie and go back to your place."

"All right." Things were looking up.

Jared said he'd come for her at eight and then their conversation ended. No sooner had Kori hung up the telephone, when it rang again. This time it was Tim, calling for Dana. Clair came home moments later, and the apartment was buzzing with activity.

"Zach is picking me up at seven," she sighed, looking at her wristwatch. "I have to shower and change. . . I'll never make it." She looked at Kori and smiled. "But I'll die trying!"

They laughed as Clair hurried into the back of their three-bedroom apartment, while Dana finished her conversation with her boyfriend. Then she and Kori shared a light supper, after which both women freshened up for the evening ahead.

At eight o'clock, Jared arrived. He was dressed casually in blue jeans and his red-and-white bowling league shirt. "Ready to go?" he asked. He didn't even bother removing his jacket, indicating that *he* was ready to go.

Kori nodded.

Just then, Clair clicked off the portable phone. She tucked several strands of her light brown hair behind her ear and placed a hand on her hip. "Plans have changed. Zach and I are staying home. . .and I'm cooking."

Kori grinned as she and Jared headed for the door. "Does Zach know what he's getting into?" she teased. "Maybe you'd better order out."

Clair gave her a pert little smile, and her blue eyes twinkled. "I am a very good cook, Korah Mae, and you know it!"

Kori winced at her given name. Only her big sister would stoop so low as to call her "Korah Mae."

Meanwhile, Jared was chuckling at them. "Well, I hope you and Zach don't mind if Kori and I come back here with rented videos."

"No, we don't mind," Clair replied. "We can watch them together. . .if you guys don't mind, that is."

"Guess I don't care," Jared said. Then he looked at Kori. "What about you, honey?"

A warm feeling flooded Kori's being at Jared's use of the endearment. "I don't care, either," she said, thinking that it really should be so easy to fall in love with him. . .

Minutes later, they left the apartment. "I've got a great idea, Kori," Jared said once they were outside. He unlocked the passenger side of his pickup truck and opened the door. "I was thinking that maybe we'd get married on a cruise ship."

"What?"

Jared closed the door before answering. Then, walking around the front of the truck, he opened the other door and climbed in behind the steering wheel.

"Yeah, these cruises are supposed to be really great," he informed her. "You go down to St. Thomas and get married by the justice of the peace."

"A cruise. . ." The idea began to grow on her. "Oh, Jared! A cruise. It's sounds so. . .romantic." *And maybe,* Kori added silently, *it'll be just the thing to make me fall in love.*

Jared looked over at her with enthusiasm shining from his eyes. "Yeah, and we could go fishing along the reef in the morning before we get married!"

Kori gazed back at him from beneath raised brows. "Fishing? On our wedding day?"

Jared shrugged. "Sure. Why not?"

Kori sighed. "Yeah, why not. . ."

"Don't you like my idea? Or don't you know how to fish?"

Kori laughed softly. "I know how. Clair and I used to fish in the little stream behind our house all the time."

"And wasn't it a thrill when you actually caught something? Now just imagine fishing along the coral reef."

"I can't wait," Kori said on a little note of sarcasm.

Jared didn't notice, however. "I can't either. This'll really be a great time." He laughed. "We'll never forget our wedding day, that's for sure—especially if we mount something we catch!"

He was as eager as a little boy and Kori softened. She wouldn't hurt him for the world. If Jared wanted to go fishing on their wedding day, that was fine with her. She was just glad that he included her in his fishing trip plans—the way Brent used to include her before he'd met his precious friends and dumped her.

"So what do you think?"

Kori brought her thoughts around to the present. "About the cruise?" She smiled. "I love the idea, Jared."

"Okay. How 'bout February?"

"A cruise in February, the same month as Valentine's Day? A cruise to St. Thomas?" Kori couldn't help a dreamy sigh. "It sounds marvelous, Jared, and the perfect thing to do in the middle of winter!"

He smiled. She smiled. And both were suddenly lost in their own, separate dreams.

Chapter 2

The bowling alley was noisy, crowded, and smokey, but Kori had a relatively fun evening. She kept an accurate running score and cheered Jared on. He was, she decided, a very good bowler.

Around eleven o'clock, they left for an all-night video shop where they chose several movies. Then it was back to Kori's place to watch them.

Sitting around the television, the three couples passed a bowl of hot buttered popcorn. Dana and Tim sat together on the sofa while Kori claimed the armchair, leaving Jared, Clair, and Zach to sit on the floor. But once the movie got underway, Clair stood and motioned Kori to follow her into the kitchen area.

"What's up?"

"I wanted to wait until everyone else was occupied with the movie," Clair whispered. She smiled sympathetically. "I hate to be the one to tell you this, but Brent called tonight."

Kori raised her brows, surprised. "Brent?" At her sister's nod, she frowned. "What did he want?"

"He wants to talk to you. Said it's important. He'd like you to call him back. He's in town. Here's his telephone number."

"Here? In Wisconsin? Brent?"

Clair nodded and handed over the phone message. "He said he called around lunchtime, too."

"So that's who called," Kori murmured, glancing at the slip of paper for a good minute. She wondered what this all meant. Finally she crumpled it into a ball and tossed it into the wastebasket. *Two points!* as Jared would say.

"I won't return Brent's call," Kori said with a stubborn tilt to her chin. "I don't have anything to say to him."

"Yeah, I figured, and I told him you'd feel that way."

"And?"

"And. . .Brent said that unless you phoned him before midnight tonight, he would pick you up at eight o'clock tomorrow morning for breakfast."

"He wouldn't dare!" Kori exclaimed, horrified.

"Well, it didn't sound like a mere threat," Clair replied in her usual, calm manner.

Kori, on the other hand, gasped. "Where's that phone number?"

"I think you're too late."

Clair laughed as Kori dug through the kitchen garbage like a naughty puppy. Then, after she found the slip of paper, she had to wipe off the food particles just so she could read the phone number.

"I suppose this is what I get for being impulsive."

"I suppose." Clair gave her a broad smile.

"This isn't funny."

"Sorry." Clair forced the smile off her face. "But I'm just dying to know what Brent wants."

"Why didn't you ask him?"

"I did. He wouldn't tell me."

Kori frowned, looking at the clock. It was 12:45.

"Like I said: I think you're too late. You didn't even get back home until 12:15."

"I'm going to call him anyhow," Kori said decisively. "Brent deserves to be awakened at this time of night. Don't you think? After what he put me through."

"You're heartless." Clair teased, and her blue eyes sparkled with amusement.

Ignoring the remark, Kori slipped into her bedroom unnoticed and dialed Brent's phone number. Her heart pounded anxiously as she listened to it ring and ring.

What could he possibly want?

Moments later, she realized that Brent wasn't going to answer. Placing the receiver in its cradle, Kori left her bedroom and reentered the living room. She caught Clair's gaze, shook her head in silent reply, and sat back down in the armchair. She pondered the idea of Brent showing up here at eight o'clock in the morning.

And then she saw him in her mind's eye, his handsome, swarthy features, his dark eyes staring back at her. She heard his voice: *I just don't love you anymore. . .*and a rush of hurtful memories flooded her being. Then she saw the smirk on his face as he walked away, leaving her heartbroken.

Oh, Brent, what do you want? she wondered once again, only this time she had to fight down a familiar wave of heartache.

Glancing at Jared then, she told herself that Brent no longer had a hold on her. She forced herself to believe that, since she was engaged to Jared now. And, of course, she had every right to refuse to see Brent altogether. However, something inside of Kori was curious—as curious as Clair's, "I'm just dying to know." After all, curiosity was a family character flaw, and Kori's mind immediately conjured up questions such as. . .What did Brent look like after two and a half years? Was he still as handsome? Did he remarry? Was it Meg? Was he still a doctor? And what was he doing in Wisconsin?

Well, maybe she'd just have to find out. Kori knew she'd be forever curious, to the point where it would drive her crazy if she didn't take the opportunity to speak with Brent one last time.

Besides, after all she'd done for him, he could at least buy her breakfast!

❧

The next morning, Kori arose early, showered, and dressed. She changed clothes three times before deciding what to wear. Then, finally, coming out of her bedroom, Kori stopped short at the sight that greeted her. "What are you two doing awake at this hour?" she asked her roommates who sat nonchalantly at the dining room table sipping their coffee.

"I'll give you three guesses," Clair quipped.

Kori lifted a brow. "Snoops!"

"Bingo!" said Dana. "And we're not even ashamed of it. What do you think about that?"

Kori couldn't help a little grin as she patted the fat french braid she'd fixed in her hair this morning. It fell to the middle of her back.

Dana was looking her over. "Nice outfit. Dressing up for the ex, huh?"

"Is it too much?" Kori glanced down at the soft, loose-fitting, emerald green sweater that hung over a full denim skirt, blue tights and brown, leather ankle boots.

"You look like you just stepped out of a Laura Ingalls Wilder book," Clair remarked. "All you need is the bonnet."

"Oh, no. . .I'll go change."

"Don't change. You look fine!" Dana declared. "Don't listen to Clair. What does she know about fashion? Besides, Brent will be here—"

The buzzer sounded.

"—any second," Dana finished.

They all looked at each other.

"Well, one of us should get the door," Clair said.

"I will!"

Dana ran for it like a little girl at a birthday party and Clair rolled her eyes while Kori stood by nervously.

"Are you sure I look all right?"

Clair nodded. "Really, Kori, you look great. I was just teasing."

"Nice to meet you," they heard Brent say after Dana buzzed him up from the lobby and introduced herself. "I'm Brent McDonald. Is Kori here?"

"Yes. She's expecting you. Come on in." A moment of silence. "Have a seat. I'll get her."

Kori and Clair waited as their friend walked from the living room, through the dining area, and into the small alcove by the bedrooms where they now stood.

"Are you guys hiding?" Dana whispered.

"Yes," Kori replied, having second thoughts about the meeting now that she'd heard Brent's voice.

"He seems very polite," Dana remarked "And he's a fine-looking man. You've got good taste in men, Kori."

She groaned. "I think I'd better change."

Clair shook her head, then looked at Dana. "You take one arm, I'll take the other."

"No, no. . ." Quietly, Kori slapped at their hands. "We're all being silly, aren't we? I mean, this is just Brent. My ex-husband. There's nothing between us anymore. He means nothing to me. He's just someone that I used to know."

"Who are you trying to convince?" Clair asked. "Dana and me—or yourself?"

Kori refused to even acknowledge such a question, and lifting a determined chin, she pushed past her roommates and marched into the living room.

Brent was sitting on the sofa, looking calm and relaxed. He wore navy-blue cotton slacks and a red, blue, and green plaid cotton shirt. He appeared amazingly the same, his thick dark hair parted to one side, except that he now wore glasses. They were a classic style and made him look sophisticated.

"Hello, Brent," Kori said uncertainly.

He snapped to attention and stood at the sound of her voice. "Hi, Kori."

She watched as he looked her over and a feeling of self-consciousness enveloped her. Kori knew she wasn't a strikingly attractive woman. In fact, she doubted that she had changed much from the day he'd left her.

But that was when Brent surprised her. "You're as lovely as ever," he said, walking toward her and smiling. "It's good to see you again."

An instant later, she was in his arms for a quick embrace, after which Brent pressed a soft kiss on her mouth, leaving Kori's senses reeling.

She never saw it coming. . .but her roommates had! They stood by grinning like two Cheshire cats.

Kori turned to them, her face flaming with embarrassment over her obvious reaction to Brent's kiss. He shouldn't have affected her like this—but he had!

"You met Dana, already, Brent," she managed to mutter. "Do you remember my sister, Clair?"

"Of course. Hi, Clair." He held out his hand and she took it. Then Brent kissed her cheek.

"So. . .are you still an ER doctor?" Clair asked.

Brent nodded. "I work for the same emergency physicians' group. We service several hospitals around the Los Angeles area. But I've taken a leave of absence until the end of January."

"A leave of absence?" Clair echoed.

Brent flashed her a charming smile. "Kori can tell you all about it after our, uh, breakfast meeting this morning." He turned to her. "Shall we go?"

Kori wanted to protest. After all, what would Jared say if he saw her dining with her ex-husband? Of course, he was probably deer hunting already. He and his friend Bob had had plans to leave for the north woods early this morning.

Clair, good sister that she was, brought over her coat and Brent helped her into it. Then, before Kori could think of an excuse not to go, they were gone.

"My truck is parked up the street," Brent said as they walked along the sidewalk.

"Your truck? What happened to your sports car?"

Brent shrugged, looking chagrined. "I sold it. It really wasn't me, I guess."

Kori didn't reply as she stepped in time with his strides. The day was cold and gloomy and the trees were bare, their limbs resembling gnarled fingers. She put her gloved hands into her coat pockets to stave off the chill.

"Why are you taking me to breakfast, Brent?" Kori couldn't help but ask.

He paused before answering. "I need to speak with you about something very important."

"Oh?" She gave him a suspicious look. "What is it?"

"Let's discuss it over breakfast. That seems much more appealing than out in this cold and on the sidewalk." His smile disarmed her. "But what I want to talk to you about is only a part of the reason I'm here. It's the biggest part, but there is something else."

"And that is?"

"Remember Mark Henley?"

Kori thought for a moment and then nodded. "From school. . .blond, blue eyes. . .nice guy."

"That's him." Brent smiled again. "Well, he's getting married next month and I'm in the wedding."

"The wedding is here? In Wisconsin?"

Brent nodded. "Actually, it's in Menomonee Falls, not too far from here."

"I see." Kori knew where it was. The community was just another suburb of Waukesha County, similar to New Berlin where she lived.

"Mark took a job as a business consultant for a large firm in Menomonee Falls," Brent explained. "There he met up with his high school sweetheart and now he's finally going to marry her."

"How nice," Kori replied for lack of a better response. But she remembered Mark, all right. He was handsome, hardworking, and smiled easily. And he was always working on that old car of his.

"Here's my truck."

Kori snapped out of her musings and stared at the handsome Jeep Cherokee 4 X 4. It was a four-door utility vehicle in a deep forest green. Impressive, but hardly flashy and pretentious like the sports car.

Brent unlocked the door and Kori climbed in. She noticed that the vehicle was loaded with every feature imaginable, a far cry from Jared's dusty but faithful pickup truck.

"You travel in style," she commented as Brent slid in behind the steering wheel. "I'm impressed."

"Thanks. I bought this 4 X 4 about six months ago."

"Business must be booming. First a sports car and now this."

Brent shrugged. "Business isn't too bad."

"Hmm. . .well, in that case, maybe I should sue you for about fifty thousand bucks," Kori said on a sarcastic note. "That's the least I invested in you. I think I ought to get it back."

"Kori, if you want fifty thousand bucks, I'll give it to you." Brent gave her a sideways glance. "My dad left me a good chunk of money."

"Oh?" She lifted a curious brow.

"You're aware that he died, aren't you? Wait, no, never mind. I know my mother wrote and told you. I saw the sympathy card you sent our family. That was thoughtful, Kori."

She shrugged. She had always been fond of her in-laws, though they hadn't corresponded much since the divorce.

"Well, anyway," Brent continued, pulling away from the curb and driving toward Mayfair Road, "Dad had been buying stock in the factory for which he worked, and its value doubled over the years. Then it doubled again. Dad wasn't even aware of his wealth until about three months before he died. He discovered it while settling his business affairs." Brent cleared his throat. "He went to see Tom Sandersfeld. Remember him?"

"Sure," Kori said flatly. "He's that *friend* of yours who took care of our divorce."

"Ah. . .yeah, right." Brent shot her a guilty-looking grin.

"Oh, I get it," Kori stated knowingly. "Since you inherited all this money, you want to settle with me so I won't come back and sue you later. Right?"

"No, Kori, I—"

She laughed, a bitter note to her own ears, yet she was sure that had to be the reason for this little "breakfast meeting," as Brent had called it. "No wonder you'd hand over fifty thousand dollars without batting an eyelash," she said. "It's probably a drop in the bucket to you now."

Brent shook his head as Kori folded her arms and raised a stubborn chin. "Well, I've got news for you, Brent," she continued. "I'm very happy with the life I've managed to rebuild after our divorce. I don't want your money. Any of it!"

"You know, I probably should have considered the money aspect, but, really, Kori, I didn't. That you would go after my inheritance never occurred to me. In fact, I'm willing to share it with you." He clicked on his turn signal and pulled off the road.

She narrowed her gaze suspiciously. "Why?"

"Well. . .because. . ." Brent gave her a wavering glance. "Say, would you mind if we ate breakfast before discussing this?"

"Before discussing what?"

"What I need to discuss with you, that's what."

Kori had to grin at the ridiculousness of his reply. Then she softened. "No, I guess I don't mind, seeing as we're already in the parking lot of the Denny's restaurant."

"This place okay with you?"

"Sure, except I thought we would be dining in elegance, now that you're a millionaire."

Brent laughed. "Hardly, Kori. I'm no millionaire, even though Dad was. He left each of us children two hundred and fifty thousand dollars—he left Mom more, of course. But if I tried hard enough, I could probably blow my entire inheritance in a year."

"I could do it in half that time," Kori retorted.

Brent laughed once more and opened the door. "Let's eat. I'm starved!"

Walking beside him into the restaurant, Kori couldn't begin to fathom what was on his mind.

Chapter 3

Kori and Brent entered the restaurant and were seated by the hostess. They both ordered cups of coffee, which arrived almost immediately. Then they gazed at the menus until their waitress appeared.

"So what are you doing these days?" Brent asked after their orders were taken.

"I'm a medical assistant."

"Really?" He smiled broadly. "I guess I shouldn't be surprised, considering your medical background. I'll bet you're a wonderful MA."

Kori was somewhat taken aback by the compliment. *He must want something awfully badly. He sure is being nice.*

Kori looked at him from over her coffee cup. "What about you?" she couldn't help but ask. "Did you remarry?"

Brent shook his head.

"Oh, that's interesting. I had imagined that you married Meg."

"Meg?" Brent pulled his chin back in surprise, but then a softness entered his eyes. "I'll admit to having a brief attraction to her, but nothing ever happened between Meg and me. Honest, Kori. We dated a couple times after you left California, but she just wasn't my. . .type."

"Kind of like your sports car, huh?"

He shrugged, but Kori knew she was right. When Brent got tired of something, or *someone,* he tossed it aside and pursued his next avenue of interest.

"You know, Kori," Brent said, tapping the zipped-up leather-bound book he'd brought into the restaurant with him—*some day planner,* Kori thought. "I felt so empty inside for years and I thought that if I was single again I'd be satisfied with life. But I wasn't. Next I thought that once I had a successful medical career I'd be satisfied. But, again, I wasn't. It seemed there was a hollowness in my soul that couldn't be filled.

"Then my father got sick and that really affected me. I wanted to be the one to help him, but I couldn't. There I was, a doctor who could save lives in the emergency room but who couldn't save his own father from terminal cancer." Brent paused. "My mortality hit me between the eyes."

Kori stared into her coffee cup. "I'm sorry, Brent. I know you loved your father very much."

He nodded. "Well, the good that came out of my dad's illness is tremendous.

Miraculous, really!" Brent unzipped the leather-covered book. "Mark Henley came to visit when he found out that Dad was dying, and he showed me from the Bible how I could be saved—he showed Dad as well."

Kori's eyes grew large. "That's a. . .a Bible!"

Brent nodded.

"I thought you were carrying around your planner." She narrowed her gaze. "A Bible, Brent?"

"I'm a born-again Christian, Kori."

She laughed. "Good grief! Now I've heard everything!" She laughed once more. "Well, at least your Christianity might keep you out of trouble for awhile."

Brent gave her a curious look. "What do you mean?"

"Oh, the doctor I work for is a 'born-again' too and he seems to spend a lot of his free time in church." Kori grinned. "Can't get into trouble if you're in church all the time."

Brent smiled. "Has this doctor shared God's plan of salvation with you?"

"All the time. But I'm just not convinced. I guess Bible Christianity sounds like everything else I've experienced. I mean, I remember when you were into discovering your Native American heritage. We even went to a couple of powwows. But that got old, so you decided to be a naturalist. Remember that? We couldn't eat anything that had chemicals in it. . . except I'll admit to sneaking a Twinkie every now and then."

Brent chuckled softly.

"And then, after you got tired of being *au natural*," she said on a facetious note, "you got into the whole environmental thing. Then it was saving the animals."

"And now I'm into saving souls. That is, I'm into sharing the Good News of salvation."

Again, Kori shrugged. "For now. It'll be something else later."

Brent shook his head. "No. It won't. Now that I've got God in my life, I don't need all those other things—even though they are important. But they can't save like Christ can. And that's what I was missing. You see, Kori, all those years, I was searching for the Truth."

And at what price you finally found it, Kori answered inwardly. *I lost my heart and you found God.*

Brent was sipping his coffee and watching her curiously. "What about you, Kori?"

"Oh, I've got my truth," she replied tersely. "I took a little bit of everything we were into while we were married and I rolled it into one. So I guess you could say that I believe in a little bit of everything."

Brent accepted the answer. . .for now. He had no choice. Only God could change Kori's heart—like He had his own.

Brent lifted his eyes from his coffee cup to consider her as she sat across the table from him. *Lord, I was so neglectful of her,* he thought, gazing at Kori's beautiful golden-blond hair. Her hair was, in fact, the very thing which had first attracted him. Like a beacon, it had signaled him from across the lecture hall at UCLA. Brent had instantly known that he had to meet the woman whose hair was the color of spun gold. Then, after he had finally gotten up the nerve to ask Kori out on what was their first date, she had looked up at him with eyes so pale green they were almost transparent. From that moment on, Brent knew he was doomed. It was love at first sight for him, just like in the books.

Years later, after they were married, Kori had given up her dreams so he could attend medical school, and she never complained. She just gave of herself freely, never expecting anything in return. Now that was love! But Brent just hadn't seen it. He'd been so blind. Moreover he had never been able to fill the void that leaving Kori had put in his heart. She had been his friend, his confidant—his one true love, and more than anything, Brent wanted her back! He only hoped the news he had for her wouldn't come as too much of a shock.

Breakfast arrived, Kori having ordered the "Grand Slam" special and Brent a steak and eggs dish.

"Would you mind if I pray before we begin eating?" he asked.

Kori shrugged. "Sure. Go ahead." She even bowed her head while Brent asked God's blessing on their food.

"I'm starved," Brent remarked, picking up his fork.

Kori shook her head at him. "I never thought I'd see the day when you'd be eating meat! You! Mr. Vegetarian Animal Lover!"

Brent grinned. "I don't eat a lot of it. Too much red meat isn't good for the heart."

"Oh, right, Dr. McDonald. Excuse me." Kori laughed softly and then began eating her breakfast.

A few moments of silence passed between them as they ate.

"Mom sends her love," Brent told her, salting his eggs.

Kori watched him in a mixture of amusement and disbelief. Dr. Health Food salting his eggs? Amazing!

Brent looked at her expectantly then, and she realized he was waiting for a reply. "Oh, yes. . .please tell your mother that I say hello. How is she doing since your dad's death?"

"Remarkably well. She's moving as we speak. Into a condo that's bigger than the house I grew up in!"

"She sold the house?"

"Yep. About a month ago."

"Oh." Kori mulled over the news as she took a bite of toast. She was happy for her mother-in-law, but thought it was sort of sad that she sold the family home for a condo. Then, again, things just didn't seem to mean anything to people anymore.

"Mom needed the room," Brent explained as if divining her thoughts. "She baby-sits for my nieces and nephews on a regular basis. Besides, maintaining a two-story house and a yard was too much for her."

Kori nodded. She couldn't argue with that reasoning.

"But as sorry as Mom was to sell the house with all its memories," Brent continued, "she's excited to move into her condominium. There she'll begin a new era of her life."

"And just like that, she'll forget about your father? Doesn't she miss him? Isn't she lonely now without him?"

"Hardly lonely with all her grandchildren to keep her company," Brent replied with a broad smile. "But, yes, Mom misses Dad very much. So do I."

"Oh, Brent, I'm sorry. It must have been terribly painful for you to watch your dad die that way."

"Thanks, Kori. You always were a very compassionate woman."

Another compliment, huh? Kori couldn't help but wonder what that meant. However, it wasn't like Brent never used to compliment her. He did. Often. Up until about their last six months of marriage, anyhow.

Several pensive moments passed and then Kori asked, "So, Brent, did you come to Wisconsin with the intention of saving my soul? That and Mark Henley's wedding?"

"Not really," he replied honestly, "but I did come to Wisconsin for you—mainly for you."

"For me? What do you mean?"

Brent chewed the last of his meal, wondering how to explain.

Then suddenly Kori pushed her plate off to the side. "Look, Brent," she said, "if you're on some kind of mission here, forget it and go home. I'll be honest. I've got my own life now and it doesn't include you."

Brent, too, pushed his plate away before wiping his mouth with his napkin. "Kori," he began, "I'm afraid your life includes me more than you think."

"Oh?"

She had a sudden frown on her face and it saddened Brent to see it there. But what did he expect?

"Let me preface what I need to tell you by saying first that I'm sorry I hurt you." He paused. "I'm more sorry than you'll ever know. I deeply regret the pain I caused you."

Kori gave him a knowing smile. "I get it. You've reconciled with God and you think you have to beg my forgiveness. Taking me to breakfast is like. . .penance. Right?"

Brent shook his head. "I need your forgiveness. That's true, but—"

"But nothing. I forgive you, Brent, so you can now go back to California and your medical career with a clear conscience."

"Please don't be flippant about this, Kori. This is serious business."

Again, that frown. "What is?"

Brent drew a long breath. "Well, you remember Tom Sandersfeld. . ."

"You asked me that already," Kori said impatiently. "Yes, I remember him."

"Okay. Well, when I went to see him about getting a divorce, he told me that if you didn't contest it and you signed the papers—which you did—that I wouldn't even have to show up in court. It was basically a done deal. Tom said he'd take care of everything.

"But then he had a streak of bad luck. He was arrested several times for driving while intoxicated, which eventually led to his suspension from the bar. He couldn't practice law for a whole year; however, by the time my father and I went to see him, Tom had cleaned up his act and was back practicing law. Except it came up that. . .well. . ."

"Yes?"

Brent took off his glasses and rubbed the bridge of his nose. He hadn't slept well last night anticipating this very conversation—even with the telephone unplugged. He had figured Kori would try to call him and refuse to see him. But what Brent had to tell her needed to be said.

"Kori, Tom Sandersfeld never filed our divorce papers before his suspension, and he kind of forgot about it. I only found out when I went to his office with Dad that one day. I just happened to question Tom about the divorce, seeing as he never sent me a bill."

For several long moments, Kori just stared at him. Finally, she blinked, looking utterly confused. "What are you telling me, Brent?"

He licked his suddenly parched lips and forced a smile. "I'm telling you that we're still married, Kori," he said. "You're still my wife."

Her hazel eyes grew wide. "What!" At her exclamation, several heads turned at neighboring tables and Kori's color heightened. She lowered her voice. "How could you have let this happen?"

"Kori, I thought Tom had taken care of everything—just as he said."

"Oh, my!" Kori turned ashen. "You mean we're still m—married?"

Brent nodded silently, allowing the news to sink in. Then, as he watched, Kori's expression went from shocked to sensible.

"Okay, we won't panic," she told him. "We'll just. . .fix it. We can file again. . .or have you already?" She smacked her palm to her forehead. "Oh, now I understand what this is all about. You need me to sign another set of divorce papers—and something excluding me from your inheritance." She nodded as though she had it all figured out. "Fine, Brent. Hand 'em over. I'll sign whatever you want."

If the situation weren't quite so desperate, Brent would have laughed out loud. Her reaction was that comical! However, Kori seemed shaken and. . .and even somewhat eager to have him out of her life by way of a divorce.

Then, again, what did he expect?

"Kori, what you don't understand is, I've changed my mind," he said bluntly. "I don't want a divorce anymore."

Her jaw dropped slightly. "You don't want a divorce?" She shook her head as if in disbelief. "Well, it's a little late for that, don't you think? Or didn't you think, Brent?"

"I've thought a lot about this situation, prayed about it, too, and my mind's made up. I want you back."

She gaped at him. "You've got to be kidding."

Brent shook his head. "It's no joke, Kori."

"But your mind was made up almost two years ago when you filed for divorce. Remember? You said you didn't love me anymore. Is it coming back to you now?"

"Two and a half years ago, I didn't know what love was. I was totally absorbed with myself. But I was the reason for my own unhappiness. It was never you."

Kori shook her head. "You can't just devastate someone and then change your mind. I won't hear another word about it!"

"Kori, please!" Brent felt like his heart had somehow leapt into his throat, except he knew that was medically impossible. "Look, I've made some terrible mistakes and I've hurt you beyond imagination. I'm ashamed of myself for ever leaving you. . .but that was before God got ahold of my heart. I'm a different man now—a better one, I hope."

"Leave God out of this, Brent," she warned him, blinking back the tears.

Seeing them nearly broke his heart, but Brent was not deterred. "I can't leave God out of this. . .or any part of my life. It's because of God's mercy and grace that I'm a new man today."

"Right. And I'm Christie Brinkley." Kori scooted out of the booth.

Then suddenly Brent saw it. The ring on her left hand. "Kori, what is that on your finger?"

As she stood at the end of the table, Brent caught her hand and held it. He was shocked to see that a gleaming diamond ring had replaced the simple gold band she used to wear.

Kori pulled away. "I'm engaged, Brent. I'm engaged to be married—to someone else."

A rush of anger rose up in Brent as he stood, facing Kori now. "That's impossible," he countered through a clenched jaw. "You can't marry someone else. . .you're already married. To me!"

"Not for long!"

With that, she turned on her heel and marched out of the restaurant, leaving Brent to flag down their waitress, request the bill, leave a tip, and pay for their meal before he could follow her out.

When he finally left the restaurant, Kori was nowhere to be found.

Chapter 4

Standing inside the gas station across the street from the restaurant, Kori telephoned Clair to come and get her.

"Things didn't go so well, huh?" her sister asked as Kori climbed into the car.

"We're still married!" she blurted.

"What?" Clair's gaze widened with surprise. "You and Brent? Still married? You've got to be kidding!"

"My words exactly." Kori leaned her head back against the seat rest. "Oh, I wish I were kidding. I wish Brent were kidding."

Clair pulled out of the gas station, heading for home.

"The worst of it is," Kori added, "Brent doesn't want a divorce anymore. He said he changed his mind!"

Clair looked at her with clouds of disbelief in her eyes. "Well, that's not nice!"

"Not nice? It's wicked!" Kori paused, collecting her thoughts. "It was so hard to adjust to not having Brent in my life and, now that it's finally happened, he says he's changed his mind! How could he do this to me?"

"Does he know about Jared?"

"Sort of." Kori turned to look at her sister. "I told him that I was engaged." She let out a moan. "I'm engaged to Jared but I'm married to Brent!"

Clair chuckled softly, but quickly apologized for finding anything amusing about the situation.

Finally she reached over and gave Kori's hand a squeeze. "C'mon. Cheer up, little sister," she said, pulling the car into the parking structure. "We'll bake some chocolate chip cookies this afternoon, go shopping tomorrow, and suddenly you'll see things from a different perspective."

Kori had her doubts.

"Really," Clair told her, earnestly now, "this isn't all that bad. A trip to the lawyer's office Monday morning will take care of everything. Just go ahead and file again, Kori. That's all. I know just the person to help you, too. Tamara Mills. She's an attorney friend of mine."

"But what if Brent—"

"Stop, Kori. You can 'what if' yourself till you're purple. Just quit moping and go see an attorney."

Kori thought it over and then nodded. Perhaps she was over-reacting. There had to be a way out of this. Clair was right.

They walked through the glass-encased, well-decorated lobby and took the elevator to the second floor. Entering their apartment, Dana immediately insisted upon being informed about Kori's breakfast with "the ex."

"Okay, so let me get this straight," she said after hearing the story. "You thought you were divorced from Brent, but you're really married to him. . .but you're engaged to Jared, only Brent doesn't want a divorce anymore. And he inherited a quarter of a million dollars. . . ?"

Kori collapsed into one of the armchairs. "That's about the size of it, Dana."

"Wow," she said, looking impressed. "This is even better than *Days of Our Lives!*"

Kori laughed. She couldn't help it. "My life—the soap opera. Oh, and did I tell you that Brent is a born-again Christian?"

Clair didn't look a bit surprised. "This too shall pass," she quipped. "He's been everything else."

Kori agreed. "Just like before, Brent will change his mind about marriage— just like he changed his mind about a divorce."

The buzzer sounded and Clair went to answer it.

"Hi, it's Brent," came the voice through the intercom. "I just wanted to make sure Kori got home all right."

"She's home safe and sound. Thanks." With that, Clair released the TALK button and walked away from the front door. "You know," she said, reentering the living room, "I've got to give the guy a little credit for that one. It was very thoughtful of him to check on you, Kori."

"Yes, I suppose it was."

But then the more Kori thought about it, the more amazing it seemed. In all the time they'd been together, Brent had never gone out of his way for her. He'd let her walk to work or take the bus while he drove their wreck of a car. He'd let her stay home and search the cupboards for supper while he ate out with his friends—on *her* paychecks. And if they argued, and if she walked away, he'd always let her go. That Brent came to see if she'd made it home all right was truly remarkable!

Finally, Kori could deny it no longer. It *was* a different Brent with whom she'd had breakfast this morning. But whoever he was now, Kori had no intention of staying married to him!

❧

Engaged! Brent tossed his car keys onto the marble-top buffet in the dining room of his rented, furnished apartment. *How could she be engaged?* He paused, deep in thought. *How could she not be? She's beautiful—more beautiful than I remembered.*

Walking into the living room, he collapsed into a large stuffed armchair. In his mind, he replayed the breakfast meeting with Kori and discouragement settled in. He had lost her for sure. Forever. Kori was going to marry someone else.

Yes, but does she love him? his heart seemed to counter in reply. *Does she love him. . .the way she loved me?*

Somehow, Brent didn't think so. He had seen something in Kori's eyes this morning when he'd kissed her hello. It was, in fact, the same "something" Brent had felt in his heart. He still loved her. He'd never stopped. He'd just been. . .confused.

And I'm willing to bet Kori still loves me, too.

Brent suddenly felt hopeful again.

☙

"What do you mean, you're not going out tonight?" Clair asked. "It's Saturday night!"

Sitting on the couch with her cross-stitch in her lap, Kori shrugged. "Jared went deer hunting this morning and won't be back until tomorrow night. Besides, I'm tired."

Clair sat down next to her on the couch. "Are you having second thoughts about Brent?"

Kori shook her head.

"About Jared?"

This time, Kori shrugged. "Sometimes." Lifting her gaze from what would be her parents' Christmas gift this year, she looked at Clair. "Jared told me last night that he wants to get married in February. In St. Thomas while we're on a cruise." Kori momentarily fretted over her lower lip. "But what is Jared going to say when he finds out I'm still married to Brent?"

Clair's expression was a mask of sympathy.

"On the other hand, maybe it's best. February will come awfully fast, and I don't know if I'm really ready to marry Jared. Sometimes I wonder if I really know him. He thinks so differently from the way I do. But he is nice and I believe he wants a home and family. . .just like I do."

"But is that a good enough reason for getting married? What about love, Kori?"

She winced at the same words Ryan had spoken to her weeks earlier. "I guess that's one more reason for waiting." She gave her sister a hopeful glance. "But, in time, I know I'll come to love Jared."

"Do you really think so—even after you consider the way Brent kissed you this morning?"

Kori shifted uncomfortably. "Oh, all right. I'll admit to. . .to responding to Brent's kiss. But he caught me off guard. That's all. Besides, Brent has a passionate nature. Jared is just more. . .practical."

"Forget practical, Kori. Jared is shallow and immature."

"How can you say such a thing?"

"Because it's true." She sighed and Kori knew that the last thing Clair wanted to do was insult anyone, particularly Jared. She was just being an older sister and Kori, for the most part, appreciated it.

"Look, I know you, Kori, and I think you'll grow tired of life with Jared because you won't really be living. You'll be *existing*. . .while Jared hunts, fishes, bowls, and shoots darts."

"There's nothing wrong with what Jared does for fun."

"No, but that's *all* he does and nothing is meaningful."

"Oh, Clair, you're mistaken. Life with Jared means stability, and I'll gladly welcome that *existence* after all the turbulence I lived through with Brent!"

"Okay. It's your life."

Kori smiled gratefully. "Yes, it is, but thanks anyway."

"As for tonight, you can come along with Zach and me if you want. We're going to his sister's birthday party."

Kori shook her head. "I appreciate the invitation, but I'm going to finish this stitching project for Mom and Dad. I've been so busy, it'll be nice to just spend a quiet evening at home. Besides, Christmas is only about five weeks away."

Clair waved off the statement. "I'll start thinking about Christmas after I get past Thanksgiving," she said, rising from the couch.

Then she headed for the bathroom, announcing her turn in the shower and Kori smiled in her wake.

❧

At six o'clock the buzzer sounded and Dana came running into the living room in her bathrobe. "That can't possibly be Tim!" she cried. Her hair was in curlers and she was just applying her makeup. "He said he wouldn't pick me up until seven!"

Laughing, Kori strode from the kitchen where she'd been creating supper. "Don't worry. I'll get it. I'll tell him to sit in the lobby, relax, and you'll be down shortly."

Dana replied with a grateful nod.

"Kori? Is that you?" came the all-too-familiar voice through the intercom. "It's Brent. I need to speak with you. It's important and it won't wait."

"Oh, great," Kori muttered. She turned to Dana. "Looks like you're off the hook. Go finish getting ready for your date."

"Well, you can't buzz Brent up here," Dana complained. "I'm not dressed and neither is Clair. And you know how our stuff is, like, all over the apartment!"

Grudgingly, Kori nodded. "Brent? I'll be right down," she said into the intercom. "We can talk in the lobby."

Releasing the TALK button, Kori grabbed her keys and left the apartment. In the lobby, she opened the outer door for Brent.

"Sorry, but this will have to do," she explained. "My sister and Dana are going out tonight and they're dressing."

"Are you going out tonight, too?" Brent asked.

Kori was momentarily surprised by the question. "That's really none of your business."

A muscle appeared to work in Brent's jaw, but he said nothing more on the subject.

Kori led him through the warm, well-lit lobby to a place where six bright, floral-upholstered love seats were scattered about. No one else was in the area, so she and Brent could get comfortable and speak freely.

"What's up?" Kori asked, settling into one of the love seats. Brent sat down beside her and there suddenly seemed to be little space between them.

He leaned forward, his forearms resting on his knees. He was momentarily pensive, before sitting back and giving Kori a direct look. "It's about your fiancé. . ."

Kori lifted surprised brows. "Jared? What about him?"

"Jared?" Slowly, Brent shook his head. "Kori, I just can't imagine you engaged to a *Jared*."

Kori folded her arms and sighed wearily. "Brent, what do you want?"

"Look at me, Kori."

She did.

"I want you to tell me that you love *Jared* more than you ever loved me."

Some undefined emotion caused her heart to skip a beat, and Kori suddenly was at a loss for words. But perhaps it was looking into Brent's dark, passionate eyes that caused her hesitation, caused her to remember. . .his kisses, his embraces, the sweet words he used to whisper in her ear. . .

At last she concluded Brent's request was impossible. Kori would never love anyone as much as she once loved Brent. However, the key word was "once," because her love for him was no more!

"Brent, you and Jared are two very different men," she tried to explain. "What's more is, I may look the same physically, but the person I am with Jared is very different from who I was when you and I were married."

"*Are* married," Brent corrected her. "And you're not answering my question. Do you love him more than me?"

Kori wanted to hurl a "Yes!" into Brent's handsome face, but the word wouldn't take form.

She stood, turning her back on him, unable to look into his dark, probing gaze another moment. "I'm going to marry Jared," she finally said with much more determination than she'd ever felt. "What does that tell you?"

Brent rose and stood behind her. Taking hold of her elbow, he turned her back around to face him.

"Jared wants a family," Kori blurted. "I want children. I want a home. And Jared is a decent man. He's got a good job—one he's been faithful to for almost fifteen years! That means a lot to me. . .stability, and Jared is a very stable man!"

"Those are fine attributes," Brent said, taking her by the shoulders and giving her a mild shake. "But do you love him more than me?"

Kori tried to twist out of his grasp, but Brent only tightened his hold. "Let go of me!" she cried in the heat of indignation. "How can you talk to me about love after the way you hurt me? I should hate you!"

"Do you?"

Kori paused. "I. . .I don't know. . ." She heaved a sigh as tears stung the backs of her eyes. "For months after you left, after you told me you didn't love me anymore, I would lay awake at night wishing upon wish that you'd want me back. Here in Wisconsin, hundreds of miles from where you were in California, I'd wish and wish that you'd call me and say it was all a mistake. But you never did."

She saw a look of guilt and remorse cloud his dark eyes and it took all her will to press on. "Finally, I had a choice to make. I could either let my depression over our divorce make me crazy, or I could get on with my life. I chose the latter. It was so hard, Brent, but I did it. I moved on. I went to school, got a job, and found someone to love me and give me all the things that you were too selfish to give."

Again, Kori struggled out of Brent's hold but, this time, she was successful. "Go back to California," she pleaded. "Leave me alone. You can have any woman you want, but I just want to be happy. . .with Jared."

A look so pained and miserable crossed Brent's face that Kori almost relented. Almost.

Brent, however, seemed to have been rendered speechless, so Kori took his hand and led him toward the outside door. "Good night," she said softly. She swung the heavy wooden, glass-paned door open wide, leaning her back up against it. But Brent just stood there, looking like a lost boy.

Finally, he turned to her. "Kori, I'm so sorry for hurting you. It will never happen again."

"You're right," she said with a tight smile. "It won't happen again because I'm going to marry Jared and I don't think he's capable of hurting me like you did."

"So my apology means nothing?"

"Your apology is too late."

Brent narrowed his gaze and any benevolence he might have displayed before seemed to evaporate before her very eyes. "Listen, Kori," he said, "it'll be over my dead body that you marry Jared. . .or anyone else!"

She gave out a little gasp of surprise at his vehemence.

"And if I have to use every dollar of my inheritance," he continued, "and every cent I ever earn, I'm going to fight this divorce."

"Brent! Didn't you hear anything I just said?"

The question, however, fell on deaf ears as Brent stormed from the apartment building.

Watching him go, Kori's heart filled with rekindled anger. *The audacity of that man! What arrogance!*

Then, pushing the button for the elevator, Kori decided that Brent really hadn't changed all that much. He still demanded his own way. He wanted what he wanted despite the cost to anyone else.

Back inside the apartment, things were chaotic. Clair was on the telephone with Zach, replanning their evening, and Dana was madly searching for her gold hoop earrings. Ignoring the goings-on around her, Kori reclaimed her place on the sofa and resumed her stitching. The angrier she got with Brent, the faster her needle went, in and out, in and out. She'd have this piece done in no time!

But when Dana left with her date and after Clair was gone with Zach, an old ache called loneliness bore down on Kori until she hurt all over. There were times, such as these, that Kori felt like she was the only one in the whole world. Suddenly she found herself wishing that Jared would phone. Hearing his voice would be such a comfort. To know that he took time from deer hunting with his friends to think of her would mean so much. To hear him say, "I love you" would erase Brent's words of love—not that Kori believed them. Brent didn't know what love was. Then again, neither did she. But Jared would show her, with kindness and patience, and one day she would return his love fully because she would finally understand its true meaning.

Oh, if only you'd phone, Jared, she wished.

But he never did.

Chapter 5

Brent paced the living room in front of the overstuffed, plaid sofa, until finally Mark Henley cleared his throat. "You're going to wear out the carpet," he teased. "Then Mr. and Mrs. Bakersfield aren't going to be very pleased with me for recommending you as sublessee."

Brent paused. "I messed up, Mark. I totally messed up. I threatened her." He shook his head. "I can't believe I did that. I mean, what right do I have, barging into Kori's life after two years and threatening her? Some Christian I am!"

"Oh, don't beat yourself up. Christians aren't perfect. . .and you haven't been a Christian all that long, either." Mark gave him a patient smile. "So you make amends by calling up Kori and apologizing. Right?"

Nodding, Brent collapsed into a nearby armchair. "I'll apologize—except I don't want a divorce. I want a second chance."

Mark seemed thoughtful for several long moments. "Why don't you try being her friend for awhile? Then you can ask for a second chance at the husband role."

"And I should just let her file for divorce and watch her proceed merrily along in her engagement to. . .*Jared?*" Brent snorted in disgust and then couldn't help but wonder how he'd stack up beside the "other man" in Kori's life.

Mark just shrugged. "Look at it this way. Divorces take awhile, don't they? Perhaps that will buy you time."

Brent considered the idea, although what Mark was suggesting went against every fiber of his being. He wanted to fight this divorce business, not stand back and allow it to happen. He was an activist at heart, not a passive bystander. "I don't know, Mark."

"Well, think about it. I know you'll do what's right." Mark stood and headed for the door. "Sure you don't want to come to Barb and Glen's for awhile? There'll probably be some homemade pizza later and Barb is a great cook."

Brent shook his head. "I don't think I'd be good company tonight. But thanks."

Mark shrugged into his leather jacket. "What about tomorrow morning? You still coming to church?"

Brent nodded.

"Good. Bible study is first at 9:30. The worship service follows at 10:45."

"I'll be there," Brent promised, seeing his friend out.

Then he strode back into the living room. He thought about phoning Kori, but decided to let her cool off until at least tomorrow. Was she with that fiancé of hers tonight? Brent heaved a curt laugh as he sat back down in the chair. Nothing like pushing her into the other man's arms by threatening her. Of course she'd run to Jared after what he'd said to her tonight. What could he have been thinking?

Brent sat there pensively for many long minutes. Finally, he decided on a hot shower. Then he'd spend the evening reading. He'd brought an entire box of books from California in hopes of catching up on the reading he had never seemed to find time for in the past. But he had the time now. He had two and a half months of time.

But will that be long enough to win back Kori's heart?

❧

"Where'd you get these roses, girlfriend?" Susie, another medical assistant, asked Kori the following Monday morning. Lifting the box and putting her nose into the flowers, the young, African-American woman, inhaled deeply. "They smell as pretty as they look."

Kori smiled, nodding. "Roses are my favorite. And these are quite a surprise. Of course, they're from Jared. He's been deer hunting all weekend. Maybe he missed me."

"I guess," Susie replied taking another whiff. "He must have missed you bad, too, because roses aren't exactly cheap these days."

A warm feeling flooded Kori's insides. So Jared was a bit of a romantic after all. Then she opened the card which had come with the roses. It read:

Dearest Kori,
    Please accept my sincere apologies for the senseless remarks I made Saturday night. The last thing I want to do is fight with you. I love you.
                                            Brent

"That man is out of his very mind!" Kori declared, crumpling the card and tossing it into the wastebasket.

"Who, Jared?" Susie stood up, her black braids swinging. The colorful beads in her hair clicked as they collided and she frowned at Kori's dismay. "What are you talking about?"

Kori shook her head. "Never mind. It's. . .it's a misunderstanding."

"What's a misunderstanding?" Ryan asked, appearing at the doorway of the medical assistants' station. He smiled when he saw the flowers. "Are those yours, Kori?" he asked with a wry grin.

"Sure are," said Susie, "but I don't think they're from Jared."

Kori gave Susie a pointed stare while Ryan's brows shot up in surprise. Then he chuckled.

Kori, meanwhile, gathered the box of flowers from her desktop and headed down the hallway.

"Hey, where are you taking those?" Susie called after her.

"I'm going to put them at the front desk," Kori replied, turning on her heel. "I think the receptionists could use some roses on a Monday morning."

"You got that right," Susie muttered.

With a nod, Kori resumed her mission. Mondays were this staff's worst days. On Mondays it seemed like half the clinic's growing population took ill and then called, demanding appointments. And, because they were feeling sick, they accepted no excuses. The poor receptionists became verbal punching bags if a doctor's schedule was full.

"Look what I brought you guys," Kori said, setting the roses in front of Vicki, a red-haired receptionist.

"For us?" she asked, her green eyes shining.

"For you. You can split them between you and Gigi."

"And where, may I ask, did these come from?" Vicki teased with batting lashes. "Or should I say, *who* did these come from?"

Kori felt a slight blush warming her cheeks. Vicki had been the one to call up and announce that a florist had just delivered a box of roses.

"Don't ask. Just enjoy. Okay?"

"Okay," Vicki said, giving Gigi a curious look.

Gigi put two phone calls on hold. "Did you and Jared have a falling-out?"

Kori shook her head. All her friends at work knew Jared. He came into the clinic at least once a week to "check on his best girl."

Kori grinned. "Look, you guys, I said *don't ask.* Just take the flowers and have a good Monday."

Both women groaned as the telephone rang again.

Smiling Kori turned and went back upstairs. Ryan met her in front of the exam rooms.

"What does our schedule look like today?"

"Booked and double-booked. We'll be here until seven tonight."

Ryan grimaced. "There's a missions' conference at church. I was hoping to make tonight's service."

"Well, if you don't chitchat with the patients," Kori advised with a teasing smile, "you might make it."

Ryan lifted a brow. "Are you insinuating that I take too much time with my patients?"

"Not insinuating, Ryan. I'm telling you. Again."

He laughed, a warm, rich sound that never failed to make Kori smile.

"Do we have any patients waiting right now?"

Kori shook her head. "Our first patient isn't due until nine o'clock—forty minutes from now."

"Good. I'd like to talk to you. Let's go into my office."

Kori acquinced and followed Ryan. "You're not going to insist that I come to your church again, are you?" she asked, taking the chair in front of his desk. A matching credenza and bookshelf lined the wall directly behind Ryan.

He shook his head. "No, I won't insist. But you're always welcome. You know that. Although, what I want to tell you sort of has to do with my church." Ryan folded his hands and, with elbows on his desk, he rested his chin on his knuckles. "I met your husband yesterday. . .at church."

"Oh, good grief," Kori said, sitting back in the chair.

"He's a friend of Mark Henley whose fiancée Julia is one of Stacie's friends. When we were introduced, I made the comment that my medical assistant's last name is McDonald also, after which Brent asked, 'Her first name wouldn't be Kori, would it?' " Ryan chuckled. "Small world."

"Extremely," Kori replied facetiously.

"Then we had dinner together, Brent, Mark, Julia, Stacie, and me."

"Lovely."

Ryan was grinning at her sarcasm. "Judging from your response to the roses, I take it he's the one who sent them."

Kori nodded, considering Ryan through a narrowed gaze. "How much did Brent tell you?"

"Hardly anything. . .just that he *isn't* your ex-husband."

The fight and sarcasm went out of Kori as the unbelievable truth once more hit her heart. She was still married—married to Brent!

"I haven't had a chance to tell Jared yet," Kori uttered before Ryan could ask.

"Any chance of reconciliation between you and Brent?"

Kori shook her head. "None."

"Hmm. . ."

"Listen, Ryan, I know Brent. He changes like the wind, blowing one direction and then another. He only wants to reconcile with me because. . .well, I figure it's because Mark reconciled with his high school sweetheart and now he and Julia are going to be married. Brent is one of the groomsmen."

Ryan nodded. "Yes, I heard that yesterday, too."

"So Brent probably got it in his head that he wants what Mark has—a resurrected love affair."

Ryan shrugged. "I guess you'd know."

Kori thought the comment had a dismissive ring to it, so she rose from the chair. "I'll go see if our first patient has arrived. Maybe we can get a jump start on the day." She turned, but at the office door, she paused. "Ryan, is this going to affect our working relationship?"

He sat back in his chair, considering her. "I don't know what you mean."

"Well, you're a Christian and so is Brent, you're a doctor and so is Brent. I'm sure you guys will soon be fast friends, and you'll take his side over mine. . .if you haven't already."

"I haven't taken anyone's *side*, Kori, and I don't expect to. But I will say that it would thrill my heart to see your marriage restored."

"Ryan, two years ago Brent said he didn't love me anymore. Don't you remember how much that hurt me?"

"Yes, you and I have had many heart-to-heart talks about how hurt you were. You know I understand, Kori."

She nodded, putting her hands on her hips. "So now after my broken heart is finally beginning to heal and I'm getting my life back together, I'm supposed to forget the devastation Brent imposed upon me and slip back into the role of his wife?" She shook her head. "I don't think so."

"It's called forgiveness, Kori."

She shook her head once more. "It's called not being stupid twice." With that, she left Ryan's office and called for their first patient, Keith Baxter.

While Ryan was in with Mr. Baxter, Kori brought their second patient into an exam room. Sara Rondel, a mother of two, had another cold and possibly strep throat. Kori logged her patient's temperature and blood pressure in the chart before hanging it on the outside of the door as she left the exam room.

As Ryan's assistant, Kori could do as much as he allowed, and Kori did everything, it seemed, except give intravenous fluids, otherwise known as IVs. Those were the responsibility of the clinic's "triage nurse" who was a licensed RN.

On to patient number three.

Little Joey Thompson was here for his six-month check-up. Since Ryan was a family practice physician, many of his patients were children. In the exam room, Kori had Mrs. Thompson undress her baby. Then Kori weighed him and logged Mrs. Thompson's remarks and concerns in Joey's chart. Everything was fine; the child seemed to be very healthy. But he'd need an immunization shot today—he'd missed his last one because of an ear infection.

"I always feel so mean when I do this," Kori told Mrs. Thompson, who held Joey on her lap. Ryan had already examined the boy. "I try to remember," she said as the needle penetrated the fat of Joey's thigh, "that inoculations save children's lives. I'm actually doing them a favor when I give them a shot."

Joey screamed at the injection, but Kori was fast and efficient and soon Mrs. Thompson was soothing away her baby's tears. Then, after advising the mother what to do in the case of fever and soreness in the baby's leg, Kori went on to the next patient. However, she was now behind, having spent so much time with the Thompsons.

Three patients were waiting and one of them was Mrs. Trumble, an elderly patient who could talk up a lather. Kori sighed.

By the end of the day, she was exhausted. Ryan left at 6:30, giving Kori instructions to call back several patients with advice. She also had some prescriptions to call into pharmacies and there were, of course, all her route slips to complete for billing purposes. In addition, Kori had to get tomorrow's charts in order—and all before she could leave for her eight o'clock appointment with Tamara Mills, the attorney who was a friend of Clair's.

Roses or no roses, Kori was still filing for divorce.

☙

"It's going to cost me. . .how much?" Kori stared in disbelief at the solemn-faced attorney before her.

Sitting behind her wide, impressive desk, Tamara Mills was a stoic professional, a no-nonsense lawyer, and Kori was convinced that she was every bit as good as Clair had said; however, this woman's fees were atrocious!

"Here's the invoice," Tamara said. "It's itemized. There's a retaining fee and filing fees."

The figures swam before Kori's eyes. This divorce business was going to cost her a thousand dollars. . .up front. Paying for it would break her savings account.

"How long do you think it will take—the whole divorce process, I mean?" Kori pulled out her checkbook.

"Divorces take about a year."

"A year?"

Tamara gave her a patient smile. "Yes. Court dates take a while to obtain." She cleared her throat. "And please be aware that the process could take longer, if your estranged spouse decides to put up a fight."

Kori grimaced. She was certain that she had the fight of her life ahead of her.

"Now then," Tamara said, "do you know your husband's address here in Milwaukee?"

Kori shook her head.

"Well, no matter." Tamara grinned. "We'll find him." Standing, the woman clad in a stylish skirt, matching jacket, and white silk blouse, extended her hand to Kori. "A pleasure doing business with you. I'll be in touch."

Kori nodded, shaking the other woman's hand. Then she wrote out the check.

As she left the attorney's office, Kori remembered that her car hadn't been running well lately. She only hoped the problem wasn't anything serious since she wasn't going to have extra money for awhile. She didn't earn a whole lot at the clinic. Twelve dollars an hour. She paid three hundred dollars a month in rent, as did Clair and Dana, and she had her share of the bills to pay.

Kori breathed a sigh of relief when her car started right up. She breathed another as she pulled into the parking lot of her apartment complex. "Just be a good car," she told it, "and don't break down on me for a least a month, okay?"

Then, climbing out of her Chevette into the frosty November night, Kori resented the fact that she was even in this position. Brent should pay for some of this, shouldn't he? He was the one who left her initially with threats of divorce. It wasn't her fault that Tom Sandersfeld hadn't filed the official papers.

But it was my fault for not following up, Kori admitted to herself.

Earlier this year when she had filed her taxes, the IRS sent her a letter stating the reasons she couldn't file a single return. She had meant to contact Brent about it—but it was just after his father died, and Kori hadn't wanted to add what she thought were mere technicalities to his grief. So she corrected her tax return, collected her refund, and put off contacting Brent until she had all but forgotten about it. Until now. Until he showed up and announced that they were still married.

But this will never happen again, she vowed. *I will never be so irresponsible in any relationship again. Never!*

This, however, brought Kori to another realization. She had to tell Jared, and she'd have to tell him soon. Tonight, in fact. She would tell him tonight!

Chapter 6

Kori drove down Cleveland Avenue, grateful to have borrowed Clair's car tonight. "Hey, what are big sisters for?" she'd said, tossing Kori the keys. Kori, on the other hand, was certain she'd developed paranoia now solely because she had exhausted her savings on Tamara Mills' fees. But logic dictated that she couldn't control whether her car broke down or where it broke down. She'd just have to deal with the problem if or when it occurred.

Reaching her fiancé's house, Kori gulped down her nervousness as she pulled alongside the curb and parked the car. Jared owned his own home, a three bedroom bungalow on Milwaukee's southwest side. The neighborhood was occupied by primarily blue-collar workers, like Jared, and kept up with hard-working pride.

Kori climbed the front porch stairs and then rang the doorbell. The window on the wooden door was too high for her to see inside, but the house was well-lit. Jared had to be home.

"Kori!" he said with surprise, opening the door. "What are you doing here?" She heard male voices whooping and hollering from inside the house. He grinned. "Monday Night Football."

"Oh, I forgot."

He laughed. "Never mind. Come on in."

Following Jared into the house, Kori took off her coat and hung it on hooks fastened to the wall in the tiny foyer. Then she entered the living room where blue clouds of cigar smoke hung in the air. Beer and soda cans littered the coffee table along with a box of Ritz crackers and an empty plate.

"Hi, you guys," she said to the five men perched on the couch, love seat, and miscellaneous kitchen chairs.

Her salutation was met with hearty words of welcome as Jared plopped back into his recliner.

"Would you mind filling up that plate, honey, with the cheese and sausage in the fridge?"

Kori smiled at the request. "No, I don't mind at all." And she didn't either.

Fetching the plate off the coffee table, Kori walked from the living room, though the dining room, passing Jared's pool table. She hoped to one day restore his billiard area into a formal dining room, and she could well imagine the dinner parties here with friends while their children slept soundly in the bedrooms upstairs.

Kori entered the kitchen where various small engine parts lined the counters. *Too bad Jared doesn't know how to fix car engines,* she mused, taking the venison sausage from the refrigerator. Slicing it, she thought about how nicely some blue-and-white country curtains would look on the bare kitchen windows. Why Jared wasn't bothered that his neighbors could see right into his kitchen, especially at night, escaped Kori. She liked pulled shades and closed draperies at night. She thought it was warm and cozy. Even more, she liked to open them up in the morning like a surprise present and see how the day had dawned. But Jared said he didn't care one way or the other.

Would he mind if I wanted new linoleum? she wondered after accidentally dropping a piece of sausage skin. *I'll bet Jared hasn't given this ugly floor a good scrubbing in all the years he's lived here.*

After arranging the sausage on the plate, Kori began slicing the cheddar cheese. She thought back to a couple of months ago when Jared had asked her to move in with him. Kori refused the offer, saying she wasn't living with any man who wasn't her husband. The same held true for giving her body to a man—Kori maintained she'd have to be married to him first. She wasn't pious. She had just been raised a conservative country girl whose parents instilled in her a high moral standard. So then Jared proposed marriage. Kori accepted. And, though she hadn't given herself to Jared physically, she had mentally. Now, if only he could win her heart. . .

"Aw, Kori, you don't have to do anything fancy with that," he said, entering the kitchen. "The guys are just going to shove that cheese and sausage into their mouths. They don't care if it looks nice on the plate." Laughing, Jared took the "hors d'oeuvres" and gave Kori such an exuberant kiss on her cheek that he nearly knocked her backward.

"Jared, I need to talk to you," she called to his retreating back.

"Okay, it's almost halftime."

With a sigh, Kori opened the refrigerator and pulled out a diet cola. Leaning against the sink, since all the kitchen chairs were in the living room, she sipped her drink and listened to "the guys" carrying on. *My word,* she thought, *but they're noisy. And funny.* Kori smiled at some of the ridiculous jokes that drifted to her ears.

"So what's on your mind?" Jared asked, when halftime came some ten minutes later. "You've got twenty minutes to tell me." He smiled, adding, "You sure are pretty."

Arms around her waist, he closed in on her for a kiss but Kori pushed him back. She suddenly envisioned Brent's face in her mind's eye, then heard his voice, saying, "We're still married, Kori." She almost felt his presence there and was repulsed by her situation.

"Oh, Jared," she fairly croaked.

He brought back his chin in surprise. "What's wrong?"

"Something horrible happened this weekend."

"What?" He actually looked alarmed now as a deep frown furrowed his sand-colored brows.

Kori swallowed. "Well. . .it's my ex-husband, Brent."

"Yeah, what about him?"

She swallowed again. "Well. . ."

"Well, what?"

"Shhh, Jared, please keep your voice down."

"Well, then, spit it out, honey," he said impatiently. "The guys are waiting for me."

Kori nodded. "Okay. Brent is in town and he contacted me because. . .well. . . well, something accidentally went wrong with our divorce papers and now we have to get divorced all over again."

Jared narrowed his gaze. "What do you mean?"

"I mean, I had to get a lawyer. I saw her tonight, and I've got to file for divorce because. . .well, because. . ."

"Kori, just say it, will you?"

"I'm still married!"

Jared gaped at her, his rugged features a mixture of incredulity and fury.

Kori lowered her gaze. "I'm sorry, Jared."

"Why?"

She looked back at him, puzzled. "Why, what? Why am I sorry? Or why am I still married?"

"Both!" Jared shook his head. "Oh, never mind."

"Jared, I'm going to fix it," Kori promised. "I've hired a lawyer, and—"

"What about our cruise in February?"

Kori tried not to grimace. She knew he'd be disappointed at the news. "It'll have to wait. You see, that's what I'm sorry about." She sighed, weary as much from this divorce business as she was from her busy day at the clinic. "It's going to take about a year."

"A year! Did you hear what you just said? A whole year!?"

Kori's heart suddenly pounded with fear. "If you love me, you'll wait," she said hopefully. "If you love me, you'll stand by me and—"

"Listen, Kori, go ask Dave out there about his divorce," he said, nodding toward the living room. "It was a nightmare. And then, after all was said and done—or so he thought—Dave's ex-wife sued his girlfriend for something really stupid."

"Oh, Brent would never sue you, if that's what you're worried about."

"Can you get that in writing?"

Kori bit her lip. *Not likely,* she thought.

Jared shook his head. "One of the reasons I got involved with you, Kori," he said soberly, "was because your divorce was far enough behind you so as it wouldn't affect me." He waved his arm. "You think I want to lose my house?"

She looked at him, her heart ready to break. "Is your house more important than me?"

"Yes! I mean, no! I mean. . ." Jared threw his hands in the air. "I don't know!"

Kori willed herself not to cry as Jared circled the kitchen resembling a caged tigar. She had been hoping for a more gallant response to this. She had been hoping to hear Jared say he loved her and he'd wait a hundred years to marry her if he had to!

However, Kori was beginning to understand that real love was nothing like the love in fairy tales and romance novels—or, then again, maybe men today weren't anything like fictional heros.

"I need some time to think about this," Jared muttered.

Kori nodded. Then she watched as he pulled a beer from the refrigerator and left the kitchen for his friends and the football game.

❧

Two days later, Brent hailed her in the parking lot of the clinic. The day was sunny, but the wind had a bite to it—and so did Kori.

"What do you want?"

Brent looked a bit taken aback by her vehemence. "I just wanted to. . ." He looked at his watch. "Are you late?"

"Yep." She pushed past him.

"Kori, wait. Please. I'd like to talk to you. I've been trying to phone you. I've left messages. . ."

She whirled on him. "Look, Brent, I don't want to talk to you. Can't you get that through your head? You are ruining my life for a second time! All I want for you to do is go away—or drop dead, whichever is more convenient."

Brent grinned wryly. "Well, I'm glad you haven't lost your sense of humor."

Kori glared at him. Then she turned and continued walking.

"Hey, did you like the roses I sent on Monday?"

She stopped in midstride. *I will not let him bait me.*

Brent was directly behind her now. He touched the shoulder of her full-length, grey wool coat. "You could just say. . .thanks. That's simple enough. Or you could say that you accept my apology for the harsh way I spoke to you last Saturday night. I'd like to hear that—that you forgive me. Or you could say you liked the roses. I know they're your favorite flowers."

Slowly, Kori turned to face him, her cheeks flaming with anger despite the frigid temperatures. "Brent, my lawyer said you'll receive divorce papers in about a week. All I'm going to say to you this morning is. . .*sign them!*"

With that, she resumed her walk to the front door of the medical clinic, leaving Brent, literally, out in the cold.

෨

Brent hung up the telephone after talking to Attorney Tamara Mills's legal assistant. She had wanted his address. He said he wouldn't give it to her. He said he was going to be very uncooperative and that Kori's attorney should consider herself fairly warned.

"We'll get your address anyway," the legal assistant replied. "I've got your phone number and we'll be able to track you down. Just thought I might save myself—and our client—some time and money."

"Guess again," Brent retorted. Then he'd hung up.

Walking through the living room now, he remembered what Kori told him yesterday. *You are ruining my life for a second time!* It pained him again to realize that he'd ruined her life even once.

Lord, I don't want to hurt her anymore, he prayed. *I just want a second chance. Am I really asking too much?*

No, he wasn't asking too much of God. He knew that. With God, nothing was impossible. But maybe. . .maybe he was asking too much of Kori.

Lord, I'm not good at waiting and I don't want to cooperate with Kori's attorney. But she's so angry with me. . . Kori won't even talk to me. How can I get her to reconcile when she can hardly bear the sight of me?

And then that Still Small Voice seemed to reply, "Love her, Brent. Just love her."

Maybe I'm not good at that, either.

It occurred to Brent, then, that he'd have to learn to be good at it. He'd have to rely on God to help him. Picking up his Bible from the coffee table, he opened it to the page he'd marked months ago. 1 Corinthians 13: "Love is patient, love is kind. It does not envy, it does not boast, it is not proud. It is not rude, it is not self-seeking, it is not easily angered, it keeps no record of wrongs. Love does not delight in evil but rejoices with the truth. It always protects, always trusts, always hopes, always perseveres. Love never fails."

Releasing a long, slow whistle, Brent thought the same thing he did every time he read that passage: It was one tall order!

All right, Lord, I'll cooperate—except it goes against everything in me. And I'll not speak harshly to Kori or threaten her any more. Brent sighed, picking up the telephone book, looking for Tamara Mills's number. *But I ask You, Lord, to intervene and stop this divorce.*

"Well, Mr. McDonald, what a surprise," the legal assistant said once she came to the phone. "I didn't expect to hear from you again. Are you calling so you can be more uncooperative?" She laughed.

"It's Dr. McDonald," he replied with all the politeness he could muster through a clenched jaw. He hated to do this—to give in. He'd rather fight; however, it seemed this battle was the Lord's.

He gave the legal assistant his address and she repeated it back to him.

"Yes, that's correct. Oh, and one more thing. . .I'd like you to document something." Brent paused in momentary thought. "I'd like you to note that I love my wife and I don't want a divorce. I've changed my mind about cooperating, but only because I don't want to hurt Kori."

"Dr. McDonald," the legal assistant began, "that's something *your* attorney should document. Not us. Good-bye."

Brent looked at the phone and then slammed down the receiver. He should have known *they* wouldn't cooperate!

With a sigh, Brent looked at his wristwatch. 6:15. Apparently Attorney Mills had evening hours.

Picking up the phone again, Brent dialed Kori's number. She wasn't home before and Brent had to force himself not to ask if she was out with Jared. He couldn't stand the thought of Kori and that guy together, yet he couldn't stand the not-knowing either. So he prayed, asking God to somehow break up that relationship so he could move in and win back his wife's heart.

"Kori's not home," Clair said once more. "She must be running late at the clinic again. Can I take a message?"

"If I leave one, will you promise to give it to her?"

"I promise." Clair paused. "Listen, Brent, just for the record, I'm not taking sides here."

Brent smiled wryly. "I appreciate it."

"So, what's the message?"

"Tell Kori that. . .well, tell her I'm cooperating with her attorney but only because. . .because I love her and I don't want to hurt her further. Okay?"

Clair was silent for a full minute and Brent didn't know if she was writing his message down or just thinking it over.

Finally, she said, "You know, that's really sweet, Brent. I'll tell her."

Chapter 7

Kori unlocked the apartment door, realizing that it had only been one week since Brent's first phone call. One week and now her life was falling apart just like her car.

"You look bushed," Dana stated, as Kori hung up her coat and walked into the living room. "Tough day?"

"Not really. I'm just stressed out."

Clair called a "hello" from the kitchen, adding, "How come you're so late?"

"My car wouldn't start," Kori replied, collapsing into the armchair. "I'm just lucky I was in the clinic's parking lot at the time. The unfortunate part is that I had to call a tow truck, which costs more money than the car is practically worth. But the driver was nice enough to drop me off here at home before taking my car to the shop." She sighed. "I guess I really shouldn't be surprised, either. I knew this was coming by the way it's been acting lately."

"I hope it's nothing serious," Clair said, coming into the room. "You know I'll share my car with you when I can."

Kori managed a tired smile. "Thanks, sis."

"Hey, have you got plans tonight?"

Kori shook her head, feeling even more miserable. "Jared went deer hunting. He'll be gone for the next week." What she didn't say was he never called to tell her good-bye. *He's still angry,* she thought fretfully. *What if he breaks our engagement?*

"Earth to Kori," Clair called to her. "Come in, Kori."

She shook off her musings. "Sorry about that. What were you saying?"

Clair left the kitchen and stood before her. "I said. . .Brent called about an hour ago. He wants you to call him back."

"Forget it."

The telephone rang and Dana jumped for the cordless phone. "Oh, hi, Brent," she said as Kori rolled her eyes in aggravation. "Yeah, she's here now. Her car broke down. Here, I'll put her on." Dana held out the phone. "For you."

"I'm not here."

"Oh, yes, you are. I see you with my own two eyes."

"A hallucination."

Dana frowned. "I do not hallucinate!"

"Oh, give me that telephone," Clair said, leaving the kitchen and giving Kori one of her long, prereprimand looks.

"Brent," she explained, "Kori is playing hard to get and she won't talk to you. Sorry." Clair paused, listening to his reply. Then she covered the phone, looking back at Kori. "He wants to come over and cook dinner for you. . .for all of us."

"Oh, say yes, Kori," Dana pleaded. "Zach is out of town till Sunday and Tim is working late so Clair and I don't have anything to do tonight."

"And you want Brent to cook for us?" Throwing her head back, Kori hooted. "He can't even boil water!"

"Hear that, Brent? She's laughing at your offer." Clair paused, smiling and listening to the response. "Okay, I'll tell her." She covered the phone again. "He says he took some cooking classes and now he's like the Galloping Gourmet, or something."

"Oh, right," Kori said facetiously. "Knowing Brent, it means he learned to turn on the oven and throw in a frozen pizza."

"Did you hear her, Brent? She doesn't believe you." Clair paused momentarily before turning back to Kori. "Brent wants to know if your favorite food is still Italian?"

"Yes, it is, but—"

"She says yes, Brent. Okay, I'll relay the message." With that, Clair clicked off the phone.

Kori lifted a brow expectantly.

"He's on his way over."

"What?" Kori stood up, glaring at her sister.

"I'm hungry, okay? Brent is offering to cook up an Italian feast!"

Dana was grinning from ear to ear. "Oh, good, I'm hungry too. Besides, I'm curious to see if Brent's a better cook than I am."

Kori groaned. "Look, you guys, I don't want Brent to come over tonight. I've spent my savings on filing for a divorce. I want him out of my life!"

Clair held out the telephone to her. "Fine. Then you call Brent and tell him that." She narrowed her gaze in serious speculation. "You're going to have to talk to him some time, Kori, be it tonight, tomorrow, or the next day. You can't just wish the man away."

"I know," Kori replied solemnly, "I tried it already."

Clair laughed.

"Hey, I've got it, Kori. Why not try being Brent's friend?" Dana suggested with a smile. "I know a woman at work who's divorced and she and her ex-husband are friends. In fact, she had some fund-raiser to attend at the Performing Arts Center and she couldn't get a date, so she asked her ex and he escorted her." Dana tipped her pretty blond head. "Now why can't you and Brent be friends like that?"

"Yeah, Kori," Clair said. "You know, a person can never have enough friends and Brent is trying to be so nice. . ."

Kori rolled her eyes. Brent was a charmer, all right.

"If you and Brent were friends," Clair continued, "you wouldn't be so stressed out. You two could settle this divorce stuff much more effectively and without lasting emotional scars."

"That's right, Kori. My aunt's divorce took years just because she and her ex kept fighting over the settlements."

"It took *years?*" Kori certainly didn't want that. One year was long enough! She quickly weighed her options. If she and Brent were "friends," she might have an easier time of things, just like Clair said, and there was no real reason *not* to be his friend. Brent had already stated that he'd cooperate. He wasn't fighting her or the divorce proceedings anymore. Maybe he'd even agree to pay half of her attorney fees so she could get her car fixed.

And if they were "friends," Brent might agree to assure Jared, in writing, that he wasn't going to sue him. Then Jared might not be tempted to break off their engagement.

"Maybe you guys are right," Kori finally conceded. "Maybe Brent and I could just be friends."

"You could at least give it a try," Clair replied. "What have you got to lose?"

Certainly not my heart, Kori thought with a shrugged reply to her sister's question. Then she walked into her bedroom to change clothes, thinking, *I want Jared to have my heart so Brent will never be able to break it again!*

❧

Brent whistled happily as he drove to Kori's apartment. He felt like the luckiest man in the world. Kori had agreed, albeit reluctantly, to let him come over and cook for her.

Thank You, Lord, he whispered prayerfully as he reached her apartment complex.

Parking his truck, Brent grabbed the two bags of groceries he had purchased on the way over. A one-pound box of pasta, cans of tomato paste, sauce, a can of crushed tomatoes, ground beef, a garlic bulb, oregano, an onion, and fresh mushrooms. Brent was prepared to make Kori and her roommates the best mostoccoli they had ever tasted. He'd also bought a fresh loaf of Italian bread, a head of lettuce, and, of course, Italian salad dressing.

Brent suddenly chuckled, remembering Kori's reaction to his cooking. He couldn't blame her one bit for laughing. It was true; he hadn't been able to even boil water a few years ago. But in order to survive as a bachelor, Brent decided he'd have to learn a few things on his own, like doing laundry and cooking. And the latter he'd had to learn by taking evening classes at a local high school.

So now he'd show her. He'd prove to Kori that he wasn't at all the helpless, demanding, self-centered man who had left her almost two years ago. Why, he could even iron a shirt without scorching it now!

Brent let himself into the small foyer of the apartment building. Rows of mailboxes lined one wall while a row of buzzers were on the other. Ringing Kori's apartment, he waited only a few minutes before Kori herself came down to let him in.

"You could have just buzzed me up," he said, entering the warm, homey-looking lobby. "You could have saved yourself a trip."

Kori shrugged and Brent thought she looked tired. "I wanted to talk to you before. . .well, I didn't want Clair or Dana to overhear our conversation." She looked at the bags in his hands. "Want some help?"

Brent nodded gratefully and handed her the lighter of the two. Then they walked toward the elevator.

"So what did you want to talk to me about?"

Kori waited a moment until the elevator door opened and they walked into the car. She pushed the button for the second floor. "Brent, I know you said you want to resume a marital relationship with me, but quite honestly, I'm not interested. Like I said before, it took me a long time to get over you but now I. . .I am!" But something in her voice made Brent doubt it. "And I'm going to marry Jared!"

Brent guarded himself against a defensive reply. He knew what Kori said was an honest response as well as a deserving consequence for him, and yet he just couldn't accept them. He simply was not a man to give up that easily.

"So what I propose," Kori continued, causing him to tune back in, "is that we commit ourselves to developing a friendship—a platonic friendship."

"A *friendship?*" Brent furrowed his brows, somewhat surprised.

Kori looked him right in the eye and nodded. "A *platonic* friendship," she emphasized once more. "Do you think it's possible? I mean, wouldn't it be better for both of us if we came to some sort of truce?"

"I don't know. . ."

The elevator opened. They both stepped out onto the floor and headed for Kori's apartment. She stopped, however, a few feet away from the door.

"So what do you say, Brent? Are we friends. . .or enemies? There is no in-between for us."

Looking down into her tired face and sad-looking eyes, Brent didn't think he could really be Kori's enemy. Not anymore. He really did love her.

Then he recalled Mark's suggestion. *Why don't you try being her friend for awhile, Brent? Then you can ask for a second chance at the husband role.*

Brent smiled, his decision made. "Kori, I would feel honored to be your friend," he said gallantly as his smile broadened. "Friends it is. Want to shake on it?" He shifted the grocery bag, then held out his right hand.

Kori narrowed her eyes suspiciously. "You're giving in awfully easily. That's not like you. I thought I'd have to at least threaten you."

He laughed, shrugging his shoulders beneath his navy-blue down ski jacket. "Yeah, well, you didn't think I could cook, either, but I can. You'll see. I hope you're hungry."

For the first time tonight, Brent saw Kori smile as she slipped her hand into his. "Friends!" she declared. "And, yes, I'm starving, so you'd better get busy."

With that, Kori let him into the apartment.

Chapter 8

Kori watched Brent create his spaghetti sauce while Clair and Dana set the table. "You know," she said at last, "if I hadn't seen it, I would have never believed it."

He grinned wryly. "And I'm not even finished yet."

"Smells great!" Dana declared, coming back into the kitchen area.

From where she sat on a tall stool beside the stove, Kori agreed. She wanted to watch Brent's every move, and she was amazed at what she was seeing. He had deftly crushed the garlic, chopped the fresh mushrooms, browned the ground beef, and added the tomatoes and spices—all by himself. A real feat for the Brent McDonald she used to know.

"So, you took some classes. . . ?"

Brent nodded, stirring the sauce that was nearly boiling. "I got sick of fast food and the hospital's cafeteria food, so I figured I'd better learn to cook."

"Oh, come on, Brent," Clair said, sitting down on a stool beside Kori. A teasing gleam entered her eyes. "You could have just found some nurses to cook for you. On the TV show I watch, those ER doctors are never without women."

Brent laughed. "Clair, a real-life emergency room isn't anything like Hollywood's. Between my patients and all the paperwork, I don't have time to act like the doctors do on television—not that I would anyway. I'll admit that occasionally romances spring up between doctors and nurses, but what you see on television, Clair, would be considered scandalous and grossly unprofessional if it happened in real life, at least it would in the hospitals I'm affiliated with."

"Well, thanks for setting me straight," Clair said with a little chuckle. "But I was only kidding."

He shrugged and turned the burner on a lower setting since his spaghetti sauce had come to a full boil. "I might as well confess that I said all that more for Kori's benefit than yours, Clair." He smiled, looking more amused than contrite.

"Oh, I get it," Dana interjected. "You don't want Kori getting funny ideas about ER docs, huh?"

"Exactly," Brent replied, giving Kori a meaningful glance.

She just turned away. "I'll get the plates out," she announced, changing the subject. Walking over to the cupboard, Kori pulled down four plates from the shelf. *I thought we agreed to be friends,* she fumed, *and friends don't give each other the kind of looks Brent just gave me.*

"Actually," Brent added, "I don't want *any* of you ladies to get funny ideas about ER docs."

Curiosity won over anger, and Kori turned back around.

"I just want to be a friend to Kori—to all of you," Brent said, defusing Kori altogether, "so I want you to know exactly where I'm coming from."

"So, doctors aren't really like they are on TV, huh?" Dana asked with a hint of disappointment. "They seem so macho and cool and like. . .they know *everything!* You'd just have to trust them with your life."

Brent chuckled. "To tell you the truth, I don't watch a lot of television."

Clair smacked her palm against her forehead and Kori laughed. Brent was laughing, too, although poor Dana just stood there looking totally confused.

"Dana," Clair said, putting a hand on her shoulder, "Brent is being a wise guy."

"Oh. . .so you really *are* like the doctors on TV."

Brent shook his head.

"Dana," Clair said, giving her a mild shake this time, "Brent's not like the doctors on that nighttime drama you watch every week, only it's funny because he's never seen the show."

"I've heard enough about it to make a judgment call, though," he said in his own defense.

"Oh, I get it," Dana said, rolling her eyes, and everyone laughed all over again.

By the time the sauce had sufficiently simmered, the pasta cooked, and dinner was served, Kori was feeling much more at ease around Brent. As they ate, they talked about movies, hobbies, and jobs—all very safe topics—and Kori thought it was a pleasant and most tasty dinner. The wall of hostility she'd set up between them seemed to be crumbling.

"I'm impressed, Brent," Kori admitted, clearing the dining room table afterward. "That was one of the best Italian dinners I've eaten in a long while."

"Thank you," he replied with a little bow and a broad smile.

"Could have used a little more oregano," Dana remarked over her shoulder on the way to the kitchen area.

"Ah, the critic speaks." Clair chuckled. "Don't worry, Brent, Dana doesn't think anyone cooks as well as she does."

Brent was still smiling. "You like to cook, too?"

Dana nodded. "Except I didn't start cooking out of necessity like you did. For me, cooking is therapeutic."

"And she needs a lot of therapy," Clair teased, "so she's cooking all the time."

"Oh, quiet," Dana retorted.

"Now, girls, better behave yourselves," Kori facetiously admonished them. "Remember, we have company."

"Yes, Mother," both Clair and Dana said in unison. Then they all laughed.

"Oh, don't look so confused, Brent," Dana told him, smiling. "Every once in a while, Kori has to practice her mom bit for after she and Jared get married and have kids. Isn't that right, Kori?"

"Right," she replied, trying to sound determined. However, some of that old uneasiness was creeping back into her heart. Jared wasn't happy about her situation and the very point of contention was standing three feet away.

With her arms full of dishes, Kori walked into the kitchen and began filling the sink.

"Let those dishes go," Clair said. "Let's put on a movie and relax before we wash them."

Kori shook her head. "You guys go ahead. I'll clean up here." She paused before adding, "I don't really feel like watching a movie anyway."

Clair shrugged. "Suit yourself." Turning, she asked Brent, "Are you coming?"

"No, I'll wash and Kori can dry. I don't feel like watching a movie either."

"Okay, then Dana and I will start the movie without you two."

Clair crossed the living room to where Dana was already sorting through the collection of classic videos.

Kori turned around and set the dishes into the sink filled with soapy water. "You don't have to help me, Brent. There's not much here."

"I insist," he said, pushing up the sleeves of his shirt. It was a brown cotton knit shirt with a collar, and it matched nicely with Brent's brown, casual pants. But Kori wasn't surprised; Brent had always been fashion-minded and coordinated to a fault.

He dipped his hands into the water and Kori picked up a dish towel. Standing beside him now, she got a whiff of his cologne. It was the same sweet, manly scent that he always wore, and Kori had to fight back an onslaught of memories. Good memories. Memories of being crazy in love with Brent McDonald.

Don't think about the past, Kori told herself, drying a plate and putting it away in the cupboard. *This is the present and Brent and I are just friends.*

"So your car broke down, huh?" he asked.

Kori nodded, but then suddenly remembered her plan.

"You, know, Brent, I'm in kind of a bind," she hedged. "I had to pay my attorney a lot of money toward our divorce proceedings, and now I don't have enough funds to repair my car. So. . .I was wondering. . .well, since we're friends now, and since you're not contesting the divorce—"

"I'll help you, Kori."

She was surprised. That hadn't taken much effort.

Kori dried some silverware and put it away, mentally forming her next request. "Would you be willing to pay half of my attorney fees?"

"Absolutely not!"

Her defenses rose and, facing him, she angrily replied, "But it's your fault that I'm in this mess, and I think it's only fair that—"

Brent silenced her by placing a wet finger against her mouth. He narrowed his dark gaze. "I am not going to help you divorce me," he told her quietly, earnestly. "But I will pay for your car to be fixed." He paused, lowering his hand and smiling. "In fact, let's buy you a new one."

"I don't want a new car," Kori muttered irritably. "Just fix my old one."

"What? And make me worry about you all winter, driving that old clunker? I'd rather just buy you a new car that's dependable and has a warranty."

Kori opened her mouth to refuse, but then thought better of it. In fact, she decided she'd have to be nuts not to take the offer. A new car—she'd love a new car!

"You really want to buy me a new car?" she asked as disbelief reared its ugly head. "Oh, you probably mean a new *used* car, right? That is, it will be used by someone else but new to me."

"No, I mean something right off the showroom floor." Brent smiled. "It's the least I can do for you, Kori."

She chewed the corner of her lower lip and gazed at Brent speculatively. This man was most definitely not the same Brent McDonald she once knew. And yet, he was the same man outwardly. The same dark hair, handsome grin. . .and then the same dark gaze looked into her eyes, causing Kori's heart to beat a little faster.

"So, are you two getting along?" Clair asked. She had come into the kitchen unannounced and now stood by the stove with arms folded in front of her. "Or are you guys getting ready for a showdown?"

Brent grinned, his gaze never leaving Kori. "No show-down here."

"Well, the way you're looking at each other," Clair said sarcastically, "I thought either you're in love or someone's going to die."

I think someone's going to die, Kori thought, tearing her gaze from Brent's and picking up another dish to dry. *It might just kill me to be his friend.*

❧

The next morning, Kori slipped out of the apartment before either Clair or Dana awoke. Brent had promised to pick her up early so they could go shopping for a car, and Kori wasn't up to any funny remarks from her sister and roommate. After Brent had left last night, they had teased her mercilessly.

"That man is after you, Kori," Clair had said. She looked at Dana. "He sends her roses, makes her favorite meal, looks at her with moon-eyes. . ." Clair chuckled. "Sounds like love to me."

"Better tell Jared he's got stiff competition," Dana had advised, wearing a silly smile.

"There is no competition," Kori had tried to explain. "Brent is soon to be my ex-husband and then I'm going to marry Jared."

"I think you need your head examined," Clair muttered without a trace of humor.

"And I think you need to mind your own business, big sister!"

After that, things had grown tense and, this morning, Kori still regretted losing her temper. But Kori thought that Clair, of all people, should remember the pain Brent had inflicted upon her when he said he didn't love her anymore. So what if he sent her flowers, cooked her favorite meal, and looked at her with "moon-eyes?" Was that really love? What was stopping Brent from changing his mind again? He always changed his mind.

Standing outside the apartment complex in the cold November sunshine, Kori wondered if Brent had changed his mind about picking her up this morning. He was late. But then she remembered that Brent's "on time" was always fifteen minutes late. *Looks like he's not such a new man after all,* she mused sarcastically.

Kori sat down on the front cement stairs and waited. . .and thought. . .and waited some more. A person could do a lot of thinking in fifteen minutes, she soon decided. The brisk air seemed to help clear her head and by the time Brent pulled into the parking lot, Kori felt ready to face him.

"Good morning!" Brent said as she climbed into his truck. He looked bright and happy.

"Good morning," Kori replied, though her greeting wasn't as exuberant.

"You think we could eat breakfast before we shop for cars?" Brent asked. "I'm starving."

"Sure."

Brent's next stop was the Forum Family Restaurant, which was just beginning its breakfast rush. Kori and Brent managed to find a table anyway and within moments, coffee and menus arrived.

"Do you have any idea what kind of car you want?" Brent asked while scanning the menu.

"Not really. Something practical, I guess."

Brent grinned at her from over the menu. "What? You don't want a sporty little Porsche?"

Kori had to smile as she shook her head. She debated momentarily whether to tell him about her future plans, but then honesty won out.

"Brent, within the next few years, I want a family. Children. So I want the car I buy today to be something accommodating. I mean, I'll probably have this car for a long time."

Brent replied with a speculative nod before setting down. Then he put down his menu, giving her his full attention.

"I was thinking before you picked me up this morning," Kori continued.

"Well, I just want you to know that I appreciate your willingness to help me this way, but it won't change anything. You're still just a friend and I'm still going to marry Jared."

Brent gave her a grin. "What's Jared going to say when you show up with a new car? Are you going to tell him 'a friend' bought it for you?"

"No," Kori replied at once. "I'm going to tell him it was part of my divorce settlement."

Brent looked thoroughly amused. "You figured that much out already, huh?"

"I couldn't sleep last night until I did," Kori muttered.

Brent chuckled in spite of himself and then the waitress came and took their orders. After she left, he looked over at Kori and sipped his coffee. "So, how did you and Jared meet, anyway?"

Kori looked back at him, surprised. "You really want to know?"

He shrugged, but his expression was solemn. "Look, Kori, I'll admit that I'm jealous you want him and not me. But I've committed myself to being your friend. . .and what do friends do? They share information about themselves so that they can get to know each other better." He took another sip of his coffee. "That's why I'm asking. I want to get to know you better."

Kori looked sadly into her coffee cup. "You used to know me better than anyone in the whole world." When Brent didn't reply, she forced herself to look up at him.

"Kori, I know I've said them before, and I know they're just words, but they're all I've got: *I'm sorry.*"

She nodded, believing that Brent was really sorry. However, Kori had felt a pain that cut so deeply, "sorry" would never, ever heal it. But real love would—and that's what Kori was sure she'd find if she married Jared.

"We met at a picnic last summer," she blurted.

"Last summer?" Brent paused, taking another sip of coffee. "You haven't known the guy very long and now you're ready to marry him? After just a few months? We dated for two years before you agreed to marry me."

"My mistake," Kori said sarcastically, her defenses on the rise.

Brent put down his coffee cup, took off his glasses, and then rubbed his eyes. He looked weary, and Kori wished she had not verbally lashed out at him like that. "Look, Brent, this isn't going to work," she said at last. "Let's just forget this car thing and you can take me home. I'll manage. I always manage. I shouldn't have asked for your help."

"Yes, you should have, and, no, let's not forget it." Brent was the one to sigh this time. "I'm struggling, Kori," he confessed in a soft tone of voice. "The Bible says that love suffers long and does not envy. Well, I'm envious. . .of Jared! And I'm not being very patient. I'm reacting out of jealousy."

"The Bible?"

Brent nodded. "It's like a Christian's instruction book on how to live, and I don't seem to be following it very well."

Kori immediately thought of Ryan Carlson and his code of ethics. She admired the man and had often wished that Jared would act toward her the way Ryan behaved toward his girlfriend, Stacie. Gallant and patient. . .

"I'm apologizing again, Kori," Brent said, breaking into her thoughts. "I'm sorry. Truly, deeply sorry."

"I'm sorry, too," she replied. "I shouldn't have gotten so defensive."

Reaching across the table, Brent covered her hand with his. "Truce?"

Kori smiled. "Truce."

Breakfast was served and the conversation stayed light and friendly. Afterwards, they left the restaurant and visited two car dealers. Kori managed to decided on the type of car she'd like—a sporty station wagon. Brent wanted to buy her something more expensive, more trendy, but Kori imagined how convenient a little station wagon would be for grocery shopping and hauling portable cribs and strollers. The best part of the vehicle, in Kori's mind, was that either side of the backseat could convert into a child's car seat.

"Mark told me about one other dealership," Brent said as they climbed back into his truck. "It's in Menomonee Falls—near the apartment I'm subleasing."

It was the last stop and had the most reasonable prices. Moreover, the salesman went to the same church Brent was attending and knew Mark Henley, Julia McGowan, his fiancée, and Ryan Carlson. Whether or not that was the reason, the salesman gave Brent a great deal on the "little red wagon," as Brent decided to call it.

The papers were signed and Brent paid in full, much to the delight of the car salesman. "You can take delivery by the end of the week," he promised.

Leaving the dealership, Brent offered to drive Kori to and from work this week.

"You've done so much already," she protested. "I don't want you to go out of your way like that."

"Kori, I've got no other plans. Driving you to work and back will give me something to do this week."

She chuckled softly as Brent unlocked the truck's door for her. She climbed in and Brent walked around to the other side.

"So, where to?" he asked, putting the key in the ignition.

Kori shrugged. "Home, I guess."

"Do you have plans with Jared tonight?" Brent asked. He quickly added, "I'm not trying to be nosy. I just wanted to know if you have to be home at a certain time."

Kori shook her head. "Jared is deer hunting."

"Oh?" Brent cranked the engine and pulled his truck out of the dealership's parking lot. "He's a hunter, huh?"

"Yep. He's a hunter, bowler, dart-thrower, baseball and basketball player, an avid Green Bay Packer fan, a true cheese-head, and couch potato."

Brent laughed heartily. "So what does Jared do in his spare time?"

Kori smiled. "He doesn't have any spare time."

"He makes time for you, doesn't he?"

"Of course," Kori replied, wishing she could think of a few more instances when he had.

"Are you a bowler, dart-thrower. . .all those things now, too?"

"Sometimes."

"And other times?"

Kori shrugged. "Other times Jared and I just do our own things."

"Separately?"

She nodded. "Uh-huh."

Brent paused. "Are you and Jared good friends?"

Kori actually had to think about that one for several moments. "No," she finally replied in all honesty. "Jared and I have a different relationship than he has with his buddies, and that's fine because I don't want to be *one of the guys*. I want to be his wife."

"I want my wife to be my best friend," Brent stated off-handedly, and Kori didn't think there was an underlying meaning in his words. He was too preoccupied with his driving.

"Well, maybe someday when you find the right woman, she will be your best friend."

Brent nodded. "Yeah, maybe someday."

Much to her surprise, Kori felt a stab of jealousy. Brent and "the right woman." How would she feel if Brent actually did marry someone else? Would she be hurt all over again? And how ridiculous of her to even contemplate such things, seeing as she was marrying Jared!

Suddenly, Kori understood Brent's "struggling," as he said at breakfast this morning. Emotions could certainly overrule common sense at times!

"Hey," Brent said, changing the subject, "would it be okay if we stopped by my place before I take you home? Remember I told you that my mother moved? Well, I had boxes stored at her house from when I emptied our apartment. . .after you left. I brought them with me to Milwaukee."

"Why did you do that?" Kori asked, amazed.

Brent chuckled. "I didn't really do it intentionally. I had forgotten all about them, but when I stopped to say good-bye to Mom the day I left for Wisconsin, she reminded me and, on a whim, I packed them into my truck." He paused. "I think we should go over their contents so I know what to save and what to throw out."

"Sure," Kori replied, though she couldn't think of anything worth saving from their apartment.

The day she had decided to move to Wisconsin, she had packed her clothes, jewelry, and other personal items, but she had left the rest. Their wedding photo album, framed pictures, knickknacks. . .even her needlepoint on the walls. She left the pots and pans, towels, sheets, pillows, and all the furniture. Then, from the airport, she had phoned Brent and told him he'd have to clean up the apartment if he wanted the security deposit back.

"What did you pack, Brent?" she had to ask. Surely, he didn't pack everything.

He shrugged. "I can't really remember, but I've got four large boxes of stuff. I barely fit them in the back of my truck."

Kori wondered over the wisdom of sorting through these items with Brent. It might stir up more hurt than she could handle. However, Kori soon decided that declaring the things they shared as "garbage" and then seeing them thrown away for good, might be just the thing she needed to do. She'd clean her heart of Brent in preparation for a life with Jared. Out with the old, in with the new—wasn't that how the saying went?

Chapter 9

The apartment Brent was subleasing was a modern bi-level with its own entrances. He showed Kori through the front door and then helped her off with her coat. He hung it on the wooden coat stand, then shrugged off his jacket, hanging it up too.

"The living room is this way," he said, leading her up seven carpeted steps.

"This is more spacious than my apartment," she observed.

Brent nodded. "It's spacious and more comfortable than a long-stay hotel would have been. I'm grateful Mark was able to get this for me. Would you like something to drink?"

Kori wasn't sure but followed Brent into the kitchen. He opened the refrigerator, revealing cans of ginger ale. Brent had never been fond of colas. He pulled two off the top shelf of the nearly empty refrigerator and handed one to her.

Out of politeness, she popped the top. "Jared's fridge is full of beer," she stated offhandedly. Then, too late, she wished she hadn't said anything.

"He's not a problem drinker, is he?"

Kori shook her head. "No, just a fun-loving guy. He can handle his alcohol."

"Hmm. . ." Brent took a long drink of his ginger ale. "Well, come on into the living room and I'll show you those boxes I was talking about."

Again, Kori followed Brent to the four brown cardboard boxes that stood in the farthest corner of the living room.

"How 'bout I make a fire?" he asked, hunkering down by the built-in brick fireplace.

"Um. . .yeah, that's fine. Which box should we start on?"

"Doesn't matter."

Kori set down her ginger ale and opened the box closest to her. "Oh, Brent, you didn't have to pack the toilet paper." She pulled out a half-used roll.

Brent chuckled. "I guess I wasn't being particular in my packing."

"I guess," Kori extracted a bar of old soap and a couple of threadbare bath towels. "We were so poor," she stated on a melancholy note, fingering the towels. "I bought most of what we had at rummage sales."

"I wasn't very appreciative of all you did back then, Kori. But I am now. Really." Brent shrugged. "Hindsight. . .you know the rest."

Kori just nodded and pulled out a roll of paper towels. Then came two plastic place mats, some cooking utensils, plates, and a toaster. "Oh, Brent," she said, shaking her head pathetically and looking into the very bottom of the box.

Brent peered inside. "Oh, yeah, and I just dumped out the kitchen drawers." Kori repacked the box. "Garbage. All of it."

"You sure?"

"Positive."

"Okay, I'll take it to the dumpster out back."

Kori sat down on the floor, her back up against the sofa, and began to unpack the next box. It contained all the pictures they'd had on the walls of their apartment.

"Garbage," she said.

"Really?" Brent pulled out one of the framed needlepoint prints Kori had made. It was the one that read "Home Is Where You Hang Your Heart" and it had hearts and flowers in the background. "None of this is worth saving?"

Kori shook her head. "I don't want any reminders of our life together." She couldn't keep the terseness out of her voice. "That's why I left all this stuff in California in the first place."

"Okay, fine," he said defensively. Then he carelessly tossed the picture back into the box.

Walking over to the fireplace, Brent stood with his back to Kori and stoked the fire he'd created only moments ago. Oh! but she made him angry. Couldn't she just be nice? They'd had many, many good years together. Why couldn't Kori remember them instead of focusing on their last six months together? Brent knew he'd hurt her badly, but he had apologized at least a dozen times. What more could he do?

Love her, Brent, that Still Small Voice seemed to whisper. *Love never fails.*

"I'd better get going," Kori said, causing Brent to turn around. She stood to her feet. "I'll take a cab if you don't want to drive me home."

Brent sighed in resignation, his inner struggle ceased. "I'll take you home, but I wish you'd stay."

She shook her head stubbornly. "You're mad at me. I can tell."

"I'm mad at myself," Brent said honestly. "If I hadn't been so selfish two years ago, we'd still be happily married."

"Married, maybe," Kori retorted, "but I don't know about the 'happily' part. I mean, you told me when you left me that you weren't ever happy. You said that was the problem."

Brent closed his eyes against a wave of pain and anger. They were hurtful words and, yes, he had said them. But how many times was Kori going to fling them in his face?

"Want to take me home now?" she asked saucily.

Brent opened his eyes and saw Kori's victorious expression. Then he couldn't help a grin. "So you think that if you make me angry enough or hurt my feelings enough I'll turn tail and run back to California, huh?" His grin grew into a full smile. "Guess again, lady."

Kori narrowed her gaze, scrutinizing him, though a little smile played upon her lips.

"And I'm not going to fight with you either," Brent added.

"You're just no fun at all," she teased him. Then she grabbed her can of ginger ale and sat down on the carpeted floor by the fire. Her back was against the sofa. It seemed that Kori had somehow been defused. She was staying.

Brent sighed, feeling a bit weary from his second major challenge of the day. The first had been their sparring at breakfast, and Brent wondered how long he could keep this up. He knew it was God who kept his patience intact, for Brent McDonald knew that he, by nature, was not a patient man.

He sat down beside Kori, his can of ginger ale in hand. "Do you have plans tonight?"

"You asked me that already." She sounded defensive. "Why do you want to know?"

"I was just wanted to make sure because if you don't have to go home, I'd sort of like to order some food." Brent grinned. "I'm hungry."

Her features softened. "No, I don't have to be home and. . .Chinese food sounds good."

"Chinese it is," Brent said, delighted that he could have Kori with him that much longer. He looked at his watch. "I'll go pick it up in about an hour and bring it back here. What do you say?"

"Okay."

A long moment of silence passed between them as the fire crackled in the brick fireplace. Brent shifted and moved a little closer to Kori. He couldn't help it. She looked so soft and huggable sitting here beside him by the fire.

Kori didn't seem to notice that Brent had moved. "Sometimes I go out with my friends at the clinic. But that's usually on Friday nights. Saturday nights I reserve for Jared, but, as I told you before, Jared went deer hunting."

"Oh, yeah, that's right."

"He was angry when he left, too." She gave Brent a pointed look. "Which is your fault, I might add."

"Mine?"

"Yes, yours—and don't give me that innocent, sweet pout of yours, either."

"I do not pout!" Brent declared.

"Yes, you do. Just ask your mom. You got out of a lot of trouble as a kid by giving her that same look."

Brent laughed. "Okay, I guess I have heard that before." He paused. "But tell me, why was Jared angry?"

"You really want to know? You don't mind me talking about him?"

"We're friends, remember?"

"Oh yeah, that's right." She gave him a skeptical look, then continued "It's simple, really. Jared wasn't exactly thrilled to learn that I'm still married." She forced herself not to cringe at the understatement.

"You told him, huh?"

She nodded. "He was pretty upset."

Brent didn't reply, but he thought that was to Jared's credit. Some guys wouldn't care if a woman was married.

Brent put his arm up along the top of the couch, resting it in back of Kori. Then, impulsively, he touched her hair. She was wearing it down today, only the sides were pulled up and secured at the top with a plain, gold barrette. Her golden hair was still as soft as he remembered.

Amazingly, Kori didn't protest his touch, so Brent let his hand get lost in her soft thick tresses, just the way he used to.

"Uhm, you shouldn't be doing this, you know," she chided him half-heartedly. "But I've got to admit, it feels so good." She paused, momentarily thoughtful. "I suppose I shouldn't be enjoying this either, should I?"

Brent smiled. Kori had always loved it when he ran his fingers through her hair. She used to say it relaxed her, and she looked pretty relaxed right now.

"Do you know that Jared never touches my hair like this? Once I even asked him to, but he said he wasn't that sort of a guy."

"Hmm. . ." Brent was glad to hear that.

"Jared isn't very romantic," Kori offered. "He doesn't like to hold hands or have candlelight dinners."

"We used to eat by candlelight a lot."

Kori's smile lingered. "Yeah, our cheap TV dinners by candlelight."

Brent laughed, too. "Ah, but they were romantic."

Kori nodded. "That's one thing about you, Brent. You're a romantic."

"Thanks. . .I think." He lifted a brow. "That was a compliment, wasn't it?"

Kori laughed again. "Yes, it was."

Brent continued to weave his fingers in and out of Kori's long hair, wondering what kind of relationship she had with Jared. She'd already said that he wasn't a romantic guy. He didn't hold Kori's hand or touch her hair. But were they intimate lovers? Brent knew that, biblically, he could go along with the divorce under those circumstances, if his wife was now physically intimate with another man; however, he almost didn't think it mattered, not to his heart. And that's when he realized just how much he loved his wife. He would gladly take her back regardless of where she'd been, though he suspected she hadn't "been" anywhere.

"In case you're wondering, I never slept with Jared," Kori suddenly blurted.

Brent lifted his brows, surprised by her sudden candidness.

"I don't know why I'm even telling you this," she continued, "except I can practically *hear* the question rolling around in your head! I mean, it's none of your business and maybe you don't even care—"

"I care very much, Kori." Brent gave her a gentle smile. "And we still know each other very well, don't we?"

Kori shrugged and a sudden silence grew between them. Brent sensed that she was wondering the same thing about him. At one time, they'd been so close they used to think alike.

"I haven't been intimate with anyone else either," he told her. "But I will confess to giving Meg a good-night kiss after a couple of dates. It never went any further, though, and I never dated anyone else. I didn't have time. My dad got sick and I was working a lot of hours, so I was forced to put my social life on hold." Brent smiled. "Then I was born-again the Bible way, and now I see those circumstances as part of the providential hand of God. Even though I didn't know I was still married, God did."

Kori turned pensive for several long moments. Her head was turned away from him and Brent thought she was watching the fire.

"What are you thinking about?" he finally asked.

"I was thinking that. . .well, I've kissed Jared a lot and here all along I've been married." She shook her head and looked back at Brent. "That doesn't make me feel very good about myself."

"But you didn't know, Kori. You aren't responsible for something you didn't know."

She nodded, but Brent could tell by the little frown of concern marring her forehead that she wasn't at all relieved by his statement. Kori always did have a good conscience. She had always been a good person, unwilling to hurt anyone.

"I couldn't bring myself to kiss Jared last week," she finally said. "I think that's what really made him mad—the fact that I wouldn't kiss him."

"Understandable, at least from his standpoint."

"Oh, what am I going to do?" she muttered forlornly, pulling her knees up to her chin. Then she wrapped her arms around them.

"You want me to answer that question?" Brent asked facetiously.

"No," Kori replied emphatically, "because I know what you'd say. You'd say I should stay married to you and forget Jared."

Brent nodded. "That's exactly what I'd say."

"Well, I won't." Kori moved away from him in one, sudden move and stood up. "If I stayed married to you, Brent, you'd probably come home one day and announce that God told you to be a medical missionary in the Amazon or something. You'd make me pack my bags and away we'd go."

Brent chuckled.

"Well, no way," Kori said seriously, though she had a smile in her eyes. "I've chased enough rainbows with you. Now I want stability. I want a house. . .a home. I want children." She paused. "And I guess I want children more than anything else."

Brent took a moment to consider her statement. "What would happen if you married Jared," he challenged her, "and then discovered you couldn't have children with him because of any number of medical reasons?"

Kori's green eyes widened. Obviously she hadn't thought of that.

The phone rang and Brent got up to answer it. "Oh, hi, Dana. Yeah, she's here." He held out the phone to Kori. "For you."

She frowned curiously but took the portable phone. "How did you know I was here and how did you get Brent's phone number?"

"He only left a hundred messages for you last week," Dana replied facetiously. "I got his number off one of them and I had a hunch you two were still together. Did you buy a car?"

"Yep. It's a small-size station wagon."

"Station wagon? Whose idea was it to buy that?"

"Mine. I wanted a family car."

"Oh." Dana paused. "So what are you guys doing over there?"

"Just talking."

"Sure you are."

Kori rolled her eyes. She wasn't up to her roommate's teasing at the moment. "What can I do for you, Dana?"

"I wondered if I could borrow your lilac-colored sweater tonight. I promise I'll take good care of it, and then I'll have it dry-cleaned when I'm done borrowing it."

"Sure, go ahead."

"Clair and I are going out tonight. She got invited to a party and I'm going to have dinner with a friend from high school."

"Okay. I'll see you guys whenever."

"Oh, and Jared called."

"He did? Is he home?"

"Nope. He said he was calling from the lodge, whatever that means. Anyway, he was kind of mad that you weren't home."

"Did you tell him where I was?"

"No way, Kori. You know me better than that. You, Clair, and I are like the Three Musketeers. One for all and all for one."

"Yeah, something like that," Kori replied with a little laugh. "So what did you tell him?"

"Jared? Oh, I said I thought you were shopping so he said he'd call back later tonight."

"Really?" Kori wondered if something serious had happened. Why else would Jared call her from deer hunting with the guys? "Well, thanks, Dana, and I'll talk to you later."

Kori shut off the telephone. Then, leaving the living room, she found Brent in the kitchen, busily paging through the phone book.

"I'm trying to find a Chinese restaurant that's close by," he explained.

"There's a good one near my apartment. We could just eat there or take the food to my place."

"Okay, let's decide when we get to the restaurant. I'm hungry."

As she left with Brent, Kori never felt so torn in two in all her life. She had every intention of marrying Jared and yet she had enjoyed so much her fireside chat with Brent this afternoon. She had talked to him in a way that she could never talk to Jared. Furthermore, she had enjoyed Brent's touch and the way he sat so close to her.

But Brent McDonald could charm the birds out of the trees, Kori reminded herself. *I cannot succumb to his charm. We're just friends,* she admonished herself. *Friends and nothing more!*

Chapter 10

Letting herself into the apartment complex, Kori stood in the lobby and watched Brent drive off. They'd had an enjoyable dinner at a small Chinese restaurant and, in a way, Kori was sorry to see the evening come to an end. It galled her to admit it, but she liked Brent's company. She always had.

Taking the elevator up to her apartment, Kori opened the door and walked into the front hallway. The empty darkness reminded her that Clair and Dana were out for the night. Kori went on into the living room, turned on a lamp, and then headed for her bedroom and changed into a long nightshirt. By the time she reentered the living room, the telephone was ringing.

"Hi, honey," Jared said on the other end. "I've been trying to get you all night. Where have you been?"

"Out with a friend," she replied easily.

"Oh, yeah? Who?"

Kori paused, wondering what Jared would think of her friendship with Brent. *He probably wouldn't like it,* she decided. *Better not tell him.* "It's no one you know," she finally replied, though her conscience pricked her for avoiding the truth.

"Oh." Jared paused. "I thought maybe you were with Joan or Cathy. . .you're still going to the Deer Hunter Widows' Ball with them on Thanksgiving Day, right?"

"Right," Kori said, glad that she could state the truth now. She, Joan, and Cathy had been planning to attend "the ball" for months.

"Sue and Bonnie are going too."

"Oh, good," Kori said. The women were wives of Jared's "buddies" and the ball was being held at a local tavern, run by one of Jared's cousins. A radio station was even going to be there, playing music all night.

"Listen, honey, the reason I'm calling is. . .well, I just wanted to tell you I'm sorry for getting so bent out of shape when you told me about your situation. It took me by surprise and I guess I sort of overreacted. But I was talking to some of the guys last night, and I realized that this isn't really such a big deal after all. You get a divorce and it's over. We get married."

"That was my plan," Kori said, wishing she didn't sound so timid. Yes! It still was her plan. Nothing had changed. So what if she and Brent were friends? She stiffened with new resolve.

"You know," Jared continued, "you could move in with me while all this divorce business is going on."

"No, Jared, I don't think—"

"Don't say no, Kori. Just think it over again. If you say you'll move in with me, we'll take that cruise in February like we planned. Just won't get married, that's all. So what's the big deal? Lots of people don't get married."

"I know, but. . ."

"Well, at least think about it. Reconsider, Kori."

She sighed in resignation. . .for now. However, she knew she would never accept such a proposition. Kori wanted a commitment that would last forever. This was her second time around with marriage and, for her, it would be the last time around. Her heart couldn't take anymore.

"I also realized," Jared was saying, "that your ex-husband. . .or whatever he is, can't sue me. I mean, it's a free country, and it's not like there are kids involved."

"No," Kori murmured, "there are no kids involved." And then it occurred to her. "But you do like kids, don't you, Jared?" They hadn't ever discussed having children before. Kori had only assumed that he would want children as much as she did. She had told him many times that she wanted a family and he'd never balked at the idea.

"Kids are okay," Jared replied. "My friends think they're kind of a burden, though."

"A burden?"

"Yeah. Well, I got to get back to the card game."

"All right." Kori shook off her sudden uneasiness. "Thanks for calling, Jared." She knew it was a big sacrifice for him to take time away from his deer camp buddies and call her. "It's nice to hear your voice again. . .and I'm glad you're not still angry with me."

"No, I'm not. And, Kori? I love you."

Kori's heart felt like it plummeted to her toes. Jared had never spoken words of love to her before. He'd merely insinuated them which, to her, had meant a lot at the time. After all, actions speak louder than words and "I love you" were just words. However, her heart had so longed to hear Jared say them. And now he was. . .yet it troubled her. But why?

"Kori, are you there?"

"Yes, I just. . .well. . .I—"

"Oh, I get it. You can't tell me you love me back 'cause your roommates are standing there listening. That's all right. I understand, honey. I wouldn't want to say 'I love you' if the guys were around."

Kori couldn't seem to choke out a single reply.

"Are you okay?"

"Yes," she said quickly, somehow finding her voice again.

"All right, then. I'm going to hang up."

"Thanks again for calling, Jared," Kori replied, trying to put a smile in her voice. "Good-bye."

Kori placed the telephone receiver back in its cradle. She felt guilty but didn't know why. *I haven't done anything wrong.* But then she remembered how Brent had run his fingers through her hair that afternoon and how good it felt. She remembered that she hadn't stopped him and how much she'd liked it. What would Jared say if he found out? Had she betrayed him?

Maybe I shouldn't be friends with Brent, she thought. However, the idea of having no more contact with him wasn't at all appealing. After today, Kori felt like a part of her had been opened to the fresh air again after a long, dark hibernation. She could talk to Brent. He understood her. She didn't want to sever their relationship—not anymore.

So what am I going to do? she wondered for the second time today. She knew what Brent would tell her. She knew what Jared would tell her. She even knew what Clair would tell her. But what did her heart tell her?

Kori just didn't know.

❧

The next day, Kori arose early. She'd had trouble sleeping, and by six-thirty, she abandoned the idea of sleep altogether.

Walking into the kitchen, she made a pot of coffee. Then she decided to make an elaborate breakfast for her roommates. Blueberry muffins, bacon, and eggs.

"What smells so good?" Dana asked, coming out of her bedroom. She yawned and stretched, still looking sleepy. "I wanted to sleep in today, Kori," she complained, "but my stomach started growling when I smelled the bacon frying."

Kori smiled. "Will you join me for breakfast?"

"Sure."

Clair woke up next. She was never one to stay in bed past seven-thirty. During the week, Clair was the first one up at five o'clock, and she was out of the apartment by seven. Therefore, sleeping until seven-thirty was a luxury for her.

"Coffee?" Kori asked her older sister.

"You bet."

Kori poured the hot, steamy brew and then dished up breakfast and they all sat down.

"Did you and Brent have fun yesterday?" Clair asked.

"I don't know about 'fun,' but Brent and I had a nice day together, yes. And, Clair, I'm sorry for losing my temper with you Friday night." Kori shook her head, feeling confused all over again. "I enjoyed being with Brent yesterday. . .maybe I do need my head examined."

Clair smiled. "Are you still in love with him, Kori?"

"No! Of course not!" She paused, setting down her fork and then relented. "Oh, I don't know how I feel about Brent." Then she murmured, "I don't know what love is anymore."

"Ah, the age-old question: What is love?" Dana laughed softly. "You know what I think love is? Love means never having to say you're sorry."

"Thank you very much, Erich Segal," Clair quipped and they all began to laugh.

"Oh, sorry," Dana said between giggles, "I just watched that movie, *Love Story*, on The Late, Late Show, and you know how much I like old flicks."

"I wish my dilemma could be solved as easily as an old movie," Kori remarked.

"It's really a no-brainer," Clair told her. "I mean, Brent is a changed man, he's still in love with you and wants to give your marriage another go, and. . .and you are, after all, still married."

"But you don't understand," Kori said softly, as if pleading her case. "I told Jared I'd marry him because I thought Brent and I were divorced. In essence, I don't feel married to Brent, I feel engaged to Jared."

"Then you're in love with Jared, right?" Dana asked.

"I. . .I don't know."

"Well, that's what you've got to figure out, Kori," Clair advised. "Who are you in love with?"

"But what is love?"

"It's that warm, fuzzy feeling you get when you're with someone special," Dana told her.

"Warm and fuzzy?" Kori had never experienced "warm and fuzzy" with Jared. But she had with Brent. Once, she'd been so in love with Brent she couldn't see straight.

"Love is responsibility and commitment," Clair said logically. "If you love someone, you make time for him. You make him your responsibility. Not that you're responsible for his happiness or for what he does or doesn't do, but you take care of his needs." She shrugged. "That's what marriage is all about and, after I marry Zach, I'll take care of him. Like sewing the button back on his shirt, making his meals, washing his dirty socks." Clair paused and smiled. "Now *that's* love!"

"But I did all that for Brent and it didn't matter," Kori protested. "He still left me."

"Just like I said, you're not responsible for what Brent does or doesn't do. Don't you see, Kori? You did right, Brent did wrong," Clair replied. "But now he wants a second chance."

"Are you going to give him another chance, Kori?" Dana asked.

"No!" she said, getting up from the table. "I'm going to marry Jared. Nothing has changed. Brent and I can only be friends." She shook her head as if to clear it.

"Look, you guys. When I even begin to consider giving Brent another chance, I hear his voice saying, 'I just don't love you anymore.' That's what he told me when I suggested a second chance at our marriage—before I left California, and I was devastated." She turned to her sister. "Clair, you know how devastated I was."

"I know."

"Dana, you remember."

She nodded. "I remember."

"So? What do I do?" Kori picked up her empty plate and dirty silverware and walked to the kitchen. She rinsed her dishes and left them in the sink for later.

"I guess what you do depends on how you feel," Clair advised, coming into the kitchen behind Kori. "If you feel like you're still in love with Brent, give him another chance. If not, divorce him and marry Jared. It's simple."

Kori nodded. Simple—oh! how she wished it were. If only she wasn't so emotional and introspective. If only she could be practical like Clair.

Chapter 11

Brent was on time to pick up Kori for work on Monday morning and she was amazed. She had thought for sure he'd be his usual fifteen minutes late. She had even called her manager to let her know she'd be late.

"I guess I've had to learn to be on time," Brent said with a chuckle when Kori mentioned it. He glanced her way. "Did you have a good day yesterday?"

Kori nodded. "Didn't do a whole lot. Read the newspaper, did some grocery shopping with Dana, washed some clothes. The usual, I guess. How 'bout you?"

"I went to church in the morning and had lunch with Mark Henley, his fiancée Julia, and some of her family. Then I went back to church and didn't get home till about nine o'clock."

"That's a lot of church," Kori remarked, wearing a curious frown. "Isn't it boring to sit in church that long?"

Brent grinned. "It's only boring if the pastor's delivery is boring, I guess. But the pastor yesterday spoke in a way that made the Bible come alive for me and I was able to apply the spiritual truths to my life."

"Like what?"

Brent thought for a moment. "Like going to the Lord with my problems and trusting Him to take care of them instead of trying to handle them on my own. Yesterday I was reminded that God's ways are perfect, mine aren't."

"Hmm. . ." Kori didn't know what to make of Brent's comments except, she thought, they sounded a lot like Ryan Carlson's. At first, when Ryan used to talk about his dependence upon God, Kori thought it was a sign of weakness. Now, however, she wasn't so sure. Ryan didn't seem weak at all. He seemed like he had his life together while hers was falling to pieces.

Minutes later, Brent pulled into the parking lot of the clinic, and Kori climbed out of his truck. "Have a good day," he told her. "I'll pick you up tonight. About five?"

"Depends on our patients. Better make it five-thirty."

"Okay."

Kori smiled at him. "Thanks, Brent. I appreciate the ride."

"Anytime," he replied, smiling back.

Closing the truck's door, Kori waked into the clinic. Already patients were lined up at the front desk and the receptionists looked harried. Diane was explaining an insurance copayment to an unhappy-looking patient, Gigi was scheduling an appointment, and Vicki was in the back, answering the telephone. A sure sign that today would be a busy one.

And it was. Ryan kept Kori so occupied that she barely had time for a lunch break. By six o'clock that evening, they had seen twenty-five patients—and that was just Ryan's practice alone. The other five family practice doctors had seen their share of people as well.

"I hate Mondays," Susie murmured as she worked on completing her route slips.

Kori was finishing up on her own. "I hate Mondays, too." The phone rang. "And this better not be one of the receptionists asking if we'll work in another patient, either!" she declared, picking up the receiver.

"Hi, Kori," Jeanmarie said pleasantly. She was a part-time receptionist. "There's a man down here waiting for you. He's been here for about a half hour. Thought you should know."

"Brent. Oh, no! I forgot about him."

Jeanmarie laughed, her bubbly personality evident even over the telephone line. "What do you want me to tell him?"

"Oh, I don't know," Kori sighed, surveying her paperwork. "I guess I can be done in about fifteen minutes. Ask him if he'll wait."

"Okay." Jeanmarie covered the receiver and Kori heard a series of muffled replies. "Yeah, he says he'll wait."

"Tell him thanks and I'll try to hurry."

Kori hung up the phone and tackled her paperwork again.

"Who's Brent?" Susie asked.

"Just a friend," Kori replied, not even glancing up from her desk.

"Girlfriend," Susie drawled, "you can't be 'just a friend' with a man!"

Kori looked over at her. "Why not?"

"Because it'll never stay just a friendship." Susie shook her head at her. "You'll be telling him your woes one day and he'll feel bad for you and hug you and then a hug will turn into a kiss and then a kiss will lead to—"

"All right, all right. I get the picture. But it's not that way. Brent is. . .well, he's my ex-husband, okay?"

Susie's brows shot up in surprise. "Oh? Do tell."

Kori went back to her paperwork, refusing to elaborate on the situation. "Ex-husband" was as detailed a description as her coworkers were going to get.

"What does Jared say about you being friends with your ex?"

"Nothing," Kori replied honestly.

"Nothing?" When Kori didn't answer, Susie continued. "Does that mean he doesn't know?"

"He knows about Brent," Kori muttered, wishing Susie weren't so inquisitive. And yet, they had been good friends for the last year. They talked about everything going on in their lives. Kori knew about Susie's children and about her mother who had diabetes and about her brother who was getting married in the spring of next year. Likewise Susie knew about Clair and Dana. She knew that Kori was divorced and was now engaged to Jared. It made sense that Susie would be confused by Kori's reticence.

However, she just didn't want to talk about it—maybe because she wasn't comfortable with her situation yet. It still wasn't resolved by any stretch of the imagination. And maybe Susie was right: maybe she would end up getting too close to Brent if their friendship continued.

Then, as if to affirm her suspicions, Kori remembered how he had stroked her hair last Saturday afternoon and she remembered how much she had liked it. . .

Kori suddenly felt a pair of strong hands on her shoulders and snapped out of her reverie. Turning, she was surprised to find the object of her thoughts standing over her. "How did you get up here?"

"I just saw Ryan in the lobby and he pointed out the way," Brent answered.

"Oh." Kori looked at Susie who was watching her expectantly, so she began introductions at once.

"Nice to meet you, Brent," Susie said assertively. Then she leaned back in her chair, crossed her arms, and considered Brent thoughtfully. "I'll bet you're the guy who sent Kori those roses last week."

He nodded. "That was me." Brent reached over Kori's shoulder and took a picture off her bulletin board. "So this must be Jared, huh?"

"Yes," Kori replied, stacking up her charts for tomorrow. She stood then and prepared to leave while Brent replaced the picture.

"Well, I don't know about Jared," he said, grinning mischievously, "but that fish he's holding looks like a great catch."

Susie grinned and turned back to her paperwork.

"Jared is a 'great catch,' too," Kori told Brent. "Are you ready to go?"

He nodded. "Just waiting for you."

They left the clinic and walked through the lot to where Brent had parked his truck. He opened the door for Kori and she climbed in. After Brent was seated and started the engine, Kori apologized for being so late.

"Hey, no problem." He glanced her way and gave her a smile. "But now you've got to make dinner for me."

"What?"

"All that waiting made me hungry. I only ate a bowl of cereal this morning."

"Well, drop me off and then you can stop at Burger King on your way home."

"But I'm sick of fast food, and I'm sick of eating in restaurants. I want an old-fashioned, home-cooked meal, Kori. Wouldn't you make that for me?" He added sweetly, "I waited over an hour for you."

Kori rolled her eyes, hating that Brent could tug on her heartstrings this way. "I was thinking of meat loaf," he continued.

"I'm sure you were," she retorted, knowing meat loaf was one of Brent's favorite dishes—at least it had been, before he decided to become a vegetarian. But he had changed his mind about food, just like he changed his mind about everything else.

Brent stopped at a red light. "What do you say, Kori? There's a grocery store right here. I'll pay for everything if you'll agree to cook. We'll go over to my place and while we're waiting for dinner we can sort through the last two boxes I brought from California."

Kori looked over at him. "I'm tired, Brent."

He turned and looked out over the steering wheel. "Okay, if you'll make the meat loaf—because no one can make meat loaf like you—I'll make everything else: mashed potatoes, tossed salad, hot rolls from the oven."

Kori thought about it for a moment and then the light turned green. "Oh, all right," she conceded. "I'll make you a meat loaf." *But it will be the last time,* she added silently. She had suddenly made up her mind that she was going to break off her friendship with Brent. And she would tell him so tonight.

❧

Kori formed the meat and put it into a glass loaf pan. Then, after washing her hands, she slipped it into the oven beside the two large baking potatoes. In the grocery store, Brent had changed his mind from mashed potatoes to baked. Typical.

Brent looked at his watch now. "About an hour till dinner?"

Kori nodded, putting her engagement ring back on her finger. She had taken it off so she could mix the meat loaf with her hands. She looked at it contemplatively, before turning to Brent. "I think we should talk."

"Sure." He leaned casually against the counter. "What's on your mind?"

"Our friendship, for one thing."

"Oh?"

Kori nodded. "At first I thought it was a good thing—us being friends. I thought it would alleviate the animosity I had for you—and it did." She sighed. "But it's not working out, Brent."

"Why?" The question was spoken softly, curiously, not impatiently or demanding and, once more, Kori marvelled at the change in this man. And yet. . . she was promised to another.

"We're getting too close."

He smiled. "We're married, Kori. Don't you think it's a good thing if a married couple grows closer?"

Kori was shaking her head vehemently. "No, we're divorced. Maybe not legally. . .yet. But emotionally. . .we're divorced."

Brent paused, his expression thoughtful. Then he stepped forward and pulled Kori into his arms. Her first impulse was to push him away, but she couldn't seem to deny herself the feeling of Brent's tender embrace. *It's just a hug,* she told herself. *It's a hug good-bye.*

Brent pulled back. "Kori, I can't make you be my friend and I can't make you love me." His dark brown eyes filled with a sadness that tugged at her heart. "Except," he added, lowering his head, "I think you do."

Brent kissed her softly and all Kori could think about was what Susie had said at work. "A hug will turn into a kiss and a kiss will lead to. . ."

Kori turned her head away, but she was already too late. She had responded to Brent's kiss more than she had wanted.

"I understand your confusion," Brent whispered, "but at least be honest with yourself about how you feel about me. You still love me as much as I love you."

"No!" Kori pushed herself away from him. "It's not love, Brent. It's remembering a time when we shared something *like* love."

Brent narrowed his dark gaze. *"Like* love? What's that supposed to mean?"

"It means we obviously didn't have a *real* love together if it failed."

Brent turned thoughtful again. "You know, Kori," he said at last. "You're right."

She didn't know how to reply. She couldn't very well argue with him if he was agreeing with her.

"The Bible says 'love never fails.' "

It surprised Kori to learn she agreed with something in the Bible, even though she didn't understand this particular topic at all. "To tell you the truth, I don't know what love is anymore."

He smiled. "Well, I do. I know what it is now. . .now that I know Jesus Christ." He stepped forward and put his arms back around Kori's waist. "Can I do my best to show you what love is?"

Kori lifted a derisive brow. "I don't think that's love, Brent. I think that's called something else."

He laughed. "No, I think you misunderstood me. If I were to show you what real love is, it would take me at least. . .oh, the rest of our lives."

Kori stepped out of his embrace. "I haven't got that long. Jared comes home from deer hunting this weekend."

"Then you've got some decisions to make. Is it going to be him? Or me?"

"A week ago, I would have said 'him,' but now I'm not so sure." She looked over at Brent who was standing there so cool and confident. It angered her. "Can't you see this is tearing me apart?"

A handsome smirk curved his lips. "Indecision will kill you."

Kori rolled her eyes in silent reply and then walked out of the kitchen.

Brent's chuckles echoed behind her.

"Say, Kori," he called, his tone much lighter now, "would you like some flavored coffee or a ginger ale?"

"No," she muttered, sitting down on the sofa in the living room.

She spied the two boxes left to rummage through. *May as well get it over with,* she thought, in spite of the fact that she'd deemed it all garbage anyway.

Chapter 12

Kori began to sort through the box and found it contained only miscellaneous items. Nothing worth keeping.

"You can throw all of this out, too, Brent," she told him as he walked into the living room.

"Okay," he replied easily, sitting down on the couch.

On to the fourth and final box of "garbage." Kori began sifting through its contents when suddenly her hand found a wad of tissue paper and, curious, she had to see what was wrapped up inside. It was something heavy, she realized, putting the object in her lap. Slowly, she began to unravel the tissue paper.

She inhaled a sharp breath once she uncovered the thing. It was a music box in the shape of a carousel. Three pastel-painted, porcelain ponies went up and down and traveled its circumference to the tune of "The Impossible Dream."

Tears stung Kori's eyes as she remembered the melody and then she just had to wind it up.

"That music box was on top of your dresser, wasn't it?"

Kori nodded and swallowed down the lump of emotion suddenly stuck in her throat.

"Where did we get that thing, anyway?"

With a sniff and another swallow, Kori replied, "I bought it."

"Oh, yeah? I don't remember."

Kori did. She remembered well. "I used to walk by a novelty shop on the way home from my evening waitress job," she explained, "and every day, I'd see this little carousel in the window. I was so drawn to it.

"Then one night I went into the store to have a better look. The clerk took the music box from out of its display and handed it to me. I wound it up, heard the melody, and it was like I just had to have it. It reminded me of you, Brent. . .it reminded me of us. You were always dreaming the impossible dream and reaching for those unreachable stars. So was I. . ."

Kori paused, fingering the treasured memento. "This was the only music box in the shop of its kind and it cost ninety-five dollars. I fell in love with it, but I knew we didn't have that kind of money. Then the sales clerk told me she'd put it aside for me and I could make payments on it. So that's what I did. Every night when I walked home, I'd stop and put down half my tip money for the music box.

Sometimes it was five dollars, sometimes it was twenty, but eventually I paid it off—without sacrificing grocery money or funds to pay the bills—and finally the music box was mine."

Kori wound it up again and gazed at it with a wistful expression on her solemn face. "I always thought I'd give this to our firstborn child. Like a keepsake." She paused and seemed to struggle with her next sentence. "I wanted a baby so badly. . .my impossible dream."

Brent just stared at her. "I never knew. . .Kori, why didn't you ever tell me how deeply you wanted to have a baby?"

She produced a curt laugh. "With you in medical school, we were scraping just to get by. We couldn't have handled the expense of a child." She sighed and her voice softened. "But I was hoping that once you got done. . ."

Brent didn't know what to say. He didn't think he and Kori had had any secrets between them while they were married. But apparently there were secrets galore. While Brent, in all his selfishness, was dreaming of being a bachelor again, Kori was dreaming of raising a family. Neither one told the other until their dreams blew up in their faces. And now, here they were, trying to put all the pieces back together—at least Brent was trying.

"I wish I would have known."

"What difference would it have made?"

"I don't know. Maybe I would have come to my senses sooner."

"Or maybe," Kori countered, "you would have left me *and* our child." She shook her head adamantly. "No. It's a good thing I didn't have a baby."

Her voice had taken on that hard-sounding tone that Brent was beginning to recognize. Instead of showing her hurt, Kori showed that she was hard. And until he figured out a way to soften her up again, she'd stay that way.

Brent heaved a weary sigh. Three steps forward, two steps back—what kind of progress was he making with Kori, anyway? Would she ever forget the past?

Lord, help me. This situation is beginning to infuriate me. I don't think I'll ever be sorry enough for Kori. Maybe she's right, this isn't going to work. Maybe there's no hope for us after all.

Once again that Still Small Voice: *Love suffers long. . .love bears all things, believes all things, hopes all things, endures all things. Love never fails.*

With another sigh—but this time one of resolve—Brent watched as Kori wrapped up the musical porcelain carousel and put it back into the box of miscellaneous items. Then she stood. "I don't want any of this stuff, Brent. Throw it out."

He stood as well. "You don't even want the music box?"

"I especially don't want the music box."

Kori looked so hurt that Brent felt sick. "I'm *so sorry*," he told her, hoping he conveyed the earnestness he felt.

She ignored the apology. "Would you take me home now, please?" Kori practically croaked out the question and Brent saw the tears as they formed in the corners of her light-green eyes and then slipped down her cheeks.

"Kori," he said, coming to her.

"Please," she implored him, holding out a hand as if to forestall him. "Please, I just want to go home."

Brent shook his head. "I can't let you go now. Not this way."

She put her hands over her face and cried in shoulder-shaking, silent sobs. "Oh, Kori. . ."

Brent closed the distance between them and put his arms around her, holding her close. She didn't fight him but instead sobbed against his shoulder.

"Shhhh, don't cry," Brent said gently. Then he realized that in all the years they'd been together, he had never seen Kori cry this hard. Oh, he'd seen her tears, tears that were easily brushed aside by his selfishness; however, he'd never heard her sob. Not like this, and in that brief moment, Brent thought he had gotten a glimpse of the enormity of the hurt he'd inflicted on her. "Shhh," he repeated, as his hold around her tightened, "don't cry. Please don't cry."

At last her tears subsided and Kori rested her cheek against Brent's shoulder. He held her until her breathing gradually slowed to its normal rhythm.

"Kori," he said, and pushing her back, he cupped her tear-streaked face, "you and I can have lots of babies." Brent smiled down into her eyes.

In spite of herself, Kori smiled.

"That's better," Brent told her, lowering his head so that his nose touched hers affectionately.

She sniffed. "I need to blow my nose."

"By all means."

Kori's rueful smile grew.

Brent brought his chin back. "There's a clean towel and washcloth in the bathroom just off of the kitchen. Why don't you go freshen up?"

Kori nodded.

"Then I want to show you something," Brent told her as she started to leave the room. "I think now's a good time."

Again Kori nodded as she made her way to the bathroom. She couldn't believe the way she'd lost control of herself moments ago. Picking up a tissue, Kori gave her nose a healthy blow. Then, looking at the mirror which hung on the wall over the sink, she shook her head in dismay at the red-eyed reflection that stared back. She lifted the washcloth from off the towel rack and began to wash her face. The cold water felt good against her swollen eyes.

As she continued to hold the washcloth against her face, Kori couldn't help but think about what Brent had said: *"You and I can have lots of babies."* Her heart pulled and tugged in every direction. Kori wanted so desperately to have a home and children; but what she yearned for most was a love that would never let her go. She had thought Jared would be the one who would win her heart and love her forever, yet it was Brent whose words and gentle touches spoke to that innermost longing within her.

Kori looked back up at her reflection. Her eyes appeared less puffy and red now. *Should I give Brent another chance?* she wondered. To even consider the question was frightening for Kori. It had taken so long to learn to live without him. Could she really forget the past and give their marriage another go? What if it happened again? On the other hand, Brent certainly seemed like a different man—like he'd learned a valuable lesson. Everyone makes mistakes. . .

A soft knock sounded on the bathroom door. "Kori? Are you okay?"

"Yes, I'm fine," she called back. "I'll be out in a minute."

She took one last glance at her tearstained face and decided it would have to do. She wished she were one of those women who looked beautiful after a good cry, but she wasn't. How-ever, the red blotches were beginning to fade at last.

With a deep, cleansing breath, Kori left the bathroom and met Brent in the living room. He was sitting on the sofa with a stack of photographs in his hand.

He patted the cushion beside him. "Come over here and sit down. I want to show you something."

"No more strolls down Memory Lane, Brent," Kori protested, thinking the pictures were some more of their past. "I can't take any more."

Brent smiled. "No more past, only present and future. Come on. Sit down."

Kori complied.

"Here. Take a look at these."

Kori took the photographs and leafed through them. They were pictures of a house. A red-brick house with white trim and a little white picket fence surrounding the yard.

Kori suddenly paused. "Brent. . .?" Hadn't they always said they'd have a red-brick house with a little white picket fence?

He smiled. "I bought it. It's. . .*our* house."

Kori stared at him, nonplussed.

"It's in Garden Grove, a wonderful little neighborhood just outside of Los Angeles. I closed on it just before I came to Wisconsin."

"You're out of your mind!"

"Very possibly." Brent chuckled and even Kori had to suppress a grin. "Here, look." He took the photos and leaned closer to Kori. "This is the living room. The previous owners painted all the woodwork yellow. It looks hideous, so you've got your work cut out for you, stripping, sanding, and staining."

Kori lifted a brow. "Aren't you being a bit presumptuous?"

"Kori, you're so good with stuff like this. Remember when you refinished that rocking chair for my sister? She still has it in her living room by the fireplace."

Kori remembered that particular project very well. She looked down at the photograph again. "What kind of wood is underneath the yellow paint?" she couldn't help asking.

"Oak—there's oak woodwork throughout the house, including the floors. Here, look." Brent showed her a picture of the dining room with its built-in corner hutch. Then came the picture of the spacious kitchen. "I know you'll want to paint and rewallpaper in here."

Inadvertently, Kori nodded. All she could think of was that the orange flowered paper didn't suit her decorating tastes at all.

"Okay, now look at this." Brent showed her a picture of the back porch, which, he said, was accessible from the landing on the stairwell going up to the second floor. "There's a little deck out here. It faces the west, looks out over the palm trees. You and I can sit out here and watch the sunset."

Kori glanced at him. "Always the romantic, aren't you?"

"Yep. Now look at this." Brent showed her photographs of the bedrooms. Three upstairs and one, the master bedroom, downstairs and, again, Brent's words rang in her ears. *You and I can have lots of babies. . .*

With an audible sigh, Kori dropped her head back against the sofa.

"What's wrong?"

"You're what's wrong. You tempt me beyond imagination." She turned her head toward him and his chocolate-brown eyes locked with hers. His held a question, hers held her heart. "If you really still love me, why didn't you come for me sooner, Brent?"

Forgetting the photographs, he gathered Kori in his arms. "I would have. . .I mean, I wanted to. I just didn't know. . ." Brent tightened his hold as Kori's arms went around him. "I only found out we were still married a couple of months before my father died. My first impulse was to go ahead and file for divorce as I originally planned—mainly because I figured it was too late to do anything else. But then I started thinking—"

"Dreaming," Kori corrected him.

"Yeah, well, once a dreamer, always a dreamer." Brent placed a kiss on her forehead. "But dreams do come true, you know."

Kori didn't argue. She was too tired and leaning against Brent this way, listening to the sure and steady beat of his heart, made her feel so safe and secure. . .even loved. But was this really love?

Brent sat up a little straighter. He cupped Kori's chin with one hand. "Let's give our marriage another chance," he murmured as his lips brushed against hers. "I promise I'll never hurt you again."

Kori turned, pushing herself away from Brent. "I won't say no," she told him in all honesty. "Part of me wants to give our marriage another chance. But I have to think this over. I mean, I don't want to hurt Jared. He says he loves me—just like you do. And whatever I feel for him, it was strong enough to agree to marry him." She paused. "I need to sort out my feelings. I need time."

Brent didn't reply, but pursed his lips, looking pensive. In that moment, Kori thought he seemed very much like the doctor contemplating his patient's diagnosis.

Turning, she sat facing him, one leg tucked beneath her. "What are you thinking about, Dr. McDonald?"

"I'm thinking about how much I hate waiting!"

Kori leaned her head back and laughed out loud. "Now there's the Brent I remember!"

He smiled back at her and then looked at his watch. "But I shouldn't have to wait too much longer for my supper."

Kori's eyes widened. "I almost forgot about our meat loaf."

"Me too."

Getting up from the sofa, Brent took Kori's hand and helped her to her feet. He didn't release her, as she expected, but put his arms around her waist. Pulling her closer to him, he kissed her with a fervency that melted the years between them.

And it was a long while later before they remembered the meat loaf again.

Chapter 13

S o. You decided to come home, huh?"

At Clair's remark, Kori blushed; it was nearly two in the morning. "I fell asleep," she muttered, hanging up her coat. She didn't, however, say that she had fallen asleep in Brent's arms as they snuggled together on the couch and watched TV.

Clair, dressed in her nightgown and robe, had obviously gotten up for a glass of water. "Okay, let's hear it," she said in her sternest big-sister voice. "Where were you and who were you with? As if I need to even ask."

Kori laughed. "The three of us, Dana, you, and I, will make fine mothers."

"Don't change the subject," Clair retorted.

"Okay, I won't." Kori knew she didn't owe her sister an explanation, but she'd give her one anyway. While Dana, Clair, and Kori respected each other's privacy, they also expected responsibility. Right after Kori moved in, they made rules for themselves—no last-minute overnight guests, no staying out all night—and if one of those agreed upon rules were violated, the offender owed the others an explanation. They had all agreed that there was security in accountability. "I'm so late," Kori began, "because Brent talked me into making him dinner tonight. After we ate, I fell asleep on the couch while Brent watched TV. I woke up about an hour ago." Kori shrugged. "Brent said he didn't have the heart to wake me up earlier."

"All right," Clair said, a little smile tugging at the corners of her mouth, "you're off the hook. . .this time."

"Thanks, sis," Kori replied facetiously as she walked with Clair to the kitchen.

"Kind of seems like you've made your decision about Brent."

Kori shrugged. "I'm no longer refusing to give our marriage another chance, if that's what you mean. But I still have to sort out my feelings. There are times, like tonight," she said candidly, "when I think I know what love is and that I'm still in love with Brent. But then there are other times when I remember how he left me and how he said he just didn't love me anymore. Then the questions start all over again. What is real love?" Kori sighed. "I know I need to sort out my feelings and make a decision soon."

Clair nodded.

"But here's the thing," Kori continued. "Feelings change. My deepest fear is that Brent will change his mind again."

"Kori, there are no guarantees in this life. Anyone could change his mind. Including Jared."

"No, not Jared."

"Yes, Jared," Clair said, pouring herself another glass of water. "A person can set his or her mind to anything, but then the circumstances change. I mean, Jared could get laid off of work or he could get a terminal illness, which could make him become a real homebody. Perhaps he'd see the value of a wife and kids. On the other hand, Jared might win the lottery and decide he doesn't want the burden of a family. He might decide to move to Key West and live like a recluse on a fishing boat the rest of his life."

Kori made a tsk-sound with her tongue. "Well, Brent could decide the same thing—as he so nonchalantly did once already!"

"Exactly my point. Circumstances change a person's feelings—Brent's, yours, mine, and Jared's."

"Okay, so how do I handle that?"

"You deal with your feelings as they change and expect that your 'significant other' will too. That's where commitment comes in. You trust each other enough to believe that you will both keep your promises despite the changes that are bound to come in life."

"But I need a guarantee," Kori contended. "I need something in this life that I can hang on to."

Clair drank her water and then set her glass in the sink. "Sorry, I can't help you there, kiddo. In my experience I've found that there are no guarantees in this life." She smiled and gave Kori a hug. "Good night."

"Good night."

Kori watched her sister walk through the living room and toward the bedrooms. She felt that abyss in her soul widen, but she couldn't figure out why. Kori had friends and coworkers who liked her, a sister who loved her, a roommate who cared almost as much as a sister, and two men who professed to be in love with her. Yet she felt like the loneliest person alive.

❧

The next day, Kori was tired and distracted. She'd sit at her desk and try to do paperwork, but then she'd see Jared's picture and feel guilty. She wanted to blame Brent for tempting her even though he knew she was struggling; however, she was the one who had curled up beside him last night. She hadn't resisted his kisses—even the one he'd given her this morning after he drove her to work. It seemed that when she was with Brent, Kori forgot all about her commitment to Jared. What kind of a person was she anyway?

By the end of the day, Kori was irritable and confused, though she tried desperately not to show it. When she was short-tempered with a patient over the telephone, she felt even worse about herself.

"Kori, can I have a word with you?" Close to tears, she looked up from the route slips on her desk. Ryan stood at the doorway. "Let's go into my office."

Nodding solemnly, Kori followed Ryan down the corridor and into his office. He shut the door and she sat down.

"What's with you today? You're not yourself."

"That's for sure." Kori sighed as Ryan sat down behind his desk.

"What's going on?"

"Oh," she sighed, "it's this thing with Brent."

"Hmm. . ." He sat back in his chair. "You can't let personal matters interfere with your work, Kori."

"I know."

Ryan was momentarily thoughtful. "You want to fill me in on the situation? You don't have to, but maybe I can help."

Kori shrugged. "I'm torn between whether I should give my marriage another chance or start over with Jared."

Ryan grinned. "You've changed your tune since the last time we spoke about this."

"I know. Brent is very persuasive and I'm very confused." Kori sighed again, this time impatiently. "Which man do I give my heart to? Which one can guarantee me he won't break it?"

"Neither one, Kori," Ryan replied in soft concern. "Men and women alike are fallible human beings."

"Yes, I know. I guess it's just like Clair said: there are no guarantees in life."

"There is one."

"Oh?"

"Jesus Christ."

Kori rolled her eyes. "I should have known you were heading in that direction." She gave him a pointed look. "Don't preach at me, Ryan."

"Okay, but let me just say this: Jesus is the answer to your questions and the solution to your problems. Jesus is the one Man you can give your heart to, and He'll never break it because He loves you with a love that will never let you go."

Kori had gotten up from her chair and was heading toward the door when something clicked. She turned. "What did you say?"

"I said, Jesus is the answer to your questions—"

"No. I mean about the love that will never let me go."

Ryan looked a bit confused. "That's just what I said. Jesus Christ loves you with a love that will never let you go."

"How do you know that?"

Ryan smiled. "It's in the Bible. Christ promised it, and being the Son of God, He doesn't lie."

Kori stood frozen. On the one hand, she doubted that any form of religion would help her; on the other, something inside compelled her to hear more.

"Sit back down, Kori," Ryan said. "Our last patient cancelled and your paperwork can wait. We've worked together for the good part of two years now and I've been your friend as well as your physician."

Kori nodded, taking her seat once more. Ryan was a friend, that was true enough, and he had helped her overcome the depression that began after she moved to Wisconsin. Ryan had prescribed some antidepressants, which Kori took for only a short period of time. Meanwhile, Ryan monitored her closely, giving her friendly advice from time to time.

"As your friend," he continued, "I want to share the good news of salvation through Christ with you. As your physician—well, I don't want you to get so down that you fall into a depression again."

"I don't want that either."

Ryan smiled. "Will you let me tell you about the Savior then?"

"You've told me about Him a hundred times," Kori said despairingly.

"But will you listen this time?"

Kori considered the request as tears filled her eyes. Would she listen? Would it make a difference if she did? She needed something. . .

"Yes," she said at last, "I'll listen."

❧

When Kori left Ryan's office, she only felt more confused instead of consoled. Now there was a third Man tugging at her heart. A Man who was God, a Man named Jesus Christ. A Man who supposedly loved her enough to give His life for her.

Gathering her belongings in preparation to leave for the day, Kori tucked the little pamphlet that Ryan had given her into her purse. Over the years, Ryan had given Kori dozens of "tracts," as he called them, all of which she had deposited in her nightstand at home. She hadn't read them before, but maybe it was time to read them now.

Kori walked downstairs, got her coat, and then punched out for the day. Brent was waiting patiently in the lobby. Seeing her, he set down the magazine he'd been reading and smiled. Then he got a better look at Kori's face and frowned in concern.

"Are you all right? Bad day?"

"Yes and yes," Kori replied with a hint of a smile.

Brent walked beside her as they left the clinic, and Kori tried to ignore the curious stares from the receptionists. They knew she was engaged to Jared, and they were probably wondering who Brent was. Rumors were probably buzzing around the clinic like pesky flies at a summer barbecue. However, tonight Kori was too tired to care.

"Would you like some dinner?" Brent asked on a tender note. "I'll cook or we could eat out."

Kori only answered his question with one of her own. "Brent, who is Jesus Christ?"

He paused in the midst of opening up the passenger door of his truck. "Who is He?"

"Yes."

"He's the Son of God."

"I know that, but. . .who is He to you?"

"My Savior."

"Yes, but—"

Brent chuckled. "Get in the truck and we'll talk on the way home. It's freezing out here and this conversation could take a while."

Kori climbed in and waited until Brent was seated and had started the engine. "Ryan and I were talking about Jesus Christ this afternoon."

"Oh, yeah?" Brent sounded pleased.

"Ryan told me that I need to give my heart to Jesus—but how can I do that if I don't know who He is?"

"Hmm. . .good question. Let me think about it for a minute."

Kori leaned back against the seat and closed her eyes while Brent pondered the inquiry.

"To me," he said at last, "Jesus Christ is like a brother with whom I am very close. He's also my best friend and, like the Bible says, He is the Great Physician, so in that way—in every way—Jesus Christ is my mentor. I can go to Christ with all my problems and leave them with Him, knowing He has the power to take care of them and me because He is God." Brent glanced at Kori. "And, being God, He expects me not to sin, though He will forgive me when I do and when I ask Him to forgive me. Christ also expects me to live up to the standards He set in the Holy Bible. He died on the cross for my sins, rose again from the dead, and now we have a relationship." Brent paused. "I hope that's not too pat of an answer, but it's the truth as I understand it."

Kori nodded, and wondered who Jesus Christ was to her. She didn't think she needed a brother or a "Great Physician." She didn't even need another friend. What she needed was a love that would never let her go. But how could she find that in Jesus Christ?

She was so deep in thought that she didn't even notice where Brent was taking her until he stopped and shut off the engine. They were in the parking lot of a Greek restaurant.

"Would you like to eat here?"

Kori thought it over and then shook her head. "No, I need to go home, Brent. I'm tired."

He nodded and restarted the engine.

"Thanks anyway, though."

"You bet."

By the time they arrived at her apartment, Kori decided that she at least owed Brent some supper for driving her to and from work. In just a few days she'd have her own new car and her independence back again.

"Want to come in?" she asked after Brent parked. "I'll make you something to eat."

"Thanks, Kori. I'll take you up on the offer."

They walked into the apartment complex and then up to Kori's apartment. Clair and Dana still weren't home and the place was dark. While Brent waited in the small hallway, Kori made her way into the living room and turned on a lamp. Then she returned and hung up their coats.

"Come on in and sit down," she said. "I'll start supper. How about a gourmet dish—like macaroni and cheese?"

Brent laughed. "That sounds great."

"Dana will have a fit when she finds out I made this," Kori told him, taking the box out of the cupboard. "Dana hates prepackaged food."

"Well, I'm not that way. In fact," Brent added, a mischievous gleam in his eyes, "why don't I make the macaroni and cheese while you slip into something more comfortable?"

"Oh, quiet!" Kori told him on a sarcastic note, while Brent laughed, sounding thoroughly amused by his own humor. Then even Kori had to chuckle.

"Oh, well," Brent said at last, "you can't blame a guy for trying."

Kori rolled her eyes and pulled out a saucepan.

"You know," Brent said, "I think you'd enjoy meeting Mark and Juli."

Something pulled at Kori's insides at the mention of Brent's friends. She hoped Brent wasn't trying to mimic Mark and Julia's reunion.

She set the pan of water on the stove and turned on the burner. "When did you want to reconcile with me, Brent?"

"What do you mean?"

"When was it? A month after you found out we were still married? Two months? When?"

Brent thought it over. "I think it was probably the very night Tom Sandersfeld told me the divorce never went through. In fact, a couple days after my dad and I met with Tom, I called him and told him to put the divorce papers on hold until I got back to him. I told him I had a lot of thinking to do.

"You see, after you moved here to Wisconsin, Kori, I had already begun to regret our separation. I had learned that being a bachelor wasn't so great. It was lonely. The dating scene was pathetic and I didn't want any part of it. And my hot red sports car certainly didn't snuggle up next to me at night."

Brent grinned meaningfully and Kori blushed. She certainly *had* snuggled up next to him last night!

Kori cleared her throat. "When did you talk to Mark Henley and find out about him and Juli?"

"Let's see. . .must have been in September." Brent gave her a smile. "I told Mark I'd stand up in his wedding and then I stewed some more over what to do about you and me. Finally I concluded that it was just too coincidental that Mark was getting married here in Wisconsin and you lived in Wisconsin. So I prayed about it and now I really believe that it's God's will for our marriage to be a success. When I told Mark that I was taking some time off to get my wife back, he really encouraged me."

"So you talked to God before Mark Henley?"

Brent nodded and then frowned curiously. "Why do you ask?"

She shrugged. "I guess I'm glad you talked to God first."

A slow smile spread across Brent's darkly handsome face but he didn't say anymore. Instead, he picked up one of Dana's banking magazines, sat down on the sofa, and leafed through it. In the kitchen, Kori added the macaroni to the boiling water and decided that there was something comforting about a man who talked to God. Like Ryan Carlson.

Then she thought about Ryan and Stacie. Kori envied their relationship, the closeness they seemed to share. Could she and Brent experience that?

Maybe our marriage does deserve another chance. Maybe my second time around should be with Brent. Perhaps we could get it right this time. . .

Chapter 14

Kori smoothed on some lipstick and then pressed her lips together.

"Where you going?" Dana wanted to know as she entered the bathroom and grabbed her hairbrush. "Have a hot date?" She laughed.

Kori was chuckling, too. "Yeah, my hot date is taking me to church."

"To church?"

Clair had been walking by the bathroom, and she paused outside the door. "Did I hear you say you're going to church, Korah Mae?"

"Yep. You heard right." Both Dana and Clair were now watching Kori expectantly. "Before I agree to give Brent and our marriage a second chance," she explained, "I decided I'd better find out if this born-again Christian stuff is something I can live with."

Clair leaned against the doorway. "Don't you think that it's just another passing fad with Brent?"

Kori bit her lower lip and momentarily contemplated the question. "You know," she said at last, "I guess I'm hoping it's not. Since Brent got religious, he's different. . .and I like the difference. If his faith lasts, so will our marriage. I'm sure of it."

"But there's no guarantee it will last," Clair said. "That shouldn't be a basis for your decision."

"True. But on the other hand, if Brent's religion is too weird, then I can't live with that, either. That's why I'm going to church tonight."

Clair nodded, looking disinterested. "Well, have fun." She walked away.

"You know, I used to go to church," Dana confided. "When I was a teenager. I was part of a youth group. But then I guess I drifted away." She paused. "But I still believe in God and I pray."

"I don't have much church experience," Kori admitted. "My parents took Clair and me to church for weddings, funerals, sometimes at Christmas, but that's it."

Dana got a faraway look in her eyes. "Wow, I haven't been to church in a long time. Seems like forever."

"You're welcome to come with me tonight."

"Yeah?" She thought it over. "Maybe I will."

"Better hurry and decide. I have to leave in five minutes. Clair said I could use her car tonight."

"Well, we can take mine." Dana smiled broadly. "I'll go change my clothes."

Kori watched as Dana bounded into her bedroom and whipped open her closet door. Smiling after her, Kori left the bathroom and walked into the living room.

"You know," Clair said, looking pensive, "maybe I should go with you. I mean, tomorrow is Thanksgiving Day and I have to meet Zach's entire family. I suppose a prayer or two wouldn't hurt, huh?"

Kori shrugged. "The more the merrier."

Minutes later, the three friends were climbing into Clair's car, since it was the larger of the two. Kori assumed the role of navigator, and within twenty minutes, they were pulling into the church parking lot.

Brent met them at the door and ushered them into the spacious lobby of the large church. "All three of you came. What a surprise."

"Yeah, well, Dana and I decided that we could probably use a little church, too," Clair explained.

Brent gave each lady a warm smile. "Great. Let's hang up your coats and go get a seat."

They followed Brent to the other side of the lobby where he solicitously hung up each lady's wrap. Then they followed him into the auditorium.

"I just love these modern-looking churches," Dana remarked as they sat down in the padded pew. Brent was on the end, Kori beside him, and then Dana and Clair next to her. "They're not so imposing, you know?"

Kori agreed, deciding that she liked the music, too. It was lively, happy. Someone played the piano while another played the organ.

Then the service began and the congregation sang a couple of hymns. After that the youth group sang.

"Oh, this reminds me of my old youth group," Dana said nostalgically.

An offering was taken then, followed by the pastor's sermon. He spoke on the power of the Holy Spirit in a true believer's life. Kori wasn't exactly sure what the pastor was talking about, though she'd heard of the Trinity: Father, Son, Holy Spirit. Ryan had explained it and, as the pastor kept talking, certain things began to make sense to Kori. So far, nothing was too weird for her.

Once the pastor finished his sermon, he asked for prayer requests. One by one church members stood and revealed problems in their lives that required prayer. Some stood and gave "a praise." They told of how God had directed them, provided for them, and answered their prayers. It was all a little much for Kori to fathom. Wasn't God too busy to be bothered which such trivial things as a new job or a new house? Couldn't these people just make their own decisions? Perhaps they were weak-minded.

Then Kori spotted Ryan sitting several pews ahead of her. Beside him sat Stacie Rollins. Kori watched as she leaned her blond head over and whispered something to Ryan. He nodded in reply.

So much for my theory, she mused. *Ryan isn't weak-minded and, from what I remember, Stacie isn't either.*

Kori looked at Brent who was writing down a prayer request on a sheet of paper. Her weak-minded theory might apply to him, but only in the way that the Brent she once knew went from one cause to the next. Could she live with this one? His religion seemed harmless enough. In fact, it seemed pro-marriage, pro-family—the very things Kori desired.

Suddenly Brent looked up at her and smiled. She smiled back and it was then that Kori realized she'd rather go to church with Brent than go to a bar or bowling alley with Jared.

The service ended and before she knew it, a small group had congregated around them, Ryan and Stacie included.

"Kori, your coming to the worship service tonight is answered prayer for me," Ryan told her, grinning broadly.

"Good," she replied facetiously. "Maybe now you won't bug me about visiting any more."

He laughed.

Stacie was smiling. "I used to think the same thing when Julia here would invite me out to hear the gospel. It sounded so. . .boring."

"I only asked you a few times," replied the lovely lady with thick, auburn hair. "And the very first time you agreed to come."

"I haven't been sorry, either," Stacie said.

A tall man with blond hair, blue eyes, and broad shoulders chuckled. He stuck his right hand out to Kori. "Nice to see you again."

She recognized him then. "Mark Henley." She shook his hand. "Nice to see you, too."

"Who would have ever thought we'd all meet up again in Wisconsin?" Mark said, giving Brent a friendly slap on the back. "Huh, California boy?"

Brent just grinned in reply. Then he introduced the group to Clair and Dana.

"The four of us are going out for pizza," Julia said, looking at Kori. "Would all of you like to join us?"

"Oh, that sounds fun!" Dana piped in. She looked at Mark. "How's the singles' group in this church. . .not that I'm interested or anything?"

Everyone burst out in laughter and Clair gave Dana a playful shove.

Mark glanced at Julia. "How's the singles' group here?" He turned back and explained, "I'm really just a visitor. I'm a consultant and travel all over the country. But I've been in Wisconsin for almost six months now. Julia, on the other hand, has been a member of this church for years. So has Ryan."

"Actually, the singles' group could use new blood," she replied with a smile. "Especially since Ryan and Stacie are an 'item.' "

"Well, I'll keep that in mind," Dana said, looking sheepish.

Clair rolled her eyes and Kori laughed.

"Let's go eat," Ryan suggested. "I'm starved."

❧

Kori put her key in the lock and opened the apartment door. Clair and Dana followed her in.

"Oh, that was fun!" Dana exclaimed, flouncing on the sofa. "I'm stuffed."

"Me too," Clair said, taking a seat in the armchair.

Kori sat in other. "I did more talking than eating tonight. Imagine that."

Clair grinned. "You and Juli were having quite the intense conversation."

Kori nodded. "She and Mark went through something like Brent and I are experiencing, only there was a child involved. Julia and Mark have a son named Jesse."

"No kidding?" Dana sat up, looking interested. "But they're not married, so. . .what happened?"

"It happened in high school," Kori explained. "Mark and Julia were young and in love and they weren't Christians. They were planning to get married after Julia graduated, but Mark got cold feet. . .on the day of the wedding. A couple of months later, Juli realized she was pregnant, but Mark had moved out of state by then."

"You know, I saw a movie like that once. What was the name of it again. . . ?"

Clair shot a pillow at her. "Will you quit with your movies already? You watch too much TV."

In reply, Dana shot the pillow back at Clair. She looked at Kori then. "So Mark and Julia just got reunited, huh?"

"Yep. Julia said she burned her bridges when she left the small town she grew up in. Mark had been looking for her, but couldn't find her. Then, finally, he met up with her at work. He was hired as a consultant and Julia was some manager or something. They're both Christians now and they've worked things out between them. And they're getting married next month!"

"What a sweet story." A dreamy expression crossed her delicate features.

"Is that for real, Kori?"

She nodded. "I have no reason to believe Julia would lie."

"I know. . .but, well, it sounds so pat. Real life isn't like that. Love and forgiveness and happily-ever-after."

"It is if you want it to be," Dana replied.

Kori decided her friend might be right. "But God has a big part of it. I mean, that's what Julia kept saying."

"Do you believe that, Kori?" Clair wanted to know.

She thought it over. "You know," she replied at last. "I think I'm beginning to." The admission surprised even Kori.

"So you're going to give Brent another chance?" Dana asked.

"I'm certainly leaning that way."

"I think you two belong together," Clair stated.

"I'm starting to agree," Dana added. "But I feel sorry for Jared."

Kori sighed. "Yeah, and I don't want to hurt him. I have to talk to him after he gets home from deer hunting." She stood. "Well, I'd better turn in. I've got a busy day tomorrow." She smiled, looking forward to her newly made Thanksgiving Day plans. "Brent is picking me up for something called a 'praise service' and then we're going to Julia's aunt's for dinner. Julia extended the invitation tonight."

"What about that Deer Hunter Widows' Ball you're supposed to attend tomorrow night?" Dana asked.

Kori shrugged. "I won't be going. I don't have a car and Brent certainly won't drive me to a tavern. I'm sure he considers it a modern-day den of iniquity, so I'm not even going to ask him for the favor."

Clair chuckled. "Brent has been against drinking alcoholic beverages for a long time. That's nothing new. Remember the time we were at Mom and Dad's for dinner and he gave us a big lecture about the effects of alcohol on the brain? He'd seen some study in one of his medical classes. There we were sitting around the table, sipping red wine. . .none of us could even finish it once Brent had his say."

"I remember." Kori laughed at the memory. "Well, in any case," she continued, "I'm sure I won't even be missed tomorrow night. Sounds like there's going to be a large crowd. I heard an ad for the party on a local radio station yesterday morning." She turned to leave. "Guess I'll trot off to bed. G'night, ladies."

Clair stood. "I'm going to bed, too. Good night, ladies," she mimicked.

"Hey, isn't that a song?" Dana cried. Then she began to sing. "Good night, ladies. Good night, ladies. Good night, ladies. . ."

Chuckling at her roommate, Kori proceeded down the hallway to her bedroom. She closed the door behind her and undressed for bed. Slipping her nightgown over her head, her ring caught on the seam of the sleeve and, disengaging it, she peered at the diamond on her left hand. Her conscience pricked her. She felt like a hypocrite.

Suddenly Kori knew she was standing on one of life's many bridges. She either had to go one way or another. Cross over to a marital relationship with Jared, or go back to Brent.

A long moment passed. Then another. Finally, Kori slowly slipped the ring off her finger.

Chapter 15

Thanksgiving dawned, another frosty November day. Gazing out her apartment window, Kori thought about the house Brent had purchased in California. She remembered its redecorating needs and decided she'd like to be the one to face the challenge. Besides, she missed California. These Wisconsin winters could be so long.

Then she thought about Jared. Kori hated the thought of breaking his heart. If only there were some other way. . .

Glancing at her wristwatch, Kori realized that Brent would be waiting for her outside in just a few minutes. She grabbed her purse and coat, called a good-bye to Clair and Dana who were just rolling out of bed, and walked down to the lobby. She immediately spotted Brent's forest-green 4 X 4. Amazingly, he was early!

"Hi," he said as she climbed into the truck, "you look nice."

Holding her coat, Kori gave him a self-conscious smile. "I wasn't sure what to wear, so I settled for this skirt and sweater."

"You look great." Brent pulled away from the curb.

"Not overdressed or too casual?"

"I think you're dressed just right."

Kori lifted a brow. "And I think you're impressed much too easily these days."

"Oh?" A little grin played on his lips.

Then she added, "But I like it."

Brent laughed. "Are you telling me that I was hard to impress during the course of our marriage?"

A little smile tugged at the corners of Kori's mouth. "No, I'm not, because you really weren't hard to impress or please. I'm just saying. . .well, I like the change in you."

He glanced over at her, a tender expression on his face.

Some twenty minutes later, Brent pulled into the church parking lot. "The service this morning," he explained as they walked toward the building, "is exclusively music and testimonies of praise."

Kori nodded. "Yes, that's what Julia told me last night."

They entered the rapidly filling auditorium and found a seat beside Ryan and Stacie. Brent was on the end, sitting to Kori's left.

Ryan leaned forward, looking at her. "Glad to see you, Kori—again!"

She had to laugh. For all the many times Ryan had asked her to visit his church, he probably never thought it would happen twice in the same week.

The Thanksgiving Day service began and Kori was impressed with the instrumental solos as well as the congregational singing. She didn't know any of the "hymns of praise," as the music director called them; however, she caught on quickly. The testimonies were interspersed throughout the service, and Kori found herself curious once more over the dependence these people had on their God. They seemed to count on Him to solve their every problem and supply their every need. Weak-minded. . . ?

Then Kori thought about her own situation—the one with Jared. She'd love to turn over the responsibility of breaking her engagement to an all-controlling God who loved her and wanted to protect her. But who was He and how did one go about getting God to do such marvelous things?

Brent suddenly reached out and took Kori's hand. Their fingers entwined and Kori sensed that he'd taken note of her bare ring finger. She stole a glance at him and nearly laughed out loud at Brent's astonished expression. He only tightened his hold on her hand and a contented warmth spread throughout her being.

Shortly thereafter, the service ended and Kori followed Brent out of the auditorium. In the spacious, well-decorated vestibule, they met up with Julia and Mark. An older couple stood beside them.

"Kori and Brent," Julia began, "I'd like you to meet Barb and Glen French. They're like my second parents."

The introductions were made and then Barb looked at her watch. "Oh, mercy! The turkey will be done in two hours, and I still have mashed potatoes to make and a table to set."

"Don't worry, we'll help," Julia assured the older woman.

Kori heartily concurred.

"Well, then," Barb replied, "let's go!"

Outside in the parking lot, Brent unlocked the truck's passenger door. Before opening it, however, he paused and the November wind tousled his thick, sable hair. "You took off your engagement ring."

Kori just nodded, looking back into his probing gaze.

"What does that mean?"

She took a deep breath. "It means I felt like a hypocrite wearing it."

"That's all?"

Brent looked crestfallen and the expression on his face plucked at Kori's heartstrings. It was then she knew that if she hadn't made up her mind before, she had now.

"I can hardly wear Jared's engagement ring," she said with an intent look into Brent's dark gaze, "when I want to give our marriage another chance."

Brent swooped her up into his arms before the last word had even passed her lips. He swung her around in a full circle and several passing church members gazed at them curiously.

"Good grief, Brent!" she chided when he finally set her down. "What will people think?"

"Who cares? I'm the happiest man alive right now!" With a lopsided grin, he opened the truck's door and helped Kori climb inside.

❧

The Frenches' home was located on the north side of Menomonee Falls, so Brent had to pass his apartment to get there. "Do you mind if I make a quick stop?" he asked, pulling into the complex's parking lot.

"Not at all. Did you forget something?"

"Sort of." Brent opened the door and climbed out of the truck. "Why don't you come on inside with me?"

"But—"

Brent closed his door behind him, cutting off her reply. *Impetuous,* she thought. *Now there's a word that describes my Brent. My Brent. . .* Kori's heart repeated those words. *Can this really be happening? Brent and I back together again?* She sighed and then realized, *If he's the "happiest man alive" right now, then I'm the happiest woman!*

She opened the door and he was right there waiting for her to exit the truck. He grabbed her hand and led her toward the front door of the apartment.

"The Frenches are waiting," Kori gently reminded him as Brent pulled out his keys. "And Barb wanted some help with—"

"This won't take long."

Brent let her into the apartment, and as Kori entered the living room, he rushed down the hallway toward the bedrooms. Shaking her head at him, Kori looked around. The boxes Brent had brought from California still lay in the corner. She was glad now that he hadn't thrown them away as she'd requested; however, she still thought the majority of their contents was useless junk.

Her gaze traveled from the boxes to the neatly stacked piles beside them. Kori's needlework was in one and their photo albums were in another. Then she spotted the musical carousel. Relief washed over her; Brent hadn't discarded it after all! Walking over to where it sat on the coffee table, Kori lifted it gently, cradling it in her hands.

Brent entered the room then, wearing a broad smile and looking like the cat that swallowed the canary.

Kori lifted a brow. "What are you up to?"

He laughed and, closing the distance between them, he took the music box. After replacing it on the coffee table, Brent looked back at her and smiled even more broadly. "Close your eyes and hold out your hand."

Kori gave him a suspicious glare. "Last time you told me to do that, you stuck something in my hand from your biology lab."

He hooted. "Oh, yeah, I had forgotten about that. Funny!"

"No, it was gross!"

"Well, this surprise isn't gross at all," Brent promised between chortles. "Really, Kori. Now, close your eyes."

Grudgingly, she obeyed. With her hand outstretched, she felt Brent set something small and soft on her palm.

"It doesn't feel slimy."

Brent chuckled again. "It's not. Okay, open your eyes."

She did and, there in her hand was a black velvet-covered box.

"Open it up," Brent encouraged her.

Kori lifted the lid, already suspecting its contents. But a tiny gasp escaped her when she viewed the sparkling diamond wedding band inside.

"I bought it a few days ago," he told her. "It was going to be a bribe. You know, the guy with the best diamond ring wins."

Kori rolled her eyes at the facetious statement.

"Here, let's see if it fits." Brent took the ring out of its satin cradle and slipped it onto Kori's finger. "It's a bit big, but we can take it back and get it sized." He searched her face. "Do you like it?"

"Yes. It's beautiful." Kori stared at the marquis diamond, set onto a gold band that shimmered from her finger. On either side of the stone were two smaller diamonds. Looking back at Brent, she smiled and teasingly said, "I guess you win."

Brent narrowed his dark gaze. "About time."

Stepping forward, he drew Kori into his arms and kissed her with all the passion of a husband.

❧

"We were beginning to think you two got lost," Mark said, opening the front door of the Frenches' home. Smiling, he welcomed Kori and Brent inside. "Here, let me take your coats."

"I had to make a stop at my place," Brent explained.

"Well, I'm glad you finally made it."

They followed Mark into the living room where a fire burned in the fireplace.

"Hi, Kori," Julia said, waving to her from where she sat on the couch.

Kori returned Julia's greeting and then said hello to Stacie and Ryan. Lastly, she was introduced to Mark and Julia's eleven-year-old son Jesse.

"So, what took you so long?" Ryan asked from the swivel-rocker in which he sat.

Kori felt a silly blush warm her cheeks as Brent took her left hand and held it up, ring side out. "Kori has agreed to give our marriage another chance."

Congratulatory cheers rang throughout the living room, adding to Kori's embarrassment. However, she couldn't deny the happiness in her heart as she and Brent sat down on the couch.

Julia, sitting on the other side of her, took hold of Kori's left hand. "I've got to have a better look here." She scrutinized the wedding band and then looked over at Brent. "Beautiful ring. You did a nice job in choosing it."

"Thanks." Brent appeared somewhat embarrassed.

Julia then had to show off her engagement ring to Kori and the conversation turned to the upcoming wedding, set to take place next month.

Minutes later, Barb and Glen entered the room and sat down. "We have a good half hour till dinner," Barb announced. "We can all just sit and relax and enjoy each other's company. Everything is done. We're just waiting on the old bird."

Kori smiled at the older woman just as Julia stood and began taking orders for coffee, tea, or punch.

"I'll help you." Kori gathered a few glasses from outstretched hands, then followed Julia into the kitchen.

"I'm so happy for you and Brent," Julia stated once she and Kori were alone.

"Thanks." Kori set down the glasses. "I'm happy for us, too."

Julia smiled as she juggled several cups and saucers. "Oh, dear, looks like I'll have to make another pot of coffee," she said, glancing at the empty pot. Looking back at Kori, she added, "You don't have to wait. You're free to join the others if you'd like. Barb's coffeemaker is rather slow."

"I'll wait, if you don't mind." Kori paused. "I'd like to ask you a couple questions."

"Sure."

Kori waited until Julia had prepared the coffee in the automatic maker.

"Why don't we sit over at the kitchen table," Julia suggested. "What's on your mind?"

"Well. . ." Kori really didn't know where to begin; however, she sensed a kindred spirit in Julia and felt that she could open up to her. "I have some. . .spiritual questions."

"All right. I'll try to answer them."

Kori began slowly. "I understand that in order to be born again, I have to give Jesus my heart. . .but I don't know who He is or how I go about giving my heart to Him—or even what that means, to tell you the truth."

"Hmm. . ." Julia nibbled her lower lip in thought. "I don't know where to begin."

"Will you start by telling me who Jesus Christ is to you?"

"Sure. He's my God, my Savior, the Lover of my soul, and the best, most dearest Friend I have."

"Even better than Mark?" Kori asked incredulously.

"Yep. You see, Jesus Christ is the only One who doesn't change. He's the same—yesterday, today, and forever. People change, but God doesn't."

Kori was very interested now. Perhaps Jesus Christ was that "guarantee" she'd been searching for.

"Mark could change, so I can't build my life around him, even though I know he is the one God would have for me to marry. And Mark has God's Holy Spirit living in his heart, just as I do, so we've got a solid foundation upon which to build our marital relationship."

"If Mark would ever leave you, or say he didn't love you any more. . . ?"

Julia gave Kori an empathetic look. "It's a scary thought, isn't it? If Mark left me, it would hurt beyond what words could tell." She paused, looking thoughtful. "But, if that happened, I'd always have Jesus. Only He is my anchor, not a man. Not Mark, though I love Mark very much." Julia smiled. "Am I making sense?"

Slowly, Kori nodded. "I think I know what you're talking about, because I built my whole world around Brent once."

"Only Jesus," Julia said. "A person can only build a life or a relationship around Him."

"And He is the. . .the Lover of my soul."

Julia nodded. "He loved you so much, Kori, He gave His life for you."

"For the world," Kori restated, questioningly.

"No," Julia said, "for *you*, Kori. If you were the only person on earth, Jesus would have still gone to the cross. *For you.*"

Kori was momentarily thoughtful. "That's an awesome idea," she said at last. "Jesus Christ loving me so much that He gave His life. . .for me."

"For you."

"But for you, too."

Julia nodded. "Yes. However, you've got to take this matter of salvation very personally, because it's strictly between you and Jesus. Once you accept Him as your personal Savior, He has your heart. That's when it happens."

Kori was beginning to understand. "But what if Brent decides he doesn't want to be a born-again Christian any more? What if this is just another passing fad with him?"

Julia was momentarily thoughtful. "Well, Brent could certainly let go of Christ, but Christ won't ever let go of him. The Holy Spirit would continue to work on Brent's heart." Julia leaned over in a conspiratorial way. "I think you're going to find that the most wonderful thing about having a Christian husband, Kori, is that if he gets out of line, God will discipline him. Brent will get a spiritual spanking from his Heavenly Father—and that's a promise from the Bible."

"A guarantee."

Julia nodded. "I've gotten plenty of spiritual spankings, and they hurt. But I'm so glad God loves me enough to show me when I'm wrong and out of His perfect will. Then, once I understand that I was wrong, I simply ask for God's forgiveness and my relationship with Him is restored."

"Well, thanks, Julia. I really appreciate you taking this time with me."

"My pleasure. And it looks like our coffee is ready, too."

Julia got up from the table and poured the steaming brew into the coffee cups while Kori filled the waiting glasses with punch. She was pensive all the while. Then, as she followed Julia back into the living room, Kori said a silent prayer: *Jesus, I want to accept You as my Savior, my Friend. . .the Lover of my soul. I don't really know what I'm doing, since I never prayed like this before, but I want to give You my heart because I want. . .no, I need Your guarantee.*

As she handed back punch glasses and took her place beside Brent, Kori sensed she'd somehow obtained the very thing she'd asked for.

Chapter 16

"Kori, I think you're a Christian now," Brent told her later. It was nearing midnight as they sat in Brent's truck in front of Kori's apartment complex. She had just finished telling him about her conversation with Julia that afternoon and now, with the dome light on and his Bible open, Brent was trying to help Kori figure out what exactly occurred afterward.

"See," he said, pointing to the Scriptures, "this is what the Bible calls it. . . being saved." Then he read Romans 10:13: " 'For whosoever shall call upon the name of the Lord shall be saved.' " He looked back at Kori. "Is that what you did? You called upon the Lord?"

"I think so."

Brent smiled and quizzed her further. "Do you believe God the Father raised God the Son from the dead. . .just like it says here in verse nine?"

"Well, if the Bible says so, then I believe it." Kori tapped her forefinger on the open Book. "This is my guarantee. Right?"

"God's Word, your guarantee?" Brent shrugged. "Sure, you could say that. I'm no theologian, Kori, and only God knows the heart, but it sounds to me like you got saved."

"I think I did," she replied, still trying to fully understand what had happened today.

Brent gave her a warm smile. "This truly has been a day of thanksgiving, hasn't it?"

"Sure, it has." Kori sighed happily. "I never thought this day would come. . . the two of us back together again. Reunited."

"Which brings me to another point I'd like to make." Brent closed his Bible, setting it down gingerly. "You're my wife, Kori, and I refuse to continue dropping you off at separate living quarters."

"I know," she replied. "I've been thinking about that tonight, too."

"And?"

"And. . .I suppose I could pack up what I have and move in with you. I really don't have any big furniture to speak of. Before I moved in, Clair and Dana used my room as a guest bedroom."

"Good. I was hoping you'd say that. You don't mind leaving Wisconsin come January?"

"Are you kidding?" Kori laughed. "January is the best time to leave Wisconsin!"

Brent grinned at the tart reply. "What about your career?"

She shrugged. "There are plenty of jobs in California."

"You don't have to go back to work. I mean that."

"Good," she retorted. "Maybe I won't."

They shared a laugh.

"Really, Brent," she continued, "some of these things we'll just have to decide later—like whether or not I go to work after we move back to California." Kori sighed, a weighty issue still pressing upon her. "Right now I have to concentrate on breaking off my engagement to Jared—without breaking his heart."

"Maybe we can talk to him together," Brent suggested. "I don't like the idea of you seeing him alone, and if I'm there, maybe emotions won't fly as high as if it were just the two of you. In the last two years I've had to handle some crisis situations concerning my patients and their families and I think, by God's grace, I've handled them well."

"I'm sure you have." Kori had all the confidence in the world in him. Brent, no doubt, was a wonderful emergency physician. Caring, compassionate. . .and she was touched by his desire to help her out of this situation with Jared. "Let me think about it," she said at last. "I don't know what the best way is—or if there even is a 'best way.' "

"Listen," Brent said in a more serious tone, "it's admirable that you want to spare the guy any heartache, but it may not happen that way."

"I know."

He smiled. "The good news is we've both got the Lord now. If we ask Him, He'll see us through this."

"Oh, yes." Kori smiled right back. "Dependence on God—like those testimonies this morning."

"That's right. . .now, give me a kiss good-bye." Brent's arm circled her shoulders as his hand came to rest on the back of her neck. "Tomorrow night, I won't be dropping you off." After a lingering kiss, he let her go.

"Oh, and don't forget," he added, once Kori was out of the truck, "we can pick up your new car tomorrow."

She smiled. "Let's pick it up right after you help me move."

"It's a date." A tender expression crossed his face. "I love you so much, Kori."

"I love you, too." The words came so easily and were so heartfelt that Kori knew she meant them. And in that moment, she also realized she knew what love was—it was there all along. "I guess that was the problem between Jared and me," she mused aloud. "I wanted so badly to fall in love with him, but I couldn't because, all this time, I've been in love with you. I don't think I ever stopped loving you, Brent."

His dark eyes shone with adoration. "I know that I never stopped loving you." He grinned suggestively. "Sure you don't want to come home with me right now?"

Kori had to think about that one. She longed for Brent the way any wife longed for her husband; but she had made a pact with her roommates. Besides, she felt she needed to end one chapter in her life—the one with Jared—before beginning another with Brent.

"Tomorrow," she said on a decisive note. "I promise."

"Until tomorrow then," Brent replied, his gaze refusing to release hers.

Impulsively, Kori climbed back into the truck and gave Brent one more kiss. He chuckled in surprise and even Kori had to laugh softly as she tore herself away from him and then made her way up to the apartment building. She felt so light-hearted and happy, and so very much in love.

Kori reached the front door, and fishing in her purse, she pulled out her keys. She never saw the other truck in the parking lot, idling in the darkness.

∽∾

"Jared was here about a half hour ago," Dana announced as Kori entered their apartment.

"Jared?" Kori frowned. "He's supposed to be deer hunting."

"Yeah, well, he came back early. He said all the guys had planned to crash the ladies' party tonight—the one you were supposed to attend. When you didn't show up, he tried to call, but of course no one was here to answer the phone. Finally, he came over. I had just gotten home."

"What did you tell him?"

"Just that your car broke down so you didn't have a ride to the tavern and that you had decided to spend Thanksgiving Day with some new friends you'd met at church."

Kori hung up her coat. "How did Jared respond?"

"Okay, I guess. I know he understood about your car breaking down."

Kori thought it over, then met Dana in the living room. "Just so you know, Brent and I are officially back together." She held out her left hand, showing off her ring.

Dana gasped. "That's the most gorgeous wedding band I've ever laid eyes on! I can see why you took him back."

"Oh, quiet!"

They laughed together and then Dana gave Kori a sisterly hug.

"I'm so happy for you," her friend said sincerely. "You and Brent. . .oh! I had a feeling you two belonged together ever since that first day when I saw him kiss you here in the living room." She paused, her delighted expression changing to one of concern. "But now you've got to break the news to Jared, huh?"

Kori nodded. "It's going to be hard, too, because I really don't want to hurt him." She looked at the wedding band on her finger and uneasiness rose up inside her.

❧

The next morning at breakfast, Kori divulged her plans to her roommates. She was moving in with Brent this weekend and, come January, the two of them would move back to California. Since all three ladies had taken the day off from work, they lingered around the dining room table, sipping coffee and discussing Kori's departure.

"I'll sure miss you, Kori," Dana told her, looking sad.

"You'll just have to come and visit me in California. Brent bought a huge house! I can't wait for you to see it."

Dana's blue eyes sparkled with the notion. "Come February, I just might take you up on that offer."

"I hope you do."

Clair sipped her coffee. "It only makes sense that you and Brent get back together. A match made in heaven if I ever saw one!"

Kori chuckled. Her sister had said that very same thing on the day she married Brent.

"I was so angry and disappointed," Clair continued, "when I found out he'd left you. I wanted to wring Brent's neck." She took another sip of coffee. "But I guess he's redeemed himself satisfactorily."

"I'm sure he'll be glad you approve," Kori quipped.

Light laughter flitted around the table.

"And, speaking of approval, I have to call Mom and Dad and let them know." Kori stood, feeling amazed at the miraculous turn of events in these past weeks. Walking over to the phone, she picked it up and dialed her parents' home in Idaho.

Kori suspected that when Brent left her almost two years ago, her father would have gladly joined Clair in "wringing his neck." However, her mother had been as heartbroken as Kori, saying she felt like she'd lost her only son. After she'd informed her parents of her relationship with Jared, neither had seemed all that thrilled, though they acted happy for her, perhaps because she was their daughter and because Kori had wanted so badly to be in love and married again. And, though her parents had readily agreed to meet Jared over the Christmas holiday, Kori surmised they'd be more than pleased to hear of her reunion with Brent.

She wasn't wrong, either. Her mother squealed with joy and then made such a fuss that Kori had to hold the portable phone away from her ear. Clair even heard the excitement emanating from their mother clear across the room.

Shaking her head and rolling her eyes, Clair said, "Korah Mae, you'll be the talk of the bridge club tonight."

"Probably the bowling league, too," she replied, with a hand over the mouthpiece of the telephone. Her father was now on the line.

They talked, Kori repeating her good news, her father's reaction a subdued replica of his wife's. Finally she gave the telephone over to Clair.

"Good morning, Dad. . .yes, it is exciting. Yes, Brent finally came to his senses." Kori watched as her older sister frowned. "What do you mean, when am I getting married? Soon, Dad. Zach and I are just making sure. No, no. . .he hasn't proposed yet. . ."

Chuckling softly at the parental interrogation Clair was forced to undergo, Kori left the living room and began packing her things. Amazingly, she discovered she'd accumulated more than she thought. Then, with Dana's help, she dug up a couple of cardboard boxes, but she'd need to find several more to get the job done.

At noon, the doorbell chimed. Kori assumed Brent had arrived to help her move, but then Clair appeared at her bedroom door, wearing a solemn expression. "Jared's here."

Chapter 17

As Clair retreated from her bedroom, Kori glanced down at the wedding band on her finger. It was as conspicuous as five lone stars in the night-time sky. She didn't dare confront Jared wearing it. Slipping it off, Kori set it in her jewelry case. Then, picking up the engagement ring, she put it in the pocket of her blue jeans, knowing she must return it, knowing the time was now.

She walked into the living room. "Hi, Jared. I didn't expect you back from deer hunting till tomorrow."

He opened his mouth to reply but seemed to think better of it. Then he continued to stand there in the little entry hall, hands inside his black, down ski vest. Beneath it, he wore a red plaid flannel shirt tucked into black jeans. Kori also noticed that he sported a new reddish-brown beard that contrasted nicely with his sandy-blond hair. He looked every bit the outdoorsman, the hunter.

"Why don't you come in?" Kori invited. "We can sit and talk." She looked askance at her roommates, hoping they'd take a hint and vacate the living room.

They did.

"I've got tons of letters to write," Dana blurted, heading for her bedroom.

"Oh, and I have bills to pay," Clair announced, taking her leave as well.

Forcing a little smile, Kori looked back at Jared.

"I've been gone a whole week and this is the kind of greeting I get?" he muttered, wearing a dubious expression.

Kori didn't know what to say, especially since Jared gave her no time to reply. He swiftly closed the distance between them, pulling her into a fierce embrace.

"I missed you," he said huskily, his whiskered chin pressing against her cheek.

Kori bit her lower lip. How could she respond?

When she didn't, Jared released her. "Get your coat. We're leaving."

"Jared, wait, I need to talk to you."

"We can talk on the way to Joe's house."

Kori frowned. "Joe's house?"

He nodded. "There's a college football game on TV this afternoon."

Kori forced a polite smile to her lips. She had no intention of spending the afternoon watching football. Jared must have read her thoughts and in one quick move, he opened the closet door, grabbing Kori's coat. Then he opened the door to the apartment.

"C'mon, let's go."

She sighed in resignation. She didn't want to break their engagement in Jared's truck, but if she must, so be it. "Let me get my purse."

"You don't need your purse."

"Jared!"

He took ahold of Kori's elbow and propelled her out of the apartment, slamming the door behind them. In the hallway, he helped her on with her coat, but never slowed his pace.

"What's the rush?" Kori asked irritably. She was irked that she didn't have her keys. When she returned, she'd have to buzz up to the apartment and ask Clair or Dana to let her in. She hoped they didn't have plans this afternoon, but then again, maybe this wouldn't take long. "Jared, slow down."

"I hate missing the kickoff, you know that!"

Kori rolled her eyes, but buttoned up her coat nevertheless. "We have to talk, Jared," she fairly pleaded. "*Before* kickoff."

"I told you we'll talk on the way to Joe's house."

"Who's Joe?" Kori asked as they entered the elevator.

"A friend from Racine."

"Racine? But that's about a forty-five minute drive from here."

He glowered at her. "Plenty of time to talk, huh?"

The elevator doors opened, and walking through the lobby, they left the apartment complex. Through the freezing rain and gloom of the day, Kori did a quick scan of the parking lot, but she didn't see Brent's truck anywhere. Too bad, since she might have been able to forestall Jared long enough for Brent to join them in the talking.

Jared opened the door, saw her into his aging pickup, and then walked around to the other side where he climbed up into the driver's seat. Kori watched him, noticing for the first time that he looked. . .angry?

Kori strapped on her seat belt. "Jared—"

"Not yet."

He pulled out of the parking lot with tires squealing and then sped down the icy street toward the expressway.

"What's wrong?" Alarm shot through her. Jared was never one to drive like a maniac. . .until now.

"What do you think is wrong?" he shot at her. "My best girl doesn't show up at the party last night, making me look like a fool. I was going to surprise you, Kori. I came back from hunting early just to surprise you."

"I heard. Dana told me and I'm sorry."

"You're sorry? How sorry are you, Kori?"

"I. . .I don't know what you mean. . ."

"Yeah? Well, let me clarify it for you. First, I felt like a fool, but then I got worried. I left the tavern and headed for your apartment to find out what happened to you. Dana told me your car broke down and that you were with some other friends—friends with a car, make that a utility vehicle. And you must have really been grateful for the ride," Jared drawled sarcastically, "because you gave the driver a good, long kiss."

Kori felt the blood drain from her face.

"I waited around and saw the whole thing," Jared muttered furiously, "so don't deny it!"

"I won't."

He glared at her, wearing an expression of incredulity.

"That's what I have to talk to you about," Kori persisted. "You saw me last night with Brent. . .my husband. Brent and I. . .well, we've decided to give our marriage another chance."

In reply, he stomped on the accelerator.

"Jared!" she screamed. "Slow down!"

Much to her relief, he did except his white-knuckled grip on the steering wheel caused Kori yet another measure of alarm. He was in a rage and driving seventy miles an hour on a slippery road.

"I didn't want to tell you like this," she said ruefully, hoping he'd relax and want to at least discuss the matter.

But Jared didn't reply, nor did he relax.

"Please," she begged. "Turn around and take me home."

Again, no reply as the pickup continued to fly down the freeway, faster than the law allowed.

Kori never knew such fear. Jared careened in and out of traffic, randomly changing lanes and cutting in front of other automobiles. Horns blared from under the palms of offended drivers, until at last he exited the freeway, forcing an audible sigh of relief from Kori. Her relief was, however, short-lived. Turning left at the stoplight, he then began to speed down Highway 20, toward the small city of Racine.

❧

Brent stopped pacing and looked at his wristwatch. "Okay, now she's been gone for over an hour." He glanced at Clair, then Dana, and resumed his pacing. "How long does it take to say: *our engagement is over, I'm going back to my husband?*"

Clair chuckled. "Take it easy, Brent. Kori's not exactly heartless, you know. She's probably trying to break it to Jared nice and slow."

"She should have waited for me."

"I don't think Jared gave her much of a choice. They were gone in a flash."

Dana nodded. "Kori didn't even take her purse."

"More's the reason I'm worried. I don't like the thought of my wife alone with that guy."

"Don't you trust her?" Dana asked.

"Of course I trust her!" Brent declared as he momentarily ceased his pacing. "It's him I don't trust. I'm worried about Kori's welfare. I don't know what Jared is capable of when faced with rejection by the woman he says he loves. All I know is that a good percentage of the assaults I treat in the ER are related to crimes of passion."

"No kidding?" Dana shook her head, amazed. "I wonder if Jared is capable of committing a crime of passion."

"He's not," Clair stated emphatically.

"How do you know?" Brent challenged her. "Look, Clair, anyone is capable of anything, given the right circumstance." He resumed his pacing. "Kori mentioned that Jared's got a fridge full of beer, so it's likely he'd have an explosive nature if he were intoxicated."

"Good point, Brent," Dana said, looking concerned.

"Will you two stop it? Kori has only been gone an hour!" Clair exclaimed, throwing her hands in the air, looking exasperated. "That includes drive time. How intoxicated can you get in an hour?" She crossed the room and turned on the television. "Stop your worrying, Dana, and, Brent, sit down and stop that pacing. You're making me nervous. Kori's fine. She'll probably be walking in any minute now."

Taking a seat in one of the armchairs, Brent looked at his watch once more. "I hope you're right, Clair," he muttered. "I hope you're right."

Chapter 18

"T his one's for you, Kori," Jared said, pulling another beer out of Joe's refrigerator. It was his umpteenth—Kori had lost count long ago. "To the love of my life," he continued in a mock toast, popping off the top. "To the only woman I ever thought highly enough of to ask her to be my wife."

Standing in the corner of the kitchen, Kori grimaced. Jared seemed so hurt and she felt awful about it. However, nothing she said seemed to eased his pain, so he chose to drown his sorrows in beer.

Jared's friends were in the den, watching the game on TV, and Kori found herself wishing—no, praying that Jared would join them so she could sneak in a phone call for help.

"I can't believe you're dumping me for him," Jared lamented. Turning, he walked toward Kori until he stood just inches away. "What's he got that I don't?"

Her heart ached for at least the seventh time since they'd arrived here over two hours ago. "Jared, don't do this. . . I've tried to explain."

"What's he got, Kori?" he demanded, angrily now.

"My heart!" she finally cried. "Brent's got my heart."

Jared pulled his bearded chin back, frowning as he considered her statement. Finally he shook his head. "That makes no sense, Kori. That makes no sense at all!"

"Hey, Jare," his buddy, Craig, said, coming into the kitchen. "You're missing the game."

"I don't care," he groused, draining his beer.

Puzzled, Craig looked over at Kori, then back at Jared. "Lover's quarrel going on here?"

"Something like that." Jarad's gruff voice seemed to fill the outdated, dingy room.

Craig gave each of them another look before trying to change the subject. He glanced at Kori. "Joe and I would have told the girls to put off their shopping trip until you arrived," he said apologetically, "but we didn't know Jared was going to bring you along this afternoon."

"That's okay. Don't worry about it."

Jared pulled another beer from the fridge. "Kori and I will be along shortly," he told his friend, and Kori noticed him sway.

"All right, all right. I can take a hint." Craig pulled a beer out for himself and left the kitchen for the football game and the four other rowdy men watching it.

Kori folded her arms in front of her. After being around Brent's friends she'd come to realize just how much she abhorred the drinking and carrying on that was so typical of Jared and "the guys." Didn't they understand that they could have fun without the beer? Kori had thought yesterday was one of the most enjoyable days of her life and not one alcoholic beverage had been served.

"There's no way that guy loves you more than I do," Jared slurred in self-pity. But then a whoop from the other room caught his attention and he sauntered out of the kitchen.

Watching him go, Kori couldn't help breathing a sigh of relief. She waited a moment to be sure Jared was thoroughly preoccupied before heading for the wall-mounted telephone on the other side of the kitchen. She dialed home and Clair answered.

"Where are you? Brent is about to have a nervous breakdown over here."

"Listen, Clair, I just have a moment. Jared is drinking. Heavily. I told him about Brent and me, but he's not taking the news very well. Tell Brent to come and get me."

"Sure. Where are you?"

"In Racine."

"Racine?"

"Yes. I'll explain later."

"I'll need directions."

"I've got them. Ready? Take I-94 and exit on Highway 20. Take that all the way through town and turn on Taylor. There's a park across the street. I'll be waiting right on the corner."

"The weather's bad," Clair informed her. "It'll take him about an hour."

"Fine. Jared should be passed out by then—I hope."

"Oh, Kori. . ."

Brent took the phone. "Kori, are you all right?"

"Yes. But I need to hang up. Jared will be even more angry if he finds me on the phone."

"I'm on my way, and Clair's coming with me."

"Good." A kind of peace flowed through Kori. "I'll see you in awhile."

She hung up the telephone just as Jared entered the kitchen. Hoping to cover her actions, she ripped open a bag of potato chips that had been on the counter under the phone.

"I was just coming to get those," Jared muttered.

"Let me put them into a bowl for you."

He shook his head at her. "No bowl, Kori. We'll just eat them out of the bag." Jared's intoxicated gaze lingered on her face. "Always thinking fancy, aren't you?"

His voice had softened. "You like the cheese and sausage all cut up real pretty and the potato chips in a bowl." He swallowed, narrowing his gaze. "You're probably the best thing that ever happened to me."

Guilt rose up in Kori, threatening to suffocate her. She wanted to say something profound—something that would penetrate his drunken haze, soothe his heart, and set her free, all at the same time. But no words would come.

"You told me you were getting a divorce."

"Jared, I've tried to explain. After seeing Brent," she said carefully, "and after thinking it over, I. . .I changed my mind."

Jared cursed and slammed down his empty beer can, causing Kori to flinch. "How can you change your mind after saying you'd marry me?"

How could I change my mind. . .? The words echoed in Kori's head. Wasn't that the very thing of which she'd accused Brent? Changing his mind?

Craig entered the kitchen then, with Joe right behind him. "Okay, break it up. Fighters to their corners."

His friends chuckled, but Jared was not amused. He grabbed the potato chips from Kori, another beer, and walked out of the room. His friends opened the refrigerator, pulled out more beer, and then they too left the kitchen.

Alone once more, Kori couldn't help but see the sad irony of her situation. She had hated the heartbreak Brent imposed upon her when he said he didn't love her anymore, and here she was inflicting a similar pain on Jared. She had never wanted to hurt him; she only wanted to do the right thing and giving her marriage another chance was the right thing to do. She was certain of at least that much.

Jesus, she whispered in prayer, *this situation is too overwhelming for me. Would You please take care of it. . .so I can someday stand up in church and give one of those testimonies of faith? Jesus, I'm depending on You. . .*

❧

Brent insisted that he and Clair take his truck while Dana agreed to stay at the apartment in case Kori called back. "I've got my cell phone," he told her as they left. "You've got the number."

"I'll call if I hear anything," Dana promised.

The roads were sleet-covered and the freezing rain continued to fall. "I'm glad we took your vehicle," Clair said as they drove past a car that had slid off the road. A police car and tow truck were already on the scene.

"This four-wheel drive comes in handy," Brent replied with a slight grin. "Even in California."

Clair was silent and seemed introspective as they continued their drive to Racine. Finally she turned to him and said, "Thanks, Brent."

"Thanks? For what?"

"For reconciling with Kori."

He chuckled. "I had no choice, Clair. I love my wife. . .even though it took me long enough to realize it."

"Then I guess that's what I'm thanking you for. . .for coming to your senses. I mean, what if Kori would have really married Jared?" Clair shook her head. "I just never thought they made a good match. He's too much into himself, always looking for a good time, and that would have bored Kori to death. She wants a home and kids and, even though she always said Jared is a stable man, he's obviously not a family man."

Brent glanced her way. "Clair, no one is stable when he's drunk, and I'm worried that Jared's 'good time' this afternoon could get someone killed. Especially if he decides to climb behind the wheel of a car. I mean, didn't you tell me that he's drinking heavily?"

Clair nodded. "That's what Kori said. But I still don't think he'd ever hurt anyone. Jared is basically a very nice, decent guy. Kori wouldn't have given him the time of day otherwise."

"Well, whatever he is," Brent replied, concentrating on the slippery road before him, "he's drunk now, and I want my wife as far away from him as possible."

❧

Kori looked at her wristwatch. It was nearly four o'clock. Brent and Clair should be waiting for her. Walking to the kitchen window, she peered out at the freezing rain that fell and pelted the side of the house. Because of the gloom of the day, it seemed dark outside already. Dark and wintery.

She let the curtain fall back into place, then she cautiously made her way into the hallway. Less than a half hour ago, Jared had poured out his heart to his friends, who, of course, took his side. Now they weren't talking to Kori when they entered the kitchen to get their beers, whereas before they had at least attempted to be friendly. Even so, Jared had refused to let her leave.

"You're staying with me, Kori," he had grumbled. He seemed to think that if he kept her here she'd somehow change her mind again, but if she left, she'd be out of his life forever. He was like a man trying to hang onto the wind.

Just outside the den now, Kori stole a glance at him. She sighed in relief at the sight of his sleeping figure, reclined on the couch. Finally! Moving quickly, but as quietly as possible, Kori entered the living room and found her coat. Putting it on, she touched the bulge in her blue jeans pocket. Jared's engagement ring.

She pulled it from her pocket and stared at it, wondering what to do. Should she leave it here for Jared to find? Stop by at his house another time when he wasn't drinking? Mail it?

No, she decided, *I have to settle this now. Any other way will only prolong the inevitable. It's over between Jared and me, but if I hang onto his ring that'll just give him an excuse to see me again.*

As she walked back through the house and rounded the corner to the den, Dave, another of Jared's friends, looked up from where he sat in a comfortable armchair. "Goin' somewhere?" he asked sarcastically.

Kori held her breath, looking at Jared, but much to her relief, he didn't awaken. Looking back at Dave, she nodded. "Yes, I'm leaving. I've arranged a ride home. But will you make sure Jared doesn't drive drunk?"

"Of course," he shot at her, his voice filled with animosity. "What kind of friend do you think I am?"

Kori didn't reply, but twirled the engagement ring in her palm nervously. She could hardly give it to Dave and expect he'd pass it along to Jared. Obviously, he wasn't going to do her any favors. She'd have to do it herself.

Stepping into the room filled with cigarette smoke and the stench of beer, Kori walked slowly toward the man she had intended to marry up until a few days ago. Relief mingled with sadness as she realized she would no longer be marrying a man she didn't love, yet she did have feelings for him. Dreams had been dashed this day, more his than hers, and Kori felt so sorry about hurting Jared.

She softly touched the rim of the pocket on his flannel shirt and then dropped the ring inside. Jared never stirred. Turning on her heel then, Kori left the room. She practically ran through the house and to the front door. Touching the doorknob, she suddenly heard Jared calling her name. Like a rumble of thunder off in the distance, Kori was instantly aware of some sort of ominous doom.

"Don't you dare leave!" he roared.

Ignoring the command, she opened the door and fled. A thin layer of ice covered the front stairs and she nearly slipped. Her heart pounded as fear rose up inside her. She'd never be able to run from Jared in this weather. Why had he awakened? But Kori suspected the answer to that one; no doubt Dave had roused him.

Reaching the front sidewalk, Kori turned left and began to half run, half slide, making her way toward the highway where she prayed Brent was waiting for her.

"Kori!"

"Go back inside the house, Jared," she called over her shoulder. Looking back, she saw he was on the front porch stairs. Then, much to her horror, he jumped and fairly skied down the ice-covered lawn. All without falling! Now he was just behind her.

With a little gasp, Kori turned and did her best to run. She nearly slipped and fell several times, but managed to maintain her balance. Jared wasn't that fortunate. One quick glance behind her showed him sitting on his backside. He glared at her, looking furious, and Kori imagined that he was angry enough to kill. But would he? Never in her relationship with Jared had she seen him drunk like this. All she knew now was that she had to get away. He obviously wasn't in his right mind, and Kori was as scared as she'd ever been.

She neared the corner of Taylor and spotted Brent's truck, but she didn't slow her pace, even though she nearly slipped on the icy walk again. Behind her, Jared was calling her, threatening her. She was so frightened, she began to cry and her tears fused with the sleet raining down, soaking her hair, her face, her coat.

Reaching the highway, Kori saw Brent get out of his truck. Through the encroaching darkness, she saw him frown. She watched as Brent looked past her to Jared, who was gaining on her.

"No, Jesus," Kori muttered in prayer, "not a fight between Brent and Jared. Jared's drunk and he could hurt Brent. . .but he wouldn't mean it, I know he wouldn't."

"Kori, stop!"

Was that Brent—or Jared? Kori's heart was hammering so loudly in her ears, but she felt like she had to keep running.

"Kori!"

That time she was sure it was Brent who called her name. She noticed the sudden look of panic and horror that crossed his dark features and then, too late, she saw the oncoming car. Braking on the icy pavement, it veered out of control. It came straight for her.

Kori screamed.

Chapter 19

B rent met his sister-in-law in the noisy waiting room of the hospital.

"Well?" Clair asked anxiously. "How is she? What's going on?"

"Kori's going to be all right," he began. "But I was right, she's got a dislocated shoulder. And we might be looking at a hip and/or back injury. She's getting X-rays right now."

Clair sat back in her chair and Brent saw her eyes fill with tears.

"She's going to be okay," he repeated.

"But I don't think I'll ever get the picture of Kori being hit by that car out of my mind."

"Me either." Brent handed Clair a box of tissues from a neighboring table. Then he sat down in the chair beside her. "It all still seems so unreal."

"Kori must have been thrown ten feet," she sniffed.

"Yes, but we're lucky that stretch of highway going through town has a speed limit of thirty-five. The driver claims she was only going about twenty miles an hour because of the bad weather. Really, Kori is fortunate to be alive."

"But there was so much blood on her face, Brent."

"That was due to the laceration on her scalp. Head wounds bleed a lot. A few stitches and Kori will be as good as new. As for her shoulder, the nurses are giving her some pain medication now and as soon as she's relaxed, the physician will manipulate it back into place."

"It sounds awful. Poor, Kori. . .getting 'manipulated.' And Jared. . .what's going to happen to him?"

"He can rot in jail for all I care!"

Clair gasped, obviously surprised by his vehemence. "Do you really think he'll get thrown in jail? I mean it isn't like he was driving drunk and hit Kori."

"It isn't? I happen to think it's very much the same." Shifting in his seat, Brent ran his hand through his hair. He knew his previous remark didn't sound very Christian-like, but his feelings for Jared Graham right now were not very Christian. Brent blamed him for Kori's accident and he had every intention of pressing charges. "I suppose the police will find him and question him. As for any imprisonment—well, I really don't know."

Clair nodded. "I just can't believe he ran from the scene."

Brent clenched his jaw, but he decided not to waste his energy on anger. Kori needed him now, whereas his dealings with Graham could wait. Then, for the first time since the accident, Brent suddenly felt uncomfortably cold and wet. His clothes were soaked from being out in the rain and tending to Kori until the ambulance arrived. Clair, too, was drenched.

"Listen," he said, leaning forward with elbows on his knees, "how about if you give Dana a call and ask her to bring you some dry clothes. I'm going to call Mark and request the same. . .and I'm hoping he knows Ryan Carlson's phone number. If Kori needs an orthopedic surgeon, I want a recommendation—"

"Oh, Brent. . .surgery?" More tears filled her eyes.

"It's a possibility. Now, go on," he encouraged her. "Call Dana." He sighed heavily then. "I have a feeling it's going to be a long night."

❧

Nearly two hours later, Kori lay relatively comfortably on the gurney in the emergency department's exam room. The laceration on her head had been sewn to Brent's satisfaction, her shoulder popped back into place. The pain medication was making her body feel light and relaxed and, despite all that had happened, she could not mistake the peace that flowed inside her. Somehow she sensed that Jesus was taking care of everything, just as she'd asked.

"Kori?"

She turned her head and smiled weakly at Brent who was leaning over the side of the gurney.

"How are you feeling?"

"Can't say this has been the best day I ever had," she admitted, "but I'm fine."

He grinned, looking amused. "Fine, huh? That's not what your X rays show."

"What do they show, Dr. McDonald?"

"Well, according to the films, *Mrs. McDonald,*" he retorted, "you've got a fractured hip."

Kori grimaced. "How bad?"

"Bad enough to warrant surgery, I'm afraid. I'm waiting for Ryan. He's agreed to come down to the hospital and recommend an orthopedist for us." Brent shook his head. "I feel so helpless because I don't know any of these guys."

"Who's the orthopedist on call?" Kori wanted to know. "I work with a lot of them when Ryan refers his patients out."

"Ever hear of Dr. Alfred Morris?"

Kori managed a nod. "He's with a reputable physicians' group. I'm sure he's fine."

"Well, I don't want 'fine' operating on you. I want the best."

She smiled up at him. "You're so sweet, Brent."

"And you're about the best patient I've ever known," he teased her. "I wish all of my patients were like you. No moaning and groaning. No persistent demands."

"Why should I moan and groan and make demands," she teased him back, "when I have you to do that for me?"

Brent laughed. "Yeah, I suppose you've got a point there." Leaning over the guardrail on the bed, he kissed her gently, reverently. Straightening, he said, "Clair isn't taking any of this very well at all."

"Clair?" Kori frowned. "But she's always levelheaded."

"This evening, she's near hysteria. She can't stop crying."

"Clair?"

Brent nodded. "I thought maybe I'd leave for awhile and change clothes so she can come in and visit with you. This hospital has a rule that only one guest can be in a patient's exam room."

"All right."

"Dana's out in the waiting area and she brought Clair some dry clothes. Mark and Julia are out there too, and Mark has clothes for me. Now we're just waiting on Ryan."

"What about Jared?"

Brent's shadowy gaze seemed to blacken in fury. "What about him?"

"I. . .well, I just wondered. . ." Kori was suddenly intimidated to ask further, given her husband's seething expression.

"What are you wondering, Kori?" Brent asked, a dark expression on his face. "Are you wondering if he stayed around at the accident site to make sure you were okay? Are you wondering if he came to the hospital, concerned over your welfare? Well, the answer to those questions is no!"

With her uninjured arm, she reached up and placed her palm against his cheek, caressing it. "I love you, Brent," she whispered. "I'm so sure of it now. But please, don't be angry with Jared. He was hurt and—"

"I don't want to talk about him." Brent took hold of her hand, placing a firm kiss on her fingers. "And I love you, too. But I never want to hear you mention the name Jared Graham again. Ever! Is that clear?"

Kori managed a nod, deciding that she was in no position to argue.

"All right then, I'm going to send Clair in, and when Ryan gets here, I'll come back."

After one last kiss, Brent left the exam room, leaving Kori to ponder over his reaction. True, Jared's actions were a factor in the accident. But it wasn't Jared's fault. Kori could hardly blame him when it was she, herself, who hadn't been watching where she was going. Surely, Brent had to know that, too. Then why was he being so hostile at the mere mention of Jared's name? Weren't Christians supposed to "love" everyone? Wasn't that what following Jesus was all about?

Minutes later, Clair walked in. Her face was tear-streaked, confirming everything Brent had said. She tried to smile. "How are you feeling, Kori? Are you in any pain?"

"A little, but it's nothing compared to what I experienced earlier."

"Oh, Kori. . ." Clair's voice sounded broken.

"Don't cry, Sis. I'm really okay."

Through her tear-sparkling eyes, Clair managed to give her a skeptical look. "Did Brent tell you that your hip is broken and you're going to have surgery? You are hardly okay."

"Yes, he told me."

"And?"

Kori lifted a brow, not understanding Clair's meaning.

"Aren't you scared? Oh, of course you must be! I'm sorry. It's just that. . .I'm so scared." More tears pooled in Clair's eyes, spilling onto her cheeks.

Kori reached out to her. "I'm not afraid of having surgery, if that's what you mean. Why are you scared?"

Clair took her hand. "Because. . .well, anything could go wrong and I. . .I just don't want to lose you, Kori. You're my little sister. You're my best friend. Stuff like this isn't supposed to happen to people like us. We're good people. This doesn't seem fair."

Squeezing her sister's hand with as much strength as she could muster, Kori tried to explain the peace that she felt. "Yesterday, Thanksgiving Day, was really that for me for the first time in my life. I realized that I have so much to be thankful for. I was reconciled to Brent, the man I've always loved—even after our two years of separation, even after trying to make myself believe I wanted to marry Jared. And yesterday was also a special day for me because. . .well, because I became a Christian."

Clair suddenly had clouds of questions in her eyes. "A Christian?"

Kori nodded. "One of those crazy born-again people I've been rolling my eyes at ever since I met Ryan Carlson." She chuckled softly. "I started thinking about it and realized that Jesus Christ is my only guarantee in this life. His promises are recorded in the Bible and the peace I'm feeling now is from Him. That's why I'm not scared, Clair. I have Christ."

"Some God He is to let you get hit by a car," she answered, pulling her hand free and wiping away an errant tear.

"But better me, Clair, than Brent or Jared. . .or you. How would I have ever lived with myself if someone else got hurt because of me?" Kori shook her head. "I wouldn't have been able to stand it. Jesus knew that about me. That's why He let this accident happen—*to me.*"

"You're not making sense."

Kori sighed as a wave of weariness swept over her. "Maybe not, but I just know that this is His way and it's the best way and. . .I'm going to be just fine. It's something I feel in my heart."

With a cluck of her tongue, Clair replied, "I think you're talking out of your head because of the pain medication."

Kori did her best to shake her head to the contrary. "I mean what I said."

Clair shrugged.

"Ryan tried to tell me for years about Christ," she went on reflectively, "but I wouldn't listen. It was only when Brent came back that I wanted to hear—because I wanted to understand the change in him. Now I know. And now I've got it for myself."

"The guarantee you always wanted."

"Yes. And a love to last forever. God's love."

Clair moved the corner chair closer to Kori's bedside and sat down. "You know," she said at last, "I feel better. I think your peace might be rubbing off on me."

Kori smiled, but suddenly she was so tired she couldn't stay awake another moment. Closing her eyes, she fell into a deep sleep.

Chapter 20

As Brent had predicted, the night was indeed long. Ryan arrived at the hospital and, after much discussion, it was decided that Kori would be transferred to another medical facility and admitted under the care of a highly acclaimed orthopedic surgeon. Once the relocation had been completed, Kori was scheduled for surgery first thing Saturday.

That morning, Brent sat in the family waiting area after a brief meeting with the anesthesiologist. He had been allowed to stay by Kori's side right up until they wheeled her off to the operating room. Looking into his coffee cup now, he found himself thinking about all the dangers of general anesthesia and all the risks involved with surgery.

"Quit worrying," Mark told him in an amused tone of voice.

Brent glanced at his friend, sitting beside him. He was grateful that Mark had offered to pray with him and keep him company this morning. "How do you know I'm worrying?"

Mark folded the business section of the newspaper and set it in his lap. "I can see it in your face. You've got great big worry lines across your forehead."

"Those aren't worry lines. I was just frowning because something's floating in my coffee."

"Sure, and now you're fibbing on top of it."

Brent couldn't stifle a laugh.

"You're not really worried, are you, Brent?" Clair asked seriously. She sat just across from them. "You said this was all standard procedure for someone in Kori's condition."

Taking one look at his sister-in-law's concerned expression, he decided he'd better not fret, if for no other reason than to keep Clair calm. He smiled. "I'm just tired, that's all." It was the truth, too!

She gave a short laugh. "Well, that's to be expected. You haven't slept all night. At least I got to go home and get a decent amount of sleep."

"I'll survive," he replied. "I've done enough double shifts at the hospital that I should be used to it by now."

"Hope you're planning to go home for awhile and get some rest after Kori comes out of surgery," Mark said in a tone of friendly advice.

Brent nodded. As much as he hated the thought of leaving Kori, he knew his limit and it was getting close.

"Yeah, I have to get some sleep," he muttered, catching the shadow of a man entering the waiting area. Looking up curiously, his full gaze rested upon none other than Jared Graham. At first, Brent was so surprised, he thought he was seeing things. It seemed too incredible. Him? Here? Of all the nerve! But, as the guy headed toward them, he knew this wasn't a product of weary imaginings.

"What are you doing here?" he fairly spat, standing so abruptly that his coffee sloshed over the edge of the cup.

Mark stood as well. "Easy, Brent," he said in soft warning, placing a hand on his friend's shoulder.

Brent shrugged it off. "You have no business here, Graham, so leave."

By now, Clair was standing also. Her wary gaze shifted between Brent and Jared, finally coming to rest on Brent. "I said it was okay for him to come," she admitted at last.

"What?"

"He phoned me late last night," Clair quickly explained. "Jared is as concerned about Kori as we are."

"Oh, right," Brent replied sarcastically, his gaze never wavering from Jared's expressionless, bearded face. "And that's why he fled the accident scene. . .because he was so concerned about her."

The man's green eyes darkened with suppressed emotion, a mixture, it seemed, of guilt and fury. Yet Brent stood undaunted. "I want you out of here. Now."

"Brent, please, give him a chance," Clair pleaded. "Jared knows what he did was wrong, but—"

"But nothing." Brent turned to his sister-in-law. "He either leaves on his own, or I call the hospital's security staff. In fact, I'm sure the police would love to know where he is."

A pained look crossed Clair's features, confusing Brent. Whose side was she on, anyhow? How could she be concerned for her sister's welfare and feel sorry for the person who caused her accident?

"I'll leave, Clair," Jared said, breaking his tight-lipped silence. "I told you he'd be unreasonable." After a scathing glance at Brent, he turned and left the waiting room.

Satisfied with the outcome, Brent sat back down in his chair. Mark slowly followed suit; however, Clair just stood there, glaring at her brother-in-law.

"I thought you, a Christian, were all about love and forgiveness," she shot at him. "That's what you expected from Kori, wasn't it? Forgiveness? And love? Isn't that what you made her believe—that love conquers all? I almost believed it, too, but obviously your faith is nothing but a pack of lies!"

Brent stood again. "Clair, I—"

"No! You never even gave Jared a chance," she railed. "I listened to him pour his heart out for over an hour last night. He's feeling terrible about causing Kori's accident. Even she said it's not entirely his fault."

"What about his disappearing act after Kori was struck by that car? Did he tell you he feels really bad about that, too?" Sarcasm dripped from every word.

"Yes, as a matter of fact, he did." Clair paused, lifting her chin defiantly. Under different circumstances, Brent might have grinned, since it was an expression he'd seen on Kori any number of times. But now, the woman standing before him was advocating for a man Brent thought he might even hate.

"He was scared," Clair said. "Jared thought he'd killed Kori. He was beside himself, wondering, worrying, and knowing nothing. He said he tried calling several local hospitals, but no one would give him any information. Then the police came to Jared's door and told him that Kori was hospitalized and in satisfactory condition. He said they questioned him, but that's all, but for the next several hours Jared said he considered his whole life, where he'd been, where he was going. He did a thorough self-examination and got in touch with his inner being."

Brent rolled his eyes. "Save your breath, Clair. I am unimpressed with pseudopsychology. It's a useless bunch of nonsense in my opinion."

"Well, no matter. My point is this: Jared needs to heal emotionally. He told me he was hurt that Kori broke their engagement, but he admitted he was wrong to get drunk. But, Brent," Clair said beseechingly now, "doesn't Jared deserve the chance to know that Kori is going to be all right and then attempt to apologize to her?"

"No!" he declared hotly.

Clair threw her hands in the air, looking disgusted.

"Listen," Mark said objectively, "she's got a point, Brent. Remember the Scriptures say we need to love our enemies and forgive one another even as God for Christ's sake has forgiven us."

"Spare me the sermon."

"Good. Then you remember." A wry grin split Mark's face. "So how about I go try and catch up to Jared? We can, at least, invite him to sit here and wait out the surgery with us. Once he knows Kori is fine, he'll leave."

Brent gave his longtime friend an incredulous look, but sensed he was fighting a losing battle. Between Mark's Scripture whipping and Clair's gaze, throwing daggers at him, he didn't have a chance. "Yeah, sure, whatever. . ." he grumbled at last. "Go get him."

As Mark left the waiting area, Brent crossed the room and stood by the window. There, he had a perfect view of the wide expanse of Lake Michigan. It reminded him of the Pacific Ocean and suddenly a wave of homesickness rushed through him. Oh! how he wished he and Kori could just up and leave this mess and start their lives together anew. He'd love to fly her home right away. If only he hadn't committed to be a groomsman in Mark's wedding.

"You're doing the right thing," Clair said, standing just behind him now.

Brent didn't even bother turning around.

"We all have certain chapters of our lives that have to be closed before we can go on living—and that's what you're allowing Jared to do."

Brent wanted to say that Jared could have closed this particular chapter of his life days ago if he hadn't gone ballistic over Kori's decision; however, he swallowed the reply, praying the bitter taste in his mouth would go down along with it.

Mark returned about a half hour later, Jared Graham in tow. Each carried a cup of steaming coffee. Brent remained at the window, doing his best to ignore the small talk that ensued after they took a seat.

"Come and join us, Brent," Clair called to him.

"No, thanks," he muttered, feeling like a grouch. And he stood there for what seemed like an interminable time, only leaving once when he walked down the hallway to purchase a diet cola from out of the vending machine.

At long last, the surgeon appeared. "Everything went very well," he announced. "No surprises." He then went on to explain how he and his staff had pinned Kori's hip and repaired several minor fractures. "It was similar to putting a broken dish back together."

Out of the corner of his eye, Brent saw Clair sway slightly. He took hold of her elbow in an attempt to steady her.

"Oh, poor Kori," she said, tears pooling in her eyes. "Her hip was like a broken dish. . .?"

"Not to worry," the surgeon replied lightly, waving off the remark. "We'll have her dancing down the hospital corridors in no time. Your sister is going to be as good as new." Turning to Brent, he added, "She will, of course, require physical therapy, but nothing extensive. I expect her to make a complete recovery."

Brent managed a small smile. "Good."

"For the immediate prognoses, she'll be in recovery for awhile and then taken back up to her room. The nurses will probably get her up this evening and in a few days, she can go home."

"Really?" Clair brightened hearing that.

After a few more exchanges, the surgeon took his leave. Brent turned to Jared, hoping he'd take his as well. However, the look of relief on the other man's face gave him pause, and Brent suddenly wondered if everything Clair had said was true. Jared really seemed concerned about Kori and, moreover, he looked quite penitent. But Brent was too exhausted to be amicable at the moment.

"I'm going back to the apartment to get some sleep," he muttered. "Thanks for coming. . .all of you. . ."

With a fleeting glance in Jared's direction, he walked out of the waiting room.

Several days later, the nurse helped Kori back into bed after another walk around the hospital wing. Kori was finally getting used to the crutches, though her shoulder ached terribly at having to use them. Sometimes she didn't know which hurt more, her shoulder or her hip, not to mention the awful muscle aches and bruises that still covered much of her body. But in spite of her physical aches and pains, Kori still sensed that sweet peace and comforting presence of her Savior.

"There now, Mrs. McDonald," the young nurse said politely. "You can rest. I heard the doctor say you'd be discharged later."

Kori smiled. He'd told her the same thing on his rounds that morning. She could go home today! She had phoned Brent earlier to share the good news, and he'd said that all of her belongings were now moved into his apartment. He had also picked up her new car. The plan was they'd stay through the Christmas holiday here in Wisconsin, and by January, Kori would be healed enough to make the drive back to California with her "little red wagon" in tow. Both he and Kori's doctor expected her to make a rapid recovery, yet there were times when Kori couldn't imagine her body healing so fast.

"One step at a time," Brent had told her and that's about as far ahead as Kori could think for now.

The nurse left the room while Kori adjusted her hospital bed so she'd recline more comfortably. Sitting straight up was still terribly uncomfortable and she could only tolerate it for short intervals, while lying flat on her back caused her shoulder to throb.

As Kori finished getting herself situated, a knock sounded at the door. Before she could even reply, Jared poked his head into the room.

"Can I come in?"

Kori hesitated a moment, fearing that Brent would show up and discover Jared visiting with her. Although he had seemed less hostile toward Jared, Kori didn't want there to be any chance for a confrontation between the two men.

"I'll only stay a minute," Jared promised, as if to sway her decision.

At last she waved him into the room.

"I'm glad to see you're doing okay," he said, looking uncertain as he walked into the room. "Clair has kept me up on your progress."

Kori nodded for lack of a better reply. She suddenly wished she were still on her crutches so she could stand and talk to Jared. She felt so vulnerable like this.

He came up to her and stood beside the bed, his hand on the side rail. He shook his head and grinned. "I practiced a big long speech on the way over, but now I can't think of a single thing to say."

Kori managed a weak smile. The sight of Jared evoked so many emotions in her. Maybe a small part of her had loved him after all. "Could I say something?"

He nodded.

"I've been doing a lot of thinking these past couple of days and. . .well, I can't change anything that's happened, but I can ask for your forgiveness. Will you forgive me, Jared?"

"What are you talking about?" he asked with a shaken expression. "Me forgive you? For what?"

Kori swallowed hard. "For hurting you."

Jared lowered himself so that his forearms now rested on the side rail. "You're crazy, you know that?"

She grinned slightly. Jared's tone was affectionate despite his hard words.

"You? Hurt me?" He shook his head in wonder. "Look what I did to you. I nearly killed you, Kori, and you're asking for my forgiveness? I came here today to apologize to you!"

Her grin grew into a full-fledged smile. "Apology accepted. I forgive you."

Jared narrowed his gaze. "Just like that, huh?"

"Just like that."

"Man, Kori, you're a pushover." Jared straightened as a trace of bitterness entered his voice. "And your husband must have known it, too. All he had to do was apologize and you took him right back with little or no thought for us. . .me."

"That's not true."

He turned and walked to the window, standing with his back to her. Kori sighed, wishing there was something she could say that would make him finally understand.

"I thought I was over him, Jared," she stated honestly. "I thought I was free to love and marry you. But when Brent walked back into my life, I realized that wasn't the case. Not only were we still married, but I was still in love with him. I didn't plan it, nor did I intentionally deceive you. It's just something that happened."

"Yeah, I know," he replied, surprising Kori. He turned and leaned against the windowsill, his arms folded across his chest. "I know you're telling me the truth, but. . ." He paused, taking a deep breath. "But it hurts so bad, Kori, that I don't think I'll ever get over it."

Tears stung the backs of her eyes.

"And look at you. You're about as banged up as anyone I've ever seen. We're two people who were supposed to be in love, but now we've got wounds to last the rest of our lives!"

A fat tear slid down Kori's cheek as she realized she'd never heard Jared talk this way before. Deep, sharing his heart with her. "We'll heal, Jared," she promised, weeping openly now.

"Oh, don't do that." He rushed to her side and handed her the box of tissues on the bedside table. "You know what's going to happen here, don't you? That husband of yours is going to walk in and hit the ceiling when he finds out I made you cry."

Kori chuckled through her tears. "Brent is going to hit the ceiling if he finds you here, period!"

Jared nodded. "It was a chance I had to take," he replied, looking more earnest than Kori had ever seen him. "I just had to see you one last time. I've got to know you're going to be happy with. . .with him."

"I'm going to be happy." Kori wiped her tears away.

"Yeah, you look real happy," Jared retorted, a teasing light in his eyes. It was short-lived, however, and then his face took on a more intent, more determined, expression. Leaning over the bed, Jared suddenly pressed a firm kiss on her lips. "Good-bye, Kori," he whispered against her mouth. Straightening again, he lightly brushed the knuckles of his right hand against her cheek.

"Good-bye, Jared."

In the next moment, he turned and headed for the door, but stopped suddenly. Kori's gaze followed him, only to see Brent standing there, arms akimbo with a smoldering look in his eyes.

Kori winced and a sinking feeling enveloped her. She closed her eyes, afraid to see what was coming next.

"Don't worry, pal," she heard Jared say. "That was good-bye forever, so don't even think about getting bent out of shape."

Not until she heard the door close did she look up. Jared was gone, but Brent still stood there, statue-still.

"Brent, I—"

"No, no. I don't want any explanations," he said, putting up a hand as he made his way slowly to her side. He put down the guardrail and then sat on the edge of the bed. "Just answer me yes or no. Was that really good-bye forever, Kori?"

"Yes," she replied in all honesty.

Pursing his lips, Brent momentarily thought it over. "Okay," he said at last. "I can live with that."

Kori felt like she would faint with relief, but when she looked back at Brent, he wore a little smirk on his face. She didn't ask what he found so amusing, just clung to him with all her might after he pulled her into a loving embrace.

"Ready to go home?" he asked, stroking her hair in long, soothing motions.

"Yes," she replied, tightening her hold around his neck. "Take me home."

Epilogue

The sun was just beginning to set in the smoggy Los Angeles sky when Korah Mae McDonald climbed out of her red station wagon and walked toward the looming medical complex. Entering the lobby, she waved to Delores who sat at the Information Center and then headed for the Emergency Room.

"Well, hello, little mama," Sharon, one of the nurses, said. She was blond, middle-aged and extremely competent—or so Kori had heard. "Looking for Brent?"

She nodded. "Is he with a patient?"

"Nope. He's in back trying to eat supper and catch up on paperwork. If he's not careful, he'll end up eating an insurance form and signing his hamburger bun." Sharon laughed.

Kori smiled, and nodding her thanks, she made her way down the outer hallway toward the office that all the ER physicians shared while on duty.

"Oh, by the way," Sharon called after her. "How are you feeling?"

"Great. . .for a whale."

The nurse chuckled. "Have that ultrasound yet?"

"This afternoon." Kori held up the large cardboard envelope she'd been carrying. "Got 'em right here."

"And?" Sharon's eyes widened curiously.

She laughed nervously. "And I'll let Brent inform you of the results. . .right after I inform him." Kori didn't add that she'd been fretting over his reaction, praying he'd be delighted. . . once the shock wore off.

"Twins?"

"I'm not saying, Sharon," she stated, doing her best to be adamant when she was fairly bursting to share the news with someone. "But it's not twins. I'll tell you that much."

The older woman frowned. "You're kidding? But I thought—"

"We were all wrong."

Sharon groaned. "You're not going to set me straight? The wait's going to kill me!"

Kori pitched another smile as she turned and walked away. Chatting any longer and she'd spill the whole pot of beans! But she simply had to tell Brent first.

He could be the one to tell his coworkers.

Rounding the corner, Kori paused at the office door. She could see Brent sitting in the far corner of the room, tapping a black pen against the desktop, staring blindly at his paperwork. Kori immediately knew he was concerned to the point of distraction and her heart went out to him.

As if sensing her presence, he looked up from his stack of forms. "Kori!" Dropping his pen, he stood and strode quickly toward her. "I've been waiting to hear from you," he said before placing a kiss on her lips. With hands upon her shoulders, he brought his chin back, scrutinizing her face. "So? What did your doctor say?"

"She said I'm not carrying twins, for one thing."

"You're not?" Brent narrowed his dark gaze. "But I heard the two heartbeats myself."

"Your diagnosis was incorrect, Dr. McDonald," Kori quipped, batting her lashes in feigned superiority.

"Oh, yeah? So what *is* the diagnosis?" Brent did not look amused and Kori immediately apologized for teasing him.

"Kori. . ."

"We're having triplets," she blurted.

"What?"

"It's true. Want to see the films?"

"Yeah." Brent snatched them and walked toward the viewing box, mounted on the wall beside the desk. He switched on the light, snapped the X-rays into place and considered them thoughtfully. At last, he turned slowly back around, wearing a broad grin. "We sure are having triplets!"

Kori returned the smile as gratitude filled her soul. While she'd known Brent wouldn't be angry at the news, she had wanted him to be just as excited as she was. From his expression, Kori realized her prayers had been answered.

"Let's see," Brent began, looking at the ceiling contemplatively, "we can get your mom to come for the first month and my mom can help with those two A.M. feedings whenever I have to work the night shift."

Kori laughed. "Clair will come and help. And Dana, too."

"I'll bet Juli wouldn't mind lending a hand for a week or so, especially if Mark gets that contract in San Diego."

"Oh, I don't know," Kori replied skeptically. "Julia's baby is due around the same time ours is—I mean the same time ours *are.*"

"Whew!" Brent said, running a hand through his hair. "Three babies. All at once." He suddenly beamed. "Praise the Lord!"

Kori nodded. They'd been praying for a baby for so long and the Lord saw fit to bless them with three! "God is certainly able to do exceeding, abundantly, and above all we ask."

"And think!" Brent added, pulling Kori into an embrace despite her protruding midsection. His eyes darkened passionately. "I love you."

With her arms around his neck, Kori murmured, "I love you, too."

"Ah-hem," came the female voice from the doorway. Brent looked up and Kori turned to find Sharon standing there. "You going to share the news about your wife's ultrasound, Brent, or keep it to yourself while the rest of us die from curiosity?"

He chuckled. "No one dies in *my* ER!" Taking Kori's hand, he led her toward the door. "I guess it's announcement time."

As she walked beside her husband to the nurse's station, an indescribable joy permeated Kori's being. This wasn't another impossible dream, this was reality! God's reality!

A Letter to Our Readers

Dear Readers:

In order that we might better contribute to your reading enjoyment, we would appreciate your taking a few minutes to respond to the following questions. When completed, please return to the following: Fiction Editor, Barbour Publishing, Inc., P.O. Box 719, Uhrichsville, OH 44683.

1. Did you enjoy reading *Wisconsin?*
   ❏ Very much—I would like to see more books like this.
   ❏ Moderately—I would have enjoyed it more if _____
   _____
   _____

2. What influenced your decision to purchase this book?
   (Check those that apply.)
   ❏ Cover   ❏ Back cover copy   ❏ Title   ❏ Price
   ❏ Friends   ❏ Publicity   ❏ Other

3. Which story was your favorite?
   ❏ *The Haven of Rest*   ❏ *Promise Me Forever*
   ❏ *September Sonata*   ❏ *Second Time Around*

4. Please check your age range:
   ❏ Under 18   ❏ 18–24   ❏ 25–34
   ❏ 35–45   ❏ 46–55   ❏ Over 55

5. How many hours per week do you read? _____

Name _____

Occupation _____

Address _____

City _____ State _____ Zip _____

E-mail _____

ℋEARTSONG ♥ PRESENTS

Love Stories
Are Rated G!

That's for godly, gratifying, and of course, great! If you love a thrilling love story but don't appreciate the sordidness of some popular paperback romances, **Heartsong Presents** is for you. In fact, **Heartsong Presents** is the premiere inspirational romance book club featuring love stories where Christian faith is the primary ingredient in a marriage relationship.

Sign up today to receive your first set of four, never-before-published Christian romances. Send no money now; you will receive a bill with the first shipment. You may cancel at any time without obligation, and if you aren't completely satisfied with any selection, you may return the books for an immediate refund!

Imagine. . .four new romances every four weeks—two historical, two contemporary—with men and women like you who long to meet the one God has chosen as the love of their lives. . .all for the low price of $10.99 postpaid.

To join, simply complete the cou~~pon belo~~w and mail to the address provided. **Heartsong Presents** roma~~nces are r~~ated G for another reason: They'll arrive Godspeed!

YES! Sign m~~e up~~ for Hearts♥ng!

NEW MEMBERSHIPS W~~ILL BE S~~HIPPED IMMEDIATELY!
Send no money now. We'll ~~bill you o~~nly $10.99 postpaid with your first shipment of four books. ~~For fa~~ster action, call toll free 1-800-847-8270.

NAME _____

ADDRESS _____

CITY _____ STATE_____ ZIP_____

MAIL TO: HEARTSONG PRESENTS, P.O. Box 721, Uhrichsville, Ohio 44683
or visit www.heartsongpresents.com